The Age of Center

Jeremy Henderson

PublishAmerica
Baltimore

First printing

This is a work of fiction. Names, characters, places, and incidents either are the product of the author's imagination or are used fictitiously. Any resemblance to actual persons, living or dead, events, or locales is entirely coincidental.

PublishAmerica has allowed this work to remain exactly as the author intended, verbatim, without editorial input.

ISBN: 978-1-4489-5733-0
PUBLISHED BY PUBLISHAMERICA, LLLP
www.publishamerica.com
Baltimore

Printed in the United States of America

This book is dedicated to my family who put up with me; present in absentia, while I wrote this story.

The Age of Center

"All the earth is a grave and nothing escapes it."
–Nezahualcoyotl (1403-1472)

Prologue

Lord Votan made his way up the steps of the stone pyramid. The night sky was clear and dark, the ceiling of stars blinking above. In spite of the night air, he felt sweat beading on his skin, the still air providing no respite. The jungle reached out to the horizon, a jagged black outline against the backdrop of the sky. A chorus of animals cried out from the deep forest, the ceaseless croaking of frogs and toads, the faint cries of bats, and the buzzing of insects. He counted each step as he climbed upwards, and his sharp eyes noted the craftsmanship of the cutting of the stones, the placement of each brick. The stone masters who had worked in the temple were the best the empire had to offer, and their quality of work was plain to see. The seams between each stone were straight and precise, the edges sharp and defined.

His ceremonial guard followed him as he ascended, a quiet watcher meant to keep watch over him during his prayers, to attend to his needs. His steps were silent, his only sounds that of his breathing and rustling beads from his necklace. His war club was held tightly in his right hand held in the middle of its length for easier balance. He was well muscled and slim, and moved with steady certainty, a seasoned warrior at the peak of his physical prowess. He followed behind at a respectable distance, surveying the grounds for danger, and only seeing campfires and stretched shadows far below. Two other guards stood at he base of the staircase, one off to each side, their backs turned to him.

Pacal had felt anxious all day, restlessness deep within his bones and muscle. He had walked through the streets of the city in silence, his Guard keeping a mindful watch over him as he wandered without purpose through the streets. He watched as women taught their daughters to weave, as masters taught apprentices their skills in stonework and metalwork. Children ran laughing through the streets, their dogs barking and yapping with excitement at their heels. Young men and women cast furtive glances at one another under the watchful eyes of their parents. He wandered the entire day, pausing only long enough to eat and drink whatever his Guards had brought to him. He felt the energy of the city and its people, felt it flowing through him and around him. The sun rose high into the sky, and eventually began to fall to the horizon, with each step and passing hour the anxiety evolved into dread. The Gods were summoning him, and he feared what was to come this evening. His visions were becoming darker, showing him a future rich with war and hunger, and unimaginable suffering. He had felt the compulsion as he awoke in the morning, and as the sun, Kinich-Ahau, traveled across the sky the call of the Gods grew louder, more insistent. With relief, he reached the summit and continued in the direction of the stone seat situated atop the center of the pyramid, catching his breath as he walked, feeling his heart hammering in his chest. He smiled ruefully, remembering from the days of his youth when he could run from the base of the temple to its peak and feel invigorated afterwards. Tonight he felt fatigue settle into his bones, his limbs protesting the climb.

Behind the seat and off to one side a sacrificial altar was prepared for him, his priests having readied the ceremony for his completion. A small table was at the foot of the altar, its legs supporting a thickly walled ceramic bowl that was painted with the fresco of a serpent. A small fire crackled from within the bowl, its glowing a fierce red and orange color. He approached the table slowly, reverently, and from his waist belt he gradually withdrew a black obsidian knife. At the tables' edge, he placed the knife in the open palms of his hands, and held it above the man tied to the table surface, whispering a prayer for the ceremony to come. He first prayed to Itzamná for strength and wisdom, then Chac, for rain for the crops in the fields, Yumil Kaxob for grain, Yum Cimil for knowledge of the Underworld. The prayers continued, each god mentioned and invited to the ceremony, each one asked for knowledge, wisdom, and their blessing. Once the gods had been honored and invited, he held the blade in both hands, and raised it high above his head, his eyes downcast, centered on the chest of the offering below him. The man was bound tightly to the underside of the altar. His eyes were blindfolded, and his mouth gagged. He was breathing quickly, his skin shiny with beads of sweat. With a smooth practiced motion, he brought the blade down and opened the chest cavity below the ribs. Acting with haste, he dropped the blade to the ground below where it chattered along the stone, and he plunged his hands into the chest. Gripping tightly, his forearms taut with exertion, he pulled out the beating heart of the victim and raised it above his head to the night sky in praise of the gods. Below him, the victim sighed with his final breath and lay still, his struggle ended. Lord Pacal took a step towards the bowl, and dropped the heart into the flames, and then spread his arms wide, his eyes closed, listening to the flesh sizzle in the hot coals. He felt the presence of the gods near to him, the offering was accepted, the gods were pleased. He gazed at the man on the table, and thanked him wordlessly for his sacrifice. His soul was now in Heaven, and would not have to voyage through the Underworld to get there, having paid the ultimate price on the altar.

He left the altar and made his way over to a small stone seat that stood alone on the summit. Once there he sat slowly, in reverence of the holiness of the location. His guard stood to the right behind him, facing the stair pathway they had climbed together. Once comfortably seated he removed his Quetzl feather headdress, and placed it at his feet, sighing quietly as he bent over with it. He sat up straight and looked upwards to the heavens, and then closed his eyes. The night air was rich with the scents of the city and jungle, a mixing of man and forest. The air was laden with the smoke of cooking, tinted slightly by the sacrificial fires slowly burning in the city. Behind those smells were the smells of the forest. The rich smells of the jungle which flooded him with memories. Memories of boyhood were the strongest, when he was becoming a warrior and building his name in the empire. He had spent much of his youth in the jungle, his father teaching him to find food deep in the forest, teaching him to track his prey and his enemies. His father taught him to fight in the jungle as well, the strategies of war and the tactics of his foes. He could small the rains in the air, the flowers and fruits high above in the treetops, the sweet odors of the forest floor. Memories of hunting and war parties, of bathing in forest streams, of standing in dense monsoon downpours as rain fell from the skies in ceaseless thundering waves. His body slowly relaxed and his mind cleared. From below he heard the cries and laughter of children, the sounds of cooking and of families preparing for bed. He allowed himself to smile slighty. The city and the empire were prospering and growing well. Children were born healthy and fewer and fewer were becoming ill and dying young. The gods had blessed this land, this people, and Pacal Votan was proud, yet humble to have been chosen to lead his people during these times. And there was a price to be paid. A price at times he would refuse, if it was within his power to do so.

He slowly opened his eyes, and kept his eyes upwards. The darkness above him was absolute, a moonless night, and the countless points of light a colored opposite the the sacred blackness. He sought guidance in the sky, hints and clues to his recent and distant visions, messages from the gods that might help him to better serve his people. The horizon to the east was faintly red, the last of sunset, a dark crimson against the horizon. Towards that red sky Quetzecoatl had vanished, promising to return to reclaim his land. He shivered at the thought of that time, of the bloodshed that was sure to come. The return of a God to rule the land of men would surely demand war and Sacrifice, and he would not care to live in those days to come. The first of his visions, he knew within his soul were of that time, and his dreams and nightmares revealed strange beasts that were half men, clothing that shone like silver, and weapons that roared like thunder. The Gods had also shown him of the death to come from sickness, of entire peoples dying, and he had prayed countless nights for deliverance from these haunting scenes, to no longer see the suffering of future peoples. The Gods had ignored his wishes and mocked him, showing him truths and fates too terrible to imagine.

Although the night air was still warm, gooseflesh arose on his arms, an unconscious reaction to his torments. He looked over to his sole guardian, and spoke quietly into the night air.

"Pachtun."

The muscled silhouette jumped slightly. He was not accustomed to being spoken to during his watch, and was not expecting it. He turned quickly and silently, dropping to his knee and bowing his head in a single smooth motion, his war club chattering only once as he laid it on the cold stone.

"What do you wish, my Lord?"

His question hung in the air for a brief moment. Lord Votan outstretched his left arm and placed his hand firmly on Pachtun's shoulder, wanting to reassure and relax him with this fatherly gesture. He looked at him in the darkness, sensing the insecurity of the moment.

"Pachtun, I need you to leave me and watch over me from a distance."

He felt Pachtun's shoulder tense, the objection to the request already rising.

"I mean no disrespect, no dishonor to you, my son. The Gods know above all else it is you I trust to watch over my in my prayers. I feel the Gods preparing to speak to me again tonight, and I fear within my heart what I will be shown. Please follow the request of an old man. Watch me, keep me safe, but at a distance this night."

He felt the tension slip from under his hand, into acceptance of the request. Pachtun rose and stood tall, bowing.

"As you wish my Lord, I will watch over you from the steps. I will return to your side when you call for me."

With that, he turned and silently marched to the edge of the pyramid, his war club by his right side, overlooking the city below. Lord Votan felt a surge of pride as he watched Pachtun stand guard. He had obeyed a difficult order with strong discipline. He prayed quietly into the night, speaking to the Ancestors.

"Your son has grown into a strong man, Tenoch. He honors your memory."

He recalled his friend, long since deceased, but whose presence he felt strongly.

"He is tall and proud, and yet quickly listens to an old man like myself. His enemies fear him, and he shows his family much devotion. I was right to name him amongst my Guard. I will not fear passing into Xibalba with sons like yours ready to lead our people."

He felt his Vision come to him, an overpowering surge of information and emotion that forced him to rise from his seat, and then dropped him to the stone, his hands clutching his head tightly, his jaws clenched.

Pachtun stood at the summit of the staircase, watching the city of Palenque below with only a partial amount of attention. Beyond the city, he could see the rows of maize growing in the irrigated fields surrounding the city, the starlight reflecting faintly between the still stalks. His focus was on Lord Votan, who he could tell was talking into the night, no doubt prayers to the Gods, or perhaps to the Ancestors of his people. Perhaps to his own father tonight. Pachtun had felt an incredible despair emanating from his King, and it was his trained instinct to want to defend him from it, to keep him safe. So he watched for the moment he was summoned, when his aid would be welcomed and not construed as disobedience or an insult.

He clenched his club tightly as his he saw the old figure rise slightly and then fall to the ground, shaking and mumbling. He saw his hands clenched to his head, and occasionally striking out into the air as if to ward off a blow. Pachtun watched the vision unfold with a dreadful fascination. There were times as a child where he had wished for such a gift, when his father had told him of the powers of their King. Now, seeing them unfold and the pain and suffering it inflicted, he felt pity for those with the gift, or indeed, the curse it became. Time passed, the night faded further into its deepest black, and finally he heard his name quietly called out from the shadows. He ran over to the shaking figure still lying on the ground, and helped lift him back onto his seat. His body was shaking strongly, either from fear, or exhaustion he did not know, and he was perspiring strongly, and gave off heat he could easily feel in the night air. Pachtun stood up and looked around the temple summit, quickly scanning the grounds for danger, staying close to his charge.

"Thank you, Pachtun. Keep watch while I rest a while."

He closed his eyes as he tried to sort the blur and emotions of his Vision. He had felt such terrible fear and suffering, and seen so many things that he could not explain, or even describe in a way to be understood easily. His memories flashed to that of the Calendar, the great Cycles that governed what would be and what would come to pass. His mind saw five blazing suns in a deep blue sky, and again a flash of the Calendar, and a confusing maelstrom of fire and water, of Earth. He saw images of people and beasts, of great cities and unknown times. The volumes of these things rose in his head until it reached a crescendo where he no longer distinguished a single isolated sound, and then the five suns disappeared and all became silent. He could hear his own heart beating, his blood flowing hot within.

He understood his Vision, this one perhaps clearer than any to date. The Gods had shown him the Closing of a Cycle; a Cycle ending so far into the future that his grandchildren's own grandchildren would not live to witness it. The Closing of the Age of the Fifth Sun. A time of cataclysm and great change, a time of an old world dying and a new one being born; the beginning of the Age of Center. He sagged to his knees and wept as he had not since he was a small child, clinging to his mother in a tight embrace.

Archie Buchanen

Archie pressed the steering column button that disengaged the cruise control of the family minivan. With a slight bump the vehicle began to decelerate, and Archie put his foot back on the gas, giving it a little to get it back up to the speed limit. Only the family dog Bunker, a sedate greyhound noticed the difference, lifting his head up from his doggie pillow and peering outside the window. Bunker stretched lazily, and with a sigh that sounded like it lasted for a minute he put his head back down on his pillow.

"Christ Almighty," Archie murmured, just slightly louder than a whisper, being careful to not wake up any of his family, and he glanced into his rear view mirror. A convertible two seater roared past him on the right, and then cut in front of him, squeezing in behind a tanker truck. It's brakes flashed twice as it rapidly slowed down. The driver was a dark haired, well tanned young man, his passenger possibly his girlfriend, her long hair streaming in the wind of the open highway. His left thumb was setting the beat of a song on his steering wheel. Based on the irregularity of the rhythm, he was either terrible at keeping the beat, or the song had no beat. Either way he was an asshole. He had been cutting off cars for the last few kilometers, weaving his way through traffic and tailgating in an apparent attempt to get himself and his passenger killed in a gory highway wreck.

Mel was in the front passenger seat, her arms crossed below her breasts, her legs resting up on the dash of the van. He looked over at her to see if she had been disturbed, his eyes quickly admiring the view of her legs up to the bottom of her jean shorts where they had yielded a better view. He felt a quick rush of heat, and then dismissed it, and looked back at the kids.

Stephanie was crashed, her sunglasses hanging askew from her nose, her book open in her lap. He adjusted the rear view mirror to have a quick look at Charlie. His mouth hung open, his one of his headphones had fallen out and lay on his shoulder, his head rested against the window glass, his head shaking slightly from the vibrations of the van. Bunker sat between the two of them, his head resting on his forepaws.

They had been following the tanker truck for more than an hour since leaving Sydney, content to set the cruise control to the trucker's speed that was a consistent pace. The trucks bright chrome tanker was polished to a high shine, and he had needed to put on his sunglasses to reduce the glare when it caught the sunlight. A comical figure was painted on the back of the tanker, with the script *I've got gas* painted underneath in a bold red print.

Charlie had shrieked with laughter when they had first read the sign, and Archie couldn't help but smile both at the commercial and his kids delight.

Steph, at the age of five, hadn't understood the joke at first, but Charlie, being nine, was quick to comprehend bathroom humor in a way only boys can, and fathers can appreciate. His mother had rolled her eyes, and then lowered her hat back down over her forehead, trying to catch some sleep on the open road. The last few days had been a blur of countless highway miles, punctuated by rest stops, pee breaks, restaurants, motels and gas stations. For the kids it was a great adventure; a great highway trek leading up to Christmas where every stop was something new, and the promise of the next day was almost intolerable. For their parents it was evolving into something that needed to be endured before it could be fully enjoyed. They had loaded their van and luggage with smiles and excitement before hitting the open road, and merged onto the highway eager to catch the horizon. For Archie in particular, the trip was the culmination of a great weight and oppression being lifted from his shoulders and the promise of a better future. A month earlier, he was a plumber for a small outfit in Canberra. He had been in trades for all of his life, beginning as a carpenter in his late teens working into his apprenticeship swinging a hammer and building roof trusses for eight hours a day. When a bum shoulder interfered with his ability to continue carpentry, he switched to plumbing and gradually earned his ticket.

His boss was a cheap son of a bitch named Cutter that worked him long hours under the continued promise of raises and a share in the business. Cutter was in his late fifties and was used to intimidating his employees.

He was just under six feet tall, and was well on his way to becoming tremendously obese. He perpetually wore wife-beaters, that had once been white but were now a painter's canvass of sauces and condiments. His stomach hung over his pants, and his body emitted a subtle but persistent foul odor that kept people from getting too close.

When he had hired Archie, he was a down-and-out carpenter that had two little kids, a mortgage, and more debt than was healthy; a financial cancer that was always present and was front and center in every purchase. It was there before he went to bed, and when he woke up in the morning, like a mild nausea that never completely went away. He had seen the hunger and desperation in his eyes for a steady wage, and the opportunity to hold him under his thumb for at least a little while. He had hired him on the spot, and immediately started to train him in the basics. Fixing a shitty toilet, stopping a leak in a kitchen pipe, whatever took the minimal amount of skill to start. He had given him an old rusty toolbox that creaked when it opened to reveal a series of rusty wrenches and other tools that had seen years of neglect and misuse, and excess moisture.

"You kin use these tools for the time bein', 'til you can afford your own. Mind you keep them in the shop at night. And if I so much as think you stole one of my tools, you'll be fired faster than you know, y'understand me boy?"

His forefinger pointed at Archie as he finished the sentence, punctuating the point with a few short jabs in the air.

"Yeah I understand."

"Glad we have an understanding, you don't seem like a dumb shit. You ain't a dumb shit, are ya?"

"No sir I'm not."

Satisfied with the outcome of the conversation, Cutter leaned back in his office chair, it's spine giving a low protesting creaking sound as he did so.

Archie had picked up the neglected tools and set off to work in the company van. And for the next few years that had become his routine. He came into the office every morning, picked up his clipboard with his days work attached to it, and made his rounds through endless clogged toilets and leaky pipes. In the evening, he would return the van, drop off his invoices, and go home. A boring existence, but it kept the bills paid and Archie had gone from being up to his eyeballs in debt to being up to his neck in debt. One fine fall afternoon he had unclogged his most recent toilet, a fine mess where some kid had put a small plastic cup in the toilet, flushed it where it got good and stuck in the toilet trap, and then his mother had evidently taken the dump of her life shortly after. And of course, it had nowhere to go but up and out of the toilet, in the same direction from which it came. He didn't gag much anymore, but this job did. The stench hit him hard, leaving his face pale and his stomach wishing he hadn't eaten breakfast. Archie was forced to clench his teeth and breathe through his mouth, to try to reduce the god-awful smell. Eventually he had to remove the toilet from the floor to remove the cup from where it was so neatly wedged. And since he couldn't easily drain the toilet, he had to dump its contents elsewhere to finish the job. Elsewhere in this case was the bathtub. He had lowered the fluid contents of the toilet as much as he could, and then down on his hands and knees, unscrewed it from the vinyl floor. As quickly as he could muster, he had pulled the toilet from its seal and poured it over into the tub, leaving a small but foul trail of liquid excrement between the drain and the tub. Grimacing, he had then turned on the shower and aimed it into the trap side of the toilet, the water pushing the small cup out and into the tub basin. He then had sprayed down the tub with soap and water, and put down a new toilet seal, affixing it firmly once more to the floor. When the job was done, he had gone to the kitchen to find the woman of the house had left with her brood. A hundred dollar bill was left on the table, held down with a small spoon and near it a note stating

"For your trouble." He left his bill and receipt for eighty dollars under that same spoon, and pocketed a twenty dollar tip.

After his shift was done, he stopped by the grocer for a jug of milk and a few loaves of bread, which he paid for with his tip. The cashier had rung up the items through the register, and the total had come to fourteen dollars even. The cashier, a skinny pimply red haired kid whose nametag proclaimed him to be Hector, had commented, "Fourteen dollars even. You don't see that happen much, an even amount."

He had smiled nervously, trying to make conversation and make his shift pass by faster with small talk, while hoping he didn't sound like an idiot. A customer behind Archie, a balding WASP, had snickered quietly, evidently thinking that the cashier was indeed, an idiot. Archie had passed him the twenty, and noticed the lottery jackpot for that Friday was estimated to be forty three million dollars.

"Do you want any lotto tickets for the next draw?" Hector asked.

Archie was wondering who the hell names their kid Hector? Figuring it was free money anyway, he had agreed and received his six lotto tickets from Hector, which he stuffed into the front of his coveralls. Hector wished him luck on the draw; Archie thanked him and went home.

He had spent that evening as he had countless others. They had dinner in the kitchen, some kind of flavored breaded chicken with various mixed vegetables and pasta, the screw shaped noodles that Archie could never recall was rotini. It was served on plain white plates, the kind that were plain and cheap and tough to break. After dinner, he and Mel had sat outside in their plastic lawn chairs, watching the sun go down while the kids played with the dog, Bunker barking excitedly as he chased his ball across the yard.

The kids were throwing it between themselves, with Bunker being the pig in the middle. Occasionally one of the kids would drop the ball, and Bunker would seize his chance to grab it and run around the yard with his prize held firmly in his jaws, smiling only as a dog can smile, showing everyone that he had the ball. Then he would drop it at the kids' feet, and the cycle would continue. Archie had sat there, drawing deep breaths to cleanse out the remainder of the memory of the afternoon smell from his sinuses. Mel sat to his right, sipping on a tall glass of iced tea, its exterior dripping with condensation. The ice clinked as she took a sip, and clinked again when she put the glass down on the table between the two of them.

"Did you finish the Christmas shopping?" Archie asked.

Mel shook her head.

"No, not yet. I'll finish this weekend. My mum is going to come with me."

Archie had nodded. Christmas was only a month away, and he liked to have the gift shopping done early so they could stick to their budget. Christmas always gave him a knot deep in his stomach. Their money only went so far, and the holidays made it stretch thinner. When Steph was six, Mel was going to re-enter the workforce, and add a second income to the family. Archie was almost counting the days when they could count on additional income. Childcare was too expensive for her to work right now, before both kids were in school, so they had agreed to wait until Steph was in first grade.

Six more months and he could stop worrying about being the sole bread winner. Of course, with the economy being in the shitter it was no guarantee that Mel was going to be able to get a job, but it was at least hope. He didn't think she would have a problem. She was smart and attractive, ambitious but not cocky. And if she had to show a little cleavage at her interview to get an advantage, then so be it.

"How long is your mum going to be here?"

"Just the weekend. Dad is on a golf tour with some school chums and she hates being home alone."

He didn't mind her mum at all. Natalie was a doting grandmother, and had helped them several times in the past when things were tight.

They had caught up on events of the day, and after having bathed the kids and sent them off to bed, had made love before turning in themselves.

The next day broke the same as the day before, the sky was clear and although relatively cool, it was growing hotter by the minute. He had got himself off to work quietly, arriving at the shop just before seven. The front door bell chimed when he had entered the building. Cutter was sitting behind the desk, working over the remains of a cigar between his lips.

"Morning, Cutter."

Cutter grunted once without looking up. An old am fm radio played quietly from the shelf behind him. He had punched in for his shift, and taken his work orders for the morning, folding them and tucking them under his arm.

"See you later, Cutter."

Cutter grunted once more.

He pushed the door open, the bell chimed again and he was off to start another day. Around noon, he had finished three morning jobs (one clogged sink, one pipe inspection complete with video camera for a local strata company, and one toilet repair) when he had stopped at a local convenience store for a drink. Fishing for change in his faded blue work pants, he had pulled out his lottery ticket, and while he paid for his Coke the cashier checked his numbers. He had placed the change down on the counter and cracked the tab on his soda. He released it slowly in case it had been shaken. The can hissed quietly and then went silent. He took a pull from the can and noticed the cashier was staring wide eyed at the lottery terminal.

The word WINNER was scrolling across the display in red LED. He leaned over the counter.

"What, I won something?" He secretly hoped for a few hundred dollars. That would see them nicely through Christmas this year. He didn't know anyone who had won more than a few thousand dollars in the lotto, and that was some retired fisherman a couple years back that hadn't even needed the money. A month later that same fisherman had gone fishing with his buddies, and in front of his friends, had clutched his chest and keeled overboard, and went straight to the bottom. His body was never recovered, and the Coroners' office had only concluded that he had suffered from a major heart attack and had probably been dead before he hit the water.

The cashier nodded, but didn't look at him.

"Good, how much?"

The day had taken a nice turn. He couldn't wait to tell Mel about it. And Cutter. See if he grunted about that.

"The whole thing…" the sentence died in the air as she obviously meant to say more but forgot what she was going to say. She licked her lips once.

"What do you mean, the whole thing?" He felt his stomach rise, as hope suddenly crawled deep into his belly. The cashier turned to him, sliding the ticket face down into the terminal where it began to print a series of numbers along the backside.

"You won the jackpot."

He felt the blood drain from his face in two quick heartbeats.

"Wha...," he croaked out before his mind shut down.

The cashier withdrew the ticket from the register, and folded it into his open palm.

"You need to take the ticket to the lottery center to be claimed. The terminal has already told them the ticket was validated, so they will be expecting someone. Keep it safe. Congratulations!"

She had smiled warmly at him, sincerely glad to be the bearer of his good fortune. He had stood there numbly for a minute while his brain tried to accept what his body already knew. He felt like he was going to throw up, cheer, cry and laugh all at the same time. A fellow standing behind him, oblivious to the event unfolding before him, muttered aloud, "Hey mister, do ya' mind? I'm in a rush here."

The cashier had grabbed Archie by the shoulder as he stood there.

"Should I call someone for you? You gonna be okay?"

Archie was coming out of his stupor, and nodded.

"Yeah I think I am okay. Thanks."

He broke out into a broad grin.

"Have a good day."

He turned about and ran to the work truck, his hand shaking so bad it took four tries to get the key into the ignition. He let the van run for a minute as he leaned his head back against the seat. He felt he could barely contain the emotion he was experiencing, and he was terrified that any second he was going to wake up in his bed from this wonderful dream. He pinched himself hard, and then shook his arm as he winced from the pain. Convinced, he had driven back to the shop. Cutter had looked up as he entered the shop.

"Wha'choo doin' back already? You ain't done yet."

Archie had placed his work orders down on the desk, with the van keys on top of the paperwork.

"I quit. Effective immediately."

Cutters eyes had bulged from his sockets.

"Whaddya mean, you quit? These people need work done!"

His fat finger stabbed the paperwork.

"Well it won't be done by me. Have a good day, Cutter."

As he turned to walk out, he saw Cutter's face go a deep shade of red, and he spluttered out "You can't quit you sunnuvabitch! Just you wait! You finish these jobs you shithead!"

Whatever else Cutter had said as the door chimed shut behind him, he didn't hear it. He had quickly got into his car, and drove home as cautiously as he could. He was taking no chances. He had pulled into the driveway, and walked through the front door. Mel came from the kitchen to investigate the sound.

"What are you doing home already?"

Her face turned from surprise to worry, as possibilities crossed into her mind.

"Oh my god, tell me your weren't fired; you didn't lose your job did you?"

He strode towards her, and he watched as her face turned from worry to curiosity as he saw his face; he was grinning from ear to ear like the Cheshire cat. He pulled her close to him and kissed her, and then broke away. He pulled the lottery ticket from his pocket and held it in the air. Her eyes went to it, and then went back to him. He saw hope glow in her eyes.

He nodded twice.

"We won the jackpot Mel, we won it!"

She screamed, and threw her arms around him, burying her face into his neck, knowing he would never play a practical joke like this; not after what they had gone through. And then she began to sob, in deep braying racks of emotion. All of her fears had come to a head and were being forever expelled. The nights of lying awake wondering how they were going to buy gas for the car, or milk and clothes for the kids, or the utility bills, and rent, all of those terrible memories were brought to the surface and exorcised. He held her close, understanding her reaction. He cried himself, burying his face into her hair, inhaling her scent and finding comfort in it. After a few minutes, she had pulled away from him, her eyes wet and red, her hands shaking, and they had kissed. They kissed as they had when they were younger, before they had children and bills and all of the weights and responsibilities of adulthood.

"Mommy what's going on?"

They heard some water splashing from upstairs.

"Is daddy home?"

Stephanie was having a bath and heard the excitement coming from downstairs.

"Yes I'm home, Steph."

"Can you wash my hair now? I want out."

"I'll be right there. Just play for a minute, okay?"

"Okay."

The splashing resumed.

They had hugged tightly, wiped the tears from their eyes, and made their plans. They finished giving Steph her bath, and then Archie had a quick shower as Mel got Steph dressed. The three of them had got into the car, and drove to pick up Charlie from school.

"Daddy, what's going on?"

Steph was looking at him from the rear view mirror. She was plainly aware that something was going on, something unusual. Archie had reached over and squeezed Mel's hand tightly.

"I don't have to work anymore, kiddo. We won the lottery."

"Oh," Steph replied. She didn't know what the lottery was, but it sounded like it meant daddy was going to be home more, so that was good.

The three of them had gone into the school office, where Archie had requested Charlie be pulled from school for the day. The secretary had inquired as to the reason for her absenteeism report.

"We have had some good family news and we are going to celebrate."

She had given a look that requested more information. None was apparently forthcoming, so she excused herself and went to his class. Minutes later the four of them were walking out to the car.

"What's going on Dad?

Mel had tousled his hair.

"We won the lottery Charlie, so we are going to celebrate."

"Oh, cool." Charlie didn't know what the lottery was either, but if it got him out of school, then it must be a good thing.

They drove to the lottery center at the other side of town, and had surrendered their ticket to the registrar behind the counter, and the let the corporate machine take over. While they waited in a backroom, the ticket was verified for authenticity, validated, inspected for fraud, and then certified to be genuine. They were given coffee and soda and donuts while they waited patiently; the kids were happy with the rare treat of junk food and pop, while Archie and Mel had simply waited for the verification to be completed, knowing that it was inevitable. An hour later, the registrar and a very friendly PR representative named Harry Jones had walked into the room.

He was all smiles, and dressed professionally. Highly polished black shoes, a black suit with subtle pin striping, and his hair combed back with Brylcreem. He offered his hand in congratulations as Mel and Archie had stood up. He had pumped each hand twice, with a firm dry grip.

"Congratulations, Mr. and Mrs. Buchanen. On behalf of the Australian Lottery Commission, it is my pleasure to inform you that you indeed are the sole winners of the most recent draw of Friday, November sixteenth, for the sum of forty four million, one hundred and sixty seven thousand dollars."

Archie and Mel had grinned at each other, feeling as though their faces would split open. Their eyes again flooded with tears. Harry had looked at them and smiled.

"Has it sunk in yet?"

"Not yet." Mel chuckled.

"But it's starting to." She wiped her tears away.

"Of course, I understand. It will take time. Before we go any further I need you to go over these documents and sign them when you are ready. If you have any questions, we have an attorney available to you."

He gestured behind him. The fellow that was presumably the attorney nodded once in affirmation. Archie and Mel nodded back.

"Here are some pens. Let us know when you are done, or if you need anything."

They had spent the next few hours reading the agreements. As they had predicted, it was the usual stuff. The lottery had full permission to advertise their winnings for endorsement purposes, they had to have their photo taken with the prize check, they had to decide where the money was to be deposited, et cetera. When they were ready, they had signed along the bottom with Harry and his attorney signing and witnessing the document as well. They had placed the pens on the desk, while the lawyer filed the contracts away into his briefcase, and then shut it with two sharp clicks.

"You are welcome to keep the pens, if you wish. They are good souvenirs."

Harry handed them to Mel, who had smiled and placed them inside her purse.

"Would you like to have your photographs taken now?"

They had agreed, and with the kids watching from behind the photographer, they were handed a large plastic check from Harry Jones, and they posed for the picture. When they had taken a picture they were satisfied with, they had been led into another back office, where they were introduced to Margaret Spencer, a tiny lady in her mid-forties who was wearing a blue dress and a delicate silver necklace. She took their banking information with a voided check, and had made a phone call to their bank informing the branch manager of the rather large wired deposit that they would be receiving within the next twenty four hours, into the account of Mr. and Mrs. Archie Buchanen. The transaction was completed via computer, and discussed over speakerphone so that all parties were witness to the conversation. The branch manager, Steven Wilcox, extended his heartfelt congratulations to Archie and Mel, and expressed his hopes that they would soon meet to go over options he could offer to invest in their winnings. His voice was quite deep, and Archie painted a mental picture of him based on it. When everything was finally complete, the kids at this point bored to tears, and Charlie wondering if the day at school might have been a better option after all, they were walked to the front door by Harry Jones.

"Please let me know immediately if there is anything I can help you with or anything I can do for you."

"We will, Harry. Thanks for everything."

"You're welcome. Have a great day, and do try to get some sleep tonight."

They had laughed, and Harry had waved them good-bye as they drove from the parking lot. And then the celebration began. By this time the family was starving as it was nearing dinner time, and the most they had eaten hours earlier was their donuts and beverages. Their bodies were screaming for solid food. They had pulled into Walters Steakhouse, a higher end steak and seafood restaurant that they had saved for rare occasions when they had some extra money to blow. They were seated at their table by a brunette named Nancy, who took their drink order. Charlie and Steph wanted root beers, Archie ordered a pint of Guiness, and Mel a strawberry daiquiri. Archie looked at the kids and told them they could order anything they wanted on the menu.

He had smiled as he saw their eyes glow, his heart swelling with happiness seeing their joy.

"I want ice cream," Steph had declared.

Mel had laughed.

"You can have ice cream after you have some real food."

"Okay." Content with the deal, and the promise of ice cream afterwards, she returned to the menu.

Charlie placed his menu on the table and proclaimed that he was having the lobster platter. This time Archie laughed.

"Alright Charlie. Whatever you don't eat we will bring home tonight."

"No way Dad, I'll eat it all; I'm starving."

"Okay, we'll see."

Charlie nodded.

Nancy returned to the table with their drinks in tow, and introduced them to their waitress and she placed the drinks in front of them.

"Charlotte will be your waitress this evening, thank you," and Nancy had strolled towards the kitchen.

"Hi everyone, how are you doing tonight?" Charlotte asked. The kids muttered they were fine as they sipped their rootbeers.

"We're fine," Archie replied.

"Are you ready to order?"

Archie looked around the table, and received three nods.

"I guess so. You go first, Charlie."

Charlie had crossed his hands in front of him.

"I'm having the lobster platter."

"With rice or pasta?" Charlotte inquired.

Charlie frowned.

"Rice!" he exclaimed, preferring the first thing that popped into his head.

"Okay, steamed vegetables or salad?"

He frowned again. This was more complicated than he thought.

"Salad!"

"Caesar or tossed?"

He let his head hit the table.

"What do we have at home, Mom?"

"Tossed, Charlie."

"Tossed!" he replied to Charlotte. She smiled and turned to Stephanie.

"And what do you want?"

"I want a cheeseburger and fries, please."

"Okay, cheeseburger and fries."

Charlie mumbled under his breath how unfair it was that her order so easy.

"And you, ma'am?"

Melanie had decided on a steak sandwich, medium rare, with a side of mushrooms and Bermuda onions, and a lemon prawn kebob.

Archie had noticed with admiration that Charlotte was taking their order with no notepad.

"And you, Sir?"

I will have the Seafood platter on rice with the tossed salad with whatever the house dressing is."

"Raspberry vinaigrette okay?"

"Sounds fine."

"Okay. Thank you for your order."

She collected the menus and went toward the kitchen. He heard her calling the order to the kitchen. While their food was being prepared they shared simple conversation and enjoyed the company of his family. He was going to charge this meal, and pay it off as soon as the received their deposit.

Before long, Charlotte brought out their dinners, her left bicep bulging holding their food as she handed out their plates with her right arm.

"The Lobster platter for you."

Charlie's eyes bulged as he saw the size of the meal on his plate.

"Cheeseburger and fries for you."

Steph followed the plate as it was placed before her, and quickly began to douse the fries with ketchup.

"Your steak sandwich."

Mel received the plate from Charlotte's outstretched hand.

"That looks fantastic."

"And your Seafood platter. Is there anything else I can get for you?"

"No thank you," Archie replied.

"Enjoy your dinner!"

Charlotte left the table, and for the next few minutes the table was utterly silent except for the sounds of knives and forks at work.

When the meal was complete, all four of them sat with their backs to the benches, the full stomachs gurgling and churning. The kids were dozing they were so full, and the concept of dessert had vanished. Even Steph had said she was too full for ice cream. They had paid their bill and left Charlotte a handsome tip, and drove home. The kids had fallen asleep during the car ride, and were carried to their beds without stirring.

Archie and Mel had lain in bed after locking up for the evening, and as Harry had predicted, could hardly sleep.

The next day broke early, as soon as the sun was up Archie had got out of bed, getting rid of the pretext that he might get some more sleep. Although they were tired, they were still rested, the vast majority of their concerns having evaporated the day before. While the kids were still asleep they showered and then prepared breakfast. Mel had logged into their bank account on their computer, and shrieked quickly.

"Archie come here."

He came around the corner, rubbing his eye with one hand with a mug of coffee in the other.

"What is it?"

She pointed to the screen.

He bent over and squinted, his eyes adjusting the brightness of the monitor.

"Holy geez," he whispered. Their winnings had been deposited during the night. Mel had her hands to her face. The number on the screen was huge.

Although they knew how much forty-four million dollars was, it looked even bigger now that it was actually there. He turned to Mel, and she had quickly hugged him. Looking down at her, he saw her looking up at him, and he instantly knew what she was thinking. Before long, they had undressed frantically and they made love right there on the living room floor, mindful to be quiet so as to not wake up the kids. They had both cried out when they were done, and they relaxed on the floor, chuckling afterwards at the spontaneity of the moment. They redressed, and began to call their family.

Later in the day, they went to the bank to meet the branch manager and to get some checks made. On the way, he had turned to Mel.

"If it wasn't for the kid at the store, I never would have bought the ticket. It's only right I help him out."

He told her how he had reminded him when he was at the till. Mel had simply shrugged in the end.

"If it will make you feel good." And so it was settled. They walked into the bank, as inconspicuous a pair of millionaires as there ever was. They both were wearing jeans and tee-shirts and sandals. Stephanie was towing behind her mother in a flowery sundress in her favorite Barbie slippers. Charlie was back in school for the day. They patiently stood in line, and asked the teller to speak to the manager. He had come out a few minutes later, calmly, and introduced himself.

"Hello, I'm Steven Wilcox. Can I help you?"

Archie was expecting a short, bald man with a portly figure. Steven instead was well over six feet tall, athletic, probably two hundred pounds, maybe two twenty, with a full head of black hair, graying at the sides. Archie smiled. So much for his mental picture.

"Yes we spoke yesterday." Archie extended his hand.

Steven frowned in concentration as he shook, trying to recall everyone he had spoken to in the previous day.

"Archie and Melanie Buchanen."

His eyes unconsciously widened.

"Mr. and Mrs. Buchanen! Very nice to meet you. I wasn't expecting to see you so quickly."

The teller abdicated to his position as he slowly pushed her aside.

"How can I help you? Forgive me! Please meet me in my office!"

He indicated a path for them to follow, and they followed him into his office. They sat down in a few fabric chairs that were within the room.

"Now then, how can I help?"

"We are going to be making some purchases over the next few days and I was wondering how we might best arrange for them?" Archie asked.

Steven nodded.

"Of course, what purchases were you planning on making?"

An hour later, they left the bank with a book of checks, an immense line of credit, and the whole day in front of them. Their first stop was a local car dealership that was festooned with balloons and neon painted signs on the showroom glass, proclaiming the great deals and selection to be had within, financing options, and a gas card for two hundred dollars with any new car. They had pulled into the lot and parked near a row of service bays. The sun was already high in the blue sky, and they had both donned a pair of sunglasses as they walked from their car into the lot. Archie walked slightly ahead of Mel, who was inspecting the cars she was walking past.

"Are we looking for anything in particular?" Archie asked.

Mel had paused for a few moments before replying.

"Mmm nope. Just something new. And not white, brown, or green. With lots of room for us."

Archie nodded.

"So a minivan, then?" He looked around the car lot. Either no one had seen them yet, or the sales staff at this dealership wasn't particularly aggressive. He didn't even see anyone yet except for a lot boy that didn't seem to be doing anything too productive.

"Yep, I don't want an SUV. Bad for the environment, and all that."

Archie nodded again.

"No SUV's." Currently the row of vehicles they were in were all SUV's. A bit further up he could see the next selection was cars and sedans.

" I think we are in the wrong section." He stopped to wait for Mel to catch up, and then they walked together. A few minutes later, the row of cars gave way to reveal rows of minivans and a few cargo vans.

"Ah hah. Bingo."

They stopped to look into the passenger side window of the first one in the row, shielding the glare off the glass with their hands over their foreheads.

"Beautiful morning isn't it?"

The salesman had seemingly materialized from nowhere, and from behind them. They both gave a start. Mel had turned around while Archie continued to look for a moment longer into the van.

"Yes it is," Mel had replied, "Going to be a scorcher today."

Archie turned around. The salesman had extended his hand to Mel first.

"Indeed. Nice to meet you both, I'm Dan."

Mel had taken his hand and shook quickly.

"Mel, and my husband Archie."

She had nodded in his direction. Dan had then shook quickly with Archie.

"Mel and Archie. Alright, how can I help you two today?"

Dans' grip was smooth and strong, Archie noted. He was dressed business casual, a white button up dress shirt buttoned up one short of the neck, creased black pants and highly polished black leather shoes that clicked on the ground when he took a step.

"My wife is looking for a minivan."

Dan had quickly and smartly averted his attention to Mel.

"Okay great. Are you looking for anything in particular? In dash DVD for the kids?"

He let the question hang in the air for a moment to see if he got a bite.

"Yes, we have two. Boy and girl."

Dan nodded quickly in acknowledgment, and continued his questions.

An hour later, they were driving off the parking lot in their new red minivan, compete with in-dash DVD screens, Captains seats, and a myriad of other options that seemed nice, but that they would probably never use. When Dan had introduced them to his sales manager to discuss their loan options, it was with a certain degree of smugness that

JEREMY HENDERSON

they had informed him that they would be paying for the van with a check. Dan had taken the news in stride, barely missing a beat and being cautious to not screw up his easiest sale of the month by showing surprise that they would be paying for the vehicle outright. He had been in sales long enough to have learned to not pre-judge his customers, ever. When it was all done, he had passed them their keys, shaken their hands again, and rather pleasantly thanked them for their business. He had even waved at them as they had driven off the lot, leaving their old car behind as a trade-in. They had returned his wave, riding the wave of euphoria of just having purchased their first new vehicle ever, and with a check. It was theirs free and clear. They both couldn't help but smile as they drove off down the road. Their next stop was the corner market where Archie had bought the winning ticket. They had pulled over to the curb, with Archie trying to see into the store to see if Hector was working. A large sign advertising Hogan's Pepperoni blocked the view of the register, and the glare off the glass obscured the rest of the store except for a few racks of soda off to the side, and a magazine rack. With Mel deciding to wait in the van, Archie had gone towards the store with the intention of seeing when Hector was working next. As luck had turned out, Archie had rounded the corner opposite the store, and he saw Hector walking up the opposite street towards the market. Looking left and then right to check the traffic, Archie ran across quickly without waiting for the crosswalk to turn green. Safely across, he walked towards Hector, who was glancing around, but not really paying attention to anything in particular.

Archie kept walking and when they finally made eye contact, he waved at him quickly. Hector had stopped in his tracks and frowned, thinking about why this guy had just waved at him. He couldn't think of any reason, so he simply waited as he walked quickly towards him.

"Help you?" he asked quizzically as Archie stopped in front of him, suddenly concerned he was about to be robbed in broad daylight. Archie had put out his hand, and Hector had replied as a matter of politeness, not recognition.

"I came into the store on the block there a few days ago and you helped me out," he said, motioning behind him with a closed fist and outstretched thumb in the general direction of the market. Hector had

32

looked over his shoulder towards the market, and nodded slightly.

"Okay." Hector was getting concerned. Who was this nut that just approached him on the street? Maybe he wasn't going to get mugged, but it was still unusual. Didn't he know how many people he saw in a day? Jeeesus. He sure didn't recognize this guy.

Archie saw Hector's eyes glaze over.

"Look, you don't remember me obviously, but don't be afraid, I'm not some kind of a nut or anything."

Hector nodded slighty, either in agreement that he didn't remember him or that he thought he was a nut, but Archie couldn't tell.

"I have to get to work mister, if you'll just excuse me...," and Hector tried to go around him quickly to the right, dropping his eye contact. Archie stepped to the left to block him, and Hector had backed one step back.

"You're starting to freak me out, whoever you are."

"Okay I know, just give me one minute; that's all I ask, and then I will get out of your way. Deal?" Hector nodded, and mentally began to count down his one minute before he intended to scream for help.

"A few days ago I came here, or to that store, after work and you were the cashier." Hector nodded. He was always the cashier.

"I got a few things and you reminded me about the lottery, because my bill came to fourteen dollars even, and you said that was weird so I should get a ticket."

Hector nodded slightly. He did kind of remember that. He usually saw only one or two customers a day that had an even bill, and so he tended to remember that more so than the rest of his shift. Anything to help pass the boredom. Archie saw a brief flicker of recognition cross his face.

"Anyway, I bought the ticket, and I won."

Hector frowned again.

"Won what?"

Archie smiled at the recollection.

"I won the jackpot. Forty four million dollars, and I am here to thank you personally."

He fished into his jacket pocket, while Hector watched. He drew out a sealed envelope, and handed it to him. Hector extended his right hand, and slowly took the envelope from him, and then began to open it with a few quick tears down the side of the seal. He looked into the envelope, and his eyes bulged in their sockets, and his mouth fell open. He had looked around quickly, and looked back into the envelope to make sure he wasn't hallucinating. His mouth had gone as dry as sandpaper, and the envelope had begun to shake in his hands. There were a lot of zeroes inside that envelope. He counted them. Six zeroes. He was looking at a check for one million dollars. He felt a cold sweat break out over his body, in spite of the early afternoon heat. Hector had looked up to see Archie smiling at him. Struggling to get his mouth working, he croaked out, "Why?"

Archie had simply shrugged.

"I caught a lucky break listening to you, and so I am paying it forward. I needed a break and got it, and I figure it's only right to give you a break. Call it karma if you like."

Hector nodded, feeling his eyes begin to water.

"Are you going to be okay? Do you want a ride home or anything?"

Hector had stood there, his hands clenched to the envelope that he suddenly feared might get blown out of his hands.

"No, I'll be okay. Thank you. That's all I can say. Thank you."

Archie nodded, feeling like he himself was about to burst.

"You're welcome, Hector."

He had patted him quickly on his shoulder, and then turned back towards the van. He had crossed the street and looked back quickly, to see Hector walking away from the store, his right hand shoving an envelope deep into his right pocket as he hailed a taxi. He got into the van, and exhaled deeply as he sat back into the chair.

"Did you find him? You were gone a longer than I expected," Mel said.

He had looked over at her, and told her what had happened. She had smiled, and kissed him quickly.

"That was a kind thing to do. You totally changed his life with that, and you didn't have to." He had looked towards her.

"I didn't have to do it, but it was the right thing to do." Mel smiled and nodded. "Now what?"

They ended up spending the next three days buying a home and furnishing it, taking countless trips to local stores finding what they wanted for each room. They had originally thought about getting a house built, but had instead settled on an existing home that wad been recently been put up for sale. It was modest in the sense that they could have purchased far more with their sudden wealth, but still extravagant for what they were used to.

The kids each had their own room, the backyard came with a large swimming pool, tiled with stonework that led from their hot tub to the back entrance of the home. The master bedroom was larger than their previous home, with a fully equipped ensuite bathroom, huge his and hers closets, and a sunken floor. They had found it by chance the evening after making Hector an instant millionaire. They were taking the kids for an evening drive in their new van, driving along the coastline when he had heard Steph make an *ooooooo* sound from the back seat.

"What is it, kiddo?" he had asked.

"Look at that house, Daddy. It's beautiful."

They had slowed the van down to see where she was pointing. The front of the home was all cut stone and tile work, with the front entrance a granite archway overhanging a stained wood door. The front yard was full of mature trees and bushes, a shock of deep green surrounded by stone and masonry. And the Pacific Ocean loomed in the background as far as the eye could see, a deep blue giant to the horizon. The front of the driveway was punctuated with a black iron lantern.

"Is that like the lantern in Narnia?" Steph asked wonderingly.

Melanie had smiled instantly. "I think so Steph. It sure looks like it, doesn't it?"

"Uh huh," Steph replied, her small mouth open in admiration of the lantern. They had next noticed the realtors sign tucked off to a corner of the driveway, partially obscured by a thickly grown palm. Mel had taken down the number and called it when they got home later that evening.

They had viewed the house the next afternoon, made an offer that evening, and had signed the purchase agreement two days later. They had paid by check, and taken receipt of the deed a day later. That evening, they had barbecued in the backyard, hearing the murmur of crashing waves, the crying of gulls, the ocean breeze rustling through their yard. They had expected the kids to be running around enjoying the open space, but instead, they had sat in their chairs staring out at the open ocean as they ate, their eyes wide as if trying to take it all in. Bunker sat below them, hopeful for a crumb to fall his way.

The following week was a frenzy of furnishing their home, getting their estate in order, and letting the new facts of life settle in. Archie had purchased a new Washburn acoustic guitar at a local music store. It had a polished ebony wood surface, and gleamed darkly in the showroom window.

The neck had been inlaid with real mother of pearl and caught the light in its silvery hue. He had walked into the store and strolled around, just looking for something that caught his eye quite like the one in the window. None did. He went to the counter and enquired politely to a well-bearded man that looked like a younger version of Santa Claus with black hair. He was wearing faded denims and a black t-shirt festooned with a spread-eagled blonde on an iron-on decal that was beginning to peel off the shirt at the edges.

"What can you tell me about the guitar in the window? The black one?"

He introduced himself to be Sam, with a voice that sounded like it belonged on the radio, a clear catchy DJ voice. The name fit him like a glove.

"Electric or Acoustic?"

"Err," he stammered, "What's the difference?"

Sam had snickered.

"Dude, there's a world of difference. What kind of sound do you like?"

Archie had put out a look that resembled a deer caught in headlights.

"Stay here, I'll be right back."

Sam had made his way out from behind the counter, turning sideways to fit through a hinged section of the counter that pulled up. He returned with the two black guitars from the front window. He sat himself on a chrome stool with a black leather seat emblazoned with *Nazareth* in a gothic script, and decorated with a few white skulls. Setting the first guitar around his shoulder, he had closed his eyes, started to bob his head to a beat in his mind, and played it masterfully. Archie couldn't help but be impressed, and a more that a little envious. He had a great singing voice, and paired with the guitar, he was evidently very talented. Sam had finished his tune, and picked up the second guitar, the one that had first caught his eye.

"Now remember what you heard first," and he began to play the second guitar. It was the same song, but the difference was instantly noticeable. The notes were a lot richer, less crisp but with better tones. Sam slapped his hand down across the strings to end the song abruptly.

"Now, what'll it be?"

He had pointed across the counter.

"That one."

Sam nodded.

He climbed off the stool.

"You ever play before?" He stopped and put up his hand.

"Forget the question."

Archie had smiled sheepishly, somewhat embarrassed about his obvious lack of musical training.

"You played long?" he asked Sam.

"Only since I was six," he replied.

"My mum was on my case when I was little. Too hyper, y'know. I always seemed to be getting into trouble, breaking things, doing things without thinking about consequences. His breathing was a little wheezy, but clear enough. One day she came home with a piece of shit instrument and I was hooked. I spent every waking moment on that guitar, and I still have it. Now, let's get you some basics before the man that made this rolls over in his grave." After getting some pointers on the guitar, they picked up probably every accessory that was ever made for one. He paid in cash, and spent the next few hours in the store becoming familiar with his purchase. He sat on a stool in the corner of the store, off the main track of the store in between a few accessory racks. While he sat there and played, he watched a younger fellow walk in the store and head to a rack of guitars leaning against the far wall. He was dressed in business casual with a white cotton shirt and black slacks, complete with leather shoes that gleamed in the lights. Archie watched him, expecting to see another version of himself do an injustice to the instrument. He had picked up the guitar, adjusted its position on his chest, and belted out a guitar solo that had Archie ogle in admiration. When he was done, he put the guitar back on the rack casually and went to the counter, shaking Sams' hand and paying for a few boxes of picks. They spent several minutes in quiet conversation before he left the counter. He walked past Archie on the way out of the store, and he stopped before he left.

"Sam is a great teacher, just don't get frustrated. Practice and then practice some more. He can make it look too easy." He wished him luck and left the building, the door chime jingling faintly as the doors shut. With firm resolve, he had spent another hour on it, with limited though gradual success. His biggest problem was his fingers were too weak to hold the strings tightly, so his notes were a little soft, and before long his fingers and hands hurt like hell. He had strung the guitar with new Black Diamond chords, getting Billy, the resident musical savant, to string and tune the guitar. They had cut into his uncalloused fingertips, leaving a deep red line in his flesh. The guitar had a deep rich sound that was magical, the notes pure and deep, when he hit the proper note. Still, it was pretty hard to strum a guitar and make a crappy sound. He had practiced for an hour a day, getting one on one tutoring with Sam from the guitar store, until his finger tips nearly bled, working as his fingers ached and grew stronger. Sam often played another instrument to accompany the guitar, to mix the sounds differently.

"Is there any instrument you don't play?" he had asked during one session when Sam had played a small baby piano.

Sam had thought about it for a moment. "I can't play flutes or trumpets." He thumped on his chest.

"Asthma."

His favorite songs to practice were classic AC/DC, music he had grown up on. The chords to *Who Made Who,* and *For Those About to Rock* struggled to break free of the guitar and waft through the house. Once the holiday season was over he was going to get longer lessons and see what that guitar could do. In the meantime, he took pleasure in small victories, one note and one verse at a time.

Mel spent her time on the garden, her hands deep in the black soil of the garden as the heat from summer gradually intensified. Her skin reddened and then tanned, even with a generous application of sunscreen, its white film fading to nothingness, surrendering to the hot tropical sun. She spent hours in the yard, tilling weeds, planting, and pruning, and came in periodically to rehydrate with another tall glass of iced tea, and to apply yet more sunscreen. When not in the garden, she had shopped for the perfect accessories of their home. Paintings, mirrors, small tables with curved iron wrought legs, whatever suited the grand scheme in her mind of how her house would look. Archie stepped aside and took no small pleasure in watching her fill their home. Local antique stores became her favorite haunting ground, and she also visited more than her fair share of yard sales and estate auctions. They fell into that rhythm, gardening, shopping, and guitar practice and the next few weeks sped by with abandon and newfound freedom.

On December Tenth they decided to go on vacation. They had woken up in bed that fine glorious morning, stretched, and the idea had popped into his head.

"We should go on a vacation. A good, long family vacation. Away from everything." He turned over to see Mel considering the idea.

"Like what?" she asked.

"I don't know for sure. Some kind of resort where the kids have a pool to play in and we can go snorkeling and fishing and go on a tour boat. Something like that. Something all-inclusive."

"Okay," she said. It was decided as simply as that. After breakfast, he had scoured the internet for a few resorts off the coast that seemed to offer what he had in mind. He had found a charter resort just north of Brisbane located on Fraser Island, a narrow spit of land just south of the Great Barrier Reef.

He had reviewed the site and showed it to Mel.

"There, look at this one. South Australis Resort." He reviewed the listing out loud, as if she couldn't read them.

"Five Star resort, all-inclusive with fishing, boat charters, pools, playgrounds. It's got everything."

"Fine. Book it then."

He had looked up at her. "You are making this too easy."

"Do you want me to tell you to look at other ones first?"

"Well…no. Not really."

"Then book it."

So he booked the trip for two weeks, from December sixteenth to the twenty-ninth. Fourteen days of fun and pampering. The kids were excited, any kind of vacation was still a vacation, and they had reacted to the news by running around the house and yard laughing and screaming until they had finally collapsed on the kitchen floor, panting and giggling weakly. They had allowed themselves two days to make the drive, plenty of time to not worry about making good time or not being able to stop a catch a few points of interest if they should cross any. Once in Noosa Heads, they would park the van in the Charter lot, and take a boat trip from Hervey Bay across the narrow strait of sea to the resort.

He finally decided to pass the tanker, getting tired of having other cars pull in between him and the truck as they leap-frogged through traffic. He pulled back, keeping his eye clear on the rear view mirrors. He looked out the drivers window to see down the highway. All clear, he thought, and pressed on the accelerator. The van picked up speed and shortly was passing by the tanker, the glare of the bright chrome partially blinding him for a few seconds as it caught the suns' reflection. He pulled back into his lane, and reset the cruise control, the open highway before him.

The family had slept for the rest of the trip as he drove, including the dog. As he pulled into Noosa Heads, the sound of the vehicle slowing down roused Mel first, who shifted in her seat, and then sat upright, putting her legs back down from the dash.

"Are we there yet?" she mumbled.

"Oh God; not you, too. It's bad enough with the kids saying that."

She looked back where they were still dozing lightly.

"By the looks of things, they haven't said much of anything."

"True enough. Not even Bunker kept me company." His ears perked up at the sound of his name.

"Didn't you, dog?" He reached back and rubbed his ears.

"Well, we are almost here now anyways. Let the vacation begin!" He took a deep breath.

"Kids!" he shouted. Steph woke with a start, Charlie blinked hard.

"Wake up! We're almost there so it's time to get up."

"Can we eat? I'm hungry," said Steph, sitting forwards and rubbing her eyes.

"Yep we have time. Our boat doesn't show up a couple of hours yet."

At the hint of food, Charlie appeared motivated to wake up, although slowly, staring out the side window with a slumbering look.

They pulled off the highway into the Charter lot, a fenced compound laced with barbed wire at the top of the fences, and a manned gate complete with video cameras and a sliding gate. Seeing the vehicle pulling in, the guard at the post stepped outside of his booth and waited for Archie to pull up to the curb, a clipboard in hand.

"Good afternoon, Sir. Ma'am. Identification, please."

Archie nodded and searched for his wallet, finding it semi-buried under a loose pile of food wrappings and an unfolded travel map. He produced his license and handed it out the window.

"Thank you. A moment, please."

The guard walked back into his booth and began entering something into his terminal at the top of the desk, while also flipping through the clipboard.

"Jesus, I didn't think we had booked a vacation at Fort Knox," he mumbled under his breath. Mel punched him on the shoulder.

"He's just doing his job. If he wasn't doing this you'd be worried the entire time we were there that someone had stolen the van."

Archie nodded, agreeing with her in hindsight.

"Do you think he'll want fingerprints?" he asked with a smile.

He got another shoulder punch.

"Now you're being an asshole," and they both laughed.

The guard came back to the van.

"Here you are, Mr. Buchanen. The Charter doesn't arrive for another couple of hours so you have some time to do some sight seeing or catch a meal. There is food on the boat but some folks like to catch the local fare."

"We were planning on it. What do you recommend?"

"If you like burgers and things like that, there is a good burger joint a few blocks up on the left. You passed the only pizza place about a block past us here, and there is a fancier place about a kilometer up the way, run by a couple of Germans that retired here a few years back."

"Okay thanks."

"Don't mention it. You can park in stall 14-F. Just drive forward and

41

take the right lane. You can't miss it. When the boat pulls in we will help you unload your luggage from your vehicle and load it onboard."

"Thanks for your help." Archie drove forward slowly, waving with a quick one sweep salute as he drove through the gate, the fencing retracting with a faint electrical humming. The gate began to close behind them.

"Well guys, what'll it be? Burgers, pizza? The fancy German joint?"

Both kids shouted in unison. "Burgers!"

"Mel?"

"Burgers are fine. I'm sure I can find something else on the menu a little healthier."

"Burgers it is, by majority decision."

He pulled into the stall, in between a Rolls Royce and a Mercedes Benz.

Looking around, he noticed all of the vehicles here were similar.

"Holy cow. We must stick out like a sore thumb in this thing," referring to the van.

Mel looked at him.

"What does this place cost for two weeks, exactly?"

Archie found an excuse to look at something more interesting lying on the floor mat as he replied.

"Um, enough."

"What do you mean, *enough*?"

He winced.

"Enough that we can afford it now, so don't worry. If I told you I would have to kill you, and that would kind of wreck the vacation now, wouldn't it?"

He opened the door, feeling his legs unbind as he stood. He couldn't help but yawn and stretch as he felt his legs loosen up.

Taking the cue she wouldn't easily get more information from him, Mel also stepped outside, and slid open the side door to let the kids and Bunker out.

Bunker hopped down gingerly, and promptly urinated on the back tire of the Rolls.

"See, honey? It's just a car!" and he laughed while the dog finished his business.

Mel shook her head.

"Let's just hope the owners don't come back anytime soon."

"Fair enough. Let's do lunch."

They found the burger place quite enjoyable, with a menu that even Mel appreciated with a variety of salads and other less fattening fare that filled the rest of the menu. The kids ate their fill and a short while later they were walking down the beach off the side of the highway towards the Charter launch. The sea had a stiff breeze flowing inland that lowered the air temperature by several degrees. Steph had kept a bag of her leftover fries and was throwing them into the air to the waiting gulls, who were floating in the wind above them like a series of white and black kites. Off shore, the waves were breaking into small whitecaps, the sea a dark blue fringed with bright white foam that washed ashore and collected into a bubbly mat on the coral sand.

"Is that ours?"

Archie turned to look out to sea where she was facing. A ship was breaking waves coming from the north parallel to the beach.

"It could be. She is big enough."

"She? Are you a sailor now?"

"Everyone knows boats are called 'she'. I'm just using the proper lingo."

"Why are boats called 'she' Daddy?" Steph asked.

"I have no idea, Steph. You can ask the Captain when we get on board, if you like."

They watched the ship come closer to shore, and it did indeed look like that was their charter. It would be right on time and was heading in the right direction. The ship was beautiful and made for cruising in the ocean, its deep V hull easily cutting through the waves and keeping her stable in rougher seas. They picked up their pace to make it to the marina with time to spare.

"That's our boat gang; let's hurry up and beat it to the wharf!"

They ran the rest of the way to the Charter yard, the kids giggling as they went, Archie and Mel making sure to give their kids the illusion that they were the faster runners. When they reached the docks, they sat on a row of benches and watched the yacht come to port, the ship taking a wide turn to starboard and then coming straight in to the wharf, correcting for the waves and drift as she went. When she was closer, her name became apparent, the Ave Maria, painted in a subtle calligraphy script. The crew brought here closer to the wharf under power, and then cut the engines, and the ship kissed the wharf, coming to a stop with a gentle nudge. Two crewmembers tossed ropes across the side, and they were tied to the docks by some waiting representatives.

"There she is guys. Quite the boat, isn't it?"

"Isn't *She*, Daddy," Steph corrected him.

He tousled her hair and she squealed and quickly ran her hands through her hair to straighten out the mess he had created.

"You're right, isn't *she*."

The Ave Maria was one hundred feet long; a two-year-old vessel immaculately maintained and designed to cater to every whim on a short trip. Her only excursions were out to the Island with perhaps the occasional day trip or two once at the Island itself, and so she was equipped to handle more short-term items. They watched as a few couples disembarked, shaking the hands of the crew as they stood ashore. One couple took a few more photographs with the ship in the background, a few more with the crew as their belongings were disembarked. Archie looked at his watch, seeing they had a half hour to go before they were due to leave for the return trip.

"Alright, let's head back to the van and get our things. We don't want to keep anyone waiting!" They made their way back to the holding yard, much to the apparent relief of the guard at the check in station. He waved at the family as they began to unload the van, getting on his radio and talking to someone with a few nods of his head, and a few checks on his clipboard.

A minute later, two men arrived with luggage carts and began to load their unpacked luggage onto them. One recorded the piece count of the items while the other loaded the cart.

"Good afternoon, Mr. and Mrs. Buchanen. Please allow us to finish unloading your van."

Archie shook his head.

"No worries guys, I have it under control."

He was met with concerned stares from both employees.

"Please, Mr. Buchanen. It is not company protocol for our guests to handle their luggage. The practice is not encouraged."

Archie paused for a moment.

"If it makes you two feel any better, I will leave a comment that you offered to do it several times, and you informed us of the policy but we chose to do it ourselves. Will that be okay?"

"Of course, Sir. We appreciate the courtesy."

"All right, then. It's settled."

Archie groaned inwardly. He didn't think it was *that* kind of a place, where you weren't allowed to do anything for yourself. He liked to be looked after, but not swarmed. Well, it wouldn't take too long for the staff at the resort to figure out that they weren't high maintenance. He imagined some of their guests were practically invalids when it came to being self-sufficient. He had seen a few of those types in his time, and he thought it unfortunate that money didn't always buy class.

The carts were quickly loaded, and they were guided back down to the wharf to meet the ships crew prior to sailing. The captain stood at the gangplank, his white uniform crisp and neatly pressed. He was just under six feet tall, his hair almost perfectly white with a neatly trimmed beard of the same color, and a golden tan. A few other men stood to his right in a line, awaiting their introduction. Their uniforms were also immaculate. He bowed very slightly as they approached the ship, and he extended his hand. Archie took it, and they shook quickly. He then took Mels hand, and politely kissed the top of her hand.

"Mr. and Mrs. Buchanen, it is my pleasure to meet you. Please allow me to introduce myself and my crew. My name is Captain Phillip Weston. To my right in order is my first officer Lawrence Smith." Lawrence was a few inches taller than the captain, with a lean slender build and an air of the second in command.

"To his right, our Chef Justin Bouchard." The chef looked like he was a man that enjoyed his food, his girth being considerable, and his face possessed a disposition that suggested he was very strict but knew how to enjoy himself, having deep smile wrinkles furrowed into his cheeks.

"To his right, our two attendants, Jean-Paul and Marcus." Jean-Paul was a wiry fellow with a thick mane of brown hair, and Marcus had a stockier build and was almost a platinum blonde with a precise flat top haircut. They progressed down the line, shaking hands as they went, doing their best to remember their names before they went to sea.

"Our ship is the Ave Maria. She is one hundred feet long, and she was commissioned two years ago. She has all of the latest electronics onboard, a hot tub, kitchen and dining area, multiple cabins, and a theater room if you care to watch a movie. It is our duty and privilege to take care of your every need, so please be certain to let us know if anything arises that we can attend to. If you please, Jean-Paul and Marcus will show you to your quarters while we have your luggage attended to."

Marcus and Jean-Paul stood opposite each other at the gangplank.

"Follow us, please," said Marcus, his voice thick with an Eastern European accent.

Steph had approached the Captain with her brother in tow, and looked up at him shyly.

"Captain?" she asked.

He adjusted his slacks and bent down to her eye level.

"Yes, my dear. How can I help you?"

"Why are ships called she? My Daddy didn't know, but he said I could ask you."

He chuckled merrily.

"Yes, of course. You can ask me anything you want to." He poked her once in the shoulder, and she laughed.

"Ships are called *she* because of the respect we have for them. Ships are like our wives and mothers. When we go out to sea, the sea is a dangerous place, and the ship takes care of us and keeps us safe, just like our mothers and wives do for us."

"Oh," she said. "Thank you."

"You are very welcome. Follow your Mom and Dad now. We have to go soon."

Steph and Charlie caught up to their parents and made their way up the gangplank, following the lead of Jean-Paul and Marcus down the length of the ship, and then into the cabins.

The ship was luxurious; the hardwood deck gleamed in the sunshine, as did the chrome and glistening white paint. When they turned into the hallway leading into the cabin area, they were shown first the kitchen. Stainless steel appliances sparkled in the sun, offset with a dark granite countertop that wrapped around the kitchen area. A multitude of pots and pans and utensils adorned every usable space in the area. Moving forward they passed the hot tub that had room for sixteen adults. It featured a built in refrigerator and liquid crystal television. The theater room was sunken with home theater seating in three rows, each level dropping a foot for the benefit of the person in the row behind. Speakers were built into the walls and hidden behind a nearly invisible screen cloth that matched the color of the paint.

Marcus demonstrated the theater lighting to accentuate the screen and keep your focus forwards.

"Please sit. I would like to give you a quick demonstration."

Archie shrugged, and they all sat in the front row. Marcus went behind a door, and the theater system came alive.

"The seating in the theater is designed to enhance your viewing pleasure by simulating motion of the movie you are watching." On the screen, two cars were racing down a dark street at night. After a few moments of hearing the cars change gears through several surround speakers, the cars turned to follow a corner. When the cars turned, the seats tilted to match the turn.

Charlie gasped.

"That is sooo cool. Isn't it Dad? We need this in our house. Wow!"

Archie couldn't help but smile, both at his own enjoyment and seeing the delight in his son.

The theater dimmed and turned off, and Marcus came back out from behind the cherry wood door.

"Forgive my indulgence. It is my favorite part of the ship."

"I know why," said Archie. "That is a nice little toy."

Marcus smiled back, glad to see their enjoyment from his quick demonstration. Jean-Paul stood silently in the background, probably having witnessed his hundredth demonstration of the system.

They went to the cabins, where they were quickly shown which one was theirs for the trip to the Island. Marcus quickly showed them the locations of the key features of the room. Archie couldn't help but notice the luggage had already made it into the suite. Very efficient.

"Please make yourselves comfortable. There is plenty of hot water if you want a shower, and dinner will be upstairs at six 'o' clock. Excuse me."

"Thank you Marcus and Jean-Paul."

They both bowed quickly, and left the cabin in the direction of the deck access hallway.

"Oh thank God," sighed Mel. "I would kill for a hot shower. I shotgun that." She began to go through her things and took a towel out from the linen closet.

"See you all in a bit." She waved goodbye as she shut the bathroom door behind her. Almost immediately, they could hear the water begin to flow.

"Well then. What are we going to do?" he asked the kids. They shrugged.

"I don't know," replied Steph.

"Charlie?"

"Whatever."

"Thanks for the great ideas."

Instead, they had stood at the bow, watching the waves break beneath the front of the ship, the distance being slowly eaten away. The kids had watched the gulls floating in the wind above the ship, as they had on the shore, using no effort to catch the wind and glide wherever they wanted to go. Steph had pointed out with awe as a large albatross glided overhead, its broad wings dwarfing the gulls as it cruised past.

"That was pretty cool, wasn't it?" Archie asked.

She had nodded her head quickly in agreement.

In took about an hour for Mel to join them after cleaning up. She had emerged from the shower, cleansed, to find the cabin empty. She dressed and then left the room, trying to find them on this maze of a boat. She had taken a few wrong turns, finding her way back to the kitchen where the Chef was all too pleased to have her sample the dinner preparations. She struggled to remember his name. Chef....J, it started with a J....Justin! Justin Bouchard!

"Follow me, Mademoiselle; allow me to give you the grand tour of my workshop. The kitchen was filled with so many different fantastic smells that her mouth began to water, her stomach roaring to life.

"Uh, excuse me, uhh, Chef, but what would you like me to call you."
He seemed perplexed.

"Je m'excuse. I am sorry; but what do you mean?"

She waved her right hand next to her face in nervous embarrassment, unsure of how to proceed. She was suddenly certain she should never have asked the question.

"I mean, do I call you Chef? Should I call you Justin, or Mister Bouchard?"

Her face glowed red.

"Ah, Madame." His arms rose to his sides as he said so, expressing the solution to the dilemma.

"You can call me whatever you like. If you prefer etiquette, then you address me as Chef. If it makes you feels more comfortable, please call me by my name." He bowed graciously, as during an introduction between honored friends.

"Is Justin, okay? I don't want to offend anyone, but this is all new and weird for us."

He was confused, his forehead coming together to show his misunderstanding.

"What is new and weird, if you beg my pardon?"

She waved her hands in the air.

"All of THIS, this lifestyle, this boat!" She sighed, her hands to her forehead. She looked up; he was still confused. She dropped her hands to her sides and took a deep breath, and prepared to explain with a minimum of drama.

"We won the lottery a few months ago."

His eyebrows raised.

"We bought a house, paid our bills, the usual stuff. But nothing fancy. THIS," she emphasized, looking around and pointing to the ship, "THIS is completely new to us. My husband booked this trip two weeks ago. We decided on a moments notice and here we are. It obviously cost a lot of money. I mean, for *chrissakes* we are the only people on this ship. I just am not used to this. I keep freaking out thinking what this is costing us. Having everyone wait on us. It doesn't feel right, having this ship and everyone on it just waiting for me to do something, or need something."

The Chef laughed.

"Madame, if I may." He sat her down on a bar stool in the kitchen, guiding her by her shoulders.

"First, please relax. Enjoy yourself, have some fun." He was very expressive with his hands, always tracing them through the air or punctuating his sentences with them, matter-of-factly, seeming to accentuate his speaking or gently adding emphasis to certain words with them.

"This ship," waving his hands through the air, "was made for enjoyment. If your husband booked this trip two weeks ago, you can afford it. The charter company verifies our passengers *very thoroughly* before taking any booking."

Mel started to speak, and he could see it was in protest. He put his forefinger over her lips, sealing them.

"*Very* thoroughly."

He turned to a pot, dipped a spoon into it, and returned to her, protecting the spoon in his hand, bringing it to her mouth.

"Please, try some."

She blew on it softly.

"What is it?"

He shook his head.

"Try it," raising the spoon to her again in emphasis.

She sipped it delicately, being cautious to not burn her lips.

The flavor was amazing.

"Delicious."

He nodded his head at the compliment.

"Merci. Do you know what my favorite movie of all time is, Madame Buchanen?"

"Please call me Mel, or Melanie. Otherwise it sounds too stuffy."

He nodded in acquiescence.

"I don't know, maybe *Gone with the Wind* or some other classic like that."

He shook his head, a small smile gracing his face, his moustache emphasizing his gleeful expression.

"*Non.* It is Beauty and the Beast. The Disney film. You have *les enfants,* you have seen it?"

"Yes, probably hundreds of times." She was sure she had the show memorized.

"I love that movie," he said, "In particular, I love a certain part of that movie. It is the part when Belle is in the dreaded castle, and the little clock and the candlestick serve her dinner. Do you remember that song?"

"Of course I do, it…"

He put his hand in the air, cutting her off midsentence. He began to hum.

"Then be our guest, be our guest, put our service to the test. Put a napkin 'round your neck, *cherie*, while we provide the rest."

He sang that much of the song in his kitchen.

"Relax, Melanie. Enjoy yourself. That song in that movie is exactly why I am a Chef. I love to cook and through my cooking, I love to please. It is my calling in life. I knew it from the first day I cooked a meal for someone, and it will be, God willing, the last thing I do. The Captain, he loves to do what he does. He is in charge of the ship and enjoys making sure you get to where you want to go safely. Everyone on this ship enjoys giving its passengers their one hundred percent attention. If we didn't we wouldn't be here. We have some passengers who are rude, or obnoxious, and we can ignore them. They know they are rude, but it won't make me act like them. Your money is new to you, and you still are unused to it. Enjoy it, do what you will with it, and stay the person you are."

Mel smiled at him.

"I think I was just paid a compliment."

He closed his eyes, and nodded once.

"Thank you, Monsieur Justine Bouchard, Chef extraordinaire."

She hugged him quickly, which he returned.

"Do you have any idea where my family is?"

He nodded. "They are on the bow."

"Which is?"

"The front of the ship." She stood still, unaware of where to go.

He pointed.

"That way, to the right."

"Thanks again."

"Enjoy your dinner, Melanie. I will have it done for you within the hour!" and he returned to his pots, humming the "Be our Guest" song cheerily to himself. As directed, she found them at the bow, watching the ocean pass and getting the occasional spray of seawater from a breaking wave. The dinner was fantastic; the kids ate in silence except for a steady stream of mmm sounds. Chef Bouchard came out near the end of the service to make sure everything was okay, taking a series of compliments on the meal. Stephanie had put her hand in the air and exclaimed that his cooking was just as good as her mommy's, to which he reacted with a practiced bow and a gratified look on his face. He had winked once at Melanie quickly after her comment, having fun with the children, showing her that this was his favorite part of any day.

They had pushed themselves away from the table, thanking the attendants for everything and retiring to their rooms. They watched some satellite tv and relaxed, feeling their copious and extravagant dinner slowly digest. Through the cabin portals it was possible to see the resort island nearing, its shape on the horizon seeming to rise out of the water and slowly become more dominant. The kids had looked out the window for a short while, eager to see where they were going, and then bored of it, not seeing it approach at any appreciable speed.

They sailed until the sun had begun to set, when the Captain had announced they would be dropping anchor for the evening. They were between the Island and the mainland, where the sea was at its most calm, and they would resume their passage in the morning. They should reach port by noon the following day. They heard the engines come to a stop, the continuous vibration suddenly stilled, and the ship became utterly quiet. There was a little motion from the waves, but it added to the relaxation effect.

"I don't think I am ever going to eat again," Archie moaned, unclasping the button on his shorts, and then burping quietly. He had been fine until dessert came out, which put him over the edge. It was some sort of thick chocolatey cheese cake, with an abundance of strawberries the size of small apples, and a chocolate mousse whipping.

"Are you thirsty?" Mel asked.

"I have no room in my stomach for water."

It was at that moment that Stephanie decided to surprise him by jumping on him. He contracted reflexively, and he felt his belly compress.

"Oh, that wasn't good for me." Stephanie was laughing and jumping on the bed with glee.

"How can she do that?"

"She didn't make a pig of herself," Mel replied pointedly, giving him no sympathy. Mel folded a few items at the bedside, putting them back near the suitcase, neatly piled.

"Bedtime guys," she announced, and received two simultaneous 'aw's.

"Yep, we have a big day tomorrow, so you will need a good night sleep." She patted Charlie on the back.

"C'mon you, time to get moving."

The kids sauntered into the bathroom mustering as little energy as possible to signify their lack of enthusiasm and protest. Mel sat into a very plush recliner, putting her feet up, and listened for the sounds of brushing teeth.

A tap turned on, and then brushing sounds. She sat in the chair, enjoying the near silence and the gentle motion of the ship. Archie lay unmoving on the bed, the only sign of life was the occasional blink and the rise and fall of his stomach as he breathed. She heard faint laughter coming from above decks. "Once the kids are in bed do you want to take a tour of the ship?" she asked.

Archie turned his head to the left to look in her direction.

"Sure." He sounded as enthralled as his kids. She listened for sounds from the bathroom. It was nearly silent, except for some faint whispering.

"Okay you guys stop fooling around in there."

"We're not."

"Then what are you doing?"

"Nothing."

"Then you can do nothing out here."

The thin veneered door unclicked and the two kids walked out, slowly getting into their beds. Mel stood up and took one of Archie's hands, trying to pull him from the bed.

"Let's go, mister."

Archie groaned. "Shoot me now."

"Later, I promise. After we take a walk."

He rolled over to get out of bed, and then rebuttoned his pants.

"Good night, kids."

"Where are you going?" Charlie asked.

"We are going to take a walk around the ship for a bit."

"Oh. Okay."

"We'll be back soon."

They left the room and stepped into the hallway, hearing the cabin door shut behind them with a click. Almost immediately they could hear the kids begin to whisper and giggle. They walked away down the hall, looking for a different way out.

"They aren't going to sleep anytime soon, you realize," he said to Mel. She smelled like sunscreen, the faint coconut odor strong in the confined space.

She shrugged.

"As long as they sleep soon it will be alright."

They walked around the ship from bow to stern in the dark, holding the guide rail just in case of a slip. A few lights were on near the top deck, and they went around the bow again, finding a ladder they had missed the first time. He gestured to Mel for her to go first. She climbed up, and he watched her legs, and then her butt as he got underneath her.

"You can stop looking at my ass," she said in a near whisper, in case anyone heard her.

"No chance," he replied, reaching up and giving her a pinch. She squealed and climbed a little faster. At the top of the ladder, she swung her leg over the side and stepped off, waiting for Archie to catch up. They walked towards the stern and came around a wall to an opening where the laughter and chatter was louder. A games table was in the middle of the area, with a narrow staircase that led to where the laughing was coming from.

"Shall we?" she asked him.

"Lead the way."

She went to the stairs and quickly went down, knocking on the wall near the bottom, Archie right behind her.

"Hello?" she asked.

There was a series of whispers and the sounds of plastic clicking together. She rounded the corner to find a few of the crew standing around a poker table, their latest hands lying flat on the table. They stood to attention as the smoke cleared, one man coughing and exhaling a small puff of smoke. They weren't only smoking cigarettes by the odor.

"Ma'am. Sir." The man nearest to them, Marcus, bowed.

"How can we help you?" The other three men she didn't recognize. They must have come onboard while they were in their cabin. Marcus looked decidedly uncomfortable, as if being anywhere else at the moment was where he wished he was.

"We're fine. We just heard laughing and decided to tour the ship. Can we join in?" he asked, indicating the poker table. Marcus looked around at his shipmates as if for a hint of what he should say. He received no support.

"Certainly, why not?" A couple of other chairs were pulled up around the table, and they sat down. Mel looked around the table and found a small black ashtray near the elbow of the man sitting next to her. A small doobie sat smoking in the cradle.

"Don't mind if I do." She inhaled, offering it to pass it around the table, holding her breath. After a moment of shock and awkward silence, the men laughed loudly, Marcus taking it from her and taking a drag himself.

"Our apologies. We never have our guests come in here after lights out. It is, *unusual*."

Melanie exhaled. "That is good shit."

There were a few more laughs. Marcus stood.

"Allow me to introduce ourselves. He went around the table, introducing the new faces they didn't recognize, starting with the man next to Mel.

"Pierre, our engineer; John, his assistant; Daniel, our onboard medical attendant." They nodded in turn at their introduction. Marcus dumped a pile of sorted chips into the middle of the table. One seat remained empty.

"Who is joining the table?" asked Archie.

"That is for the Chef. He is getting the snacks from the galley while we play a round." He began to push piles of chips out the each spot.

"We cannot play for money, Captains policy, so we play for bragging rights." He sat down, and quickly sorted the chips, pushing a small pile out to each player. Pierre began to shuffle the deck, the cards a blur in his hands. He tapped the shuffled deck down loudly on the table twice, and dealt, the cards flying from his hands and landing on the table with practiced ease. They played the hand, John winning with two pair, while Mel and Archie folded quickly. They heard someone coming down the stairs, singing to himself. Chef Bouchard came around the corner, both hands full of bags of chips and a bowl of steaming dip. He looked around the table and stopped cold in his tracks, seeing Mel and Archie seating with the crew.

"Mon Dieu."

Seeing the table was proceeding normally, he came forward and put the food on the table.

"Monsieur, Madame."

Marcus lit a cigarette.

"Relax, Justin. They are playing with us. These two have created a precedent. Sit down."

Chef sat down, looking unsure of how to proceed.

"We are having fun, Chef Bouchard," said Melanie. She took another drag of the joint that was now much smaller. He smiled, recalling their earlier conversation in the galley. He smiled and shook his head at the same time, laughing a little.

"You certainly aren't like our normal guests." His face hardened.

"Now you see my poker face. Prepare to lose your chips."

Daniel spoke up loudly, leaning into the middle of the table.

"The way you play poker Monsieur Bouchard you should be glad we don't play for money!"

The crew laughed, poking fun at the Chef who smiled, accepting his place as the butt of the joke. He leaned forward, his finger pointed at Daniel.

"I recommend you let the man who cooks your dinner win once in a while."

They played into the early morning. As predicted, the Chef was cleaned out first, while Pierre amassed a huge pile of chips. Archie and Mel stood from the table. Mel was swaying as she stood, more than a little drunk.

"Thank you for a wonderful evening, but we better call it a night." He looked at his watch. They had enough time to get some sleep before the day began. The crew raised their drinks into the air.

"Goodnight, then. We will see you in the morning. We will have Chef put some aspirin on your wifes' breakfast plate!" said Marcus. Archie laughed.

"That would be a good idea." Melanie looked at him, and then nearly fell over a chair.

"Why? I'm not drunk." She said drunk like Der-unk, with a lot of emphasis on the K. He waved goodnight to the crew, who saluted back, and he led Melanie back to the cabin. The kids were sound asleep, snoring quietly.

Mel had put her fingers to her lips, pushing them harder than was necessary, pushing her lips.

"SHHHHHHHHH. Quiet. The KIDS are shleeping." Charlie turned over at the noise. He laid her down on their bed, and she fell asleep instantly. He undressed to his skivvies, and pulled the sheets over himself, and soon was sleeping soundly.

They arrived at the breakfast table as scheduled, Archie's stomach rumbling loudly after having eaten so much the night before. The kids seemed anxious to see what kind of meal was going to be spread before them, remembering the experience the night before. The table had been filled with a series of various drinks from coffee and tea, water, and several juices. A small bottle of aspirin was planted strategically in the middle of the table. Melanie had opened quickly and downed two pills while Archie had watched her with a grin.

"What's so funny, Mr. Poker champion?" She massaged her temples, trying to make the slow dull pain fade away.

Breakfast ending up being a large buffet offering, with fresh croissants and English muffins, all still piping hot and steaming. There was a large bowl of scrambled eggs that were so light and fluffy that they were more whipped than scrambled, and a plate of eggs done over easy and sunny side up. There were plates of fruit, hash browns, and sausage and bacon ranging from done to extra crispy. There was even some sliced breakfast ham, pancakes and Belgian waffles, and real Canadian maple syrup. He wondered how the hell Chef Bouchard could put a feast like this together with maybe four hours of sleep under his belt. The man was a genius, of that there was no doubt. They ate heartily and with gusto. Even Mel found her appetite restored with the variety of well-prepared food laid out before her.

The horn blasted twice, making Mel wince, followed by the anchors being raised with the noise of the winch and the occasional clang as a link bounced against the guide. The steady vibration underfoot returned, and the liquid in their cups leaned towards the stern of the ship, as she got underway. The day was already warm and cloudless, promising to be a real scorcher.

"Next stop, South Australis Resort!" The remaining few hours went by quickly, seeing the island growing in the distance quickly gave a better measure of time than the previous day when it had largely remained invisible. The island was a mix of topography, with forest and clear areas, wide-open pristine beaches, and a few shipwrecks laying deep in the coral sand. Development of the land was strictly controlled to keep its value as a destination resort, where human presence was limited and kept to a minimum. They circled the island, coming to the dock that had been built out at the end of a long expansive pier. Looking through the water, it was easy to see why. Leading up to the beaches were corals and sand dunes in varying depths of water, their close presence changing the color of the water from the deep blue of deep water to the lighter colors of the shallows. The ship could not come any closer to the resort, so the pier had to be built to give it a place to dock. The disembarkation was the same as they had witnessed the day before, with the crew shaking hands and exchanging pleasantries with the passengers, handing off to attendants from the resort itself that were there to make sure the trip had been to their expectation.

They were greeted by Paul, and slim man of average height who was darkly tanned, the sun seeming to have bleached his eyes a very clear shade of blue. He squinted continuously, the wrinkles at the corner of his eyes permanent.

Paul was evidently in charge of maintaining high standards aboard the Ave Maria, and was anxious to know how they had enjoyed their trip.

"Everything and more," replied Archie.

"Really great, thanks for asking," said Mel.

Paul had positively beamed, delighted to hear they had enjoyed themselves. He had called two younger boys from the resort to come and retrieve their baggage from the dock, loading the suitcases onto the baggage carts. They had waved to the crew as they had walked towards the resort, knowing they would be seeing them in about another two weeks when it was time to return home. Paul had walked with them at the front of the procession, reviewing some brochures and pointing out highlights of their stay, as well as a map of the island with all the main interests clearly marked with a black anchor within a small circle. The kids came next, followed by the baggage boys pushing the carts, their thick rubber wheels hitting the gap between each plank with a thump sound. When the wheels weren't hitting the gaps in the pier, they were rumbling along the planks, the sound carrying down the length of the structure.

"We are so glad you have decided to stay with us on your vacation," gushed Paul. He had an interesting accent.

"Food and drink is available twenty four hours a day, as is room service should you prefer." Rumble rumble thump. "There are several island tours via horseback or jeep depending on the length of the tour you may like to take. We offer massage services, several gymnasium facilities, indoor and outdoor salt water pools, fishing excursions, and a host of other entertainment options that are listed in our items list."

He handed them each a copy. Rumble rumble thump. They came to the end of the pier where the wooden beams met with a concrete sidewalk, flanked with decorative paving stones.

The rumble rumble thump was replaced with the steady grind of the wheels on the pavement. The shore yielded to a flat but slowly rising landscape that was green with flowers and shrubs and young trees. Further in to the development and resort the foliage was dense, leaving vast areas of cool shade. The heat on the sidewalk was intense, the sun overhead with no shade, and a salty wind blowing up from the bay. If not for the breeze, the heat would be incredible. They continued to follow the path as it wound towards the shade, where several accommodations became visible.

They saw another family sitting on the beach, the kids playing in the surf while the parents sat under two large striped solar umbrellas, one blue and white, the other red and white. Bunker whined in his doggy carrier, eager to be out exploring. Paul brought them to the door of the first house they saw on the beach. It was larger then the home they had owned before winning the lottery. He produced a pair of keys, handing one set to each adult.

"Here are your accommodations. I trust you will find it to your satisfaction.

There is a pool in the back area, as well as a restaurant just up the beach about fifty meters." They could smell the grill smoke in the air, something delicious cooking.

"If you need anything, please call the services desk by pressing the One key on the phone.

"Thank you, Paul," they both said.

"My pleasure, of course."

He smiled and turned, giving instructions to the baggage carriers, and walked away down the sidewalk path towards the direction of the restaurant.

He slid the key into the door, unlocking it with a faint click, and entered the home. It was beautiful, the floor all marble tile throughout, leading to a sunken living room exquisitely furnished. The kitchen table was a wooden monstrosity, probably solid cherry wood with enough space to sit twelve people easily. A large flowery gift basket sat atop the table, several bottles of wine clearly visible protruding from the wicker, as well as a few boxes of dark chocolates. The baggage was unloaded at the door step upon the insistence of Melanie, who thanked the boys for their help. The rumble of the carts was audible for several moments as they were pushed away, the sound of the surf and wind blowing through the trees gradually overwhelming them. The luggage was put away, and each room inspected and admired. The level of detail was astonishing, with no detail left forgotten.

"So who wants to go to the beach?" he declared. Stephanie yelled.

"Yaaaaaaay!" and unzipped her suitcase, finding her bathing suit and closing the door to get changed. Charlie got ready quickly as well, without the same degree of vocal enthusiasm. Before long, the four of them were on the shoreline, their sun block still wet and sticky on their skin. The waves were mild, breaking slowly over the coral sand with a repetitive shhh sound of the coral sand rolling over itself. The sound was hypnotic. He walked straight into the surf, going chest deep and enjoying the feel of the warm water buoying his body. The kids went up to their necks; Mel went in only partially, sitting in the water where the waves crested upon her stomach. He swam around for a short time, diving under the surface to look around in the clear water. A small orange fish investigated him, and then swam away with the furious beat of its fins.

They spent the day at the beach, their skin absorbing the hot rays of the sun, their pores opening under the deep cyan sky. Whatever stress they had melted away and evaporated under the tropical sun and the refreshing tang of the salty air. Before long, the succulent smells that wafted down the beach from the restaurant became irresistible. Archie had finished swimming, his hair slicked back over his head where it had quickly dried, fixed into a swept back position. He sat besides Mel, leaning back, his hands digging into sand for support. For the first time in a long time, he felt completely at ease. His breathing was slow and relaxed, his heart beat was slow and steady, and his mind was utterly free of thought. He sat on the beach looking outwards across the horizon, just *looking*. The smell of the food cooking carried past them, making his stomach gurgle. He ignored it, finding that even the rumble in his belly felt relaxing. He was just too content to be bothered with eating at the moment. Moments like this were too rare, and he wanted to prolong it as long as possible.

"Penny for your thoughts."

The sound went in one ear and out the other.

"Archie?"

He came back to reality hearing his name.

"Hmm?"

"What were you thinking about?" asked Mel.

He thought about it for a moment, struggling to think about what he had been thinking about.

"Absolutely nothing." He smiled.

"The kids are probably getting hungry."

They were splashing each other in the surf, their arms beating the surface of the water.

"Probably." He didn't want to disturb them; when they were hungry enough they would stop playing. In the meantime, he was enjoying watching them laugh and splash, carefree.

"I'm hungry, too." He knew where this was headed, but wanted to extend the time at the beach just a bit longer; even by a minute if he could.

"You must be hungry," she said.

"No. Not really, actually," he lied, his stomach growling a protest.

"Well, I am; and the kids must be."

Time was up.

Mel cupped her hands to her mouth and yelled.

"Come on in kids. Lunch time."

They kept splashing, ignoring her. Archie had seen Charlie look over, so he knew they had heard her. He chuckled under his breath.

"Steph! Charlie! Lunch time!"

"Awwww, do we have to?" Charlie whined, letting his hands fall into the water.

Stephanie saw her chance, and splashed him furiously while his defenses were down.

"You turd," he said, splashing her back.

"I'm not a turd. *You're* a turd," she replied, smiling, satisfied with her retort.

"A bigger turd than me."

Archie laughed, surprised by her comeback. Her brother laughed, too; enjoying the lowbrow humor from his little sister. They stuck out their tongues at each other, each trying to get in the last gesture of defiance.

"All right, you two. Game over; time for lunch," said Mel, standing up and brushing the sand off her legs and backside. Seeing her stand and wait, Charlie and Steph knew she was serious, and they grudgingly made their way to the shore. Archie sat still, watching them come slowly, wanting to sit where he was for as long as possible.

"That means you too, mister."

Archie looked up to see Mel looking down at him, hands on hips.

"Nuts."

He stood up as the kids stepped out of the water onto the beach, water dripping from their swimsuits. His stomach growled again. The surety of lunch had aggravated his hunger, although he still felt like he didn't have to eat. Mel had grabbed their beach towels, and was patting down Stephanie who had her eyes closed, rubbing her hair dry, while Charlie wrapped his towel over his shoulders. Archie held his in his hand, preferring to dry as they walked to the restaurant.

The restaurant was small, built and designed to cater to relatively few diners but to serve them in high class with all of the best that could be offered. It was an open air concept, with an enclosed dining area within for those that wanted to get out of the sun or wind and enjoy some air conditioning. A blue and yellow sign, with fluorescent backlighting was situated above the main entrance, the large block capital letters of Charlie's Grill standing out from the stone façade of the exterior wall. Charlie smiled, thinking it funny that the restaurant shared his name.

"Guess they named this place after you," said Archie, tapping him lightly on his shoulder.

"Pretty sweet," agreed Charlie.

"Pretty gross," replied Stephanie; not too impressed at all by the coincidence. Mel smiled, but kept quiet.

They walked past the outer dining tables, into the central area through a pair of thick wooden doors, stopping at a sign indicating to wait there for service. The air conditioning hit him like a cool wave, making his skin goose pimple in contrast to the heat outside. A hallway led off to the left from where they stood, a door on each side of the hall. One was labeled 'Blokes, and the opposite door 'Sheilas'. He didn't expect to see the terminology in a place like this, but then he supposed it also had to appeal to the tourist trade.

The kids had decided to have a hamburger platter for their lunch, served with bikkies for dessert and a side plate of home made chips with all the fixings. The waiter had taken their order with a degree of surprise, not expecting to order a meal as simple as a hamburger.

Archie noted his watch, seeing it was already early afternoon. The earlier part of the day spent at the beach had gone by faster than he had realized.

"What time is it, Dad?" asked Charlie, seeing him check his watch.

"A little bit after one."

"That means this isn't lunch," said Steph, matter-of-factly.

"Lunch is at noon."

"What is it then?" asked Charlie, a little annoyed, hungry and tired from the hot sun.

"It's dunch!" she exclaimed, suddenly giggling and covering her mouth with her hand.

Charlie rolled his eyes.

"Or how about lupper?" asked Mel, smiling, enjoying seeing Steph laughing and enjoying herself.

Steph laughed louder, and even Charlie grinned a little, although he was careful to make sure that it wasn't too obvious. He took a sip of his drink.

Their waiter came out from the kitchen, three plates balanced expertly on one arm, and the fourth held in his hand. The meal was fantastic, although if not the standard fare of the kitchen. Archie and Mel had ordered a large plate of barbecued prawns to share between the two of them. The prawns were flavorful and burst with juice when bit into, the flesh tender. The plate was surrounded by cut wedges of rock melon, the orange color serving to accentuate the plate as well as add a nice dash of fruit to the meal. The kids hamburgers smelled fantastic, and were evidently spruced up by the chefs to at least resemble something they would normally prepare, refusing to let something like a simple burger leave their kitchen without a flair of creativity. They had just started to eat when Archie noticed the ceiling fans were beginning to slow, and that the lights in the kitchen seemed to have gone out.

Dak-ho Seuk

Dak-ho walked through the airport entrance, deferring to an older couple and their son who was carrying their luggage. The terminal was bustling with activity, full of people travelling over the holiday season. The sun was just coming up, filling the building with long shadows and the yellow light of dawn. Dak-ho walked around the family towards the departures gate, his black leather soled shoes clicking on the glossy stone tile floor. He carried only his briefcase as luggage, a classical style black and aluminum Samsonite model that he had purchased several years earlier, when he had first begun to travel extensively. The briefcase held his laptop, his wallet, some travelling money, and his toothbrush. He had no need to carry any other luggage; his apartment in San Francisco had everything else he would need before his board meeting.

He sighed when he arrived to the ticket counter; the line up of travellers meandered through a series of guides for several hundred feet. The line was typical of the early morning; mostly business class with a few early rising families that had hoped to beat the line they were now stuck in. The line moved slowly, the people within shuffling slowly forwards, a few feet at a time. He glanced down at his watch, straightening his arm so his jacket would pull back and reveal the watch face. He put his arm back down. As usual, he had plenty of time to spare. He watched the people in the line up, studying their habits and analyzing their behaviors, taking pleasure in watching normal behaviors, and being able to guess what they were like. A young family half way to the counter was frequently checking the time, their child of no more than four half-dozing, leaning against the leg of her mother. Their faces betrayed their stress and exhaustion.

Further ahead, an older fellow, probably in his early sixties stood straight and unbending, his eyes forward, his demeanor matter-of-fact. His hair was meticulously styled back, combed into place in a simple sweep, easy and fast to maintain. He was relaxed and in no rush, a veteran of travel. Behind him, a young woman in her early twenties. She was well dressed in a navy blue business suit and skirt. It was inexpensive but stylish. Her hair was tied back in a medium length pony tail, professional and clean. Her skirt was knee high, conservative and business style. She was nervous, perhaps her first flight. She had smiled shyly at him when she saw him looking at her, and had quickly looked away, her nerves distracting her focus. Outside of the line lanes of people were walking to and fro, some quickly, some slowly, some relaxed, some anxious. An airport was a great place to watch people, very nearly a human zoo where in a short period of time you could expect to see a wide range of personalities, all brought to the surface in this particular environment.

His habit of watching people was developed over time, and had crossed over several of his prior occupations. He had always been interested in psychology and sociology, and so in university they had been his majors. He was quiet and introspective, with a minimal need for human interaction. He was not anti-social, he simply was very independent and self motivated.

On the contrary, he very much enjoyed talking to other people and helping them, he just didn't require the interaction as so many other people do. The behaviors of people fascinated him, and he strove to find the consistencies of the human animal, the core reactions of the species that could be relied upon as normal behavior within certain conditions. While many people thought of themselves as being independent, they were actually highly dependant upon the proximity of others, that their self-perceived independence was in fact confidence derived from being accepted into a group, of feeling safe within peers. Time after time his thoughts were validated by observation. Very few people could function at a high level for any length of time while being truly alone. The human animal was a herd animal, just like any other.

His focus on observation led to study on body language, the often unseen and unconscious communication between people.

Facial expressions, body position, gestures, they all spoke loudly of opinion and thought and decision, but very few people were aware of it at a conscious level, it being a largely subconscious way of communicating. As such, it was very honest. Body language being very primal and instinctive was therefore very difficult to lie through. Words could say one thing, while the body screamed the opposite. Body language was very consistent across all cultures, the straightening of the mouth showing anger or fear, the narrowing of the eyes during a smile to reveal a true smile, or watching a good salesman sell his wares.

His expertise in behavior and body language, with his naturally confident style made him a natural salesman, and he found great success in sales throughout school and afterwards. He often went home mentally exhausted, his body not needing sleep, but his mind unable to think any further. Each customer was a study, from the initial greeting to the final sales transaction, every moment of the process he studied and analyzed, body language, visual cues, dealing with the differences between single men and women, and to the differences in couples. Couples were often the most personally satisfying due to the challenge involved, determining who wanted what, and who was in control of the buying decision. Which he had found was very consistently the woman, regardless of the attitude and machismo of the male. He had used this knowledge to his advantage whenever possible, always making sure to spend enough time with the woman to sell her on the product, while stroking the mans ego enough to make him feel important.

His sales career had begun with selling electronics for Rizio Electronics, initially a small Korean firm that was localized within a few small stores. As the company grew, and began to focus more on production and supplying other companies, he rose through the ranks, from running his own store, to the manufacturing of the liquid crystal panels, to managing the plant, to being responsible for the development of international sales markets, specifically, North America. When the market grew more and more competitive, they had sold their manufacturing capability, choosing to outsource their panels to lower costs and investment needs. As the market grew, profit margins decreased, and so inventories were gradually shifted from a twelve week supply, to ten, to eight, and now down to two.

A few years ago this short supply would have seemed unthinkable, to be certain business suicide. Instead, it had proved to allow them to be more flexible to changing costs, and it had only improved their bottom line and profits. Some of their competition had faltered and failed, whereas they had steadily grown market share in a business that was saturated.

He finally approached the ticket counter. The counter person was an attractive woman in her mid-thirties.

"Good morning, sir. Any bags to check with us today?"

She made direct eye contact with him, she was confident and comfortable. Her shoulders were square to him. He had her attention.

"No just the briefcase, thank you. It is carry on."

She nodded in affirmation.

"Of course. May I please see your identification please?"

He opened his briefcase with two loud snaps as the locks released, and provided his drivers license and passport for her to examine.

"Thank you Mr. Seuk. Do you have a preference for a window seat or the Aisle?"

He thought about it for a moment.

"Window seat please."

He was less likely to be disturbed if someone needed to go to the washroom.

"Window seat."

She deftly began to type in the information, and then waited briefly as the boarding pass was printed. She efficiently folded the pass along its perforations, circled two points on the ticket, and passed it to him.

"Here you are, Sir. Your plane will be boarding in approximately one hour in Gate 24. Your seat is 12A, at the window as you requested. Can I help you with anything else?"

She smiled broadly, her eyes narrowing as she did so. A genuine smile. She sincerely liked her job.

He confirmed the information on the ticket as she pointed to it.

"No, thank you. Have a good day."

He examined the ticket, noted his seat 12A Gate 24, folded the ticket and slid it into his breast pocket, and then snapped his briefcase shut.

"Thank you; I hope you enjoy your flight," she replied.

He smiled quickly, nodding in confirmation to her comment, and made his way to the security gate. The line up moved quickly, he could see through the door that several security stations were processing travelers to keep the lines to a minimum. He reached the security attendant, who had quickly looked him over from head to toe, verified his boarding pass, and then directed him to a station to the left. He removed his jacket as he walked over, and placed it inside the waiting plastic x ray bin.

He quickly looked to the security team in place. The x ray technician was leaning on the monitor, her eyes scanning the baggage passing through the machine, a greatly disinterested look apparent on her face. The guard at the gate was scanning another customer, running the sensory paddle over his body.

The third attendant was verifying all metal goods were placed in the x ray bins, her voice a monotone of someone who was tired of saying the same thing over and over again, shift after shift, week after week. He removed his watch and belt and placed them into the bin over his coat, and placed his shoes in another bin with his briefcase.

The attendant came over to him, and quickly itemized the contents of the bins.

"Do you have any other metal objects in your pants, sir?"

"No," he replied.

"It's all in the bins for you."

"Please open the briefcase, sir."

He snapped it open for her, and opened up his laptop.

"Please turn on the laptop, sir."

He depressed the power button, and with a quiet whirr the screen brightened and displayed his desktop and background, a red dragon on a white backdrop; his icons surrounding the periphery of the screen.

"Thank you, sir."

He stood at the front of the line, watching the airport employee run the x-ray paddle over the previous person to check in. The paddle beeped almost instantaneously as it was held past his arm. The employee pulled back the sleeve to reveal a large wristwatch.

Dak-ho rolled his eyes, *Jesus Christ – who forgets to take off a watch?*

The watch was removed and placed in a grey plastic tote, and he resumed his body survey. It beeped again on the other arm. The subsequent search revealed a medic alert bracelet. It went off again over a pocket in his pants, and this time a set of keys was placed into the tray. Dak-ho almost laughed aloud. *Where the hell was this fool from?* Passengers behind him were not so amused. He caught the tail part of "…ucking idiot," being whispered from a well tanned couple a few behind in the line up. Eventually, after his other pockets were emptied to reveal some change and his belt was removed, Dak-ho was gestured through. The guard was waiting for him to walk through the metal detector, his arms crossed at the waist and the sensor paddle loosely held in his right hand. He didn't appear to be too amused from his previous passenger either.

He stepped through the gate.

As he had expected, nothing triggered the gate, and the guard motioned him to his belongings which were sitting at the end of end of a declined ramp with aluminum rollers, with a stack of empty bins off to the side. As he collected his belongings, he noticed a lady arguing with another station attendant over the bottles in her purse. She was dressed in a black cotton dress with a floral print, with matching heels, and she wore a scarf with a matching pattern wrapped around her neck. Her sunglasses were sitting on top of her head, ready for use. It appeared as though several bottles of expensive perfume were destined for the garbage can, and the lady was trying her best to argue her case. Predictably, she lost and the small glass vessels were dropped into the can with a series of dull thunk sounds. The lady in the dress put her sunglasses on and marched away angrily, her heels punctuating each step on the hard floor, her lips mumbling what could safely be assumed to be a string of expletives. He wondered where these people came from to be so unaware of travelling reality. Perhaps a cave?

After collecting his things, he made his way past security where the room opened into a foyer that branched off to several gates. He went to the right, and made his way down the wing of the terminal towards his departure gate. He purchased a newspaper at a small café, handing the cashier exact change and made his way to a row of seats sitting perpendicular to the attendant kiosk.

The seating area was filling quickly, already half full with a number of seats claimed in absentia, the territory marked with a jacket or magazine. The loading ramp was flanked by two large windows where the aircraft sat outside. It was a Boeing 777, its' two large engines sat turning lazily in the low morning breeze.

The underbelly was painted white, the top in the light blue of Korean Airlines. He could see the flight crew inside the cockpit, going though the motions of a preflight checklist while seemingly engaged in a friendly and active conversation, the crew laughing frequently. A desk attendant was busy entering something into her desk kiosk.

Spotting an available seat at the back wall of the lounge, he made his way over to the aisle. The seats were covered with a medium grey cloth, and had no arm rests. Across the lounge area, in another departure terminal, an exhausted traveler was sleeping stretched out covering several seats, his head resting on his jacket that he had folded and put over his briefcase. To his right a few seats down, a discarded newspaper was left for the next reader. The sections had been separated and piled one atop the other, in the sequence they had been read by a previous person. Looking about quickly, he saw that no one else had an interest in the paper, so he quickly made his way to the paper, retrieved it, and returned to his seat. Settling into the spot, he put the paper into his lap and opened the first section, resting the spine of the paper on his crossed leg. It was the daily print of Chosun Ilbo, a Korean newspaper that printed in several languages.

He wasn't particularly interested in the paper. He would browse through it, looking for articles that would be to his liking, but primarily it allowed him to watch his fellow travellers from behind at least a partial mask of impartiality.

The front articles were the usual fare, how the President was faring in his efforts to repair the US economy, developments in Afghanistan, more disputes between India and Pakistan – the fare that he could pick up again next week and see re-hashed in another publication.

Without putting his paper down, he glanced at his watch to note the time. Another thirty minutes to his boarding call, give or take a few. So far there wasn't really anyone that was too interesting in the lounge to observe. An executive sat in the far corner next to a large potted plant, that certainly looked real enough but was probably artificial, maintaining a conversation on his cell phone with a friend or colleague a few decibels louder than was necessary. As a result, anyone in the lounge that cared to listen was aware of his past day, and what he had told so-and-so, and who had said what. Typical conversation.

A family sat a few rows ahead of him, the wife was trying to catch a few moments of relaxation keeping her eyes closed resting in her seat, while her presumable husband kept their young daughter entertained. She stood in his lap, pointing out items of interest, saying what they were, and continuing to the next item. Passerby's were smiling at her, especially older people that were probably relating to her as a grandparent would. One lady waved at her with a subdued motion, and the child waved back, smiling openly and turning her body to follow her as she walked away, still waving as she departed.

Dak-ho smiled, enjoying the innocence she displayed, knowing that within a year it would likely be replaced by a taught fear of strangers.

The counter attendant put on a headset, cautious to not cause harm to her hairdo. Satisfied with its fit, she turned to her co-worker and pointed at something on her monitor. They both nodded, and the lady with the headset began to speak, the PA system suddenly drowning out the chatter around him.

"Attention ladies and gentlemen; Korean Air Flight 893 has has now arrived on schedule. Once the flight has disembarked and refueled we will begin with pre-boarding. Thank you."

With that, a line of people began to appear from the ramp, disgorging into the terminal. Several people went directly into the washrooms, a few made their way to a small coffee shop, and the rest wandered away down the terminal wing towards the baggage claim areas and exits. Looking over his right shoulder he could see the tanker truck near the wing of the airliner, and large red hose connected to the wing, a vein of jet fuel. The maintenance worker stood on a ladder supervising the procedure. He rubbed his arms and hands several times to generate some body heat while he waited. It wasn't too cold out for nearing the end of December, but it was humid and the moist air stole away body heat quickly. A few bags of garbage were removed from the plane, and two flight attendants had appeared from the ramp, discussing something at the counter. Their dark blue suits were well pressed, the white collars of their shirts contrasting sharply with the deep blue.

"Attention ladies and gentlemen, this is a call for pre-boarding of Korean Air flight 893. At this time any children traveling under our supervision, or those in need of boarding assistance are asked to come to the boarding counter. Thank you."

Dak-ho lowered his paper and scanned the seating area. No one apparently needed extra assistance with the plane today. A few people were looking around the Gate, for some reason very curious as to who may need extra help. The counter attendant waited her mandatory time, and then made her next call.

"Attention ladies and gentlemen, this is a boarding call for Korean Air flight 893. At this time we would ask that those passengers with seats from rows thirty to forty-four please register at the counter as we are loading the back of the plane first. Please have your boarding pass and photo ID ready for verification. Thank you."

Dak-ho noted that her pages were very precise and polished.

A large line up had quickly formed, and then slowly proceeded past the counter. He could hear "please's" and "thank you's" from the desk as identification was presented and verified.

"Attention ladies and gentlemen, this is a boarding call for Korean Air flight 893. At this time we would ask that those passengers with seats from rows ten through twenty-nine please register at the counter. Please have your boarding pass and photo ID ready for verification. Thank you."

Dak-ho looked around and watched as the line up to the counter swelled. He folded the newspaper and put it down to the right of him, ready for the next traveler that would be in the area. And then he waited patiently for the line up to shorten. It was always amusing to see how everyone lined up, just to go nowhere. Just like when the plane was unloading. Everyone would stand up and wait, although it would take another several minutes before the door was even opened. He laughed inwardly at the predictability. The man with the cell phone was telling someone named Jasper that he was now boarding and had to go, but that he would call him once the flight landed. His phone closed with a sharp click, and he made his way to the line. When it was down to a handful of people, he stood up and made his way to the counter, his boarding pass in his left hand with his briefcase, and his passport in his right hand.

He presented his ticket and passport to the lady with the headset.

She typed his confirmation number into the terminal, glanced at his face and then to his passport photo, and returned back to the terminal screen.

"Thank you Mr. Seuk. Have a good day." Her smile was as polished as her announcements.

"Thanks. You, too."

He closed up his passport and slid it into his jacket pocket, and made his way down the flight ramp. He showed his boarding pass to the flight attendant directing passengers at the door.

"Hello. Window seat to your left."

He nodded in confirmation, and walked slowly through the Executive section in the forward end of the plane. The line up of people slowly made its way forward as people found their seats and stowed their carry on baggage.

Shortly he passed by the curtain separating the front and middle sections of the plane, and was pleased to realize his seat was in the first row of the middle section. He secured his briefcase into the overhead compartment, and made himself comfortable in his seat. He watched out the small window to his right as a few passengers filtered past him, and the executive section began to fill. The fuel truck had disengaged and was leaving the gate, its yellow strobe lights flashing in caution. He sat in comfort as the rest of the flight boarded, a steady stream of people slowly proceeded down the length of the plane, the low murmuring of polite conversation constant. He checked the information in the seat pouch in front of him. The usual things. A barf bag, an airline magazine, the safety features of the plane they were on. In case of an emergency landing, place your head in between your legs and kiss your ass goodbye. Instead, of course, it showed a drawing of a jet floating in a body of water, in one piece, with people in life vests deploying down bright yellow emergency chutes. He wondered what the odds were, of a plane touching down in water and remaining in one piece.

He was sure they were astronomical. He remembered the footage of a jetliner that had tried to make a landing in the sea near some Caribbean island. It had approached smoothly, going in level, and then one wing had clipped a wave that seemed to just jump out of the sea, and it all went to hell from there. The wing was sheared off the plane, and it had begun to spin like a giant broken toy. It had spun a half circle above the waves before hitting the water, where it seemed to disintegrate like a model that suddenly had all of its glue removed, and pieces flew everywhere, shattering like a glass bowl. He didn't see that photo in the guide. He looked up from the seat and found the stewards and stewardesses walking up and down the plane checking the overhead luggage and verifying seatbelts were properly used. The typical pre-flight stuff. The no smoking light above was glowing steadily, and he noticed the fan was on slightly.

He could smell the faint odor of jet exhaust coming through the fan, and he inhaled deeply. He had developed a liking for the smell.

With a small lurch, he felt the parking brake disengage, and the plane began to roll backwards, the whine from the engines increasing in volume. The plane turned, and made its way down the line, bouncing softly as it crossed a few cracks in the pavement. The flight attendants made one last inspection, walking up the aisles checking again for seatbelts and improperly secured luggage.

"Flight attendants, please prepare for take off." The broadcast ended with a faint click. He looked down and gave his seatbelt one final pull to make sure it was secure, and leaned back into his seat to get more comfortable. The middle seat in the row was unoccupied, and a lady with a bright red head of hair was trying to read a novel, quite obviously uneasy with flying. She was very fidgety, and easily distracted, her eyes moving constantly from one source of sound to the next in rapid succession. A stewardess pulled the curtain shut in front of them, turning around to draw the fabric tight. He admired her backside as she was busy, and then quickly averted his eyes when she turned around. She unclasped a seat from the wall that faced backwards towards the passengers, and sat down on it, drawing her seatbelt tight. He watched her sit; her movements were efficient and smooth, and she sat in a practiced motion, probably an airline training process. She sat fully upright, her knees held tightly together, her skirt smoothed out and pulled down to minimize her exposed legs.

He admired her legs as discreetly as he could, and then looked up to see that she was watching him watching her. Her face held a suppressed smile, and he quickly averted his gaze, slightly embarrassed to have been so obviously caught. He made the conscious effort to look outside the window.

"Where are you two travelling to today?" He tried to ignore the question, pretending he didn't hear it. The red headed passenger answered first.

"I am going back home to Saratoga. It's outside of San Francisco."

"Were you on vacation in Korea?" the stewardess asked.

The redhead shook her head. "No, well, yes. Kind of, I suppose."

The stewardess smiled, a quizzical look on her face.

"I was visiting my son in Seoul. He teaches English there. He has been there for a few years now and I came to visit him."

The stewardess nodded in understanding.

"I was born in Seoul. It's a very pretty city. Did you like it?" she asked.

The lady nodded in agreement.

"It is very nice. More crowded than I am used to, but everyone I met was very friendly."

The stewardess nodded and smiled.

"I am glad to hear you enjoyed yourself. My name is Jeong."

The red head smiled back.

"Madison."

The plane turned in a steady motion onto the runway, and the engines whine began to turn into a powerful rumbling. A moment later, he felt himself being pulled back into his chair as the plane accelerated down the tarmac. He smiled with the familiar feeling of the power of taking off.

The plane bounced slightly twice, and then was aloft, his stomach dropping as the plane began to climb steeply.

He looked outside, watching the buildings below quickly shrink in size, seeing the full scale of the airport and city revealed as they gained altitude.

"You obviously enjoy flying."

"Yes," he replied, still looking outside. He answered the question without thinking about who had asked it.

"I like feeling the power. It's amazing, every time."

"And where are you going?"

He looked over and realized it was Jeong who had asked the question. She was looking at him expectantly.

"To San Francisco. I travel back and forth."

"For business, then?"

He nodded in agreement.

"Both. I live in San Francisco and Seoul. It depends on what I have to do."

"So what are you doing in San Francisco this time?" she enquired, leaning her head slightly, crossing her legs, her left over her right.

He fought to keep his eyes in contact with hers, while using his peripheral vision to admire her legs.

"I am meeting with several clients and their buyers."

She nodded.

"How long have you been with the airline?" he asked.

She looked up as she thought briefly.

"Almost three years now."

"And do you like it?"

"Yes. Every flight is different. Different people, different places. I don't like to be bored."

He nodded, understanding how the variety could be appealing. It was for a similar reason he liked sales.

"Do you find you get sick a lot, being in a small workspace, with recycled air?" It was a question he had been burning to ask of late.

After he said it, he wondered if it was an appropriate question to ask.

He wasn't overly proficient at more social conversations.

"I was at first. The first six months I was ill a lot. Then your immune system gets used to it. I haven't had a cold now for over two years."

Interesting, he thought.

"So is that normal for a new hire?"

She nodded in agreement.

"In the first year we are expected to be ill for several months. Then the body gets used to it and the immune system is very strong."

He thought that was fascinating, and it made perfect sense. He recalled reading in a science magazine where kids that grew up in very clean homes with no pets had a much larger incidence of allergies and sickness, because their bodies had built up no resistance. Kids growing up in Africa in the opposite study in quite opposite conditions had no allergies whatsoever, their immune systems being on high alert and exposed to a variety of challenges.

He felt the plane begin to level off, hearing the engines being powered down into level flight.

Jeong unclipped her seatbelt, standing and securing the seat back into place. She turned around, looking at Dak-ho.

"Nice to meet you. Maybe we can talk later?"

He felt his pulse quicken, and he smiled back.

"I hope to."

She turned to Madison.

"Have a good flight, Madison. Let me know if you need anything."

Madison put her book down quickly into her lap.

"Thank you, dear."

She brought the book back up, trying to forget where she was within its dog-eared pages. Jeong discreetly waved to him, and then disappeared behind the curtain. He settled back into his chair, wondering where things might lead with his very friendly and attractive stewardess. He looked down at the ocean below.

He could see the white caps of breaking waves far below, and puffy white clouds, like giant cotton balls, floating past. He watched as they overflew a large freighter, its deep wake settling into a wide V shape on the ocean surface. He turned to his flight-anxious neighbor.

"Do you mind if I close the window?"

"Please do. Then I can't see how high we are." She chuckled nervously. He drew the plastic slide down.

"My husband could fall asleep on a plane during take off. I never got used to it. I know all the studies that say it's the safest way to travel. For me, it's just the height."

"Does your son know how afraid you are of flying?" he inquired.

"Yes, normally he comes to see me because of it. I did the trip this time because I wanted to meet his girlfriend. They are expecting my first grandchild and she is on bed rest. Difficult pregnancy, poor thing. She has to lie down for three months. Anyways, this was the only time I could get off from work, so here I am."

"Well, congratulations, then."

She smiled.

"Thanks. I would feel better if they were married. But I'm from a different generation and I know you kids see things differently."

She reached out a hand and patted his left hand on the armrest.

"I'm sorry; I hope I didn't offend you by calling you a kid. When you get to my age everyone younger than me I see that way."

Dak-ho laughed quietly.

"No offense. I understand perfectly. I see people in my company the same way." The fact of his increasing age had hit him the year before. The company had hired a series of interns to do market evaluations to study buying decisions during the summer. He had asked one of them their age in the course of conversation, and when she had replied she was seventeen it hit him that he was seventeen twenty years ago. He was rapidly getting to the point where some of his youngest sales people could be the age of his children, if he had any.

"Well, thank you. You are a nice young man. See? There I go again."

He smiled back. At first glance, she didn't appear to be as old as she was claiming to be. The red hair helped that effect. She had some smile wrinkles around her eyes and mouth, a few spots, but nothing that gave the first impression of someone who must be in her fifties or maybe early sixties, based on what she said. He shrugged mentally. Surgery was a possibility, or she was one of the genetically blessed that aged gracefully. He had noticed he had started to go grey, but it didn't bother him in the slightest. He felt it gave him a more mature look. The cabin speakers suddenly came on with a faint crackle.

"Good afternoon, everyone. I would like to thank you for deciding to fly with us today. My name is Yeon Gaesomun, and I will be your pilot for this leg of the flight. Your co-pilot is Kim Gu, and he will be taking over later this evening. We have reached our cruising altitude of forty-one thousand feet. We have turned off the seatbelt lights at this time and would like to remind you that if they come back on it is for your safety so please buckle up. The skies are clear and sunny and we are expecting to see only great weather for the duration of the flight. We will be passing over Japan in a little bit, and you will be able to see the main island of Honshu to the rear of the plane, with Hokkaido at the front. The weather in San Francisco today is mild, about fifteen degrees Celsius with light winds from the west. Our flight time today is approximately ten hours and fifteen minutes as we have some wind pushing us along just a little bit faster, so we should get you landed on the ground about fifteen minutes earlier than scheduled, at about eight o'clock in the evening, Friday night, San Francisco time. On behalf of the flight crew, I would like to thank you for deciding to fly with us today, and we hope you have an enjoyable flight."

The pilot had a very radio friendly voice, Dak-ho mused. If he ever tired of his airline career, he could probably go into radio or broadcasting with minimal effort.

Madison had settled into her book again, so he sat back in his chair, and watched the small monitor in the headrest of the seat before him. Out of habit, he critiqued the screen for its quality. He looked for the contrast differences, how dark the black was, if he could see any shadowing effects or stair casing. It wasn't too bad. Not the cheapest option for the airline, but certainly not the most expensive either. It was a commercially available product, nothing he sold. He fished for his headphones, digging them out of his inside jacket pocket, and inserting the end into the jack built into the armrest. Touching the monitor, he selected the movies option on the menu. The hard drive took a moment to respond, finally displaying a series of viewing and listening options. He looked down at his watch, noting it was already noon. He would have time to watch a few movies before the plane landed. Sitting on board a plane was one of the few chances he had to catch up on watching shows he had wanted to watch. He selected a cartoon for the first movie, and settled back into his chair to enjoy the show, adjusting the volume up to keep outside distractions to a minimum. He didn't like to be disturbed while he watched a movie, a large reason why he didn't go to the theaters.

Madison glanced over to see what he was watching for a moment, and then she returned to her book, slowly watching the time pass on her wristwatch, wishing she was already home.

Try as he may, he fell asleep watching the first movie. It began all right, the story line of some lost insect in a bug version of New York, where small humans scattered into cupboards when lights were turned on, and then he began to yawn. They began small, and grew into the yawns that everyone around you catches in some sort of communal telepathy. He looked over apologetically to Madison as she covered her mouth to stifle her latest one, which caused her to laugh.

"Contagious, aren't they?" he asked.

The gentle humming of the Pratt and Whitney turbofan engines was very relaxing, and he soon found himself fighting to keep his eyes open, occasionally letting them close for a few minutes to see if he would be more awake after he opened them. Instead, he found opening them harder and harder. Eventually his eyes began to fight to close, and it took conscious effort to keep his eyelids from slamming shut. Eventually he gave up and let them close, and he sat there listening to the movie before finally falling asleep.

When he woke up, he found himself leaning against the cabin wall, his headphones still lodged within his ears, the in-flight menu of the monitor patiently waiting for his next selection. He woke up quickly, hoping he wasn't drooling or doing something in his sleep that would prove to be embarrassing. He stretched, and realized he felt great. He must have been more tired than he thought.

"Good afternoon," said Madison.

"We already had lunch, but you were sleeping so soundly we didn't want to wake you." She produced a wrapped sub sandwich.

"I selected this for you in case you were hungry when you woke up."

"Thank you." His stomach growled.

She pulled out a digital camera and punched a few buttons, and turned the view screen to him, showing him a picture of himself sleeping soundly against the wall, the headphones dangling from his ears.

"I hope you don't mind I took the picture. I thought it was too good a picture to pass up."

He shook his head, smiling, and unwrapped his sandwich. It looked like something with a bunch of deli meat of some sort.

"No, it's fine. I'm just glad to see that I wasn't yelling or something."

Madison laughed as well.

"I'm glad you didn't yell also. I am so jumpy on a plane I probably would have screamed."

They laughed together at the image of him yelling and then her screaming. He looked at his watch, amazed to see it was coming up on three o'clock.

"Wow. It has been awhile since I had a nap that long," he said to anyone that was listening. He pulled up the shutter of the window to see the Pacific stretched out underneath him, seeing nothing but blue ocean from horizon to horizon.

"I guess I missed Japan."

Madison nodded.

He took a bite of the sandwich. It was old, the bread a little spongy having soaked up some moisture from the meat and lettuce, but it tasted fine. He took a few more bites, chewing in silence, taking the edge off his appetite. He would have to have something hot when they landed, maybe a pizza.

He pressed the monitor back to the home setting where it showed an icon of the plane on a GPS setting. According to the display, he was travelling at eight hundred and fifty kilometers per hour. Looking outside where the clouds barely seemed to be moving and the ocean was an unchanging sheet of deep blue, it seemed hard to believe. The plane icon was well over the Pacific, flying near to Kamchatka nearing the ring of

Aleutian Islands that fanned out south of the Bering Strait. He continued to look out the window, hoping to glimpse the shadow of the aircraft on the waves below. As the pilots had predicted, the flight was smooth, the plane hadn't hit any turbulence that he was aware of. The clouds below were light and diffuse, stretched out thinly between the layers of atmospheric wind, like cotton balls pulled apart with giant delicate fingers. Almost at the height of the wing, the quarter moon hung in the blue sky.

A stewardess walked past handing out newspapers and airline magazines to those that were interested. He kept alert, watching as she made her way towards his row, the selection slowly thinning out as she handed out copies. When she reached him, the pile was down to half. He anticipated her question, so when she stood in the aisle to the left of Madison and made eye contact, he quickly said," I'll have a paper, please." She took the top issue, and passed it over Madison, excusing her reach to which Madison had replied there was no problem. Thanking the flight attendant, he unfolded and opened the paper to its front page, scanning the headlines for things that might catch his interest. The global economy was still growing according to the International Monetary Fund, showing steady gains as the world continued to recover from the recession a few years ago.

The ice sheets in Antarctica continued to melt, although so far it was still sea ice and not land ice, so there wouldn't be an immediate problem with a rise in sea levels. The arctic could expect to experience an ice-free summer for the first time in thousands if not millions of years. Polar bears were faring better than expected as seals were forced to have their young on shore, making for easy meals for the bears. The concern was now shifting to the welfare of the seals as bears were decimating newborn seal pups. At the bottom of the page, a small article made comments about the coming of the next day, and its significance to the Mayan Calendar. He made comparisons to the unfounded fear over Y2K and its results, claiming history was repeating itself. A small photo was above the article, showing a step pyramid somewhere in Central America, surrounded by thousands of people waiting to usher in the Winter Solstice, and a Mayan priest in full ceremonial gear atop the structure. He checked the date of the paper. December Twenty-first. Of course, that was a Korean paper. The day would not dawn fully upon the world for about another half-hour or so. The Chinese space program had made firm plans for a manned landing on the moon, with a follow up plan for a manned Mars landing. Israel and Palestine were still in negotiations to settle their dispute, hosted by Syria with representatives from all of the Arab nations, as the hopes of Middle Eastern peace seemed to be finally realistic. Iran was the sole holdout, and it was losing influence rapidly as its religious rhetoric towards Israel had begun to fall on increasingly deaf ears. The next Iranian election held promise for change as the upcoming generation was proving to not be satisfied with the status quo, the earlier Iranian revolution holding no significance to them. The Terrestrial Planet Finder funding had been approved by a United States Senate subcommittee, with an expected launch date of 2016. The article was brief, stating in summary of its goal to locate earth-sized habitable planets relatively close to our solar system. He turned the page where it showed a giant Chinese car factory mass-producing electric vehicles for the world markets, and then a huge wind farm off the Chinese coast, where the turbines seemed to stretch forever, their sheer size obscured by the lack of anything to compare them too. Having seen them in person, he knew each blade was over thirty meters long. The Chinese government was putting up wind farms as fast as they could be produced, wherever the wind was strong enough, in a massive effort to eliminate coal consumption for electrical production. Entire villages were being moved, if necessary, to achieve the Party's goal.

So far, it was working with huge success. The air in Beijing was becoming cleaner, and it was becoming a source of huge national pride. The Century of the Dragon was unfolding rapidly, a strong comparison being made to the previous century and the United States, who had been displaced as the worlds' top economy.

Gischane Camara

Gischane Camara lay on his cot, his blanket pulled up tight against his neck to keep the cool air out. Bright sunlight already filtered through the window of the trailer, the wooden slats doing a poor job of darkening the interior space. The air was still cool in the room, but would begin to warm quickly as the sun rose. He could hear the steady mountain breeze coming from the east, rustling the branches and leaves of the trees that surrounded the camp. The camp generator was chugging along, a huge red monstrosity that he barely heard anymore. When he had first come to the camp, it had kept him awake for his first two nights, forcing him to toss and turn, placing pillows over his head, and eventually, using bright orange foam ear plugs to keep the sound to a more tolerable level. Now, the only time he really noticed it at all, was when it was shut off, and the silence of the forest and hills returned. He had been back in his country for nearly a year, and was slowly acclimating back to the heat and humidity, although not without a bit of suffering. He had spent the several years in Paris, earning his bachelors degree in Geology at J. Fourier University, and then completing his Masters degree at the Ecole Nationale Supérieure des Mines de Paris.

He had shivered nearly his entire time there, the cold settling deep into his bones that he had tried to minimize with multiple layers of clothing. His only reprieve was that of a rare hot summer day, where the locals would be parked in front of air conditioners with a tall glass of something cold. He was a minority in the school, but he found several friends in the Islamic neighborhoods of Paris where he lived. He had quickly paired up with a slender Moroccan student named Sayid. He was almost six feet tall, and was wiry thin with a thick stand of straight black hair that he kept relatively long, in an effort to help him feel warmer. They both studied hard, and were not entertained by many of the fancies that offered distraction at the school or in the city. They had come here to study, and one hundred percent of their attention was bent to that end. Gischane was funded through a government scholarship earned through recognition of his abilities back home in Guinea. His country paid for all of his expenses, as long as he maintained his high grade results. His motivation to not shame his family and return home without a government paid-for education kept him on the straight and narrow. Sayid had been sent to Paris to study by his father, who was a fairly well off merchant who had made his money investing his family funds in Libyan oil speculation. When Libya struck oil with the development in the Elbouri Offshore Oil Fields, he had seen his investment pay off handsomely. The newfound wealth kept him focused on making certain that his children did not become lazy, and could be self-supportive. Sayids' older brothers had been sent to school in the United States to study engineering, and his sisters to medical school. Sayid had decided upon geology, simply to further a boyhood interest he could now pursue with the blessing of his family. His father came to Paris monthly to check in on his son and his studies.

The first time Joseph had met Yusuf, he was struck by the physical difference between the two. Yusuf was short and stocky, nearly bald, with a mind and eye that was always wandering, not satisfied with being in one place always looking for something else, in contrast to Sayid who was quiet and studious and did not like a great deal of external stimulation.

Gischane and Yusuf had hit it off immediately; Gischane being reminded of his grandfather, and Yusuf being impressed by the work ethic he displayed. When school had ended the previous summer, Yusuf had been present at the graduation ceremony, strutting about the school with obvious pride that his son had graduated. After the degrees had been presented, Yusuf had found them both in the crowds of intermingling people and families, and he had immediately hugged Sayid in a rare display of affection. Yusuf had then turned to Gischane, his eyes still moist, and given him a firm two armed handshake, congratulating him on his degree.

"Congratulations, Gischane. Sayid told me how hard you were working to graduate this year. I know it was hard being here without your family. We are both very proud of you."

Yusuf gripped his hand so tight he feared it may break, and he fought to not wince.

"If you need any help, please call me. I will always help people that are friends to my family. Allah has blessed me, and I would be a fool to not spread my blessing to others."

Gischane had been momentarily dumbfounded at the offer, and struggled to reply.

"Thank you, Yusuf. I will keep your generous offer in mind."

He could feel his eyes begin to water with emotion. At that point, Yusuf had turned to face both of them, and proclaimed loudly, "That is enough emotion for one day. We are talking like women! Let's go enjoy this day with a feast fit for the occasion!"

Yusuf had grabbed each of them with an arm over their shoulders, and together they walked away from the school grounds. They hailed a taxi to a local restaurant where Yusuf took control over the menu, ordering a little of everything and making the waiter struggle to keep up. At the end of the meal, the three men sat leaning back upon their chairs, their stomachs bulging. Yusuf had undone his belt and loosened his pants with a great sigh of relief. The evening drew to a close, with Yusuf hugging them both and then taking another taxi to the airport to catch his flight home. Sayid and Gischane took a taxi back to their apartments where they spent the next week tying up loose ends and prepared to return home.

Gischane had spent a few weeks at home enjoying the company of his family before he set to his work. He had first gone to the National Library where he had investigated mining and mineral rights in the highlands and mountains in central Guinea. The strata and content of the ground was what he expected to find, mostly comprised of granites and quartzites. His main source of frustration had been the lack of detailed information.

He could find topographical relief maps of the area, and only the most very basic of geological results. He found an area deep in the mountains where there were no existing mining claims, and he got busy. Filling a large backpack with basic supplies and sleeping gear, he bought a bus ticket to the central city of Dabola, where he could hike the remaining distance through the forest. His bus left Conakry while the morning was still dark, and it was crammed full of everyone and everything possible. The top of the bus was piled high with luggage and freight, live poultry and a large spare tire and fuel cans. The front and rear of the bus was festooned with bicycles of all shapes and sizes.

Inside the bus, people sat three to a seat, shoulder to shoulder, with others standing in the middle aisle holding onto handles for balance as the bus roared down the uneven roads.

It took two days to reach Dabola, where he was grateful to stretch his arms and legs from the cramped seats of the bus. He had been dropped off to the side of the highway at the crest of a hill. He had thanked the driver, and given him a quick wave as the bus drove off, belching diesel at it picked up speed downhill. He had stretched luxuriously for a few minutes, feeling the blood return to cramped and restricted muscles, and then put on his backpack, cinching it tight to his chest. Taking a deep breath, he walked off the highway and into the forest, his machete in his right hand. He had trekked steadily for a week through the deep forest, stopping frequently to mark his progress on his laminated map and verifying his bearings with his compass. He had chosen the long route to where he wanted to explore, opting to follow the winding valley bottoms for its relatively flat land instead of walking up steep hills only to face a steep decline on the other side. It doubled his distance, but it was an easier march. It also kept him closer to a source of water. He had made his way from one valley to the next, following the creeks and rivers as they merged and split, spending his evenings sleeping in a hammock under a draped mosquito net. He had brought a large amount of dried food that he ate sparingly, preferring to find food in the forest as he went. He had made an arrangement with a local trapper to bring him food once a week, providing the old hunter with a map of where he could leave the food, hoisted high into the treetops to prevent forest animals from feeding on his supplies. Eventually he had reached his target area.

For the most part, it looked like any other hillside in the forest. It was covered in trees and vines and smaller foliage, with a small plateau of perhaps ten acres that was almost perfectly flat. Sunlight filtered down through the layers of the canopy, the forest floor almost perfectly shaded. Small pockets of light that made it to the ground supplied younger plants with the energy to rapidly grow upwards in fierce competition. He found himself taking deep breaths of the clear air, enjoying the lack of exhaust fumes and dust he had grown accustomed to in the city. Birdcalls replaced the constant honking of car horns. He had pitched his tent nearer the middle of the area, next to two large lenge trees where he had hung his hammock. He spent an hour emptying his pack so everything was easy to find, and then built a small cook fire. He ate a small lunch of dried fruit and jerky, washed it down with some water from his canteen, and then made ready. Finding his rock hammer, with his map and compass in his pocket, he slowly made his way along the hillside, his trained eyes examining every stone that he passed over. All through the afternoon, the sound of his hammer cracking and chipping against stone carried into the woods. He spent his days working methodically along the hillside, his face covered with sweat and dirt, his hands blistering from the hammer grip as he cracked stone after stone. He kept a careful record of where he was sampling as he progressed, labeling each piece with a number and letter to designate where he had found it. At the end of the first night he had collapsed into his hammock, exhausted, and fell into a deep sleep only moments after unveiling the mosquito net. He awoke late the next morning with the sun already high in the sky, its bright light piercing the tree canopy.

He ate breakfast quickly, eager to make up lost time. He had quickly washed in the stream below, the cold water invigorating him, and he methodically began to trace his path set the previous day. Joseph worked his system, his bag slowly filling, his map filling with a series of marks and lines.

He emerged from the forest a month later, his bag filled with stones, his clothes torn and covered in sweat and dust. His face was streaked and lined from exhaustion. He sat at the side of the road, and waited patiently for a bus to pass by. When it did, he paid for passage back to Conakry. He slept the entire ride, his bag between his legs. Once home, he washed his samples and viewed each one with a small hand held magnifying eyepiece, his trained eye looking minerals blended into the stones. He made two piles, discarding one out his back door when he was finished. The other pile he sorted and brought to Guinea University, where he had access to a geology lab with is degree. He spent the next month crushing his samples in a small ceramic bowl with a pestle. Once ground into a fine powder, he analyzed each baggie of dust. They were subjected to acid washes, more examination under microscopes, spectrometers, and gas chromatographs. Each test revealed a story and the make up of each stone and its history over time. Each test and result was printed, Joseph meticulously filed each test under its location on the map, and as he went the results began to draw a picture. He was at the University from dawn until dusk each evening, his pile of stones slowly growing smaller. Once his testing was done, he carefully removed his samples, spreading the dust and fragments out over various areas and sometimes into the trash to prevent anyone from studying his work.

Two days later he strolled into the Ministry of Mining and Development, with a small crumpled map held tightly in his right hand, squished together like a small oriental paper fan, and a black folder brimming with papers. He found the claims desk after quickly scouring the signs hanging from the suspended ceiling, and approached the lady behind the counter, and waited. She continued to file some paperwork as he waited, looking up once quickly to acknowledge he was there. A small plastic tag on the shelf proclaimed her name to be Mary. Her hair was long and tied back in a tight ponytail that not one hair had managed to escape. Her office attire was bold but simple. A white cotton shirt underneath a deep blue sweater, and black slacks. Once her filing was completed, she rested on her elbows as she looked up at him.

"Can I help you?" There was no enthusiasm in the question, her voice monotone and flat.

"Yes, I am Gischane Camara. I have an appointment with Mr. Membeki, thank you."

She waited for a further moment to digest this bit of information, and then reached over to her phone and pushed a quick sequence of numbers.

"Sorry to disturb you, Sir. There is a Mr. Camara here to see you? Alright."

The phone clacked briefly as it was laid back into the cradle.

"Mr. Membeki will see you now. His office is in room 201 to the right of the hallway."

She motioned in the general direction of her instructions with her right arm.

Gischane nodded and smiled. "Thank you, have a good day."

"You too, Mr. Camara," Mary replied.

Gischane quickly strolled down the hallway, and found room 201 to be the third door.

A small painted sign on obscured glass declared it to be the Mining and Claims Office, Interior Region, of Guinea. He knocked twice quickly on the door, and winced as the glass rattled loudly, loose inside the wood frame of the door. He then turned the brass door knob and entered. The air was very cool, the air conditioner hummed loudly in the secured window frame of the opposite wall. An extraordinarily obese man in a suit sat in a mahogany desk adjacent to the air conditioner, his thin framed glasses hanging onto the bridge of his nose.

"Mr. Camara, I presume? Please have a seat."

When Gischane reached the desk the extraordinarily fat man outstretched his hand, and they shook in greeting. Gischane pulled a matching mahogany chair to the desk and he sat quickly.

"Nice to meet you, Mr. Membeki."

Mr. Membeki leaned forward on his desk, resting his upper body on his elbows, and Joseph felt the uneasy impression he was being studied.

"How can I help you today, Mr. Camara?"

"I need to register a claim with the land office for mining rights in the interior."

Mr. Membeki wheezed.

"And where is it that you wish to claim, Mr. Camara?"

Gischane quickly produced his folded map, and spread it out over the surface of the desk, trying to minimize the worse of the creases in the paper. His forefinger followed a bolded topographical line along the map as he outlined his area.

"This area here. It is approximately fifty square kilometers near the feet of the interior mountains. Very hilly, very forested."

Mr. Membeki remained silent and studied the map with only his eyes. His upper body remained motionless. He wheezed again. Then he looked up at Gischane.

"This area is directly in between two other mining territories, one to the north, and one to the south. Are you certain there is no pending claim to this land already?"

"One hundred percent. Before I examined the area I checked existing records to make sure I wouldn't waste my time."

Mr. Membeki nodded in acknowledgement.

"And what do you have in the folder?"

Gischane passed it across the desk. Mr. Membeki took the folder and leaned back into his chair, the folder resting on his belly, reading the papers through the lower part of the bifocals hanging low on his nose. He read each sheet with care, the minutes passing slowly and quietly. Gischane sat in nervous silence, leaning forward in his chair with his hands intermixed. Finally, after at least twenty minutes, the chair creaked loudly in protest and Mr. Membeki leaned forward, placing the closed folder on his desktop.

"You certainly came prepared, Mr. Camara. Are you certain about the figures?"

Joseph nodded once.

"Yes I took hundreds of samples in the area and analyzed each one. If the numbers are right, this could be the highest yielding mine in the country."

"Quite remarkable."

Membeki sighed as if it was anything but remarkable.

Gischane produced an envelope and slid it over the desk. Membeki raised an eyebrow and accepted the envelope. He raised the flap of the envelope and peered inside, his thumb expertly separating the bills as he made some quick calculations.

"F-f-for your time," Gischane stammered. Membeki looked up at him quickly and then returned to the envelope. In a few moments he pulled open a desk drawer, slid the envelope into it, and pushed it shut with a faint click.

"It's a very interesting proposition, Mr. Camara. Your findings are complete and seem to be in order and merit further inquiries."

Gischane was confused. "Inquiries? Inquiries to whom?"

"The established mining facilities that are in that area for starters. It must be verified that there is no existing claim to this area that I may not be aware of. It is highly irregular they would miss an area that seems to hold much promise."

Gischane felt his stomach drop.

"But if they are contacted they might claim the area. They have enough money to buy officials to give them the claim!"

"Nevertheless, this must be looked into. Your donation was most generous for someone from your modest family means."

Gischane felt like he would throw up.

"If the mine companies get even a hint at what I found I will lose it! All of my studies and work will have been for nothing!"

Membeki leaned forward across his desk.

"They may not be so unappreciative, Mr. Camara. I am sure that with the right phone calls, they would offer you a high position to compensate you for your efforts."

Gischane sputtered, his voice raising as he felt the walls closing in on him.

"A high position? I didn't go through all this work to be a foreman or a supervisor! I want the chance to run my own mine!"

Membeki stayed silent as Gischane vented his frustration, patiently biding his time.

"You are young, Mr. Camara, and your enthusiasm and hard work is appreciated and is to be considered. However, there are processes to be followed that I do not have the luxury of omitting. I will extend your claim for another thirty days before I make any inquiries. In the meantime, should you find the means to increase your donation to my office, I will reconsider investigating the claim validity, in light of your generosity."

Gischane's eyes nearly bulged out of his head in outrage, but he managed to keep his voice down to a controlled whisper.

"You mean to say that if I give you a larger *bribe* that I will get my claim, and if I don't you will sell this information to someone else? That envelope is my life's savings! My family is poor, there is no way I can raise more money, you son of a bitch!"

Membeki replied calmly.

"Profanity is not productive here Mr. Camara, and it will not aid your situation. Consider your options carefully. If I grant you your claim, your competition will instantly be very interested in your area. You have little funds available to you. How did you expect to proceed if I granted you this title? The land would sit while opposing interests did some exploring of their own, as you cannot hire anyone to keep the area secure, and I shouldn't wonder that you may meet with an unfortunate accident that would be beneficial to their investments."

Gischane slumped back into his chair, defeated.

"If you wish, I can contact these interests and negotiate on your behalf, for a modest fee of course. Like I said before, freely volunteering this information can secure you a lifelong position in these companies. You will be able to provide well for your wife. You can send your children to school. Many are not so fortunate."

He leaned back into his chair, crossing his hands across his chest. "Consider your options, Mr. Camara. You have my word I will not proceed for thirty days. If you cannot raise the necessary capital to develop this land, you have options, and I am the man that can make them happen for you. I bid you good day, and look forward to hearing from you. My secretary will see you to the door."

Membeki pushed his intercom button and summoned his secretary.

Gischane stood from his chair, and blankly and mutely followed her to the door, not hearing her as she wished him a good day. He squinted briefly as the sunlight flashed across his face, and he felt the hot air open his pores. He walked slowly back to his home, his face the picture of concentration and deep thought. By the time he got home, the sun had risen further overhead, eliminating his shadow altogether, and the heat and fresh air had cleared his mind. He knew what he had to do, and he wasted little time.

Mr. Membeki was a busy man. As the sole representative of the Ministry of the Interior in the area, everything related to development or exploration had to come through his door, unless it involved the army. If that were the case, he would receive a brief notification of what paperwork to file, for what area, and a brief memo saying thank you for your assistance in the matter. He had spent nearly his entire adult life in the civil service, getting his first job as an assistant to a local bureaucrat. His father had been a local farmer who had been generous with his surplus crops, hoping to win favour with someone in authority to give his children an advantage as they grew into adulthood. He had been working in the fields with his family, bent over black volcanic soil with the heat of the sun baking his back, when a white Mercedes has driven up to the family home. His father went to investigate, telling his children to mind their own business and to keep working; everything was fine. He kept working, finding a reason to somewhat face the home so he could see at least a little of what was happening. His father had quickly washed his hands under the water pump, and he went toward the car. The car looked amazing. There were only three in the entire town at the time, and so this was sure to create some excitement amongst the neighbors.

When he father reached the car, the driver opened the door and walked around the back of the car, opening the right rear door to a husky man in a suit. He had slowly exited the car, and then stood to meet his father, while the driver shut the opened door when he was clear. The man and his father were the same height, but he could see his father bend over a little, to be respectful of this man in the Mercedes. Membeki remembered feeling anger seeing this. His father was a successful farmer and did not need to bow to this stranger! By this point, he had stopped working and simply watched as his father had guided him into his home, mindful to open the door for him, and to close it behind him. The next several minutes were mental agony. What was happening? What was being said? Was there trouble? His mind raced from one idea to the next, the hot sun forgotten. Minutes passed, and he eventually returned to his work, albeit keeping one eye on the home. He slowly progressed down the field, his hand shovel turning under weeds with expert efficiency and smooth motion. He settled into the routine of the labor, his mind drifting off from thought to thought. With a start, he realized he heard his name being called.

"Phillipe! Phillipe!"

He stood and turned to the sound, wondering if he was imagining things. In the fields, it was sometimes hard to hear anything if the wind was blowing just right. The sounds of insects, of soil being churned, and of leaves rustling could and had overpowered his father yelling from the house before. His father *was* standing at the doorway, the door being held open with his left hand as he used his right to gesture his son to come to the house.

"Phillipe come now!"

His eyes had squinted with thought as he wondered why he was needed at the home. He drove the shovel into the soil, and began to run back to the house, his forearm wiping the sweat from his brow. His father stood still, watching him approach. When he got to the door, his father had placed his muscled arm around his shoulder, and looked him directly into the eyes.

"We have an important guest, Phillipe. He works in the city, and he would like to meet you. Whatever he says, remember your family." With that, he had clapped him hard on the shoulder, nearly knocking him over.

"Let's go."

Together they had entered the home, the door creaking on rusty hinges. Phillipe entered first and his eyes tried to adjust to the darkness of the room. He saw his mother sitting at the side of the table, with their guest sitting at the head of the table, one hand extended and open to him. He wore a bright white shirt and a gold tie, his jacket was slung over the chair behind him. His smile was broad and went from ear to ear, but his eyes did not fully convince him the genuineness of the smile. He felt like he was being evaluated, and he went on guard.

He approached him quickly, extended his hand and then shaking firmly, two quick pumps and release. His hand was dry and strong, and he smelled some mild sweet fragrance coming from him. His mother had cooked him a quick lunch, some meat stew with flatbread, the empty bowl sat in front of him on the table, a nearly empty cup of coffee on the side.

"Phillipe, it is good to finally meet you. Your father has told me many things about you over the years we have known each other. He says you are a good worker. Is he telling me the truth?"

"I am a good worker. My brothers are stronger, but I am faster. They are getting too big to go as fast as I can."

The man had laughed deeply for a few moments.

"An honest answer, Phillipe. Your father tells me you like to read. Tell me, when do you get the chance to read, working on a farm such as this?" He had shrugged quickly, responding quickly.

"I read at night after dinner. I have a small candle next to my bed, and I like to read a bit before I go to sleep. Sometimes I read during breakfast, if Mama lets me."

"What do you like to read, Phillipe?"

"I am reading an encyclopedia."

"An encyclopedia?" the man exclaimed, raising his thin eyebrows in surprise.

"I had expected you to be reading books like other boys, about pirates and girls and such."

"I have books like those," Phillipe had replied, "but I have already finished them and like the encyclopedia."

"Why?" he inquired.

"I like to learn about things from everywhere, I think it's good to know about other things."

"And what was the last thing you read in your encyclopedia?"

"It was about a Greek named Eratosthenes. He tried to measure the circumference of the Earth. He knew the angle of elevation of the sun at the summer solstice in Alexandria, and he calculated the angle in another city at the same time. His calculation was off by less than one percent, and that was almost two thousand years ago."

"Very remarkable. Remarkable, indeed. Phillipe, it was a pleasure to meet you. Your father and mother and I have more to talk about."

They shook hands again, and his father had led him outside. They both squinted as they stood in the bright sunlight. The driver of the car looked over his shoulder as he leaned against his door, exhaling his cigarette, then turning his head back to face forward.

"Go back to work, Phillipe. We will call you if we need you."

Phillipe nodded once.

"*Oui,* Papa."

He ran back to where he had impaled his small shovel into the ground, and quickly settled back into routine. The other children in the field watched him, hoping for an explanation of what had happened in the home. Sensing nothing was forthcoming, they too settled back into their rhythms. Phillipe kept his eyes to the ground, and focused on working. His mind was racing. What did that man want to see him for? His questions were strange. Why should he care if he read? And why did his parents serve him lunch? Why were his parents so deferential to him? He had never seen his father act that way. He was always respectful, but he had sensed his father hanging on every word he had said, how he had carried himself. And his mother seemed to scarcely breathe, tense and ready at a moments notice to serve some more food and drink, or to remove it from the table. The entire thing was very strange. Time passed, and his mind gradually eased into a more relaxed mode. He ignored his siblings working near to him, not wanting to answer the thousand questions he expected to be bombarded with if he showed even so much as an interest in talking. A while later, he heard the car doors being slammed shut, and then the sound of the diesel engine as the car slowly drove away down the road. His parents remained in the house, and he stayed in the field until the bell began to peal for dinnertime.

Seated around the table, the entire family remained quiet. His father sat at the head of the table where the man had sat that afternoon, and his mother went around the table scooping a meal of hot stew onto everyone's plates. Her spoon chattered loudly as it tapped against the tin plates, knocking any food that stuck to the spoon onto the plate.

In the center of the table, another plate was filled with a stack of flatbreads, and several bowls had been filled with cut fruit. His mother sat across from his father at the other end of the table, and she lowered her head. Her children immediately copied her, and his father began the evening dinner prayer. After several hushed "Amen's," the kitchen was filled with the sounds of people eating, people that had worked hard in the fields and had built up a furious appetite. There was little talk, mostly just the sounds of chewing and grunts of satisfaction and of cutlery tapping against plates, or scraping against plates to get the last piece of stew that stubbornly refused to hop onto a spoon. Phillipe had eaten a normal amount, but had done so without zest. He ate his dinner robotically, filling the void he felt within him, but realizing no satisfaction in doing so. His mind had begun to work hard again, creating plausible solutions to the reason of the visit. The problem was none of them seemed plausible under further scrutiny. Dinner progressed as normal, the family cleaned their plates and utensils and stacked them away neatly into the cupboards. His mother and father were quieter than usual, but to outside eyes the evening carried on as had dozens of evenings previously.

A month passed uneventfully, the curiosity of the visit that had remained sharp for a few days faded quickly into distant memory, and in some cases was already forgotten. The routine of the farm returned to normal and everyone went about their business. One evening Phillipe sat on a chair near the house. He was watching the sun set over the distant hills, the horizon turning into a myriad of oranges and reds. A few chickens pecked at the ground around him, scratching as they went, and their dogs were chasing birds from the fields, barking excitedly as they flew off into the sky. His brothers had retired into the house, and were settling into bed to be ready for the fields the next morning, while his sisters helped their mother in the kitchen before they too went to bed.

He could hear the occasional bang as a pot was hung from the ceiling, or the clap sound from a wooden cupboard being closed too firmly. All the sounds blended into the evening, and he found them relaxing. He didn't hear his father pull up beside him until his chair thumped into the dry ground beside him. A couple of hens looked in his direction at the sound, and then quickly returned to their foraging. He looked over at his father as he had settled into his chair with a sigh, the wood joinery creaking as it took his weight. He rested his arms on the sides of the chair and crossed his hands on his lap.

"What are you watching, Phillipe?"

"Just the sunset, Papa. I find it relaxing."

His father had nodded.

"When I was a boy about your age, I used to sit out here with your grandfather, and watch the sunset at night."

Phillipe barely remembered his grandfather. He had passed away when he was just four, and his memories were disjointed and random. He mostly remembered the smell of his pipe tobacco, and the feel of his calloused hands lifting him onto his lap for a story with his brothers and sisters. He remembered he was very wrinkled, but that his eyes held a kind of magic in them, the gleam of the memory of youth.

"He was still building the farm when I was small. He had built the house with your grandmother and his brother. It took them many years to get the farm going. The field was only half as large as it is now; the forest was still close. We would sit out here at night, and we would just look at the sky as the stars came out, relaxing a bit while we could."

Phillipe smiled. He was proud of his farm, mindful of the work his family had put into creating it. He hoped his grandfather was at peace. He was buried next to his grandmother at the foot of a large palm tree, two wooden crosses marking their spots simply. He visited them infrequently, paying respects if he was near the area.

"I received a letter from Mr. Youla today."

Phillipe frowned as he tried to remember who Mr. Youla was.

"He is the man that visited us recently, who you spoke with in the kitchen."

Phillipe had felt the flame of curiosity relight in an instant. He struggled not to show it, to appear indifferent to the news.

"What does he want, Papa?"

"He wants you to work in his office in the city."

A knot of uncertainty began to grow in his belly.

"Work for him? What can I do to help him? I don't know anything about the city!"

He struggled to keep his fear of the unknown under control.

"I have known Mr. Youla since I was a young. He comes from a good family, very respectful. Your grandfather helped his grandfather many years ago. His family had very little food, and they were very sick. He kept them here on the farm as they got better, and he helped him get back on his feet. His family has never forgotten this debt."

"So why me? Why not Robert or Jean? They are older and stronger than I am."

His father nodded, understanding the confusion felt by his youngest son.

"Your brothers will take over the farm when I am gone, to raise their families here when they marry and have children of their own. They are farmers to their very soul. They feel the earth, feel it breath and will do well here. You are different, Phillipe."

Seeing the protest rising in his eyes, he had countered quickly.

"Yes, you can farm, but you have more potential, and I see it, and Mr. Youla sees it. You love the land as do your brothers and sisters, but your mind is elsewhere. You are always hungry to learn. Your brothers do not care to read unless it helps the farm. You read because you like to. How many people here know of that man you remembered in the kitchen? Eratos?"

"Eratosthenes?"

His father had smiled.

"Yes, the Greek. No one here knows of him but you. Mr. Youla needs someone like you, and because of our family debt, he first inquired to me. I told him of you nearly a year ago, and last month he finally came, to see you for himself. He was very pleased. And so was your mother and I. We couldn't be more proud. You are going to work in the city, to go to school, to be someone important."

Joseph understood. The choice was already made. A great cold lump of fear had settled into his stomach like a tumor, fear of the unknown, and the fear of leaving what was known. He felt a lone tear drip onto his nose.

"When?"

"In two days. He will come in two days. You will live with his family in Conakry. You will work with him in his office in the morning, and go to school in the afternoon."

"Will I come home sometimes?"

His father reached an arm to Phillipe, resting his hand in the middle of his back, patting him in a soothing motion.

"You will come home in the summer, and on some holidays. You will be missed, Phillipe. Your mother cried for hours when she read the letter, but it is a sacrifice we are willing to make, for your future, for our family."

Phillipe fought back what felt like a great braying sob, his throat had constricted tightly. He wiped his tear away with his forearm.

"You will do us proud."

Phillipe nodded.

His father stood and pulled him to his chest in a tight hug. In that embrace, Phillipe wept.

The car arrived two days later, as promised. Mr. Youla was absent, but it was the same driver as before. He had placed his small suitcase in the trunk of the car, all of his worldly belongings stuffed inside it, and then made the rounds with his family. He hugged his brothers and sisters goodbye first, making his way to his mother, who had held him tight to her chest, crying quietly as she did so. He hugged his father briefly, before he had broken the hug softly, and then shook his hand, as he would to another man from the village. "Remember what I said to you that day, Phillipe. For our family."

Phillipe nodded and smiled, the anguish of leaving being fought moment by moment with the excitement of what lay beyond. Taking a short look at the farm and homestead, he stepped into the backseat of the car. The driver closed the door behind him, got into the front and started the engine. As the car turned and drove down the road, he sat up and kneeled facing out the back window, and waved goodbye, his family all waving back, his father holding his mother, until he could no longer see them.

It took several hours to drive to Conakry, and Phillipe spent most of his time looking out the window at the countryside passing by. He had never been more than a few kilometers from his home, so the drive west was full of new sights. The land slowly became less hilly and mountainous, and the smell of the ocean air became more noticeable. The driver spoke infrequently, only asking him if he needed to go to the washroom when he had stopped for gas, or if he was getting hungry or thirsty. Otherwise, the only companionship was the sound of the radio, which was full of noise and static as they drove through the winding hills. By the time they had reached Conakry, the hiss had cleared up and the radio came in clear as a bell. The city was the first that Phillipe had seen, and the commotion and volume of people amazed him. He had seen photographs in his books, and heard stories from his father and others in his village, but they had not prepared him for the reality of what was now passing before him, street by street, block by block. Eventually the car pulled into a narrow side street, and then paused at a driveway, waiting for an iron gate to slowly swing open. It whirred quietly, and then clanked once loudly. The car slowly proceeded past the gate, and then parked at the end of the driveway. Phillipe had looked around, taking in the surroundings while the driver had left the car and popped the trunk. While the driver was behind the car, a tall woman in a colorful dress came out of the house towards the car. She came to the side, and opened the passenger door, leaning over with a broad smile.

"You must be Phillipe, come out of the car, dear, so we can get a look at you."

Although he was shy, and a little afraid, her smile was genuine and he could not help but do as she asked. Once out of the car, she held him by the shoulders, keeping eye contact with him and continuing to smile.

"Aren't you a good looking young man?" she asked, and he could feel a deep blush settle in from the roots of his hair down to his neck.

"I am Marie."

She placed one hand on her chest to emphasize her name.

"It is a pleasure to meet you, Phillipe." He smiled back.

"It is nice to meet you, Marie."

With that, she pulled him close to her, chuckling.

"Thank you, Phillipe. Come, let me show you our house." She looked back to the car.

"Antoine, please bring his things to the house and leave them in the hallway."

Antoine nodded his head once quickly, a hand going to the rim of his hat as he did so.

"Yes Ma'am."

"Thank you, Antoine."

She placed an arm around Phillipe and led him to her home. It was a simple home, but elegant, with many touches that Phillipe could see had been the personal flair of Marie.

Pruned rose bushes had been spaced equally along the length of the fence, a spot of color against a fence that itself was simple and clean. A red brick walkway led to the front door, curving in a lazy S from the driveway, its sides decorated with small bushes and grasses. The front door was simple in design, but fit into the stucco design of the home perfectly. It was a dark stained hardwood, framed with obscured glass sidelights and a clear glass transom highlighted with wooden divided lites. The interior of the house was painted a light shade of brown with white highlights, accented with ornately framed mirrors and small pieces of darkly stained furniture that matched the front entry way.

Phillipe was dumbfounded by the extravagance and display of finery. Phillipe spent the next few years in this house, feeling accepted as an adopted member of the family if not truly as one of their own. As promised, he returned to his home in the summer, and on several holidays through the year. It was easier for him to understand the desire of his mother and father to go to the city and take the opportunity he was given. Before he left the farm, it seemed everything he could ever hope for. In his universe up to that point in time, it was the sign of success he was accustomed to. A large acreage, with fertile land and several more acres of fallow land, with land still uncleared for the future. In the city, the concept was different, and to a young man, very appealing. His training began the very next morning, driving in to the government office with Mr. Youla himself, dressed in a conservative and office-appropriate white cotton shirt, black slacks and black shoes. He had never had clothes like that at home, and he had spent several minutes looking at himself in the mirror of the home before Marie had ushered him patiently outside to the waiting car. He started at the very bottom, delivering messages from office to office, running errands for various other officials and their assistants, and other day-to-day tasks that were inglorious but necessary. All the while, Mr. Youla kept an eye in his activities, monitoring his work and progression with oversight that was anything but subtle. In the afternoon, he went to school that was a block from the ministry offices, where he indulged in reading and learning as much as he possibly could. The resources of the library were limited, so when he read a book he dedicated it to memory, knowing he may not be able to refer to it in the future for some time. He impressed his teachers with his work ethic and skills, who forwarded their views to his caregivers in due course. One by one the years passed, one blending and fading into the next. He was promoted from one position to the next as his skills developed and his education was completed, rising with slow and steady sureness within the ministry.

Phillipe double clicked the icon on the screen, and waited for the screen to open.

"Thirty nine emails?" He shook his head.

"How can I get thirty nine emails in one night?"

He spoke to no one in particular; it was a habit he developed from working alone in his office over the years. Listening to his own voice was better than listening to no one. Music was too much of a distraction when he was entering information in triplicate and each entry needed to be perfect. He worked best in utter silence, where he could concentrate and focus on what needed to be done. His quirk of talking to himself, of thinking aloud had been the side effect. He seemed better able to make a decision if he heard himself say a problem out loud, instead of thinking about it. He spent a few minutes reviewing files and applications from the previous two weeks, shuffling paper from one folder to the next, humming to himself. He saw the claim application for Gischane Camara, and quickly recalled the particulars. He had expected the young man to be back in the office all ready to settle the matter of the territory he wanted to mine. He supposed that maybe he was going to take the entire thirty-day window to exhaust his options. He sighed and shook his head. The amount of his offered bribe was sufficient to to get anyone in the government to take his claim seriously. He had hoped that by educating the boy about the costs necessary to develop his stake that he would relent and tell him to proceed with contacting his other sources. No such luck yet. He had several investors that would pay Gischane handsomely for his information, and provide him with a steady well-paying job for life. And Phillipe a nice little kickback, of course. Money he could send home to his family farm. Still, he had to respect his stubbornness. When he was young he likely would have felt the same way, if he had been given the chance. No matter, in another few weeks the boy would be in his office, they would conclude the agreement, and they would both be the richer for it.

The screen opened and he began to go through the list in his inbox, one email at a time.

His intercom made a quiet buzzing sound. He depressed a red flashing button with his left forefinger.

"Yes?" He heard Yvette through the speaker.

"There are two men here to see you, Mr. Membeki. They said they have an appointment."

Phillipe frowned. He opened his appointment scheduler and opened it to today's date. It was blank except for a meeting in the afternoon. Well, no matter, his calendar was open; perhaps he had forgotten to make a note.

"Very well, Yvette. Please send them in."

The intercom connection stayed open for a moment, long enough for him to hear Yvette say "He will see you now." It cut off as she directed his appointments down the hall. He waited patiently, quickly making sure everything on his desk was organized and neat. A desk told you a lot about a person. He heard two sets of footsteps coming down the hall, and then a light knock on his door.

"Come in, please." He spoke loudly so he would be heard. The door creaked open, and two men entered quietly. His eyebrows went up in curiosity. Two Arabs, if he was not mistaken. Very interesting. He did not often see Arabs in his country. He was intrigued. One of the men was tall and heavily built, his face very masculine, with dark intelligent eyes. The other man was shorter, maybe five and a half feet tall, very thin with aquiline features, wearing thin black rimmed glasses. Both men wore suits, the taller Arab in a black suit, the shorter one in a tan suit. He stood to greet them, extended his hand. "Salaam, gentlemen. Please sit."

They both shook his hand in turn, returning the customary reply before sitting down. The shorter of the two sat nearest the door. "Now how can I help you? You have travelled far, and so must be here on a serious matter. I know everyone important in our government and army, and so I am sure I can facilitate your business interests here very efficiently."

The tall Arab sat forward.

"I am glad to hear that. We are here to make certain our business interests are handled promptly."

The shorter one nodded. Phillipe was intrigued further. He had expected the taller man to be the bodyguard of the shorter.

"Do not be mistaken, Mr. Membeki. We are here on behalf of our client, and we prefer to see our work handled quickly. You see, we work on a contractual basis, so the faster we get results, the faster we can proceed to our next job. Our reputation is very important to us. Doubtless you perceived my presence as that of a strongman. I can assure you it is a common misconception. My partner is stronger than he looks, and he also has more training in the ways of being, shall we say, persuasive. I, on the other hand, move faster than you would expect."

Phillipe was growing concerned. This seemed to be a strange partnership, and stranger still, was why these two would be here to see him.

"Forgive me," said the taller one.

"I should explain our position further. My name is Navid. My partner is Darius. As I mentioned earlier, we are here on behalf of our client who seeks a resolution to an issue that you are involved with."

"Resolution?" Phillipe asked.

"I can assure you, I have no matter that is in dispute. There must be a misunderstanding."

"There is no misunderstanding. My client was quite explicit with the situation, where you were described in detail."

Phillipe pushed the intercom button on his phone.

"Yvette." There was no answer. He looked at his watch. She should be at the desk.

Navid smiled thinly.

"Your secretary is not at her post, I am afraid, Mr. Membeki."

"What? Wha...what have you done with her?"

Phillipe stammered.

"I can personally assure you that Yvette is quite fine. We paid her a small sum to be elsewhere for the time being. I presume she is shopping. We gave her a cell phone, and when we phone her, she will return. We understand you are accustomed to receiving sums of money for favors?"

"Of course, it is customary in all levels of our country. It is the way we do business."

"Good, then I am correct in assuming you will bear Yvette no ill will?"

Phillipe had planned on firing her the minute she returned. He shook his head to the contrary.

"Good. We would be displeased if she were to meet with repercussions for something you do on a regular basis. Nevertheless, we will follow up with her to be certain you kept your word."

Phillipe swallowed hard. This conversation was rapidly going against his favor. Whoever these two represented had moves planned ahead.

"Would you mind discussing what brought you here?" Phillipe inquired.

Navid turned to Darius.

"Do you mind if I continue?

Darius shrugged. "I don't mind at all."

Navid nodded and turned back to face Phillipe.

"Excuse us. We usually take turns, but Darius is quieter than usual."

"You have in your files a mining claim filed by a Gischane Camara, do you not?"

Phillipe began to fidget.

"I may."

Navid chuckled, amused.

"You do. He met you by appointment just over one week ago, where you advised him to surrender his business interests, or return with a larger bribe. Quite despicable, don't you think? Ransoming a mining claim for a bribe?"

Phillipe immediately went on the defensive.

"The boy does not have the money to develop his claim fully."

He slapped an open palm down on the desk.

"I am merely trying to protect his interests by making him see he cannot proceed. If he takes my advice, I can get him a good paying job."

Navid leaned forward.

"I can assure you, my client does not see it that way."

"Your client?" Phillipe asked.

"How can Mr. Camara afford your services?"

"You assume too much, Mr. Membeki. Mr. Camara is not our client. Our client is rather fond of Mr. Camara, and of relevance to you, he *can* afford our services. It is very doubtful that Mr. Camara is even aware of our presence here, our client preferring to operate with a minimum of fuss."

Phillipe felt a bead of sweat run down his spine.

"What do you want?"

Navid laughed quickly, a broad smile flashing brilliant white teeth.

"I like you, Mr. Membeki. I like you a great deal. So many of our visits with our customers are more difficult to resolve. You understand your situation clearly, and seek resolution. You are a pleasure to deal with. Quite simply, you will immediately process for approval the mining claim filed by Mr. Camara. There will be no holds, no delays."

Phillipe nodded, his face blank.

"You will use the contacts you previously mentioned to facilitate the approval, if necessary. There will be no unfortunate leaks to opposing interests; the application will proceed quietly.

"I can process the approval first thing tomorrow morning," said Phillipe. His tongue felt dried to the roof of his mouth.

"I have another appointment this very afternoon."

"Not acceptable, Mr. Membeki. We arranged our meeting this morning so we can personally supervise the approval today. I can assure you we will not interfere. We are here to simply witness the transaction so we can report its completion to our client. The later appointment you speak of has already been moved ahead one day. We have made the necessary arrangements. He was most understanding."

"And if I cannot?"

"Then, Mr. Membeki, one of your family will meet with an unfortunate farming accident. One phone call is all it takes. If you continue to protest, we can find other means of motivation more personable to you."

Darius drew from inside his jacket a nine-millimeter handgun, brightly chromed, with a large matching silencer, and he began to thread the two together.

Phillipe dug into his folders, quickly producing the mining claim filed by Gischane a week earlier. With his hands shaking, he opened it, and spread it over his desk.

"I see we have reached an understanding," said Navid.

Darius grinned. His teeth were bright white and perfectly spaced.

The two sat patiently across from Phillipe all morning. The two sat quietly, at times paring their fingernails, or simply staring forward as he completed the file.

Two hours later he pressed the SEND button on his screen, and the dot matrix computer on the shelf whirred into life, the printer clacking loudly as the form was generated.

Phillipe gathered the form, stamped SENT and APPROVED on the cover page with two large red stamps, and handed it over the desk to Navid. The large sweat spot under his armpit had grown appreciably, and the stack of papers shook as it changed hands.

"Relax, Mr. Membeki." Navid and Darius reviewed the stack of paperwork without expression, examining each page thoroughly. Phillipe sat nervously, quite certain that these two men knew exactly what they were reading, and what to look for. He only hoped he hadn't forgotten something from his nerves. They might be understanding, but then again, they might not. He felt like he was going to be sick. Minutes passed, and finally Navid collected the paperwork together, and sorted it into a neat stack, placing it down near the keyboard.

"Everything appears to be in order, Mr. Membeki, well done. Sometimes people attempt to slip things past us. You apparently took us seriously. Fortunately for you. I…"

"Now what?" Phillipe interrupted.

Navid sat back in his chair, opening his palms outwards as if he was going to catch a ball,

Navid did not appear too upset that he had been cut off. Phillipe regretted it immediately.

"Now? Now we go about our business. You can keep the funds Mr. Camara paid you. We have a few more arrangements to make before we are entirely done with our client, but our time with you seems to be at an end. Unless of course, complications arise after our departure."

Phillipe had the strong impression that if complications arose after their departure they would be back quickly, and their company would not be wanted.

"We appreciate your cooperation in this matter, Mr. Membeki, and we wish you a pleasant afternoon. We will see ourselves out, if you don't mind."

Navid and Darius stood quickly, and within a few moments Phillipe was listening to their footfalls echo from the hallway, and then a jingle as the office door was opened. He exhaled deeply, not realizing he had been holding his breath. He quickly rubbed his hands over his face as he collected his thoughts. He gathered up the printed file, and slid it into a folder tagged APPROVED. He closed the file quickly, happy to be rid of it as it slammed shut with an abrupt click sound. He sat in the quiet for several minutes, just thinking. Who the hell was Gischane Cama associated with for him to get a visit like that? Phillipe suddenly had to grab the garbage can from the side of his desk. Wheezing, he puked up his breakfast into it in heaving gasps. His knuckles went white as he gripped the edge of the can, feeling his stomach contract in waves. Afterwards, he leaned back in his chair, wiping the sweat from his face and wishing he could get that sweet sickly taste out of his mouth. It was even in his nose. Grimacing, he spat into the can to try to get rid of the taste, wiping his mouth with his forearm when he was done. He didn't notice an improvement. The intercom buzzed faintly on his desk. He depressed the button.

"Mr. Membeki?"

"Hello, Yvette." He groaned softly, hoping he sounded normal.

"Can I get you anything?"

He wondered what would happen if he did fire her, and then thought against it. His mind remained blank.

"No, Yvette. I will be going home for the remainder of the day."

After he cleaned out his garbage can, that is. Maybe he should just throw this one away. The thought of rinsing his puke out of the can made his stomach turn.

Yvette watched as Phillipe left the office. She was concerned, as he rarely had sick time. Still, there was a bug going around. He was decidedly pale, and his eyes bloodshot. She hoped that whatever he had wasn't catching. She hated being sick, and she hadn't been sick in four years. The worst thing about being healthy was that you forgot just how shitty being sick was. Oddly, his shirt sleeves had been rolled up to his elbows, and were wet at the edges. Maybe he had washed his face. After she had watched him drive away, she glanced down at the bag under her desk. She had spent the morning shopping with the money the two businessmen had given her, purchasing two new dresses, some make up, and some dried fruit and a nice lunch, with some money left over which she had cached in her bra. She hummed pleasantly to herself, happy with the unexpected good fortune of the day.

Gischane sat in his apartment, feeling the heat of the midday sun slowly bake the interior of his room. The last few days he had spent in deep thought, wondering where and how he was going to get enough money to get his claim approved. The rage and despair he had felt when he had left the office the other week had faded, and was replaced with a dull feeling of failure. Thinking the conversation through, he realized that Membeki was right. He didn't have the money to develop his claim. The chances of him vanishing in the woods were not so unlikely, after he had thought it out. Some upstart university grad goes into the jungle, files a mining claim, maybe cashes out a few ounces of gold or so, and then he gets followed back to his camp, and is never seen again. He wanted to think that this couldn't or wouldn't happen, but he had to be realistic. This was worth perhaps millions of dollars, and far worse had been done for much less. The sonofabitch in the claims office was probably right. He could sell the rights to his claim, get some money out of it and a good job. The more and more he thought about it, the more and more it seemed what he would be forced to do. It sure beat the alternative of being a rotting corpse dumped in the jungle. He could not bring himself to go to the phone and call Membeki. Not just yet anyway. He had emailed Sayid when he had returned from his appointment, and he had had the good fortune to find him online as well. They had chatted for a while, where Gischane had vented his dilemma to him, telling him what had happened, what he had found, and how he seemed to be screwed. He couldn't bear to tell his family, so his friend from school was a good option. Sayid had asked a few questions about what he had found, trusting enough in Gischanes field and lab work to not ask more. They had chatted online for a couple of hours, after which Gischane had felt better for getting it off of his chest. They had agreed to chat again in a couple of weeks. He had spent some time walking through the city, deep in thought, trying to find a solution. He walked through the streets, watching children playing football in the back alleys and lanes, young and old chasing worn out balls in giant mobs. He smiled fondly, remembering his times of playing with his brothers and other children from neighboring farms. He had spent entire days playing football, and imagined these kids did as well. He had spent one day at the beach, throwing rocks into the deep blue of the Atlantic ocean from the breakwater, a large construction of boulders that had been dumped in a nearly straight line parallel to the beach. It helped to keep large waves from eroding the beach, which was popular with tourists. He had spent the day by the seashore, watching old men string out their fishing lines into the receding tide, or others in their boats pulling up nets and lines strung out from rods tied to the sides like large antenna. He found the sea relaxing. The near constant sound of the waves breaking against the shore, echoed with the pounding sounds of the larger waves smashing against the breakwater was rhythmic, drowning out almost everything else. A few gulls and terns cried out overhead, but otherwise the sound of the water dominated all. He had enjoyed feeling the sun bake into his skin, the smell of the salty air, the feel of the smooth beach sand on his feet. He had mostly simply stared out at the distant horizon, towards Brazil, seeing where the ocean met the sky in a fusion of blue. It was said the Pacific Ocean held no memories, and he wondered if the same was true of the Atlantic.

He had returned home late in the evening, his skin dry and a deep-seated thirst beckoning him. He had removed his sandals and had gone into the kitchen for some water when he heard a quiet but sharp knock at his door. He looked at his clock, wondering the hell would be knocking at his door this late at night? He hid a knife in his front pocket, concerned about being robbed, and approached the door. He opened it partially to the extent the brass security chain would allow. Two men in suits stood in the hall.

"Gischane Camara?" the tall one asked.

"Yes?" Gischane answered questioningly. The two were well dressed and well groomed, both with black briefcases.

"May we come in please? We have some business to discuss at length with you."

They must be from a mining company. Those bastards. It had only been a week and that shithead Membeki had already told them where to find him. He felt the dull anger rising.

"You can tell Membeki to kiss my ass. He gave me a month, I will take my month!"

The two men looked at each other, and then back at him with a patient stare. At least, he assumed from their body language they were staring. He couldn't see their eyes through their sunglasses. The short one sighed.

"We do not represent Mr. Membeki, I can assure you. I am allowed to divulge that we did speak with him earlier today; however, pertaining to your application."

Allowed? What did he mean, allowed?

"Who are you and what do you want?"

"My name is Darius, my friend here is Navid," the short one said, gesturing with a turn of his neck.

"We were hired by your Libyan friend Yusuf to attend to matters here that were brought to his attention. Let us in, Mr. Camara, unless you want your neighbors to hear our entire conversation."

Yusuf? Gischanes' eyes widened as he digested the sentence. He closed the door, and fumbled with the chain briefly as he slid it out of the lock. What did Yusuf do, he wondered? He opened the door widely, gesturing with a sweep of his arm.

"Come in, please."

The two men nodded in agreement, stepping forward quietly and in unison. He closed the door behind them, peering out into the hallway to the left and right first to see if anyone else was out there. The two mean had seated themselves at the kitchen table, their briefcases each leaning against a table leg to their right. Taking a deep breath, he sat at the table, his hands crossed together on the table top.

"Can I get you anything? Some water?" Gischane asked, suddenly remembering his own deep thirst.

"Water, please."

He poured two tall glasses of water from his tap, and handed them to the two men.

"Thank you, Mr. Camara." They drank from their glasses. Gischane poured himself another tall glass, drank it, and then poured another before sitting down.

"Thirsty?" asked the short one, Darius, whose name he suddenly remembered.

"Yes, I was at the ocean all day. You mentioned you were hired by Yusuf?"

"Straight to the matter, Gischane. My colleague and I were hired by Mr. Yusuf Nasser to attend to settle your claim application that you had discussed with his son."

"Sayid?" Gischane groaned.

"Sayid told Yusuf?" He shook his head.

"That is apparently correct. Judging by your reaction it was not your intent. Regardless, Mr. Nasser is quite fond of you and mentioned he was acting on a promise he made to you in France."

Gischane quickly drank the rest of his water. *His promise in France?* He remembered the conversation. He had no intention to ask Yusuf for money, he would have been mortified to ask for help!

"But I didn't ask for his help!"

"Mr. Nasser expected your reaction, and so acted without your request. He said you were too proud to ask. Mr. Nasser is a very insightful man. He was correct about you, as well."

"So what are you two here for?"

"We have been hired firstly to verify your mining application has been approved. Secondly, our services have been contracted to provide you with the necessary security and resources to develop your claim. The first portion of our contract has been completed."

"What?" Gischane exclaimed, not believing his ears. "What did you say about my application?"

"It has been approved. The land is yours to develop as you applied for."

"But how? How did you...?" The sentence trailed off as Gischane realized he may not want to hear the answer.

Navid predicted the question.

"Mr. Membeki was most helpful in approving your claim within a few hours. He was convinced that it was in his interest to proceed. He is very efficient when pressed."

"He will kill me! Once he gets a chance…"

"He is not your concern, Mr. Camara." Navid interrupted surgically. "He is under a very clear understanding from our visit with him today. You are very unlikely to ever see him again, and if you do, I feel confident he will be most helpful."

Gischane paled, understanding what Navid was saying. Then he felt a bubble of elation rise through him. He clapped and jumped around his apartment with a release of energy, laughing with happiness. All of that work wasn't going to be wasted! He spent a few minutes being overwhelmed with the thoughts of everything he was going to have to do. When the immediate thrill had passed, he returned to the table.

"What next?"

Darius answered.

"Tomorrow we will make the necessary arrangements to supply your operation and locate to the area. Once provisions and equipment have been secured, my partner and I will secure the talents of a reputable security group that will be in charge of your safety as well as of the claim area. From there, Mr. Camara, you will hire as necessary the people you need to proceed with your mine. We have access to whatever funds we require, under the review of Mr. Nasser, to see this operation underway. Mr. Nasser for his investment will see a fifty percent stake in your operation. He did not anticipate any protest with this expectation."

"No, of course not. It is quite fair." Joseph agreed. He would have agreed to a minority share if that was the offer. He couldn't believe his luck.

"Very well, then. We will return tomorrow at noon to begin making the arrangements. We will contact Mr. Nasser to advise him we have reached the expected agreement. At this point, he wishes to remain anonymous and so asks you to not contact him until he states otherwise."

The two men rose from the table.

"Congratulations, Mr. Camara."

"We hope to be of great service to you."

They shook hands, and with their briefcases in tow, left his apartment. Gischane locked the door behind them, and then he laid in bed wide awake until four in the morning, unable to sleep as his mind raced with plans.

The next two weeks passed quickly as the arrangements were made.

Gischane hired a few miners to start the operation, a cook, and his new accomplices hired his security team. They secured transport from an old olive green Huey helicopter, a United States military model sold off to the highest bidder. In this case, the bidders name was Kamil, a muscular Kenyan with silver sunglasses who had found a good market for his machine and services in the area. Although the helicopter was old, it was fastidiously maintained. If Kamil wasn't sleeping or flying, he was working on the Huey, the skin under his fingernails perpetually tinged with oil and grease. His Huey was his baby, and he knew its workings by sound. Darius and Navid had introduced Kamil to Gischane at the airport, where he kept his helicopter off to a secluded corner of the facility, far from the runways and nearest buildings. They had driven up to the pad, where Kamil was sleeping inside the passenger compartment, his feet hanging out over the edge of the chassis. When the car had pulled up, Kamil had awoken, swinging himself out of the machine and standing next to it, waiting to see who was coming. He stood leaning against the cockpit, one hand shielding his face from the sun. Kamil did not seem concerned in the slightest. Darius and Navid stepped out from the car, and Navid opened the door for Gischane, closing it behind him when he had stepped out. The three of them walked towards Kamil, stopping a few meters away from him.

"We have come here to hire your services," said Darius.

"You know my rates and conditions," replied Kamil.

Darius nodded.

"That is why we came to see you. Our client, Mr. Camara, requires you and your helicopter for an unspecified amount of time." Darius gestured to Gischane, who was standing in between and slightly behind them. Kamil looked at him, and nodded.

"When can you be ready?"

"Where are we going?"

"Flying inland to the foot of the mountains; there is no landing pad as of yet so it will be a return flight. You will be dropping off a few men and supplies. We will provide you with the coordinates when you are ready."

Kamil nodded.

"She will be ready tomorrow. I will replace the fuel filters before we go. How is eight tomorrow morning?"

"Eight is fine. Until tomorrow, then."

Darius and Navid shook his hand in turn, and then Gischane did as well, sealing the arrangement.

They returned to the car and drove away. Gischane watched as Kamil watched them drive away, and then open a side hatch on the fuselage.

"Can he be trusted?" Gischane asked.

Navid nodded.

"He has worked with us before. He is very loyal, and dependable."

"How do you know he can be trusted?"

"We pay him well, and he is somewhat of a mercenary."

Gischane nodded, having to trust their knowledge of the man. They returned to the airport the next morning to find Kamil fueling the helicopter and loading on some full jerry cans as well.

A large pot of coffee was brewing on the tarmac, attached to a solar powered inverter that was providing the power.

"Coffee, my friends?"

Darius and Navid shook their heads no. He shrugged, and turned to Gischane.

"Coffee?"

"Yes, please."

Kamil strolled over to the pot and poured a large mug full, handing it to Gischane.

"Sugar?"

He nodded, and Kamil poured a few teaspoons into the mug, and handed him a small stirring stick. He sipped at it gingerly. It was hot and very rich.

"The beans are from my home. My brother plants a few acres. We have the best coffee in Kenya."

Gischane nodded. "It is very good."

Kamil nodded and smiled, and looked over at Darius and Navid.

"You see, *he* likes my coffee. I will have you try some one day," pointing his forefinger at them.

He returned to the helicopter, walking as if listening to an unheard song, whistling as he went. He topped off the fuel hose, and returned it to the pump, and then closed the hatch.

"There, my friends. We are ready to go," he said expectantly.

Darius looked at his watch. It was ten to eight.

"We are waiting for a few other employees. You will be dropping them off at the destination."

Kamil nodded, and hopped into the cockpit, going through his pre-flight checklist. A few minutes later, Gischane had nearly finished his coffee, and an old rusty Lada pulled up to the pad, parking next to their rented Mercedes. Four men stepped out, and began to retrieve various gear from the trunk of the car. Kamil noted the arrival, and had begun to warm up the Huey, its rotors beginning to slowly cut through the air as its motor warmed up.

Darius gave him a thumbs up, which Kamil returned. He then placed a headset on, adjusting the mike and earphones to a comfortable fit, and began talking to someone. The first three men stowed their gear onboard the chopper, several bags being piled on top of chainsaws and axes and shovels and lengths of rope. The fourth kept his belongings close to him, a duffel bag slung over his shoulder, and a briefcase held tightly in his right hand. He stood close to Darius and Navid, presumably another former acquaintance newly rehired for this contract. Darius remained on the ground while the other men climbed into the helicopter and strapped themselves in. Gischane was directed into the co-pilot seat by Kamil, who was talking to the control tower. Kamil looked back over his shoulder, and received another thumbs up. He nodded, and increased power to the chopper, the blades swirling through the air. With a small bump, the Huey began to lift off, and then climb forward. Picking up speed, it traced a smooth half circle over the corner of the airfield, and then straightened out its path towards the east. Kamil handed Gischane a set of headphones. He put them on, fitting them snugly over his ears.

He was amazed at how efficiently they blocked out the sound of the helicopter.

"So where are we going, boss?" It was Kamil.

Gischane dug out a map, unfolding it and spreading it over the control panel. He pointed to the near center of the claim site, where the ground was the most level. Kamil looked at the map, and nodded.

"Okay boss. On the way. Enjoy the ride." Gischane folded his map back into his pocket, and looked over the side at the ground passing by below. Kamil was smiling from ear to ear, flying being the love of his life.

They arrived over the site a few hours later, hovering over the thick forest canopy that was swaying in the wind being pushed down by the Huey. It was tough to recognize from sight alone, save for the distinctive landmark of the small cliff face where had explored. The lack of concealing undergrowth on the bare rock face made it easy.

The four men tied their ropes to the undercarriage of the helicopter, and rappelled themselves and their supplies into the forest, disappearing as though swallowed by the trees. Navid untied the ropes when they were safely on the ground, allowing them to fall to the men below. The chopper turned around, and flew for home.

They returned a few days later, to find a neatly cleared landing pad cut out of the forest, standing in stark contrast to the dense jungle around it. Kamil smiled.

"It looks like your boys have been busy!"

Piles of cut logs had been stacked to one side of the clearing, with small burn piles taking care of the dense underbrush and branches.

A few of the logs had been squared off to use as support beams and cross members once they were needed. He flew the Huey over to a smaller cleared area, and positioned the chopper squarely over it. Once satisfied with his positioning, he pushed a release button, unhitching a cable from the undercarriage of the chopper, allowing the bundle of supplies to settle onto the ground. He then went over to the larger area, where he touched ground to let Gischane off, and his newest security employee.

"I'll be back in two days, Boss."

Gischane gave him a thumbs up, slapping his hand against the warm

THE AGE OF CENTER

body of the helicopter, and then he turned around, and ran crouching out of the landing area. Kamil took off, the wash from the rotors blowing loose vegetation everywhere. Gischane stood and watched the chopper rise and finally disappear over the crest of the nearest hill, the echo of the rotors rattling through the valley.

He turned to his newest employee, a fellow highly recommended by Navid for his skills.

"Quaashie?" he asked, hoping he pronounced it right.

"Did I pronounce it right?"

"Yes, sir."

"Good. Petiri has set up his security operations center over next to the tamarind tree." The center, as of yet, consisted of a small desk with a few maps showing the local area and topography. The map was marked showing where he patrolled regularly, not too far away from the camp where he was provided good cover.

"Get yourself organized, and when he comes back I am sure you two will have a lot to talk about."

Quaashie nodded, and walked briskly over to the small desk, placing his belongings under a camouflaged tarp that had been stretched out from the tree to the ground. Gischane walked over to the supply dump clearing to see how it was going over there. A few of the crates had already been opened, revealing cans and bags of dried foodstuffs and preserves. Gischane sat down briefly to wipe some sweat from his brow. He watched Quaashie unclasp a dark metal briefcase from his belongings, and swing it open with care. The inside was molded foam, matching the color of the exterior shell. With finesse, he quickly removed the components of the case, snapping and twisting them together in an efficient manner. Within a minute he assembled an AK-47, albeit one that was chromed and had the look of a prized possession. He inserted a clip into the underside, and chambered a round. Attaching the shoulder harness to the rifle, he slung it over his shoulder and began to review the maps. Gischane was beginning to think Navid and Darius had hired ex-Special Forces troops as his security team. He mentally shrugged, thinking that extra talent could come in handy. Navid and Darius seemed to think that might be needed, and so he had to trust their judgment.

121

Returning to the crates, he found a pry bar and began working on the sealed boxes. A few nails gave easily, and a few as per normal refused to cooperate, splintering the wood as they reluctantly gave ground. Two of the three men that had been dropped off in the initial forest drop emerged from the bushes, coming from the direction of the cliff face. When the wind shifted, he could hear a pinging sound, something metallic that was striking at a regular interval.

"Abdalla and Zalika?" The two men nodded. Zalika, the taller of the two, spoke first.

"Madu is at the rock face, beginning to dig."

"You have been busy, I see. Thank you for your hard work."

The two men nodded, accepting the compliment silently. Together the three of them unpacked a few more crates and assorted the items in similar piles. So far they had one for tools, another for food, and another for clothing and shelter. A few oil drums stood in the center, sealed and labeled, with a hand pump and hose tied to the top of one of them. They spent the next two days working through the pile of crates, eventually dispersing the pile until only a stack of empty crates remained. He had met Madu the evening of the first night he was there. He had started a sizeable hole in the cliff face. It wasn't yet deep enough to require bracing, going only a couple of feet into the rock. A sizeable pile of rubble had been dumped to the outside of the hole. Madu was a stocky man, short but built heavily, his arms thicker than some legs, his legs thicker than some waists. His chest was broad and inset, with deep muscle that did not seem to tire.

He enjoyed the hard work of swinging the pick axe into the stone, the work a challenge he measured through the progress into the stone.

He was quite content to have Zalika and Abdalla unload the supplies. Both men were of lighter build, and did not begrudge Madu the work he liked. There was enough hard work ahead for everyone.

As expected, Petiri and Quaashie spent considerable time together, testing each other's abilities and building a level of trust and camaraderie important to their responsibilities. They did no physical labor at the camp. Their responsibility was to keep the area secure, and so they did. They patrolled frequently, sometimes together, sometimes as a team on opposite sides of the valley, keeping in contact with personal radios.

After seeing them work together, the rest of the camp settled into a regular routine, confident in their mutual skills.

As scheduled, Kamil arrived in two days time, the steady beat of the helicopter rotors echoing through the canyon minutes before the chopper itself was visible. He dropped off another large bundle of supplies, this one having a few larger crates. He contacted him via the camp radio while he was still overhead.

"Come in, Kamil."

"Yes, Boss." Gischane smiled. He was always just Boss to Kamil.

"When are you going to more frequent deliveries?" He knew some supplies and specially ordered merchandise would be available shortly, so Kamil would have to make more frequent runs to the camp as the supplies became available for delivery.

"I have another tomorrow morning, and then it looks like about two per day for a while." Gischane nodded.

"Do you know what is coming?"

"Uh, I think a generator, drills, a trailer, some pumps, fuel, and lots of heavy shit."

"Thank you, Kamil. Have a safe flight and see you tomorrow. Over."

"Thanks Boss. Out."

They exchanged waves and he returned to his tasks.

The next week was busy, with the team trying to put away the supplies that Kamil was dropping off, or assembling the machinery that was in the crates. By the end of the week, they had run a pump down to the creek to keep them with a good supply of water, and a large industrial Kubota generator. Madu had assembled a Sterling water cooled mining drill and was cutting deep into the rock face, preparing to blast his way into the cliff side and make some real progress. The drill was attached to the water pump and sprayed water everywhere as he bore the cutting edge deep into the rock. He was covered with water and rock dust, and he smiled every minute of it. Abdalla and Zalika had constructed a basic sluice, and ran the debris that Madu was creating through it in their off time. Their work had paid off already with a few ounces of gold. Most of it was small flecks, but a few larger nuggets were already produced, increasing the already high morale of the group of men.

Gischane had a small work trailer delivered, which became his work area as well as sleeping area. It was positioned under the shade of a palm tree, to keep the thin tin structure from getting too hot to make being in it unbearable. As it was, the door to the trailer was open nearly all the time, a mosquito net draped over the door to keep the bugs out. He had considered getting a trailer for the camp workers to sleep in, but after seeing how warm the interior was in his, they exclaimed they were more than happy to sleep in their tents, or under their hammocks and nets.

The camp had started to fall into place, with the generator being positioned near the edge of the camp, but highly visible and easy to watch over and refuel. Before long they were accustomed to its noise and most of the time had forgotten it was there. The rest of the camp was situated in a semi-circle around the cliff face, with the area around the early mine shaft being cleared and leveled to make for easier work conditions and removal. A small rail track had been laid down in preparation for when the mine became deeper, and a rock crusher positioned further down in a straight line near a water source.

A large box of dynamite and fuses had arrived the day before, and Madu had spent the day gingerly sliding sticks of dynamite down into a myriad of holes he had bored into the rock, pushing them down gently with a smooth stick. His face the look of extreme concentration, his body tense with caution. The rest of the camp had stood clear as he laid the charges, and watched nervously, fearing a giant explosion and the death of Madu. It would be a bad omen to lose someone so early. Madu finished laying the charges, and ran back to where everyone had been watching him from. He stripped the ends of the two wires in his teeth, and connected them to a small yellow hand detonator, screwing them down tightly. After a quick head count to make sure everyone was accounted for, they had inserted their earplugs, and Madu began to count down aloud.

Five…four….three….two…one….and he pumped the detonator handle twice. For a split second nothing happened, and the camp collectively held their breaths, and then the wall of the cliff exploded outwards in a gigantic roar. Abdalla fell backwards in surprise from where he was sitting, and everyone else flinched as they felt their insides shake from the explosion. A huge dust cloud poured form the opening, billowing out and then collapsing back to the ground, where the slight forest breeze gradually carried the thick dust away. They could hear the dust falling on the leaves, like static on a radio. When they could see the cliff face again, it looked as though some mountain creature had belched forth a tremendous pile of stone from its lair, leaving it scattered across the hillside. Rocks and boulders of all sizes were everywhere, and a neat shaft had been cut into the hillside. A collective cheer rose from the group, and more than a few people had patted Madu on the back congratulating him on his blasting. They milled around the opening, waiting for a few scattered rock falls to come to an end before they got too much closer, no one wanting to wear a rock on their head. Satisfied the worst was past, Gischane and the others found some flashlights and cautiously entered the new mine shaft. The mine had been blown fifteen feet into bare rock, the hard stone yielding only grudgingly. Gischane had shone the light on the mine wall, carefully holding the light to the surface, rubbing dust away with his hands to better his view. The crew grouped their lights together to where he was looking, effectively illuminating a good portion of the wall face. Meter by meter he crept down the wall towards the back of the shaft. Half way down, he stopped, and tried to rub more debris out of his view.

"I need some water."

Quaashie returned moments later with a full canteen. He passed it into the group of men, who passed it hand by hand down to Gischane.

"Thank you." he replied to everyone.

He unscrewed the cap, and slowly poured the water down the wall.

The dust first absorbed the water, and then clumped together, and then slowly washed down the wall into the ground. He poured the water cautiously, scrubbing at the wall and peering closer. As the water trickled down, a faint yellow line became apparent in the stone. It ran in a nearly horizontal line, thickening and waning as it went, disappearing into the earth. Gischane screamed and began to holler, pointing at the vein of soft metal weaving through the stone. The men cheered, seeing the gold embedded in the hard rock. They had spent the rest of the day clearing the rubble out of the shaft entrance, and then Madu began to erect the support structure, hauling the cut and squared off logs to the entrance. Abdalla began to hammer the boulders and rocks with his sledgehammer, washing the remains clean and then sifting through the gravel for the precious metal. Zaliki and Madu measured and cut the beam lengths inside the mine, nailing them together with six-inch spikes. There were a few more small rock falls from the roof of the cave, so Madu had taken his sledgehammer and struck away pieces of ceiling that seemed weaker than the rest. A few more blocks had fallen, but no more after that. Once the beams and struts were in place, the remaining detritus was slowly cleared and crushed by hand. Gischane began to look forward to the arrival of the rock crusher. The larger boulders still had to be reduced to smaller sizes by hand, but the thick steel rollers would take care of the vast majority of the rubble they had produced.

When Kamil arrived in the afternoon, he had delivered the components of a small furnace, so they could smelt the resulting metal into more manageable ingots. There was beginning to be enough work around camp to be done that he needed more men.

Further development was being slowed and impaired. He sent the information back with Kamil, with an update for Darius and Navid on the progress being made. The next helicopter brought another eight men, more than doubling the amount of men at the camp in one fell swoop. Kamil had made three deliveries that day, the first for the new crew, and the remaining two the awaited rock crusher.

For the next month, the infrastructure of the mine was assembled with the completion of the rock crusher at the end of a large belt. The smelter was constructed on a separate platform that was built in another clearing, and a few trailers were brought in for the crew after all, complete with small air conditioning units that ran in the evening after the large camp generator was shut down for the day. The security detail had grown to four individuals, two for a day patrol and two more for a night watch. The miners had begun to work in shifts and specific teams were now involved in the actual drilling and blasting, and others for the removal of the debris. The mineshaft extended over a hundred and fifty feet into the bedrock, following the vein of that gold that had thickened as they went deeper into the hillside. The vein had also begun to produce silver and smaller quantities of platinum. Everything was beginning to go as he had hoped from the very beginning. Except he felt a cold coming on, and a damned good one by the feel of it. He had kept the blanket on the entire night, making sure every draft had been sealed, and he still felt cold. The sunlight coming through the window burned his eyes and made his head feel like a chisel was planted in his forehead. His joints ached. Every one. His fingers, his shoulders, his toes, his spine, everything. He could feel his sinuses filling up with snot, the kind that you can't breathe through and that gives you a sore throat in the morning. He lay there, feeling everything, and tried to convince himself that he was imagining feeling this bad, it couldn't be real.

Maybe he had eaten something bad the previous day. Maybe it was heat exhaustion. Except that he had felt that before, and this wasn't the same. The last time he had felt this bad was his first winter cold in France, when the winter chill had crept into his very bones and settled there, threatening to make every moment of life an unbearable hell. This felt a lot like that. Eventually, he managed to get himself into a seated position, the wool blanket wrapped tightly around his body and neck, scratching his skin, making him want to itch it fiercely.

Except he felt too crappy to move his arm to scratch the itch. Judging by the light coming through the window it was probably around eight in the morning. His watch was sitting on top of the small plastic table sitting near the bed, but he didn't feel like stretching over to check.

He managed to catch a small sunbeam where he was sitting, and he felt the heat warm his skin through the blanket. It made the rest of him feel colder. He sat there, eyes closed, trying to feel better, trying to feel warmer.

He could hear the camp activity picking up as the days work was about to begin. The generator was in the background, its familiar loud hum drowning out most of the background sounds. He could hear men talking and laughing, and then the faint sound of the water pump further down the hillside. A moment later, the generator gurgled and then quit. The water pump was quiet also. The sounds of the men became much more apparent, and the deep silence of the forest seemed to amplify the camp chatter. *At least I still have an appetite* he thought. The worst type of cold was when you didn't even want to eat. He could feel his stomach grumbling, and even heard it make a faint wheezing growl. He suddenly felt a little better, realizing that at the very least, he wasn't nauseous. He stood slowly, feeling his muscles and joints protest the effort, his headache flaring briefly and feeling more than a little dizzy. He made his way to the table where he had a little food, a soft granola bar with a fruit filling and a little chocolate. He washed it down with some warm water, and felt a little better. The taste of the food had reduced the awful taste in his mouth. He opened the trailer door, and felt the warmth in the outside air soak into him. It was going to be a hot day. He stared about the camp for a few minutes, taking stock of what everyone was doing. A couple of men were looking at the generator, apparently discussing what the problem could possibly be. A few others were sitting around a smoldering fire, tying their boots and preparing for another day, where a few more were going into the mine, their tools slung over their shoulders. If the generator couldn't be restarted, there wouldn't be too much progress made today.

Ibrahim al-Sadr

Ibrahim climbed the stairs of the tower slowly and methodically, his sandals making a slight scratching sound against each step as he went upwards. The still morning air was cool on his skin; the rising sun had not yet broken the dark line of the horizon, although off to the east the dark sky was yielding to a dawn palette of blues.

The city was quiet and awakening but was waiting for the call to prayer to begin the day. The muezzin of the mosque, Mohammed, was certainly at the top of the tower already, waiting for Ibrahim patiently. He cleared his mind as he climbed, preparing his intention for the morning ritual. He allowed his right hand to trace the wall as he went upwards, feeling the roughness of the plaster and stone on his fingertips. He found the speaker wire that had been secured into the wall, and opened his palm to it as he walked. The wire ran from the top of the minaret down into the mosque and surrounding courtyard, here and there spliced off to speakers mounted on rooftops or under eaves. The minaret was a relative rarity in the sense that he insisted the calls to prayer were made from the top platform of the spire. Many mosques simply ran speakers to the tops of their towers to broadcast the call to the faithful. Ibrahim rejected the concept, feeling deep in his heart that to be lazy in a place of worship was an affront to his faith. God was difficult to sense in the modern world with its speed and haste; from the tower top he felt closer to what he sought. So he and his muezzin climbed the spire five times a day. He was feeling his years this morning, his joints were sore and aching, although not so sore as other days.

Ibrahim had recently and quietly witnessed the passing of his sixtieth birthday. He had stared at himself in the mirror for seemingly an eternity. He had noted the wrinkles on his brow and face, his hair becoming more white than black. He did not recognize the old man staring back from the bathroom wall. His eyes still shone with wit and intelligence, his mind sharp and focused. He had little to regret in his life, and inshallah, *god willing,* he had many good years remaining.

He reached the top of the minaret and found Mohammed waiting for him, as he had thought.

"As-Salaam-Alaikum, Ibrahim."

"As-Salaam-Alaikum, Mohammed." *Peace be with you.*

For a few moments they both gazed out over the city, enjoying the quiet and peacefulness of their surroundings. The evening stars were beginning to fade from the sky, only a handful of bright ones still shone clearly in the fading sky.

"It is time, my friend."

Mohammed nodded and turned around, flicking a switch mounted on the inner wall of the spire, turning on his microphone. A faint snap of static broadcast blurted from the speakers following the high whine of feedback, and then all went still again. He turned up the volume of his microphone and returned to the outer walkway of the spire. He cleared his throat quickly, took a deep breath, and began.

"Allahu akbar Allahu Akbar
Allah is great Allah is great
As ha du Allah illaha illaulah
I bear witness that there is no God except Allah
As ha du Allah illaha illaulah
I bear witness that there is no God except Allah
Ash-hadu anna Muhammadur rasulullah
I bear witness that Mohammad is the messenger of God
Hayya alas-salat
Make haste towards prayer
Hayya alal-falah
Make haste towards welfare
As-salatu khayru min an-naum

Prayer is better than sleep
As-salatu khayru min an-naum
Prayer is better than sleep
Allhu akbar Allahu Akbar
Allah is great Allah is great
La ilaha illallah."
There is no God except Allah

As Mohammed sang the call to prayer, Ibrahim closed his eyes and listened to his voice carry over the square and neighbourhoods below. His voice was clear and strong, and carried well. He often thought that Mohammed had great talent, that his voice was a gift from Allah. With his eyes closed and his mind focused on the beauty of the call, his mind recollected earlier days and times. Ibrahim was transported backwards in time to 1979. He smiled to himself at the memory, a young man just graduated from university. He had travelled to Iran to reconnect with his homeland, Persia, the cradle of civilization and the home of his family. His mother and father had immigrated to the United States when Ibrahim was very young, and he had no recollection of his birthplace, save smells and sights that he could only now place. The scent of jasmine in the courtyards, the noise of the selling and trading of the market place, the musical calls to prayer that pierced the sounds of the city.

His first day in Tehran he had walked the streets alone, tears in his eyes and a grin on his face, in love with the city and its people, reawakening to his culture and his people. He had been taught about the Middle East in school, and from his parents who had made certain that he was fluent in Farsi as his first language, and English as his second. He was grateful to them for his education and teachings, making certain that he did not forget his roots. The sense of history all around him overpowered his imagination.

He had read about Persia, the Middle East, and histories relating to his culture, but here it was in front of him, an open book flooding his senses and begging to be read. The smells, the sounds and the sights. It overloaded his brain, had reset everything to zero, as if he had crashed into a wall and had reopened his eyes now aware of his surroundings in a way that he had ignored before, a rebirth of his mind. In America he was used to the timeframes of history spanning decades, perhaps a century, and if stretched, two centuries. He was now walking through streets and villages that had been populated in some cases for over a thousand years, sometimes two thousand. Through these streets had walked Alexander the Great on his conquest to the East, the armies of Persia; history made real, not read from the flat tomb of dry dusty pages from a book. The wonder of it all made him want to scream into the streets that he was home, his mind wanting to explode.

He stayed in rented apartments from town to town, having no family in Iran; his friends were back in America. He strolled through the bazaars and street shops for his groceries and other necessities, taking time to absorb whatever he could from each passing moment. He was new to the area, and instantly identifiable as a stranger, his odd American-Farsi accent unfamiliar in the old streets. As such, he was initially kept at arms length, as no one knew of him or his character. Tradition compelled and custom demanded open arms, and he slowly won over the locals as a trustworthy young man. He befriended a short portly vendor named Mahdi, from whom he shopped regularly, a man quick to smile and laugh, and deep in observance of his faith. Mahdi had one day asked him what mosque he attended services in, and Ibrahim had quietly replied that he had not attended any services while he had been in Iran. Mahdi had nodded in patient understanding, his wise eyes showing he was aware of the challenges a young man in a foreign country might face. He passed no judgement. Instead, he extended his right arm, clasped it firmly on his shoulder, and invited him to prayer at the mosque he attended.

"This way you will come with a friend, and not be surrounded by strangers."

Ibrahim had nodded and smiled gratefully for his understanding, and accepted the gracious and sincere offer.

He had met Mahdi for the Friday service at his shop, and together walked to the local mosque. It was an old building, its white plaster faded and cracked from the hot sun overhead. It was simple and functional, the entryway a wide arch that opened into a wide corridor that divided into separate walkways, one for the men and one for the women. They left their shoes at the entrance and walked in together, solemn and in reverence. An old Imam, whose skin was a deep brown and set with deep wrinkles on his forehead and cheeks, wrinkles of study and mirth, led the service. He walked with a shuffling gait, his back slightly humped over with age, but his eyes bright with life, clear and sparkling. The eyes of a young man trapped in an old body. His presence and demeanour commanded respect and deference; the mosque was utterly silent. His service was simple, brief points of information from the world at large, and quotes and wisdom from the Qur'an. Ibrahim had paid rapt attention throughout his service, as his discussion ranged from dealing with strangers, the promise of forgiveness, and finally the Shah. He had felt the tension in the mosque, a tangible emotion that was a raw undercurrent emanating from the people gathered in prayer. His voice was clear and carried with authority throughout the mosque. The Imam worked to ease his congregation, to remove the unease. His had begun keeping his voice low, making the congregation work harder to hear his words. As he progressed, his began to raise his voice, to punctuate and stress his session. He played the congregation with skill, a master orator that read the mood of his audience. When he needed the mood to change, or wanted to emphasize a point, he did it with his voice alone. He kept the vocabulary simple, the lessons clear, and the message unmistakeable.

At the end of the sermon, Ibrahim was introduced to the Imam. He was introduced to him by Mahdi, and was offered his hand in greeting. Ibrahim took his hand, and was surprised to feel the strong grip. He looked up at the Imam, and was surprised to see a small grin cross his face.

"I am old, but Allah has not yet taken my strength."

Ibrahim had quickly chuckled, his involuntary response to being caught in the truth. His eyes quickly widened with horror, and he dropped his eyes and head with penance.

"Please forgive me, Imam. I meant no disrespect."

He felt his heart thudding in his chest, his face growing red.

"There is nothing to forgive. I am an old man, but I remember what youth feels like. Come, and let us share tea."

Ibrahim had exhaled with relief, feeling his shoulders lift as a perceived weight was removed. He followed the Imam to his study, a small room furnished with an old blue carpet, and two small tables. The walls opposite the door was lined with books, from the new to the very old. Simple shelves lined the walls from the floor to the ceiling, old cedar wood that had been hand hewn, the planks bearing the scars of hand saws, the cuts from the blades visible in the tight wood grain. In the middle wall, a small shutter less window was open to the street, allowing a faint breeze to flow through the space. He was motioned to the carpet, and together they shared tea while they talked into the night.

Over the next several years he had spent a good deal of time with the Imam, and became familiar with the books lining his walls. He became a familiar sight with the old man, a mentorship between the Old world, and the New. Ibrahim was fascinated by Alim, as he was allowed to name the Imam in private. He was tutored in his sermons; he studied the Qur'an in depth, eventually memorizing the Holy Book, and was impressed by the depth of wisdom that seemed to flow from his being. One day following an examination of the Qur'an, Alim had wandered over to his books, and with a slow rasping sound, had drawn it from its neighbours. A thin cloud of dust was blown from the cover with a quiet gentle exhalation. He returned to his carpet, and placed the book in Ibrahims hand. Ibrahim had studied the cover quickly. It was a thin black leather, old and faded and worn, with cracks running through the thick grain. The pages were yellow and worn, the paper thin and nearly transparent. He felt Alim's eyes on him, studying him as he examined the book. He closed the cover, and read the typeset centered on the cover in thin silver leaf. His forehead creased as he frowned, and he had looked up quizzically, and with question.

"You want me to read the Christian Bible?"

His eyes sought for a long answer, a reason for the direction. Alim had replied simply.

"Yes."

"But I don't understand, why…"

He was quickly and surgically cut off, a raised arm in the air calling for his silence.

"Because you must."

He looked into his eyes, and saw there was no room for negotiation, only acceptance. Ibrahim sighed quietly, and accepted the book. Alim poured some tea. Another year passed, and together they observed the fall of the Shah and the rise of the new government and Ayatollahs. The sermons had shifted from those primarily of teaching the Koran and explaining the wisdom of the prophets, to calming his congregation, diffusing the confusion and uncertainty. Ibrahim watched the role of the Imam change from one of a wise teacher and spiritual leader, to a leader of the community. His presence was a calming force, a guiding hand to followers. He had his greatest challenge with the youngest men of the congregation, those that were most susceptible to the messages of others. Others who preached not patience and perserverance, but violence and intolerance. Ibrahim witnessed Alim struggle as he fought for the minds of those young men and boys.

Ibrahim gave Alim back the Bible. Alim had nodded, and then went to his books. He returned with another book, this one even more worn than the previous, it's cover clinging to a fine coat of dust like an old favourite and worn blanket. He glanced down at the cover.

"The Talmud?"

Alim nodded, and returned to his tea. Ibrahim had nodded in reply, and sipped his tea, placing the Jewish Holy Book off to his side. The weeks passed and he gradually completed his latest assignment. During the weekly services Alim had begun to have Ibrahim sit nearby him, and occasionally he would read the Qur'an to those attending the service when Alim required a quote to use in context. At first it raised a few eyebrows in the congregation, but as time passed and Ibrahims' reputation grew, it became an accepted practice, and newcomers to the mosque would see an Imam and his studious pupil. He was known to be studying with the Imam, and had displayed strong character in the community, and was properly deferential to his teacher.

After the latest service, a day that promised to bake the city in a sweltering blanket of dry air, he returned the Talmud to Alim. It was accepted with a nod and it was placed back in its spot on the bookshelf, where a small rectangular hole had been present in its absence. Ibrahim had waited in silence while Alim returned the book and then returned to the small seating area. Alim poured his tea, took a cautious sip, and sat the cup back onto its saucer. He looked up at Ibrahim with his faded grey eyes.

"Now ask me the question." His voice was quiet but clear.

Ibrahims' mind raced with questions. He settled on the most likely.

"Why would you have me read the books of the Jews and the Christians?"

Alim sat upright, keeping his hands palm down on the tea table.

"Why do you think I wanted you to read them ?" he replied quizzically.

Ibrahim sighed inwardly. He hated answering a question with a question.

"To know their faiths better, to know what drives them and how we are different."

"NO!" Alim yelled, emphasizing his dismay by slapping his hands down hard on the table top.

Ibrahim jumped, not expecting the sudden outburst.

"Not to see how we are different but how we are the same! Did you not see the thread of likeness that runs through our faiths?"

Alim sighed deeply and quietly, nodding his head in understanding.

"You have already been influenced by those fools that undermine and lessen our faith. When you were in America, you had friends that were Christian, did you not?"

Ibrahim nodded in agreement.

"You probably had friends that are Jewish."

Again Ibrahim nodded.

"Were they so different, to be your friends? To be your friends you must have had respect for them, and they for you. You were friends because you had similar interests and similar beliefs. You may have even loved them."

"But they are infidels! Unbelievers! I understand that now!"

Alim's posture sagged visibly.

"Infidels, you call your friends. They would be ashamed of you to hear you discredit them. They believe in God, and so they cannot be infidels."

"But not Allah!" Ibrahim protested.

"Are you so close minded to twist the words of the Qur'an to suit your needs? They have faith, and through that faith they earned your

136

friendship, perhaps giving you too much credit. They do the work of God through a different name. A name! And because of a name you would abandon them. Open your mind, Ibrahim! You were raised in the West, so you can see through the lies and falsehoods of the Ayatollahs. You know deep within you, you know better than most the truths of the world. In this neighbourhood where we are now, people will be born here and die here, never leaving to see even a fraction of the outside world, to gain perspective and knowledge. Because of that they can be manipulated and mislead, knowing no better. There are those in the West with the same blindness; they will never understand or see the truths as they are also mislead and manipulated. But you are from both worlds, have seen both sides, and you can continue to do so if you choose to. Think of your friends back in America. Did they love and honour their families? Did they help those that needed help? They welcomed you, were cherished by you, and they respected you. Does that sound so different than what Allah commands us to do?"

Ibrahim bent his head towards the ground, ashamed of his thoughts. He recalled his friends vividly. They were as Alim had described, and he was embarrassed. His closest friend was Alex, a self-described dork that was well on his way to a medical career. His hair was always a mess, and he wore thick-rimmed glasses that were always sliding down his nose. Alex had been his campus guide, showing him the campus during orientation. He was intensely likable, being quick to smile at anyone and to give anyone help or directions. He had met Julie in his calculus class. She was a stunning blond with ice blue eyes, and a mind that was incredible. She could find a solution to a problem by *looking* at it. He had been jealous of her talent, and envied her for it, before he knew the cost she had paid for her skill. She was the only female in the engineering program, an outsider in a boys club that saw her as an anomaly. She was frowned upon and chastised, even by some of their professors who saw her presence and ability as a challenge or threat to the status quo. Mathematically gifted, she was socially awkward and had been forced to become self-reliant and to display outward strength. Inwardly she was insecure and full of doubt. Naturally, they had developed their friendship slowly, walls slowly coming down, and over the course of time, became inseparable.

"Remember the similarities of our faiths, Ibrahim. If there is one lesson you need to learn, this is it. Keep your mind open to possibilities. Once it closes, it stagnates and rots, and it will not be able to change. And so as time passes, your views will become more and more irrelevant, as the world and reality changes around you. Do you wish to know what I think?"

Ibrahim looked up at his mentor, nodding slightly in the face of his chastisement.

"You will need to keep your mind open, to hear what I have to say."

Ibrahim nodded silently. Alim began to speak quietly.

"Think of the similarities of our faiths. The messages in the Holy Books are virtually the same. The messages are those of love and honour, to be respectful, to not steal, to show the disadvantaged favour, to show the fallen hope, to help the misled find their way. The stories are also shared. The Flood, the book of Job, Moses, Creation, Abraham, Jesus. I believe that the reason they are so similar is because they are from the same God."

Ibrahim inhaled quickly in surprise. What Alim was saying was blasphemous. He forced down his feelings, intent on listening. Alim saw the shock in his pupils' eyes and watched him struggle with his feelings, and gain control over them. Satisfied, he continued.

"I have though about this for many years, Ibrahim, and it is the only conclusion that satisfies me as the truth. The great faiths have so many common points because they are trying to tell the same message. One God, call him whatever you like, trying to teach us over the ages through different vessels. Moses, Abraham, Noah, Jesus, all of them prophets of God."

Ibrahim posed a question.

"Then why are the faiths different?"

Alim was satisfied with the question, it was a logical response.

"The faiths are different because the vessels that deliver the message are impure, they have faults. Those that receive the message are also impure, and can change what they hear, if the message disturbs them. So it is bent to suit their motives. I do not pronounce to say I completely understand His message, but only to say I understand the minds of Men are easily corrupted. The prophets were born in different times, to different regions, with different situations. Because of this, they had biases, and the word of God that they were meant to deliver was diluted and changed. And people changed the message as well. Perhaps this was Gods' intention, to test his Creation."

Alim leaned forward across the table, staring deeply into Ibrahims' eyes.

"If we choose to read between the lines, I believe in there we will find the message that God wants us to hear."

He sat back to an upright posture.

"I fear that too many of us read the wrong message. The Israelis and Palestinians kill each other for reasons so far buried in the past as to be forgotten, and they should be forgotten and the mindless slaughter end. They have killed each other for decades, and will continue to do so long after I am gone from this earth. Mankind kills in the name of God, although it is expressly forbidden by God. We modify the Holy books if it serves to provide power or fame or wealth. I fear the Devil has influenced the world, and shown God how imperfect we truly are. I will speak no more this evening. Think of what I have said. I don't expect you to agree with me. I do expect that you will think about what I have told you, and I expect you to listen to my sermons deeper than you currently have been."

Alim slowly rose to his feet, his legs stiff from sitting so long, and he made his way to his bedchamber, leaving Ibrahim to sit in silence, lost in his own thoughts. Ibrahim sat there, alone, for fully an hour before leaving. His mind was a maelstrom of ideas and thoughts, all fighting for dominance as he struggled to sort out what Alim had shared. What the Imam had shared with him could have him killed by the Ayatollahs for blasphemy. And yet he was amongst the most pious of men he had ever met. He went home, and could not sleep.

Over time, he had listened intently to the sermons at the mosque, hearing the same words but finding different meaning in them. The teachings were well prepared, enough to satisfy the Mutaween, the religious police, that he was compliant with the Revolution. Hidden within the message, skilfully enough to fool the zealots, was a deeper teaching of the will of God. Weeks passed and he felt his mind open to new and wondrous ideas, and his heart opened and was filled with a joy he had never felt before. He found Alim alone one afternoon in the mosque, he was sweeping the floors with an old straw broom that was frayed and broken at the end. He had approached him quickly, and Alim scarcely had turned around before he found himself being embraced by Ibrahim. After the moment of surprise had passed, he had returned the gesture. Ibrahim had pulled away first, and had quickly rubbed damp eyes. The old wizened Imam had looked at him in understanding.

"Come see me this evening, and we will talk."

Ibrahim had nodded, embarrassed by his display of affection, and left the mosque quickly, while Alim held his worn broom and watched him leave. After a moment, he began to sweep, the weathered straw on the floor making a soft whispering sound.

Later that evening they had met as planned, and sat once again in the study, the evening air still hot and dry. They prepared their tea, and sat facing each other. Alim broke the silence.

"How much do you know of the past, Ibrahim? The history of Islam?"

He sat for a moment thinking, shrugged lightly, and replied.

"I know of Muhammed; of Mecca, the assassination of his successor. I know of the prophets..." Alim had raised a hand cutting off his sentence.

"Yes yes, but what do you know of the *history* of Islam, the role it has played in the world?"

"Very little, Imam."

Alim sipped at his tea, and place it down on the table without making a sound.

"Islam is responsible for the world as it is today. When the Roman Empire fell, it's knowledge became lost to ancient libraries and monks that failed to have the understanding of what was in those libraries. The technology and science from its centuries of rule was lost to time. As our faith spread across the Middle East and Africa, scholars came across those libraries and translated them and copied them and spread them across the realm. That knowledge built our cities and made our peoples strong and powerful. When monks from Europe visited Morocco, they did not want to leave and return to Christendom. Why? Because in

Morocco they found bountiful food, clean towns, paved streets, healthy people, education and a desire for more knowledge. If they returned to Europe, they were faced with scurvy and disease, muddy towns, and ignorance of the world about them.

When at last the Renaissance came about, all of the knowledge that our culture had preserved was ready to be applied, and the Dark Ages came to an end with the rebirth of science. After that, we slowly fade from view, decade after decade our power atrophied and waned, until we became the society stuck in time. The technology in the world today exists because it had the platform of knowledge of the Greeks and Romans to build upon, wisdom we preserved. Now, we are stagnant, stuck in the past, stymied by dogma and controlled by the elite few that cling to power. We have become a new Dark Age, where we opened the world to light. We await our Renaissance."

Alim sipped his tea.

"We must do what we can to bring light back to our faith."

Ibrahim was startled.

"We? How can I help you? You are the Imam! I help Mahdi in the market!"

"I am getting old Ibrahim. My joints ache and I feel tired *within*. My time is coming to an end, and I need a successor, someone that will help guide our peoples through the times ahead."

A creeping horror dawned upon Ibrahim.

"ME?" he exclaimed.

"How can I succeed you? Become an Imam? The congregation would not have me."

He swallowed reflexively in near panic. The Imam chuckled softly, humour flickering in his eyes.

"Do you not see what is around you? Oh, Ibrahim you are the best kind of leader, because the thought of leading frightens you. You do not lead because you want to. You lead because it is something in your nature that you are born to do. And that is the right reason. You do not seek power, you do not seek recognition. All you seek is a place to call home. And I think, because you are still here, that you in your soul have found your home."

He took a drink of his tea, letting his words sink in.

"Mahdi informs me that you are fond of his eldest daughter."

Ibrahim had blushed deeply to his very core; he felt it rise from his neck to the very roots of his hair. He had seen Yasmine bring her father lunch at the bazaar on a few occasions, and she seemed to be coming by more often. He had been struck mute the first time he had seen her, truly at a loss for words. He had fumbled, trying his best to appear calm and in control, when in reality he was anything but, stuttering his sentences and uncomfortable in his own skin. Alim laughed aloud, his strong voice making his laugh carry far into the mosque, echoing in its empty places.

"Mahdi is very fond of you, and I can tell you that he is happy and approves of your interest in his daughter. And of her in you. I think you will be seeing more of her."

Ibrahim had wished he had a hole in the floor he could crawl into and disappear.

"So you see, the man you work for approves of your interest in his daughter. The congregation has accepted you into its very inner workings. When you sat near me as I led the sermon did you hear any protest? Any questioning my decision to place you there? When I had you read from the Qur'an before them, they listened. When you walk through the mosque do you not see the respect in their eyes as you pass? You are the American Persian that has come home, and they love you for it. If you let me teach and guide you, they will accept you as their Imam."

The old memories faded from his mind; his youth quickly blurring into his adulthood. Mohammed continued with the *adhan*, the call to prayer. He recollected his old friend with fondness. Alim had passed away years earlier, peacefully in his sleep, at the ripe old age of eighty-seven. Until the very end, he remained sharp and astute, only his body betraying him, a vessel incapable of carrying the intellect it had harboured for so very long. Ibrahim passed into the role of Imam seamlessly, his marriage to Yasmine completing his acceptance into the community. Their daughters were both now married, with children of their own, their husbands' respectful businessmen that honoured their families properly. His mother and father had stayed in America, finally acquiescing to his permanent move to Iran, the only one of his siblings to remain in Iran. They were proud of his community position but did not say so in words, but in acceptance of his home. They had travelled to Iran for his wedding to Yasmine, and been present at the births of each his daughters, proud grandparents eager to meet the next generation and provide their blessing.

As he stood atop the minaret, he recalled the prophetic wisdom of his dear friend Alim. The Israelis and the Palestinians were still killing each other, and various organizations twisted the words of the Qur'an for their own purposes, in conflict with the teachings of Islam. It seemed that every religion had those fringe groups that gave the faith a black eye. Christianity, Judaism, and Islam all suffered from the taint of those that sought their own prerogative. For the Imam and his responsibility, it was his mission to impair those groups from recruiting from his congregation. He was mindful and watchful of youth that seemed prone to violence or suggestible to direction. On occasion, he was introduced to children by their parents who were concerned of the path their children were taking. His sermons on occasion became tactical if needed, attacking specific actions that needed addressing directly. When the twin towers had fallen in America, there were a few in his congregation, much to his dismay, that seemed to take delight in the act. His sermon had been direct and specific, reminding his congregation of the fact that those killed in the attack had been non-combatants, and therefore the attack was not, and could not, be sanctioned by Islam. That it was in fact, criminal. He denounced the offenders as cowards and criminals, and not martyrs as others would have the youth believe. He completed his sermon, to realize that in the end, he had been shouting his lesson, gesticulating wildly, his face red with anger. His followers sat quietly before him, and he saw in their eyes the same shame he felt. They had led a prayer in memory of those victims of the attack, and prayed to Allah to punish those responsible. It had been the toughest sermon he had ever had to deliver, or reflect upon.

Alim had been right; his faith needed strong leadership that was true to the message of Allah. His fears were that the silent majority of Islam that did not condone the terrorism would remain silent. It had happened previously in history, in modern times, where the violent minority had succeeded in their plans, only because the majority, due to apathy or disbelief that the radical cause would actually prevail, failed to act. It had happened in Germany, where the minority Nazi following had wrestled power as the population watched, gaining legal power as it remained unchallenged. And again in Russia, where a minority Bolshevik revolution had risen to the surface and taken control as millions watched. There was some hope for the future. Egypt was taking a strong role in settling the Arab Israeli issue, and *inshallah*, they would finally know peace. The next generation was showing a growing disinterest in the past, with inter-faith marriages that would have been unheard of twenty years earlier, and the growing strength of Muslim populations in the West, with their different perspective of old animosities seemed promising.

Mohammed completed the adhan, his voice fading away in the morning light. They had walked down from the spire together, retracing familiar steps downwards into the welcoming courtyard. He had promised the old Imam that he would fight, one person at a time, to rejuvenate Islam, and it was a promise he intended to keep. What he had not foreseen was the internal struggle that began with the last election. The current ruling generation of clerics that had taken power with the overthrow of the Shah had become more and more irrelevant with the next generation, more isolated in their way of thinking that had created the Velvet Revolution. As they struggled to remain in control, the needed to use more and more physical power, thereby becoming what they had originally rose against. Ibrahim could feel the anger and resentment in the youth of his mosque, the feeling of a need for change. He only hoped it would not lead to violent change of power.

He walked through the streets of his neighbourhood, being greeted by the shopkeepers opening their storefronts, and by those walking past. He needed to think of how he could be most effective. The time went by quickly, and he could feel the heat of the sun beginning to warm the air. He stopped at a goldsmith, where a young boy of perhaps twelve was linking together a thick necklace with skill. He stopped to admire his handiwork, watching him use his tools with precision, his focus and attention on the metalworking. He did not notice that Ibrahim was watching him.

"Salaam, Imam."

He looked up to see an older man watching him. It took him a moment to recognize him.

"Salaam, Jafar." They shook hands over the top of the working boy.

"Is this your son, Jafar?"

"Yes, Imam. My youngest; his name is Abbas."

"He is very talented. I have been watching him and his concentration and skill, especially for one so young, is impressive."

Jafar beamed.

"Back in America, my family knew a Persian goldsmith. We went to his shop sometimes and I would watch them working while my parents visited. Seeing Abbas working reminds me of watching them. He is very talented. See? Even though he can hear us, his concentration does not waiver."

"You are too kind, Imam. Please, tell us what he can make for you. It will be a gift for your wife."

Ibrahim smiled and shook his head politely, so as not to offend.

"Thank you, Jafar. That is not necessary. It is enough to watch your son work. I appreciate the offer. I will remember his work when I do need something."

Jafar bowed his head quickly in thanks.

"Salaam, Imam. Please excuse me, I have work to attend to inside."

"Salaam, Jafar. Thank you for visiting with me."

Jafar turned and returned inside to his shop, leaving Ibrahim to watch Abbas create a gold necklace as he watched. His brow was furrowed with concentration, his tongue sticking out of his mouth as he worked a link, applying heat to the metal and bending it to mate with the other end, and then joining the two ends. His small hands moved deftly and with confidence. Ibrahim thought to himself that when Abbas was a man, and was stronger, his goldsmithing skills would be among the very best. He couldn't help but smile watching him work. He watched him for several more minutes, and then crouched down and placed a coin near his feet.

"This is for you."

He held up his finger to his lips, making a quiet shushing sound.

"Our secret?"

Abbas grinned and nodded, palming the coin in his shirt. Ibrahim tousled his hair, and then stood and went on his way. After watching Abbas work, the day seemed brighter. And then he noticed that the streets had become just a little bit quieter. The vendors were still hawking their wares, and customers were haggling, and children were playing, but a familiar background was missing. He looked around the street, wondering what it was. An old man, probably in his late sixties, was sitting at an outdoor café, a small cup of hot tea steaming in front of him. He was fidgeting with a small portable radio he had on the table in front of him. As he watched, the man tried smacking the unit a few times, before he set it back down in disgust. At a spice shop next to the café, a woman was yelling at her son to look at the television that was mounted on the wall. It's screen was black. He was yelling back at her, obviously upset that it was off just as much as she was. That was it; the power was out. The hum of the power lines, the constant babbling of the radio and music in the background was gone. He listened, enjoying the change. He could even hear the crackling of the fine gravel under his sandals as he walked over the flagstones. He looked up into the blue morning sky, seeing the white straight line of a jet contrail. He could see the jet was further ahead of the exhaust stream, leaving no further contrail behind it. It must be descending, the warmer air not condensing into the familiar white cloud behind the engines. The jet was a faint pinprick against the sky, only the glint of sunshine from the fuselage made it easier to see. He walked around the corner, where a man was struggling to get his car started. The hood was popped, latched open, and another man was inside the car in the drivers' seat, turning the key over as he watched under the hood.

"Nothing!" he yelled into the engine compartment.

"You piece of shit! Today of all days you decide to not start."

Further down the street a young man was trying to kick start his motorcycle. It wasn't co-operating either. He was pushing down furiously with his leg, trying to force it to come to life. He finally quit, sitting back on the seat, taking a deep exasperated sigh, holding his hands to his forehead in disbelief that his bike wouldn't start. He saw no other cars or bikes running either. He couldn't even hear any other running vehicles. Not a single one.

Ixtab

Ixtab stood atop the pyramid of Chichen Itza. He had climbed the steps of the stone structure with Bacab shortly after noon to mark the ending of the old Age. Bacab stood silently behind him, off to his right, tending the smoldering incense and sacrificial offering. They both remained utterly silent while they stood and waited, inhaling the smoke of the offering, and silently praying to their gods. On the well-kept grounds below, the stone statues of jaguars and Chac-mool bore silent witness to their attendance. The two men were dressed in full ceremonial attire, in remembrance and honor of their ancestors. The feathered headgear fluttered silently in the light breeze. Below them, on the pyramid grounds, thousands of people had gathered over the previous weeks and now occupied virtually all of the space below. Ixtab was pleased at the gathering below, for the most part. The crowd represented a gathering of peoples from all over the Americas, and a lesser group from around the world. Here and there, a van sat at the edge of the crowd from news stations, eager to try to make a story, interviewing those who had made the pilgrimage to this site. The people had come for many different reasons. The reporters were their to do their jobs, some people were there to see what this fuss was all about, and others were there to mark the holiness of the day. Tribes from all across North and South America were represented in the peoples below. Each had performed and were preparing to perform sacred ceremonies to mark the sanctity of the day yet to unfold, the tribal Elders and priests bearing the most holy of items from tribe to tribe, eagle feathers from the Northwest, buffalo hides from the Plains, whatever was held in highest esteem. One group had travelled with a white buffalo, a great honor to bring to the pyramid, a sign from the gods of times to come. The buffalo had been adorned with the jewelry as those who had come to the site paid their respects to the animal, and what it represented. Smoke from hundreds of incense fires wafted over the grounds, dozens of sweet and aromatic smells mixing and flowing over the grounds and into the air and forest around them.

The day had remained relatively cool as they had stood on the pyramid. It had taken them several hours to climb the steps, marking each one as they went upwards, Ixtab making a quiet prayer, thanking the gods for their blessing, and Bacab quietly repeating it, carrying the incense urn slung over his shoulders. They were both breathing heavily when they had reached the foot of the pyramid, flush with the exultation of the sacrifice performed to recognize the end of the Age. They had performed the ritual hidden in the surrounding forest, the deep cover of the trees and the night providing ample privacy. It was not ideal, they would have preferred to have utilized the top of the pyramid, but necessity demanded caution. The throngs of people surrounding the pyramid would likely have not looked kindly upon their religious observance. Bacab had selected the individual two weeks earlier, shortly after they had first arrived at the site. They had made their way into the area as they had made their travels together everywhere, on foot, with a bare amount of essentials held in fiber bags slung over their shoulders. Ixtab had begun his journey almost forty years ago, as a young man who had found his path and now sought to fulfill it. As a boy, he had wandered with his mother and father, their only child and their sole focus in life.

They were full-blooded Mayan, a fact they had driven into Ixtab early in his life, something to be fiercely proud of. They had earned their living wherever they had went, his mother as a seamstress and cook, his father as a mechanic to a lesser extent, his primary calling as a priest. Mechanically, he was very talented, able to solve most issues by first witnessing how a machine operated if it still did, and if not, by simply looking at the inner workings and deducing its trappings from there. He had once explained to Ixtab that he could simply *see* how it was supposed to work, he could explain no further. His reputation grew however not from his skill with tools, but instead from his other passion, as a priest. He himself had seen the Christian impact upon the peoples of the Americas, but his faith was not in Christ, but in the gods that preceded the arrival of the Spanish. He was a Mayan High Priest, and he worshipped the Old Gods as they had demanded. As Ixtab grew, he instructed him on his faith, teaching him the intricacies of his rites and rituals, and the stories of the gods and man. He sacrificed small animals to the gods, goats and birds, offering their hearts in burning urns. He himself had been taught by his father, across many generations from father to son, and from surviving priests that worshipped hidden in the dark forests. He read the Popul Vuh, one of the very few surviving texts from the Mayan civilization, and memorized it, savouring every word and every story, a direct link to the past and his people, feeling the ghosts of the Dead reading it over his shoulder, repeating his words. They had travelled from village to village across their ancient homeland, teaching and worshipping their faith as they went, encountering in village after village the blend of Christian and Mayan faith. His father had spent most of his time with the village Elders, to learn of old stories so that they would not disappear from the memories of his people, and he would then write them down feverishly into a worn notebook with a thick leather binding, terrified he would not record the story precisely as he had been told. The book grew thicker and thicker, full of stories about Rabbit and Jaguar, Crab and Deer, and many other animals from the woods.

Ixtab spent hours reading the stories with his mother, and she explained the unseen story behind the written story to him. When Ixtab neared manhood, his father had taken him deep into the forest under the light of a full moon. Ixtab had followed him without question deeper and deeper into the forest, until they had come to a small clearing. In the center of the clearing, a goat lay tied to a small stake that had been pounded into the earth, near to a small fire concealed behind a small wall of stones. At the edge of the forest clearing, barely visible in the flickering shadows, sat several dozen elders and other priests. They remained silent, and watched them as they emerged from the forest.

"Stand by the fire, Ixtab, and wait for me," his father said quietly.

Ixtab stood by the fire, glad of the heat from the flames that reached upwards from the wood like small yellow fingers. He watched as his father was dressed to worship. His face and body were painted with many glyphs, and he was passed a feathered band that was placed on his head. A thin obsidian knife was tied to his waist, and he was then passed a small clay bowl. His father had stepped forward and faced Ixtab, raising the bowl to him.

"Drink," he said simply.

Ixtab took the bowl from his father and raised it to his mouth. He inhaled deeply, the liquid in the bowl was sweet smelling, with the sharp small of fermentation. He sipped from the bowl and swallowed the concoction, and started to lower the bowl.

"Finish the drink, Ixtab."

He raised the bowl again, and finished the drink, handing it empty to his father. His father then handed it to another priest who was standing behind him. He felt the drink burning in his throat, and he began to feel unsteady on his feet. His father took a step towards him and raised his arms wide, the quiet and low murmuring around the gathering becoming utter silence. Ixtab had begun to feel distinctly nervous, but the drink had made him feel detached, like he was also witnessing it himself from afar.

His father then spoke, his voice clear and with complete authority.

"Tonight we gather to honor my son, Ixtab. He has learned the ways of our people and he honors our gods and ancestors. He has much yet to learn, and there is much he does not yet know, but he will do his duty when the time comes."

The gathering remained utterly silent.

"I name Ixtab to be my rightful heir and student of the priesthood, heir of the Mayan people. The rest of you know the truth, Ixtab alone among us does not. His grandfather of many generations passed was Pacal Votan, High Priest of the Mayan civilization and King and Lord of our people. Through generations our family has learned and preserved the memories of our people, to mourn and satisfy the ghosts of our ancestors to allow us to live on the land. The time now comes when our Age will end and we will be made to account for the sins made upon this land. Ixtab Votan will represent our people as descendant of Pacal Votan, to accept the will of the gods in the coming of the next Age!"

150

The priests around him bowed. He was confused and shocked, not trusting his ears. His father stood proudly, his arms extended from his sides, his face upwards looking into the night sky. He turned one complete circle, and lowered his arms.

"Tonight we will honor our ancestors with sacrifice, and ask the gods to bless you in your task, my son."

The forest parted, and a group of four younger men carried a struggling shape from the undergrowth. Their faces were painted fiercely, their bodies marked with warrior tattoos. The men carried the shape towards the stone table, and holding it down, tied it to the surface. Ixtab watched, mesmerized as they backed away from the table and revealed a man tied to the stone. They kept their heads bowed, and quietly went to sit behind the ring of priests and elders.

His father beckoned him towards the table with an outstretched hand and a solemn look upon his face.

"Taal waye', in paal." *Come here, my child.*

He approached the table, where his father put his hand on his shoulder, and guided him to the side. The man on the table was blindfolded, and was bare except for a loincloth over his waist. He was covered in sweat, and his tendons and muscles struggled against the ropes binding him down. He felt his father place a cool object into his right hand, and he closed his left over it, both hands holding it tightly. He looked down at a black obsidian blade, its sharkskin hilt in his palms. His father guided his arms upwards into a strike posture, and he moved to the front of the table, his arms outstretched upwards.

"This night we offer a sacrifice to the gods, his heart for our favor and blessing. Tepeu and Gucumatz, we come together in the darkness, in the night."

Ixtab saw his father nod slightly, and he tensed, and then drove the blade down. He felt it pierce bone and sinew, feeling the man on the table stiffen, hearing his muffled scream through his gag.

He drew the blade down to open his chest, and spread the chest wide to reveal the heart. He quickly cut the heart free, and then dropped the blade onto the cool forest floor, plunging his hands into the opened chest to pull out the beating organ, holding it aloft in the night air. The men around the table bowed forwards, their foreheads to the ground. His father picked the beating heart from his shaking hands, and he placed it into smoking brazier. The heart sizzled and the odor of burning flesh wafted through the clearing. The bowed men sat upright, their arms outstretched upwards, seeking favor. Ixtab had felt his legs begin to weaken, and then give under his weight. He fell to the ground and knew no more.

He woke the next morning with his father by his side. He had a irritable headache, and he felt like he was going to throw up his empty stomach. He tried to rise, but his father pushed him gently back down.

"Rest, Ixtab. You need food and drink before you stir. I will have your mother get them for you."

Ixtab had grabbed his fathers arm as he had began to stand.

"Wait. What happened last night? I barely remember."

His father nodded, and sat back down.

"We made an offering to Tepeu and Gucamatz and the Forefathers. We were blessed by the Creator and the Maker."

"The man, on the table?"

"His soul has passed to the Underworld. His soul is blessed for being the sacrifice. His journey to the Underworld was unchallenged for his selfless offering."

Ixtab had nodded, understanding the special passage the soul of the sacrificed received when crossing into the Underworld.

"You said that our family ancestor was Lord Pacal, that we are his heirs. How can that be?"

"When the Spanish came to our land and destroyed our people, the high priests and their families fled into the deep jungle, where the Spanish and their diseases could not follow.

There our families hid for generations, passing our knowledge from one generation to the next, waiting for the coming of the next Age. The next age is nearly upon us. I may not yet live to see it, but you surely will. And you shall usher out this Age, and welcome in the next."

"But how? Why?"

"That," he smiled, "is my task to teach you."

As the Age drew to its end, Ixtab made his preparations and selected Bacab as his witness from the ranks of the priesthood. The word had spread amongst the townsfolk that he was coming to mark the new Age, and the word had spread further, so that when he had arrived he was welcomed with open arms by hundreds of people. Local bureaucrats had initially tried to prevent him from worshipping upon the pyramid, until intense pressure from the locals had forced them to change their minds. They had made the preparations at the summit of the structure, cleansing the stone and offering prayers and incense to appease the ghosts that dwelt there, seeking their acceptance. They had found their sacrifice in a small town near Chichen Itza, Bacab had selected the man, and, when the opportunity was right, had captured him, taking him deep into the forest and binding him to a tree. Together, they had performed the sacrifice, and his heart now burned in the brazier hanging from his shoulders.

He had fielded many requests for an interview from reporters covering the celebration, and allowed Bacab to select one.

Cindy Hawkings had been in the business for nearly ten years, and she wasted no time in what promised to be an interesting story. She had covered international interests, selling the stories and rights to media giants that were too large to be able to send proficient people of their own, or who could not. She was aggressively ambitious, and she was known to push the line between what was or could be perceived as appropriate.

Her camera operator, Greg, was bred from the same A-type personality, and she could count on him to keep filming when other crews would have turned and ran, or turned their cameras off. He knew, as she did, that is was the original story that made the money, and the crew that filmed the longest had the most original story. He had invested earlier than most in a high definition camera, and his van was stocked with the latest in satellite telecommunications and recording equipment, all with multiple back ups and redundancies. He liked the fact that she wasn't afraid to cover a good story longer than her peers, and that she never told him when to turn the camera off. He let her ask the questions, she let him do the recording. They were both career focused and had no time for relationships being on the road all the time, with no fixed address short of a rented out mailbox in Beverly Hills. He liked the assumed social standing the posh postal code provided him. She was in her mid-thirties, a shapely brunette that knew how to use her female persuasion to open otherwise closed doors. She was also possessed of a photographic memory, so prior to doing a story she would read as much as she could on a topic, often amazing her interviewees with the depth of her knowledge on a subject. When she had heard a local official was to make the decision about who would be selected to interview this Mayan priest, she was there first in line. When she spoke to this official, she made certain her blouse buttons were undone just a little bit lower than usual, and her skirt was raised just a little bit higher than usual. That and the money she had palmed him during the initial handshake had secured her position one step further than many of her contemporaries.

She had discussed the forthcoming interview with Greg as they had lain in bed that evening. She had stretched one smooth bare leg across his hips.

"This should be relatively easy. Maybe not as easy as you, but easy."

He had chuckled, and then gave her body a quick squeeze.

"Lucky for you, I am that easy."

With their busy work schedules, and mutual interests, they had become lovers early in their working relationship.

"Why do you think this will be easy?" he asked.

"Come on. These two guys come from nowhere. They have spent their lives in whatever godforsaken forest it was, practicing a religion the Spanish all but wiped out centuries ago, and now they are here to pray to a calendar that says the world is supposed to end in a couple of days?"

"Just because they aren't technical it doesn't mean they are stupid."

"I didn't say they were stupid. They just have no idea of the outside world. Remember when the turn of millennia was coming. Nuts were popping out of the woodwork faster than you could keep track of. All of their stories were the same. End of the world this, judgment that, and the sad thing is, people bought it. People spent their life savings to go flee into the woods, quitting their jobs, all because of the religious hysteria these frauds perpetrated. And then do you remember what happened?"

He shrugged.

"Nothing. Nothing at all. And all of these fear mongerers disappeared, back to where they came from after getting their five minutes of fame. And the really sad thing is that everyone let them.

One minute they were ranting and raving about the certain doom about to fall on everyone, like Chicken Little, and the next they went back to life in suburbia drinking their cappuccinos and chatting on the internet. They should have been strung up by their thumbs, but instead they were forgotten. People let them forget. Probably too embarrassed to go after them. And here we are again, twelve years later, another so-called prophecy coming due, and the nuts are coming out again."

She shifted in bed, laying flat on her stomach, her chin on her forearms crossed under her.

"What are you planning on asking them?" he asked.

"I don't really know yet. Well, more like I have to figure out where to start. I'll get a better idea when I meet them."

She was generally a good judge of character, very astute at picking up signals in the interview, using eye contact or fidgeting as clues that could give her the opening to go in for the kill and really start to ask hard questions.

"Where are we meeting them?"

"In the Rose Room," she said, and she scratched at her shoulder.

"Still at ten?"

She nodded.

"So we have lots of time to sleep in, then."

"Why are you concerned about sleeping in?"

"Because I'm not planning on going to sleep yet."

He rolled towards her, running a hand up her smooth thigh to her bare buttocks.

She turned to face him, her eyes intent and focused.

"Then you better hurry up, because I'm getting tired."

He laughed quietly, and then pulled her to him.

The alarm clock went off at eight, loud static playing in the room.

Cindy never set the clock to music. Random noise was much more efficient at getting her out of a warm bed.

155

"Fuck."

Greg moaned, stuffing his head under a pillow. His voice was muffled.

"That time already?"

She laughed, pulling the pillow away from his head, and then hit him with it.

"You wouldn't be so tired if you had left me alone."

"If you weren't naked I might have."

"I doubt it."

She walked around the bed to get a towel draped over the wooden chair. She was still naked, and he watched her get the towel. He was too tired to do more than watch, although he appreciated the view, saving it for mental playback later on.

"Call for room service when I'm in the shower. Get me the usual."

She went around the corner, a door clicking shut behind her. A moment later, he heard the shower spray and the squeak of the curtain hangers as she got in. He fumbled for the room phone, almost dropping it off the dresser as he rubbed his eyes and yawned.

He dialed O, and waited. The line clicked.

"Room service."

"I'd like to order breakfast for room 512."

"Certainly. What would you like?"

He found the voice was incredibly chipper for eight in the morning.

"Two eggs, scrambled, with a side of whatever fruit you have and sourdough toast, two slices, no butter."

"Is that everything?"

His stomach suddenly rumbled at him.

"For me, a stack of pancakes, with real syrup if you have any."

He heard the voice repeat his order, a pen scribbling on paper in the background. Anything else?"

"A pitcher of cranberry juice, diluted fifty-fifty."

"Sir?"

Half water, half juice. Otherwise it's too sweet."

"Thank you sir. It will be up to room in about fifteen minutes."

"Thank you."

He hung up the receiver into the cradle and laid back down in the bed. He thought about joining Cyndi in the shower, but then thought against it. She was getting ready for an interview, already playing it through in her mind, trying to predict how it would flow. His advances would not be welcome. He closed his eyes, enjoying the darkness and trying to doze for just a little bit longer. Breakfast arrived within moments of the shower turning off. There was a faint knocking at the door, a brief staccato rhythm, and a muted, "Room service."

Greg answered the door and signed for the meal, handing over a tip to the young woman who had brought up the meal. Gratuities were built into the price of the meals, but he always tipped when he was in an area that was economically vulnerable, aware of the impact even a few extra dollars could make for a family. It was an awareness he had quickly developed when he had gone into the business, and something he had tried to help where ever he could. Resort hotels paid their employees a pittance compared to the revenue their guests brought in, so he always found some extra cash to give to the employees that helped him.

"Gracias," she said, stuffing the cash into her uniform gratefully.

He wished her a good day and brought the food into the room.

He inhaled deeply. He loved the smell of pancakes. He leaned into the bathroom door, hearing Cyndi toweling off in the room.

"Breakfast is here," he said.

He put her food on the night table on her side of the bed, leaving it covered, as he propped his plate of pancakes on his lap. There was a small glass bottle of genuine Canadian maple syrup on the side of the plate, that he emptied over the pancakes, keeping the bottle upside down, getting a few more drops out. He screwed the lid back on, and threw it into the recycling can by the wall. It fell in with a swish of plastic and a dull plastic thud.

"Two points."

The pancakes were perfect, a golden brown, steaming hot, with a certain flavor to them that he had never been able to reproduce when he tried to make pancakes himself.

When Cyndi had finally come out of the washroom, he was nearly done.

"God, you eat fast," she said.

He shook his head, chewing, his fork held in one hand waving in the air as he disagreed.

"Mmm mmm." He disagreed, and swallowed.

"The truth is that you were in the bathroom forever."

He cut himself another mouthful.

She let it lie, and sat on the bed, the thick white towels she had wrapped around herself impeding her ability to move easily. The towel on her head stood a foot high. She ate her food stiffly. Greg went to shower when he finished, taking only a few minutes from start to finish. He packed his own body wash, not liking to use soap. He had never tried it before, until he had showered with Cyndi. He had always felt a certain machismo that using body wash was somehow feminine, and then when he had tried it, after a certain amount of chiding and taunting from her, he had never used soap again. He had dressed quickly, donning a white cotton short sleeve shirt and khaki shorts. Cyndi was still at the mirror, applying her make up, when he left the room to go set up the recording equipment.

"See you at ten," he said to her.

She waved back, and the door clicked shut behind him.

Cyndi applied her make up, imagining the interview in her mind, trying to guess how it could unfold, trying to be ready for any circumstance that might develop. She had another hour before the interview, so she had plenty of time to be thorough. By the time she was ready, Greg would have set up the room, and they would be ready to go.

She dressed in a beige suit, with a moderate skirt that had an appealing slit up the side of the thigh, and a taper in the suit that accentuated her waist. She wore her hair in a neat ponytail, keeping her look neat and crisp. Smoothing out the fabric over her hips, she gave herself a once over, and satisfied, made her way to the door.

The Rose Room was a relatively small business room, comfortable for a small meeting where you did not want to feel too close, or too far apart. Greg had set up his cameras at opposing sides of the room, with the backlighting and microphones at the other side where their guests would be sitting. He had run the cabling alongside the base of the wall, minimizing the overall look of the set up. Her laptop was on a small wooden table placed to the side of her chair, and a case of bottled water sat on the floor next to it. The chair was positioned opposite to where Ixtab and Bacab would sit together, with a slight angle so as not to be facing them directly.

There was a knocking at the door. A hotel employee opened the door slightly and poked his head through the opening.

"Excuse me, ma'am. Your interview is here. Should I send them in?"

She glanced down at her watch. It was a silver Rolex, the wrist band a dark brown leather strap. She didn't like the feel or weight of a metal strap.

They were five minutes early.

"Are you ready, Greg?" she asked.

"Whenever you are."

She nodded.

"Yes, send them in." The hotel employee went back outside. She heard his voice faintly through the door, but couldn't make out what he was saying. The handle twisted, and the door opened.

She had expected to meet with a small timid man that she could easily bully and coerce. She had arranged for the hotel room, as per her request, assuming the location would put him off guard and make him uncomfortable. Two men entered the room, one before the other. The door closed behind them, and for a moment they had both stood still, appraising their surroundings. The slim old native man she expected to see was instead quite young, probably only in his early thirties. His body was thick and naturally muscled, and his eyes held her own, a proud presence she came across rarely. He was very sure of himself. The other was slightly taller, perhaps an inch or two, and a little older, maybe his late thirties. He had the same demeanor. She refused to show her surprise, and came across the room with her usual commanding presence, her hand out in greeting.

"Hello. It's so nice to finally meet the both of you."

They each shook her hand in turn, their hands soft but strong. Their faces were warm and inviting. Greg did the same, introducing himself to the pair.

159

"We apologize for being early for your appointment," the shorter man said. His English was perfect, his voice clear and in total control. He spoke slowly, picking his words carefully.

"Bacab and I were waiting, but both felt the time was right, so we came to see if you were ready."

Ixtab was the shorter, and younger of the two.

"Shall we?" He indicated the chairs with his hand.

"Yes of course," Cyndi replied. "After you."

The two men smiled and nodded, sitting themselves.

"Water?" she asked, untwisting one for herself.

"Thank you, no," Ixtab replied.

She sat down, purposefully crossing her legs to provide him with a good view, the slit in the skirt revealing a lengthy portion of upper thigh.

She noted that they did not break eye contact with her, keeping their focus on her. She abandoned her strategy and adopted another.

She looked back at Greg, who gave her a thumbs up. Both cameras had a small blinking red light. They were recording.

"If you don't mind, I'd like to get right into it."

"Yes, so would we. Time is short."

This time Bacab had replied.

She cleared her throat once.

"I understand, Ixtab, that you are considered to be the High Priest in the Mayan religion."

Ixtab nodded.

"What position does Bacab hold?"

"Bacab is a High Priest as well, and my guardian."

"What makes you a higher rank?"

"Our families have held different traditional duties for our people. My ancestors led our people, and so by birthright I am the High Priest. Bacabs' family holds high honor in our people, a family that serves and guards the High Priest. I am honored that he is here with me. I understand where your questions lead. He is not my subordinate. He must fulfill another role, one equally as important. Our tasks are different, but no less vital."

"How do you know what roles your families held in your culture?"

"After the Spanish destroyed our civilization, and burned our books and written word, we relied on word of mouth to pass on our knowledge to our children. And so it has been for centuries, passed from one generation to the next."

So your father was High Priest, and Bacabs' father was his guardian."

"Yes."

"Why stay hidden for so long? Why come out now?"

"It was crucial to maintain the purity of our faith. We saw what your priests did to our people, trying to convert them to the Christian God, destroying their culture and identity. We remained secluded to remain pure, lest we too fall victim to the White God. We are here now to witness the end of an Age, to welcome in the next."

"What do you expect to witness?"

"We do not know. It has been many generations since this Age began, and any knowledge of the passing of the last Age has long been lost to us."

"What is your role, in being here for this new Age?"

"We are here to appease the Gods, to show them that our people are still here, that we are still connected to the Earth. We seek their favor and blessing."

"How do you mean to appease them?"

"Through prayer and offerings."

"Why do the Gods need to be appeased?"

"If we anger them, they will need a reason to be satisfied with us; that we can do better or that we understand and have learned from our mistakes. They seek pious and subservient creation."

"How have we made mistakes?"

"We have forgotten that we were given our place on the world to look after it, to care and nurture for its plants and animals. We were made to guard creation."

"And if the Gods decide that we have failed?"

"Have you studied our faith, Miss Hawkings?"

"Only a little, I am afraid."

"When the world was created, the Gods were eager to keep their creation safe, and so they made other creatures to watch over the world. Over time, those creatures were found to be ill-suited for their task, and they were removed from the world. There were beings made of mud, and of wood, and found to be unworthy, and so were destroyed. We were made to take their place, as the caretakers of their creation."

"How do you think the Gods will judge us? Do you think the world will be destroyed, as some are saying?"

Bacab spoke up.

"We cannot presume the minds or will of the Gods. We can only abide by their will, and leave our judgment to them. Our actions will have to be left to speak for themselves."

"And the destruction of the world?"

"The destruction of the world is a concept created by those who see themselves as the ultimate creation. The world will surely not be destroyed. The world will continue to orbit the Sun for countless Ages to come. The question you seek an answer to, is whether or not we will continue. That question, I cannot answer."

"There are those that say we have lost our place in the world, that we have become disconnected with nature. What would you say to that?"

"I agree. We have only to look at the peril of species around the world; the destruction that has been wrought on the land. We have surpassed the worlds' ability to heal itself."

Ixtab then took a turn, continuing the conversation smoothly.

"We also need to only look at the concept of time in the modern world. The different calendars are attempts by Man to fit the world into an artificial concept, a concept of our imagination. Our calendar flows with the movement of the world through space, a true reflection of our place within a greater design."

"So our concept of the calendar is an example for you of how we have forgotten our way?"

"It is a symptom of a greater illness."

"Are there any indications that you look for; something that we can look to as a warning?"

"There are no warnings. You are right; there are signs of the importance of the time we live in. As an Age draws to its end, there is a brief period of time where the transition occurs. The new Age dawns at the end of that transition."

"What indicators have you seen, as we come to the new Age?"

"It is the change in consciousness in general that people are having about the world. The growing knowledge and acceptance of people that have been harming the world, of the changes that people are beginning to make; those are hopeful signs that we are returning to a point where we understand that we are part of the world."

"And if we don't?"

"Then we will surely be destroyed."

"The Gods will destroy us?"

"Yes, directly or indirectly."

"You think they will come down and snap their fingers, and end us?"

"They could, if they wished it. Or they will let us destroy ourselves, through our own hands."

"What makes your end of the world prophecy different than the Christians? When the year two thousand approached, we were hearing the same thing from them, and nothing happened."

"Again, the calendar. The Year Two Thousand was an artificial construct; an arbitrary date chosen from people who tried to attach significance to a number."

"And your calendar is different?"

"Our calendar follows the cycle of the Earth, based on observation of the skies and the rotation of the galaxy."

"And so then the world will end, based on your Cycle?"

"The dawn of a new Age does not signify the end of the world. It signifies a time of great change, of completion of a journey. What the new Age will bring, I cannot say. Our world, the human world, may end, or change, but the Earth will remain."

"Isn't that why you are here? To mark the end? Those hundreds of people, those *thousands* of people outside, isn't that what you want? You have become a powerful figure."

"You have been listening without listening. I hear your skepticism, and understand. I am here to fulfill my duty to my people and my Gods. I do not seek wealth, or fame, or power. The people outside have come of their own free will, without my guidance. If they look to me, then I will provide aid in whatever form I can. We will provide aid however we can."

"And if nothing happens, then what? You will return to the forests and villages, doing what you have always done?"

"We never said anything will happen, nor do we expect anything to happen. We are here to mark the beginning of the Age of Center. We will observe for one day, on the building of our forefathers, praying to the Gods and making offerings, and then we will return to our homes."

Cyndi sat in her chair, quiet for a moment.

"Thank you both for your time. I think I have enough to do what I need to do."

Ixtab leaned forward in his chair, and he stretched out a hand.

Cyndi mirrored him, placing her hand in his open palm. He closed it gingerly over hers.

"I understand your doubt. It has been bred over time, and you seek answers that are dramatic. I cannot provide you those answers. I hope you find what you are looking for."

He stood, and Bacab followed him. They both shook Gregs' hand before leaving the room without looking back.

Cyndi sat in her chair, reflective and silent. Greg turned off the cameras and lighting, reducing the glare in the room down to the normal fluorescent lighting.

"So do you still think they're nuts?" he asked.

"It went differently than I expected."

"You were expecting some crackpot that had chewed more than his fair share of coca leaf, weren't you?"

"Perhaps."

She stood up, taking a sip of her water, which was now stale and warm.

"I was hoping to get something more sensational out of him, but it is still sellable."

"He doesn't strike me as the sensational sort."

"We'll have to get him tomorrow, when he goes back to wherever it is he came from, with some close-ups of them on the pyramid. We have this room for another hour. Let's get this cleaned up and go to the pyramid. We should get some good clips out of the crowd over there."

He nodded, and began to unscrew the cameras from their tripods, wondering about what the day would bring. Once the room was back to normal, he stowed the gear in the van, bringing a camera he could comfortably carry over his shoulder, with a few extra batteries and digital tapes just in case.

It proved to be difficult to get the van close to the pyramid, and so they had to ditch it, walking the kilometer to the site through groups of people that had collected along the way.

Cyndi had decided to ditch the high heels in the van, and wore flat shoes that she had stored for just such a situation. By the time they reached the press area, it was early afternoon and the area was filled with people. Greg set up the camera on a tripod, and aimed it on the steps of the pyramid, where they could see Ixtab and Bacab slowly making their way to the summit.

"Hey, I heard you guys got an interview with them?" He looked over his shoulder, towards the voice.

He nodded.

The voice was familiar, a former anchorman turned independent reporter named Chris Hatzenberg. He had quit to go reporting instead, finding the inside of a news studio too boring. Greg had thought being away from a desk would have helped him drop a few pounds, but he hadn't appeared to. He was sweating profusely, his large body size not designed for the heat of the area.

"What were they like? Are they a couple of weirdos? Are they queer for each other?" His voice was raspy and high, not what you'd expect from looking at someone so big.

"No, in fact they were pretty ordinary. If you exclude the fact they claim to be Mayan High Priests."

Chris looked disappointed. He tended to go for the more extreme stories, liking the bizarre and unusual. He even had a website where he saved his favorites. It was followed by a group of small but dedicated fans that drove him to find even more fodder for his site.

Some singing had started near the base of the structure, where a group of indigenous people had formed a circle, and were dancing around a smoking fire at its center. A few men were on drums, holding a steady and soothing beat. Cyndi had removed her shoes and was sitting on a chair another reporter had volunteered. She was waiting for something else, not the circus atmosphere that was currently around them. They settled down, and waited.

Kuljit Parmar

The forest floor was covered with litter making the tracks difficult to follow. The tree canopy filtered in the light from above, creating a blend of shadows and patches of light that mixed the hues of the vegetation and earth below into myriad shades of browns and greens. The leaf litter was dense and had been covered by a recent blanket of fresh fall, the old brittle leaves cracking atop the old decaying leaves below. The old leaf litter kept the ground moist; the smell of the rich and fertile earth below permeated the forest. Above the decaying leaves, the heat of the summer sun had dried the forest. Thick patches of grass stood in dense patches of beige, the green of their stems long ago bleached out and faded. Twigs became brittle and easy to break, berries dried to small purple shapes on their branches. Birds flew amongst the trees, and insects burrowed into the grasses and leaf litter, but larger creatures sought the shelter of shade and water. Kuljit and his team advanced slowly into the forest. They had abandoned the Jeep a kilometer back on the park trail, where the vegetation had become too dense, and the tracks led into an area they couldn't normally follow.

The five men stepped with caution, their eyes wide attempting to peer into the deep shade of the forest, looking to find a pattern in the jumble of colors. Normally they would have marched through the trees at a faster pace, but they had lost the track they had been following, and so they proceeded with extreme caution. They had followed the trail into a small gulley, where the bushes had thickened considerably and proved to be a formidable obstacle. Their thin lithe bodies slowly made their way through the thicket, albeit slowly. They knew they were relatively safe in the tangle of bushes; the animal they were following was too large to have gone through them herself. The concern was that she may be hiding near them, or using them as an ambush point to conceal herself from her prey. They took some solace in the fact that there was no running or pooled water in the gulley, and so it was less likely to be used as a hunting ground. A branch cracked ahead of them, and Kuljit's arm quickly shot up to warn the rest of the troop. They had stopped instantly, listening intently, scarcely breathing in case the sounds of their own respiration would cause them danger. They had stood in place for five minutes before his arm lowered. He looked back at them and smiled nervously, his white teeth bright against his skin blackened by the dust and soot on his face. He gave a silent thumbs up, and received four back. Sweat ran from the faces of his comrades, a combination of the exertion of working through the underbrush, and fear. He nodded once, turned around, and slowly moved deeper into the bushes, twisting his body as necessary to avoid branches that might reveal his location. Thirty minutes later they emerged from the thicket where the gully turned upwards into a more densely forested plateau, with thin grasses and bushes where the ground was largely visible and clear. They walked in single file to the top of the gully, and then stood as a group surveying the forest in front of them, looking for tracks. The thin covering on the ground concealed the passing of animals well. The local forest was abundant with deer, and even their tracks were difficult to find. Jaswinder, the heaviest man in the troop, cried out in discovery.

"Look, over there!" pointing towards a stand of mahogany trees. Jaswinder walked quickly over to the trees, mindful and cautious of the shadows. Everyone followed him, hopeful of good news. The base of the tree was heavily scored with a series of scratch marks, long grooves running up and down the tree bark. Jaswinder ran his hand along the scratches, spreading his fingers to fit the cuts in the tree.

"She is big." The base of the tree revealed several large prints, each distinct and precise in the dry soil.

"Janesh, make a cast of these prints."

He nodded and began to dig through his pack for his supplies. He laid four sticks in a square around each pug mark, pressing each firmly into the ground so they would not move easily. Satisfied with their position, he removed a small bag of plaster from his pack, and scooped some of the powder into a small ceramic bowl. After returning the mix to his bag, he retrieved a water bottle, and poured a small amount of liquid into the bowl, mixing it slowly.

He patiently stirred it as it turned into a thick pudding-like slurry. Satisfied with the mixture, he returned to the paw prints and poured the plaster into each cast, being cautious to pour the mix slowly and evenly, sparing enough for the other molds. Each paw print was unique to each animal, and would verify which one had been visiting this tree. Having emptied the bowls, he stood and bent his head towards his right shoulder, and was rewarded with a satisfying crick in his neck.

"Now you two oafs watch your steps," he said, pointing with his stirring stick at Kuljit and Jaswinder.

"Or I will leave my scent on your tents when you sleep tonight."

They both laughed quickly, imagining Janesh pissing on their tents in the dark. He then laughed as well, and turned back to clean his bowl as the plaster set. Returning to the tree, still grinning, Kuljit and Jaswinder examined the scores in the bark while the other two kept a watch into the forest.

"These are fresh, a day or two old, no more."

Jaswinder nodded in agreement. The disturbed bark was still slightly moist, the sap becoming congealed. Jaswinder looked over his shoulder.

"Pawan, do you have the map handy?"

Pawan nodded, and removed the pack from his shoulders, unslinging his rifle and leaving it leaning against the base of a small banyan tree. Kuljit removed his pack as well, and sat on the ground.

"Let's make camp here for the night. It will be dark soon."

The others nodded in agreement and removed their packs.

"Amit, when you are settled, photograph the tree markings. Janesh, you can start the fire tonight." Janesh snickered as he removed his bag.

"I think I start the fire every night. Maybe we should have brought our wives to teach you how to make a fire, Kuljit." A chorus of good natured laughter burst from the men.

They had been working together in the preserve for nearly five years, and had become good friends, relying on each others strengths daily. Janesh walked over to a nearby palm tree.

"I will start the fire once I finish some business." He stopped at the base of the tree, and a moment later urinated on it.

"Jas, make sure you pee on a tree this time." Jaswinder laughed.

"Maybe I will use your rifle next time." A month earlier, Jaswinder had mistaken Amits' rifle for a small sapling, and had relieved himself on it during the night. Amit had taken his camera out, and was busy snapping pictures of the tree markings. Jaswinder and Pawan had unfolded the laminated map on the forest floor and were tracing their path. Kuljit and Janesh were gathering kindling and small twigs together for protection, keeping within eyesight of the other men.

"How is Aishi doing, Janesh?" Kuljit asked, stooping to pick up another stick. Janesh was stuffing handfuls of dry grass into a small bag at his waist.

"She is doing well. She is getting big."

Janesh drew a half circle in the air in front of his stomach.

"She can only sleep on her sides now. When she was carrying Vikram she was sick all the time, but with this baby she isn't sick at all. We are hoping for a girl this time. We will name her Rupi."

Kuljit smiled and quickly patted his friend on the back.

"That's a good name for your daughter. I'm glad Aishi is doing well. When we get back we will have to have supper together again, before she delivers. When is she due?" Janesh paused stuffing for a moment.

"In six weeks, already."

They continued to work through the underbrush, catching up with the lives of their families and children, while the other three back at the campsite did the same, their laughter plain to hear.

Later that evening they sat in a circle around a small fire. The perimeter of their camp was set with alarms and noise makers in case something came too near, and they had all urinated in the trees nearby so animals would easily find their scent, and hopefully stay away if the smell of the wood smoke did not. Their pup tents were grouped together near the fire, their food stuffs tied high and hung into a tree for safe keeping. Their jackets were done up to the neck, and everyone was grateful for the heat of the fire, now that night had fallen and the evening temperature was dropping quickly.

"Pawan," Kuljit asked, "Where are we on the map now?"

Pawan reached into his back pocket and pulled out the map, unfolding it and turning it out facing everyone around the fire.

"This is where we are right now." His finger pointed to a small black x marked on the plastic.

"We covered approximately five kilometers today from our last camp. We last saw Aryana here, near the creek that flows into the Malik Talab Lake. We confirmed the deer kill upstream where Amit found the remains buried near the old den site. We have crisscrossed her known territory like this," moving his finger across the map in a small zig-zag pattern, "while we were looking for fresh tracks. The gully we entered yesterday is at the foot of this plateau, where we are on the edge of here. If she follows her normal pattern, she should circle through to her main den within a week or so. Tomorrow we will pass a small lake; if we keep to the right of it we can stay on more level ground, and have a better view. She normally keeps to this side, so unless she has gone deeper into her territory we should find tracks. We will have to be cautious. We know she uses the pond to hunt deer, and she has been successful here before." A red line outlined a rough circle in the center of the map, where the lake was near the edge to the left.

"Dakshi's territory is to the west of the lake. He shouldn't be in the area for another week." He folded up his map and slid it back into his jacket.

"Amit, what do you think?" Kuljit asked, keeping his eyes fixed on the flames. Amit shrugged.

"Pawan is right. We have seen her here before and she likes to hunt here so our odds of finding tracks are good. She is pregnant and so will be a little more temperamental and cautious than normal. In a month or so she will probably stay closer to the main cave, if she chooses that one for her cubs again. Her other den is nearby, and she raised her litter previous to last years there. It is a small cave that is well hidden and deep. We should look there for her tomorrow."

Kuljit and the others nodded in silence, listening to the wood embers crack as they burned.

"Jas, tell us a story tonight," Janesh said. Jaswinder was the story teller of the group, skilled in remembering stories and being able to faithfully recall them years later, every nuance and flair recollected.

"Very well. I told this story to my little Suhky before we left for this tour. It is the Ungrateful Tiger." He cleared his throat and stood before he began, slowly walking around them in a small circle, his friends listening expectantly.

"A long time ago, the people of a small village came together to decide what to do about the tigers that were wandering near their homes and eating them.

"We must do something! With all these tigers wandering around we're too scared to go out of the village" said one.

"Yes! We have to do something. Last week a tiger ate one of my parents."

After much discussion and arguing they decided to dig deep holes to trap the tigers. Everyone helped, including the old men and little children. They dug deep holes near all the tracks leading to the village that the people used.

A few days later, a young man came to visit his father and heard loud howling sounds as he walked along a path to his home in the village.

"What's making all that noise?" he asked. "Whatever it is it doesn't sound very happy."

The man followed the terrible sounds until he saw a deep hole in the middle of the path. He looked over the edge, and saw at the very bottom a tiger in it. The tiger tried to jump out and each time he fell back and roared.

"Hello Mr. Tiger" said the young man. "How did you get down there?"

"I don't know" cried the tiger. "I was walking along this path in t e forest, looking for something to eat, when suddenly I fell into this deep hole."

The tiger pleaded with the young man. "Please, please help me get out of here. If you help me I'll be very grateful."

The young man was a very kind person. He found a large tree branch that had fallen near the path, and he pushed and pulled it to the side of the deep hole.

"Watch out Mr. Tiger" yelled the man as he pushed it. The branch fell into the hole, allowing the tiger to climb out of the hole in the path.

The tiger sprang up the branch and out of the deep hole.

"Much better," said the tiger, happy to be free.

The young man felt suddenly very nervous, standing next to the large tiger.

He decided it was time to go.

"I must be going now, Mr. Tiger," he said.

"What?" said the tiger. "Not yet; I'm going to eat you."

"But you said you would be grateful if I helped you," cowered the man, kneeling on the path.

"I am," said the tiger. "But humans dug that hole to trap me and since you're a human I am going to eat you."

"That's not fair" cried the man, wondering if he should try to run.

"I'm a tiger and that's what tigers do," snarled the tiger, coming closer.

"I helped you and now you're going to eat me just because I'm human," said the man.

"I think we should ask some one else to judge if that's fair or not. If they agree with you, you can eat me."

The tiger thought about it for a moment, and then agreed. They went to look for someone to be their judge.

They first found a cow. "I think it's fair for the tiger to eat you," said the cow. "Humans treat us very poorly. We're made to work all day and when you want to, you kill us and eat us."

The tiger moved closer, growling to the young man. He yelled "Let's make it two out of three!"

The tiger agreed after a few moments, and they went to ask the most colorful bird in the forest. "I think it's fair. Humans trap us and kill us for our colorful feathers."

The tiger looked pleased and very hungry and showed his big teeth as he smiled at the man, licking his lips with his big tigers tongue.

The man was so scared his legs began to tremble. He saw a rabbit hopping along the path near the tree. "Please Mr. Rabbit, help judge if Mr. Tiger should eat me."

The rabbit then also listened to their story, and then said "Before I can judge I must see exactly what happened."

They all went to the deep hole in the path where the young man had rescued the tiger, the branch still sticking out of the deep hole.

"Now show me where you were" the rabbit said to the tiger. Hungry and wanting to eat the man, the tiger quickly ran back down into the hole.

"Was this branch in the hole?" asked the rabbit.

"No," answered the tiger. The young man and the rabbit pulled the branch out of the hole, pushing it back into the forest.

"My judgment is that it's not fair for you to eat the man" said the rabbit. "Just because it was humans who dug the hole doesn't make it fair for you to eat him. You should have been grateful for his help."

The rabbit hopped away and the young man ran home to the village, leaving the tiger howling in the deep hole in the path, furious at having been tricked.

Jaswinder stood bathed in the firelight, bowing deeply to his audience before sitting down on his bare patch of ground, listening to their applause for a story well told.

"I hope Aryana proves to be grateful," Pawan muttered.

The rest of the evening was spent with small talk, men talking about their wives and children, trying to push away the thoughts of their homes as they sat in the cold air around their small fire, while their families slept in the comfort and security of their homes. They wondered if their wives were up late, concerned about their husbands who patrolled the Ranthambore Tiger Preserve, charged with keeping her tigers safe from poachers. They talked deep into the night before turning in, under a dark curtain of southern stars.

The next morning broke cool and crisp, the sky was clear and blue and the forest was utterly still. The team slowly roused from their tents and quickly threw some wood onto the embers in the fire pit. The wood smoked heavily and crackled, but would not catch flame. While Amit attended to the food, Janesh leaned into the fire pit and blew softly into the ashes, closing his eyes as white ashes flew into his face. On his third breath, and finger of fire caught the sticks and began to spread. The thick white smoke slowly cleared as the flames rose from the ashes and began to consume the wood.

Amit returned with enough provisions for breakfast, and hung a pot of water over the fire. With the sounds of morning activity, the rest of the group stirred and awoke, and eventually gathered around the morning fire, cradling their cold hands around their tins of hot tea. They ate breakfast quietly and efficiently as they slowly woke up, and then began the quick process of tearing down their camp, folding their tents into their packs and dividing the remaining stock evenly. Janesh retrieved the print casts from the base of the tree, and slid them into his pack wrapped in linen. When this trip was complete, he would clean the prints, identify them with their location, and send them to the ministry lab in Mumbai. Once the fire pit was buried, they aligned themselves with their map, and made their way through the trees westward towards the small lake. Kuljit began to whistle a familiar morning tune.

"Kuljit, didn't your mother teach you any other songs?" asked Pawan.

Kuljit laughed and replied.

"The only songs I know your wife taught me."

The five men laughed, and began to whistle again, breaking trail westwards.

By noon they had reached the lowlands that surrounded the lake. The ground began to grow soft and boggy, and they had to keep a slight track east to keep to the drier ground. The area surrounding the lake was lined with thick reeds that thrived in the marshes, and where the ground became drier, the reeds were replaced with dense stands of grasses that in some places concealed the shoreline. The grasses were replaced by shoreline that was kept low and clear by grazing animals. Just beyond the flat areas the forest slowly took over, one or two trees gradually gave way to larger stands and thick bushes and undergrowth. They broke trail where the forest became thick, where a predator would be restricted in its view. They hoped to stay behind where they expected their quarry to travel, and so to catch her trail as she left the lake. They proceeded slowly, and slowed near clearings or where underbrush wasn't thick enough to impede an adult tiger from stalking. Kuljit frequently turned around to make sure they weren't being stalked from behind. Her stripes in the dappled shade of the forest allowed her to vanish into the undergrowth and watch unseen. The knee-high grass would conceal a tiger lying on the ground from a very short distance. Pawan took the lead, followed by Amit and Jaswinder, with Janesh and Kuljit in the rear. They were careful to not stray too far apart, while also not keeping too close in case they needed to use their rifles for defense. The sun rose in the sky, providing little warmth in the shade of the trees. They did their best to keep a constant pace, being mindful to not stop and give a tiger an opportunity to advance. Experienced tigers would advance on their prey when the prey had stopped for a moment. Of course, this would not help them if a younger animal was stalking them, but the odds were in their favour. As the day progressed, a slight breeze picked up that added the random rustling of leaves to the sounds of the forest. They rounded the curve of the lake, having covered half of its distance shortly before noon, when Pawan quickly scurried to a disturbance in the ground that bisected their route. He knelt to it, and motioned the others to come forward as he looked around.

"Got her," said Amit. A large tiger foot impression lay in the ground before them. She had stepped in a small patch of the forest floor that wasn't rocky, or dry, or covered with leaf litter. The mud that held her footprint was dark and firm, and it held no water. The pads of her foot were clearly distinct in the earth. Her path led closer to the shoreline, toward a dense growth of trees slightly raised from the lowlands of the shoreline a kilometer distant.

Her path came from the ridge above, from a course that would have paralleled their own trek in the morning. They all felt uneasy at the knowledge that the animal they were following could have been above them holding the high ground while they were looking in another direction. Amit took a measurement of the print, and Kuljit recorded it in his logbook.

"We will go higher around the hill towards her den. She is closer to the shore than we expected, so if we keep to high ground we should have an easier time spotting her. She is hunting, so be cautious," Kuljit whispered in hushed tones. The group nodded, and silently made their way up the hill to its ridge, where it still provided a partial view of the lake and shoreline. The top of the ridge was relatively bare of vegetation, so their progress was better than expected, and they made less noise. Pawan took notes as they crossed the tracks of a small group of wild boar. The leaf litter had been churned up by their snouts and tusks as they foraged through the underbrush.

The forest remained silent. They had seen a few gulls swimming along the shore line, and a lone woodpecker had flown overhead, searching from tree to tree. It had vanished from sight, but the distant rap-rap sounds of it searching for grubs amongst the trees were still audible. Off in the distance, a chorus of bird calls carried across the lake, and then just as suddenly faded into silence. By mid-afternoon they had reached a small delta on the north shore of the lake. A small stream lay within a larger creek bed, meandering down into the lake itself. In the wet season the stream would grow and overflow its banks, but now in December it was a mere shade of its full potential. Along the banks of the channel animal tracks had churned up the soil, leaving dark black prints in an otherwise grey surface. The game trail emerged from the forest where it followed the stream down to the lake. From there, the tracks had spread out as animals separated into smaller groups and individuals to drink at the shore line. Pawan led them to a small clearing along the ridgeline that gave them a concealed view of the watering spot. Kuljit noted the time on his Timex wristwatch, and the men settled into positions to survey the area. Kuljit stood watch over the group as they broke out their binoculars and searched the lower lying areas. Pawan put his binoculars down onto his backpack with disgust.

"I don't see anything. Nothing at all." He shook his head with dismay and frustration. Jaswinder kept his binoculars aimed at the shoreline.

"There are deer at the waters edge," he whispered.

"Where there are deer, she can't be far away." He glanced down at his watch.

"Let's give her some time; maybe she will come to us."

Jaswinder and Amit kept watch while the others prepared a small meal of dried fruit and meat. They had noted they were downwind, but dared not risk a cooking fire. The faintest scent of smoke would disturb their quarry. A small herd of four sambar deer made their way to the waters edge, their ears swiveling to catch the slightest sound as they slowly made their way forward. The lead deer kept her nose high smelling the wind for danger. When the others were done their meal, they took watch while Jaswinder and Amit began to eat. Janesh held his binoculars to his eyes with his left arm while he used his right to slowly feed himself a bag of dates. He chewed slowly as he watched the deer near the water. He trained his binoculars up the slope where the deep grasses yielded to the forest, perhaps one hundred meters to from the lake. A small patch of grass was slowly being pushed aside. Janesh stopped chewing. The tops of the grass moved again, but not with the breeze that was waving the rest of the vegetation. He dropped his date and shook his hand vigorously in the air, pointing to where he was looking in an approximate direction. He heard Jaswinder and Amit put their food down and scramble to their binoculars.

Kuljit took up position to his left, his right hand on his shoulder as he tried to see where Janesh was looking.

"Where?," he muttered under his breath. Janesh took a slow deep breath.

"A hundred meters to the north, where the reeds and grasses are thickest. Maybe twenty meters from the forest. Nothing is happening now."

Four pairs of binoculars aimed towards his directions in near unison.

Amit struggled to focus his set, missing the knob in between the lenses as he tried to find it from feel alone, not wanting to peel his eyes away from the view below.

"Shit." A moment later he found it.

"There we go." For several minutes they stared in silence, scarcely daring to breath for fear it would somehow cause them to miss something crucial. The minutes passed slowly. They watched the deer drink and move to and from the watering hole in a slow and steady procession. Eventually, the grass began to move again. The tops of the stems betrayed the motion below, being pushed aside in a cautious advance. The birds flying overhead to drink at the lake shore raised no alarm, having seen no threat. For another twenty minutes the path through the grass worked its way towards the waterhole, slow progress being interrupted by minutes of inactivity and tension.

"There she is!" Janesh whispered excitedly. Sure enough, just barely visible through the stems, Aryana's head was in sight. The stripes of her fur concealed her well with in the grasses, and their trained eyes had difficulty in spotting her. Her ears were pointed directly forwards, and flickered to the left and the right to catch the slightest rustle of sound from the shore. Her lips were pulled upwards in a grimace as she smelled the air deeply for the scent of her prey. The mid afternoon breeze was blowing off the lake, carrying the smells to her in the grass. As they watched she lowered her posture nearer to the ground, her eyes intent on the path in front of her, her body taut in a crouching position, her forepaws under her chest, with her hind legs dug into the hard earth. They could feel their hearts pounding in their chests as they watched her stalk the deer. They had seen enough tiger hunts in their jobs to know she had less than a fifty-fifty chance of making a kill, but on this day, the odds were stacked in her favour. Aryana was an experienced hunter. Her every step was measured and calculated, placed onto the ground in absolute silence. She was downwind of her quarry, in cover that perfectly utilized her natural camouflage. The orange and black stripes of her fur blended into the moving tall grasses, and her large wide paws muffled the sounds of her muscled weight moving through the undergrowth. More time passed, and they watched her watching the deer. Her patience was excruciating. From the woods, a Sambar stag appeared following the game trail to the shore. He limped slightly as he made his way down to drink, his left fore leg injured in the breeding season. He was heavily muscled, his three hundred kilograms of weight evident in his thick body. The light scar on his foreleg revealed where skin had healed over, but his injury was deeper and caused each step to drag slightly.

With a silent explosion of power, the tiger burst from her cover in the tall grasses and charged the lame stag at full speed. Birds took to the skies in a cacophony of alarm calls and beating wings, and deer leapt into action, pumping their legs as fast as possible in any direction in a bid to outrun anything that might be chasing them. A few boars squealed into the underbrush, and a sole deer swam into the lake making for the opposite shore. The stag reared backwards in an attempt to reverse direction, but his injured leg failed him, and he only succeeded in turning partially around. In the next moment, Aryana had closed the distance and using her immense paws, swatted his legs out from under him, using her body to push him towards the ground. As he fell, she leapt for his neck, closing her jaws over his throat and sealing his windpipe. Satisfied with her grip, she settled to the ground, using her immense strength and mass to hold the deer down as he struggled to break free of her grip. His legs and hooves beat at the earth as he tried to run and loosen her grasp. The kicks slowly became weaker and less energetic, and then ceased, laying upon the ground.

Aryana kept her eyes on her surroundings as her prey breathed its last, cautious of another tiger that may try to steal her prize. Her sister sometimes visited the lake as her territory bordered on her own, near to their mothers, and she was mindful she may try to claim some of her meal. When at last she sensed its death, she released her grip and stood over the deer and breathed deeply and quickly, taking oxygen into her body exhausted by the quick pursuit and struggle with her prey.

A minute later, she bit into the neck and began to drag her victim into the woods. The men sat in wonder at the scene they had just witnessed. The Sambar stag was equal to if not greater in weight than Aryana, and she had knocked it to the ground, held it there, and she was now carrying its dead weight through the forest. The men sat in silence as they watched her carry the deer up into the bushes. They sat in awe of her power, in reverence of her strength and spirit. The men compared notes and transcribed them into their journals, and then made their way down to the creek bed to document the kill site. The lake shore was silent and calm, the larger game having fled into the forest. The birds were returning to the water to drink and bathe, but as of yet, nothing larger had returned to the watering hole.

"Her den is what, five hundred meters from here? " Kuljit asked to no one in particular. Pawan shrugged.

"About that. We will have to follow the ridge to where it plateaus. Her den is just west of there, by the old statue."

An ancient marble figurehead of Vishnu had been placed in the forest long ago. It was covered in old leaves and few vines that had managed to gain a foothold. There was nothing else near the statue, no ruins, no foundations, so they could only guess the carving was an old grave marker to someone held in high esteem that was placed to rest in the forest. Kuljit nodded.

"Okay then. We will give her time to feed and rest before we continue to her den. I need a quick wash in the lake. You too, Jaswinder. You smell like shit."

Jaswinder chuckled, and extended a one-finger salute.

"I may smell like shit, but you look like shit."

They laughed good-heartedly, and then took turns bathing and washing in the lake while the others kept alert. Aryana may be fed, but her sister may not have been. They washed quickly, rinsing their clothes in the water as well while they had a chance. They would dry quickly enough once they were wrung out and walked around in for a little bit. The afternoon breeze they were familiar with settled in, cooling things off a little, and making the underbrush rustle with falling leaves and shaking branches.

Jas looked around at the group, feeling the direction of the wind with his arm up in the air.

"There are no taxis to ride here," said Pawan, smiling, seeing a good opportunity to make a joke. Kuljit and Amit smiled with him, and Janesh laughed. Jas kept looking around, watching the trees blowing softly.

"The wind is blowing in the wrong direction. It normally comes from the west in the evening. This is from the east."

They looked around for a few moments, confirming the observation.

"It is unusual," Kuljit agreed.

Jaswinder lowered his arm into the water, finishing his bath while looking around into the bush. He was rinsing off when Pawan shouted down at him coming out of the lake.

"It's about time. You bathe longer than my daughter."

He smiled and came out of the water, trying to think of a good zing, but instead he let it lie, running his hands over his body in long sweeps to get the excess water off his skin. His clothes were slung over his left shoulder, twisted from ringing them out over the surface of the lake. Amit had strung a branch over a small fire, where clothes had been hung over to dry. Jaswinder unfolded his shirt and pants, hanging them over as well, walking around the fire in his underwear. The others were looking up into the woods, pointing out which way they were going to go up into the hillside.

They wanted to avoid the taller grasses where tigers would be prone to stalking, and stick to clearings where they would not like the exposed views.

As a group they were more likely to not be attacked, especially in a population of healthy cats. With the abundant deer population in Ranthambore, it would be an uncommon occurrence. The breeze continued to pick up, sending a endless stream of small wavelets of the surface of the lake. Jaswinder flipped over his clothes, finding they were drying quickly, and that the other ones were already done.

"Amit, Janesh. Your clothes are already dry. Yours too, Pawan. I know you like to walk around naked in the bush, but I need the space over the fire."

"Finally!" exclaimed Amit.

"The bugs were starting to get to me." He quickly came over and pulled his clothes off the branch.

"Ouch! They're hot." He danced around as he put them on, waving them in the air trying to cool them down faster. He held up the sleeve cuffs to the air.

"Look; they're burned!" The cuffs were blackened at the edges, and smoking just a little. He laughed, showing everyone the cuffs, their edges crispy.

"We should make a camp near here, further up the trail," said Kuljit.

"Then we can go take a look for her in the morning."

"You don't want to go check in on her now?" asked Janesh.

Kuljit shook his head.

"By the time we found her, it could be getting late, and I don't want us to get caught in the dark trying to set up camp at dusk, or later."

Janesh shrugged.

"We could separate; a few of us going to follow her, and a couple set up camp."

"There is safety in numbers; if Aryana's sister is in the area, or a rogue male, there is more danger to us. No, we need to stick together."

Looking around the hillsides, they settled on an embankment that was overgrown with rows of thick bushes, full of thorns, and dense with branches. It wouldn't be easy for a tiger to get into it, and it wouldn't be too easy for several men either. The embankment jutted out from the hillside, and hung out over the lake partially, in an area where the water was deep, and the hillside steep and rocky, a nearly vertical bluff. Once behind the bushes, they could only be reached by the crest of the hill, their backs safe to the lake below.

They spread their small fire out, kicking dirt over the few embers, and then dumping some water in the pit where they had built it. The coals hissed angrily, released a puff of smoke, and went out. Satisfied, they marched up the hillside and then fought their way through the scrub onto the bluff, each bearing a few cuts on their hands, arms, and faces from sharp branches that fought back stubbornly before yielding to their advance. It took them just over two hours to get settled and create their barrier, piling high and interweaving the bushes that had resisted their approach. When it was done, they had a clearing about ten feet by fifteen feet, with a fire near the edge, off center from the camp to keep it further away from the dry vegetation surrounding them. Most of the outcrop was a topped with a flat slab of granite that had been exposed from under the dusty surface. In the later part of the day, sitting in a patch of sunlight, it was pleasantly warm to the touch.

"I've got my bed," said Pawan, slapping the granite surface with his palm, looking forward to sleeping on the warm surface.

"You go right ahead," said Janesh.

"I can't imagine it will be too warm come morning."

Pawan's eager smile suddenly slipped a notch as he thought it over, the seed of doubt planted by Janesh taking root.

"We'll keep a spot open by the fire for you." Janesh laughed, patting the soil.

From the forest floor, they pulled a series of logs and lined the perimeter of their camp with them, a makeshift windbreak to block the night breeze.

The birds that had gathered back at the lakeshore took flight, their wings beating the air furiously. Their calls were loud and sudden, carrying across the water and into the forest. Pawan looked over to the lake, looking to see what had caused the birds to take flight. Birds were good at giving warning, so they took the disturbance seriously.

"I wonder what..." started Kuljit, before he was interrupted by a loud roar and a trembling rush that rose from the very ground, like a dragon fighting to free itself from a deep cavern. He was driven to the ground as the earth buckled beneath them. The granite slab Pawan sat upon cracked loudly with a deep internal snap, and shifted downwards. Pawans' eyes grew wide, his hands searching for any kind of crack or protuberance to hold onto. He leaned forward, trying to push himself forwards and get off the overhang. He was too late. With another crackling sound, the rock split from the shore and plunged into the lake. They heard Pawan scream as he went down with the stone, and then heard the tremendous splash as it hit the lake. A column of water breached the sky, and then fell back to the lake. Everyone struggled to keep their place as the ground shook, clutching at the ground for a root or branch or half-buried stone. A flurry of dead leaves fell from the tree canopy, sounding like rain as they landed on the forest floor.

Kuljit saw that Amit had been fortunate enough to cling to the stump of a tree, while the rest of them were spread over the ground. Janesh had taken hold of Jaswinder, bracing against themselves. They couldn't hear anything from Pawan; their ears were filled with the sounds of the quake and the birds shrieking overhead, watching the calamity below. The shaking stopped, and for a moment, nobody moved. They kept their hands dug into the earth or whatever purchase they had found, waiting for the shaking to resume.

Kuljit was panting for breath, swallowing hard.

"Is everyone okay?" He looked around. Everyone seemed to be all right.

He took a breath to calm his nerves, exhaling loudly.

"Holy shit," he whispered under his breath, relaxing his muscles and laying flat on the ground, letting his tense and aching muscles go loose.

He heard Amit let go of the tree, the bark rustling against his shirt as he laid his back to it, sighing loudly.

"I think I shit my pants," he exclaimed, to no one in particular.

"Huh," muttered Janesh.

"I know I did."

Jas began to laugh.

"Good thing we are close to the lake, if we all crapped in our pants."

He was laying on his back, arms outstretched, looking up at the sky.

They all began to laugh.

"Hey!"

They heard the shout, going silent as they listened for where it came from.

"Hey up there!"

"It's Pawan," Kuljit said, getting to his feet. He walked gingerly to the edge, where the granite slab had separated itself from the outcropping. The exposed rock was bright and crisp, in stark contrast to the old weathered stone he stood upon. He kicked a loose stone off the edge with his boot, watching it fall to the water, vanishing in a series of ripples.

"Well look at you!" he shouted down to the lake.

Pawan was treading water ten meters out; the slab he had fallen in with was gone from sight, deep under the water.

"Fine time for a swim, Pawan."

He laughed at the sight of him, his wet hair plastered to his head.

The others came up beside him in turn, watching Pawan in the water.

"I don't know about the rest of you, but I need a bath now." Janesh pulled off his shirt and boots, and jumped into the lake.

"Hey!" yelled Pawan.

"Who's going to help me out?"

Amit pointed in the direction of the shore.

"Surely you can swim to there?"

Pawan spat out a mouthful of water.

"I was hoping to get a rope tossed down to me so I can climb up." He swam closer, to where Janesh had landed. He had swum near the shore, and was in the process of taking off his pants.

"What are you doing?" yelled Amit.

Janesh looked to him, scrubbing his pants in the water.

"I wasn't kidding about shitting myself."

Amit hollered, bending over in laughter. The rest joined in, laughing in surprise and in good spirits, while Janesh flushed with embarrassment.

"Laugh all you like, but if I don't get this washed out you won't want to sleep next to me tonight."

"That's true," replied Amit, who was wiping the tears from his eyes.

"Take your time." He chuckled a few more times, smiling broadly, feeling good.

Jaswinder fed a few sticks and some grass into the fire pit, hunching over and blowing deep and slowly into the grey ashes. The earthquake had shaken the hearthstones away from the fire, allowing it to spread out and die down, a few embers all that remained in the center of the pit. He had recollected the stones that were still warm to the touch, pushing them back together into a rough circle, before spreading the tinder out over the ashes.

He was quickly rewarded with a burst of orange flame that spread up into the grass and across the sticks, spreading outwards. He fed some larger sticks over the flames, angling them across each other, building them atop one another. The grey smoke of the grass cleared as it burned away and the sticks began to catch. When the larger sticks were burning nicely, he placed two logs across the fire, and then two more on top of them in the opposite direction. The fire crept upwards, and was soon putting out a comforting heat.

Pawan and Janesh emerged from the scrub a short while later, damp and very much looking forward to drying off around the fire.

"Amit, help me get some more wood."

Jaswinder stood up, heading into the woods to gather enough fuel to keep their fire going through the night.

Amit grimaced slightly, enjoying the warmth of the flames on his skin, reluctant to leave it for the coolness of the forest in the evening. He got up slowly, and then walked briskly along the same route Jas had taken, deciding that if he was going to leave the fire, he could go quickly and so return sooner. Kuljit watched them go, making notes in his journal as Pawan and Janesh dried themselves as best they could.

The evening wind had continued to pick up strength, and was making their wet clothing uncomfortable.

"Well, you won't be forgetting this trip anytime soon, will you?" said Kuljit, watching the two shiver and rubbing their arms and hands.

"Not likely," replied Janesh, who had taken off his shirt and was wringing it out over the coals, holding it out by the sleeves to help it dry faster.

"What's up with that damn wind? I'd feel okay if it wasn't blowing at my back."

Pawan nodded, agreeing with him as he stared into the embers, his eyes tired. Kuljit finished making his notes and clicked his pen closed, placing the cap over the tip and sliding into the coiled spine of his journal. The journal slid into his pack, which he tied shut, making a quick loop in the drawstring to keep it secure.

"We'll keep busy tomorrow, and you will forget all about today," he said to the two of them.

"We'll go check out her den. If we can confirm she is there, we'll head back to the Rover and file our report."

Their eyes brightened at the prospect of going home, even if it was going to take them a few days to walk back to where they had left their vehicle. At the present, they weren't enjoying themselves.

"Sounds good to me; I'm looking forward to some home cooking. No offense, Pawan."

Pawan elbowed him back lightly, smiling at the lightly barbed insult.

"Even I am getting tired of my own cooking," he replied.

"But at least you didn't have to suffer with Amit's cooking!"

"Only Amit could burn paan bread!" Janesh said, recalling how Amit had tried to brown the bread over some hot stones, and then forgotten about them, leaving them to catch fire the previous summer. They had peeled off the rocks in brittle black chunks, dry and flakey.

Amit and Jas returned a moment later, each carrying a tall pile of wood held at their chests, their arms underneath. The wood was dropped unceremoniously into a random pile, and then Pawan made sure to reposition the thorn bushes into place, blocking access to their ledge.

Amit looked at Janesh and Pawan, sensing some humor between them.

"What?" he asked, trying to see what was so funny at the moment.

"We were just discussing last year's paan bread," replied Pawan.

Amits' face dropped a bit, when he found out he was the source of the humor, recalling the burning bread all too well, and the joking that had come of it at his expense. He let it lie, and soon enough they were all gathered around the fire, watching the flames and feeling their tiredness seep into their bones.

"Well, I'm done," announced Jas, rolling over and placing his back to the fire. "Goodnight." He stuck his hand up into the air and gave a quick wave, before pulling his blanket over his body and curling into a fetal position.

They all muttered their goodnights, and then inspired, began to do the same.

Amit was next, and then Janesh, followed by Pawan. Kuljit was the last to bed down, watching the stars coming out in the night sky over the lake. The half-moon sat above the lake, just above the tree line, reflecting jaggedly in the water with waves driven by the wind. He watched as they all fell asleep, their snores and quiet breathing around the fire. He got up as silently as he could, taking several pieces of thick wood from the pile near the bushes, breaking a few into pieces long enough to fit inside the ring of stones, and a few thick short logs. He fed the sticks into the pit, and laid the logs down on top, watching them catch and begin to burn. The logs were wet and steamed over the hot coals, and only slowly began to burn. Satisfied, Kuljit laid down, his head on his pack. He fished for his blanket at his side, pulling it over him to his neck line, feeling it break the wind that was flowing through the forest in gusts. He turned over, face to the fire and soon slept.

Adelle Bäcker

Her eyes were closed tightly, and she watched as the colors and shapes in that self-induced blackness folded, disappeared, and changed. It was a way to escape from reality, a reality that was unavoidable with open eyes. Denial was a powerful instrument, a strong mechanism to avoiding a change in reality that was not desired. A strong imagination could keep reality at bay a little longer if the need existed.

She knew it was early in the morning; she had always been an early riser and today was no exception. Except that maybe it was exceptionally early. The sounds from the hospital were still low and quiet. The hum of the fluorescent lights and the sounds of the equipment in her room were the consistent and predominant sound, easy to ignore once she adjusted to the rhythm. The nurses station had no phone calls; the one nurse on duty was doing her best to stay awake after switching over to nights just the previous evening. She had the room to herself so there were no sounds from other patients that were close by. The previous evening a patient alarm had sounded and she had heard the commotion from down the hallway as nurses and the attending physician worked to delay the unavoidable. So for now the silence allowed her imagination to not be distracted. She allowed her mind to wander, her face sometimes betraying her thoughts with a smile or a frown, but at the moment it gave no insight. Her face remained calm and emotionless as she thought of better times, recent times. Movies with friends, meals with family at holidays, visiting the countryside for the weekend. The sharp ding of an elevator arriving on her floor echoed down the hallway. She frowned at the distraction, and concentrated, ignoring the sound of footsteps shuffling down the hall.

Her mind returned to memories. Joseph and herself spending the weekend traveling through Poland. They had planned the trip for over a year, picking destinations and sites of interest as time had passed, and creating a route to follow as the trip slowly and magically unfolded before them. She had met Joseph early in school, when they were both only ten. Their friendship had been continual throughout school, where they had spent time together doing homework and discussing their life plans and their parents and their siblings and other friends and those tense and always changing relationships. Over time, they had spent more and more time together, and the friendship had evolved into something further. Their interests had remained the same, their goals similar, and so perhaps it was only natural that as they matured into adults so did their interest in one another. She distinctly remembered the Saturday night when she had first found him attractive. They were sitting together on a fountain ledge, the rushing noise of the water behind them drowning out the sounds of passerby's, giving a sense of privacy in a public square. He had asked her to look at his new book, some story about time travel and the Roman Empire, and when she saw him, the old familiar Joseph was gone. She looked at him and was no longer seeing the boy that he was, but instead the man he was becoming. Something primal within her stirred, and she had looked at him and realized how good looking he was. His sandy brown hair was made darker by the street lamps, and the slight evening breeze was playing with a few strands of hair. She had looked into his eyes and looked at his face in a way she never had before, and she found herself compelled to want to kiss him, a strange heat flowing through her body. He had seen the change in how she looked at him, and had become instantly awkward, sensing somehow that their friendship was changing, but lacking the experience to know how. His tongue was stuck to the roof of his mouth, his mind completely blank of ideas. Instantly nervous, he had fumbled with his book and it fell from his suddenly clumsy hands with a wet *plop!* into the fountain. They had both looked at it for a moment as it sunk to the bottom, the unexpectedness of the moment relieving the sudden tension in the air, before he reached for it, and shook it in the night air.

"Oh shit," he had cried, and with that they had both laughed sincerely, laughing as friends, the strange moment partially forgotten.

Over the next few weeks and months the feelings had continued, until finally they had kissed, an awkward clumsy experience, but one nonetheless that had validated their mutual interest. They became inseparable, much to the concern of their parents who had not yet relinquished acceptance of the maturity of their children. She had listened to her mother argue with her father on a few evenings about their dating, her ear pressed firmly to her bedroom door. Her voice had started calm, and became shrill with emotion as she saw that her concerns were not wholly shared with her husband.

"They are too young Helmut! They need to be seeing other people, she needs to see other boys!"

Her father had remained quiet, and replied calmly.

"They are not so young anymore. Adelle will be in university in a couple of years. And I think she will be the one to decide if she wants to see someone besides Joseph."

Adelle had smiled, thankful for her fathers understanding. A few weeks prior she had come to him in his study, wanting to talk but not knowing what to say. She had sat on his leather sofa across from his desk, the thick leather creaking as she had settled into the cushion, leaning back into the thick padding. The room was paneled in a red cherry veneer, a deep rich grained color that she found made the room very warm and inviting. He was sitting behind his desk smoking his pipe, the sweet tobacco smell filling the room, and his glasses hung half way down his nose, his face a study in concentration as he read. She had cocked her head to the left to read the binding. A collection by Ray Bradbury. His wall was lined with hardcover novels, every single one in the science fiction genre. A collection of his favorites in the field. Arthur C. Clarke, Isaac Asimov, and numerous other authors. He brow had furrowed as he tried to maintain his concentration and read, but finally he gave up, surrendering to the quiet but insisting presence of his daughter. The book was silently closed and placed on the desktop, a tassled book mark keeping his place noted.

"Yes, Adelle?" The question leaving it up to her to open the conversation. Her mouth had gone instantly dry, her courage gone like the pipe smoke hanging in the air. In theory her planned conversation had gone smoothly, reality was a disaster. She struggled to free her tongue from the roof of her smooth, and she fidgeted on the sofa, her eyes dropping to her lap.

"I wanted to talk to you."

"Yes, about?" The question hung in the air for a few brief moments that passed like hours, each measured by a heartbeat. Sensing she would not be able to continue easily, he had gone first.

"Is it Joseph?"

She had nodded slowly in agreement. She had swallowed hard as a lump of nervousness materialized in her stomach and her palms began to sweat. The brevity of her answer raised his concerns, and he asked the next logical question that would be second nature to any father of a teenage daughter, fearing the possible answer.

"Are you pregnant?"

She had looked up quickly, her face turning a deep crimson. She had never talked to her father about sex, and so to hear him discuss this possibility was decidedly uncomfortable.

"No, Papa," shaking her head.

This time it was his turn to lean back into his chair, sighing in deep relief at her answer, dismissing possibilities that had become irrelevant.

"Then what is it?"

"I think I love him," she had blurted out, and she waited for his reaction, her hands clenched together, her knuckles white. He had sighed deeply again, and then smiled at her in a way that dissolved the tension in the air.

"Oh Adelle, is that all?" He had chuckled briefly, and then rose from his chair to sit next to her, the leather on the sofa creaking loudly.

"You had me imagining the worst."

She had smiled at that, understanding his perspective, but still not knowing how to proceed.

"Are you here asking for my approval of him?"

She had looked at him and shrugged her shoulders. She honestly didn't know.

"I don't know Papa. I needed to talk to someone."

"And you came to me instead of your mother?"

"Mama doesn't want me to see him. She wants me to see other boys. I see how she looks at him…she *hates* him. She won't understand." She felt tears rise to her eyes, but could not, would not wipe them away. He had nodded his head slightly, but only as far as accepting her reasoning.

"Your mother is only concerned for your comfort. We have talked about this before, her and I. She wants you to be secure in your future, and so she wants you to marry someone that can give you that security."

She nodded softly, absorbing his words. Her family had done well through investments and connections, and she knew her father was considered wealthy.

"For your peace of mind, I like the boy. His family works hard, and there is no shame in that. And besides, I can see how he looks at you, and how you look at him. And your mother sees it, too, and that is why she is afraid. She is afraid of what two young people in love can do that can harm their futures."

Adelle felt another blush coming on, rising to her cheeks.

"I think you two are smart enough to not make that mistake, and so I have to trust your judgment. Believe it or not, I was once your age and I still remember what it feels like to be young and in love."

She smiled, her nervousness fading away. He opened his arms to her, and they had hugged deeply. The argument downstairs slowly faded away, her mother conceding the battle but not the war.

The next two years had passed with relative calm, her mother ceding the presence of Joseph like a stain on a rug. Something that was there but that could be ignored, and that one day may be gone. With secondary school completed and university beginning the fall they had finalized their plans to travel across Europe that summer.

They had loaded his yellow Citroen with their luggage, hugged their families and delivered promises to stay in touch and left Frankfurt, occasionally looking back fearing something would rise up from the ground and prevent them from getting away. They had driven in near silence for the first few minutes, each savouring the freedom of the open highway, gazing at the scenery of the countryside as it sped past. Adelle had then turned on the radio, breaking the quiet. They had begun to tap out the beat, she on the edge of the door panel near the window, he on the top of the steering wheel. They had looked at each other simultaneously, and then had begun to sing together, in a chorus of missed notes and dropped words that would have made the songwriter cringe. They ended up laughing at their mistakes, caught up in the moment and enjoying every second. They drove slowly, stopping at every small burg they drove through, looking at souvenir shops in no great rush. By night fall, they had only driven as far as Stuttgart, where they had decided to stay for the night. They had checked into the room, both slightly nervous with the knowledge they would be together all night, with no fear of parents of friends. They had unpacked to the minimum extent that was needed, keeping most of their things in bags so leaving in the morning would be easier. They had gone out for dinner in a small tavern that was built hundreds of years earlier, where thick wood beams crossed the ceiling and the air had the scent of uncountable memories long since forgotten. They had eaten a light meal with a few drinks, sharing pleasant conversation and the company of a very plump charismatic waitress. They had retired to their room where they had prepared for bed, with a strange awkwardness that they hadn't experienced in a long while. They had slipped under the cool covers, their skin shivering and covered with goose pimples. They had looked at each other for a short time.

"What are you looking at?" Adelle asked.

"You." he had replied simply. She had smiled back.

"It's strange isn't it? Being here together."

"What do you mean?"

"After all that planning and time waiting to go on our own, we are finally here. Pinch me in case I am dreaming."

He saw her arm move under the covers, and she pinched his bottom soundly. He yelled, and then went with the moment, over acting and playing up his grievous injury. She looked at him with false sympathy.

"You told me too."

"Yeah okay, but my ass?"

She laughed, and then leaned towards him. His nose was filled with the sweet smell of her perfume, and it took all of his control to not let his eyes drop to her chest.

"What else would you have preferred?"

He felt his heart thump in his chest a little harder. She normally wasn't so forward or suggestive, and his mind leaped a few steps ahead. The awkwardness had vanished, and he pulled her to him, feeling her warmth and soft skin under the thick blankets. They made love twice over the course of a few hours before falling into a deep sleep. Adelle had woken up first at ten in the morning. She had simply opened her eyes and seen that it was very bright outside. Normally when she woke up the morning light was still faint, so she knew she had slept in. Joseph was snoring quietly. She had got out of bed, wrapping a loose bed sheet around her body, and had gone to the window. A faint dusting of snow had fallen overnight, but the ground was already wet where it had begun to melt. She glanced over at the clock and saw the time, frowning as she wondered what that would do to their schedule. She would have to call ahead and book their next hotel.

They had begun to climb into the mountains, driving south into Switzerland, stopping only to fill up in Zurich at the side of the highway at a small gas station. They drove through the afternoon on the highway to Lucerne, where they had booked a hotel for the night. The Alps grew as they drove, avalanche barriers becoming a more frequent sight bordering small mountain towns at the foot of steep slopes.

Large pines and spruce slowly shrank into smaller alpine species with narrow trunks and stunted branches, small copies of the giants that grew in the valley floors. The traffic had been slight with few cars on the road, and they made good time. The highway branched out into a passing lane to the right, where the side of the road surrendered to a deep valley with a small glacier fed lake at the bottom. A logging truck had come up fast behind them picking up speed to tackle the incline of the road before them. The truck was fully loaded, two flatbed trailers of cut lumber strapped down and covered over with bright blue tarps tied down to the corners of the trailers. The truck passed them quickly, Joseph looking over his left shoulder as the truck roared past. The truck passed the small car, and further up the road it began to signal to turn into his lane. He flashed his lights twice in quick succession to acknowledge the driver, who flashed his lights back and then merged into the lane. Joseph downshifted and began to pick up speed up the hill, closing the distance between the truck. Adelle was enjoying the music, her body swaying with the rhythm, looking out the window and not ahead. Joseph looked over his shoulder to pass, and in that moment the right rear tire of the trailer blew. There was a tremendous bang and then a rain of tire fragments flew outwards in all directions.

Adelle heard the explosion, and turned forward in time to see the pieces of tire flying towards the windshield. She screamed in fright, her hands flying up instinctly to cover her face. Joseph swerved quickly as a piece of tread flew under the car, and drove directly into the path of a larger piece that tore into the windshield. The glass fractured with a dull thud, and he rose his arms to shield his face. The Citroen weaved twice, and then cut to the right, smashing into the rail guard. The metal squealed and protested as the car ground against it, sparks and paint chips flying into the air. Another truck driver further down the hill watched in horror with his mouth open as the car continued to ride against the rail, his eyes not believing what he was seeing, hoping he was imagining the scene unfolding before him. Adelle continued to scream in fear as Joseph tried to push the collapsed windshield off his face. In the moment before he grabbed the steering wheel, the rail guard collapsed, a rusted beam that had been missed in a maintenance inspection buckled and tore, and the small car had shot through the gap in a split second, leaving the highway and taking air as it flew over the bent railing. It began to roll, and struck a large pine at an off angle, pitching the car violently to the side.

The windows in the car shattered, and Adelle felt herself pinned to the side of the car as it spun in mid-air. Joseph clung to the steering wheel to the moment the car hit the tree, his eyes wide with disbelief as everything had so quickly went wrong. A moment later he was shot out of the window when his seatbelt failed, the locks tearing free from the car with a series of cracking pops, sending his body flying into the open air into the valley and trees below. The truck driver behind them stomped on his brakes, locking up all eighteen tires with a loud squeal of rubber and dense grey smoke. He brought the truck to a stop just in time to see Joseph being flung from the crumpled car, his body loose and spinning in the air, only to disappear as he went below the ridge. The truck driver they were following was slowing down to see what tire had blown, feeling the pop as he was driving, but as of yet unaware of the tragedy unfolding behind him. The car spun off the side of the tree and dropped from the air to the steep decline of the highway, rolling end over end down the hillside. Adelle was aware Joseph was no longer in the car, and was being tossed around the inside of the car like a small toy. Her hands were still held up to her face, and her head was banging against the side of the car as it rolled. She felt her right leg snap sharply as the front of the car folded behind the engine compartment. She felt her head thump sharply against the side of the door as it rolled again, a wave of pain flowing through her body and her vision blurring. She felt her head hit the side again, and a slight crack from the base of her neck. She felt no more pain, and the world mercifully went black.

The driver jumped out of his truck and ran to the collapsed rail guard, the bent piece of white aluminum pointing out into the valley as if to show where the car had gone. He peered over the edge and saw a thick cloud of dust rising into the air, and through it, about one hundred meters down, he saw the yellow car wrapped around the base of an old tree. A trail of destruction led the way with pieces of car and railing and forest strewn to all sides, shattered bits of everything telling a small story of the energy of the accident. Below the tree where the car had been brought to a violent stop the mountainside had become steeper and treeless, a gravel and stone slide that led to the valley floor a kilometer below. The driver wiped his forehead with his forearm, licked his lips once, and ran back to his cab as fast as he had ever run in his life. He had fumbled for his radio, his hands slick with sweat, and he had called for help.

She woke up replaying the accident in her dreams, her hands raised to protect her face. Except that her hands were still by her sides. A chrome rack with a few bags of something hung near the bed side, a few tubes combined and funneled into her right arm where a needle protruded with a dull metal gleam. Her mother was asleep in the chair next to her bed, her fathers' overcoat hanging from the chair next to her. Her nose suddenly itched, and she moved to scratch it. Except her arm didn't move. It didn't so much as twitch. She tried again. Her mind *felt* her arm move, but it refused the order and lay there, flat on the sheets. Then she heard the machine behind her compress, and she felt her lungs fill with air. She looked around, paying more attention as her panic began to set in. A bluish tube was coming from her neck, and it led to the side of the bed. She looked as far to the right as she could, to see it led into a machine with a black pump at its center. The valve compressed downwards, and she felt her lungs fill with air again. She tried to scream, but couldn't.

She tried to move her body any way she possibly could, and nothing happened. She couldn't even move her head. All she could do was blink and move her mouth, that was all she could *feel*, was her head. The horror crept up from deep within her insides and settled like a cold splash. She fought to remain calm, her emotions threatening to overwhelm her. She frantically retraced her memories, the accident. She remembered feeling the terror of seeing the windshield collapse into the car, the shaking and impact of striking the railing, feeling Joseph fight to regain control of the car, seeing the terror on his face, the tendons in his arms bulging as he fought the steering wheel.

Then she remembered the feeling of falling, of flying, the car suddenly still and smooth, for the split second before she saw the tree rushing up to meet them, the metallic crunch as the car bit into the wood, the tree refusing to yield, and the feel of the car spinning wildly, being tossed through the air. The sound of glass shattering, seeing Joseph being torn from the car, her scream, and then everything coming to a stop in a split second. A cracking sound, and then nothing. *No, Joseph must be okay, he had to be okay.* And she remembered seeing him ejected from the car like a ragdoll, his arms and legs extended in a gross parody of flight. She realized her mother was awake, and was looking at her. She hadn't felt her place her hand on her arm. Her mothers eyes were filled with a mothers fear and worry, something only a mother could feel, deep in her heart and mind. A nurse had been foolish enough to suggest they leave for the night, to rest and return in the morning.

The verbal barrage she had received in a ceaseless torrent drove her to flee from the room, crying. Her mother had unloaded everything she had, point blank, all guns blazing, venting her fear and anger and love and loss in a verbal eruption.

Her father had reacted much differently. His instinct was to protect his daughter. His reaction was one of anger and hostility and indignant outrage. The hospital administrator had strode down the hall after hearing about the outburst, purposefully to admonish them for what had occurred. He had rounded the corner into the room, mentally reviewing his prepared speech in his mind, and he saw the look on Helmut Backers face, the expression of restrained fury. His conviction evaporated instantly, deciding that with another possible confrontation he would be risking his own personal safety. He instead made sure they were okay, seeing if he could get anything for them and offering his condolences to the situation, and his hopes for her recovery.

They had driven the distance to the hospital in such a short time that it was evident they had exceeded by a large margin the recommended speed. Helmut drove the car as if he own very life depended upon it. In a way, it had. His wife had sat quietly, not making a comment about the speed at which they were passing by other vehicles on the road. In fact, she had hardly noticed. Every moment was an agony that threatened to tear out her throat. He barely came to a stop at the few red lights or stop signs they came to, instead slowing down just long enough to verify the road was clear, followed by rapid acceleration. If they had seen a police car, it was highly doubtful they would have stopped, and God himself help the officer that may have tried to restrain the pair. The existence was entirely occupied with the purpose of getting to their daughter.

Adelle saw her mother awake, holding her arm tightly, as if she would be torn away from her. She didn't feel a thing.

"*Hallo mein Leibling.*" Her voice was thick with emotion, fighting back tears of joy and sorrow.

"Hallo, Mutter." She had to fight to get the words out, waiting for the respirator to fill her lungs with air. Her mother had wiped her eyes, only to have them fill with tears a moment later.

"Ich liebe Sie."

The words were tender with worry, and she stroked a finger through her hair as she said it, remembering doing it when she was a small baby.

"I love you too, mother."

Her mother leaned over the bed and held her close to her bosom, her body racked with sobs as the grief washed over her yet again. After a few minutes she let go, standing over the bed to regain her composure. She

walked slowly to the door, and leaned into the hallway, holding the door
jamb for balance with one hand.

"Helmut!" she yelled down the hall.

"Sie ist wach!"

Everyone in the hallway knew she was awake now, not just her father.

He arrived a moment later, pale faced and ashen, his strong body
seemingly weakened and frail. When Adelle saw him, she knew how he
would look when he was much older. He rushed to the bed, and repeated
what her mother had just done. She had never seen her father cry, not
once, even at the funeral of his own parents. He had remained tight-
lipped and his eyes were strained and red, but he had not relented. Feeling
him cry against her, like a small boy, released a flood of emotion pent up
within her, and they had cried together, his face buried in her neck next
to her ear.

"Es tut mir Leid."

"Why are you sorry?" she asked.

"Ich war nicht dort für Sie."

"You couldn't be there, father. There was nothing,"…the respirator
hissed … "you could have done. It was an accident."

"Meine Tochter." *My daughter.*

He held her close for a few more minutes, her mother sitting at her side
holding her hand as he did so. He needed to hold her close, to feel her and
smell her and convince himself she was not lost to him.

He kissed her once on the forehead, softly, and pulled up a chair next
to the bed, taking her other hand in his, his thumb rubbing the top of her
hand in small slow circles.

"Vater?" she asked him. *Father?*

"Wie ist Joseph?"

His already pale face sunk in a little further, and she saw the pain
constrict in his eyes. He looked once at his wife for strength; she saw her
nod to him out of the corner of her vision. If she could, she would have
felt his hand tighten around hers.

"Joseph ist tot."

He cleared his throat, and lowered his head.

It was her turn now, to feel the grief and loss and pain well up within her, and explode in wave after wave of uncontrollable sobbing. She felt her chest constrict and tighten, *she could feel the pain,* and she could not stop the outburst that followed. All of their promises together, the life they were to have, their dreams, gone and torn away in a moment. After she had collected herself, feeling drained and exhausted, her parents wiping away her tears from her face, she had to ask another question.

"War es schnell?" She felt the question nearly stick in her throat. He nodded, his eyes deep in concern for her.

"He died very fast. The doctors told us he probably didn't feel anything."

"What happened to him?"

"Are you sure you want to know?"

"Yes."

"He was thrown from the car. The seatbelt harness broke, and he was thrown from the car. He died from his injuries sustained when he hit the ground."

He tried to recite the words *verbatim,* as the doctor and police had described to him. He hoped it didn't make him sound cold.

"And his parents?"

"The police notified them. The local police called the authorities back home, and they were notified personally."

She imagined the police coming to their door, having to tell his parents that their son was dead.

"How are they?"

"They are destroyed."

He shrugged his shoulders in sympathy and understanding. "There is no better word for what they are experiencing. They send you their love and want you to know they pray for you."

His voice hitched, nearly unable to say the last few words, knowing how close he came to suffering their level of grief, which he could not imagine, which must be unbearable.

"They will see you when they can. Right now, they are in too much pain."

"I understand."

They sat in the relative quiet of the room for a few minutes, enjoying each others company, the nearness and comfort of family.

She had come to know the nurses rotation, and was getting very good at knowing the names of who could be expected to be on shift at a given time, barring emergencies or unexpected shift changes. Winter had deepened, the early snows melting and then freezing, and being replaced by the permanent snow of winter that would become brown and grey before finally melting with the coming of spring. When she had stabilized, she was flown back to Germany, and placed under care in the Johann Wolfgang Goethe University Hospital, in the Spinal Cord Injuries ward. Her mother and father visited daily, staying past normal visiting hours, a nurse there almost making the same mistake as the one in Stuttgart.

This morning she woke alone, her mother not coming in early as she had a doctors appointment of her own that morning. In spite of the comfort of having her parents there, today it was a welcome reprieve from the routine. She needed some time alone. Christmas was coming fast, being only four days away, and there was no doubt that she would not be enjoying the holiday at home this year. And there would be the conspicuous absence of Joseph this year. That she was not sure how she was going to cope with. She could feel the pain subsiding, the acceptance of his loss internalized, but on special days the emotional scars were torn afresh, and she felt as if she was back to square one. The nurse had changed the wall calendar during the night to December 21. It was the type of calendar where the date cards were slid into a narrow sleeve, the card that fit into it large, and the typeset bold and easy to read. A handy feature in a hospital where you never knew when having most things easy to read was a plus.

The morning nurse Elise, had come by and checked on her, wishing her a pleasant morning, making sure her blankets were on properly. Adelle didn't see why that part of the routine was checked. It wasn't like she was able to move the sheets off by herself. She sighed, exasperated. Of all the morning nurses, Elise was her favorite. All of the nurses smiled and knew their business, but not all of the nurses liked their jobs. Elise was one of them that did. She was very maternal, and so the nature of taking care of people in the routine of her occupation was a natural fit for her. And her patients could tell. She walked with energy all day long, taking satisfaction in doing her job, and so not really feeling tired. The hand on the clock moved slowly forward, showing about six forty five and about seventeen seconds. She wasn't expecting her parents until probably noon today, so she could even watch some television shows without interruption. Her favorite was a nature channel that specialized in showing people living off the land in bizarre survival situations. The episode she had seen the other day had the shows star being air dropped onto a glacier. From there, he wound his way down the ice field, navigating around deep fissures that promised a cold and painful death to the unwary. He had found himself entering a high pine forest and struggling to make a fire to pass the night with a minimum of discomfort. Other episodes had him eating spiders that surely wiggled furiously in his mouth before he bit down on them with a series of satisfying crunches, or drinking handfuls of urine in desert situations. Each episode generally had something uniquely gross or disturbing to it, and that was part of the appeal. She hoped to catch the show while she was still alone. In the meantime, Elise had put the television onto a news channel, giving her something to watch as she did her morning rounds, before she came back and attended to her. The news channel covered a variety of headlines from around the world instead of primarily focusing on local news. Since it was coming up on eight in the morning, the top stories had already been covered, and the last bit of the hour was covering stories that were more special interest. A Russian billionaire had invested a sizable share of his money in a wind turbine factory, with the hopes he would secure a contract that would enable him to cover large swaths of the tundra with wind farms. A Japanese biotechnology firm had made great progress in extracting viable DNA from a series of Tasmanian tiger fetuses that had been stored for decades in a laboratory in Perth. The company was hoping to be able to clone the animals and reintroduce them into the wild within ten years. To round out the hour, it highlighted a large group of people in Mexico somewhere, around an old Mayan pyramid. Thousands of people had flocked to the site and surrounded the structures, all watching two men on top of the largest pyramid burning incense and praying. She thought they looked very striking, with their ceremonial clothing. The reporter covering the story had said they were there to witness the fulfillment of their calendar, the culmination of thousands of years of history.

According to the reporter, time was divided into a series of ages, each age signifying some kind of change or revelation. Once the entire cycle had completed, it started all over again. She showed a few clips of her interview with the Priest and his aide, where she asked him a few specific questions. The microphone was off camera, and the interview had been held near the pyramid grounds based on the background scenery.

"Do you think the end of this Age will mean the end of the world?" The reporter sat in a comfortable looking reclining chair, while the two native men sat on the bare Earth. They sat quietly for a moment, and then the Priest, a man named Ixtab, had spoke in quiet and subdued tones.

"The world will not end. The Ages and the Cycle are measurements of time that we all must travel through. It means nothing to the Earth. The Earth will be here forever."

"So what is the significance of the ending of this Age? You called it The Age of the Fifth Sun."

"The ending of this Age is to bring alignment back to the Earth. Mankind has distanced itself from the world, disconnected himself from nature. The next Age will correct the imbalance."

"There are many people that believe this new Age means the end of civilization. What do you think?"

"I do not know the will of the Gods. We were created by them to guard over the things of this world. Their judgment will determine our fate. I am here to show that there are still people in touch with nature, that the failure of Mankind is not absolute. I am here to witness."

"Do you plan to be here all day?"

"We will be observing the entire day, from midnight to midnight."

The interview came to an end, the reporter signing off, with a last view of the two men standing atop the pyramid, their hands raised upwards in supplication. The news anchor reappeared, to tell her audience they were going to a commercial break. Adelle rolled her eyes as a very familiar commercial was replayed. It felt like the hundredth, no, the *thousandth* time she had seen it.

"Get some more sponsors."

She sighed, tired of the same commercials repeating over and over again. She looked down the hall while the commercials ran, doing her part to protest from seeing them again. She might be forced to listen to them, but she wouldn't watch them. Besides, staring down the hallway was infinitely more interesting than a super absorbent cloth advertisement. Hearing it wrap up, she turned back to the set, in time to watch the anchor happily welcome her viewers back, and she began to review the top stories.

"Top stories we are following this hour…" and the lights flickered, the fluorescents humming loudly, and they went dark.

Dr. Clive Parker

The transport plane touched down on the icy landing strip. He noted the pilot had to make some wind adjustments for his landing, which was not unusual for the Antarctic plateau. The giant plane had touched down with a quick cloud of snow marking contact, and then rapidly decelerated as the planes flaps were deployed. Clive adjusted his thick gloves over the second pair, and zipped his parka up to his nose. In another minute, the Hercules would reach its unloading location, and it was crucial that he minimized his time exposed in the open air. He glanced over to the barometer and weather station outside the crew trailer, and ruefully noted the outside conditions. Minus fifty degrees Celsius, wind speed of forty-nine kilometers per hour. A quick mental calculation gave a wind chill factor of minus eighty-eight degrees Celsius.

"Christ that's cold," he mumbled to himself. He quickly thought of his apartment in Miami, where it was a hell of a lot warmer. He glanced over his shoulders to see if everyone else was ready to go. Dr. Jessica Owens was to his right, a stunning green-eyed brunette with more Masters and Doctors degrees in meteorology than he thought existed, and possibly a knock-out body. With the layers of clothing they were always wearing it was hard to tell for sure. Dr. Neil Jakobs was to his left, a lanky red haired Dane who specialized in geology, and as a hobby, meteorites. He smiled to himself and chuckled at their appearances, how they must look, with so much outer gear on.

They looked like giant marshmallows of various colors, and would look more comical once they donned their goggles. The distant drone of the Hercules engines whined down as the pilot parked the huge craft. This was it. Clive turned around to face his two associates, gave a thumbs up, received two thumbs back, and with a last breath of warm air, they quickly filed outside towards the waiting plane, closing the door behind them.

The first breath of air, even through the thick clothing, was a shock to their systems. At an altitude of almost four kilometers above sea level, the air was utterly devoid of moisture, and bitterly cold. The sky was deep blue and piercingly bright, without the goggles visibility would have been extremely difficult and limited. The glare off the snow was painful and blinding. The three doctors ran towards the unloading ramp of the Hercules, which was beginning to descend. Clive saw the pilot wave at the threesome, and he quickly gestured back. A quick and informal salute would have to suffice. The ramp touched ground, and the skids of camp supplies began to descend the platform. A treaded forklift from the Russian Vostok Station began to remove the first skid. Clive thought it either Igor or Petr on the forklift today, but he simply couldn't be sure - the clothing masked anything he could use to distinguish an identity.

Vostok station was the original science settlement on the plateau, built in the late 1950's. East Camp was an American base placed next to Vostok Station in the late 90's. Together, the two camps had an average settlement population of about forty souls, and specialized in earth studies, from ice core drilling for atmospheric research to magnetism. Vostok Station was built over the South Magnetic Pole, specifically to study the pole and the magnetic field of the Earth. The miscellaneous driver waved hello, Clive waved back, and they went up the ramp into the belly of the plane. In the rugged isolation of their studies, camaraderie was strong and cooperation vital to their research. Antarctica did not favour individualists.

Further into the plane, Clive saw two individuals coming towards them with several large duffel bags. He noted with approval that they both were fully geared and dressed to go outdoors. Which also meant he couldn't identify who was who.

"Doctors Grewal and Tucker, I presume?" extending his right hand out. The blue parka shook his gloved hand, "Dr. Grewal." The yellow parka then shook his hand, "Dr. Tucker."

"I'm Dr Parker; pleasure to meet the both of you."

They both nodded.

"Dr Owens to my left, Dr. Jakobs to my right: welcome to East Camp, Antarctica. Please follow me," gesturing towards the off ramp and the base just beyond.

From above, the base looked like a dump half buried by windblown snow. The living quarters were the equivalent of a series of modified mobile homes, linked together with constructed walkways and access ramps. Just beyond the homes were dozens of full and empty fuel barrels, stacked neatly in rows. The camps generator sat next to the fuel dump, thereby keeping the distance needed to walk to refill it to a minimal level. The generator ran day and night, a steady roar in the background of the environment. Everything in the camp, one way or another, ran off the generator, and so it was at the center of a spider web of power cables that spread out in all directions from its center. The vehicles were parked next to the generator as well, and when not running were also plugged into a bank of power outlets. The oil in their engines would quickly freeze if they were not kept running, and so had to be plugged in, in order for their block heaters to keep the engine oil warm. The heart of the camp was the Earth Sciences lab, a larger well-insulated structure where the large majority of their research and work was completed. It consisted of computer labs, communications arrays, and sufficient space to store hardware and supplies to support the ongoing research at the base.

Around the ground area of the base mini weather stations peppered the complex, and antennas sprouted from every structure, resembling a frozen metallic insect in the ice below. The landing field consisted of a smoothed out length of snow and ice, bordered by fuel barrels for a visual outline of the area. Before a scheduled flight, the camps would remove any new snowdrifts that had accumulated on the field. They were utterly dependant upon the outside world for their supplies, and so the airfield had to be kept in good condition year round. Next to the American base was the Russian base, each indistinguishable from another except for the U.S. flag mounted on one pole, and the Russian flag on another.

An hour later, the new camp inhabitants had been suitably introduced and shown their living areas, and then given some time to unpack and settle in for the evening. Clive nursed a small glass of rye and Coke, rotating the glass in his hand as he examined a photograph on the desk. The office was shut behind him, the thin veneered door providing a modicum of privacy.

"Do you see all of these fractures, Jessica? Christ Almighty the ice sheet is disintegrating before our eyes!" He frowned in concern and thought, and then looked upwards. Jessica was nursing a cup of coffee, both hands holding the cup. She was wearing a deep red woolen sweater, her lower half was hidden behind the desk. The steam rose from her cup a good foot into the air before disappearing. She was nodding in agreement.

"These photos were taken a month ago. If this pace continues, the shelf could calf another iceberg within a year or two. One that would make the 2003 event look tiny."

Clive agreed. In 2003 an iceberg larger than some European countries had broke free form the glacier, hundreds of square miles of ice breaking off and floating off into the sea. She collected the picture and filed it back into an old yellow envelope, and then leaned back into her chair.

"I guess we knew something was up. Everyone that has been here for more than a year has heard more cracking than before. This just confirms it."

Clive nodded, and quickly imagined her naked in the office, her hair down over her shoulders and waiting for him. He felt his pulse rise and then regretfully he forced the thought from his mind. His tongue felt stuck to the roof of his mouth. He felt confident in his paranoia that one day he would actually say aloud what he was thinking, and he would be socially humiliated when she turned him down.

"Are you planning on taking the newbies up to the core drilling site tomorrow?"

She nodded in the affirmative. "The Russians are drilling a little deeper tomorrow, and this would provide a good opportunity to introduce them to the Russian team. While we are out there we are also going to release another weather balloon. The Russians have an extra experiment module they want to attach to the next launch, so the timing works out pretty well."

"What experiment?"

"It's a particle collector. It's going to sample the atmosphere at preset elevations to measure particulates. It'll drop off in a day or two and parachute down. Then some lucky team gets to dig out a GPS and go find it."

Clive laughed aloud.

"Poor bastards."

He had been at the camp for 13 months and still hadn't adjusted to the cold. If anything, he had become more resentful of it, and more firm in his resolve to never go anywhere cold again. Jessica smiled.

"Not my idea of a fun time either. What is on your itinerary for tomorrow?"

Getting you liquored up my dear so I can lower your defenses. STOP IT! He felt himself flush, and he hoped she attributed his color to his drink.

"Jakobs and I are going out into the field to do some collecting for the day. The Geminid meteor shower was a pretty good one this year, so he is hoping to find some meteorites out there."

"Wasn't that like a week ago?"

He sipped his rye and Coke.

"Yeah but the snowstorm covered anything new that would have fallen. The wind over the last couple of days should have taken care of that problem."

"Ah. And you call the Russians poor bastards. It looks like you might have drawn the short stick. At least they have a GPS. You get to look for small rocks on top of a glacier."

Then she laughed heartily for a moment.

"Be sure to take pictures for souvenirs."

Clive swallowed. Her laugh was sensual, something he imagined it would sound like in a post-coital interlude, warm and inviting.

"Thanks for the reminder, Jess. Just what I needed to hear."

Then he too laughed, more out of pity than humor. As with the rest of the base, the rooms and offices were small and so crammed with everything possible. The smaller rooms were easier to transport to the base, and also easier to heat in the deep chill of winter. His office wall was lined with a single string of tinsel that was his contribution to the seasonal decorations of the camp. It was also cheap and easy to put up, and take down when the season was over in a few days. He had always found holidays to be an inconvenience. He disliked the time needed to comply with seasonal expectations of decorating. Jessica had decorated her quarters with a few seasonal paintings, some Norman Rockwell and scenes of that nature. He admired her simplicity. Pictures were also easy to put away. He looked down at the desktop and remembered their game of cribbage. He had forgotten they were playing a game, distracted by their conversation. Jess had not reminded him to cut the deck, she was very patient and was in no rush. There was no where to go to, so it didn't matter how long it took to play the game. He cut the deck and frowned when he looked at his cards. This round was not going in his favor. He glanced up quickly, and saw Jessica smiling slightly at her hand. He frowned, annoyed at her luck. She beat him handily most games. Her luck with cards was funny at first, but was becoming ridiculous. He wondered if she would be so lucky at another game, one involving a wager of clothing. A few minutes later, she had moved her pegs another thirty spots down the board, to his twelve. It looked as though he was due for another skunking.

Jessica watched him frown at his hand, and it was difficult not to laugh at his expressions. He gave away everything with his face, his gestures very transparent. It was not so much luck with her cards that helped her win, instead her willingness to use his transparency against him. He had no poker face. And that is why she knew she liked him. When she had first come to the base she had been put off by his rather open discomfort around her. After the time they had spent working together in a close environment, she had learned that his behaviors were not intentional, or meant to be so plainly visible. He was a creature of study, more at comfort with books and computers than with people. His social skills had suffered at the hands of his passion for learning, and as a result he was uncomfortable and awkward. She frequently had to begin conversations with him in order to get him talking. If she didn't, he was apt to simply sit there wondering what he should say. She could see him thinking about what to say, except there was a disconnect between his brain and tongue. And so she ignored the social faux pas that he frequently committed, and as they worked together in the confined settings of Antarctica she began to find his awkwardness appealing. He was a good looking man with a strong jaw line and a husky build. He looked the role of a lumberjack or blacksmith, and not a scientist. What he lacked in social attraction he made up for in physical appeal, notwithstanding his obvious intelligence. As she sat across from him she could sense his awkwardness coming through the surface. He had blushed repeatedly while talking to her, his couple of drinks loosening his tight control, but revealing his discomfort. She had felt her attraction to him growing over the last month, a heat that was settling deep within her that she was more and more compelled to act upon. She knew he would not, could not. She put her crib hand down on the desktop.

"Fifteen four and eight are twelve."

He looked at her cards. Two sevens, an eight and a nine. Jesus. *In a crib*. He hadn't scored any more than four points in any of his crib hands. She moved her peg down the board and into the final hole. Game over. His pegs were both still behind the skunk line.

"Good game Clive," she said politely.

"You're just being polite," he protested feebly.

"Yes, but you are getting better ."

She put out her hand across the tabletop for a shake. He extended his and they shook on the game. After the obligatory few pumps, he went to let go of her hand, but she did not. She held firm, and rose from her chair. He looked up at her, confused, and she returned the gaze with a confident and knowing stare. He felt his mouth dry as with ash, and his arm felt weak. He dropped his eyes as she walked around the table. He felt his pulse quicken, and his mind began to whir into a panic of disjointed thoughts. Out of all the thoughts, he heard his mouth croak, "What?" before failing entirely.

She pushed his chair back, and sat down on his lap.

"I know what this room needs to feel more festive," she said, looking into his eyes. He felt as though her eyes were boring into his skull. But he did not break the stare. He could smell her perfume and hair, the scent was almost narcotic. She brought up her other hand over his head, and he followed it upwards, as she revealed a twig of mistletoe held between her fingers. He only had a moment to look back at her before she descended on him. Her lips were soft and tasted like cherry, and for a few moments, their kiss was tentative and cautious. His hands, free of the constraints of his mind, instinctively roamed up her body and cupped her breasts. Her kiss at that point became more urgent and needy, and she removed her sweater in a few deft motions. She broke the kiss, leaning back and enjoying the power of seeing him stare at her, seeing him want her.

"Merry Christmas, Clive," and she released her bra. They had kissed urgently for a few minutes, while his hands ran over her chest and back before she had put her sweater back on.

"Your room."

He nodded in understanding, his body not wanting to wait.

If there was any awkwardness the next morning, it was felt only by Clive. He was unsure of how to handle himself around Jessica after the previous evening. They had gone from the office to his room, trying to remain calm and walking without creating suspicion, while their hormones had them feeling anything but calm. He had tucked her bra under his shirt as they walked quickly to his room. Knowing she was naked under the shirt was driving him crazy. When he woke in the morning she was already gone, and he had laid there for a few minutes not believing what had happened. He was nervous about how to react when he saw her later in the morning. He showered and dressed, releasing the blinds that had covered the window during the night. With the sun not setting, he found his sleep patterns were terribly disrupted if he did not keep his room as dark as possible. Outside the window, the construction crew were busy working on the new habitation complex, a large building constructed on stilts and funded by the National Science Agency. The only time it could be worked on was during the Antarctic summer when the temperature was relatively warm and the continuous sunlight made for fast progress, if everything went according to plan. In the cold weather, things rarely went according to plan, and the building had slowly taken form over a period of several years. From what he could see, it might be done this season. The crews were now inside, working on the interior of the building sheltered from the unforgiving outside climate. Once it was done, it could house a significantly larger crew and run far more experiments than was currently possible, all within one large building. Over the next few decades, Antarctic research was going to flourish. He left his room and went to the breakfast area where a dozen people had already arrived. The new crew from yesterday was seated at the table, both looking exhausted and worn.

"How was your first sunlight night?" he asked the two.

He received a series of headshakes.

"Terrible. I imagine it takes some time to adjust."

Clive shook his head.

"You can't adjust. The sunlight triggers your melatonin levels to increase so it keeps your body clock confused. One good trick is to wear glasses when it would be night, to stop your eyes from getting any sunlight, or stay away from windows."

Tucker nodded.

"Sound advice; I'll remember that for tonight."

He rubbed his eyes and yawned. A minute later everyone else in the room had yawned as well.

"You bastard," laughed Grewal.

"I hate contagious yawns. I already feel another one coming on."

He yawned again.

"See?"

"Good morning, everyone."

He felt himself tense, hearing Jessica come into the room. There was a series of *good mornings* from everyone, and a couple of Russian versions as well. He turned to greet her.

"Good morning," he said, trying to remain as nonchalant as he could muster.

"Good morning," she replied, and then she bent over and kissed him soundly on the lips. A few catcalls broke out in the room, and a few whistles. Clive felt himself blush furiously, his face growing warm. She broke the kiss and smiled at him, walking over to the buffet. He fought to stop his growing erection. He cleared his throat and tried to reface the table as calmly as he could. He saw a series of broad grins from his peers, a few of them still chuckling.

Jakobs patted him on the back.

"Well, at least *two* of us had a good evening."

Jessica returned with a plate of her breakfast, and sat down next to him, winking once. He didn't know how she could be so calm. He needed to move.

"Excuse me please while I get my breakfast."

The remainder of the morning went normally, with everyone discussing the plans for the day, with the one exception of Jessica placing her hand on his thigh. They cleaned up, the teams agreeing to meet in a half hour at the south door.

A half hour later, Jessica and Jakobs were fueling their snowmobiles, a pair of rugged Arctic Cats with wide fairings, heated seats and handles, and a large storage compartment for their supplies. Each snowmobile also had a small sled attached to it, hauling extra fuel and equipment. Each unit was fitted with a CB radio, and a GPS device, set with the base as the home location.

"Where can we expect you guys to be for the rest of the day?" Clive asked to either of the two of them.

"We are going straight inland for probably two hours, we'll stop for a bite to eat, refuel, and come back," replied Jakobs. "If we find more meteorites it will take us longer. We'll keep in touch with base station if the plans change. We aren't expecting any other weather than clear skies so everything should be fine."

Clive nodded.

"All right. Good hunting."

He waved at the two of them as they climbed onto the snowmobiles, their engines starting quickly with a high-pitched roar. Jakobs and Jessica fit their goggles and helmets to fit, and then looked back, each waving a quick farewell, and then the snowmobiles revved up and pulled away from the camp, picking up speed quickly as they drove away. The Cats had been fitted with special tracks to help them grab onto the thick ice of the glacier, which was as solid as concrete. Thorough topography of the immediate area had shown there were no crevasses, so they could travel very quickly for the first hour, before they needed to use more caution. Clive turned to Grewal.

"Okay then, now that they are away, we can go introduce ourselves to the Russian team. They will be getting ready to launch another balloon shortly." They trudged over the ice, the thin snow layer crunching like Styrofoam under their boots, the thin screeching crunching sound unavoidable with each step.

They walked around the corner of the station, and then proceeded up a slight incline where a few people could be seen moving some equipment around, and unpackaging some material, just outside another small series of buildings. They covered the ground quickly, and soon were with the other crew.

"Dobraye utro!" *Good morning.*

A tall blonde man with a square jaw and welcoming grin turned around from his crate.

"Dobraye utro, Clive. Kak pazhivayete? *How are you?*"

He shrugged.

"Nevazhna." *So-so.* "It's too damn cold."

The man laughed loudly, his breath condensing instantly in the cold air and drifting away.

"This is like a winter day in Moscow, my friend." He breathed in deeply, exhaling out another white cloud of his breath.

"I wouldn't recommend you visit my country, except maybe in the summer."

"I wasn't planning on it, to be honest. Ivan, I would like you to meet Doctor Grewal and Doctor Tucker. They arrived last evening."

"Rad tebya videt!" *Nice to see you.* He shook both their hands in turn.

"I am Doctor Ivan Petrenko of the Russian Institute for Applied Sciences. My colleagues are Svetlana Chernenko, and Anastasiya Voronkova. Both are completing their doctorates at the Academy specializing in Meteorology."

They all shook hands in turn, and when they were done, Clive turned to Ivan.

"So how can we help this morning?"

"You can help us launch this weather balloon."

"What are these things made of, Doctor Petrenko?" asked Grewal.

"Please, call me Ivan. I prefer a first name basis."

"In that case, my first name is Amarjit."

"Thank you, Amarjit. The balloon is made of rubber, very simply.

The day before we launch it, we dip the balloon in ATK, Aviation Turbine Kerosene. This coats the rubber, helping it withstand greater pressures before exploding. These ones just arrived," pointing to the crates at their feet.

"We fill the balloons in the building, where we have a hydrogen compressor inside a special fire resistant room. When the balloon is filled, it is moved outside with the scientific payload attached, and we release it. Simple. Let's get these inside and we can launch the next balloon. Anastasiya will be launching this next one."

It took them twenty minutes to bring the new supplies into the first balloon building, where the crates where piled neatly against one wall, keeping the room free of debris and orderly.

"Yzumitelno!" *Marvelous.* Ivan stood near the door.

"Nice to get that out of the way. While Anastasiya prepares let's go outside to the balloon launch."

A few minutes later at the far end of the building a pair of doors opened and the balloon was pushed out attached to a large table, Anastasiya dressed from head to toe in protective gear, meant to shield her from an explosion if the hydrogen in the balloon somehow ignited. A large cable was attached to the balloon, where small boxes of scientific instruments had been affixed.

"Wow," exclaimed Tucker.

"It is impressive, isn't it?" agreed Ivan.

Anastasiya gave a thumbs up, which Ivan returned.

"She is going to release it now."

She released a few moorings, and the balloon rose quickly, the cable twirling slightly underneath.

"It will rise about three hundred meters per minute," Ivan explained.

"And how high will it go?" asked Tucker.

"In excess of twenty-five kilometers. Somewhere around there it will explode. There; you have witnessed your first Antarctic balloon launch. Now we can go to the drilling station."

Jessica and Neil flew over the glacier in the snowmobile, sometimes at speeds nearing one hundred kilometers an hour when they knew the terrain well enough. They could still feel the bite of the wind, the heated seats and handles just enough to keep it from getting too uncomfortable. The glacier was a bright blue white, the sunlight reflecting off the surface like a giant mirror. Their goggles were specially designed to reduce the glare and prevent snow blindness, allowing them to see the terrain clearly. So far, they hadn't seen any meteorites. At least, none large enough to spot from a moving sled. Neil wanted to travel further inland before they would dismount and search on foot. The sky was incredibly blue, a deep color that Jessica had noted only seemed present in the winter. It must be psychological, a combination of a blue sky and a white ground that made the cyan look more vivid. There was no other reason why the sky should be a different color in the winter. She thought back to breakfast, smiling a little thinking of the obvious unease that was plain to see on Clive's face. She thought it was cute. The previous evening had unfolded not as she had planned, but still quite pleasantly. She knew his awkwardness would fade once he had accepted the reality of the situation. He was simply too shy to move quickly past that first step. She would have to help him with that later that evening.

She caught a sudden glimpse out of her peripheral vision, and immediately allowed the sled to slow down, before turning back in a gradual arch.

"I saw something Neil," she radioed as she turned.

He slowed and turned to follow her, as she back tracked her path in the snow. She found it a minute later, a black rock the size of a softball lying on the surface of the glacier, a small pocket of windblown snow stretched out alongside it over the ice. She dismounted and crouched down to look at it, leaving the Cat running. It was better to leave a machine running out here than risk turning it off. It might not start again. Neil pulled up behind her and hopped off, eager to see what she had found. The rock was charred and black, pitted with lines of cooled melted rock that looked like drips of melted wax on the surface. It had melted into the glacier a couple of inches.

Neil bent over to take a closer look, removing his goggles for an unobstructed view.

"Fascinating."

Jessica could see this was an iron meteorite; the colors of the melted metal and crystals unmistakable, especially when compared next to a chondrite, or stony meteorite.

Neil gingerly grabbed the stone, and began to coax it out from the ice that held it dear. He twisted it a few times, before the ice released it with a faint cracking sound. He held it up to the sky to get a better look, twisting it around to see all sides.

"Beautiful specimen. Good eye, Jess. How did you manage to spot it?"

"Lucky break."

"Whatever, I'll take it."

He unfolded a thick Ziploc bag, and placed the stone inside, sealing it tight and folding it into the compartment at the back of his sled.

"Well that already made my day. Anything else from this point is a bonus!"

They got back on their sleds, and turned back in the direction the direction they were originally going, doubling back on their original tracks. She heard his voice crackle over the radio.

"We'll get off in another thirty clicks or so."

"Sounds good."

"Do you have any music we can listen to?"

"What do you like, Neil?"

"Just no shit, okay?"

"Okay, I'll try. She fumbled with her iPod that she had playing, connecting it to the sleds FM transmitter. She was currently listening to an album from Enya. She found her voice worked well with her mood while travelling over the empty landscape. And if Neil didn't like it, tough shit for him.

The drill site was a mass of cables and drill bits and steel and rumbling machinery. Shattered cores lay strewn around the ground, some nearly complete lengths of blue ice several feet in length, and others were incomplete shards and broken piles. They were walking towards the actual drilling hole itself.

"This is where we have been drilling over Lake Vostok," Ivan declared.

"The ice sheet here is approximately four kilometers thick, where it lies over a currently dormant volcano. We hope it stays dormant. An eruption would be very bad for us." Ivan chuckled.

"The Lake is approximately thirty-five hundred meters beneath us.

We are not allowed to drill into the Lake itself. The scientific community fears it might introduce something into its environment, a d disturb its current condition. So, we have to study it by drilling around it. We use seismography and radar to get the best images we can, and then we drill around the surface of the lake, within about a hundred meters or so. When we drilled the last core, we came up with a new find, and I believe that is why you are here, Doctor Tucker."

"Simon, Simon Tucker," he replied, providing his first name for Ivan. He nodded in acknowledgment.

"Come, see for yourself." The drill was silent, the bore stationary inside the machine, plugging the hole that led deep into the ice. Around the shaft, a reddish-brown stain marred one side of the hole, and led away for a meter in the direction the water had flowed when it had first come to the surface. Simon crouched down to examine the stain, trying to loosen some of the material with his hand. It remained stuck in the ice. He looked up at Ivan.

"So what happened exactly?"

"The team was drilling normally, Mikhail and Marco were doing the work that morning. They continued drilling above the lake as I had mentioned for another six meters, and when the core was brought up this came out with it,"he said, pointing at the coloration. The core itself is clear for the first few meters, and these colors begin to appear in the deeper part of the core, as specks and thin veins and lines in the ice."

Simon nodded, recalling the precise story from the article he read before he was sent to the drill site to examine the recovery. He needed to find out of they had drilled into a pocket of dirt, or maybe something more interesting. In the field, it would be very difficult to tell. He needed to get into a laboratory and get his hands on a thawed sample and a microscope, for starters.

"Where are Marco and Mikhail now?"

"They are in the lab, cutting the core for your analysis."

"Let's go have a look."

Under the microscope the sludge was altogether more exciting. Mikhail had produced the first slide to examine when they had shown up, and had slid it under the scope for study, clasping it into place.

The microscope was high quality, something that you would ordinarily only see in a well funded research lab. Simon had settled onto the stool, sliding his glasses up onto his forehead to hold them in place, before peering into the eyepiece, adjusting the focuser to zoom in on the material on the slide. He looked at it for a minute, adjusting the magnification in silence. "Well? What can you tell us?" asked Ivan. He leaned back from the microscope, blinking as his eyes readjusted to his glasses.

"Was there any chance of contamination of the equipment at the drill site?"

"Nyet," replied Mikhail.

"The equipment was sterilized. The sample is untainted."

He whistled quietly, allowing his mind to organize his thoughts.

"The sample is bacterial life."

"We have confirmed that as well," said Ivan.

"And it has profound implications," replied Simon.

"It means there is a significant colony of bacteria under this glacier that does not use photosynthesis to survive. Very likely, a form of chemosynthesis. Which, at this point, I cannot say. Perhaps copper, perhaps sulfur, maybe iron.

Mikhail, can you do a DNA profile on a sample? I would like to see if we could match it with anything currently known. We can run the results through our database and cross reference it."

"Do you expect to find a similarity?" asked Ivan.

"No, I expect this will be a new species altogether. Perhaps one of many. All drilling at the site will need to stop until we know more."

"Of course, comrade. Good news! Prepare what you know, and I will issue a memo to our respective agencies to announce the discovery."

"Thank you, Ivan. I will have something for you by tomorrow; is that okay?" He nodded.

"Clive, I will be here if you need to find me."

"Okay, Simon. Best of luck. We will let you know when dinner is ready." Amarjit and Clive left the Russian team with Simon in their lab to study the samples, and returned to East Camp.

They entered the camp, and Amarjit began to unzip his parka.

"You might as well leave that zipped up; I am going to show you where to find your cores for your research." He zipped it back up.

They went through a small maze of corridors before coming to a large flat door with a flat horizontal handle with a large push button at the clasp. Clive pushed the button and pulled the handle. It unlocked with a loud click, and he pulled the door back, opening it. He held the door open, motioning Amarjit inside, and he followed him in. The door shut mutely behind them.

"Don't worry, it can be opened from the inside."

Amarjit nodded.

The room was lined with row upon row of ice samples; cores running from floor to ceiling from front to back of the room.

"Excellent," breathed Amarjit.

"The cores were obtained by the Russian team as they were drilling down into the glacier. You have almost four kilometers of ice samples in here to study, going back a very long time. Is there anything in particular you are looking for?"

"I am looking to show the rise in carbon dioxide levels in the atmosphere with the rise of human civilization. Specifically, to tie into major civilizations. The Romans, the Greeks, the Chinese. All leading up to modern times. Did you know ice cores show a large increase in lead deposits during Roman eras? Romans used lead in their pipes, and as a sweetener, and the metal shows up in ice during the relevant periods of the empire."

"Hmm. I didn't know that about the lead. Very interesting." He waited while Amarjit walked through the rows of ice, his eyes glowing with satisfaction. When he was done looking at the ice, trying to take it all in, he came back to the door where Clive was waiting.

"Good enough for now?" he asked.

"Yes, thanks. Now you know where I will be tomorrow."

Clive laughed.

"So I've already lost you and Simon, and you both just arrived. The Russians have already dated the cores, so all you will have to do is find out their filing system. I think Marco keeps track of that, along with Ilena. We haven't seen her yet. She is around here somewhere."

They left the room, pushing the thick insulated door shut behind them.

"That's enough for me; I'm starving," said Clive.

Amarjit nodded, his hand going to his stomach.

"I'm hungrier than normal."

"It's the cold. Your metabolism has increased to keep you warm. When I go back to Florida I'm sure I'll gain twenty pounds just from eating out of habit."

"You better have a lot of Twinkies in the pantry, because I am craving junk food in the worst way right now."

They both laughed, retracing their steps back into the camp and towards the kitchen.

Jessica looked over to where Neil was walking, his face to the ground. They were just finishing their search grid, covering a few square kilometers where the ice was the most clear. Neil was jubilant, having recovered several fresh specimens. Unusually, the majority of the samples were iron meteorites with only a couple of small stony ones. Jessica was wrapping her samples into the compartment under the seat.

"You almost finished, Neil? It's getting late."

It was tough to tell time when the sun never set. She had to make an effort to check her watch regularly.

"Uh-huh," he replied.

He didn't look like he had heard her, replying out of habit rather than an actual response.

"NEIL." She raised her voice to a level to break his concentration.

He looked up at her.

"What?"

"We need to get going." She tapped her watch face for emphasis.

"Oh. Right." His face looked like that of a kid who was being told it was time to leave the carnival.

He sighed.

"Well, I guess we can head out this way in a couple of days again."

"We?" she laughed.

"You'd prefer to be cooped up in a cramped building instead of being out here in fresh air?"

"If the air was warmer, I'd have no problem with it. I'm going to need a long shower to feel even semi-warm again."

She undid the gas cap, and tipped up the jerry can, waiting until the contents were drained and the red and yellow can was empty.

"How's yours? I have another jerry can with a few liters still."

"It's good. Good enough to make it back to base."

"Then you better top it up. The last thing you need is a fuel line freeze."

"Humph."

"Hey; it wouldn't be me walking back."

"Okay, fine. Give me the damn jerry can."

She pulled a small one out from the netting on the side of her sled, handing it out to him.

"Why the hell do they call these things jerry cans anyways?"

"It's from the war. World War Two, I mean," she replied, watching him unscrew the black cap.

"What, really?"

She nodded.

"The Germans used small cans on their convoys to transport gasoline. The Allies adopted the use, and the slang stuck."

"Huh," he replied.

"I'll bet you've been saving that one for months."

She smiled.

"I've been known to hang on to an obscure fact or two."

He handed back the empty can, and sat on his sled while she stuffed it inside the netting. He zipped up his jacket and strapped his helmet under his chin, checking the mike before they got underway.

"Can you hear me now?" he asked, keying the mike.

She gave a thumbs up, repositioning her goggles as he drove up beside her. Neil waited for her to be done, his hands on the handlebars.

"Gentlemen. Start your engines!" he said, revving the sled up.

She nodded, and suddenly accelerated away, the track kicking up a fine spray of crystals that hung briefly in the air, making for a short and small rainbow.

"Hey!" he protested.

"That's cheating!"

He accelerated after her, hearing her laughing in his headphones.

She wasn't going full speed, and he soon caught up with her, driving alongside following the tracks they had made earlier in the day. He looked over at her, shaking his hand at her with a pointed index finger as if scolding her. She returned a middle finger in quick fashion, laughing again.

"That's not very polite," he said.

He saw her shrug, and then press a button on her dash, filling their headphones with music.

He nodded his head to the beat, some catchy rock and roll tune playing in his ears instead of a bunch of flowery woman music he had been forced to endure earlier.

Dr. Sam Tse

Doctor Tse bent over the stalk, looking closely at the stem, examining it for signs of weakness or decay. The plant was suspended in a vast hydroponic facility, grown indoors year round to enable the researchers to grow and test new varieties on a continual basis. The left side of his lab coat came free, and interfered with his arm movements as he looked at the plant. He found the weight of the cloth on his arm an irritant when he worked, a distraction that obscured his focus. He stood, handing his clipboard to his lab assistant, a twenty five year old student named Kim. Kim fumbled with his own clip board for a moment when Doctor Tse had suddenly passed him his own board to hold. He had pushed back his lab coat to his waist, and held both ends of the drawstring tightly, tying them in a loop and a series of knots. When he was done, satisfied with the tightness of the belt, he held out his hand, waiting for his board. Kim handed it back to him quickly, nodding as he did so. The Doctor took the board without comment, and bent back over the specimen.

"Subject H8 shows a potentially brittle stalk with moderate root growth. Leaf structure is moderate, so far the seed production seems adequate."

When Doctor Tse was done talking, he paused, listening to make sure the assistant had written down his observations. He had little patience for students that were not attentive, and did not like to repeat himself. He heard Kim scribbling furiously on the sheet of paper, and waited for him to stop. He stopped.

"H8 was crossed with D2 for its drought resistant characteristics; the apparent brittleness of the stalk remains to be tested to verify as a flaw of this specimen, or merely a cosmetic coloration variant."

He couldn't tell if the stalk was weak yet; he wouldn't know until the variety had completed going to seed and it could be analyzed for its quality of seed production. So far, its seed quantity production was good, with an abundant growth. The seeds would have to be tested for mineral and vitamin content, their quantity, and then again for how well they grew and could survive a variety of stresses, lack of water being just the beginning. If they proved to be efficient at utilizing water, they could then be subjected to pest experiments, as well as exposed to a variety of potential diseases. The stalk on H8 was a little brownish in places, and so needed further analysis. With a little luck, the discoloration would be a normal part of its life cycle and would have no bearing on its ability to grow and reproduce.

He listened as Kim finished writing his last observations, hearing the pen click as he pushed the top of the pen to retract the roller. Kim was better than most of his assistants; he learned quickly and did not have a problem in acknowledging his inferiority in the experiment. Some of his previous assistants had come from the same university and walked into the facility as if they were the saving grace of the program, as if their few years of book studying and pitiful classroom experiments would provide them the insight to revolutionize genetics and food modification technology. He had sent a few away in tears, berating them publically for their lack of attention or respect. Others had completed their day after such a scolding, and then not returned in the morning.

Doctor Tse had no respect for such students; how could they expect to make a contribution in the world when they failed to show respect for the professors and scientists whose work their education had been based on? They were fools, spoiled fools. He would not admit it to Kim, but he liked him. He was quiet and he was attentive, and did not speak unless spoken to. If he kept his nose in his books, and learned from watching real science taking place, he would definitely have potential in the field. A year involved in the facility experiments was worth four in the university, and would establish a variety of valuable contacts in multiple fields, any of which could turn into a career. The Doctor went to the next specimen, adjusting his glasses to get a better view as he bent over the plant.

The facility was funded by several large foundations and businesses, the largest of those were food companies and multi-national investment interests seeking to firstly make a profit, and secondly develop new strains of plants to feed the worlds growing population.

It was a large multi-winged building, all using hydroponic labs for optimal growth environments, all built under a large greenhouse structure to add natural sunlight to the plants growth cycle wherever possible. In the summer, the greenhouse utilized the sunlight almost exclusively. In the winter, it provided a warmer climate than that outside, while also providing a little natural light. It helped to keep the costs down. Even now, in the later part of December, the interior of the building was hot and humid, the atmosphere enriched with carbon dioxide to aid in the plants growth. In the ceiling, honeybee nests hummed and buzzed year round, natural pollinators that were far more efficient than any human could be at fertilizing plants. With the vast abundance of plants being grown in the lab, the bees always had a good source of nectar all the year round. The nests were examined periodically to remove new queens from enciting a swarm within the facility. In the spring or summer, the queens were released into the outdoors. In the fall and winter, they were quickly dispatched.

Each wing of the building stretched for a hundred meters, each subdivided as necessary depending on how many variant strains were being grown at any given time. The primary plant strains being tested were all staple food crops with the potential for high yield growth, or specific ability to survive in areas not normally conducive to their growth. Doctor Tse specialized in rice modification, and his experiments had yielded variants that required far less water than their natural counterparts to grow successfully, and whose seed production was double what was currently being achieved.

He went to the next batch, a different variety that was being bred for drought resistance. At this stage in the experiment, seed quantity was not important. They goal was to see how efficient they could get rice to grow in a water starved environment; possibly even to grow in similar conditions as wheat, where planting in water was not necessary. So far they were only a few generations into the test, and had not actualized anything particularly hardy. There were some promising patches where the seedlings were growing faster then their peers, and were going to be watched carefully as they matured. Doctor Tse examined their root structures, making note of how deep and spread out the roots were in this plot. The seedlings were sending roots deep and wide; a crucial step to drought resistance. The plants needed to find water, and catch as much of it as they could when they did.

"What do you think of genetically modified foods, Kim?" the Doctor asked. It was a blunt question, meant to force Kim into a quick answer. He replied quickly.

"Everything we eat has been modified already."

He laid the pen on top of the clipboard, sensing he would not need it for the immediate term. The Doctor decided to dig further.

"So what do you think of groups that seek to ban our work? Those that would seek to stop our research?"

Kim knew this was coming. He had been warned from other teachers and students that he liked to see how his assistants answered this type of questionnaire. Now that he knew it was happening, it didn't make it any easier. His answers would determine if, or perhaps how long, he would study under Doctor Tse.

"I think they are misinformed, or do not understand what it is we are doing."

"Explain."

He continued to examine the roots, content to make observations while questioning Kim.

"Many people do not understand genetics, and think that by directly inserting genes into plants we are creating unnatural forms."

"How is what we do different than nature?"

Kim swallowed. The Doctor was replying immediately after he was done talking, making the discussion progress rapidly, giving him little time to think.

"Nature modifies genes over time through random selection. It is evolution. Those plants, or animals, that are best suited to their environment survive and reproduce, passing on their different genes to their progeny. Those that are less successful die, or reproduce less

228

efficiently. We, on the other hand, insert the genes directly into upcoming generations, and so can accelerate the evolutionary process. We can breed and select for certain traits, and selectively strengthen that adaptation in a shorter timeframe. We do in a few short years what might take nature a millennium."

The Doctor nodded as he inspected his plants, not replying quickly as he had previously. Kim stood silently, feeling his heart pound in his chest. He was suddenly very thirsty.

"Do you think we are playing God?"

Kim shook his head.

"We are doing more efficiently what might take farmers many generations to achieve."

"And what about taking genes from one plant, and transferring it to another?"

Kim would have killed for a glass of water.

"Those genes are still natural, and very possibly would have eventually evolved in the other species over time, given the right conditions. Parallel evolution. Something that has happened many times in the course of life on Earth."

"What would you say to those who refute our work?"

"I would say to them that they are condemning millions to death by starvation."

The Doctor was silent, inspecting another seedling whose roots had grown deep into the hydroponic tank. He had taken out a cloth tape measure, unrolling it from the base of the stalk to the approximate end of the root tips.

"Fifty-seven and one-quarter centimeters."

He re-rolled the tape measure into his palm, standing up.

Kim stood there for a moment, his mind processing what the Doctor had said without fully understanding him. Suddenly it clicked.

He grabbed the pen and clicked the top, writing the measurement down furiously on the paper.

"Specimen Fifteen B."

"Fifteen B."

Kim repeated as he wrote.

Doctor Tse nodded, and then moved along to the next plot. With his back turned to Kim, he smiled thinly, satisfied with Kim's answers.

He did well under the pressure, answering quickly. His questions were designed to make his students think fast, with little or no time for thought. The faster someone answered, the greater the chance or likelihood that the answer was genuine. If his assistant did not answer quickly, he answers would be subject to further scrutiny. Kim had answered quickly, to all of them, and so it was very likely that his answers were sincere. Time delay indicated that answers were being thought out, which diluted complete honesty. He walked onwards, towards the next plot in another room. He looked outside as he went through the various corridors to get to where he wanted to go.

The entire facility was under the greenhouse glass, so he could see the weather outdoors wherever he went, at least in the areas where plants were being grown. The day had been a mix of sun and clouds, the giant fluffy type of clouds that blew past quickly, allowing the sun to shine through for a few minutes before once again being obscured and throwing a dim shadow across the building. It made it difficult to read small print, Doctor Tse found. The older he got, the harder it was for his eyes to adjust to changing light conditions, especially in dimmer light. He adjusted his black-rimmed glasses as he walked, pushing them up high onto the bridge of his nose. He squinted as he did so, trying to get the glasses higher. He really needed to get new frames, he would admit only to himself. He just couldn't justify spending the extra money on new frames when the actual prescription was fine.

Another cloud passed in front of the sun, dimming the hallway and removing the heat of the light that so easily penetrated the glass. One of his favorite sensations was the feeling of the heat from a bright ray of sunshine on his body, a fondness acquired when he was a young boy sitting in front of a window on a cool winters day, when the sun would briefly come out, and he would feel the warmth soak into his skin through the glass. In the steady heat of the greenhouse facility the temperature was highly regulated, but the direct heat of sunshine was still a feeling he relished, finding it deeply relaxing. In a few places on the exterior of the building small patches of snow were quickly melting, the earlier snowfall of the day nearly gone while still coating the ground outside in a bright white finish. Where the snow had already melted, large beads of water had collected where the angle of the glass did not allow for easy drainage. When the sun came out again, the light passed through the water, giving sections of the interior a brightly colored hue as countless numbers of tiny rainbows formed. Judging by the position of the sun in the sky, it was getting on past dinner time, the sun dropping to the horizon and the sky gradually getting darker. He walked faster; he wanted to check on the pest control variants before he called it a day.

They were currently trying a few strains to reduce losses through pest damage. The first plot was a test to develop non-preference types of rice, where insects would simply find the plants uninteresting and move along, sparing the crop from damage. The second plot was dedicated to antibiosis, where the consumption of the plant would cause death in the insect population, and the final plot was trying to develop tolerance, where a plant would continue to develop good growth and yields despite a high insect infestation. Each test was subdivided into various insect types, the gall midge, the leaf folder, and weevils. It was a large subsection of the experiment. The overall challenge was to develop plants that were drought resistant as well as able to grow well despite insect attack, or to be ignored by insects altogether. Some variants had been developed that were highly effective at growing in dry conditions, but that insects found irresistible. Other specimens were avoided by insects, but needed an environment rich in both water and nutrients, something not practical in most situations. The challenges were daunting, but they were also what made the work so interesting and satisfying. Each generation produced new variants, each of which required study and presented a unique result. A few people he had worked with over time had wondered how he could continue to work after failing time after time.

His response in each situation was a quote he had learned from Thomas Edison, the inventor, who had said that he had never failed, only that he had succeeded in finding many ways that didn't work. That generally shut them up. Research was not an occupation that harbored pessimists for long.

Doctor Tse and Kim finally arrived at the section, and had to go through a decontamination routine, making sure that none of the pests escaped into other plots where their presence could seriously affect the outcomes or development of other variants. The rooms were vacuum sealed, and sprayed with insecticides with each entry and exit. They could take no chances. When they had finally passed into the wing, they were looking forward to examining the plots. They hadn't checked on the strains for a few days, wanting to give the insects time to work on the plants, and vice versa. Some variants had failed to resist; their stalks or leaves were brown and dying, while others were still vibrant and green. Doctor Tse checked the first green one they came to, examining the plant for insect infestation as well as overall growth and health. He frowned quickly. The plant was healthy, and seemed to be avoided by insects, but it had produced virtually no seeds. Kim recorded the variant. It could be crossed later with a specimen that produced a bountiful crop, with the desired result that the progeny would inherit the non-preference trait of one parent plant, while also gaining the abundant seed production of the other. The two men bent over the first plot, reviewing each plant systematically. The sun dimmed again, passing behind another cloud. In the later stages of the evening, it made some observations difficult, as subtle colors were lost in the shade, or insect damage could be obscured completely. They waited patiently, examining what they could while waiting for the sun to reappear. They would not have time to examine the rest of the plots today; the dimming light was going to be a problem with the cloud cover. Kim looked at his wrist watch to check the time, coinciding with Doctor Tse looking at his. They both frowned. And then the light began to come back, and they checked out another specimen. The room lit up, and the men took the opportunity to look at plants that were further inside the plot, where there was more shade. In the brightness, they wanted to take advantage of the situation while they could.

Kai Kwong Mok

"These are fantastic," he said, flipping slowly through the results of the latest test batches.

"How about software glitches?" he asked.

"Very few," the engineer replied. He was very happy with the latest results, and was eager to share them with the Program Director. Success meant prestige and funding. Funding meant job security.

Chief Engineer Xu had been in charge of the program since its inception, and was entirely responsible for its development and ultimate realization.

"What were they?"

"One unit was unable to calibrate its sighting system; another failed to go into defensive mode. It apparently did not recognize a potential threat and so failed to react. "

"Very good. So two units had issues out of how many?"

"Twenty four, Mr. Mok."

"And did any have hardware issues?"

"None whatsoever. The gelatinous muscle tissue is proving to be extremely reliable."

"And the joint motors?"

"We replaced them completely from the last generation. The motors were proving too costly in terms of energy use. We found that by having the latest models simulate a human walking motion, where each step is a controlled fall, we were able to eliminate the motors entirely, and the prototypes had to learn how to walk, as we do. It is much more efficient."

Mr. Mok had seen the initial prototype tests, where the units were learning to walk, and then run. It was very amusing to see them struggling with something so basic, at least something that looked so basic. When he had seen the work that had gone into developing the balancing systems, it was a wonder that it was feasible at all.

"And how are the batteries systems coming along?"

He nodded quickly.

"Current battery lifespan is twenty four hours, under moderate use. Once we enable the units with fuel cell capability, we expect to see a much more reasonable lifespan within a field of operations."

"When we have our nuclear battery prototypes off the line, we expect to have settled the range issue."

The entire operation was enclosed with the high rise; a thirty-story apartment building that had been slowly and covertly renovated to suit the needs of the research. Below ground level, the building continued for an additional ten levels, where the actual unit testing took place. The above ground floors were strictly for programming and analysis. The sublevel floors had been modified to simulate combat conditions to test the prototypes, where others had been converted into assembly lines where they were built piece by piece.

He had been to the lower floors only once, when the facility was deemed fully operational. At that time, the program had only one prototype that had been built, the others were in various stages of construction. The primary unit, whose systems were based on artificial intelligence and learning, was built atop a desk, nothing more than a head piece attached to its main computer, with limited mobility but with access to a wide degree of information. They wanted the thing to learn, so they gave it the access it needed.

For physical abilities, dummies were created that were nothing more than functional endoskeletons with the same weight and height characteristics that the final combat models would possess. They were attached to basic computers and programs that were taught to simulate basic human bipedal movement. The first models fell frequently, the programs not yet being sufficient to coordinate a walking or running motion. But it was smart, and it learned, and very shortly the chassis units were running and walking through the simulation course with proficiency, leaping over obstacles that would impede all but the most skilled of human athletes. The machines wrote their own programming code as they built upon their successes, each line of code building upon the last. When the prototypes no longer stumbled or fell, the code was finalized and downloaded into the main unit, for use in programming the next generation. The same procedure was used for climbing stairs, and each program learned faster than the last; the experience of the previous lesson accelerating the adaption of the next. Mental abilities were the final procedure; teaching the machines what they would need to survive in a real combat situation. They needed to be be programmed with an instinct for self preservation, and the ability to recognize a potential adversary. He was confident that would not take long.

"Programming?"

"The team is currently working on specific facial recognition algorithms. We want to enable the units to be able to examine a facial pattern and from there determine a reasonable course of action. For example, we want to create a test where a unit is placed in a situation where it faces imminent attack, although it may conclude otherwise based on speech and weapons positioning."

"How do forsee the test as an example?"

"Something simple. The foe will verbally surrender, which the unit will recognize and normally then remove that individual as a perceived threat. We will try a few varieties where the foe has a weapon, or not, to see how it learns to recognize a threatening facial characteristic, or aggressive body posturing. Something that our units currently cannot perform."

He nodded, closing the report and sliding it back to Mr. Xu.

"Continue current operations, and please keep me informed of any progress or delays you encounter."

"Yes, Sir. Thank you, Sir."

He bowed quickly and formally, leaving the office with the report folder held tightly to his chest, dear to his heart.

Mr. Mok would have to prepare a report early in the next month for the Central Military Commission, who oversaw the program and would be critical in continuing its funding. The autonomous robot infantry was but one branch of its investments, all of which were based on artificial intelligence weapons systems. The Chengdu J-20 was already being fast tracked for development and deployment goals were set for 2020. A photograph of a scaled down J-20 was on his desk. It was half-scale, and so far in testing in had proven to be extremely efficient. Full scale prototypes were now in production, and would be coming off the assembly line with the year. The jet was extremely aerodynamic, looking like a sleek torpedo even just sitting on the tarmac. The benefits of pilot-free warplane were considerable. There was no expenditure in training, the plane could actually perform to mechanical specifications and not be hampered by the frailties of the human pilot, and if it was actually shot down, everything it knew could simply be downloaded into a new aircraft. Everything it *learned* could be downloaded into a new aircraft.

A few test flights had been performed where the plane was crippled due to enemy fire, and so far none of the planes had been lost. The onboard computer had quickly calculated its new flight characteristics, and had brought itself home for repair. What's more, they had learned from the previous mission, and when the sequence was initiated, the computer had reacted defensively, preventing a repeat of the original simulation. The Military Commission had quickly seen the benefits of the armed drones currently being used by the United States Air Force in the field, and wanted a version of their own. It was no secret that the U.S.A.F. was also investing in a pilotless craft, and they did not want to play catch up with this technology. It would prove invaluable in future conflicts, and had high potential in the nation's space program.

He turned around in his chair, holding in his hand a plastic model of the Robotic Autonomous Soldier. The program was also in high gear, and he expected to see real results with a few short years. They had solved all of the basic hardware issues such as walking and running, or going down stairs. The skeleton was simple; a titanium frame modeled after the human skeleton where the energy systems could be stored within an armored chest cavity, as well as additional computing power if necessary. Two stereoscopic cameras in the head provided for accurate depth perception, and a much more sensitive ocular design meant the combat units could perform using the visible light spectrum, or infrared, or microwave. Once the units had been calibrated to their weapons, they never missed, and their shots could be programmed to kill, or wound specifically, or to take whatever shot was available. He had seen a movie based on such a creation, and he smiled to think that reality had almost caught up with science fiction. He knew that if he were an enemy soldier and he saw a platoon of these units coming down the street towards him, he would likely surrender immediately. He put the figurine down on his desk, in a standing position, facing towards his door like a plastic sentinel.

Randy Palmer

The air inside Edison's mill was cool, and filled with the fine sawdust that covered everything under a thin layer of light beige. The deep hum of the machinery penetrated everything, the metal catwalk vibrating underfoot, feeling much like walking on the deck of a ship at sea. The air was filled with other regular sounds; the clanking of large chains, the whisper of rubber belts, and the shriek of saws biting into wood. He barely noticed any of it anymore. It rather vanished into a general category of background noise that no longer caught his attention. Unless he was working in an area where he had to be especially cautious. The mill was built between Osborn and Parkers Ferry, off the State highway 17 to the south. A wide gravel road off the highway was the only sign there was something further off the road, and it had to be followed for several kilometers before you could actually see the operation. It had been built in eighteen ninety-seven by Seamus Edison, a rough and hardworking Scotsman with a passion for working with wood. At first it had been a normal sawmill, cutting logs and producing lumber for the growing cities around it, Charleston being not too far away to the northeast. Times began to change, and the lumber market became very competitive. Before he could be squeezed out of business, Seamus had begun to specialize, gradually retooling the mill to produce more finished product that he could sell at a higher price, and more importantly, that had less competition. The plant had gone from cutting rough two by fours and two by sixes, into planed baseboards and other finished woodwork, supplying the area with value added products. The mill thrived, and before Seamus had died at the ripe old age of eighty-seven, he had seen it supply the entire eastern seaboard, and even ship some product out as far as California from time to time.

At the far end of the yard, very near where the original mill had been built, the wood came into the plant to be cut down into workable pieces, running down a long green chain, a few rip saws, and eventually a baler where it was sorted and stacked according to grade and species. After some time in the kiln and running through the planer, it was processed into the specialty products like flooring and edging that kept the mill profitable. A tall wall of logs surrounded the mill that kept coming in by the truckload, all bought at a higher grade to maintain a high level of quality. The yard was separated by species, with pine and spruce taking the majority of the yard, and fir and other less common soft and hardwoods taking the difference. The mill would run through the wood in share, making sure it kept a variety of products available to the chains of home building centers that bought from them.

Randy had started at the mill at the age of fifteen, when his father had been a yard foreman and pulled some strings to get him his first summer job. He was hired to work with a bunch of negroes and a few other school kids to start entry level, which meant clean up. He had spent the summer cleaning the yard, picking up broken lumber and debris and piling it all on a two-foot wide belt that ran directly into the chipper. The white kids had stuck to themselves, and the black kids were forced to stick to themselves, only working together when the job had no other option. The segregation at the mill was not official, it just was. When you went on break, the break room divided cleanly into a white side and a black side, something that a newbie could see quite plainly. When the yard had been cleaned he was set to work with a shovel and a wheelbarrow, to go into the nooks and crannies of the plant and dig out the piles of sawdust that had been accumulating under the walkways and machinery. It had taken him a month to dig them all out, the shovelfuls coming slow and awkwardly. The sawdust and bits of wood stuck together in thick clumps that Randy had thought would come out easily. Instead, the clumps really stuck together, and resisted coming free from the pile. It turned out to be a bitch of a job, and more than once he had thrown the shovel aside and scooped the debris into the wheelbarrow with his own hands, taking huge satisfying clumps out of the piles one at a time. He took each barrowful and dumped it onto a slower belt that ran underneath a magnet, lifting nails and small pieces of metal and solder free from the pile that could ruin the saw teeth cutting above him. He would angle the barrow up to the railing of the belt, and rock it back and forth, spilling small amounts of the sawdust a bit at a time. He couldn't believe how much metal came flying out of the piles, sticking to the magnet with a sudden click, the larger pieces like nails and screws hitting it with a satisfying *thunk* sound, like a bug hitting the windshield on the highway, spreading itself over the glass in a thick yellow smear. Once past the magnet, the sawdust continued down the belt under the bowels of the mill, finally being swallowed by a burner that ran the kilns, heating the oil to dry the wet lumber. He worked hard, and found the labor to be extremely gratifying, watching the piles of wood under the mill disappear by the wheelbarrow full, and the yard grounds as clean and neat and they could be, furrowed by the thick grabbing tires of the forklifts and log pickers. When the summer was over, and school loomed on the horizon, one of the bosses offered him a permanent job at the mill, impressed by the work he had done in cleaning up the place in a couple of short months. He was ecstatic, and couldn't wait to tell his father when he got off shift a few hours later. He received the opposite reaction he had been expecting. He had come into the house, untying his boots dropping them in the front closet, the laces strewn about tongues folded outwards, the leather soft and broken in. He had met him in the kitchen to break the good news.

"Burns offered me a job at the mill today, for after the summer."

His fathers face, already tired from his shift, dropped further, his mouth becoming a thin straight line across his face.

"You mean during school."

He had nodded back, agreeing.

"Over my dead body are you going to quit school at fifteen."

His voice was deadpanned and flat.

"But we can use the money!"

He protested, visions of a car of his own and money to spend suddenly becoming less likely.

"I can pay rent, and help with the food."

240

His fathers face had dropped even further, the reality that they could indeed use the money striking him a hard blow. They had nearly lost everything after his wife had died of cancer, the doctor's bills eating up their life's savings and forcing them to sell their home. In the end, all for nothing. The cancer hadn't even blinked twice at the treatments; it had raced through her body, doing everything but killing her until it had no where else to go. The doctors couldn't explain why she wasn't dead yet. She was gaunt, hairless and feeble, but alive. The cancer was in her lungs and bowels, her skin becoming lumpy with the tumors growing just underneath the skin. In the end, she had died of pneumonia, but by then there were financially ruined.

"You are going to finish high school, and that is the end of that!"

He could see the rage bubbling just below the surface, the tendons in his fathers' neck tight under his skin.

"But...," he tried to begin, and was cut off, his fathers finger pointing at him like a sword.

"Goddamit you are going to finish school! If you want to work at the mill after you are done, then fine, but the very least you are going to do is graduate!"

In the end, he did the least he could do. He finished high school, working his weekends and summers at the mill for extra cash, the only compromise his father would make on the subject. He started full time at the mill the day after school ended.

His father had died a year later in a fluke accident. He had been walking in the yard doing inventory on the baled lumber stacked outside the planer, checking off the quantities and grades of lumber. He had gone in between one of the several rows stacked five high, when the baling strap on the top pile let go. The sudden release in tension freed a two by ten on the edge of the pile, and it fell to the path below, where his father had been scratching his head, removing his hard hat to do so. The board had struck him squarely on the head, and he was dead before he hit the ground. A forklift operator had found him an hour later, spying a hard hat lying on the ground between two stacks of lumber. He had gone to investigate, and had found him on the ground in a pool of drying blood.

Randy had used the life insurance money to buy himself a small house near the mill, free and clear. He could almost walk to work if he wanted, but he chose to drive his old blue Ford instead. The next few weeks at the mill were awkward, with everyone giving their condolences and saying how god-awful *bad* they felt, what a terrible tragedy it was. He took it quietly, which people took as respectful and heartfelt, but instead was actually sheer boredom. He didn't give a shit what these people thought. He couldn't believe how these people couldn't let go. Compared to how his mother had died, he had taken a good measure of comfort in knowing that his father hadn't felt a thing. That's how he wanted to go, how he hoped to go someday. Something quick where he had no idea of what happened. One moment he could be cooking breakfast, and the next he was standing at the Pearly Gates wondering where the frying pan he was holding in his hand had gone. Eventually it passed, and the mill resumed its normal day to day routine. He befriended William, a former acquaintance from the local high school that shared a similar opinion of minorities. He had curly hair that he couldn't do anything with, and a slight case of Tourettes' that always had him fidgeting and unable to sit still, with the occasional facial twitch if he was stressed. They frequently smoked together during their breaks, discussing their political and ideological views.

"Now, I don't have anything against a nigger," he said as he exhaled.

"It ain't his fault the way he was born. But it ain't right that he can take the job of a white man."

He grimaced as he said it, as if he had taken a bite of a particularly sour apple. Randy had nodded in agreement.

"I understand they was slaves once, and that it wasn't their fault neither, but then they should all just go back to Africa."

They kept the discussion low, keenly aware that their own beliefs were not shared by everyone they worked with. Their discomfort had been generated by the hiring of a new executive at the mill, who happened to be black, who had been hired to analyze and optimize the efficiency of the mill. He was just over thirty years old, fresh with a MBA in business, and younger than any other of the management, and a good portion of the veteran employees.

"You coming over this weekend?" Randy had asked.

"Yup. We gotta get that shelter built sometime don't we?"

He nodded back. They had been building a bomb shelter, after a fashion, in Randy's back yard over the past several years. When it was still exposed to the elements it had been a bitch, as they had been going slowly on it year round, but now that it was enclosed it wasn't so bad. A few years back they had seen a travelling preacher, a Reverend Parker, in a local tent, who had been warning everyone of the coming of the end of the world, and to make preparations for the End of Days. He spoke with enthusiasm and passion, and had little old ladies fainting in their seats, warning about the impending Day of Judgement. He had seen the Gulf War as a sign of the end, and Y2K, and the year 2000, and Hurricane Katrina. In fact, pretty well everything in the news he saw as proof of the end of the world. And he convinced Randy and William of the same thing. After the end of his latest sermon in the area, they had asked him what they could do to better prepare themselves.

"Well!" He had said, with a huge exclamation, "What have you done so far?" They explained their bomb shelter. He had nodded as they had described it to him.

"And what do you have to arm yourselves?"

They looked at him quizzically. Seeing the confusion, he clarified himself.

"What do you have for self protection? Guns and that sort of thing?"

William and Randy had looked at each other before looking back at him.

"We don't have any guns."

"Well that's going to be a problem now, isn't it? How do you boys expect to be able to hunt for food and protect your interests without any kind of firepower?"

They stayed silent for a moment.

"We hadn't really thought that far ahead, I guess."

"That's what God had put me on this Earth to do. To help his children prepare. Come by here this evening, say around ten?"

They had agreed and returned later that night to find the Reverend standing against a green Ford Econoline van, the kind used by couriers with no windows in the sides or back.

"Glad to see you boys. Now let me show you what I kin offer ya'."

The Reverend, still dressed in his collar, unlocked the van and opened the rear door with a loud click. The twin doors opened revealing an assortment of firearms hanging from every available nook and cranny of the van. There were AK-47's, Uzi's, M-16's, and a huge amount of other assault style weapons, handguns and rifles and the ammunition to go with them organized in a cubby hole of neat white boxes behind the front seats. The Reverend Parker was wanted nationally on weapons smuggling and racketeering, and only dumb luck had so far kept him ahead of the FBI. The two men had whistled in awe of the weapons selection in front of them. After much debate and aid by the Reverend, they selected two AK-47's and a few hundred rounds of ammo for each one. They paid in cash, and stowed the weapons in the back of Randys' Ford, covering them in a faded orange tarp.

The Reverend shook their hands after counting their money slowly and methodically, using his tongue to moisten his finger periodically as he flipped through the cash. They each drank a beer as he counted.

They had driven back to his house, parking the truck behind the house, near the bomb shelter. It was nearly impossible to see from the driveway, the shelter having been built underground, and then all but covered over with a layer of soil and sod, leaving only the door way exposed. Three ventilation shafts protruded from the ground, placed in thick foliage to help conceal their existence. Overall they two men were very pleased with the way the shelter had come together. They had found some designs and plans on the internet, and dug the space out of the backyard with a co-workers back hoe, paying him in beer and some framing lumber bought at their employee cost.

They opened the door, and walked down the staircase, flicking on a light switch that still took its electricity from the grid. In case of emergency, it would be switched to the generator in the bunker. On either side of the bunker were thousand gallon drums, one full of water, another full of gasoline. The bottom of the staircase revealed an eight-inch thick blast door that sealed against the inside of the frame and a thick gasket, keeping it waterproof. The door opened outwards, and opened into a narrow room eight feet in width, and forty feet long. There were beds and counters built into the walls at various locations, leading to the end of the room where another door was shut. It opened to yet another room, this one another twenty feet long. It had been filled with foodstuffs, enough to last for a considerable amount of time, depending on how many occupants were using it. Beyond the food stores, there was clothing and medicine, and books on every imaginable topic. At the end of that room, they leaned the new guns against the wall, piling the boxes of ammo on a shelf nearby. Over the next few months, the Reverend had stopped by a few more times, and they added to their stockpile a few hunting rifles, some shoulder slings full of hand grenades, and a few more AK-47's just in case they happened to need parts.

The shelter itself was nearly done, requiring only a few more items more for creature comforts than to aid in survivability. They wanted to add a deep freeze, but hadn't yet decided on if it was worth it as it would impact the longevity of the fuel they had stored. The generator was stored in a separate room built into the wall itself, ventilated into the bushes overhead. If they needed to access it, it could be reached by breaking through some cinderblock, but that was an unlikely scenario. The generator had been directly attached to the fuel tank, and was turned on or off from the inside wall of the bunker.

The next day at the mill had started just like any other, the shift change announced with a shrill double blast of the horn, a hoarse sound that carried for miles. The mill ran from eight in the morning to four in the afternoon, with the night shift going from four until midnight. In the summer, it was the best shift you could hope to get. It was hot in the afternoon, but by the time you were off the night had cooled the air nicely and it was easier to sleep. The saws momentarily fell silent, giving an eerie calm to a place that generally was always loud. The men had put their lunches into their lockers or the old fridge, a dirty old ivory colored thing that should have died ten years earlier. It kept food just on the slight of cool, the compressors and coolant no longer able to keep the interior actually cold.

It was adorned with more than a few cutouts from some girlie magazines, a pornographic wallpaper. Management had tried to remove the pictures to keep in accordance with its human resources policies, but eventually gave up after the fridge always had a new collection the shift after it had been cleaned up. The shift had punched in and the men had gone to their duties, Randy getting his hardhat and visor placed on his head, and lowering it to shield his eyes from the dust he would soon be blowing around with the air hose. He went to the ground level, and felt the saws start up, the vibration running up his legs and rumbling deep in his guts. He couldn't even hear himself breathe once everything was running full tilt. The smooth concrete floor of the foundation was covered with the ever present film of thin wood dust from the nightshift. When he had first begun the job, years earlier, it had pissed him off furiously that it was always dirty. After a brief time, he had realized it was not going to change, he worked in a sawmill for Christs' sake. It was like expecting a toilet to not get dirty after an endless stream of people had pissed in it and shit in for a day. Once he had come to realize that it was going to be dirty every morning, he had really come to enjoy the routine. His day would start first with him hosing the floor off with the air hose, blasting what he could outside where the wind would carry it away. The rest would accumulate in dense piles in the corners of the mill, where he would come by later with his shovel and wheelbarrow, scooping up the little piles by the shovelful, making trips to the waste belts that would run the dust into the sawdust piles or the kiln furnaces. Once the dust was caught up, he could go for the bigger pieces of wood that had fallen from the chipper, or the debarker, rooting them out of the crevices they always got stuck in, and then feeding them into the chipper all over again. He had divided the mill into days, so the entire mill was cleaned over the period of a week. The mill hadn't failed a fire safety inspection since he had gone into clean up. He made doubly sure the fire hoses were clean and stored properly, and the hydrants were flushed regularly. The fire extinguishers were everywhere, brightly marked so that even a moron, which the mill was sometimes apt to hire, could find.

He sprayed the floor with the hose, kicking up a cloud of sawdust, keeping the flow going, pushing the debris out towards a large venting door at the side of the building. The hose had a huge reach, a bright blue thing that never seemed to get stuck around a corner. The air hissed loudly, kicking up a spray, and he kept it moving with further bursts. He kept his head down so the visor was the most effective at keeping the dust from his eyes. Wood dust was the worst. One moment you could be working away, and the next minute you would drop the hose, clutching your face and swearing when it felt like sandpaper was being dragged over your cornea. The hose hissed, and he took another step forward to the opening. He saw the shadow cross the floor, the bright sunlight casting into the mill. Being December, the light wasn't too warm anymore, but it sure beat a cloudy day. He thought nothing of the shadow, and depressed the valve on the hose, getting another loud hiss of air and another rolling cloud of dust. By now, the amount of dust in the air was immense, the sunlight glittered in a myriad of fine specks that filled the air, floating almost magically in visible waves of particles. He looked up, suddenly wondering what the shadow was. He saw someone standing in the vent, his face bent down into cupped hands, a cigarette held in his lips. It was a new kid they had hired as Christmas help now that school was out for the holiday season, one the morons they had recently brought onboard that so far had managed to keep a low profile, avoiding being caught doing nothing. His name was Danny. He had recognized him, and then shook his head in disgust that he was already slacking off, not more than ten minutes into his shift, and he was taking a smoke break. Another fucking moron. He sprayed the hose again. He was taking a smoke break in the mill, standing in the vent and the cloud of wood dust he was blowing outside. Trying to light a cigarette. His eyes widened as his brain finally connected the dots, and he dropped his air hose to the ground. The copper fitting clacked loudly on the concrete, but under the rumble of the mill, it was muted.

"Fuck Danny nooooo!" he yelled, just as Danny flicked the lighter again.

The spark caught, issuing a small orange flame to the tip of the cigarette, and he inhaled. The flame jumped into the wood dust in the air, just as Randy hit the ground, his arms covering his head as he fell as flat as possible. Danny took a drag, just in time to see the air around him fill with a bright orange glow, before it went WHOOMP! with a loud clap and the dust in the air caught fire and exploded, blowing him clear out of his boots and away from the wall. The air decompression popped Randys' ears, and he could feel the flames flowing over him, licking at his

247

coveralls, burning in the air over his back, blowing outside. He scrambled back, on the ground, when he heard the fire klaxon ring in the mill. A millwright working on the floor above had seen the gout of fire blow outwards from below, and had immediately pulled the fire alarm on the wall next to him. Randy reached a stairwell, and he had pulled himself up, looking back to see the fire had already blown itself out, the wood dust suspended in the air ignited and spent, now just thin ash in the air. A "No Smoking" sign hung on the wall, the white paint blackened and bubbling from the short but intense heat, bubbled at the edges.

He looked around, seeing no residual fires, just thin ashes floating down to the ground. His back still felt warm from the fire that had surged over him, and the smell of smoke was heavy in the air, the sweet campfire smell of freshly burned wood. He jogged outside, stopping at a smoking boot that lay on the ground, sole down, the waxy end of one lace burning slowly. He looked around, seeing more workers getting out through the fire exits.

"Get the First Aid Attendant over here now!" he screamed, hoping someone would act on it. He looked around the grounds, finally spying another boot just over the edge of a small crest on the grounds. He ran over, and stopped at the top. The smell of burnt flesh was overpowering. He gagged reflexively, covering his mouth with his hand as he looked at what remained of Danny. His hair had been burned off his body, his head a mass of burns and blisters lined with peeling black skin. Angry red burns covered what was not blackened or blistered. His ears were mostly gone, and his eyelids seemed fused to his face, a single sheet of skin. His nose was melted, his lips a bloated shape of tissue. His coveralls had patches that had burned through, or were blackened nearly to ignition in the sudden fierce heat. His hands were on his chest, twitching convulsively. It was then he saw he was still breathing. Jesus Christ the kid was still alive.

"For fuck sakes I need first aid over here NOW!" he screamed even louder, spit flying from his lips. He saw a few people run back to the mill, and a moment later the siren from the ambulance parked at the end of the logyard.

He bent low to the ground, near one of Danny's melted ears. He knew enough first aid to know there was nothing he could do for the kid. He needed a hospital, and right quick, or he was going to fatally dehydrate from his leaking burns.

"Help is on the way, Danny. You hang in there," he whispered into his ear.

Danny whimpered softly, mercifully unconscious. He heard boots behind him.

"Holy fuck what happened?" he heard someone say. It sounded like Robert, an electrician from the planer that Randy had caught going into a debarker a month earlier without locking it out. Not too bright.

Someone else replied," It don't matter. Look at that kid. Ain't that Pauls' boy? Jesus Kee-rist. Shouldn't someone go tell Paul?"

There were voices everywhere all talking at once, and so hard to recognize in the chatter.

"Merry fucking Christmas."

"Why don't you go tell Paul if you're so keen?"

"I saw the fire, I did. Hundred foot high it was, just blew outta the mill like BOOM."

Randy was glad a moment later when the ambulance pulled up behind him, the tires biting into the pea gravel. The first aid attendant, a retired military medic named Ben surveyed the scene quickly, and took a deep breath. He was getting used to deep slivers and the occasional eye cleanse. He hadn't seen anything like this in years, and for a moment, and it was just a moment, his mind cleared, unsure of what to do. Then everything came back and he stepped into action, taking control and directing who was to do what and when. Randy was suitably impressed. He didn't think the geezer had it in him, not knowing his background. Whenever he saw him he was sitting in his first aid booth reading books, making those grey plastic models you buy from a hobby shop, or watching some educational television program. A weird duck, from what Randy was used to, and so very possibly queer. A few minutes later, Danny was lying on a stretcher in the back of the ambulance with Ben giving him an IV line. Vern, the senior forklift operator drove the ambulance, doing one hundred east towards Charleston, siren screaming.

It was pretty strange going back to work after that. The smell of the smoke and flesh lingered in the air, and the memory of the gore was fresh.

It took a good hour for the routine to wash away the surprise of the accident, to get to feeling normal again. At lunch break the room was quiet, filled with men that were eating and deep in thought.

"What happened, Randy? You was there first. You musta seen somethin'."

He chewed his sandwich, and swallowed, feeling the eyes of everyone in the room on him.

"I was spraying the dust outside. The wood dust from the floor."

He had everyone's attention, no one was even eating anymore. Only the clock ticking on the wall made any other sound.

"He walked by the vent and lit a smoke." He used his hands to show an explosion.

"And that was that. Game over. Right by a fucking no smoking sign, too."

"We're fucking lucky the mill didn't explode."

"If there was enough dust it woulda."

A lone whisper rose from the room, and then faded.

"Whaddya think is going to happen to that kid?"

"His chances are fifty-fifty. If he inhaled when the fire took it might have burned his lungs. Pretty tough to breathe with burned lungs."

The room was quiet a moment longer, and then one by one everyone started to eat again, their initial questions satisfied.

As is turned out, Danny's chances were considerably lower than fifty-fifty. He had taken a deep breathe at the moment of the explosion, and the heat and raced into his throat and lungs, blistering the tissue. His breathing began to rattle badly about halfway to Charleston, and twenty minutes out from the hospital he quit breathing, drowning in the fluid his lungs were putting out from the burns. Ben tried CPR, but only succeeded in squeezing some of the liquid out of his lungs, where it pooled in his mouth. He had tried to swab it out, but it just kept coming. He worked until he felt the pulse quit, sweat beading on his forehead. He told Vern to cut the siren, and they drove the rest of the way to the General Hospital in glum silence.

Back at the mill, while Danny was breathing his last, the crew had gone back to work with a certain amount of zest gone from the day. The planers and saws were started back up, and the familiar rumbling helped them to forget, or at least take the immediate edge off their memory. Grading length after length of lumber helped, the mental concentration needed to arrive at a quick decision bringing things back to normal. Robert had gone back to his tool room to sharpen some saw blades, the nudie calendar on the wall didn't even catch his eye. Normally, the brunette with the big jugs and long bare legs that didn't seem to ever stop that was Miss December would catch a noteworthy glimpse, but not now. He grabbed his saw file, and ran it between a few worn teeth, his mind trying to push the recent events from his mind. He was gonna go home after his shift and get right drunk, he decided. Just drink until he would lay on the floor clutching it, feeling it spin under him, the empties on the floor next to him. He tried to think how many beers he had in his fridge back home. At least four. But four wouldn't be enough. He would have to stop by Larry's Liquor Mart on the way home and pick up another dozen or two, and maybe a bottle of rum while he was at it. Not dark rum; that stuff gave him a terrible headache and a deep nauseous feeling that would last for days. He liked white rum; that stuff he could drink until he forgot all cares.

Donald had gone back to the stripper, a green painted lump of iron into which he fed handfuls of wooden slats in between each row of lumber, before it was hauled away by a forklift and brough over to the drying kilns. He had felt sick to his stomach, his eyes moist with tears that he refused to acknowledge. His limbs felt weak, like they did after puking up, when your eyes were bloodshot and your mouth was full of that sick flavor that made you want to puke a few more times, if your stomach had anything left in it. He had put on his thick leather gloves, and dug his hands into the slat bin, forcing his muscles to cooperate, making them listen to him, trying to work the weak feeling out of them as fast as he could. When he was ready, feeling his heart beating deep in his chest, the adrenaline flowing, he turned around and gave a thumbs up to the guys on the chain behind him that sorted the rejects before they got to him.

They saw him signal, and in turn signaled to their lead hand who got the chain rolling again. The two by sixes came rumbling towards him in a ceaseless flow, and he turned off his mind, feeding the stripper handfuls of wooden slats as fast as he could shove them into the guides, feeling his muscles work loose and the sweat in his gloves dampening the leather. He got into the rhythm quickly, feeding the first guide until it was full, then the second, then third, and lastly the fourth, and then returning to the first one that was nearly empty again. It was an endless cycle; a good routine that cleared the thoughts from his mind, freeing him from the unsettling memories that wanted to haunt him, that wanted to settle into his mind and disturb his dreams. The boards slammed into the iron guide, shaking the foundation as they piled against one another, the feeding chain underneath them clanking and rolling over the thick cogs of the gears. When the row was done, the hydraulics hissed and pressed down four slats, the stack dropping a few inches, waiting for the next row of boards to feed into the open mouth of the stacker.

Randy had returned to his compressed air hose, giving the lever a few quick squeezes and being rewarded with two blasts of hissing air. The smell of the burned sawdust was rich in the under floor, a sweet wooden scent nearly masking the corruption of the burned flesh and hair that lingered in the dark spaces in the mills labyrinth of belts and corners. For him, he could find no such escape that his co-workers had escaped into. There was no real routine he could lose himself in; no thinking process that would overwhelm the images of a ball of fire exploding outwards into the evening air. The hose laid where he had dropped it, when he had clung to the smooth concrete floor to save his life, feeling the fire biting at his backsides. He aimed the hose at the floor, and held the trigger, pushing the sawdust outside into the evening wind that carried it away. The trees at the border of the yard were beginning to become nothing more than dark shapes against the night sky as the day came to a close; the ground nothing more than a shapeless shadow. A few lone stars had already appeared in the sky, and for a moment, hose forgotten, he stared up at them, twinkling in the sky. He realized he wanted to be home, away from the mill, surrounded by his things. The remaining hours in his shift stretched before him, each minute a drab and pale eternity.

By midnight, he had sprayed most of the foundation floor clear of dust, getting into the nooks and crannies with his shovel and wheelbarrow, feeding the results onto one of the several belts that ran underneath the main floor. The evening air was getting very cool, and he had to keep busy and active to stay as warm as he liked to be. He had decided to change his schedule and go under the planer, where thick piles of itchy sawdust were always springing up. Shoveling sawdust seemed easy, if you had never done it before. It looked light, and there shouldn't be too much too it. Except that it wasn't too easy. First of all, it was itchy as hell, and it always seemed to find its way under a shirt cuff or into a boot and settle into somewhere that was hard to reach, driving you insane with the persistent scritch scritch feeling when you moved. He had removed his boots on more than one occasion, blasting them with compressed air to remove a speck that was driving him up the wall, sure as shit. When you tried to drive a shovel into sawdust, you quickly found out it was spongy; he had tried to explain it to someone once who had asked him what he did at the mill, and he figured he was only partly successful at the attempt. When you dug your shovel into a thick pile of sawdust, all of those little edges of wood that were so good at making you itchy stuck together, on all sides, and there were thousands of the little buggers. So when you tried to slide your shovel in, the blade would never get very far before all of those little pieces of wood came together and refused to budge any further, and when you tried to push the shovel in deeper, you could see the entire frickin' pile move with you, sponge like, all pushing back at the shovel. And if you did manage to bury the shovel in the pile, all that wood dust was still stuck together, so lifting it out was a bitch.

It came up in thick matted clumps, resisting all the while, bending the shovel this way and that as it broke free with clumps of dust falling off, which fell back to the pile kicking up great piles of itchy dust that hung in the air forever. The tiny pieces of wood hung in the air, and if the sun was just right, they would sparkle. Damned if he knew how would could sparkle, but it did, and when he would come by in the morning, all of that fine dust would have settled onto the ground and machinery in a thin grey dust. That dust looked soft, but was course and grainy, and if it got stuck in the skin of your neck or your armpit, or worse, in your crotch, it would rub you raw, just like fine sandpaper.

There were wheelbarrows full of sawdust just waiting to be carted out and dumped, and this seemed like the night to do it. He wanted to stay warm, and the pile of dust would surely do that. He laid his shovel into the barrow, the metal blade grating in the bucket of the barrow, clanging as the soft front tire bounced on a bump on the way. He stopped the barrow short of the pile, arms length from the base where he would be shoveling. Then he could turn around and just dump the shovelful into the barrow without having to make another movement. Just a twist of the wrist, and it would fall into the bucket. He adjusted his gloves, pulling the sleeves down over the cuffs, trying to make a tight fit to keep that dust out as long as possible. It was inevitable, some always got stuck by the elastic at the wrist of the glove, but he hoped to delay it for as long as possible. He gripped the shovel, and thrust the blade into the pile. It dug in halfway with a thick grinding feeling, and it stopped cold, the pile flexing as he tried to push it deeper.

"Fuck," he said to no one, venting some frustration. He scooped the bit out, watching some of it fall back to the pile, and dumped it into the wheelbarrow. When it was heaping full, he speared the shovel into the pile, and carried the barrow thirty feet away where a two-foot wide belt spun set into the floor. He lifted up the handles, and shook the bucket, sliding the dust down onto the belt where it was carried away towards the beehive burner a few hundred feet away. In the evening, the beehive was a great dark shadow that loomed over the yard like a massive idol, the fires within setting it aglow with a deep red glow, like it was placed over the very gateway to Hell itself. The ground between the mill and the burner was bare and desolate; not even the hardiest of weeds could survive in the dry baked earth surrounding it. A few tried, in the spring when the ground was a little more damp from the melting snow, but by late spring they were nothing but dried brown husks that were stuck in the ground, any green they once had long since gone.

He kicked a bit of wood that had missed the belt, and watched it get carried away, careful to make sure that he didn't end up falling on the belt and wind up well done himself. He spun the barrow around, and went back to where the shovel was sticking out of the pile, leaning slightly. He parked it, grabbed the shovel again, and took another chunk out of the pile. It would take him a few hours to finish the pile, and by then it would be time to call it a day. He got busy, working under the sodium light that hung from the corrugated aluminum ceiling. He could hear it humming, even through the bright orange foam earplugs that were stuck in his ear canals. It was strange how some sounds always seemed to be noticeable, he thought. Must have something to do with the frequency. The deep booming sounds of the operation were muffled very well, but the bite of the saws not so much. The edge was taken off, but they were still easy to hear.

Ryan Speer

The loud zip zop sound of his snow pants was almost hypnotic, a powerful sound in the dead chill of the winter air. The only other immediate sounds were the crunching of his boots as they broke and sank into the knee-high snow, and his breath. He didn't know where particularly he was walking to, his grandfathers property was a few hundred acres, but he kept the home in view, although sometimes it grew very small, less than half the nail on his little finger if he had held up his hand to compare the house in the far distance. Today he was walking west, towards a grove of willows that flanked a stream barely a yard wide that wove like an old root through the property. Deep into winter, they rose from the frozen ground like skeletal hands, bare branches reaching to the sky. *Zip crunch zop crunch zip crunch zop crunch* as he plowed ever forwards. If he tried to run, the sounds became *ZIPCRUNCHZOPCRUNCH* as he worked his way furiously over the white field, and the loud staccato of his progess halted as he stopped to catch his breath. His breath came out in large clouds of white vapour that dispersed upwards quickly and vanished into the deep blue sky, carried away by a cool breeze that kept his cheeks and nose a shade of red. He continued to walk to the west, squinting his eyes from the glare off the fiercely white snow, raising his gloved hand to his forehead to reduce the brightness of the day. Zipcrunchzopcrunchzipcrunchzopcrunch. From behind, came the sound of running feet. He smiled to himself, and moments later, as the sound grew nearer and nearer, his grandfathers dog flew past him to the left, eating up the distance that took him twenty minutes to walk in less than two.

Lucy was a purebred Husky, and felt none of the cold that he did. As she ran past him, she glanced over as if to show off her prowess in the winter conditions, and then kept running.

Ryan watched her run a little further, and then shouted.

"LUCY WHERE YOU GOING?"

He watched with amusement as her ears caught his voice, and she abruptly came to a halt in the field, and turned to watch him, her tongue hanging from her mouth and sides pumping from her fast breathing.

"LUCY!" he yelled again, and he watched her launch back in his direction, her feet barely touching the ground as she ran at full speed towards him. He could not help but feel instinctual intimidation watching her bear down on him. She weighed a solid eighty pounds, not that much less than he did, and she was far stronger. Lucy covered the distance in no time, and when she reached Ryan she did a quick lap around him, and he ran his gloves over her back. He bent over and quickly patted her head with affection, as they walked in parallel.

"Good girl, Lucy."

She wagged her tail to agree that she was indeed, a good girl.

"What you doing huh? Having fun?"

She bent down and bit into a mouthful of snow, crunching it and swallowing the result. He pet her back again, and with a quick look up at him, she began to run away, heading for the willows and a pair of ravens that were watching her run towards them with dismay. The ravens cawed their annoyance as she reached the base of the willow tree they had chosen to roost in. She stared up at them, barked twice, and ran in between the trees, her nose close to the ground sniffing for a trail to follow.

The ravens cocked their heads in her direction, but otherwise did not move, saving their energy and fluffing their feathers out to keep warm.

Ryan kept on towards the willows as well. Looming high in the distance the Rocky Mountains stood tall over the land, seemingly coming straight up from the ground. On some days their peaks were cloaked in clouds, but today the sky was clear, and their tops reached high into the deep blue. His grandfatehr had recently given him The Hobbit to read, a book he felt he was sure to love with his active imagination. Hewas proven correct, as he was quickly taken in by Bilbo and the troop of dwarves. He had read the book in a week, no small feat for a ten year old with school and chores and friends to interrupt him.

Watching the mountains as he walked, his imagination ran wild. He thought with surety that when Tolkien had envisioned the mountains of Mordor, he must have had these ones in mind. Smaug would have loved these mountains, and he imagined dwarves digging their cities deep into them, following veins of mithril and fighting goblins and orcs in their vast dark keeps. Somewhere, he felt sure, from a high peak or concealed cave opening, Gollum was watching him, anxiously keeping his Precious near to his heart. Lucy barked again and followed a rabbit trail to its ending under a tree, where she sniffed furiously. He walked over to the dog, bending some branches out of his way with his arm as he made his way through the stand of trees. Lucy looked up at him, and put her head back into the rabbit hole. He saw the rabbit tracks all over the snow, in between the willows and the gnarls of deadfall.

"Hey Lucy; you have a rabbit in there?" he asked.

She again looked at him, with the big smile dogs have, and barked, agreeing that she did indeed, perhaps two or three in fact. She could hear them breathing down deep in their holes, chewing their pellets, their warm scents rich in the cold air.

"Come on pup, unless they're the dumbest rabbits ever you won't get them now."

He patted her back again, and began to follow the stream back in the general direction of the homestead. Lucy poked her head up from the hole to watch him go, and then after relieving herself outside the rabbit hole, she ran to join him. The stream was twisted and gnarled, and followed a course that was not even close to straight. Its banks in most places were deep, about 6 feet down to the water and steep, covered in bullrushes, small willows, and other bushes and trees. Ryan followed its path for another hundred feet before coming to a stop with Lucy at his left side. She was tiring and was no longer in the mood to run, although she still had enough juice left to break her own trail. Ryan observed this with a grin. They frequently took these long walks together, and he knew before they got home she would be following behind him, allowing him to break the trail through the snow for her. He stopped to look down at the ice covering the stream. It was thick and able to bear his weight, at least a foot of solid ice covering a cold flow of water. He could see the water flowing under it, air bubbles bouncing under its surface gurgling quietly. In this spot the stream faced the sun, and so was exposed for most of the winter. In other spots snow drifts concealed the entire channel, hiding the very existence of the stream altogether. Lucy made her way along the edges of the vegetation, sniffing rodent trails as she went, going through the undergrowth if it was sparse enough. He felt the breeze shift direction against his face, and smelled the smoke of the fireplace. He looked towards the house, and he could see the smoke rising from the chimney. It was too cold for the smoke to continue to rise, and instead it curved downwards towards the ground only a short distance from the home. Together they followed the stream until its direction strayed away from home, at which point they changed their path and followed the smoke trail backwards, the sweet wood burning smell slowly becoming stronger. Thirty minutes later he stomped his cold boots up the stairs onto the wood patio deck and opened the door. Its hinges creaked in the cold, and he immediately felt the heat from the living room flow past his face. He held the door open just long enough for Lucy to get inside, and he shut the door behind her. He sniffed loudly as his nose began to run from being indoors. His cheeks and nose burned in the warm air as he struggled to remove his snow pants and heavy winter jacket. Lucy had walked over to the fireplace, turned around two times on her doggie bed, and curled up into it, and lay there watching Ryan remove his cocoon of winter outerwear. Once he had hung up his jacket and pants, and put his boots on the drying rack, he went into the kitchen to make some hot chocolate. It was turning out to be a pretty good day. The inside of the home smelled richly of pine and baking. The kitchen was to the immediate right of the home past the door, and was largely accented with dark slate and stained wood. The kitchen led directly into the living room, which was dominated by a seven foot tall pine tree, adorned with Christmas ornaments. The tree had been cut down a few days earlier from a local stand near the homestead. To the right of the living room the fireplace dominated the wall. It was built of smooth river stone that had been gathered from the property. Candles and family knick-knacks were displayed atop the mantle, a single beam of oak that had been expertly incorporated into the fireplace. Christmas day was only four days away, and each day seemed an eternity to him, as in the way of children. School had let out a few days earlier for the break, and so now he had home to himself, until his grandfather returned in the evenings.

Lucy barked twice, and he heard the crunching of cold snow, and a vehicle driving towards the home. She ran to the door, looking upwards at it, her thick tail waving and thumping loudly on the floor.

He heard the vehicle turn off, the diesel sound unmistakable, a door slam shut, and then the crunching of feet on the packed snow. The feet echoed up the stairs, and then the door began to open. Lucy leaped up on it, nearly pushing it shut again.

"Move, you stupid dog."

Lucy backed away as the door was opened.

"Hi, Grandpa." Ryan called from the kitchen, he hands wrapped tightly around his mug of chocolate.

"Hello."

"What are you doing back so early?"

"I found everything I was looking for faster than I thought. The perfect shopping trip. Especially with all the fools out there buying for Christmas. You have to be crazy or just plain stupid to like shopping at this time of year."

He came into the kitchen, eyeing the hot chocolate.

"Now there's a good idea."

His eyes scoured the countertop.

"Got any more of that?"

Ryan pointed towards the stove top, his lips pursed shut with a mouthful he was trying to swallow.

"Ahh, bingo."

He poured himself a mug, a took a quick sip. It was perfect, hot enough to feel good, without burning your mouth. He took a few gulps, and then refilled the mug with what was left. Lucy stared at them both briefly, and then went to find her chew toy, a heifer thigh bone from the local slaughter house. She positioned it between her forepaws, and set to work on it, her sharp teeth gnawing away at the bone.

"What have you two been up to?"

"We went for walk out past the creek, and then came back. It's too cold out to walk further."

His grandfather looked out the window over the kitchen sink. The mercury had sunk to minus thirty seven Celsius. The sky was clear and cloudless, which meant it was going to stay cold.

"I guess. I'm going to check the fire."

He went into the living room, and sunk down on his knees, both of them crackling faintly as he settled down onto the floor.

"Christ I think I am getting old."

Ryan laughed. His grandfather had looked over his shoulder at him.

"You think it's funny, do you? Wait until you are old and grey like me, and your knees are forever popping whenever you move around."

He grabbed the fire poker from the rack, and stuck it into the fire, moving aside a few nearly done logs and stirring up the embers.

"Yep, ready for more."

He reached for some wood, grabbing one piece at a time from a small pile stacked neatly to the right of the fireplace. He threw them into the coals, one by one, stacking them upwards as he built them up. The coals began to blacken the bottom pieces, sending small tendrils of fire licking upwards into the wood. Then they caught, and the fireplace was quickly crackling and snapping and sending out intense heat into the home. Lucy grabbed her bone, and settled herself near the fireplace in a sweet spot where she could warm up without singeing her fur. He stood up, both knees crackling again, and went towards the sofa, where he parked himself down on the leather where it creaked and took his weight.

"Ohh, that's much better."

He reached forward and took the paper from the table, resting his legs on the table top, crossed at the feet.

He unfolded the paper in his lap with a few quick jerks to get the creases out of the middle.

"So what do you want to do for the rest of the day?" he asked while he scanned through the articles.

Ryan shrugged.

"Dunno. Maybe watch some tv?" he asked hopefully.

Watching television was not a usual pastime in the house, not with its sprawling acreage and recreational amenities nearby.

"Sure, why not. It's only four more days to Christmas, and it is cold enough to freeze the balls off a brass monkey." He winced as soon as he said it, forgetting that Ryan was only ten. Steve had worked in the oilfields and the outdoors for most of his life, which meant his language at times could be course. It had improved drastically as of late, but he still made the occasional slip up. He hadn't planned on raising any more kids this late in life, but it was something that had just happened out that way. Truth was, he was only in his mid fifties, but he enjoyed playing up his age to sound like a Shakespearean tragedy, that he was nearing the age of Methuselah himself. He was fit, healthy and good looking, and retired to boot, and he was immensely satisfied with the way things had turned out. The way most of the things had turned out. He was an only child that had gone into the oilfields as soon as he was strong enough to do the work. He saved his money, not spending a dime on anything unless it was necessary, and when the time came, invested his money with a friend in an undeveloped field that seemed to be screaming that it was full of oil. His rigger instincts were right, and he had cleaned up, clearing his first million before he was thirty. They kept on investing, and he cleared his next million a year later, seeming to have a nose for where oil was buried, or for finding companies that just needed some funding of their own. The business flourished, and began to grow into leasing heavy machinery and forestry, and even potash mining. It expanded exponentially until it got too big for his comfort level and ambitions. His friend Richard had sensed the unease and offered to buy out his share, an amicable splitting that left Steve with more money than he could ever spend, and a lot of free time on his hands. Richard spent a lot of time in the Middle East and Russia growing his business, and from he had heard, was now worth a few hundred million dollars, and was one more surprise or coup away from a lethal heart attack or stroke that would kind of make the entire value of his fortune meaningless in no time flat.

Steve had taken his opportunity to travel the world for a year. He had met his wife in Miami while touring Disneyland by himself just to see what it was all about. He retained his frugal means, driving a modest car that he had bought used with low mileage, dressing in jeans and not eating out very often. They had married a year later, Carrie had been clueless about his wealth until they had planned their will, her belly beginning to grow with their child. She had nearly fallen of the couch when she saw his net worth, but she didn't let it go to her head, it was just one less thing to worry about. They looked forward to the start of their family, and settling down in a family way with some property where they could enjoy themselves. She had found the ranch after looking for only a week, and they had driven up to take a look at what it had to offer. They had fallen in love with the area, complete with a creek and pasture for horses or cattle, and the awe inspiring view of the Rockies out of their windows.

Once the deal was done, they had leveled the old homestead that had been on the property, and old farmhouse from the early nineteen hundreds with shiplap walls and a peeling white exterior. They had their home built on it in record time, offering bonuses to contractors who could get the job done before their child was born. They had delivered, once again proving that money is a helluva motivator. They had kept an eye of the construction to verify the workmanship maintained a high standard, and watched the home come together. The completion bonuses were paid out, and they moved in just a month short of her due date, and she had spent that month furnishing the home in every room, right down to the collectibles on the shelves and the toys in the baby's room.

She had died after childbirth, just long enough to see her baby and hold him for a few short minutes before her uterus tore delivering the placenta. The blood had poured from her body, the doctors and nurses working frantically to stem the bleeding, but it was all over in a minute. It seemed like it happened even faster. He had seen birthing before in livestock, and he had never seen so much blood, and it seemed impossible that all of it, lying on the bed and the floor in deep red thick pools could possibly be all hers. One moment he was taking his son into his arms, and the next his wife had bled to death in front of him, her l ft hand holding her baby as she expired, his small hhopand gripped tightly around her forefinger. He took whatever comfort he could in knowing she had seen him born and healthy. He raised his son alone, fortunate that his money had enabled him to easily do so, and he bore the societal stigma of raising his child alone, once telling an obtrusive and overly zealous housewife in the local food mart to mind her own God-damned business. Her face had paled, being spoken to in such a manner. She had tried to recover, explaining that surely it was Gods will, and it wasn't right to raise a child without a mother. He had exploded at her, screaming that if it was His will that He should murder his wife on the delivery table, then it was His will that he should raise his son alone as he wanted to. He wasn't overly proud of venting his anger at a woman, it was the only time he would ever do so in his life, never mind one with such a restricted view of life to begin with, but it was done, and when the air cleared he didn't hear any more gossip about how he chose to raise his child. He was certain there was, but his explosion had made the local gossipmongers more cautious, and no one had the courage to say anything to his face about it ever again. He had chosen to not remarry, and only had dated a few times before he realized he was just not interested.

He had raised John as best he could, using his money to make sure he wanted for nothing, while keeping him working hard on the farm so he learned the value of money and hard work. He had seen him off to school, and the years passed faster than he could have ever believed. He sold his cattle, nearly three hundred head to his farmhands at value pricing, the revenue from the sale irrelevant in his scheme of things. He kept every acre of his land, allowing it to go wild and fallow, keeping only the immediate few acres around his house clear with a bright green John Deere riding mower to reduce the fire hazard. With the land lying unused and relatively quiet, deer became a common sight out his windows, and he would spend his time quietly watching them feeding as he nursed a warm coffee or meal. He took special delight in seeing the young fawns following their mothers through the fields, their small bodies so out of proportion with their gangly legs, their spots slowly fading as they grew. On occasion, he saw a few large bucks come through the fields. Even a ten pointer one season, standing in the field as though claiming it for his own. He had shot it, with his Nikon camera and had the print enlarged and framed, the buck standing proud in the dusk. The season after that he had planted a series of apple trees to give the deer something extra to attract them to the farmstead.

His son went out into the world, got married, bought a house, had his own child, did the usual expected thing. Steve had felt his life progressing down the path he had expected, becoming a grandparent and then hanging around until his time was up and he went on to whatever came next. Instead, about two years ago now, (god how time flew by), he got a phone call at just after three in the morning.

He had heard the ring, and had integrated it into his dream. He was fishing somewhere warm an a fourteen foot aluminum boat with a nice little outboard putting away in the hot summer sun, when he heard a phone ringing in the forest. At the second ring, he woke up, still half way between actual consciousness and imagination. On the third ring, his hand had scooped the phone from off of the nightstand, his thumb pressing TALK, and had pressed the handset to his ear.

"Mmmf. Hello."

"Mr. Steven Speer?"

"Yes." He had then farted, and had to scratch himself.

He heard, "This is Constable Mark Hammond of the Coquitlam RCMP. I'm sorry to inform you that…."and the rest of the conversation was a blur of phrases that he could barely recall of tragic accident, first on the scene, fatalities, terribly sorry.

He was out of bed and out the door in less than twenty minutes, just enough time to finish the notification of next of kin phone call, have a shower, grab a few things, and ho pinto his truck and drive to the airport. He had caught the first flight out of Calgary, and was in Vancouver before breakfast. Not that he had any appetite, or would for days. He felt sick to his stomach and had given no thought to food. Booze maybe, but no food. A few days in NeverNeverLand riding a good buzz seemed to be the answer, but he knew it wasn't. Getting off that buzz would be like peeling a gorilla off his back, with another one waiting to jump back on.

He had taken a taxi to his sons' house. What used to be his sons' house. He tipped the cabbie, a Pakistani national with a PHd in aeronautical engineering an extra fifty to get their as fast as he could.

He made record time. Muhammed, being a thorough cab driver had inquired about his visit, and nothing in the world prepared him for the story he heard from Steven. His eyes had swelled in sympathy tears, which he dabbed away as inconspicuously as he could, and his left foot pressed down just a little bit harder to add some extra speed. They pulled into the driveway, and he had already opened the door. He took his bag from Muhammed, thanked him for the fast drive and walked towards the house. Actually seeing the house made the reality of the situation that much more real, and for a moment he just stood there, the house like a dark idol daring him to come in. Come in to this little shop of horrors. See wait awaits you. Muhammed had broke him from his stupor.

"Go in. He needs you, more than anything he needs you right now."

He had looked at him, took a deep breath, and pressed forwards. He heard Muhammed behind him.

"I will pray to Allah to give you strength."

He had nodded as he walked away, not turning back, but he knew Muhammed had seen it. He walked past the police cruiser sitting in the driveway, up to the front door, and walked into the house. The constable was sitting at the kitchen table with Ryan, who was eating a bowl of Lucky Charms. At least, it looked like Lucky Charms. It had a lot of colorful marshmallows in it, whatever it was. The constable looked as nauseous as he felt. *Christ, imagine doing this as part of your job.* His opinion of policing went up a few notches that morning.

"Hi Grampa! What are you doing here?"

He had ran from the table, still chewing his mouthful of cereal, and thrown himself into his arms to receive a giant hug. He held him close for a minute, not daring to let him go, wondering how the hell he was going to break the news to this kid. He felt a lump in his throat the size of a football. He had put Ryan down gingerly, and patted him back towards the table.

"I'll tell you in a minute, kiddo."

His voice was rough, his throat constricting something fierce.

The constable stood from the table, and shook his hand, offering his genuine and sincere condolences, while Ryan sat there watching them, eating his cereal. He had offered to stay and provide support while he broke the news. Steve was sincerely tempted, but after a moments thought declined the offer, thanking him for it. The officer had patted him twice on the shoulder, a gesture of support, before leaving the home. He heard the cruiser fire up, and the police radio chatter, doubtless the constable telling the dispatcher the grandfather had arrived at the home of the previous nights victims, leaving him in custody of his grandchild.

He stepped towards the table, sat in the chair, and with a quick decision and a hail mary, he told Ryan the bad news, his hands shaking so badly that he had to sit on them to keep them still. Anyone that has told a child something terrible knows how completely kids give themselves to emotion, and Ryan was no four year old that couldn't comprehend death, that didn't know what it meant. He was nearly eight, and he knew what death meant. He knew what *your mom and dad are dead* meant. His face had gone from that of a normal boy eating his food in one instant, to a face of unrestrained grief and agony the next. His small body shook itself to the core, his very being devoted to mourning the passing of his parents. There were no learned inhibitions to hold him back. He cried hard for minutes, but when he was done, he was done. He finished his cereal, and asked if he could watch some television. He had sat him on the couch and gave him the remote control, letting him figure out what he wanted to watch, feeling the last of his control melting away as the minutes passed. When he was settled, he went down the hallway to his sons' room, seeing his wedding picture on the wall, the pictures of his daughter-in-law Marjorie on the night table, the pictures of Ryan as an infant, and then toddler, and then little boy.

He shut the door behind him and turned to sit on the bed, feeling his hands shake worse than ever. He put his hands into his palms, and felt the tears come. He cried quietly, trying to slake some of the pain he was feeling, to remove the overwhelming emotion back to a manageable level. He did his best to not have Ryan hear him, to try to look resilient and strong for him. He spent a month in the house with Ryan, pulling him from his school permanently, knowing he would not be coming back. He had gone to the morgue and identified the bodies. He had decided there was to be no funeral, and since Marjorie had been an orphan, and his own side of the family was down to just him, there was no one to contest his decision. He had the couple cremated, the ashes dispersed by air over the ocean where they had met on a kayaking excursion. The home went on the market well below appraised value, much to the consternation of the realtor.

"But Mr. Speer," he had protested, "You could get another hundred thousand or more with the right buyer."

He normally was a patient man, but times were not normal. He had poked his finger into the realtors' chest.

"You listen to me, and listen good. I want this house sold as soon as possible. Not in a month, not in the spring. I am not waiting for the perfect buyer. We are never coming back to this godforsaken city, so I want it sold, and if that means we are the cheapest listing you have, so be it."

"Y-yes Mr. Speer."

They had signed the agreement papers, and a week later the house sold, furnished, to a couple that couldn't that couldn't believe their good fortune, bubbling and gushing about the great deal, wondering aloud how *anyone could sell it so cheaply.*

When the agent informed them of the double traffic fatality and the sole surviving child, they shut up faster than a mafia snitch in court, embarrassed at how they probably had come across. Steve had opened a bank account in Ryan's name, and had the sale proceeds of the house sale and two life insurance policies deposited into it.

Eight years old with a net worth of just over a million dollars. He had kept the account a secret, making sure that Ryan had no access to the account until he said so. When he was thirty or so, likely married with kids of his own, he planned to deliver the bombshell to him. Until then, it was earning him twelve percent annually.

They had returned to his homestead west of Sundrie, where they settled into a routine. They had spent a lot of time indoors that first winter, getting to know one another better than they ever had. He had not gone back to school that year, but had already registered him for the upcoming school year, and so the local school board was satisfied. They had taken many long walks through the deep snow, teaching him the property, where everything was, just in case. He didn't want Ryan to get lost and not be able to find his way home, or to fall into some abandoned well, so he showed him where everything was. There would be no accidents if he could help it. As winter was coming to its close, and the ground was getting mushy with the runoff, he had a neighboring breeder deliver Lucy to the home. She was a little over two months old, and still couldn't walk perfectly straight, as all young puppies are liable to do. It was love at first sight, and from that moment forward Lucy and Ryan were inseparable. Steve watched carefully as Lucy grew and matured, taking her to obedience classes, and making certain that Ryan was seen as the superior packmate. He wanted Lucy to listen to him.

He wanted to be sure that if Ryan and Lucy went out for a walk, that Lucy would be an effective guardian. He was going to leave as little as possible to chance. He was pleased with the way she was developing, but hadn't yet really felt confident with her, until one day a salesman had come soliciting to their door. He was well off the beaten path, and must have been in the area, figuring it was worth a shot. Steve had been in the shower when the doorbell had rang, and Ryan had let him in. As far as he could deduce, Lucy had not seen who had entered the home, and had come out of the hallway from her doggie bed to investigate. She had immediately inserted herself between the salesman and Ryan, growling from deep within her belly and baring her fangs, not in fear, or mock aggression, but in a real threat display. Her ears were laid back, her tail rigid, her legs poised to spring, and she refused to let Ryan come between them, pushing him aside. Steve had heard the growling in the shower, and knew something was wrong. He had leapt out of the shower, wrapping a towel around himself with the barest of coverage, and ran into the living room to see what was happening. The sales man was leaning flat against the door, down on his knees, his portfolio held tightly in both arms pulled to his chest. When he had seen another adult enter the room, his eyes had bugged out.

"Pl-please mister, don't let the dog on me. I wasn't going to do anything, honest."

It looked as though he had wet himself.

He had called Lucy to heel. She had waited for a moment, and then retreated, sitting on her haunches at his side, her incisors bared. She still growled, and her eyes were daring the man to make a move.

"Oh god, t-thank you."

He never did say what he had come to try to sell. He had stood up, and left the house as fast as he could, running to his car and leaving the driveway with a spray of gravel and dust. After that, Lucy had his full trust.

He went through the paper slowly, keeping an eye on what Ryan was navigating through the channels. There really was shit on. It took him about five minutes or so to select a show after narrowing the field between a few shows. He had finally settled on a SpongeBob Squarepants. According to the information guide, it was a marathon special. He read his paper, listening to the show in the background. He would never admit it, but he actually had a partial liking for the program, and he had on occasion had to really struggle to not laugh out loud and give away any indication that he was paying attention.

His stomach growled, the low type of grumble that makes you think a cat somehow got stuck in your belly.

With a heave and the squeak of the couch he got up and went into the kitchen, Lucy momentarily forgetting her bone to see what was happening.

"You hungry Ryan?"

"Sure."

"What do you want?"

"Whatever."

He wondered how kids could give such incredibly vague answers and still have the gumption to be unsatisfied with an outcome.

"So liver and onions are okay?"

It was a test to see if he was listening. Ryan had looked over at him and grimaced.

He took out some bacon and laid a few strips down in the pan while it warmed up. They were the thick slabs, not the thin stuff that curled up like paper in the heat. He filled the pan with it, using a spatula to squeeze the pieces together and get an extra one in there. Lucy was at his side, looking up at him hopefully. He felt generous, and slipped her a slice behind the counter. She practically inhaled it, giving it a few quick bites and then it was gone. She licked the floor to get any crumbs she may have dropped, and then resumed the position, hoping for more.

"Don't think so, dog."

She heard the tone in the mans voice, and knew she wasn't going to get anymore. She wasn't hungry, but she did so like the taste of bacon. After a few minutes, she relented, and went back to her bone.

Steve cut up a few tomatoes and threw some bread into the toaster, making sure the settings were right to get the bread just a little golden, enough to make it crispy. He didn't understand how people could ruin bread by setting it so high that it came out black and smoking. That wasn't toasting, that was burning. The bacon was sizzling nicely, and he flipped the slices, the pan sizzling loudly as the meat was flipped. Everything else was done, so he stood there waiting for the bacon to be ready, watching a little bit of the adventures of SpongeBob and his snail Gary, who happened to *mew* like a cat.

He didn't think it was going to be an active day. It was frickin' cold outside. You knew it was cold when snow made that squeaking sound when you stepped on it, the crystals crushing together and fracturing, but not melting. When he had left for town in the morning he had taken a deep breath on the front steps, and had felt the cold air rush into his sinuses and surely freeze whatever was up there. Once he climbed into the warm cab of his truck, everything that had frozen up his nose began to thaw, and then run. His windshield had been covered with a really fine layer of crystals that had proved a bitch to scrape off. After a few attempts with moderate success, he had went back inside his truck and set the defrost settings to blast the windshield. He watched the ice evaporate into the cold air in tiny whisps of steam. He didn't want to use his wipers and smear the windshield with water, knowing it would quickly set into ice. He had sat patiently for about five minutes, watching it disappear, before leaving. He tried to think of what they could do, being stuck in the house not appealing to him. Ryan had already tried to go for a walk, but had turned back early from the cold. They could go sledding.

The new Cats had heated handles and seats, but he knew the fairings would be pretty useless to keep their faces warm. The wind chill would be extreme. They could always shoot off a few rounds at the targets out to the side of the field, before their hands got too cold to hold the rifles. Dammit. It looked like it was going to be an in day.

He had got lunch together, calling Ryan over to the island where his BLT sat waiting for him. They ate in silence, only the crunching of the toast and snapping of the fire contributing to any appreciable sounds.

"Milk?" he asked.

Ryan nodded yes, so he added a second cup to the one he had already taken out. They finished eating and cleaned up the kitchen quickly, and then topped up the fireplace with two more logs.

"Can you split some more wood for the fire?" Steven asked.

"Sure. How much?"

Steven measured a distance in the air with his arms.

"About that much."

"Okay. Come on, Lucy."

She licked her muzzle, watching him go to the side door. She dropped her bone and ran over as he opened it up, and went through.

Inside the carport against the far wall they had stacked a wall of wood from the floor to about five feet in height at the tallest, tall enough that it was easy for him to help out. The carport wasn't heated, but its proximity to the house kept it relatively warm, and much warmer than it currently was outside. The storage inside the room allowed the logs to dry out, making them easier to split and burn. He didn't even put on a jacket, knowing he would soon be even warmer. He grabbed a log from the tall point of the pile, and positioned on top of the cutting block. He centered it just so, and went over to the wall, pulling off a two headed axe. He swung it in his arms, feeling the weight and liking how it felt. He stood in front of the log, and looked around to make sure Lucy was at a safe distance. She was laying against the wall, watching him warm up. He swung the axe over his head in a practice swing, bringing it down in a controlled chop where it stopped on the top of the log. He brought it back up, and this time let the axe fall. It bit into the wood with a satisfying *THUNK* and the log split cleanly in half, one side falling off the block onto the floor. He repositioned the remaining half, and quartered it with a series of swings. He picked up the remaining half, and did the same. He was very satisfied with his wood cutting, noticing how he was improving.

It still wasn't unusual to have the blade get caught in the log, but he was getting stronger, so his swings were coming down with more force. His practice was also improving his control, so he was also getting better at cutting consistent pieces to feed the fire. He fell into a routine of splitting a log, and then quartering the halves, placing the pieces near the steps to bring into the house and stack near the chimney. He knew his grandfather was likely in the washroom while he was cutting. He used to watch him, until he was satisfied he wasn't going to cut off his hand or injure the dog. He didn't like being watched anymore doing it. It made him nervous for some reason. It disturbed his focus. He cut for about a half hour until he felt he had filled the quota. He rehung the axe in the brackets on the wall, and loaded up an armful to bring to the fireplace. It took him ten trips to resupply the wood pile, and afterwards he got himself a glass of water from the sink, feeling the cold water chill his throat as it went down. He really preferred cold water, and in the winter, there was no shortage. Sometimes it got cold enough, that if you chugged enough of it, you could give yourself a brain freeze. He would fill the glass, and take a deep breath, and pour the water into his mouth as fast as he could swallow it. He could feel his head begin to ache, and just when he would finish it the headache hit him hard, and he would run around the living room with his thumb on the roof of his mouth to make the headache go away faster. He still did it sometimes, but more often when he was younger. Usually if he did it now it was to show a school friend that it could be done. His Grandpa would watch them drink, knowing what they were doing, and then shake his head in disbelief that people would knowingly do that to themselves and call it fun. He drank two glasses, but didn't give himself a *braino,* it was less fun alone, and returned to the couch in time to hear the toilet flushing down the hall.

"Do NOT go in there for a few minutes," he said, waving his hand theatrically in the air as he came out into the hallway.

"Something die in there, Grampa?"

"Yeah, I almost died in there."

They both laughed at the bathroom humor, and Lucy came over to get her head scratched.

"Monopoly?"

"Sure."

Ryan went to the closet and got the board game out from the games shelf. The usuals were in there. Battleship, The Game of Life, chess and checkers, Snakes and Ladders.

Ryan got the board ready while Steven counted out the money, doling out their share to begin.

"Racecar or Shoe?"

Steven thought about it for a moment.

"Racecar."

Ryan moved the pieces to the starting square, and they rolled to see who went first. He rolled nine, Steve rolled eleven.

"Ha-ha." he chortled.

"Lookout, the dice feel hot today."

He shook the pair in his closed hands, and dropped them on the board. His face fell as his hot dice had just rolled him two squares.

"Well, that sucks."

Ryan laughed. He always though it sounded funny when he heard his Grampa say something sucked. It didn't fit into his stereotype of who used that word.

Ryan picked up the dice, and rolled, blowing into his palms for good measure. Ten. He moved his Shoe across the board with authority, liking the way the metal piece sounded as it clicked along the heavy cardboard.

"I can see you're using the cheating dice again."

They played for a little over three hours. By the time they called it a draw, Ryan owned the entire right side of the board, and Steve had owned the other, complete with Hotels on every property. Every piece of property and utility and railway was owned, causing a frequent exchange of money that so far had not claimed anyone due to attrition. They shook hands over the board, calling the game done.

"What should we have for dinner tonight?"

"Food." Ryan replied.

"What kind?"

"The kind you eat."

It was nearly a nightly ritual.

"Burgers it is."

Steve took a package of hamburger out of the fridge, and mixed it up, tossing in two eggs, a few shakes of garlic, some barbecue sauce, some finely diced onion, some onion powder and a little Worcestershire sauce. He mixed it all up, kneading the mixture into itself, and then washed his hands. The grill was outside on the deck, surrounded by a two foot tall clearing of snow around it. They used the barbecue year round. It was just a bit easier in the summer.

He pulled on a pair of white Thermopac boots that went up to his knees, and his winter jacket. He held the butane lighter in one hand.

He stepped outside into the cold, sliding the door shut behind him and pulling the cover of the grill. A white cloud had risen from the house when the door was open, the moisture in the warm air condensing rapidly in the dry winter air. He could see every breath Steve took outside. He was back inside a minute later, sliding the door back open with urgency and closing it again just as quickly.

"Woo it's cold out there."

He blew into his hands and stamped his feet in his boots. Ryan noticed the tops of his ears had already gone red.

"You better throw a few more logs into the fire while I'm at it."

He waited in the warmth of the house while the barbecue warmed up, and with as much efficiency as he could muster, he ventured back outside with the plate of raw burgers, placing them on the cooking rack as quickly as he could to get back inside. Ryan put a few more logs into the fire, and stayed close to the fireplace while the burgers were cooking. The draught when the door was opening and closing wasn't nearly so bad close to the flames. Lucy paid no heed to the cold, and rolled into the snow on her back, taking a few bites out of it while she slid through it. Her thick Husky coat kept the cold out, the bite of winter never touching her. He watched as the fire consumed the wood, enjoying the sweet smell and being hypnotized by the bright embers within. The heat on his face made him feel sleepy.

"Burgers. Are. Done."

The patio slid shut behind Steve, steam rising from the burgers stacked high on the plate. He slid the plate down onto the counter, and removed the boots and parka, rubbing his hands together for warmth and sniffing a few times to keep the condensation in his nose, in his nose. The burgers were perfect, hot and juicy, and Ryan was tempted to have seconds. When he was bigger he was sure he would eat two at a time. He just didn't have enough room yet. While he was finishing up, Steve had fed Lucy, mixing up a can of wet food into a cup of dry food, and then spooning out the mixture into her food bowl. She watched patiently, if not intently. If her bowl so much as scratched the surface of the countertop, she knew the sound and would be there in a moments notice, ready to eat. Steve took pleasure in trying to be as quiet as possible. So far he had met with little success. Either he was just too klutzy or her hearing was just that good. He supposed it was a little of both. The bowl slid onto the floor, and Lucy ate with gusto. He was never sure why she ate so quickly. He supposed she might be concerned he would come for a portion one day, and so wanted to make sure there wasn't any left for him if he did.

After cleaning up, they spent the rest of the night watching a comedy on television. Some kid named Ralphie was doing his best to get himself a Red Ryder BB gun for a Christmas present. The movie was hilarious, and they had both enjoyed it while the fire kept them warm.

When it was finally over near nine, Ryan could barely keep his eyes open.

"Time for bed, Bucko."

He had risen slowly, each motion needing specific concentration.

Steve had stayed on the couch, giving Lucy a belly rub.

He made his way into his room, and pulled his bed sheets over his body, feeling their coolness after having sat in front of a fire for a few hours.

"Did you brush your teeth?"

"Yes," he mumbled.

He heard him get up and go to the bathroom.

"Why is your toothbrush dry?"

Busted. He dragged himself out of bed, and plodded to the bathroom where he saw his Grampa holding his toothbrush out ready for him.

"Nice try," he said, returning to the living room where Lucy was waiting for her scratch to resume. Steve sat down and started to scratch her belly. Lucy sighed contentedly. He noticed that her belly seemed a little bigger, or maybe her nipples were more pronounced. Christ, he wondered. Was the dog pregnant? It was not a big deal; he had always meant to get her fixed but had never got around to it. He would have to bring her to the vet after the holidays and have her checked. Ryan brushed his teeth without enthusiasm, obeying the letter of the law if not the spirit. He finished brushing, and gargled a mouthful of water, spitting it into the bowl with a loud *Pitoo* sound.

"Floss yet?" he heard Steve call.

Instead of answering just yet, he weighed the odds. He decided they weren't in his favor tonight.

"No."

He pulled out his floss and measured out a string, cutting off a piece and weaving it through his teeth. He tossed it into the garbage can.

Going into the hallway, he flicked off the light and made a beeline for his bed.

"Goodnight, Ryan."

"Goodnight, Grampa."

He hit the sheets, and felt their coolness envelope him. After being denied sleep to brush and floss his teeth, they felt even better. He turned over a few times to get buried in his blanket, and then fell into a deep sleep. Steve stayed up for another hour relaxing by the fire and scratching the dog, the television was on but he wasn't really watching it. All of the lights were off, the fire in hues of yellow and orange sporadically illuminated the room, casting long shadows against the floor and wall. He eventually turned off the set and walked over to the large window overlooking the field. The night sky was dark, the stars were bright and crisp in the cold winter air. The moonlight cast down over the snow gave it a faded white glow in the dark. This kind of view was the reason Carrie had liked the property. He found the view very relaxing and peaceful, the night calm and quiet, and he thought he could still feel her on nights like this one. Lucy found her way over to her bed, and stood in it, curling around a few times before lying down, covering her face with her tail. While he stood in the window, she fell asleep. He returned to the fire, filling the pit with a stack of fresh logs to keep the embers hot until morning. They caught quickly, and he slid the chain mail spark guard across the fireplace opening. There was nothing flammable within eight feet of the fire, but peace of mind and safety made him close it anyways. It was an old habit from when he was a boy, and his old house had carpet right up to the fireplace. He wondered how that was ever allowed by fire code. Stifling a yawn, he stretched where he stood, and went to bed.

Robert Nestle

From an altitude of three hundred and thirty-nine kilometers, the view was still amazing, even after six months. It was a soothing way to pass the time, watching the world below pass by with silence. Not that there was much time he could spend gazing outside the window. Between the low gravity biological science experiments and metallurgical experiments he had been running there were precious few moments to spend looking outside, and frequently the times he had planned were cancelled due to restocking launches, or critical parts of the experiments that needed his extra attention or finesse. But for now at least, he had an open window of opportunity and he was taking advantage of it.

The Amazon basin came into view below, and he could see the outflow of the river emptying into the Atlantic ocean, the mixed colors of sediment laden fresh water swirling far into the salt water of the sea. Slightly to the west, smoke patches from the burning rain forest rose into the air, bordering the clearings were some families were etching out a living far below, unaware of his watch from above.

The deep blue of the Atlantic stretched away to the horizon, where its waves crashed against Africa. Only from space had he truly comprehended how vast in scale the oceans of the world were. Fully two-thirds of the world passing below him was covered by water, and the majority of that water was untraveled by people, restricting themselves in large to shipping lanes and major currents. He mused to himself that Earth was misnamed; it should be called Water. The world below him passed by silently at a rate of eight kilometers per second.

Captain Robert Nestle removed himself from the window, and with his arms pulled himself through the docking ring into Module B. He took some amount of personal pleasure from the quick efficiency of the motion; he had been in orbit long enough that he was becoming adept at locomotion through the space station. His legs were a relatively useless appendage in zero gravity, and despite hours of exercise he could see the muscle mass dwindle in them.

He knew that his return to Earth in a few months time would be challenging as his body had to re-adapt to a one gee environment. He personally rued the time he would need to get back into shape. At forty-five it would not come fast or easy, as it had when he was in his twenties. He was totally gray already, more of a family trait than a sign of old age. His hair had begun to go gray in his late twenties, and by his late thirties, a dark hair on his head was a rare and infrequent sight. His mind still though he was in his twenties, and that was the important thing. He saw enough people that thought they were old, and that thought had displayed plainly on their bodies. Get busy living or get busy dying was a favorite saying of his, something he had picked up from a movie he had once seen, and that phrase had stuck in his head ever since. There was a lot of truth in such a short sentence. He was busy living, and he kept in good shape, and in good spirits.

He had been born in early 1963, just outside the town of Arlington, Washington. His father William had been a real estate developer after spending a few years building homes for a local investor. He was a small stocky man who had seen big things coming a little further south in Seattle. He was also personable, and made strong ties with those he had come in contact with. He remembered faces, and he remembered names, and he remembered the names of wives and children. A handy strength in the sales business. He was from the area, had seen combat in the Korean War where he won a Medal of Valor. His father had never spoke much about his experiences in the army and had given the his son the impression that he felt his medal was unnecessary. He was assigned to hold his position, and he had. The truth, which went to his grave with him, was more complicated. His platoon was ordered to keep a hill that overlooked a narrow windswept valley. It was the high ground for the area, holding a commanding view of the neighboring plateau. It looked like any other valley in the winter. A blanket of snow covered the fallen leaves, and black twigs protruded from the ground, shaking in the steady wind. His foxhole was twenty feet upslope from Jimmy Faltons' hole. Jimmy was from Florida, a 6 foot tall 150 pound skinny white kid with a mane of black hair on his head, and he was not acclimated or prepared for winter. His idea of winter was the mercury hitting 75, not 10, and so he had bitched endlessly about the weather, stomping his boots and rubbing his arms to keep warm. As far as Jimmy was concerned, the goddam commies were welcome to this part of the world; if they wanted this bleak, godforsaken plateau he would throw them the keys and thank them for coming so soon. Despite his complaining, he did his duties without question, and was a crack shot, a natural with a rifle, and he was fiercely loyal to his friends and platoon. There was no doubt that you would share a foxhole with Jimmy Falton. Bill was glad to have his back, and he knew Jimmy was a solid asset to his troop. Early one dark morning they were again stationed on the hillside, and Bill was watching Jimmy stomp his boots in his hole, no doubt muttering something about the fucking cold Korean winter, when the saw movement just over the nearest hilltop. Jimmy had seen it instantly as well, and brought his riflescope up to get a closer look. Bill had watched him scan the area through the scope. It really wasn't necessary. The down slope a few kilometers from them was positively crawling with troops, all making their way down to the valley floor, where presumably, they would begin to come up their hillside. "Holy fuck Bill! You seein' this?" Jimmy yelled from his hole.

"Oh my god lookit them all!"

Neither of them had seen actual combat yet, or fired a live round at another human being, but the reality of the moment had crept up on them and hit them in the head like a large frying pan. William felt his testicles creep up as a sudden knot of fear and dread suddenly dropped into his stomach.

"Yeah I see them Jimmy, are you ready buddy? I got your back."
"Ready as I'm gonna be ... whattheFUCK."

The whole platoon saw them. All over the hill side rifles were being loaded and cocked, sounding like a giant knuckle cracking contest. The lieutenant could be heard screaming over his radio operators' back into the phone, calling for artillery and air support RIGHT FUCKING NOW THE OPPOSING NORTH HILL IS CRAWLING WITH GOOKS ! Jimmy had his M1-D sniper rifle out, and was patiently training his sights on the body of troops coming towards them, still a kilometer away but closing fast. From overhead came a loud WHOOSHing sound, everyone instinctively ducked so precisely as to have been choreographed, followed by the faint popping of an artillery piece behind their lines. A large clump of frozen ground erupted in the distance, along with a few troops. The lieutenant yelled into the phone that the range was good, repeat the range is good. More whooshing sounds came from above, and the valley began to explode, the echoes rolling across the hillside.

At about six hundred meters, Bill had seen Jimmy butt the rifle into his shoulder, followed by a quick CRACK as he snapped off a shot. The range was pushing the ability of the rifle, but his aim was true. A silhouette in the distance fell to the ground. Bill had smiled. Jimmy, confident in his weapon and skill, cold forgotten, calmed down and began to fire into the masses of men, reloading every eighth shot in a practiced and smooth motion. His fear was tempered now by his training and discipline, turning him into the machine his drill sergeant had so carefully and skillfully crafted.

At three hundred yards, the platoon opened up, the sounds of carbine and rifle shot cracking in the cold still air. Then they were at two hundred yards, and then one hundred yards and then they were right on top of them, mixed fighting from hand to hand and pistol fire. He had held his position while wave after wave of troops came up the hill at him and his platoon. His company had fought furiously, hugely outnumbered by the forces thrown their way. If they hadn't had high ground, they would have been screwed, and he knew it. It wasn't that his platoon had more training, or that they were more convinced in their cause, it was the hillside they were on. Lady luck, or the gods, or a cosmic toss of the dice had given them the good fortune to have a defensible position. As it was, he had fired his rifle so many times at the wall of soldiers running towards him that it overheated, and then he had quickly switched to his machine gun, fumbling with shaking hands to get it into position. He opened fire with it, spraying the field below, before it too decided it was too hot to work, and jammed.

Feeling his stomach drop with fear, and his face pale, he drew his service revolver. The ground in front of him exploded, and when the dirt and smoke cleared Jimmy was stunned and unconscious, but alive, halfway out of his foxhole. And being dragged the rest of the way out by some Korean soldiers. Momentarily confused, he watched as the two men started to drag Jimmy down the hillside towards their lines.

Snapping back to the situation, he felt a surge of irrational rage course through him. *What did those gooks think they were doing? They can't do that!* Much like a make believe playground battle fought between second graders, William was consumed by the irrational thought that this wasn't right. No way. Shooting was fair. Grenades were fair. Artillery maybe cheating a bit because you couldn't see them, but if they had them too, then maybe it was OK. But this was against the rules. *Just what did they think they were doing ?* Going to bring him back for interrogation, you dumbass, he heard a little voice say on his shoulder. Gonna ask him just where your foxhole is, and if he is stubborn gonna mess him up a bit until he squeals. We will make him squeal UNCLE like you have never heard before. His face paled and with a roar he screamed.

"NO GODDAM WAY YOU TAKIN' HIM NO WAY!"

He jumped out of his foxhole and ran downhill. The two Korean soldiers that were dragging Jimmy downhill looked up at the same time to hear what some fool was yelling, just in time to catch several bullets apiece in the chest. They fell where they stood. William reached his friend, holstered his pistol, and with a heaving grunt draped him over his right shoulder, and staggered back up the hill, impervious to the fighting happening around him. And since Fate was not ready just yet to close the book on either of them just yet, he made it. Jimmy would later be heard to say, if he was asked, that his name was on the list that day, that his time was up, but God simply hadn't got around to attending to him. Working with his reputation, he took his savings, partnered with Jimmy Falton, took out a loan from a banker who also seen big profit potential in his proposal, received some investment capital from a few other close Army friends he had served with, and bought land. For the next few years, they had worked feverishly, subdividing lots and building homes on the speculation market. And his vision paid off - the housing market in the Pacific Northwest took off, and so did his financial situation. His investment group spent the next twenty years developing properties and land in the area before finally selling off their interests, and retiring very comfortably.

His mother was a small wiry woman who was extremely cautious of the family financial situation, a trait developed from her own mother and her experiences during the Great Depression. The day that her husband had gone to the bank seeking his investment loan, she had spent throwing up with worry and angst over the debt the family had become liable for. During the next several years that worry had slowly faded as the financial rewards had begun to roll in. She had also taken a firm control and interest in the monetary affairs of the family, prudently and precisely giving her opinion and advice. She had not married a fool; her husband knew better than to ignore her, as all husbands know better internally, but may deny in the presence of other men. Her caution and business intuition had proved sound, and together they had built their business.

By the time Robert was six, his parents were financially comfortable, and able to entertain their only child as his interests developed. When Neil Armstrong took his first awkward lunar step, the Nestle family was watching it on their twenty inch color television set in style. That blurry, choppy image of a man standing on the surface of another world was ingrained in his mind from that point forward, inspiring his career path ahead.

The interior of the module was typical of the rest of the compartments on the Station; largely white with dozens of instruments attached to the walls with sections of Velcro. The only sounds consisted of the air filtration system, the occasional chatter from a ground control center far below, or the latest set of science experiments. He stopped himself at his work station and quickly reviewed the notes he had scrupulously taken in the last twenty four hours. He flipped through the plastic sleeve covered sheets quickly and efficiently, and then stopped, slapping his palm on the sheet to emphasize to himself that he had found what he was looking for.

"Going a little cabin crazy, are we?" he muttered under his breath, and then, "Here we are." Robert had found he was talking to himself on a more and more frequent basis, a realization that he missed hearing people talking. Listening to ground control teams wasn't an effective substitute as the voices were full of static and tinny. Taking the notes under his arm, he pushed off slightly towards a bank on the far wall. By mission standard procedures he was required to have a companion in the station anything simply for the safety of another human being should there be an emergency, either with the vessel or one another. As it was, his crew member had begun to develop appendicitis, and so was forced to leave the station with the last Chinese resupply mission. Mission control had determined that he was of sound mind and body, and he was capable of seeing through to completion the experiments that had been running for the last several months. Investment companies were unwilling to sacrifice their projects due to an unfortunate case of appendicitis. Should he have a physical emergency the docked emergency Soyuz capsule was available for his own re-entry, should it be necessary.

Coming to a stop, he logged on to the computer in front of him, and began to take notes on the current experiment. This station was monitoring the efficiency of a new class of solar cell arrays. The cells were made of several layers, each sensitive to a different wavelength of light. As light hit the panels, more energy could be absorbed by each accumulated layer than could the traditional one layer panel. The technology seemed promising. Having taken the necessary notes, he moved over to a biological experiment. Peering inside the glass tank, he tapped his pencil on the glass twice. Charlotte reacted instantly, contracting her body on the web to appear as small as possible. Charlotte was a common garden spider, one of those big fat orange ones you were likely to find on your fence in the summer time. She sat in the middle of her web, a perfect creation as any you would find on the planet below. The first three times she had tried to make her gossamer trap in orbit, the design had been seriously flawed, the web was irregular and laid out in a deranged pattern. The team responsible for the test was struggling to explain how zero gravity would make her instinct unable to replicate a web that she was intrinsically designed to do. On the fourth day, Robert had come to the experiment to find her web perfectly created, the spider hiding neatly in the top corner of the aquarium, her long foreleg resting on the thicker string of webbing that would carry vibrations of struggling prey to her. The geometry of the web was perfect. She had simply gone from being unable to make a normal web one day, to making a completely normal web the next. He secretly was delighted by the result. Now her experimenters had to explain how she had adapted to zero gees to make a perfect web, where before she could not.

While she was still in her protective posture, he retrieved a mealworm from a plastic container, and lightly tossed it towards the web. It floated the short distance quickly, and then quickly became trapped in the web. Charlotte remained motionless as Robert watched avidly. A moment later, she had extended a leg in the direction of the struggling insect. Sensing the vibration, she extended her opposite foreleg and given the web a quick tug. Satisfied with whatever information she needed, she had quickly crawled down the structural part of the web to her prey, and after the shortest of pauses, began to wrap the worm in spider silk. Mission Control was scheduled for a download of the latest batch of data before he signed off later in the day, so he also verified the information was compiling for data transfer. While the information was readied, he gazed out the nearest portal, where China was passing silently below. The sight of the vast nation passing by far below brought a quick and slight smile to his face; a memory of recent friends and mutual respect. During the last several months the station had two dockings from the Chinese space agency, where the testing of hardware and crew functionality was increasing in importance and scope as that country rapidly geared itself towards the landing of its citizens on the surface of the moon, a declared national goal. Robert had found himself pleasantly surprised when he had met the two crews. He had gone into the meeting with a note of caution, and had emerged firstly disappointed in himself and secondly profoundly happy to have met them. When the Chinese government had requested use of the space station to test its developing hardware, he had found himself coerced into politics on a national scale, something which had never appealed to his nature.

He was briefed extensively on what to say, what not to say, how to act, and what to expect, to be cautious of potential repercussions in the face of a nation that was rapidly overtaking the space program of the United States and that of the rest of the combined world. Coming from that preparation, he was ashamed at his expectations by the warmth of the crews that had shared the station with him for a brief period. He had found them hard working, as expected, but also quick to humor and to find happiness in day-to-day activities. They were extremely talented and proficient in their skills and professions. The benefit of having a population of over a billion people, was that when you needed people with talents that were rarer than one-in-a-million, it meant that China had over a thousand candidates to choose from. He had expected to find a sense of competition between the two crews to be selected to go to the moon. Instead, he had found only a mutual understanding of the importance of achieving the national goal, and that the reason for having two trained crews was simply efficiency; if one should perish in an attempt another team was prepared to raise the flag and try again immediately. From those meetings he could see the strength of their space program; it was one that possessed the vigor of youth, understanding that risk was inherent, but also the only way through which to achieve success.

In the opposite corner, NASA represented a tired warrior, obstinate in taking chances and preferring to play the game safely, and as a result not making notable progress. Where China had accepted a potential fatality rate of ten percent as acceptable in a moon mission, NASA was paralyzed by that statistic into delay, committee, and inaction. Below him, those six brave souls trained feverishly for events coming in the next few years, and deep in his heart he felt a sense of jealously in what they were to accomplish, and also a feeling of pride that he would be able to name those souls as friends.

A quick series of beeps confirmed the data was compiled, and the Captain refocused on the tasks at hand. Abruptly, in the silence of the confined quarters, a burst of static roared into life.

"Mission Control to the ISS Freedom, please respond."

Robert smiled at hearing a familiar voice, and pushed himself through the air to the far wall, where he had left his headset. Before he reached it, the voice came through again,

"ISS Freedom, do you copy?"

Robert placed the headset in position, turned it on, and replied.

"ISS Freedom copies your transmission, Mission Control. All is well. You are on the switchboard earlier than I expected Mike."

Mike had been stationed in Northern Australia, and he was not due back in the U.S. for another month.

"Good to hear from you Bob; the goddam spiders creeped me out so I cut short my vacation time. How is your vacation going?"

Vacation was his buzzword for his latest assignment.

Robert laughed aloud, and replied, "Likewise; my vacation is going well. The neighbors are really quiet up here, but the food sucks."

This time he heard Mike chuckle through the speakers. "Sorry Robert; we had no room in the food budget for your Liebfraumilch. Maybe next time."

Their friendship had begun more than twenty years earlier, just after they had both completed basic training and were into Officer Training. They had been assigned the same room through their program, and had instantly become friends through shared interests and a sense of humor, mostly involving practical jokes on one another as time permitted. Mike had developed his spider phobia directly from Robert, where he had placed a tarantula in his shaving kit. It had been discovered dark and early the next morning as it ran up his arm, glad to be free of its leather confines. Robert had heard the shriek clearly, and he had immediately fallen to the floor, clutching his stomach laughing loudly. By the time Mike had come to his room, he was ashen faced and trembling, Roberts' laughs had faded to chuckles, as he wiped the tears from his face.

Mike had slowly walked over to his bunk, sat down, and placing his face in his hands muttered, "You are a fucking asshole," which immediately sent Robert into another fit of laughter. After that experience, Mike had never again used a shaving kit bag, instead choosing to keep his razor, blades, and gel in plain sight on the countertop. Mike had given Robert a hard time over his preference of fine dining, and the necessary accoutrements involved in that experience. His jokes had therefore revolved around food, doing what he could to widen the experiences of his good friend and his palate. Their mutually inspired nicknames had arisen from their experiences. Mike had become Flanders, after the popular Simpsons' character and his scream, and Robert was the Swedish Chef, from the Muppet Show.

"Roger that Flanders, a 1948 would be great with the freeze dried stroganoff."

"We copy your request Robert. The engineering team wants to know how the P4 truss solar cell array is functioning."

Robert gathered up his notes on the array for reference.

"The electrical current has diminished by five percent but otherwise is stable; whatever caused the damage was too small to really make things FUBAR."

Two days earlier a small meteor had punched through the solar panel, no larger than a grain of sand, but traveling with enough speed to be potentially lethal. It had left a hole in a solar panel the size of a dinner plate. The lower reaches of Earth's orbit was becoming congesting with space junk; bits and pieces of earlier missions that had come free and drifted away, and now posed a serious risk.

"We copy Bob; are your notes on the impact in tonight's download?" "That is confirmed Mike; the photos and power history are in there for them, over."

"We have a team looking into replacing the array if it becomes necessary. We are hoping we can get away with something simple and just replace a segment of the array. We'll keep you up to date on whatever they conclude."

The space station had recently suffered some other minor damage from objects in orbit around the Earth, all of them small so far, but also all travelling much faster than a fired bullet. Anyone of them, in the right location, could cause fatal damage. A window had been scarred when another smaller object had smashed into it, making a small crater in the dense glass. They spent the next twenty minutes discussing the other events in the station and the status of the experiments.

"Alright Bob; sounds good. We are signing off for the day, then you are on your own time until 0:700 hours tomorrow. Don't let the bed bugs bite. Mission Control out."

"Goodnight, Mike. Talk to you guys tomorrow. ISS Freedom signing off."

A moment later, the system beeped again. On the computer screen, a cursor flashed impatiently. ENTER ENCRYPTION CODE:_

He positioned himself at the keyboard and typed in the sequence of numbers and letters. He had to have so many numbers, so many letters, so many capital letters, all committed to memory. He pressed the ENTER key.

The signal transmission was not direct to the ground, but would pass through a series of military satellites, each time being encrypted and transmitted to another to guarantee the security of the data.

The screen flashed once as the data was transmitted, and then the intercom system came alive once again, only this time it wasn't NASA.

"Captain Nestle."

The voice was clear and precise, and authoritative.

"Sir."

He replied quickly, acknowledging the call.

"I understand there was a power disruption. Should we expect complications with the project?"

"No, sir. The power loss was minimal, well within operating parameters."

He heard a quiet sigh of relief from the general.

"Very well. It is fair to assume that testing will commence as planned?"

"Yes, General."

"Should there be any other further issues report them immediately through authorized channels. I will reestablish transmission in forty eight hours."

With a quick snap of static, radio contact was broken. Robert removed his headset, fed it through a velcro loop on the station wall, and then pulled himself through the Columbus module, around the corner through the Harmony module, and down into the Destiny module. He glanced out the portal, watching as the electromagnetic tethers gradually lowered down from the station into the atmosphere below. These tethers were the primary reason he was onboard the station alone, and why had not been allowed to leave or have further astronauts join him. The project secrecy was utmost, and no one else with sufficient understanding of the science involved had yet been granted clearance to join the study. He enjoyed working with the spiders and growing the plants that NASA had assigned him to, but it was not his real mission, and it was the source of the concern when the Chinese taikonauts had been onboard. He had to verify that any trace of the military projects he was involved in would not be inadvertently exposed during their presence.

The tethers were lowering themselves into the atmosphere at the rate of one kilometer per day, and hung like black strings from the Earth side of the station. They were made of a nanotube composite that was superconductive that gave no electrical resistance whatsoever. As the tethers passed through the electrically charged atmosphere below, they would conduct an immense amount of power into the station project. An earlier test in 1996 had failed when trapped air bubbles had caused that tether to melt and break away from its satellite. Before it had broken, it had generated significant data, enough to merit further military investment. Redesigned, the new tethers had been brought to the station over time, kilometers of cable wound tightly and shipped in secret. It was inventoried as supplies for military purposes, and so kept from NASA. Robert had spent much of his initial time installing the tether machinery on the station with the robotic arm. Now that they were all installed, he could spend more time with the life sciences experiments that NASA had provided, as well as his photography. The tethers themselves would not provide enough energy to run the project, but they would generate enough power to begin the work.

Once the cables were deployed to a length of fifty kilometers, he would initiate the power systems and harness their combined electrical generation into the Xerxes module. The module was huge, and had been installed in secret, launched on a shuttle mission that had been claimed to be launching a new global positioning satellite for the military. Instead, the module had been brought up and installed by Robert and his associate, who was now on the ground with a surgical scar on his abdomen. Once the cables were ready, the power would channel into the Xerxes module, which was adorned with a series of highly compact lasers, all focused on a relatively small structure that housed a core of helium three, within a highly magnetized outer sphere.

The module was the culminating result of nearly twenty years of fusion research based at Groom Lake, or Area 51 to the public culture. If there were aliens there, he hadn't seen them, but then he was only one of several projects that had been ongoing there during his time. If there was such a project, he had no way of knowing about it. Each project was isolated and secure from the next. Robert had been highly involved in the research, beginning work on the project shortly out of school with his doctorate degree freshly signed. His time on the space station was the culmination of decades of intense, secretive work. If everything went to plan, the lasers would ignite the helium three at the core of the structure, held within the magnetic field of the containment chassis, and a small sun would burn, a man-made sun that would promise untold energy. If this test worked, the second stage of the project would begin. The extra power flowing from the fusion reactor would be channeled into a series of modules built into the underside of the Destiny module, the "floor," if a module could be said to have a floor. This part of the project had been designed by his associate, and had been his specialty. These modules could harness the electrical power of the reactor, and through a process he only vaguely understood, should be converted to having the effect of mass, and through that, create a gravitational pull. If it worked, he, and everything within the field of the compartment, would be pulled to the "floor" of the module.

He felt his stomach growl with hunger. Preparing dinner was a mundane task. His enjoyment of fine dining consisted as much from the preparation of the food as much as from the actual eating of it. Taking a freeze dried package out from its storage compartment, he added a little more water than was required, and let the microwave do the rest. A few minutes later, along with a beverage package, his feast was ready to be served. Afterwards, tired from his day and with his belly full with his meal, he brushed his teeth, dimmed the lights, and velcroed himself into a sleeping bag which itself was attached to the wall, and he soon fell asleep.

He awoke the next morning at 0:700 hours to the familiar repeating beep of the alarm clock. After completing a rigorous stretch, he unzipped the sleeping covers, and made his way to the stations bathing facilities, rubbing the sleep from his eyes as he went. With a long relaxed yawn, he undressed, entered the shower facility, and turned on the water. His mind was largely clear of thoughts during his shower, he knew what needed to be done, and so had given the days events little attention. Fifteen minutes later he was dried and dressed and went about the business of preparing his breakfast. He looked at his freeze dried choices, and went with scrambled eggs and bacon, with OJ to wash it down. While it was heating, he prepared his communications center and activated systems that had gone dormant while he slept, which consisted largely of some lighting systems. Everything else was set to an internal timer, with multiple redundancies. He glanced quickly at his wristwatch to make sure he was on schedule, which he was, and verified he would have fifteen minutes of free time after his breakfast to look outside his portal. After that, he would have his morning communication with Mission Control to verify his day ahead, afterwards which he would sign off and work in isolation, lost in his thoughts and procedure.

Another beep broke him away from his watch, signifying his eggs and bacon were done. He opened the packages, watching the steam quickly disperse inside the cabin, in all directions in the zero g environment. Eating his breakfast quickly and methodically, he cleaned up the packaging, went about relieving some bodily functions, and took up his favorite seat to watch the Earth below, camera in hand ready to photograph whatever caught his fancy. His camera was his personal luxury, a Canon that had cost him well over three thousand dollars. He had left his film camera, his favorite, back in his home in Maine, and had purchased this unit for the flexibility a memory card offered him in space. From here he could download his photos and purge the card, ready to take another several hundred photos. Once he returned to civilian life, he was going to compile his photograph collection and have them published, his visual record for the public to see what he saw on a daily basis.

Settling into a comfortable position, he raised his camera and snapped a few shots of the Himalayas that were breaking over the eastern horizon. The sunlight was breaking over the highest white peaks, and were contrasted with the limb of the world, partially silhouetted by the glare of the sun. Shifting position to face the edge of the world going into night, he was able to catch a photo of edge of the Middle East, mostly Afghanistan with a beige sliver of the eastern border of Iran quickly fading from view.

Nemesis

It was born of extreme heat, immense pressures and cataclysmic explosions, and yet it now lay dark and utterly cold. Its' black surface reflected virtually no light, absorbing what little light came to its dusty crust. The shallow carbon surface blanketed a mantle of rock several kilometers in depth, which itself covered an irregularly shaped mass of solid iron. It was a small remnant of a giant star that had once burned blue with intense heat billions of years earlier. This giant star itself had existed for only a few millions of years before it had exhausted its supply of hydrogen, and once its rapid pace of fusion could no longer be sustained, the immense pressures that had once been balanced by gravity became unequal, and the giant star blew itself apart in a titanic explosion. The shockwave from the initial explosion was refocused to the center of the dying sun, the energies involved crushing lighter elements into heavier ones, creating heavy elements and metals. The shockwave then again expanded outwards, this time tearing the star apart in a giant release of energy.

Over billions of years, the remains of the explosion dissipated and cooled, sometimes seeding the births of smaller stars as its shockwave traveled through vast clouds of interstellar gas, and sometimes to coalesce into small clumps of leftover debris. Some of these remains were incredibly small, to be measured in terms of millionths of a centimeter, and yet others grew from repeated collisions into objects many kilometers across.

The giant star had recycled itself, releasing its hydrogen and other newer elements like oxygen, carbon and iron born from fusion and its death, out into space. From its death, it had seeded the potential for life. Over the course of time measuring tens of millions of years large amounts of gas thrown out from the initial explosion had come together again, and over time collapsed onto itself as gravity drew the matter together. Eventually, the center of this gaseous mass became hot and dense, and eventually, with a flash of light burst into nuclear fire, a new sun born of its parents remains. Unlike its blue parent, this infant star was far smaller, and burned with a cooler yellow light, and would live a life to be measured in the billions of years.

This one piece of a long dead sun now distantly orbited this small yellow star, both offspring of the same explosion, however dissimilar. From its dark surface the sun it orbited was so far away it was indistinguishable from the millions of others shining in the black sky, merely another cold unblinking mote in the curtain of night. Very seldom its path through space led it inwards towards the star, where it picked up great speed, and it traveled around the star at the narrowest part of its orbit in a period measuring mere months. During this infrequent time its surface became incredibly hot, and it boiled away to the void of space any exotic ices that had accumulated on its surface since its last voyage through the inner solar system. It was not like a comet whose bright tail of vaporized ice and ions revealed its very being with a tail millions of kilometers long. Its small collection of ices boiled away before it came close to the star, and so it passed without notice or distinction, a small piece of hot rock and metal largely invisible, rapidly speeding again into the cold backdrop of night.

It was now deep into another orbit around its distant relative; it had spent many tens of thousands of years traveling inwards, and had recently shed its newest coat of ice, and was traveling ever faster. In times past the object had only come as close as the largest gas planet before returning to deep space. This time it passed too close to the failed sun, and its gravitational influence altered its orbit, sending it towards the center of the solar system. Months passed, it was now closer to the star than it had ever been before; its opaque surface was growing ever hotter. It passed close to a small moon, which itself was orbiting a small planet; and the gravity well pulled it downwards. Within the next day it had traveled the distance between the moon and its planet, and was inexorably rushing towards it.

Robert Nestle

Coming from the terminator, he spotted a dark object moving rapidly into the light. He had to again shift his seat to keep up with its velocity. It was about the size of a dime and he could see it was slowly spinning around its axis. Fascination rose as he realized what he was seeing, and he couldn't believe his good fortune. The asteroid had obviously not been detected by ground means, which was in itself not unusual. Usually one or two asteroids that were new to science passed near Earth annually, but not this close. Most discoveries passed outside of the orbit of the moon, and only seldom came between the pair. He lifted his camera to the window and began to photograph the asteroid below. This one was large, and it was passing below him, which meant it was very close to Earth. As he watched it through the viewfinder, his fascination began to quickly turn to fear, and then to dread.

He could discern the leading edge of the body was beginning to glow, with occasional flash of white, from it skipping across the top of the atmosphere. He knew it was plowing through the upper echelon of the Earths atmosphere, and he began to pray in his mind that it would skip its way out of harm, like a stone bouncing over the surface of a lake, the density of the atmosphere and its own speed preventing it from descending any lower. It was moving in a course nearly parallel to his own orbit, and he watched with rising dread as the edge of the object shifted from red to orange, and then to an increasing white and blue. He considered radioing in to anyone that was listening, but quickly dropped the idea; it was simply too late to let anyone know what he was witnessing, and the photographic record he was taking could prove invaluable for later study.

As the body sped away to the East, towards the island of Kyushu, Japan, he was forced to crane his neck to keep it in sight, and then his dread turned a cold lump deep in his belly as he saw the asteroid trail flare into a white orb. He instinctively rose his hand to cover his eyes from the inevitable, while he used his other to keep taking pictures as fast as his camera would permit. The interior of the module suddenly was lit up by a strobe of blinding light, and he saw the red of his flesh through his hand. A moment later, everything in the station died, and the lights went out. The electro-magnetic pulse from the explosion had destroyed the electronics of the space station.

He hoped it was an atmospheric explosion; that the heat and pressure of the atmosphere had caused the object to explode high in the sky, far above the ground. Glancing to his left, he watched as the clouds below were suddenly dispersed by a massive shockwave. He waited a moment longer, for the white light of the explosion to fade, and then he lowered his arm. A giant red and orange fireball was unfolding, while the shockwave was spreading outwards, a ring of white vapor expanding across the globe. He shock turned to horror, and then to rage, and then loss, as he wailed aloud in solitude, his screams echoing loudly within his narrow confines. He continued to watch, speechless, as the destruction unfolded before him. He passed over the impact site a moment later, and watched the explosion spread outwards in all directions, and upwards into the atmosphere.

Fearing the worst, Robert quickly sped from module to module, frantically sealing the access ways between each segment. Each door sealed with a faint hissing sound as the modules were isolated. There was no verification light that flashed when the seal was completed. It's circuitry had been destroyed. With the modules isolated, Robert quickly floated back to his observation window, wiping the sweat from his brow with his right forearm. The fireball dominated his field of view, and it had now gone entirely through the atmosphere. Robert jumped over to the extra vehicular space suit, and with shaking hands, he began to put it on.

"C'mon, c'mon," he muttered furiously.

The suit was difficult to put on in the best of times. His increasing panic was complicating the procedures he had memorized and practiced countless times. The light through the portal was becoming red as it diffused into space. He knew he was a man on borrowed time. His education and common sense both told him he was dead. His professional training had detached a normal response to imminent mortality. For now, it was in control and he busied himself with the tasks of data recording with pen and paper, and analysis of what he was witnessing. His radio was utterly dead. His camera was dead. He knew he would be soon as well.

An extinction level impact had occurred suddenly and without warning. Robert was a lone and silent witness to the death of civilization. As he passed over the world the familiar lights of cities were gone, everything was dark. The electromagnetic pulse that had so efficiently disabled the space station had done the same to the power grids and electronics far below. He worked diligently as he wept silently, tears drying on his face. Below he saw nothing more than a black world, where flashes of lightening and flame were the only light from below. The clouds and soot were spreading rapidly, and would cover the globe within two days.

The initial blast cloud had quickly passed from the northern to the southern hemisphere, disrupting normal atmospheric circulation. Raging forest fires added to the smoke cover, and new impacts from around the world seeded new fires and clouds. The world was being wrapped in darkness, covered in its own death shroud. He had lost his appetite as work overwhelmed his immediate bodily needs, and he worked with unsteady hands and shaking limbs as exhaustion and hunger took its toll. Eventually his body stopped cooperating, and he fell into a deep sleep.

Robert awoke to a dimly lit cabin. He roused quickly, his body partially recharged from his slumber. His stomach roared in its demand for food, and his weak limbs protested as well. He opened the food packets and ate them cold. He finished eating and dropped the empty packages to simply float in the cabin. He spent the next hour slowly making sure his suit was on properly, and that his helmet and gloves were nearby. It was precautionary and mostly futile. Nothing on the suit worked any longer, it was simply an emergency back up in case of a loss of pressure. He wrote of his friends and co-workers below; people that he knew were either already dead, or struggled to survive. A survival that he knew was very much in question. Ironically, the asteroid had crashed into the part of the world that was most equipped to survive such an event.

Western civilization was so dependant on the transportation and mass production of its food that he knew it was doomed. Hundreds of millions would simply starve to death or perish from exposure. The hunter-gatherer societies of the far east were the most able to survive where food needed to be gathered from the environment, in small groups of families. And from what he could tell, these peoples had been vaporized from the immediate impact, incinerated from the pyroclastic wave, or crushed in the huge tsunamis generated from the impact. The ecology of the planet was in for a major restructuring. If the Cretaceous extinction was any indicator, large creatures were doomed to extinction. Small birds, small mammals, insects, and some reptiles would be the only survivors. The slate of life on the world was going to be set back to almost square one. He spent some time gazing at the stars, much more visible now that the albedo of the earth was all but gone. And eventually he slept. Robert awoke in blackness, breathing in cool air.

The station was utterly black and silent, His exhaled breath had begun to condense on the walls of the station, and was now faintly visible. Shaking off his slumber, he made his way to the CO_2 meter. With the power off, the air scrubbers were no longer cleaning his atmosphere. The indicator was now at the half way point, meaning he had several more hours before CO_2 poisoning would begin to impair his thinking abilities, followed by unconsciousness, and then shortly after, death. Feeling the edge of hunger creeping up on him, he returned to the refrigerator, ate a quick meal, and returned to his workstation. He collected the CD's that held the record of the experiments onboard, the station hard drives, his memory cards and camera, and any loose information that he was able to carry, and stored them inside the Soyuz escape capsule.

Several hours later the task was complete, and he sealed the hatch between the station and the capsule. Satisfied the information was safe inside the capsule, he returned to his sleep area and settled into his bedding space. He was trembling with exhaustion, his body fatigued with the extra effort of increasing his metabolism to keep warm, and moving through the cramped quarters while loading the capsule with its cargo of knowledge. Closing his eyes, he focused on his breathing, and concentrated on slowing his respiration and reducing his stress. As he steadily relaxed in the darkness, he watched the lights that flashed in his closed eyes. The flashes were caused by cosmic particles that were travelling through his body in the numbers of millions per second.

A small percentage of these particles interacted with his retinas, which translated the energy interaction as a flash of light. Enjoying the lightshow, his mind and mind and body relaxed as endorphins travelled through his system. He heard a rustling sound, like leaves blowing across concrete. He pushed himself towards a window, scraping the frost off the glass with his palm while trying not to exhale on it. He watched the limb of the world coming into view, the rays of the sun obscured by the thick cloud of ejecta lying in the path of his orbit. The cloud he was now entering. He went to where his helmet was fastened to the plating of the station, removing it with a few rips of velcro. He pulled it over his head, twisting it into its fastener, and then locking the clasp to secure the seal. He felt the suit pressurize, feeling his heartbeat speeding up as he heard the sound outside getting louder and louder, the scraping becoming a steady hiss, like sand being poured into a tin can. He held onto the side, looking around the cabin as the sound grew louder and louder, more insistent. The hissing grew into slight pings and knocks, a faint rattling and knocking like something scratching trying to come in, trying to find a way past the welds and rivets to get at what was inside. He watched, feeling his body tense, his breath coming slowly, his body beginning to sweat.

And then the air inside began to swirl, the edges of paper lifting as if blown with a gentle breeze. The knocking became louder, and Robert flinched as a hole was suddenly punched in the side in front of him, another hole punching through the opposite end nearly instantly. The cabin became a flurry of loose objects being blown out into space, flying through the air before getting close enough to one of the holes to disappear a moment later.

He felt the wind pulling at him, trying to pull him from his handhold on the wall. Robert felt the station trembling as it was bombarded from outside, the multitude of impacts shaking the structure. He could feel the station gyrating under the stresses of the impacts, and more objects shooting through the thin metal of the station. A few more punctured his cabin, and he felt himself pulled violently outwards as the compartment decompressed, exploding its remaining pressure into space. He struggled to keep a hold on the tether while the section out gassed.

Once the atmosphere had vented, he could stay inside and utilize the minimal shelter it provided. Later, he might be able to find a section that wasn't breached and use it as a lifeboat.

He didn't want to re-enter in the Soyuz capsule just yet. The events that were unfolding below were too violent; he needed to stay in orbit as long as he could. The compartment began to buckle, tearing where the debris had punctured the station.

"Shit," he muttered, being forced to move. He pulled himself along the wall, pulling himself into the airlock section where the structural part of the pod was the greatest, offering him the most protection.

He sat in the narrow gap, and watched as a section of a solar array drifted past, twisted and crumpled. He could see the debris from the impact floating around him. It was going to slow his orbit, pushing the station down into the atmosphere from the friction of so many small impacts. The view outside began to twist, the station going into a slow uneven roll. He was going to have to get to the Soyuz capsule now. The rapidly degrading state of the station was forcing his hand.

If the station began to spin quickly, it would tear itself apart, and there was the very real risk that he might lose consciousness if the g forces became too strong. The module was beginning to look like it belonged on a firing range; its skin was riddled with holes, with a steady stream of new impacts adding to the damage. He took hold of the manual door release, checking the pressure of the other module. It was also at zero. He twisted it counter clockwise, lefty loosey, disengaging the hatch, and pushed it inwards. The next module was nearly destroyed, the shell a patchwork of holes and cables floating in space. He pulled himself through, cautious of any sharp ends that might tear a hole in his suit. He reached the next hatchway, and found the indicator was still reading a pressurized atmosphere beyond. The impacts began to get ever louder, the station was vibrating ominously, the twisting station beginning to spin a little faster. The section behind him suddenly sheared away with a large bump, spinning off into the distance, falling lower into orbit. He dared not look behind him, not wanting to see the remains of the station falling away. He removed a small panel, and pushed the large button within. The pressure gauge began to lower immediately, the air being vented off into space through a series of valves on the exterior of the module. He waited until it read zero, and then unsealed the hatch, pulling himself inside. A series of panels lined the walls, behind which were a bank of pressurized canisters filled with oxygen and other gases needed for the station to function.

The station continued to roll over, exposing shielded components to the debris cloud. Robert felt the impacts hitting the component almost immediately, and he reached forward to pull himself through the area as fast as he could. The hull began to be breached; holes ripping through the thin metal. He kept going forward, striving to reach the capsule beyond the next hatchway. He never felt the explosion that tore apart the station. An oxygen tank was impacted, the pressurized gas releasing its pressure in a moment, spraying the module with shrapnel and breaking loose the other containers. Robert was thrown against the wall by the explosion, feeling himself pushed forward by a force he had no time to counter. His eyes widened as the bulkhead loomed in front of him, coming too fast to react. He struck the metal beam hard, and was knocked unconscious and left floating. The next series of explosions killed him; when the other tanks were struck and exploded, ripping open his pressurized suit. His body swelled in the zero pressure, and exploded in a moment. The spark of a ruptured fuel cell caught a jet of pressurized oxygen, and the flame tore through the small space, until the inner pressure shattered the wall, tearing it open and damaging the hub of the station. Destabilized, the core of the station tore itself apart, sending pieces spinning in all directions. The orbiting cloud of debris destroyed the surviving pieces of the station, shooting it full of holes and driving it down into the atmosphere, where it began descend to the earth below.

Archie Buchanen

The light from the outdoors was bright and strong, and there were enough windows to make lighting not really necessary during the day in the eating area. The kitchen staff had come out from behind the spring-loaded doors, propping them open to allow more light into the kitchen. There were a few windows there as well, but not as many, so although the kitchen was not dark, it wasn't clearly lit like the rest of the establishment. The fans came to a halt, and it didn't take long for the bite of the air conditioning to lose its edge, the air beginning to warm quickly.

"The power must be out," said Archie, taking a bite out of another prawn.

"Really?" said Charlie, looking over his shoulder, trying to find a light that was out. Stephanie kept eating, and Mel paid him no attention, her focus on eating lunch. It was still cool in the restaurant, and it was early afternoon so it didn't really matter if the lights were out.

Charlie made a quick 'hmm' sound when he saw the fans were still, pointed out to him by Archie, and then he returned to his burger, trying to open his mouth wide enough to stretch over the thick bun and take a bite. He squeezed the burger together with his hands, compressing the bread flat, before successfully taking a bite.

The power was still out when they finished lunch and left the restaurant. When they opened the doors the heat from outside came over them in a wave, momentarily stealing their breath. In the coolness of the air conditioning, they had felt full but alert; the heat of the afternoon sun began to make them feel groggy. At least Mel and Archie felt groggy.

Charlie and Steph were eager to return to the surf, pulling their parents back towards the beach where they had spent the morning.

"To have their energy again," stated Mel, being pulled along by Stephanie who was gripping her hand tightly, trying to get her to walk faster. The kids seemed to be immune to the effects of the heat; their full bellies giving them more energy to play.

"All right. We surrender," said Archie. "Go where we were earlier."

Steph and Charlie took off down the beach, their feet padding the sand as they ran along the shoreline, running through the waves that were breaking and sliding up the sand. Archie and Mel watched them run, their towels hanging over their shoulders, making sure they returned to where they had spent the morning. It took them a few minutes to catch up to them, stretching out the towels back over the sand in front of their beach house.

Mel sighed as she laid out on her back, pulling her hat visor down over her eyes for the shade. Archie laid down on his right side, his head supported by his arm, watching both the kids play and Mel breathing quietly in front of him. Charlie and Steph were splashing each other furiously, eyes closed, their arms a blur as they beat at the water. A few gulls and a couple of terns flew overhead, wings outstretched, checking out the scene hoping for a scrap of food, hovering in the offshore breeze. He could feel his brain mellowing out by the second. If the time continued to pass this slowly, and it was this relaxing, the two weeks they had booked were going to be life changing.

He looked out at the kids, who had ceased their frothing spray and stood bent over the water, hands cupped around their faces, looking down into the water. He guessed they were watching for fish, by the way they were pointing here and there and then trying to follow a certain direction, walking slowly. He looked out beyond them, out to the sea and the horizon, where a few boats were making way. He turned over onto his stomach, straightening his arm that was beginning to cramp, when the sand beneath him suddenly roared and then surged, throwing him off his towel. His ears were full of the sounds of screaming and a deep ferocious rumbling sound that he felt as well as heard. His hands dug into the earth, clawing for something to hold onto as the ground beneath him waved and

305

bucked. The kids had reflexively pulled up their legs; and were doggie paddling in the water, not able to stand. They watched as Mel and Archie were shaken around the beach, unable to right themselves, the trees lining the beach shaking furiously, a few falling over, kicking up a spray of leaves as the trunks crashed through the underbrush. The windows in the houses lining the beach exploded out of their frames, the walls shaking and cracking. One by one, the houses fell apart, collapsing, releasing clouds of dust as they crumbled to the ground.

The ocean waves quivered into a series of ripples that danced along the surface. The earthquake continued for minutes; and then stopped nearly as suddenly as it began, the rumbling fading and then ceasing altogether, the rushing sound of the waves on the beach resuming its methodical rhythm.

Archie found himself spread out on the beach, his muscles aching from the effort of trying to hold his ground. Charlie and Steph came ashore, crying and scared, Charlie going to Mel who also lay crying on the beach, and Steph to Archie who was wide-eyed and tense. He took her in his arms protectively, holding her tight to him as she cried into his neck.

"It's okay baby," he whispered into her hair, rubbing her back, trying to convince himself that everything was okay. He stood up, carrying Steph who was clinging to him with all of her strength, and went over to Mel and Charlie who were also sitting together in a tight hug. They sat in shock for minutes as the fright and tears worked their way through them, trying to comfort each other.

"We're okay guys. We're okay." Archie repeated it a few times, feeling Steph loosen her grip, and seeing Charlie move to sit on his own, wiping the snot from his nose and the last of the tears from his eyes. Mel leaned against him, whispering and talking quietly into Stephanie's ear. She eventually began to nod at whatever was being said to her, and after a little more coaxing sat between her parents, who had their arms around each other.

"Let's get off the beach guys. There might be other people who need our help," said Archie, standing and pulling Mel up with his arms. He was looking around, seeing the ruins of the villa around the shore. The restaurant was burning from what he could tell. At least, the pile of rubble that was in the area of the restaurant was burning. There was nothing left standing but a few utility poles and the forest itself, which had also suffered casualties.

"Come on."

He held out his hands, Steph taking one and Mel the other, while Charlie took his mothers' left hand, and they made their way off the beach, taking a straight line in to where the houses were, onto the sidewalk. The sidewalk was shattered and lay in a random broken line, cracked and spread out along its former path. An older couple dressed in bright floral tropical patterns stood in front of the remains of their beach house, arms around each other, scarcely aware of their presence walking towards them.

Mel reached out to touch the lady's shoulder.

"Are you alright?"

She didn't move, but the man turned his head and nodded to her, a small grateful smile on his face.

"We are going to continue down the beach," said Archie. "If you need us, we'll be down further along."

The man nodded again, but this time didn't turn to face them. He stared forwards, holding his wife to him.

They went on down the beach, passing others who sat on the shore, close to the water, not wanting to be near the houses that so easily could have been their tombs. They had been extremely lucky so far. The quake had struck when it seemed that everyone was outdoors enjoying the afternoon. They neared the cloud of smoke that was climbing into the sky, a thick black sooty smoke that was fluffy and billowing. The employees stood around the ruins, watching the place burn. A broken gas pipe stuck out of the cloud, a bright flame spraying outwards into the debris, feeding the flame and keeping the temperature high. The gas was fed from a large white cylinder the size of a truck about ten meters away. The fence around it was twisted and distorted, but the tank itself seemed to be in good shape, although it was broken from its foundation. The fire would continue to burn as long as there was gas in the tank.

Their waiter from lunch saw them approach, and walked over to them, the genuine concern on his face heartwarming.

He took Mel's hand in his, looking the family over from head to toe.

"Is everyone okay? No one is hurt?" he asked.

"We're all fine, thank God," replied Archie.

"We were all at the beach when it happened. Did anyone get hurt?" The waiter shook his head.

"We got out just in time. Just when it fell in. The line snapped a second later. We heard the gas hissing inside, so we ran like hell. A second later the place went up."

"Incredible," said Archie, shaking his head slowly.

The waiter nodded.

"There is a boat launch further down the beach, a few klicks or so. Some of the staff are moving people down there. I don't know what is left of the pier, but the boats can always anchor."

"Is there a place to stay? A building?"

He shook his head.

"Just boats, but it's a roof over your head tonight."

Archie had to agree; it was better than walking around trying to find somewhere to spend the night.

"Okay, thanks for the advice. We'll head over that way. Do you know if there are any supplies over there?"

"A bit. Some water and some food. Nothing too fancy but better than nothing. Here, wait a moment."

He went away for a moment, rustling through some boxes that lay in a heap near an old boat that was flipped upside down, her hull half free of barnacles.

Archie thought it over for a second, taking stock of the situation. If worse came to worse, they could always sail to shore anyways, although with a quake of that size it was sure to have caused some big damage elsewhere, so they might be better off where they were. Their waiter returned with four bottles of water, an island brand and still sealed.

"You better take these for the walk. The kids might need a drink or two before you get there."

Archie was touched, and by the looks on Mel's face, she was moved as well.

The water was warm, almost hot, but it was fresh.

"Thanks so much."

They shook hands quickly, and began to make their way in the direction the waiter had indicated.

"Daddy, are we going to sleep on a boat tonight?"

"Probably, Steph. It depends on how many people are there already."

"They might even send the Ave Maria over to us. It has a lot of room," said Mel.

Archie agreed. The ship could send their lifeboats to shore if need be. Her hull was likely too deep to get near the pier. He had imagined it as a small wooden fishing dock, probably built when the island was first settled on to be developed to get supplies ashore, or perhaps built by local fishermen even before that. All they had to do was get there. If it was a few klicks away, with the kids, it would take them an hour or two to reach it. The kids were still wearing their swimsuits, their clothes and shoes tucked into a khaki colored bag that Mel had bought specifically for that purpose. Their towels were draped over their shoulders, keeping the sun off their skin. They were already dry, and the kids hair was blowing in the light wind.

"How long until we get there?" asked Stephanie.

"Around supper time, kiddo."

She nodded, looking down at her feet as they walked over the beach.

They had abandoned the pathway; the broken up concrete was a little too unsteady for his liking.

"You should put your sandals on."

She shook her head.

"Then I can't go in the water. Can I go walk in the water?"

He couldn't think of a reason why not, and so he agreed.

"Just stay at the shore. If you go deep you won't keep up."

"Okay."

She let go of his hand, and trotted across the sand, demarcated between a high tide and a low tide line with a series of deadwood and seaweed. He watched her go down to the shore, with Charlie following shortly after her.

Something didn't seem right, but he didn't know what it was. Archie and Mel walked shoulder to shoulder, watching their children walk in the surf, kicking up the water with their feet and getting some more fun out of their situation. They seemed to have already brushed off the terror of the earthquake and moved along. They walked along slowly, the beach becoming a smooth flat expanse of sand with a gradual decline. As they walked, it seemed as though the beach just grew wider and wider, further out to sea, the shoreline further away.

The resort was crazy to not have built facilities on this side where the beach was so expansive. Where they were playing earlier in the day the beach was a strip of sand maybe ten meters at its widest. Here it was at least fifty, maybe more. This beach could be filled with people with room to spare.

"Daddy."

The high tide mark was the same; the beach just seemed to go on forever.

It would be interesting to see high tide come in, and cover all that sand up. He wondered how long that would take.

"DADDY."

He snapped out of his thoughts with a jab in the ribs.

"What was that for?" he asked Mel, the owner of the elbow that had jabbed him.

"Steph is calling you."

"What?" He was surprised. He didn't hear her at all.

They stopped walking and faced the beach.

"What?"

"The water keeps going away from us."

"The water keeps going away from you?" he mumbled under his breath, wondering what she meant.

"What?" he yelled back, hoping for a better explanation.

"The water keeps going away," she tried to explain, flustered, her arms waving to make the point.

He didn't know what the hell she meant, so he stood and watched, seeing her standing where the sand was still wet from the breaking waves, but where they were no longer reaching her toes. He stood there, watching her looking at the waves. He felt a chill race up his spine when he saw what she was talking about. The waves were retreating, the ocean itself pulling back as if draining away in some far off faucet. The beach wasn't normally this wide, like he thought. The beach he could see was normally under water, and now lay exposed to the air as the sea pulled back. He quickly glanced at Mel, who seemed to not notice what was happening, or did not attach the significance to what was happening. He looked down the length of the beach, where at the farthest edge he thought he could see something that might be the pier.

"Mel, we need to get to that pier as fast as we can. Can you run that far?"

Hearing the tension in his voice, her stomach filled with butterflies, butterflies the size of pigeons, suddenly afraid at why he was saying what he was saying.

"What? Why do we need to run there? You're scaring me." She looked off to where they had to go.

He felt her grab his arm, feeling her shaking as she squeezed him.

"Can you run that far? Yes or no. We don't have much time."

"Y-yes, but why? Why do we..."

He cut her off, satisfied with her answer and not wanting to waste any more time discussing it. He felt the need to move, the urgency pressing down upon him. He didn't know if the kids could run that far, but goddamit he would carry them if he had to. He had no choice.

"Steph! Charlie!" He yelled as loud as he could, instantly getting their attention. He pointed down to the far end of the beach. It was the pier. He could see a boat or two for sure.

"Let's have a race. You kids against Mom and Dad. We'll race to the pier over there."

The kids looked down the beach, their faces dropping when they saw the distance they would have to go.

"Awwww, geez that's not fair," Charlie complained.

"There's no way we can race you that far and win."

"All you have to do is run that far; it doesn't matter who finishes first."

He saw them look at each other, analyzing the terms of the deal.

"If you make it, you each get whatever dessert you want."

That did it. They looked at each other one more time, nodded slightly, and then started to run, their little arms and legs pumping them forward. Charlie and Steph ran side by side, their gaze focused on the dock off in the distance.

"Let's go, Mel, now."

She started, running with him, her eyes creased with concern.

"What's wrong, Archie? Tell me!"

He looked over at her, seeing she was deadly serious. He kept running slow, making sure the kids were ahead of them, seeing them look back to check on the distance between them. Stephanie's ponytail was swaying back and forth as she ran, working hard to keep up with her brother who was staying back for her.

"The ocean is retreating."

"Yes, so what?"

"It means a tidal wave is coming, a tsunami."

"How do you know that?" The voice was questioning, but her face was fearful. He clenched his jaw, not wanting to have to explain it to her; just wishing she would listen and do what he said.

"When the water pulls back like that, it's because it's being pulled back to fill a gap. It happened in Indonesia; remember that? All the tourists went out to play on the beach when the water retreated. They were the first ones killed when it came back."

"What caused it?"

"The earthquake, I guess. Something moved, pulling the water with it. And it's going to come back really fast."

She looked out to sea, not seeing anything like a wave other than what looked normal. There was no huge wave coming that she could see.

"I don't see anything."

"That's because the wave is in deep water, so it's still low. When it gets close to shore, the energy pushes the wave up and out."

He looked at her, seeing if she was getting it.

"As long as we don't see anything, or the water keeps going out, we have time. When it comes back in, it will come quickly."

"Shouldn't we go for high ground then?"

He nodded.

"If we weren't on this island, yes. The whole island isn't more than a few meters high. The wave is probably going to sweep right over the island. The whole island."

He looked at her, seeing the tension in her face, wishing he didn't see it.

"There isn't anywhere on this island high enough to escape to."

"So what are we doing?"

He looked for the pier, seeing they had covered about half the distance. The kids had slowed; their initial energy spent, they were now running on will power and the sheer energy of their youth.

"We need to get to a boat."

"A boat? Won't a wave push a boat over?"

He shook his head.

"Maybe not. If we get on one, and get out to sea, where it's deeper, before the wave starts to rise, the boat might ride it out. The wave passes under it."

"If it gets in water deep enough."

He didn't feel like saying that if they didn't get to deep water, then the wave would carry the boat along like a small fragile bathtub toy, picking it up and smashing it to pieces along the shore when it came crashing in. Along with anything inside it. By the look on her face, he thought she understood.

"Maybe not," she said.

"Maybe not."

He could see there were in fact five boats floating near to what was left of the pier. A few boards clung to them, the rest lost to sea. One boat was still moored to a post, stranded on the sand left by the retreating water. He could see the boat nearest to them, a two-hulled open catamaran, was beginning to unfurl her sails. The man who was working with the rigging on the ship saw them coming, and stopped what he was doing, waving them forwards. Only a few hundred meters to go.

He went to the stern, watching them come, looking around out to sea periodically.

"He's waiting for us, Archie," Mel gasped, her lungs burning.

Archie nodded, waving back at him.

"Keep going, Mel. We're almost there."

"Get to the big boat kids!"

Charlie looked back at him, frowning.

"That's not the dock!" he yelled back.

"The race is to the boat now. The man is waiting for us."

The kids went into the water, quickly thigh depth, and then they began to swim out to the boat, where the man had lowered a rope into the water and was waiting by the side with a ringed life preserver that was tied to the aft mast. When the kids were in the water, Archie and Mel caught up to them quickly, and soon were swimming right behind them.

"Come on!" the man yelled at them. He was the biggest man Archie had ever seen, easily six and a half feet tall, and a thick wall of muscle. It didn't appear he had neck; his shoulders just seemed to blend into his jaw.

"Grab my neck, Charlie. Hold on to me."

Charlie was gasping, doing his best to swim out to the rope. Stephanie had already latched onto Mel, who was doing a brisk breast stroke to the ship.

He felt Charlie grab onto him, and then Archie went forward, making up time. The side of the boat grew nearer and nearer, and finally he could hear the lapping of the water on her hull, and managed to grab the thick hemp rope sitting in the water. Lady was thinly stenciled and painted on the side in a flowing calligraphy script.

"You go up first, Charlie." He felt him let go, and move to his side.

"Give me your hand, lad."

Charlie put out his hand, and was lifted straight up out of the water, landing on the deck with a thud and the sound of dripping water.

Stephanie was next, pulled from the water a little faster than her brother.

Mel started up next when Archie nodded her forward.

"C'mon, Sheila. Up you go." She took his hand, and then the other, and he lifted her out of the water, the muscles in his arm bulging, but not appearing to have any great difficulty.

"While I get your man, be a dear and raise the anchor."

Archie was starting up the rope, struggling to get a solid footing while the rope swayed in the water. Mel went to the bow and begin pulling up the anchor rope, turning the crank to raise the anchor.

"C'mon, mate; give me yer hand."

He looked up to see the open hand waiting for him. He took it, and felt it clamp tight around him, and begin to pull him up. He straightened his legs, and pulled up with his other arm, and soon was on the deck, his hand still firmly clasped in a tight grip.

"Welcome aboard. Now I reckon we'd better catch some wind and get the hell outta here. Whaddya say?"

Archie shook his hand, feeling a surge of relief to be on deck and on the water.

"Sounds like a fine idea...," the sentence was left hanging.

"Paul's my name."

"Archie's mine. Thanks for waiting for us, Paul."

"Don't mention it. I'd be a regular son of a bitch if I left a family stranded on a beach if I had time to save'em, wouldn't I?"

"I think you're a saint."

Paul laughed, a deep hearty sound that made him smile and the kids see who was making such a racket.

"We're not out of the pan yet, mate. Do you know much about sailing?"

"Not a lick, I'm afraid."

"Then take yer missus and kids between the hulls into the rigging."

The space between the two hulls was connected by several akas from the vaka, the main hull, to the ama, the outrigger. Between the akas, a narrowly spaced rigging had been secured, where Paul had placed some of his supplies.

The four of them sat on the rope, watching Paul raise the sails and get his ship going. He paid them no attention, keeping his mind on the task at hand, his focus on getting out to sea.

The sails caught the wind quickly, snapping tight, pulling her forward with an acceleration that surprised Archie. Paul caught the wheel, cheering.

"Wooohoooo! There goes my Lady. C'mon, let's go." He was smiling from ear to ear, obviously taking great pleasure in his ship and what she could do. The catamaran surged forward, cutting through the waves like a knife and riding the sea smoothly. Paul stood at the wheel, his legs shoulder width apart, his hands controlling the wheel with finesse, giving the rudder a little leeway to play with. Periodically he would reach over to a lever or pulley, and tighten or slacken the lines, pulling the sails into different angles.

Archie watched the shore line rapidly fall away.

"Where is everyone else? We were told other people were meeting at the pier."

Paul nodded.

"They went inland to tour the forest. There is an old wreck from world war two in the trees. An old bomber of some sort. A Liberator, I think it was."

"Why didn't we wait for them?"

"They were going to be gone for a couple of hours, and had left earlier. Then the surf started to go out. They wouldn't have made it back in time."

Archie nodded, understanding. If Paul had waited, he risked his own life for the slim chance the other people would have returned in time for him to get further away, when he had no reason to expect them to come back earlier than they had planned. It was their own good fortune that they had arrived near the pier when they did, or they might have seen him sailing away without them.

"So when do we get our dessert?" Charlie asked.

Mel laughed.

"We'll have to see what our friend Paul has onboard. Otherwise we can wait until we get to another restaurant later."

"Okay."

"I'm thirsty," said Steph in a low voice. She was tired, and had laid down on the netting.

Mel still had her water from the beach restaurant stuffed in a deep side pocket of her shorts. She fished it out, and twisted the lid, snapping the seal with a few faint cracks.

"Save some for your brother." She handed her the bottle, and Steph quickly raised it to her lips, drinking it slowly but steadily.

Charlie watched her drinking it, making sure she didn't drink it all.

Steph lowered the bottle with a loud 'ahhh', and passed it to Charlie, who quickly emptied it, finishing with a quiet belch. He handed the empty bottle to his mother, who stuffed it inside a plastic mesh bag, pulling the drawstring closed at the neck.

Mel laid down, Steph joining her to her right, and Charlie to her left, snuggling into her and closing their eyes. Archie made his way over off the netting, one shaky step at a time, and then planted his feet on the deck, walking towards Paul with his landlubber gait.

"The family is relaxed?" asked Paul, keeping his eye on the horizon. Archie nodded.

"Good. Worrying does nobody any good."

"Seen anything yet?"

Paul looked over at him, moving his head only slightly.

"You mean like a wave?"

He nodded again.

"Nothing yet, but she's coming."

Archie secretly hoped they had already sailed over it, but knew that was a false hope. Even in the deep sea a tidal wave will still appear as a swell several meters higher than the average wave, and so far nothing had been out of the ordinary.

"What were you doing when the earthquake happened?" asked Archie, curious about him.

"I was fishing. I was sitting on the dock sipping a nice bottle of rum when the whole world went upside down. And I lost my bottle of rum."

He seemed more upset about his lost bottle than anything else.

"And I lost my fishing rod in the drink, to boot. A nice carbon-fiber job.

I only just bought it. Son of a bitch. So I jumped off the dock before it fell apart and I swam over to my Lady here." He patted the wheel with affection.

"You?"

"We had just finished lunch and were going swimming. Do you live on your ship?"

"Yup. I surely do."

"So you live around here?"

"Mm mmm." He shook his head. "I sail around the coast, putting in when the weather gets rough, or I need a little rum."

He smiled lightly.

"Right now I need a little rum."

"You and me both."

They laughed together, feeling a little better.

Archie saw Pauls' face slacken, his smile droop and slide off his face.

He looked forward, and saw the swell on the horizon, a crest running higher than the rest of the surrounding sea. He glanced down to the netting, seeing his family still lying down, eyes closed, oblivious to the incoming wave.

Archie kept his voice low, whispering to Paul.

"Are we far enough out?"

"I don't know. The wave is already big."

They watched it coming towards them, a rolling crest already meters taller than the rest of the sea.

"Is it normal to be moving that fast? I mean, do they normally?"

Paul shook his head.

"I don't know."

They watched it moment to moment, able to see it rushing towards them, and then, it began to climb into the sky, the surge pushing upwards.

"Oh Jesus," Paul whispered, his hands gripping the wheel, his knuckles going white, the blood being squeezed out of them. He released his grip on one hand, making the sign of the cross across his chest, slowly and methodically, his finger pressing into his body at each point. He gripped the wheel again.

Archie gripped the bench at the helm, looking over his shoulder to see if Mel had noticed anything. They were dozing, unaware of their situation.

The wave continued to rise, a wall of water pressing towards them.

"How much longer, do you think?" asked Archie.

"Maybe a minute, maybe less."

Archie figured it would be less. They stood quietly, not wanting to create a scene, powerless to stop what was coming. All they could do was hope they would rise over the crest of the wave back into smoother waters. With each passing second it seemed less and less likely it would be so easy.

They stood and watched, Paul steering the Lady onwards, silently. They felt the trough of the wave reach them, the ship dropping in the water, and then rising, the wave carrying them forward in the advancing swell. Mel opened her eyes, feeling her stomach dip and then rise.

When the tsunami reached the Lady, it had risen to over three hundred meters, and was continuing to grow as the wave swept into waters less deep. The Lady was picked up, and pushed up the wall of the wave, carried in the curve of the swell. The screams of all aboard were lost in the roar of the wave, caught up in the fury. She was pushed up the swell, towards the crest, where she tipped over and fell into the trough as the wave reached the shore of Fraser Island. Paul gripped the wheel as long as he could, seeing the family he rescued tossed into the churning waters. The Lady was first snapped in half, the akas shattering like toothpicks, the outrigger and main hull dashed in the surf, finally forcing Paul to release his hold on the wheel when his body was crushed in the rolling wave. The tsunami swept over the narrow strip of land at a height of over five hundred meters, scouring the island down to bedrock and dashing everything on it to pieces, sweeping over it in seconds, leaving behind an incalculable scene of destruction. It maintained its course towards the mainland of Australia, where it would breach the coast at a height of just over eight hundred meters a minute later, sweeping inland faster then the speed of sound, tearing the city of Brisbane apart and washing its remains inland for hundreds of kilometers.

Dak-ho Seuk

A flash of light caught his eye from the rear of the plane, the light shining through the window as though the sun was coming out from behind a dense cloud. He looked out the window, and saw only clear skies, and a bright western sky. He folded his paper and tucked it inside the pouch of the seat in front of him, and then looked outside again. A thin line of white vapor seemed to be forming and flowing through the air, coming from the west towards the plane. The thin cotton clouds behind it disappeared in an instant, to be dispersed in a much thinner spray of white. He watched it with a frown, his concern growing as he wondered what the hell he was seeing. He looked over his shoulder, and saw a few other passengers also looking out their windows to see what the glare was from. *What the hell?* He frowned in wonder, seeing the ring come towards the plane at what must be great speed if he could actually see it moving. As it neared he could see the air before it was clear, and that the thin clouds were appearing *before* the ring, that something was making water vapor condense out of the thin cold air. The ring itself was an illusion, merely where the clouds were forming. He looked across the horizon, seeing the thin white line stretched as far as his eyes could discern the subtlety of the formation.

It's a shockwave, he suddenly thought. His mind raced for possible solutions. It's from behind the plane. Did someone light off a nuke in North Korea? If it was a nuke, it must be a freakish huge one. He had seen the video archives of atomic and nuclear tests, where the shockwave had spread out from the core of the explosion, travelling in front of the explosion itself. It would be upon the plane in moments now, the speed of the approach terrifying. What was even more scary was that he had absolutely no control over his situation, all he could do was sit here and wait to see what happened. He sat utterly still, not wanting to scare his nearby companion, yet his body was rigid and tense. He knew this could not be good. The line rushed towards the airliner, and he blinked once before he knew it would reach the plane, using his left hand to secure the buckle at his waist.

The flight sensors of the plane blinked and sounded their alarms, the turbulence light instantly flashing on. A split second later everything went dead. Nothing turned off, they just *went off.* The lights, the fans, the monitors, *everything* lost power. The interior of the cabin dimmed, the only illumination came through the windows. He could feel the throttle of power from the giant engines suddenly reduce. If it wasn't a shockwave, then what the hell was it? He had expected to feel the plane surge and then be tossed through the air like a plastic toy. Looking out the window, the strange line of light continued on through the atmosphere.

"Excuse me, excuse me, *Miss*?" The voice came from the rear of the plane.

"What happened?"

"I don't know, Sir. I will go ask the pilot and see if I can an answer for you." Her voice sounded stressed, but in control. A moment later she walked past his seat towards the cockpit. More and more people were beginning to talk, the volume increasing as more and more people began to question the loss of power. He felt the plane begin to bank to the right. It was slight at first, his stomach revealing the change in direction before his eyes could even see it. The sound of the engines continued to fade to a dull drone, the turbines spinning from the wind flowing through them. He clenched his armrest again, his stomach knotting as he realized that something very bad was happening.

The plane continued to dip to the right, the wing tip now below the horizon as if in a slow turn. He then felt his stomach rise as the jet lost altitude. So far, no one else on the flight had voiced a concern, although he was sure that someone else must be aware of what was happening. The wing bumped as the jet hit a pocket of turbulence, and it couldn't recover. It suddenly dropped, tilting the plane into a tight turn. He

clenched his teeth as the plane carved through the air in a tight curve, and
people began to scream. He managed a glance outside, and saw the wing
pointed straight down towards the ocean, a nearly perfect ninety degree
angle. The plane continued to turn over, the cabin turning upside down.
The screaming rose into shrieking and yelling. Luggage and belongings
began to fall through the cabin, adding to the unfolding chaos.

The plane began to spin. The rotation began slowly, and then
increased in speed as nothing countered the effect. The g-forces so far
were slight, but were increasing in strength. He could feel his body being
pulled into the seat and feel the vibrations course through the fuselage.
An overhead compartment burst open, spilling its contents onto a row
of passengers. A piece of luggage struck one elderly man on the head,
instantly causing blood to flow as he grimaced in pain, holding his hand
to the wound.

Yeon Gaesomun thought furiously. In all of his years of piloting and
testing, he had never experienced anything like this. His co-pilot was
relatively inexperienced but his training was coming through. He was
following orders without delay. He had worked through simulations of
power loss before, generally with an engine shutting down or the loss of
instrumentation. This was new altogether, he had lost every onboard
system. The cockpit was utterly silent save the sounds of the command
crew struggling to bring their plane back to life. He couldn't even try to
restart the engines as the panel was without power. So far, the plane was
carrying itself forward on its own momentum. It was only a short matter
of time before their situation would grow more perilous. He felt a bead
of sweat run down his temple.

"Kim, try that restart again."

Kim reached over, and pushed the button. Nothing, not even a click.
Yeon noticed that Kim was beginning to look particularly grey.

"Shit."

They heard a knock at the cockpit door. Kim looked at Yeon, who
nodded at the unspoken question. Kim unlocked the door and opened
it. His voice was abrupt and terse.

"Yes, Mia?"

She wasn't expecting his tone, and was momentarily taken aback.

"Come inside, quick." He reached for her hand to get her into the cockpit faster, and locked the door behind her.

"Um, some of the passengers are wondering about the loss of power." It was then that she noticed the cockpit was completely silent as well. And she noticed the sweat and apprehension on the faces of the flight crew.

"Oh God, what's wrong?"

"We don't know, Mia. The plane has lost all power and…"

The plane bumped through some turbulence, and they felt the plane begin to dip to the right.

"You had better sit down."

Her eyes widening in fear, she nodded and sat down in an unfolded chair, clicking the seatbelt around her waist.

They felt the plane dig into a steep bank, the horizon becoming a ninety degree angle through the windows, and then the plane going inverted, edging into a downward angle.

"Fuck, Kim try that restart NOW!"

They heard the screams of passengers mutely through the door.

Yeon tried his radio again.

"Mayday, Mayday this is Korean Air Flight 893. We have lost all power, repeat, we have lost all power. Does anyone copy this transmission?" He clicked the radio off.

Nothing. The radio remained mute. The nose of the plane had dipped noticeably towards the ocean, the jet continuing its slow corkscrewing motion through the air as it dropped altitude with increasing speed. They continued to check and recheck the panel, waiting for the plane to power up before it was too late.

Dak-ho kept his eyes forward, not wanting to look outside and confirm what his senses were telling him. The plane was spinning downwards out of control. Madison was pinned into her seat, her hands clutching her chest as she evidently was having a severe heart attack. Her face was grey and sweating, her breathing shallow and rapid. No one could move as the plane turned end over end, pieces of luggage falling through the cabin like balls in a lottery drum. Passengers that were not wearing their seatbelts struggled to get to any seat they could. The screaming was putting him on edge. He wanted to shout SHUT UP AND STOP SCREAMING IT WON'T HELP but he didn't. The panic level was getting too extreme.

People were beginning to question their very survival and were getting past the point of rational thought. The hum from the turbines was getting louder as the plane picked up speed. He wondered how much longer the plane had. He closed his eyes and waited.

The *Ulysses* sat dead in the water. As dead in the water as a ship could sit out on the open ocean, anyways. The ocean swells were at eight feet, so it was a relatively calm sea this evening. The previous night the swells were breaking ten feet over the bow, washing the decks in a continuous spray of nearly frozen water. She was one hundred and thirty feet from bow to stern, a twenty-year-old crabber that had seen a couple of owners in her time, and the loss of more than a few of her crew in rough seas. The deckhands were struggling to secure a crab pot that was sliding around on the side of the ship, hanging from the arm. Derek stood back from the controls, waiting for the pot to be relatively still, timed with a wave when he could secure it with a line and tie it down. There was no time yet to figure out what had failed. One minute the ship was breaking through the swells and the pot was being hauled in, the crew ready to secure and empty it, the next; she had just died. He could see the captain, Leif, struggling in the Captains Lookout to go the ship back under control. He had signaled with the sweep of his hand across his neck that the ship was dead, so as Senior Deckhand he took control of the situation. He had ordered the rookie below decks before he got hurt, or killed. He had stood on deck frozen as the crab pot spun around out of control, his lack of experience freezing him where he stood.

"Michael get the hell out of here now!" he had yelled. He hadn't moved, probably not hearing him over the roaring break of a swell over the ship. *Sonofabitch* he swore under his breath, and ran over to where he stood, grabbing him by his shoulders, leaning his face into his right ear.

"Get below decks NOW before you get killed!" The deck roared as another wave broke across the hull. Michael nodded and a moment later was closing the bulkhead behind him. Derek pointed to Clyde, an experienced crabber with only one month less experience than he had. He signaled to wait, motioning where he was going. He got a thumbs up in reply. Both men were in their mid thirties and from Kodiak Island, thickly muscled from working on ships all their lives.

Their mutual experience had saved each other on more than one occasion from serious harm, maybe even death, and so their mutual respect was deep and hard earned. Both had lost friends to the sea, and did not care to lose another if they could help it. Clyde stood opposite Derek, braced against a stack of pots, watching for him to make his move. When he tied his line through the mesh he would pull on his, taking up the slack and tying the pot down to the deck.

Derek paused. The Ulysses climbed the swell of a wave. Nearing the crest when she would be most stable he lunged forward, feeding the loose line from his left hand through to his right inside the pot. Grabbing it quickly, he pulled back and ran with the line towards an eyehook on the deck. He clasped the hook down, hearing the eye close over the metal loop, and looked over to see Clyde furiously pulling his line. His rope drew tight, and he looped it around an anchor tie three times, and then drew the loose end through another eyehook, drawing it taut with a quick knot. He signaled with a thumbs up. Both men went towards the pot, giving it a quick pull to test it. It moved, bit only slightly.

"What the fuck happened?" Clyde asked, breathing deeply.

Derek shook his head.

"We have to figure it out. Leif isn't having any luck by the looks of things." Paul nodded.

"Well, I am going to have a breather before I go see what we can do. All that excitement added another grey hair to my head."

Clyde laughed. "I thought they were all grey already."

"Fuck you, Clyde. Every grey hair I have on my head is because of your fuck-ups."

They both laughed together, relieving the stress.

Clyde stood tall, looking out over the sea.

"What is that sound?"

Derek listened. "I don't hear anything."

"Wait, between the waves."

They both listened, waiting for the quiet points between the waves breaking on the ship and next one.

Derek heard something, his eyes widening.

"What is that?" The sound was whining, a quiet drone, but it was getting louder.

Clyde shrugged.

"It isn't the ship."

They both listened for it, trying to hear where it was coming from. The sound was getting louder by the moment. The ship decks remained motionless, no engine vibrations, save for the waves.

"It sounds like...like a jet. Like a jet engine."

Derek nodded. The sound was closer; they could hear it over the sound of the waves now. They started to scan the sky for the source of the sound, the whining becoming louder and louder.

"Oh sweet Jesus," Clyde murmured.

Derek turned and saw Clyde looking up into the sky. He followed his gaze, and saw it. An airliner was coming down fast, corkscrewing as it flew towards the sea. They watched powerless as it screamed overhead, covering their ears as it passed them by in an instant. Derek saw Leif looking skyward through the windows and then drop from view as he must have hit the floor, thinking something was going to fall on him. Derek counted the seconds. *One Mississippi, two Mississippi, three Mississippi, four Mississippi,...* he nearly got to ten when the ocean erupted into a boiling wall of water. The jet drove towards the surface when a wingtip caught a wave, and was sheared off. The plane pivoted sharply in the air and slammed into the surface with a giant clap and the shrieking and tearing of metal. The roaring turbines exploded as the fan blades tore themselves to pieces in the water. Derek made the sign of the cross on his chest, and prayed in silence for those that had been onboard.

Clyde had expected to see the tailfin of the plane rise from the explosion and sink like a torpedoed ship, but there was nothing. The plane had been torn apart from the impact, and the surface of the water was littered with fragments no larger than a pillow. They floated in the open sea, helpless to do anything but watch.

Gischane Camara

He stepped down onto the ground and made his way over to the men at the generator. He walked slowly, very conscious that the way he felt was coming through in the way he was walking. He didn't like looking sick, and he knew he did. He passed one man who was re-lacing his work boots.

"You're looking rough this morning, sir."

He smiled faintly, and waved weakly at him as he passed by.

"Thanks. I feel rough."

"Hope you feel better soon."

He nodded in acknowledgment, and kept going. He didn't dare stop, thinking he might not get going again anytime soon.

"What's wrong with it?" he asked the two who were looking at the generator. One of the men shrugged, the other shook his head in frustration, his brow furrowed.

"I don't know. I mean, this thing is brand new. Nothing should happen to it. It just up and quit. The fuel filter is clean as a whistle. The hose isn't plugged."

"Well, keep trying. Something is sure to come up, probably something simple." He turned around and began to make his way to the mine. He stopped at the entrance, allowing his eyes to adjust to the darkness inside the mine. A metallic gong sound came from deep within the shaft, like a bell being rung. The interior blackness gradually yielded and he slowly walked into the mine, keeping near the left metal rail of the rail track in the floor where the path was more clear. He could hear the crew at the back of the shaft talking, and the sounds of stone and tools. The helmet flashlights cast an irregular illumination as the men moved about, sporadically illuminating their surroundings. Near the front of the cave he passed a stockpile of supplies, a rail spike had been driven into the support beam, and from the end of the spike a miners helmet was hanging. He reached forward and took the helmet from the member, and placed it on his head, tightening the plastic clasp at the back for a snug fit. Satisfied with the fit, he reached up to the front of the helmet and found a small switch. With a sharp click, the light came on. Another metallic bell sound came from the far end of the cave. The path in front of him suddenly became much clearer, and he had to squint as his dark adjusted eyes were overcome with the glare from the lamp. With his helmet lamp, the crew were now aware someone else was walking towards them.

"Haamid, is that you? You're late, you fat goat!"

The men laughed heartily.

"No, it's not Haamid." The crew recognized the voice.

"Our apologies, sir. We were just having some fun."

Gischane continued to walk towards the men, raising his hand to ease their minds.

"No apology needed. In this dark you can't see your own hand.

Is everything going okay in here?" One of the men dropped a large stone into a cars resting on the rails. When it hit the bottom, another gong sound filled the narrow space of the cave.

"With the generators down we have no power or water for the drill, so we are just cleaning up a bit."

Gischane nodded, satisfied they were finding something to do in the meantime. The men had been dumping rocks into the rail cart to push them outside for crushing. The useless power drill lay stuck inside the end of the shaft, its cutting drill buried within the rock.

"Well, you can go outside the cave until the generator is fixed. You have been working hard." They looked at each other, wondering if he was serious. Seeing the looks on their faces, he settled the matter.

"I'm serious, go outside, have a cigarette, write a letter to your wife, or your girlfriend. There will be time to work hard later."

"Thanks, Mr. Camara." They leaned their tools against the wall, and began to make their way outside, all save one. Gischane winced.

He preferred to be called by his first name, to keep the operation on a more intimate level. With more and more staff coming into the camp it was becoming increasingly difficult to do. The new hires saw him as the boss, and so were very deferential towards him, unsure about how to act around their young boss who walked around the camp and helped them out from time to time. They were used to people who sat in chairs all day, giving orders and never lifting a finger in manual labor. Even being called *sir* got on his nerves, but it was better than *Mr. Camara.*

"Excuse me sir, I just want to finish cleaning this pile up. I will go crazy if I leave it here." He recognized the voice in the near dark.

Gischane nodded. "Here, Farid, let me help."

"No sir. That isn't right. You are the boss. I will clean this up."

Gischane sighed.

"Ridiculous. I have two hands and a strong back, and there is no reason I can't help you pick up some rocks."

Between the two of them they developed a steady pace, and had the loose pile of stones steadily disappearing into the car cart, the metallic echoing lessening as the cart filled. He enjoyed the labor, feeling it loosen his muscles as he began to sweat and warm up. He looked over his shoulder to the mine entrance in time to see the silhouettes of the other workers as they went outside into the bright daylight. He wanted to start up a conversation with Farid to get to know him better.

"Where are you from, Farid?"

"I am from Kenya, sir."

"It is a beautiful country. What part are you from?"

"Near Kisumu, a small village to the west."

Joseph nodded, doing his best to remember his geography classes.

"Near Lake Victoria, then?"

"Yes, sir."

He smiled, obviously pleased that Gischane knew the area.

"How did you end up in a gold mine in Guinea?"

Farid wiped his brow, and sat against the rock wall. Gischane threw the two stones he held into the cart, and then did the same.

"I was a fisherman in my village, but there are too many boats, and not enough fish to go around. I was hoping to marry a girl from Nakuru, but to get married I needed more money. I came here to make more money, so I can go home and marry her."

"Well, Farid, that is a fine reason."

"And you, sir? Are you married?"

"No. I haven't had time to look for a wife. I have to get this mine working first. When I am comfortable with it, then I will look to start a family."

"Man without woman is like a field without seed," said Farid.

"Hmm?" asked Gischane, not quite hearing what was said.

"It is a proverb my grandfather taught me. Man without woman is like a field without seed."

Gischane nodded.

"My grandfather told me a story once, after he had told me that proverb. When he was younger, there was a man in our village that thought only about having more boats, and more fisherman working for him. He was always buying more boats and looking for men to fish for him. He was never satisfied with what he had. He became a very wealthy man, but still he wasn't satisfied. One day, many years later, a snake bit him in his home, and he died alone and without family. All of his boats and all of his wealth meant nothing, and soon everything was gone. If I may be bold?"

Gischane nodded.

"Do not be like this man, Sir. Don't let this place take your soul. We see the kindness in your eyes. You are not like other men we have worked for, who beat their men or are cruel to those around him. You treat us like men, and so we will work hard for you. Get what you need from it, and find your wife, or let her find you. Children are the reward of life. Without them, when you die, you will be forgotten. Only through your family will you be remembered. You will not be remembered because of a hole in the Earth, because of a camp in the forest. They sat in silence for a few moments, the sounds of pebbles grinding under their boots dominant.

"I appreciate your honesty, Farid. Thank you for saying what you felt."

Farid exhaled; deeply concerned in the previous silence that he had overstepped his bounds.

"I think our pile of stones is okay for know. Let's go outside."

Gischane stood, and Farid began to rise, and then stopped, listening.

"What is it?"

"Listen."

Gischane heard something. It was deep, a faint rumbling.

Farids' eyes grew wide.

"WE MUST GET OUT NOW!"

He grabbed Gischane by the shirtsleeve, and together they ran for the daylight ahead. Gischane didn't know what was happening, but seeing the fear in Farids' eyes made him run. The rumbling became louder, and he could see dust begin to fall from the ceiling.

"What is it, Farid?

And a moment later it felt as though the floor was pulled from beneath his feet, as if a wave had thrown him forwards. An immense roaring sound filled his ears and the earth shook violently, and he felt himself collapse on top of Farid. He saw the opening of the cave fill with dust and then the bright daylight vanished as the ceiling fell, the wooden beams shattering like dry toothpicks. They screamed as the tunnel went utterly black, and they felt a wave of dust from the rock fall sweep over them. Their helmet lamps were covered in grime and faded. The shaking continued, the ground vibrating and buckling around them, the stones grinding and shattering like china plates all around them. He heard something crack, and then felt something solid fall on his head and fall over him, stars and bright dots filled his vision, and he felt no more.

When he woke up, he saw Farid looking at him, the light from helmet shining on his face. He squinted in pain, feeling the light burn into his eyes and trigger a wave of pain in his head.

"Sir, sir, stay awake!" He felt Farid slapping him lightly on the face.

He opened his eyes again, and saw the dust caked onto Farids' face, the dirt stuck to his sweat and creased into his skin. The mine was utterly dark except for the lamp, and from what he could see, it was nearly destroyed. The walls that had been relatively smooth were jagged and pockmarked, where the walls had collapsed and shattered. Wooden beams lay splintered, the thick wood crushed and twisted under the immense weight of the rock. He looked about slowly, feeling his neck twinge painfully. The front of the cave was sealed shut by a large rock fall. Countless small rocks had filled the cavity, effectively closing it from the outside.

He licked his dry lips, feeing the grit on his skin.

"What…what happened?"

"Earthquake, sir. We are lucky to be alive. If we had been a little faster the entrance would have fallen on us."

"Where are we?"

Farid smiled.

"God granted us mercy. We are by the supplies cache. We have food and water and tools. Enough for two weeks if we are careful. Surely enough to last until we are rescued."

He relaxed his back, not realizing he had tensed it trying to look around. The pain left him quickly as he relaxed, and he lay on the ground.

"Can you hear anything from the outside?"

"Yes, sir. The men outside are trying to reach us. It has only been about a half-hour since the quake, and I heard their tools on the rocks trying to get to us after the quake stopped. They know we are here. I banged my shovel on the rocks, and they banged back. You don't have to worry, they will get us out."

He listened hard, and he thought he did hear the faint clanging of metal on stone.

"What fell on me? It felt like a house."

"It was the wall beam. It cracked and fell over us. Again, God helped us. If it had not fallen over us, we would have been crushed by the stones that came from behind it. I saw the stones roll over us. I prayed to God for our souls when I saw them falling, and they rolled over us. I didn't know if you were Christian or Muslim, so I prayed to God and Allah. And we are still here."

Gischane smiled and took Farid's hand, squeezing it.

"Thank you, Farid."

"There is no need to thank me. You would have done the same."

Gischane nodded, closing his eyes.

"I need to sleep, Farid." He felt his cold coming on stronger, his illness taking advantage of his injuries.

"Sleep, then. I will be here when you wake up."

He awoke later in the day to find himself in pitch blackness. He could hear the distant ringing of tools on the stones outside the mine, and Farid breathing. He felt his face with his hands, wincing when he found an injury on his forehead and another over his right eyebrow.

His face was covered in dust that he could feel sliding off of his skin when his fingers brushed over it. He sat up awkwardly, not knowing where anything was, trusting his sense of feel only. He moved slowly so he wouldn't hit his head against anything unexpectedly. He sat in the dark, eyes wide open, seeing only black and the myriads of colors and swirls being generated within his own eyes. He wrapped the blanket around himself, holding it tight to his chest, and just sat and thought.

A short while later, Farid woke up in fits and starts, his breathing coming faster, and then coughing as he cleared the dust from his throat. Joseph heard him stretch out and yawn, and then fumble for something. He wondered how Farid could have been sleeping so soundly. He was stretching and yawning as if he had just woken up in his own bed. He heard a click, and was blinded when the helmet light suddenly shone in his face. He covered his face quickly, his vision seeing nothing but purples and reds as the intense light overwhelmed his vision. As he covered his eyes, Farid roused and stood.

"Sorry, sir. I didn't know you were awake."

Gischane couldn't help but laugh.

"Just promise me that the next time you do that, you'll say something to warn me, just in case."

"Agreed."

He slowly lowered his arm and opened his eyes slowly to have a look about. Farid was walking around inside the cave, looking at the walls, and seeing if he could see anything yet through the rubble at the sealed entrance. A good portion of the mine had not collapsed. There had been falls here and there, but by in large the cave had survived in good condition, the only exception being the front entrance.

Once this was all sorted out he would have to have the shaft inspected before any work was continued. All he needed after this was for an unseen fissure to open up and kill his crew as they mined. A series of the wooden braces had supported and restrained some rock falls from coming down completely, the stone wedging itself neatly against the supports. He stood slowly, feeling his body pains stabbing at him, and he walked down the shaft slowly, taking stock of the damages. Satisfied, he returned to the cache where he had been resting to see what they had. Farid was pumping some water into a canteen from one of two large drums of drinking water, the other of which was still sealed and unopened. Water was not going to be a problem. He felt better seeing that; he had read and heard about mining accidents where trapped men had died of thirst, a painful and terrible death, where those that had died and those that had survived had been forced to drink their own urine in order to get some type of moisture into their bodies. That, it seemed, would not be his fate. Next to the drums were several wooden crates. They had all been opened, probably by Farid, and stacked into several neat piles. One pile was canned goods. He sorted through them, seeing canned fruit, preserves, and soups and stews. His stomach growled unexpectedly. He didn't like the idea of cold soup, but at least it was food. In the other crates, he found flat breads and crackers, as well as some dried fruit and spices.

He leaned against the wall. Farid was right; they had food and water enough to last for an extended rescue, so that was something he didn't have to worry about. He was concerned about his cold; he didn't relish the idea of being underground for who knows how long while he got over it. And for the matter of personal hygiene, they didn't have to many options about where to go to the bathroom. It would be unpleasant, but tolerable. Farid took a long draught from his canteen, and then passed it to Gischane. He drank deeply as well, the cool water feeling great as it washed down his throat, cleaning the grit from his mouth. They resisted the idea of using any water to wash; they had a lot, but they didn't want to assume too much about their rescue timeline. Farid spent a little time picking some rocks from the entrance collapse, and carrying them to the end of the cave.

"I might as well do a little, right? Maybe we will meet them halfway through."

Gischane agreed, and paid little attention as Farid busied himself with the stones. He picked up one in each hand, and walked to the end of the cave, where he dropped them into the rail cart. Each landed in the cart with an echoing *bong*.

Coming back from the latest trip, he had looked to the side of the wall where a generous slice of rock had cracked from the wall face, the large piece being evident that it was going to break off, but not indicating that it was about to anytime soon. Farid kicked it once at the far end of the break, and it shifted slightly. Encouraged, and with nothing really better to do. He kicked it again. Each kick was rewarded with a slight shift of the stone, but it refused to yield to the flesh. Fixated on the task, Farid came back to the cache where he retrieved a large black pry bar, nearly three feet long. He returned to the wall, smugly, to use iron where flesh had failed. He carefully slid the thin end of the bar into the widest fissure around the rock, and wiggled it down to make sure it was secure, and he pulled. The stone shifted and then stuck again. Not dismayed, he redoubled his effort, placing one leg against the wall where it was solid to brace himself, and he pulled again. The stone first stood firm, refusing to yield. And then, as if on second thought, it suddenly popped free of the wall, the grating sound of stone on stone as it slid off and fell over. Farid had stood over it for a moment, acknowledging the stone for the resistance it had given him, much like honoring a fallen warrior. He then wiped his brow, and looked at the wall where the stone had fallen from. The pry bar fell with a teeth grinding clanging sound on the rocks of the floor, bouncing off the rail track once for good measure. Gischane watched him, and wondered what was so interesting. Farid had dropped to his knees, and was tracing something on the wall with his hands. Gischane watched as Farid rose and ran over to him.

"Get up, get up. You have to see this." He rose slowly, and put out his left arm for help. Farid took it and pulled him up standing and they walked briskly to the wall. They would have ran, but Gischane resisted that, electing instead to be pulled in a brisk walk. Farid pointed at the wall. Gischane stopped and looked, not seeing anything in particular but seeing everything instead. It was like when a professional goes to look for a tool that he needs to finish a job. He knows where it is, or where it was, but when it comes time to find it, he can't. After minutes of fruitless and frustrating searching, the missing tool suddenly and magically reveals itself, in plain sight and right in the middle of where he had been looking. Gischane experienced that at this particular time. He saw the rock lying on the ground, he saw the wall, he saw where Farid was pointing, and he even saw the vein of gold that ran through the wall, just as he had seen it many times before. Eventually, his mind cleared and he saw what he had been looking at without seeing. It was a massive gold nugget, lying buried in the stone. Nugget wasn't the right word for it. It was a boulder, a gold *boulder*. His eyes boggled at the recognition of it, and Farid smiled broadly when he finally saw the lights go on in Gischane's face. It was huge. He took a tape measure from his pants, and unrolled it across the floor, from one tip to the other. Farid held one end of the tape as he unraveled the other. One hundred and ninety seven centimeters in length. He repositioned the tape and measured the height. Almost one hundred centimeters. He sat down forcibly, his teeth clicking together. Farid sat there quietly, clearly enjoying the shock on his bosses' face.

"That is the biggest single piece of gold ever *found, ever.*" They sat there for minutes and simply stared at the mass of gold in the wall.

Finally Gischane broke the silence.

"Farid, time to have dinner to celebrate!"

They celebrated with cans of cold stew and bread torn from the loaf, but it was the best meal he had ever enjoyed. The sounds of the crew working outside were coming ever closer; it sounded hopeful that they were making good progress on the rock slide. A little bit of light seemed to be coming through the very top of the cave, and they could feel a small breeze as fresh air was coming through the stones. When dinner was done, he checked his watch. It was nearly four thirty in the afternoon already. He was amazed at how the time seemed to go by without another frame of reference. He looked at the empty can lying on the floor, and suddenly wished he had something cold to wash it down with besides water. He heard a small sound of pebbles sliding down, bouncing and clicking, and looked over to see a small metal rod pushing its way through the stones. He got up quickly with Farid who saw it coming through as well. Farid took hold of one end, and pulled on it with a few quick jerks. They both heard a faint cheer come from the other side of the stones.

Farid let go of the stick, and they watched as it was quickly pulled back through. They hugged each other quickly to share in the good news, patting each other on the back with a few loud slaps that all was going to be well.

"The first thing I am going to do tomorrow when we get out of here is to have the longest shower of my life!" Farid declared.

Gischane laughed.

"Only if you beat me to the showers first!"

Farids' face went suddenly solemn.

"We need to thank God for our deliverance."

Gischane nodded in agreement. It seemed a little premature, but he decided it was a good idea, in light of how things could have turned out. They knelt together, Christian and Muslim, and prayed.

Afterwards, Farid had found a deck of cards neatly tucked into one of the crates, and they had agreed to play a game of poker. Farid shuffled the deck with difficulty, the smooth and stiff cards from the new deck being quite different that the old cards he was accustomed to playing with. As he dealt out the first cards, he suddenly stopped.

"Do you feel that?"

Gischane tensed, suddenly wary with the recollection of how Farid had felt the earthquake coming as well. A noticeable breeze had sprung up with the cave. Through the helmet lamps, they could see the dust being drawn to the entrance of the cave. The air was being sucked *out*. The faint wind whispered through the stones. They noticed that the outside work had stopped as well, the sounds of tools suddenly stilled. As they listened, they heard the sound of the wind increase, from a faint whisper into a steady breeze. The breeze began to intensify, like the sound of a sudden gust of wind pushing through leaves and branches. A moment later, the wind clapped outside like a storm had broken against the cliff wall. Farid and Gischane watched as their clothes fluttered in the wind howling through their cave, the dust swirling and being blown through the narrow space. The rocks shook, and the sound was unbearable, as they covered their ears to try to block it out. They listened, terrified, in wonder of what was happening outside. They heard the gigantic cracks of trees being torn down, their thick trunks protesting and then yielding with fierce explosions. The wind slowly abated, and several minutes later they were able to lower their hands from their ears. It was still loud, like a summer thunderstorm, the wind howling like an enraged beast that could not get at them inside the mine. The wind faded and then gradually ceased, and the two men listened for sounds from the outside world. They could hear nothing but that of their own breathing.

They listened patiently for hours, and heard nothing. Morosely, Farid turned off his helmet light shortly after ten 'o'clock, after they had decided it was best to try to get some sleep. The light dimmed and then went off, plunging them both back into isolating darkness.

They lay in the dark, and feared for what was.

They woke early, their nerves refusing to let them go back to sleep.

There were still no sounds from the outside.

"We have to dig." Farid said, without emotion. His voice was flat and tired. And so they began, piece by piece, stone by stone. The work was exhausting and painfully slow. They knew the stick had been pushed through to them, but they didn't know if it was four feet, or eight, or twelve. At the end of the first day, Gischane lay on the ground, his fingers curled in pain. His skin had dried and cracked in a few places from the arid dust, and several fingernails had been broken, splitting under the nail into the sensitive skin. Farid had fared no better, and he had begun to wrap his hands in cloth to keep the dry dust off his skin. The next day proceeded as had the first, with slow progress that was hard to measure. The rail cart had been filled with stones, and they had begun to pile the debris against the far rear wall. They agreed to work slowly to reduce the amount that they were sweating. They had a lot of water, but did not want to go through it rapidly. At the end of the third day, Farid had climbed through a body sized hole at the top of the pile, and dug himself through it with much discomfort. Every move he made seemed to get another sharp rock into his ribs, or elbow, or back. Gischane had sat on the ground, shaking with fever as he watched Farid worm his way into the stone. He had begun to cough, but it did nothing to improve his congestion. His throat was sore, and his breathing was shallow.

Farid had to see what had happened outside. Nothing he knew of could explain what they had heard and felt. He knew he had the best chance of success by climbing through the top of the pile to get to the other side. Gischane was getting very sick, and so could not easily do this himself. There may be pockets in the stone that would make his way possible. He also knew he risked being crushed from a rock fall that would pin him to the stones, but his brain tried to push that unpleasant outcome out of mind. He had climbed to the top of the incline, searched for what seemed to be a hopeful path, and had begun to dig his way into the stone. The progress was slow and difficult to measure, and intensely claustrophobic. He felt the stones on him at all sides, with just enough space to keep moving forward.

After considerable effort, he began to feel more air reach his face, but he could not see any sunlight. He pressed forward, and after a few more meters, the stones suddenly fell away before him, and he could see outside the cave. He could not believe his own eyes, and he stared at the desolation not comprehending what he saw. The day was black, as black as night. He could see thick clouds rolling overhead, but no moon, and no sun. A giant black sackcloth had been pulled over the sky. Of trees, all of them were gone save a few thin spires that protruded into the sky. All of the mature and old thick trees were gone, blown flat across the ground like play sticks. The stream at the bottom of the valley lay concealed under a dense blanket of trees and vegetation. He knew it was there, but he couldn't see any of it. Shattered trunks dotted the ground, in some cases still clinging to their trees that lay twisted and shredded on the ground. The few trees that remained standing had been stripped bare, not a leaf or branch to be seen. Of the camp, Farid could see nothing. Everything was gone. Only the massive red generator lay nearby, on its side and tens of meters from where it had been installed on its platform. It looked as though it had been abused by a giant as a plaything. In some places, the powder coating had been stripped from its surface, leaving bare metal. It was covered with massive dents and gashes. The ground of the camp had been stripped to bedrock.

All of the soil and undergrowth was gone, only bare rock remained. There was nothing else. Of his friends and co-workers, he could see no trace, and so he prayed in silence, hoping they were at peace.

About an hour later, Gischane saw a pair of feet working their way backwards through the top of the rubble, kicking some loose stones down the incline before them. He watched as Farid slid slowly down the incline feet-first. He remained hopeful, until he saw the look on his face. His tears had dried into nearly patches of clear skin, and his eyes were red and haggard. Gischane felt his stomach drop, and he feared the worst, feared asking what he had to ask.

"Tell me, Farid. A blind man could see the look on your face and know something terrible has happened. Tell me."

Farid sighed, as though wishing he could keep a great secret, or wake from a dream and find all of it untrue, his friends still outside.

"Everything is destroyed. *Everything.*" He clenched his fists as if trying to hold on to a great loss.

"There is no sky. Although my watch tells me it is the afternoon, there is no sky. It is as black as night, the blackest night I have ever seen. It is dark, like within this cave. I could see no moon, and no sun. The trees have been blown down. The *forest* has been destroyed. I looked to the farthest hill I could see, and almost every tree is gone. Those that remain have no branches or leaves. I could see only bare hills against the sky."

"The men? The camp?"

Farid shook his head slowly.

"They are surely all dead. The only thing I could see from the camp was the generator, and it looks like a soda can left lying in the street after children have played with it. No, they are all surely dead. I can only hope they died quickly."

They sat in utter silence. Farid sat in despair, his mind trying to digest the entirety of the horror he observed, and Gischane sat trying to picture the description he had heard. They did not try to dig any further that day.

When they awoke the next morning, they ate their breakfast and began to work again at the pile, enough to widen the top to allow them both to crawl through with greater ease. Gischane worked as long as he could in intervals, as long as his cold would permit before he felt too ill and needed to rest. Farid climbed back into the hole the rest of the time. By the end of the day, they were both satisfied with the size of the hole, and planned to make their way out the next day, along with their supplies.

"Does it feel warmer to you?" Farid asked Gischane.

Gischane only looked at him and shook his head. With his fever that had come back that night, he felt cold, although his body was pouring off waves of heat. When Farid was at the mouth of the tunnel, the air outside felt warm, like on a humid summer day when the air felt thick.

It was still black outside, and he could see nothing move. It just felt warmer. Before retiring for the night, he placed a few larger stones in the opening, angling them snugly into the cracks in case an animal tried to enter the cave during the night. He climbed down, and soon fell into a deep and dreamless sleep.

The next morning they were hopeful to be on the move, and yet concerned about what they might find. Farid was beginning to think that they shouldn't go anywhere until Joseph was feeling better. They had enough supplies to hold out for some time, the cave was good shelter. They ate breakfast, contemplating the day ahead, and then Farid unstopped the hole and climbed into it to see if anything had changed overnight. He came back through quickly. Gischane could sense his urgency.

"What is it?"

"Something new is happening, something else is wrong. It's hot outside. Much hotter than yesterday. I could feel the heat in the stones when I went forward, and when I got to the edge it felt like my head was near a stove. We can't go anywhere today."

He stopped up the hole, deeper than he had the night before, and they sat, playing cards, and talking.

"What do you think is wrong, Farid?"

He sat in silence for a moment, chewing his lip, thinking.

"I think we are witnessing the End of Days, my friend. I think we are witnesses to the judgment of God upon Man. The sky is as black as night. It was foretold."

Gischane was absorbed in thought.

"What do you think our loved ones are doing out there?"

"I think they are mostly dead. I have begun to pray for their souls. Every night and every morning, I pray for different people I have known. If you tell me people you know, I will pray for them tonight."

They talked through to the early hours of the morning, finding consolation in their beliefs.

Farid tried to go outside the next day, but only got half way through their tunnel. There was light coming through the tunnel that morning, but it was not warm yellow sunlight. It was red and orange, and the air had carried with it the smell of fire, of burning leaves and wood. The rocks he had placed in the opening were warm to the touch, and the air inside the cave was warmer as well. Gischane had stopped shivering, and looked to be recovering, as he was also coughing up phlegm. He stayed in the hole only a few minutes, before coming back down and plugging the cave shut.

"There are only flames outside. The world is burning. I couldn't get too far, but the little bit I saw, was on fire."

The next day the flames had died down, and the red light that had come through the rocks was gone. The sky was still black, and the air thick with smoke and soot. It was still hot, and they could not venture outside. The next several days were spent trapped inside the cave. Gischane's health had returned, and Farid rested a bit more than he had the previous few days while Joseph worked on the pile of stones.

They had begun to organize their foodstuffs to make them easier to fit the hole when the time came. They weren't too sure how to move the water, but they had time. The pile of stones came down, piece by piece. As it turned out, the rock fall was only eight feet wide at the top, and fourteen at the base. They were able to measure it once the outside temperature had dropped enough to become tolerable, and they renewed their attack on the rock pile, making steady progress as the hours passed. It took three days for them to clear the path through to the outside. On the second day it had begun to rain, and they could smell the air clear of soot and dust, a fresh smell that buoyed their spirits. They were not thinking long term, just the prospect of escaping the cave renewed their spirits and gave them hope. They slept their last night in the cave, satisfied that they were now able to move about upon their own free will.

They had ventured briefly outside to where the forest once stood, and found themselves standing deep in charred ashes. Of the forest, there was nothing. A few charred stumps sat on the ground, and nothing smaller had survived the firestorm. The generator was a blackened husk that had exploded when the diesel fuel within it had reached critical temperature, splitting the metal frame like tinfoil. The sky remained black, and walking about was a slow and cautious process as it was difficult to see where they were stepping. They used their helmets sparingly, using the batteries cautiously now that they were no longer stuck in the cave. They had tried to drink some of the rainwater that was collecting in pools on the ground, only to find it was bitter and sulphuric, leaving an awful taste in the mouth and an increased thirst, so they avoided it. It was a little brighter outside, enough to see shapes and outlines and get about, not like the deep blackness of the mine. They spent the evening dividing the food between the two of them, portioning what they liked and didn't like to keep it as fair as possible, and then pumping water into their canteens and a few plastic containers. The second barrel would remain untouched, as would the food still in crates that they couldn't carry.

"What are you planning on doing?" he asked Farid.

"I am going east. I have to try to get home, to see if anyone survived. You?"

I would like to go west, for the same reason. I fear I already know the answer." His eyes filled with tears, which he wiped away.

"My family is dead, I know it in my heart, I feel it in my soul. They are beyond this world and its worries, so I must rejoice for them, as certainly as they mourn for me. I have nothing here anymore."

He remained silent for a moment, looking at the ground.

"I will go east with you, if you will have me. Together we are stronger than if we go alone. I will help you seek your loved ones, for better or worse."

Farid put out his hand, and Gischane put out his, they clasped their hands and shook them, gaining strength and confidence in the gesture.

"We will go together, as men and brothers."

"*Inshallah*," whispered Gischane. Farid nodded.

"God willing," whispered Farid.

The next morning dawned as dark as the previous. It seemed a little brighter, the certainty of leaving, of seeing what was beyond had cheered their spirits, even among the desolation and ruin they faced.

They had begun the day with breakfast, and a morning prayer where they asked for blessing and strength to see them through the challenges ahead. They wrote their names deep within the mine on the smoothest part of wall they could find.

Gischane Camara and Farid Gharani
Departed December 29, 2012

They pulled their bags over their shoulders, two worn packs encrusted with dust and mud left behind after a previous days work.

Gischane carried a third pack that they agreed to take turns carrying. They did not know what to expect, and so brought everything they could carry. Gischane had wrapped his itchy wool blanket around his shoulders, the pack keeping it securely around him and off the wet ground. The longest journey begins with but a single step, and they took that step together out into the ruins of the land. The rain had abated, relenting into the occasional drizzle that was enough to keep the skin cool although it evaporated quickly from their body heat. The ground was black, soaked with the ashes and coals of the fires that had raged over the ground. Here and there they saw small whispers of steam issuing from the ground. Farid kicked at one, throwing up a pile of ash and soot before uncovering a pocket of white-hot coals still baking in a sheltered pocket in the ground. A flurry of glowing embers floated up into the sky where the moist air quickly doused them, the coals in the ground hissing and turning red as they cooled.

They saw nothing else moving on the ground. A few birds flew overhead from time to time, going from the burnt husk of one tree to another. The sight of other life cheered them, giving them hope of finding more. They stuck to higher ground, trying to stay on the top of the ridges to keep clear of the deepest pockets of debris that they had no hope of easily navigating. The valley floor was buried in burned trees and ashes, the gullies packed with the remains of the forest, piled where the fierce wind had piled everything like a irresistible broom. The hilltops were stripped bare, denuded of anything larger than a charred patch of grass. The walking was treacherous, the ground slick and greasy. After a few missteps and near falls, they had tied a short rope around each other's waist for added support. Farid took the lead position for the first while, his helmet the only source of bright light as they were keen on preserving their batteries for as long as possible. Where the ground had not been stripped bare and was cool, mushrooms and other fungi were sprouting and growing under ideal conditions. They could feel them popping under their feet where they could not step around them, the rubbery stalks crushing easily. As they walked, they had recognized a few that were edible, and so added to their diet that one fresh food source. The view from the tops of the hills was the same, nothing but darkness in all directions, the earth barren and charred. At each crest there was the inward hope of seeing something hopeful, only to see more of the same. There were still some birds, and insects were about. They were attracted to the helmet lamp, and flew around it, landing on their shoulders and heads or flying straight into them. If the ground was clear, they began to keep the light off for short periods to gain a reprieve from the bugs that would fly away, having nothing more to attract them. Without their watch, they would have had no concept of time. The first day they had walked until midnight, an experiment to see if there was a difference in brightness between the sky during the day, and at night. It was slight, but the day was a little brighter, enough to see shadows and outlines better, but little else. Everything in the world was shades of black without the lamp.

They had spent their first night under a windblown palm that had been covered over with other large trees, creating a small charred cave. The trees were burned through to the core, the charcoal remains holding fast, but brittle. Gischane had stuck a knife into a deep fissure of the tree, the sound like twisting Styrofoam, a squeaky shrill sound, and twisted the blade. A large piece had come free, crumbling into bits under his fingers as he ground it in his hand.

The fires had been intense, the heat incredible, to have burned so deeply. The shelter and protection provided in the cave had been fortunate. They passed large boulders that had once rested in the forest shade that had split in the heat, the sharp shards lying around the stony core that had blackened in the heat. The night under the palm passed quickly, their bodies collapsing in exhaustion from their long walk of the day. They were also mentally tired, from being continuously scouring the land with their eyes, trying to see things and find their way. They roused late the next morning, having no sunlight to tell their bodies to wake up. They ate quickly, and got underway, climbing back to the top of the hill and slowly working their way to the east. The next few days saw more of the same. They found whatever shelter they could in the ruins when it was time to sleep, they ate whatever mushrooms they could find, and they rationed their supplies. The rain was consistent, it was either drizzling, or it was pouring; it hadn't stopped for days. The lightening storms were incredible, the clouds discharging electrical displays as they had never seen before. Huge white bolts cracked from the sky, the ground trembling with deep waves of thunder. Their eyes flashed with the image afterglow, unused to the bright light that would suddenly illuminate the landscape. Other times, the lightening seemed to dance in the sky, a colorful web that crossed from one cloud to another, tracing overhead light bright spider webs. The lightening was beautiful to watch, but it made their passing more hazardous. When they were on the top of a ridge, they were the tallest things on them, and so were naturally the shortest distance for a lightening bolt to trace from the sky. When there was a storm, which was common lately, they were forced to get below the ridge for their own safety. Tied together, they would both likely perish in a lightening strike. Even worse, one might survive. Walking in this land, they were glad to have the companionship. To walk alone would seem to be walking through Hell itself.

The air was getting colder. Gischane had commented that morning to Farid.

"Good for us we brought the blanket. Last night I found myself getting chilled."

Farid had agreed. The first few nights they had slept alone in the dark, the warmth in the air still present and comfortable. The previous evening they had come close in the night to share body heat, and instinctual reaction and seeking for warmth. Only then were they warm enough to sleep deeply without waking feeling cold.

The mushrooms had also begun to slow, the ground was covered with their caps and root systems, but they were losing the vitality of their earlier spread across the ground. The bugs were more sluggish as well, and small burrows could be seen where the insects were digging themselves into the ground.

"If it keeps getting colder, we are going to be in trouble." Gischane said aloud. Farid stayed quiet, but had heard him clearly, his concerns echoing Gischane's. It kept getting colder, by matter of a little bit every day. The cumulative effect was more noticeable than the daily effect.

"Did you realize we spent Christmas in the cave? I had completely forgotten about the date when we in there. It came to me this morning."

"Yes I thought about that as well. I also forgot."

He had meant to get gifts for his camp for the holiday, something to recognize the Christians that worked for him, and something to give his Muslim workers to show his appreciation as well. It didn't matter anymore, it seemed.

"How far do you think we have walked so far?" Gischane asked.

Farid was silent for a moment, as he listened to their footsteps over the ground.

"I would think we have gone about one hundred and eighty kilometers. We have been walking twelve hours a day, or more, for five days, so if we average three per hour, that's an estimate. I don't know if we have been doing three kilometers an hour. And since we are not going due east, but following the hill tops, we haven't travelled that distance at all. We are probably getting close to Mali. We should reach the Niger River if we can recognize it. We can follow it north into Mali, and then it goes east. When it turns south, we can keep east, or follow it south through Nigeria to the ocean."

"What do you think we should do?"

"Let's follow it east as far as it goes, and decide then."

It sounded good, and they needed a plan to give them purpose.

The terrain slowly flattened out as they left the interior of the country, the hillsides yielding to countryside more amenable to walking.

They reached the river two days later. They cold hear the water flowing, but it was difficult to see. The surface was a chaotic jumble of dead trees jamming the length of the river, creating huge log jams that cracked and groaned in the dark like gunshots, only to be replaced by the roaring of released water. They could not pass, but were forced to follow the western shoreline. They had hopes to find a passable bridge, but were not optimistic. The heights of the log jams were likely to have undercut any bridge, tearing it down into the river with it. Where the water had pooled, they had stopped for a drink. The water was bitter, like the rain, and left the mouth feeling dry.

The shoreline was littered with dead fish and the occasional crocodile. The corpses were raw and bloated, having escaped the fires that had torched the land.

"What do you think got the crocodiles?" Farid wondered aloud.

"Some were probably killed by the logs in the river, others the fire probably did kill but the bodies sunk."

The fish evidently could not tolerate the water. Most fish. They did not see any catfish or lungfish. Around the fish and bloated crocodiles, small scavenging birds had collected, and feasted on the scraps. They had even passed by the crushed body of a hippo, its bodily mutilated and pummeled, bloated and distended as it decomposed. They were tempted to try some of the meat, but had no means to cook it, and they did not want to risk food poisoning.

They noted there were no large birds. Typically, large animals were covered with vultures and other large birds of prey. Their conspicuous absence confirmed what they had assumed in their walk. Nothing large had survived the disaster, except what was sheltered from the wind and fire. Their own survival was fortunate, a blessing in what otherwise could have been a tragedy. Farid no longer had faith that his loved ones had survived. He had wept for their loss the previous night, mourning their passing while

Gischane had been there to lend his support and understanding. Their walk had become more of an expedition to find somewhere that was better, more habitable than where they had come from.

They walked for three more days, and came to the point where the river curved off in a southerly direction. They had found nothing. The sky remained black, and they had found nothing living beyond insects and a few smaller birds. They had slept near the shores and wondered what to do next. Their food and water was down to half of what they had packed with them. It was becoming difficult to keep optimistic. They had decided to retrace their steps back to the mine, where at the very least they knew there was more food and water. It was not a permanent solution, but they would last longer there than they would out in the countryside.

Fixing their bags across their backs, they had turned and began to retrace their steps westward. They felt better for the decision, knowing they had somewhere to go where they knew there were supplies. They walked silent in the dark, absorbed in their thoughts.

Farid, by turning around, had settled in his mind that his loved ones were dead, and so a large part of his silence was due to his grief that he kept bottled up, refusing to let it vent for the time being.

"What are we going to do once we get to the cave?" he asked.

"We will rest a bit, and refill our supplies. We should continue to go west, to the sea. There at least we may be able to fish for food."

So they walked, each step blending in with the last, forgotten in a long procession. It took them four days to get back to where they had originally found the river, the path westward slightly uphill and more tiring with their subdued spirits. When they returned to the hippo carcass, it had burst, its internal gasses finally becoming too much for its weakened rotting flesh. The stink was enormous, and they had to cover their noses from the stench. A logjam had burst since they had last passed, and they had walked into a narrow rivulet where the logs had finally come to rest, blocking their way. The height of the logjam had surprised them. They had merely walked, seeing the logs at their sides, slowly growing higher, until they could go no further, the pile blocking their way.

Gischane climbed his way up the first log, going cautiously and feeling for a secure footing before he went further. He kept climbing, reaching the highest log on the crest. Two trees had come together at the top, forming a bridge leading down to safer ground below. He could barely see Farid on the ground.

"Come on Farid. I can see the way from here. Take your time."

He sat and waited at the top, listening for Farid to make the climb. He enjoyed looking out at the view, finding the height pleasant. There was little to look at that he hadn't already seen, but the perspective was interesting. He heard Farid scrabbling up the side beneath him, a few loose pieces of burnt wood cracking and breaking off. He put down his arm, felt Farid grab it, and he pulled while Farid climbed the remaining distance. They stood together, looking at the view below.

Gischane had gone first down the tree bridge, keeping his feet on the wider of the two trees, using his arms outspread to balance his walk. The trees were not burned through owing to being in the river, and were still quite springy. He walked down the slope slowly, sliding his feet along the surface as opposed to taking steps, fearing slipping off and falling into whatever he could not see in the shade below. He reached the end, and jumped off the tree onto a dirt pile at nearly the same height. His feet sank into the dirt a few inches, and he stepped out feeling it cling to his boots, the suction of the earth letting go grudgingly. He found another tree lying on the ground and sat down, waving Farid to follow.

"Go slow, Farid. Don't step, slide your feet."

Farid waved, and began. Gischane could see the tree bend under his weight as he made his way across. His arms were also out for balance. He noticed that he was walking on both of the trees, instead of just one, his legs spread partially, each tree taking his weight as he shuffled down the length. Something seemed dangerous about that to Gischane; there was some reason he didn't do it that way. He shuffled across, and he could see more pieces falling away from the logs as he went.

Farid was a little over half way when it all went wrong. He had shuffled a little further, his right leg on the right tree, his left leg shuffling on the left tree, when the trees suddenly pushed apart.

The sideways pressure of his steps found a weak point, where the springiness of the trees and his weight overcame what held them close together. For a split second he watched as the trees began to roll apart, Farid waving his hands frantically for balance and then falling forward to grab something, anything, before he fell. He managed to grab hold of one tree, and he clung to it desperately.

"HELP GISCHANE HELP ME IT'S SLIPPERY!"

Gischane made his way to the tree and began to walk up it. He could hear Farid frantically trying to keep a hold onto the wet tree, loose bits coming free in his grip, his breathing was panicked and gasping. He made it halfway to Farid, when he suddenly dropped into the dark below, screaming as he fell. There was no desperate grab, no last second scramble for a better hold. His hands simply slipped from one moment to the next, suddenly holding onto nothing but air. He heard a sickening crack as he landed, and the scream stopped suddenly. He heard nothing else.

"Farid!" he yelled into the dark.

"Farid!"

Nothing.

He shuffled down the log hastily, nervously certain he was going too fast and would suffer the same fate, falling headfirst to the ground below. He pulled off his pack, leaving it on the log he was sitting on, and went back to the hole. He turned around, and lay on his belly, and began to slide backwards down the slope. Anyone knows how terrifying it is to go down a hill backwards, feeling for purchase with your feet, hoping to God there is something below and you aren't going to get stuck hanging from a precipice, only to eventually let go from exhaustion and fall to your death. He went slowly, kicking his feet out to find a purchase, holding on to the ground with his hands, peeling back a fingernail with exquisite pain. He reached the bottom covered in sweat and shaking with exhaustion. He couldn't see anything.

"Farid?" he whispered.

He reached forward, trusting his hands where his eyes failed him. He felt along several smaller trees and logs, a few rounded boulders, and then cloth. He felt upwards, following what must be a leg, up to the head. He felt his chest for breathing. It did not rise. He ran his hands upwards, and felt his neck loose in his grip, feeling the grinding of broken bones through his skin.

He felt his hands over his face, closing open eyes that did not see. "Be at peace, my friend."

Feeling around, he found a small clearing of ground. He pulled the body from the tangle of trees, and laid Farid to rest on the earth. It did not seem right to leave him lying where he fell. When he had positioned the body in the opening, he crossed the arms over the chest, and covered him as best as he could with a larger shirt from inside his bag. He did not want to sacrifice his blanket with the cool nights ahead. He stood above the resting place for a few minutes to respect the dead, praying for his soul and blessing. Satisfied he had done all he could do, he pulled his bag over his shoulders and began to seek a way out.

He first tried the edge of the hill itself from where he had slowly slid down. The steep and wet earth gave him no purchase, and he quickly realized he would not be climbing up the way he had come down. He felt back into the tangles of trees and debris, and looked upwards against the slightly brighter backdrop of the sky. He could see patches of sky, and dark lines where trees lay piled one on top of the other like a pile of pick up sticks.

He stepped up, and began to pull himself upwards through the tangle. At first, he had made good progress, climbing up and finding good clearings where he could get his body through with ease. Then the debris pile thickened, or gave no areas where he could get a decent enough grip to feel comfortable and proceed without falling himself. He was forced to crawl horizontally and diagonally through the pile, pushing and pulling himself in between the holes in the logjam. He could feel cuts burning in his skin where sharp pieces of broken wood scratched and lacerated his skin, and he became more and more afraid that he was going to get himself into a corner that he could not get out of, and starve to death trapped in a maze of wood. He had to stop and eat when he came to a larger pocket that he could pull his entire body into in a squatting position. It was not comfortable, sitting on a few hard pieces of wet wood with his knees crammed up to his chest, as he fed food into his mouth, and chewed in the dark. He felt his strength slowly returning, and his confidence when the hunger passed. After a struggle to put the bag back on, he straightened out his body and resumed his struggle. After what seemed like hours, he could feel more wind reaching his face, and the thickest parts of the piles seemed to be behind him; the openings becoming easier to navigate, with a few spots where he was able to pull himself directly upwards.

And then he had found himself on the top, his face free, the feeling of clear sky overhead. He paused there for a moment, feeling the relaxation come across him that he was not going to die trapped in the logs. He squirmed his way to the top, cutting his leg again as his patience gave out and he had fought against a snag, just pulling to get out. The pain felt good.

He stood on top of the pile to allow his muscles to stretch and bend after being confined for so long, and he looked for a way off the pile back onto solid ground. He walked across the top like a crab, using all fours to keep a solid footing as he searched to make sure he wouldn't fall into a hole he couldn't see. He finally came to a large thick palm that had popped to the surface of the jam, and its top had come to rest leaning on a slight incline to the crest of the hill. There were no other logs near it, so he didn't feel comfortable to stand and walk up the tree. Instead, he lowered himself and crawled as long as he could along the thickest part of the base, eventually sliding himself along the narrowing mid and top section, hugging the tree as his legs and arms wrapped around it as far as they could and he pulled himself along on his belly. It was slow going, and after a while his testicles ached from the constant pressure, but he could see his progress. Eventually he came ot the end, and he awkwardly pulled himself off the tree back to solid ground. He walked along the crest, and after ten minutes found his bag at the top of the hill that he had slid down hours earlier. He emptied Farid's bag into his own, and then folded it neatly into his own, not wanting to discard it. He looked into the pit one last time, and then turned around, and continued to the west.

Without company, the time passed slowly, each step crunching into the earth, the sound of his own breathing driving himself slowly but surely mad. Almost as if he needed proof he was, he began to talk to himself, hearing his own voice far better than nothing else. He sang a few songs he had learned from his university days to pass the time, coming to a few verses where he had forgotten the lines and hummed his way to the next verse that he did remember. The worst part about being alone was that he found his mind could not, or would not, stop thinking. And his thoughts tended to swing into more pessimistic thoughts, the devastation around him contributing heavily to his negative miasma.

He had seen no other human beings, alive or dead, or any other large animal, and he was beginning to wonder what his actual odds were. And he had to wonder to what had happened to cause the destruction. The earthquake had saved his life, he knew that for certain; the rubble pile that had trapped him so neatly in the cave had sheltered him from the wind and the firestorm that had burned everything to charcoal. It must be a volcano. Some freakish huge eruption had taken place, something with no warning that had wiped out large areas. It made sense; it explained the windstorm. It must have been the pyroclastic flow from the explosion.

The earthquake was the eruption itself, and the firestorm was the fallout from the sky. The darkness of the sky could also be explained by the eruption cloud climbing up into the atmosphere and then spreading. Still, for a volcano, this would have to be one of the worst that had ever happened, and no one had any kind of warning about it at all. There were huge volcanoes in the world that had this kind of potential; Yellowstone in the United States was a prime example. There was a volcano that covered hundreds of square kilometers; its' magma chamber swelling the ground by meters, fueling the Old Faithful geyser, and very few people gave it any kind of thought as to what would happen when it finally erupted. After all, it was not an extinct volcano, only dormant. Only it was too far away to burn, what seemed to be, a large piece of the African continent. Yellowstone would destroy a large piece the United States, but it would have much less impact across the Atlantic. Therefore, that must mean that a similar sized volcano had been dormant in Africa, and it had finally blown its top. It just didn't seem right, though.

He knew the enormity of it was difficult to comprehend with little or no frame of reference. How can you think something like this could be possible, unless you had lived it? Well, he was living it, so it was obviously possible. There had been an eruption far back in the history of Earth that was probably similar to what this was like. It was massive;

another word not existing that could describe it better. He remembered it from his geology classes, an eruption almost a quarter of a billion years ago, in Siberia. In that case, a magma plume had worked its way to the surface, and then had come through, the resulting explosion releasing huge amounts of ash and steam, and over a million cubic kilometers of lava over the area. He remembered that over ninety-five percent of the life on Earth had perished from the eruption, in the Permian and Triassic era. The extinction of the larger creatures at that time opened the niche in biology that allowed the Dinosauria to emerge. There wasn't a great deal of consensus about how long the eruption took to occur, perhaps over a hundred thousand years, to upwards of a million years. Either way, it was fast geologically speaking, and most forms of life couldn't adapt. It was the only eruption scenario that made sense to him.

He thought about it for days as he trekked west. He had to make it to the coast. In the ocean, at least, there was a better chance he could find food. Whatever he had faced earlier, he had come to settle on a few new priorities. He had to find food and shelter. Some food was at the cave, enough to last a little longer, certainly enough to get to the coast.

Once there, he needed to find shelter, and once established, find other people. He wondered what the survival rate had been from the explosion. The survivors would have had to survive the earthquake, which meant ideally not being indoors. Secondly, they had to survive the fires, which meant they needed shelter for days. To have survived this long, they would have needed to find food and water, that had been sheltered from the fire. The percentages rolled in his head like dice, the chances of survival getting lower and lower as he did the calculations.

One thing in particular troubled him, and that was he had not seen any planes or indications of people at all. Assuming an eruption of Triassic proportions had occurred in Africa, it meant that Europe and Asia and the Americas should be relatively intact. They would be dark, and concerned about how to feed millions and billions of people when crops were certain to fail, but they were still there. He couldn't accept mentally that those parts of the world had seemingly abandoned Africa. It would make sense to occasionally see a plane fly overhead that was perhaps there to document the eruption for history, to take samples and look for survivors as the research took place. However, he hadn't seen anything. Not so much as flashing lights in the sky from a distance. The only light he saw in the sky was lightening. That part didn't make sense. He wondered what was going to happen to civilization. He knew what was going to happen in the short term; he was wondering long term.

Millions and possibly billions of people were literally going to starve to death as the world ran out of food. Probably every large animal in the sea and on the land would go extinct. The world was going to experience a fundamental shift in biology and ecology. All of a sudden the oil crisis, the global warming crisis, the population crisis was solved. Mother Nature had taken care of everything, nearly overnight. For humans to survive, they had to find food, wherever they could, and that likely meant cannibalism in some areas. The thin veneer that covered the primordial ape was going to be pulled back, revealing the beast underneath, with survival of the fittest becoming the dominant factor. Or, survival of the most ruthless.

People that were able to abandon caring for their fellow man, and focus on themselves and their families were the ones most likely to survive. People that would kill other people to feed their families, nature red in tooth and claw. Sociologically it would be very interesting, to see how survivors reacted with other survivors. Initially there would be happiness, as people are gregarious, we don't like to be alone. That would last as long as food and water was available; the basic needs of survival were being met. Once those ran low, conditions were likely to change.

The old and the infirm would be the first to go. Unless they had skills that aided in survival, they would be seen as a burden very quickly. The human race was going to be reset to a time when its most valuable members were younger, smart, and of prime breeding age.

If survivors were able to find each other and form groups, these groups would be very wary of others, and highly suspicious. It was likely that the human penchant for murder and war would not be resolved by the disaster; it would be nurtured and fed. The groups would have to remain small, to be able to forage for enough food. When the skies cleared, and seeds began to germinate, the groups could become farmers again, and civilization could once again take hold. He wondered if he would live long enough to see that happen. His specialized education suddenly meant very little. His net worth to the species was his youth and intelligence.

In the darkness it was very difficult to see what kind of progress was being made; only dark outlines of hills on the horizon gave any noticeable indication of the distance or bearings. He kept the highest hill in the distance as close to the center of his path as he could, knowing it would lead him back into the foothills that turned into the winding valley that led to the mine.

He arrived at the cave a week later, his bags empty and his stomach growling for food. He still felt strong, and the long walk and self-reflection had motivated him, giving him strength to push forward. He knew what he had to do. Whatever had happened, whatever the conditions were elsewhere, he had to survive. At all costs, he had to survive. He stumbled into the cave, the blanket wrapped around his shoulders to help keep him warm. It had begun to snow lightly, the ground covered with just a light dusting, enough to look beautiful after staring at the dark ground for so long. The cave floor was dry and dusty, and he could see small tracks in the fine dirt. Small tracks that led to the back of the cave.

He pulled his helmet from his bag, and turned on the light. He squinted painfully for a minute, his eyes already unused to the brightness. He walked quickly, following the tracks. They were very small, from rodents most likely, and he was suddenly very concerned about his food supply. The tracks led to the pile of wooden crates, and small piles of sawdust where the crates had been chewed through to get at the food inside. He quickly unstacked them, piling the canned food to one side to get at the dried food. Every case of dried food had been chewed into, rodent droppings littering the insides of the boxes. The dried fruit was nearly gone, and the other foods had also been looked into. The flour and bread, the seeds, sugar, all had been spoiled. He groaned and then yelled.

"NOOOOO!" he screamed, the narrow cave amplifying his voice and carrying it outside. It was not ideal, but he could not waste the food regardless of what he found. He would have to risk the rodents had not contaminated what was left. Food had become too scarce a commodity.

He spent a few hours organizing what was left of the cache, refilling his canteens, and sorting through the food to prioritize what was left.

His ideal supplies were canned, and whatever had the most fat and carbohydrates. He needed whatever could give him the most energy possible. Afterwards, he made a large meal out of what was left, which was still too much for him to carry alone. He ate until he felt he was going to burst, his stomach more full than it had been for several weeks. He rested a while, letting his large meal settle, staring at the carving on the wall made only a couple of weeks earlier when he had left the cave with Farid. It seemed now a cruel reminder of the situation, whereas before it had been a symbol of hope.

He went through the food one last time, putting aside enough for a large breakfast the next day. Taking the remaining food stores, he went to the mouth of the mine, where the ground remained dry under a small ledge in the ceiling, and he dumped the food onto the ground, opening cans and shaking out the contents in neat small piles. The dried food he left in their crates, figuring if they had already chewed through the wood, they could use the holes they had already made. Maybe it would provide something with a little shelter or nest, if it came to that.

"Eat up, little guys," he said aloud. He had decided that if he was not going to benefit from the food, it would be a shame to leave it sealed so nothing else could use it. It made him feel a little better inside, knowing that he would be helping something else stay alive, even something as little as a rodent. He had thought about saving the food in case he had to return, but he had decided that he could not return. To return was fatal. There was no food nearby, so he would certainly die here. When he left in the morning, he would leave for the last time. To remove the temptation, he had to make sure there was no food to return to. And if it benefitted something else that was alive, then so much the better. This done, he returned to a deeper part of the mine, and piled up some clothes on the floor, and settled himself into it. He felt his warmth seep into the pile quickly, retaining his heat. He quickly nodded off to sleep, and what he dreamt of he could not remember.

The next day dawned, as had the previous. He had simply woken up when he had enough sleep, to the sky that must be day because it wasn't totally black. He had to urinate terribly, and he ran to the outside, where he took aim against the outside cliff and relieved himself. He shivered once, feeling the heat of the clothes he slept in dissipate in the cool air. No sooner was he done, than he needed to do other business. He looked around out of habit, and remembered that no one was going to be watching him. It was then he saw how much snow had fallen as he slept. The cliff had kept the opening of the mine relatively free of the stuff, but farther away, it was now a few inches deep, with only the sides of larger rocks still being visible on the ground. Using his hand, he scooped out a little cavity and squatted. He finished, covering the product with some snow, and went back to the cave. He noticed there were a few more tracks in the dust, the small piles of food having been found and nibbled on in the night. There weren't many, only maybe a couple, but it was better than nothing. He wasn't completely alone in the dark. He couldn't see them, but he felt better knowing they were out there.

Gischane ate his breakfast down to the last morsel and scrap, emptying the can entirely and licking his spoon, which he then threw into the dust. He wrapped himself in the clothes on the floor, stuffing the remainder that would fit into his bag, or tied around his waist. He then wrapped the blanket around his body, adjusting his bags, and then he left the cave without looking back. He strolled into the darkness purposefully, feeling confident and with a mission. The sound of his footsteps quickly faded in the wet snow, and he soon vanished from sight.

When the sound was gone, the mouse came out from behind the rock where it had been dozing. It sniffed the ground thoroughly, smelling food and making its way over to where the scents were coming from.

It found the piles, and ate its fill, grooming itself with its forepaws when it was finished, not stopping until it was satisfied that it was clean. It ran back along the wall, and followed its path on the ground to its burrow. It followed the narrow run quickly, the small hole filled with its scent and comfortable.

Coming to the end, it dug itself into a small pile of feathers and grasses, uncovering its pink hairless young, who squeaked excitedly at her scent. They crawled to her warm body and began to nurse as she lay on her side, and slept.

Gischane kept going. He couldn't afford to stop. He had been walking for days and the snow had continued to fall. Sometimes it fell in sporadic amounts, and other times it fell thick from the sky. The snow had begun to accumulate in significant amounts, deep drifts concealing depressions in the ground. He would be walking along, breaking trail in snow up to his shins, and then the next step cloud have him buried up to his waist. The initial beauty the snow had in concealing the dark ground was gone, long forgotten. The temperature continued to drop, and he was always cold. It was difficult to find places to sleep in that could provide shelter, or some degree of dryness from the wet ground. Other times he was forced to sleep on the ground, exposed to the elements. He tried to find a snowdrift or log to break the wind or retain some measure of his body heat to make the night pass just a little more easily. He always felt cold. The wool blanket had been a lifesaver, keeping moisture away from him that otherwise would have soaked through to his skin. As it was, he didn't feel good. He couldn't remember how many days it had been since he left the mine. Was it the third or fourth day he had come across the car? His memory was foggy and incomplete. The car had been a burned out shell, the roof sagging in from the heat that had burnt it down to bare metal. If there had been people inside, they were ashes lying in the remains of all that was around it. He thought it was the seventh day he had come to the road. The road was flat and covered in snow, and it made walking easier. He had come across the wreck of a bus, although he did not know it was the same one that had driven him to the roadside months earlier, depositing him into the jungle to begin his mining adventure. The bus lay at the foot of a hill, where the roof had been crushed in, the bus nearly bent in half. It looked as though it had been picked up and thrown against the hillside, and bent around a rocky outcropping before being dropped to the ground and then burned. He looked around the bus out of curiosity, and peeked under the undercarriage.

A charred skeleton greeted him, the darkened ribcage silhouetted against the snow. The skull was shattered, having exploded as the brains trapped inside had boiled feverishly, and then blew outwards from the pressure within. He stopped looking, and kept going, his lone footprints the only mark on the road.

He felt like he was getting another cold, and that really scared him. Sleeping outside in these kind of conditions could eventually lead to him suffering from exposure, but he had hoped to reach the coast where he could find shelter and recuperate. If he caught a cold, he risked pneumonia or something else that wouldn't wait for his plans.

He thought back, trying to think of where he must be.

"Six, or seven?" he mumbled, trying to remember something in particular that would give him an idea of where he was. He left the hills and began to descend into the lowlands where the snow fall was lighter, and his pace a little faster. He could feel he was going down slope, so he knew he was getting closer, he just didn't know how close. In the distance he could see the ground became very bumpy and cluttered, with mounds of debris piled wide and deep over the end of the valley, where the foothills began. When he came to the area, he found it was a huge mixture of rubble. There was bent metal beams, piles of shattered brick and concrete, huge stones, and vehicles of all makes, all piled together and mixed in with one another, like someone had taken a huge broom and swept everything together. He walked past a few boats that had been near the top of the piles, seemingly randomly thrown into the mix for good measure. It took him two days to navigate the field, but he was thankful to sleep inside the ruins of vehicles for the two nights, as rough as the form of shelter was. He had actually been walking for two weeks, the days and nights blurring into the next until they were indistinguishable from the next. And so he was surprised when he looked up from the road and found the ruin of a shattered wall to his left. He looked around further, and everywhere he looked he saw the remains of houses and buildings, piles of rubble buried under a blanket of snow. There weren't too many cities on the coast, and he had no way of knowing which one he was in.

"HELLO?" he yelled into the dark. There was no response; only the distant sounds of waves washing ashore. He kept walking, but now with his head up, calling into the remains of the city. He passed a taller building that had so far resisted collapsing. It was surrounded by mounds of twisted metal and jagged concrete that had surrendered. The standing building was a hollow shell, twisted and bent on a slight angle to the right, to the east. The ends of the metal beams sagged, bearing mute witness to the intense heat that they had experienced. As he walked further, he began to notice that there was nothing small on the ground. Whatever remained of the city was in large pieces, and seemed to be piled high against structures that did not fail. The base of the building that was sagging was littered with a few buses and cars, all stacked on the seaward side.

The thought hit him quickly, explaining the strange deposits he was seeing. Tsunami. The city had been hit by a tidal wave, washing and tearing the city to pieces, depositing the remains wherever objects had held. It also made sense why he had walked into the city and hadn't noticed. Most of it had been carried away, and lay buried under snow. He was seeing the protruding foundations of larger buildings that had enough reinforcement to bear more violence and destruction. He remained vigilant, and at last came to the sea. It broke upon the shore as it always had; the washing sound of the rocks and water together comforting, a familiar sound. The ocean gave no indication of its former fury, the waves low and quiet with only a light wind coming ashore. Looking up and down the lengths of the beach, he could see a few places where some wood pylons barely protruded above the waves, the anchors of docks that had been peeled away in the surge. Fish littered the beach in all sizes, some bloated and rotten, others still fresh. Birds were feeding on the remains on the beach, keeping a wary eye on him as he walked along the shore, never letting him get too close. He coughed a few times, feeling his lungs ache, and he spat out a mouthful of mucous. He needed to find somewhere to sleep, to rest. He walked back towards the ruins of the city, leaving the beach behind him. He was tempted to get some of the fresher fish, but he didn't want to eat them raw. He had to try to build a fire if he wanted to cook something. His food stores were getting very low; he had just a few days worth left in his bag. He shuffled down the street, looking for the remains of a building that offered some shelter from the wind and falling snow.

He came across a metal sign that was banging against its post in the wind, twisted slowly like a kite on its chain. The sign was dented and bent, having been twisted around the post at some point with huge force.

362

The paint had been nearly burned off the metal, but the sign had left an imprint on the thin metal. He could read *spital,* the remains of a large H still faintly visible underneath. The large foundations had been neatly stripped away, the hospital removed from the ground leaving only the footprint of its base, with a few small corners that had resisted the destruction. He inspected the corners, finding them low and not providing a break from the snow. He kept on walking, a few hundred meters later coming to a corner where the former building had been built on an angle, so the structure had been able to resist the waves better. The remaining brick was a few feet tall, and covered a few feet to either side. Hopeful, he climbed behind the walls to test it. He found quickly it was very open to wind, the breeze swirling in the gap where he sat. He moved on, coming to a few high rises that had not yet fallen. The outer walls had come off and been carried away, exposing the structural skeleton within. Here and there the concrete floors had broken, revealing the rebar within, the thin steel hanging down and twisted. On the surrounding blocks he could see where other buildings had already come down, some apparently in the tidal wave itself as the wreckage was leaning away from the shore, the waves pulling the falling building with them. Other piles were rounded and straight, having collapsed afterwards and falling straight down, the floors pancaking as they went. He could see nothing else large in the distance, nothing worth checking out.

Against his better judgment he went towards one of the buildings that stood straight, examining it as he approached. If he wanted out of the rain and snow, he had no other choice but to shelter in the standing ruins. He walked into the ruins, and into the dry ground floor. It felt warmer already, proving to be a windbreak as well as giving cover overhead. He went to the middle of the building, where the elevator shafts were, the doors partially open. He tried the first door, trying to push the doors apart and get inside. The doors were only wide enough apart for him to get his hands in between them, and they refused to budge. He went to the second shaft, where the door opening was wide enough for him to get his body in between the two doors. He braced himself, and pushed, groaning with the effort. The doors moved slightly with a squeal, then stopped. He took a deep breath and pushed harder. The doors suddenly relented, and he fell back against them as they slid in their track. He had no way of closing them, but this shelter was better than anything he had seen.

He put his bags down, and snuggled into the corner, feeling his muscles ache and burn. He was getting sick, he could feel it. His body ached and he felt stuffy, his thinking unclear and foggy. He lay in the dark, his eyes closed, trying to sleep, feeling his body shiver.

When he slept, his dreams were feverish, and he woke several times screaming into the dark.

"Farid!" he yelled, sitting up abruptly, swearing he could see him sitting in the elevator next to him, or walking around in the ruins.

In other dreams he was at school, or in his apartment studying. The dreams were incredibly detailed and vivid, and he woke up more than once dismayed, convinced they had been reality. He was hot, he could feel his head burning, and his body shivering. His nose was full of snot, and his breathing was thick and raspy. When he coughed, he could hear and feel the mucous snapping in his lungs, and he spat out what came up. He could feel he was incredibly tired. He would sleep for what felt like long periods, wake for a bit, staring into the darkness and shadows, and then his eyelids would grow heavy, forcing themselves shut, and he would sleep again. He was thirsty.

He had drained the last canteen, and thrown it out into what had been the foyer. He feverishly saw his friends bringing him tall glasses of cool water and iced tea and juice, only to have them vanish just as he was to grab the glass from them.

"Sayid! Yusuf!" Sayid did not come back with his drink, and he slumped down to the floor, feeling his dry throat and mouth with his tongue. They had been dead for over a month already, their bodies burned to ash and spread into the wind.

He didn't need to urinate anymore. The last time he had, he had stood against the outside wall, shaking. It had burned when he relieved himself, and he could smell the urine thickly. If he could see it, he knew it would be a dark orange. He was getting badly dehydrated, and the cold didn't seem to be getting any better. Occasionally, if he breathed deeply, if could feel a small twinge of pain in his left side, but he passed it off as a stiff muscle from lying on the floor of the elevator for so long.

Gradually, his dreams became more and more vivid, and he seldom woke and was conscious. When he was awake, he saw people and things that were not there, talking to them and sometimes pleading with them for help, or food, or water. Sometimes he laughed as they told him a good joke or shared a clever story. His nose ran freely, and his breathing was labored and shallow. The pneumonia raging in his lungs spread.

In the night, he woke briefly, pulling his blanket over his head, and spat out another mouthful of phlegm. Coughing hurt terribly, and he winced in pain. He settled back down, wishing he had a glass of water. He died two hours later, his chest rising one last time, and then slowly falling as his rattling breath was released. His hand fell from his forehead with a dull thud on the elevator floor, the clenched fist relaxing into an open palm.

Ibrahim al-Sadr

He kept walking, enjoying the deep quiet, suddenly realizing how much background noise there always was, how much sound he was always ignoring.

He was reminded of a time when his parents had gone camping for a weekend in the mountains. Up to that point, they had been strictly an urban family, his parents never showing the slightest interest in nature or the outdoors. He had come home from school one Friday, anticipating a normal weekend at home with his friends, walking around the neighbourhood, and watching some television. The family car was packed full, with just enough room to sit, and a small U-Haul trailer attached to the rear of the car with a newly attached hitch, the bright chrome blinding in the sunlight.

"What?" he wondered aloud, seeing that something was planned out of the ordinary. He had walked up the driveway, and entered the front door, placing his schoolbag on the coat rack.

"Ibrahim?" he heard his mother shout from down the hallway. He didn't reply yet, he walked upstairs into the kitchen.

"Ibrahim!" He heard footsteps coming down the hall towards him.

Like all teenage boys after school, he opened the fridge. His mother rounded the corner.

"Ibrahim!" She placed her hands on the sides of his head, pulling him down to her so she could kiss him on the forehead.

She kissed him on the forehead.

She was just over five feet tall, he was fourteen, and she had to already pull him down to her. He was going to be tall like his father.

"What are you doing?" she asked.

"I'm hungry. I was going to make a snack before dinner."

"Always eating!" she exclaimed. "Where do you put it all?" She complained regularly about how much her son ate, to anyone who would listen. Deep down she was gratified he had such a healthy appetite, finding maternal satisfaction in watching him eat. She slapped him lightly twice on the cheek, a sign of her affection.

"Here, you go pack your clothes, and I will make you a little something." What qualified for a little something for her would pass for a sizable meal in most households.

"Pack? Pack for what?"

"Your father wants to take us camping for the weekend."

"Camping? Like in the forest?"

He was appalled.

"We have never gone camping before," he said, stating the simple truth.

"And that is a reason to not go?"

"No, it's just we have never done it before."

"Go pack your clothes for the weekend. Don't forget your toothbrush!"

His mother would be satisfied if he packed nothing but his toothbrush. She was fanatic about oral hygiene, making sure he brush·'d after every meal, flossing, and never missing a dental appointment.

He surrendered, and went to his room, digging out his bag and quickly stuffing a couple days worth of clothes into it. He didn't know quite what to pack, so he also threw in a few magazines, some popular science and some comics, and a crossword puzzle. He didn't pack his toothbrush yet, because he would have to brush after he ate. He went back into the kitchen with his pack, where his mother had already laid out a steaming plate of khoresht that had been poured over a bed of white rice. The stew was his favourite, and so she always seemed to have some on hand, in one bowl or another. He sat down and began to eat, conscious of his mother watching him for his first few bites. Satisfied he was going to eat, she returned to her packing. Ibrahim heard the front door quickly open.

"Mahvash!" his father yelled.

"Mahvash, are you ready yet? Where is Ibrahim? We should be going soon!"

Ibrahim heard him run up the stairs, where he stopped at the kitchen.

"Ibrahim! Why are you eating? We need to go soon."

His mother came down the hall.

"Hush, Sohrab. Your son was hungry. I made him something before we left." He did not argue, knowing it would be a futile struggle. He rolled his eyes in surrender. He searched for another solution to speed up the process.

"Is he packed?"

Mahvash picked up his bag and gave it to his father.

"And you?" he asked.

"In the bedroom."

He nodded, and went to retrieve the rest of the luggage. If he was going to be forced to wait, he would do what he could to get everything else ready. He took the extra bags, and disappeared outside, where he fought to find room for the remaining articles.

Ibrahim finished eating just as Sohrab came back in the house.

His mother motioned him to go brush his teeth as she picked up his plate to rinse it clean.

A few minutes later, they were driving down the road towards the interstate, destined for a small park a few hours away. His father was anxious to get there before the sun had set, while he still had time to set up the brand new tent that lay surgically packed inside its box in the trunk. The drive passed quickly, until the road that led to the campsite was blocked by a logging truck that had spilled its load across the lane. Traffic was blocked in both directions until a loader could come and clean up the mess. It took two hours, and by the time they reached the camp, dusk had fallen and the campsite was thick with dark elongated shadows, and the bugs were starting to come out in droves in the cool of the evening. Sohrab had insisted they both stay in the car while he set up the tent. He had initially tried to set it up in the twilight, but the light failed him, and quickly vanished. He propped a flashlight in the V-crook of a thick fir tree, aiming it more or less in the area where he was struggling with the tent. Its supports were spring loaded and thin, and for a first-time tent builder operating by flashlight, the process did not go smoothly.

"Haramzadeh!"

It was the first and last time Ibrahim had ever heard his father swear. He heard his mother gasp. She rolled down her window and quickly berated him. He ignored her, his mind focused on getting the tent up as soon as possible. He bit his tongue, and whispered another colourful string that he alone heard. An hour later, the tent was up, the orange fly neatly stretched overtop, suspended by rope tied to a few neighbouring trees. They cooked a quick, if unsatisfying dinner over a small green Coleman stove, and retired to the tent for the evening, now nearing midnight. His mother applied some cream to the insect bites his father had sustained while putting up the tent, and they soon were asleep. Ibrahim had lain there in the dark, his senses *underwhelmed*. Once the light had been switched off, he had never been in an environment that was so devoid of sensation. His eyes remained open, and he still couldn't see anything. If he didn't know any better, he would have said for a fact that his eyes were shut. He couldn't see his hands in front of his face, and the forest canopy and tent had blocked out the starlight, so there was no light at all. Combining with his lack of vision, was the almost complete lack of sound, asides from the whispering of his parents breathing. There was nothing to hear; he could hear the blood flowing in his body, it was so silent. He wanted to scream! His senses that had grown up with a constant barrage of light and sound cried our for stimulation, and for a few minutes he felt as if he was going to panic, his heartbeat speeding up and the dark becoming a frightful enemy.

The quiet he had heard then was very nearly the same amount of quiet he heard now. The only sounds were people talking, or walking down the street. He could hear dogs barking clearly, and even birds. He walked down the lane, much as he had done as a teenager, observing and enjoying the life around him. He would be expected home with a few hours, where he could share the company of his wife and youngest daughter over a planned lunch. He walked back to the mosque, where he would sweep the yard with an old straw broom. He found it relaxing, the simple task giving his mind time to think while his body was busy, a habit acquired from Alim. The wooden handle was old, worn smooth by the steady use of many hands. He entered the yard, and retrieved it from the corner where he always leaned it. The mosque was empty and serene, his second home. He went to the far end of the yard, and began to sweep, the brittle straw smoothing the fine dust as he went back and forth in a constant motion, each movement timed. He went across the yard from right to left, working towards the mosque entrance where he would lean the broom back in its place. It took him a little time; time that he found sped by as his mind worked. Mohammed would be inside, practicing with his swords. He owned two antique scimitars, their curved blades etched by time, the hard steel scratched and pitted with use. They no longer were used in battle, but were admired instead as family heirlooms, polished and maintained by Mohammed. He would spend hours bent over the blades, rubbing oil into the steel, keeping the metal free from corrosion and decay. When they were clean, he would practice with them singly or doubly, duelling against imaginary foes with deft skill, the blades cutting into the air with sharp precision, his hands turning the blades over from one to the other, behind his back, over his head, each swing precise and measured over countless hours of practice.

When he was done, his lithe body would be covered with sweat, his chest rising and falling quickly from the exertion of the exercise. He drove himself to exhaustion, only stopping when his hands and body shook from fatigue, the final sword strike taking the last of his energy to not drop it, his mental control over his body the final test. Mind over body; spirit over flesh. He knew the practice was mental as well as physical, each motion being carefully measured by a strong body taught to accurately handle a heavy blade. He frequently garnered an audience, who came to admire both his skill, and the beauty of the swords made centuries earlier. In the hands of a novice, the swords were impressive; in the hands of Mohammed, a sword master, they were beautiful. Afterwards, he would sheath the blades and pray, practicing his mind as his body rested, the physical exertion making his mind as sharp as his swords. He paused in his sweeping to listen. He did not hear the swords cutting through the air. He must be polishing them. He resumed his sweeping. Looking around, he was surprised to see that he was nearly done. The sun rose into noon, the air dry and warm. He paused to stand, turning his face into the light for a minute, enjoying the feeling of the warmth on his skin.

His stomach rumbled, and he suddenly felt thirsty. He swept up to the entry, satisfied with the yard, the ground smooth and free of debris. It wouldn't last long, but for the first few people who came to the grounds the yard would be neat and clean. He knew children often would run around the grounds after he had swept, to see their footprints clearly in the dust. Initially a few parents were upset to see his work be quickly undone with footprints, until they saw that his reaction was pleasant, taking joy in the delight of the children as they played.

He leaned the broom against the wall, the wood tapping once against the stucco wall. He made his way to the study where a pitcher of water stood on his table. He drained a glass, setting it down next to the pitcher. He heard a tapping sound. He turned to see Mohammed holding a wicker basket.

"Our breakfast."

Ibrahim was surprised.

"I was supposed to meet my wife at home today."

Mohammed nodded.

"She came by while you were out earlier this morning. She told me that she was taking your daughter shopping and didn't know if she would be back in time."

He felt disappointed; he was looking forward to their plans. It was likely she would visit the mosque afterwards in any case, to get the basket, and he could visit with them later. He sat down at the table, moving the pitcher to make room for the basket.

"Well, then. Let's eat."

Mohammed came over, placing the basket on the table. There were two bowls of white rice, and a large pot of his mothers' khoresht stew recipe. He smiled, and Mohammed took a deep breath.

"It smells delicious." He portioned out the food, each getting half. They ate in silence, both hungry and enjoying the hot meal.

"Do we have any power yet?" he asked Mohammed.

He shook his head in reply as he chewed a mouthful.

"Nothing at all. It seems like everything is out. I can't even get the radio." He shook his arm.

"Even my watch is dead."

"What? Your watch?"

He nodded.

"It stopped at a little after nine thirty this morning."

He frowned in thought, thinking that was about the time he was walking in the street. Strange coincidence? He wasn't sure.

"So, about a half hour ago?"

Mohammed thought for a moment.

"Yes, about that."

He heard something fall in the entrance, and went up to investigate. The broom had fallen over, and lay flat in the doorway that opened to the yard. He stood it back up, and saw birds take to the sky.

A moment later he fell to the ground as though he feet were pulled from beneath him. A deep rumble filled the air, and the earth shook violently. Finding himself under the arch, he crawled the rest of the way outside into the yard, the ground buckling like a wave. Objects on the ground were bouncing around, being thrown about as the ground shook, smashing into walls and doors.

"Mohammed!" he yelled as loud as he could.

"Mohammed, get out!"

He felt himself rolling on the ground, himself unable to stay in one place, realizing that Mohammed was probably trying to, but likely couldn't. A moment later, his worst fears were realized as the brick and mortar building fell in on itself with a roar of its own, in a thick dust cloud. All around him, buildings collapsed, and walls fell over, shattering on the ground. He watched as a power line snapped and then went over, crashing down on the remains of a home. He clung to the earth, feeling the seconds pass unimaginably slowly. He tried to dig his fingers into the hard ground, wanting to cling to something.

When the shaking stopped, the silence was terrible, the air filled with dust that slowly floated past, settling on the ground. He lay on the ground, relaxing his body in one tremendous sigh, his face pressed to the dry earth, eyes closed. He was safe. He feared for his family, praying they were not trapped indoors when the earthquake hit. He took a breath, and got to his knees, and then stood upright. He didn't see a single building that had survived; everything had collapsed into great piles of heavy brick and stone.

"Mohammed!" he called.

He rushed over to the remains of the mosque, a mound of rubble, trying to remove bricks as fast as he could. The bricks had been shattered by the quake and the fall, and he could only remove small handfuls at a time, frustrating him. He crawled over the pile of brick, searching over the spot where his study had been, trying to get deeper into the pile. He threw a few handfuls of brick away and came to a wooden beam that had been buried in the wall. Propping himself under it, he leveraged it up, opening a gap in the ruins. Cautiously, he went into the hole, feeling with his hands as his eyes tried to adjust to the darkness. He waited for minute, and could make out the frame of the couch. The couch was flat, nearly parallel to the ground. Squinting, he saw a hand protruding from under the frame. He took hold of it, trying to get a response.

"Mohammed! I have you!"

The hand did not move. He traced up to the wrist with his fingertips, and then pressed down, searching for a pulse. He could find nothing. He tried over and over, convinced he was putting his fingers on the wrong spot. From under the couch, a red stain slowly grew in the dust, spreading outwards, soaking into the ground. Taking control of his hope, he looked around, and saw that the couch had been flattened, the top of the frame buried under the wall that had collapsed over it. Mohammed had sought cover under it, only to be let down when the wood frame failed under the weight of the falling wall and ceiling. He sagged, and dropped his head, fighting back tears that fell into the dry ground, being swallowed in the dust.

"Baradar asodeh bekhab."

He climbed off the pile of brick, his arms keeping him balanced, making his way cautiously to solid ground. As the dust cleared from the air, he could make out more and more people standing in the narrow corridors of the streets, surrounded by collapsed buildings on either side. Some were running down the lane, dodging debris in the lane, while others simply stood there, mute and transfixed, their eyes not focused on any one thing; their minds in shock. A few people were crawling over the rubble of their homes and businesses, yelling names and hoping to hear a response of any kind.

The tallest thing he could see standing was a thin metal spire, a radio antenna that had not fallen over or been struck by a falling building. He blinked, suddenly feeling the layer of dust that was caked to his face, making his eyes itch and burn. Everyone he saw was covered in dust, sweat and blood gluing it to their skin in a fine crust. No one noticed, their wide concerned eyes saying everything. He left the yard of the mosque, to make his way home, trying not to make eye contact with anyone else he came across. There were too few survivors to help everyone. He saw people pleading with their neighbours, who themselves were trying to dig through the remains of their own home or business, desperate to find someone they knew was trapped inside.

Other piles of debris had no one searching through it, the owners either all vacant, or all inside when the walls and ceilings came down. In the homes, it was late enough that people who had jobs to go to were out working, but the worst of it was the women and children. He wondered how many women and little children had been at home, having breakfast or a quiet morning moment when calamity struck. He forced the image out of his mind, not wanting to imagine the tragedy that was unfolding before him. There would be thousands dead. Thousands. And the lack of power meant that there would be no organized rescue or relief attempt. Whatever miracles would be performed, they would be on an individual basis.

He prayed quickly, as he marched through the streets, that power returned quickly. Without it, those who survived but were trapped would also perish, in a few short days at the most. The streets looked entirely different to him, familiar landmarks had been destroyed or so badly altered that they were no longer easily recognizable. He was surprised at how much of his sense of direction was defined by familiar objects he was looking for. He knew the streets, could walk through them blindfolded he was certain; but the ease of finding his way through the city was gone. The spice shop was gone, its yellowed stucco an easy reference in a sea of white buildings, or the magazine stand with its red and white striped awning, all landmarks that marked progress on the way around town.

He knew where he was going, but the ease of navigation was gone, as was the ability to easily measure his progress. He knew he would be halfway home when he passed the bank, and a quarter of the way there at the apartment complex. He didn't know how long he had spent staring at the apartment buildings. At first, he didn't recognize them; couldn't recognize them. He had been walking past a large multi-storey building that had collapsed; the floors pancaked one on top of the other, the top floors broken and hanging around the ones below.

Twisted rebar poked through shattered concrete walls and floors, the broken bones of the building. The concrete clung to the twisted metal supports, making recovery even more difficult. The floors and walls may have shattered, but the rebar held the remains together like a heavy torn blanket covering the destruction underneath. He had been nearly past the apartment when he recognized the black iron fence sticking out awkwardly under a portion of wall. Most of the fence still stood, undamaged, the falling remains well back of the perimeter. His memory of the fence included the building, and without it, the fence was just a fence. His mind clicked the puzzle together, the missing pieces suddenly making a whole. And he had stopped in his tracks, just stopped cold, the enormity of the situation starting to really sink into the cracks. He had stood there, his eyes seeing everything, his mind trying to peel away the edges. There had been hundreds of people in the apartments, *hundreds* of them. He saw no one walking around, trying to get inside, or trying to get out. The apartment had become a tomb; a giant mausoleum where everyone had been neatly buried by the building itself. He watched birds land on the edges of the walls and the remains of the rooftop. Small bits of rubble broke free randomly and crashed down to the earth below, while small bits of paper fluttered to the ground. All was quiet. He came out of his stupor, and continued to make his way home, trying to see less and less of the destruction as he walked by. He passed an old woman, kneeling on the street, screaming at the remains of her home. She tried to cling to his legs as he went by, begging for his help.

"Please, my grandchildren and daughter are inside. Help them please. In the name of Allah, help us!" She wailed, the depths of her soul already knowing the truth.

"I cannot," he replied, a lump in his throat that threatened to burst. "I have to get to my own family." He held her hand quickly in remorse. "I am truly sorry."

She continued to scream as he walked away, her voice slowly fading away into the distance. Her few visible neighbours ignored her, searching through the remains of their homes, the pain on their faces visible.

He saw a thick pall of black smoke rising though the dust, only becoming visible as the breeze blowing over the city cleared the air. Whatever was burning, had been burning for a while. The smoke rose into the sky, and it was black and sooty. He kept an eye on it, watching as it grew nearer. His mind tried to think of what it could be; what building was near to his home. He had walked for a few kilometers so far, and not seen a single building remaining standing.

One government building had seemed to stand up relatively well; as he approached it the corners were still straight, the walls upright. The window glass was gone, covering the street in a layer of reflecting shards, but it looked like a beacon of hope amidst the ruins. He walked past the building, to have his hopes crushed. The opposite side of the building had collapsed, the floors falling into themselves towards the center. Steel girders were twisted like licorice strings, jutting from the rubble. He stopped to look up into the building, at the opposite side of the walls that were still standing. The insides of the walls were skeletal; the interior side of the wall showing where everything had been, before falling down together. He had seen a building like this in Germany, a remnant of World War Two.

A building had also collapsed like this, only two joining exterior walls remained standing, a few partial floors in between them. The exterior had been riddled with bullet holes and shell craters, testimony to the furious battle that had taken place outside it. The city had left it standing as a memorial to that event; now this building in his town reminded him of that same ruin. He watched as paper floated down from the ruins, or from the pile itself. He looked upwards to the upper floor, where a sheet seemed to be waving in the wind, in a small narrow pattern of movement. He ignored it, taking in the rest of the destruction. The sheet kept moving, and he looked up at it again. It wasn't a sheet. It was a man, in a white shirt. He was stuck up on the upper floor, confined to a narrow ledge of floor that had so far not succumbed to gravity. The man was pacing on his narrow ledge, trying to find a way he could get down. He was clearly panicked, his hands on his head. He saw Ibrahim, and waved for help. Ibrahim shrugged back, trying to tell the man there was nothing he could do for him. The ledge he was trapped on was perhaps two feet deep at its widest, and no more than eight feet long. It alone remained attached to the wall, its undersides smooth with little to hold or to find purchase. Ibrahim wondered, by what grace, this man had survived. He must have lain next to the wall, or had fallen next to it, when the floor behind him had fallen. He was fortunate enough to have not rolled back and fallen into the pit, but now was trapped on his high ledge, with no certain means of escape. He counted the floors upwards. Fifteen. God help him. He turned, and continued down the street, watching the cloud of black smoke rise into the sky.

Rashid stood on his narrow ledge, trying to figure out what he was going to do. He couldn't believe what had happened, and his mind still reeled in partial denial that this could be anything but a dream.

He had been sitting as his desk, going through his inbox, organizing his day. He had taken a call from the Oil Ministry, talking to someone whose name he couldn't yet recall about the progress of a series of new wells and pipelines, when the power had failed. The lights had gone out, and not even the emergency lights came on. Even the phones were dead. Taking the opportunity to work without interruption, he began to sort through his paperwork by sunlight, enjoying the novelty of the situation. He had worked for a few hours like this, by pen and paper, eating his lunch at his desk, when all hell had broken loose. He had been thrown from his chair against the wall, where he had cracked his head soundly while the building around him swayed back and forth. He didn't know if it was in his head or a dream. He sat there, holding his head, feeling for blood which he was sure must be coming. He had heard scalp wounds were bad bleeders. He watched as the chair rolled around the floor, the desk skidding around the office. His filing cabinet, a four-door horizontal monstrosity, shook and rattled, and then fell over with a metallic smash, spilling folders of papers all over the floor. He sat there, his legs straight out on the floor, when the floor suddenly dropped away from him in a smooth motion. It didn't crack or splinter. One moment it was there, and the next it fell away, leaving his feet dangling over the edge. He watch it fall, stopping briefly as it crushed the floor below it, and then continuing downwards, smashing its way down relentlessly. Half-way down, the walls opposite him began to fall inwards. He watched in horror as they fell toward him, only to plummet down onto the floor he had formerly been sitting on. As it went, the roof came with it, peeling itself from the walls with a shearing groan. He watched it all come down around him. He closed his eyes, waiting for the sensation of falling, knowing it was coming. But it didn't. His wall stayed upright, continuing to sway until the quake stopped, when it came to rest, seemingly as solid as before. He looked around, amazed and dumbfounded. The narrow bit of floor that he rested on was covered in glass from office windows that had exploded. He swept the shards off with his hand, off the ledge into the pit below.

He looked down, seeing the shattered remains of the building roof mixed in with the building wall. An immense dust cloud billowed out of the shell of the building and was carried away by the wind, and he squinted on his ledge as bright sunlight poured into the ruins. He took stock of the situation, staring out into the void that was before him, seeing the walls that supported him standing in empty space. Nothing else was standing. He could see for kilometers around, and it looked like every building had collapsed. He twisted to his side, standing cautiously so as not to slide from his narrow perch. He kicked off his shoes, watching them fall into the pile below. He made it to his feet, and walked the length of his ledge cautiously, testing the strength of the floor. It was solid. He laughed insanely, wondering how it held. He looked around the wall and ledge, looking for some way he could make his way down safely. He didn't see anything that would make it too easy. The wall was full of nooks and crannies, but he would have no way of knowing how secure any of them were, until his full bodyweight was already on it. At fifteen floors up, that would be a fatal error.

He paced back and forth slowly, trying to see a route down the wall from his ledge. He wasn't in a panic, feeling relatively secure that he would get down safely, either on his own or once the authorities came with a rescue team to assess the damages. They could get him by a helicopter quite easily, once they knew where he was. He looked up and saw a man in a white robe down in the street. He seemed to be looking up at him, seeing him there on the ledge. He waved at him, to make sure he was seen. The man waved back, and then shrugged. There was no way he could help him. He gave a quick wave back, grateful that at least someone knew that he was there.

He sat back down on the ledge, and waited.

Ibrahim walked away, making a mental note of the man in the building. When help came, he would have to tell them about the poor soul trapped up on the ledge. He continued down the lane, scouring the horizon for any form of help, be it a plane or helicopter or bus. He couldn't see anything moving except for birds and people, and a few dogs that were sniffing around the ruins.

When he came to the source of the black smoke, it had cleared somewhat, and was now burning a whitish grey. It was a school that had collapsed, formerly a few stories high, now no more than a few meters of rubble. Burning rubble. A large tank of natural gas had been stored near one of the walls, a wall that had fallen down on the tank, evidently puncturing the tank and sparking, igniting the compressed gas. The bottom of the tank was still visible, a white semi circle of metal. The sides and top were gone, blown away when the tank had exploded, leaving shredded fragments dangling on the blackened ground. The explosion had set the remains of the school on fire. The flames had travelled easily through the fallen building, finding the narrow confines between brick and wood a perfect avenue to spread, the gaps in the pile insulating the flame and acting to draw air into the building. If anyone had survived the collapse, the fire or the smoke had certainly killed them. He hoped mercifully it had been the smoke, or lack of oxygen that had killed them. To burn alive while trapped was a fate he did not care to wish upon anyone.

He was nearly home, and did not see anything else that was enough to draw his attention. His mind had quickly become numb to the destruction, ignoring those he saw crying on the street side, or even the few bodies that by this time had been pulled free of the ruins. There was nothing to cover them with, so their loved ones had begun to pile bricks around them in a makeshift burial cairn. It would keep the crows from the bodies, and hide the flies and disfigurement of those that had been killed. He arrived home, grateful to see his car was not there. Wherever his wife and daughter was, they were not at home. He could only hope they were not in a building when the earth had shook. He could only wait for them to come home. He dug through the pile, seeing none of his neighbours. He gathered some bricks, and fashioned himself a bench to sit on in the street, or lay on, if he had to. When he was done, and satisfied he had somewhere to rest when he wanted to, he returned to the pile of his home to look for items, nothing in particular; whatever he could find. A breeze had begun to pick up, the moving air refreshing in the otherwise still afternoon. He was surprised to see the sun was already getting down towards the west. It had taken him a lot longer than he had thought to walk home. Thinking about it, he wasn't surprised. He had been at the mosque for a while looking for Mohammed, and he had walked slowly, stopping more than once for extended periods of time.

He crawled over his home, pulling at a few two by fours that stuck out of the pile, causing a large heap to come loose, crashing down and sliding flat over the yard. The top of his fridge was visible, badly dented, but still closed. His stomach suddenly rumbled. His mind had been so busy that he had been able to ignore his stomach earlier, to push down the feelings of thirst and hunger. Now that he was home, his immediate concerns returned, and the sight of his fridge was a powerful reminder. He made his way to it, and began to clear the area as best he could, just enough so he could get inside it. He would have to be fast once he opened it. It had been without electricity since the morning, and by opening it he would compromise whatever cold air was still in the unit.

Once he was ready, he had to open it quickly, get what he wanted out, and close it again to keep the air inside as cool as possible. He threw the bricks aside one by one in a steady pattern, finding he was making good progress. The wind had picked up a bit more, and was now gusting occasionally. There was normally an evening wind as the air cooled, although this was getting a little stronger than normal. Perhaps the flattened skyline helped the wind keep more of its strength, he surmised.

He kept digging, finally making his way down far enough, clearing enough of a gap, that he would be able to get to the side of the fridge, and open the door about a foot, enough to see where things were inside it and then remove them. He stepped to the side, and took a steady footing, determined to go as quickly as possible. He grasped the handle, and pulled. He felt the cool air on his feet, and he quickly reached inside. There was always a container of water on the top shelf. He found it, taking it out and putting it on the ground where had made it as level as possible. He reached back in, finding a block of cheese and some left over chicken. He took out whatever meat he could find, leaving the more resistant food like fruit inside for later. The meat would spoil quickly, so he wanted to take advantage of it while it was still edible.

He sat in the gap he had created, and bit into the food. It tasted delectable, and his hunger gave way to something more primal. His body started to shake he was so hungry. He ate the chicken down to the bone, even chewing the gristle at the ends he would normally ignore. He then ate the few slices of lamb that were left, the cold meat tasting wonderful. When he had swallowed the last piece, he unscrewed the plastic cap on the top of the bottle, and raised it to his mouth. The water was still cold, and he felt it pour down his throat. He drank it slowly, not wanting to waste any of it. He downed nearly the entire bottle before he refastened the cap.

"Hello there."

He jumped, pre-occupied in his meal.

It was a policeman. He raised his hand in greeting.

"Hello."

He stepped out of his pit, going towards him.

"Are you doing alright? Is this your home?"

"Yes, thank you. It was."

He looked around the mess.

The officer nodded, spying the container of water. He licked his lips.

Ibrahim saw his eyes go to the bottle. It was perhaps a quarter full, only a few cups worth. There was more in the fridge, and some juice and milk still.

He handed the container out to him, and saw his eyes widen in thanks. He stepped over some of his former front wall, and took the bottle from him cautiously.

"My thanks."

He unscrewed the lid, and began to drink from it, slowing down as he came to the final cup.

"Finish it, if you want. I've already had my fill."

He tilted the bottle higher and finished it, holding the bottle end up to get the last few drops that fell. He sighed, handing it back to Ibrahim.

"Thanks again."

"Have you heard anything from the authorities?"

The officer shook his head.

"No, nothing. There is still no power, so we decided to do some foot patrols. Help where we can. Was anybody... I mean to say, did you...," he looked very uncomfortable.

"No, my family was out when the quake happened. I was fortunate. You?"

"I am not married, and my parents and sisters live far from here, in the north. I am sure they are fine. Once we get the power back on, I will call them. I am sure they are worried sick about me."

Ibrahim nodded.

"We are fortunate, compared to most."

The officer nodded.

"Well, glad to see you are okay. I'd like to stay and talk, but I have to cover more of my area tonight. Salaam."

"Salaam."

Ibrahim watched as he walked away, happy for the company and the news that he, at least, was well. He also felt better knowing the police were out on the streets. He was concerned about looters coming in the night. The sky was slowly changing color, changing into its evening hues. Ibrahim went back to his hole in the debris.

It would make a suitable place to sleep, should it come to that. He went back over the pile, stopping at the top to look around at his highest vantage point. In the east, a large wall of dust was coming over the horizon. It looked like a giant desert sand storm, with a definite wall of churning air that reached high into the sky. He watched it, it seemed to be moving as he watched it, from so far away. He stared, confirming he could see it moving, coming his way.

If he could see it covering ground at that distance, it must be moving very fast. He looked around, to see if he could shout at the police officer, to warn him to find some shelter before the storm broke over them. He was already gone; vanished in the maze of ruins.

The wind gusted from its direction, lifting a cloud of dust up from the ground and swirling it into the air. He turned to get into his hole and as much shelter as he could. He would have to cover his face in his gown so he could breathe when the storm hit. He sat in the hole, turning his back to the oncoming cloud to hide his face as best he could. He sat, counting the seconds and minutes as it came towards him. He saw the sky darken, and felt the wind blowing through the ruins. It began to howl in between the cracks of the bricks, and then he could feel the wind pelting his skin, seeing objects flying in the air over him. Lots of paper and cloth, and plastic bags, and more than a few branches and leaves. The volume continued to rise, into a furious shrieking sound he had never experienced, the wind sounding like a jet turbine. He covered his ears, and lay on the ground, keeping his face sheltered as he stole ragged breaths from the fast moving air. He felt a large clap like a thunderstorm breaking directly over him. He screamed out in fright, unable to control it. He felt the air around him being sucked away, and then felt it pummelling his body. Bricks were blown down over him, and his small shelter collapsed around him, the rubble beating him with stabs of pain. Each breath was a struggle to draw, and even with his ears covered the sound was intolerable, threatening to drive him mad. He knew he could not escape, so he fought to endure, calling on the depths of his mind to get through this, whatever it was. He knew it was no ordinary sandstorm; the savagery and violence was unlike anything he had ever witnessed. Through the bricks he could hear the ground being scoured and pelted, the rubble of houses blowing away. He could not see it, but he heard a car being blown across the ground, the metallic crashing sharp and distinct in the maelstrom. He knew if he didn't have this rough shelter, he would be dead already. He gave a prayer for the policeman he had talked to earlier, certain of his fate. Anything outdoors that was not sheltered was doomed.

Something sharp dug into his hamstrings, and he screamed in pain. Then the wind began to lessen, his breathing coming easier. The shrieking air quieted, and slowed, and he was at last able to uncover his ears. Shaking and trembling, he let his stiff and tense body relax on the ground, as much as he could. His body was full of adrenaline, his heart beating fiercely, his muscles wanting to run, run to anywhere except for here. He felt like he could run for miles. The wind fell further, the gusting wind reduced to a heavy breeze, and then to almost nothing; the normal soft wind that blew over the city at night, just enough to make curtains lift away from the window with a rustle of cloth.

He looked around his brick shelter, feeling the bricks that had fallen on him dig into his body when he moved, grinding against each other.

As he turned, a few fell onto the ground, freeing up more space for him to move. More bricks fell, a few on his back, making him wince, and then he was able to move freely. Looking up, he saw the bricks and other debris had formed a rough roof over his body, enough light coming through the cracks that he could see his surroundings and the dust eddies in the ruddy evening light. Taking a piece of wood from the ground, he pushed upwards against his ceiling. It gave reluctantly. He heard brick and stone sliding down something metallic, some cracks, and the grinding of brick against brick. He put his back against it, and stood, pushing back and upwards. The weight was incredible, but eventually it gave, the pile of rubble having no real strength. He stood, pushing a wider clearing free around his head. His leg was throbbing in pain, but it didn't feel like it was bleeding too badly. He crawled out of the hole slowly, being cautious to not injure his leg even more, and then stood in the remains of the street.

The city had been scoured. Piles of rubble that had once been houses had been blown across the street, spread thin or piled into brick dunes. The street was no longer recognizable or distinct, debris was everywhere. It was like a giant had come along with an immense broom, and spread the city across the ground. He could no longer see the standing walls of the fallen office building. They had come down in the wind. He whispered another prayer, this one for the man that had been trapped so high above the ground, unable to escape. Looking down at his leg, he saw a strand of straw poking out from his flesh, neatly driven through his robe. He lifted his robe slowly, feeling the straw pulling at the cloth.

"Ahhh," he gasped, feeling the pain as it pulled.

When it was free, he placed his fingers around its base, squeezing it, and then with a deep breath, he pulled it out. He felt it pull out of his leg, and with a gasp he fell onto the ground. He felt like he was going to vomit; the pain darkening his vision as he gasped for air. He lay on the ground, feeling the wound bleed freely, taking deep breaths as the nauseous feeling slowly faded. The sharp pain in his leg faded into a throbbing sore, and it felt better. He looked down at his clenched hand that still held the straw. It bent easily in his hand, crackling and dry, brittle like winter grass. The wind had blown it into his body, as surely as if it was a knife. The end of the stalk was bloody, for a few inches. It looked smooth and complete. He could only hope he had pulled the entire length out, fearing a slow death from infection that a remnant stuck deep in his leg would cause. He dropped it to the ground, where the evening breeze twisted it lazily along the ground.

He stood again, favouring his injured leg, looking back at his house. The storm had blown a pile of ruins on top of his home, a few lengths of corrugated aluminum lay twisted and buried in the mass, covered and dented by countless objects that had blown against them. The remains of his home had trapped enough windblown debris around it that it had sheltered him from the very worst, keeping him alive. Along the far horizon, a dark cloud was spreading in all directions, a distinct front in the evening sky. In the fading light he walked around a short distance in what used to be his street, hoping to see someone else.

He walked down the partially buried road, to where a power pole stood leaning in the sky, its cables hanging limp like giant black overcooked noodles. Stopping there, he went in another direction in the same distance, completing a perimeter walk around his former home. At the south end, he came across a pair of legs protruding from under a pile of stone, the rest of the torso covered over. The exposed skin was flayed and raw, pelted in the wind. He could not see who it was, but they were certainly dead. Flies were already lighting on the open wounds, searching around the flesh in small circles. He left the body, going back to his house.

The sky continued to darken, the dark cloud spreading over the night sky as the sun sank to the horizon, red as blood. He turned at the sound of fluttering wings, to see a raven perch on the power pole, flexing its wings and preening its feathers before sitting calmly. He watched it settle onto the pole, and it watched him as it preened, keeping an eye on him as he walked slowly. When it was satisfied, it sat calmly, scanning the ruins, looking down and around with the tilting of its head. He reached his home, and walked into the hole near his fridge, preparing to settle down for the night. He prayed his family was safe, wherever they were.

The raven suddenly leaned forward, its claws digging into the wood, and cawed, its call causing him to jump in surprise. Another replied in the distance. He wondered if he would see his wife again. *Nevermore*, the raven seemed to taunt. Of all the poems he had ever read, The Raven was his favourite, the vision of a large black bird perched above a chamber door for some reason staying in his head. The raven sat on his perch above the ruins, watching Ibrahim watching it, its eyes glinting in the dimming light, *having all the seeming of a demon's that is dreaming.*

He shivered uncontrollably, the vision of the bird above the ruins completing an apocalyptic scene, something dreamt of in a forgotten nightmare. He settled into the shelter near his fridge, drawing his legs up into his chest for warmth. The small cavity soon took on some of his warmth, and he closed his eyes, and he slept. And the raven, never flitting, still is sitting, still is sitting…

When he woke up, all was dark. He felt around his space, feeling his way up and out, blinking and rubbing his eyes, getting the grit out of the corners of his eyes. His lashes were thick with dust, and he could feel it crumble in his finger tips. His leg was sore, but it didn't feel too bad, and he was able to move it normally, the wound scabbed over.

He could smell smoke, and dust, but he couldn't see anything. He stood in the hole, trying to make out some form or shape. He crawled slowly to the top of the pile, seeing a faint glow in the distance. A fire was burning in the rubble, the red and orange light was all he could see in the darkness. The firelight amplified the darkness, giving the shadowy and shapeless lumps in the dark a supernatural flavour. He returned into the hole, and opened the fridge. The air inside was only slightly cold. He left the door open, no longer concerned about keeping the insides cold. He found the remaining water bottle and fruit, and ate his fill, throwing the fruit cores out into the street. He bundled the left over fruit in his clothes and made his way out into the street, stepping carefully, his arms cradling the food and water. He walked slowly down the street, towards the ruddy light in the distance. It was difficult to measure the distance in the dim light, the stretched shadows playing tricks on his eyes.

Ibrahim walked slowly, trying to avoid spraining his ankles on the ground he could barely see. In the first kilometre he had stepped on a loose stone, feeling his sore leg buckle under his weight, and he fell to the ground, his food and water rolling into the dark. He had sat on the ground, his hands on his ankle wincing in pain. He sat for an hour, waiting until the pain subsided, the throbbing lessened. When it felt better, he crawled in the dark, feeling for his dropped food with his hands. When he had collected it all, he rebundled it, and stood slowly, testing his ankle slowly, making sure it would carry his weight. It was sore, and he limped, but he could walk. He shuffled his feet as he went, not stepping, but sliding his feet over the ground, kicking objects out of his way. He stubbed his toes a few times, stopping to let the pain pass, but it was better than risking another injury to his ankles. Limping and shuffling, he made his way forward. He heard the ravens calling in the dark, once catching the glimpse of wings and movement fluttering over something in the street. He did not stop to investigate, but kept plodding onwards, seeing the fire getting closer.

He walked for hours, feeling sweat bead on his skin. He could begin to see shapes in the dark, moving against the light. Other people. In the darkness, instinct took over, and the survivors had sought light. Instinct brought them to other people, driven by the same basic need for comfort and companionship. There were six people that he could make out by the shapes; a few men and women, but no children. One shadow had stopped moving, watching him come forward from the darkness. The rest milled about, restless, ignoring him but aware of his approach.

"Hello."

The shadow moved, but did not reply. It lifted a hand and waved.

He moved towards him in the dark, stopping short.

"You are hurt," the shadow said. Ibrahim nodded.

"My ankle. I stepped on something in the street." The shadow nodded.

"How many are you?"

"There are eight of us; nine, including you now."

"I only see six." The shadow nodded again. The others had grouped together in the light, watching them talk.

"The other two are behind us. They are badly injured." He paused, drawing a breath. "I don't expect them to survive much longer. Do you have any food? Any water?"

Ibrahim was cautious, unsure of how much to reveal. He knew that his supplies were precious, and his own instincts told him to keep them to himself, to save them for later. He should have hid it before he got close. He struggled against his teaching, his mind telling him to help, his body telling him to stay quiet. He decided to keep quiet for the time being.

"I have some fruit back at my home. Not very much, but it is some."

Ibrahim sat down on his good leg, settling into a sitting position. When he was comfortable, he carefully dumped his fruit into a shadow, hiding it in the dark. He moved the water bottle last, slowly, making sure it made no noise as he set it down. The shadows hid his movements, concealing his actions. The man came forward, and Ibrahim tensed, suddenly anxious and worried. He sat to this left, opposite to where he had cached his food. He relaxed. The man sat down, the firelight illuminating his face and high cheekbones. He was older, perhaps in his early fifties, younger than Ibrahim but in better physical condition. From the shadow his body was strong, a wide upper body that made Ibrahim think he was a young man. Sitting next to him he could see the gray in his hair, and the wrinkles of age, the worry in his eyes. Ibrahim suddenly felt very guilty looking at him, having hidden his food. In the dark, he reached into his cache and took out a piece of fruit. He pretended to draw it out from under his clothing, and handed it out to him. He saw his eyes widen, and then he reached for it, looking at him as he did so.

"Thank you."

He bit into the fruit, cautious to be quiet. The others in the group were not looking, sitting looking into the fire of the flattened building. He ate quickly, hungry, eating the fruit down to the core, nibbling out whatever flesh he could from the fruit. Finished, he threw the core out into the dark. Ibrahim watched him eat, glad to have shared at least some his stores. The man turned to him, his posture softened, his hand out.

"Afshar."

Ibrahim took it, and they shook hands lightly, their hands clasped.

"Ibrahim."

Afshar nodded, and pointed to the fire.

"I walked for three hours to reach this. It was the only light I could see."

"Where were you, when the wind came?" Ibrahim asked.

Afshar rubbed his hand down over his face, and down his neck, before resting his arm over his lap.

"I was working on the city water lines, in the sewer mains. When the power went out, and the earthquake was over, I was sent to look for problems underground. I was underground when the wind came. I heard it." His body trembled at the memory.

"It screamed over me; I could hear it, screaming. It pulled the covers off the manholes. Solid iron covers. They were sucked out of the street like paper. And it was pulling at me."

"How did you make it?"

"I tied myself to a ladder. I wrapped a leg through the bars, and I tied myself to it. If I hadn't, I wouldn't be here. The wind tried to pull me out of the tunnel; I was floating in the air; only the rope held me down."

"The others?"

"I don't know. I haven't asked them. Allah has spared us from something terrible. For now, at least. How about you? How did you survive?"

"I was lucky; luckier than I can believe. I was hiding in my house, in the ruins, sleeping under a pile of bricks I had dug out. The wind blew more over me, covered me."

Afshar chortled, and then fell quiet.

"Very lucky," he said.

They sat together in the dark, watching the fires burn, enjoying each others companionship.

"The others, the two that are injured. Can you show them to me?"

"Are you a doctor?" he asked.

"No; I just want to see them."

Afshar nodded, standing with a sigh.

"Come with me."

Ibrahim stood, limping after him in the dark, around the corner of the building. Two people lay in the hollow of what was a floor, motionless and unconscious. Ibrahim knelt down, inspecting them. The first was a teenage boy, perhaps seventeen or eighteen. His head was covered in dried blood, his eyes still under their lids. He breathed slow and shallow. Ibrahim ran his hands over his head wound, feeling the skin depress under his palm, the fragments of bone loose under it. A quarter of his skull had been crushed, the skin holding his head together. The other was a middle-aged woman. A beam of wood penetrated her chest, piercing her ribs. Her breathing was fast and rattled, a thin bloody foam collecting on her lips. She was already dying, drowning in her own blood.

"You see? We can do nothing for them."

Ibrahim prayed over them, granting them their last rites. Afshar remained silent and respectful, watching over the ceremony. When Ibrahim stood, Afshar placed a hand over his shoulder, aiding him.

"You are an Imam."

It wasn't accusatory, he was just pointing out his observation. Ibrahim nodded.

"Then maybe your survival wasn't so lucky after all. He may have kept you for another reason." Ibrahim nodded. The thought had crossed his mind, but only fleetingly.

"We may all have our reasons, yet," he replied. He took a breath, looking into the fire. It was slowly dying, the fuel burning away. If they let it fail, they would be alone in blackness.

"We have to find wood, before the fire dies."

"I will ask the others for help." They walked back around, to where the others were sitting, their expressions morose and beaten, without hope.

"We need to collect wood, before the fire dies. Who will help us?"

At first, there was no answer, each person lost in their own thoughts and concerns. Two older people sat in their place, shaking with exhaustion, but the four others stood.

"Just bring back whatever you can find, and put it in a pile here. Be careful, and go in pairs, in case someone is hurt."

The four split into pairs, walking off into the ruins, while Ibrahim and Afshar did the same in the other direction. There was plenty of wood in the wreckage; the difficult part was getting at some of it, and finding it. The darkness made visual recognition less reliable, and they were finding when they reached for a piece of what they thought was wood, it was actually stone.

"We need to work slowly, so we don't sweat. I don't know where we can find any water yet."

Ibrahim felt guilty about hiding his bottle from him, but didn't feel the need to reveal it just yet. He would have to be careful.

After a few hours, the six of them had collected a good-sized pile of timbers, and had piled them together in a haphazard fashion. They continued in pairs, taking breaks to keep the pile steadily growing.

Meanwhile, Afshar built a small ring of bricks and stones, stacking the wood into it in a triangle shape, filling the bottom and insides of the pile with kindling and smaller shards, lining the outside with the larger and thicker lengths. By the time he was satisfied with the pyre, the flames within the building had died down significantly, now only visible through a few open spots in the ruins. White and red coals still glowed, sheltered and insulated in the pile. Afshar selected a suitable length of wood, and slid it into the coals, where it quickly caught fire. When he was satisfied with how it burned, he pulled it out of the building, and slid it into the pyre, where it quickly spread in the dry kindling he had laid out at the bottom. It crackled, smoked, and then caught, a growing sheet of flame that licked its way upwards into the heavier boards. Soon, the fire was burning hotly, and the group gathered around it.

"Why is the sky so black?" an older man asked. They were the first words he had spoken since they had found each other, and everyone at first was too surprised to answer him.

"It should be daylight, and we can barely see each other."

No one replied. No one had an answer. The windstorm and the sky was somehow related, perhaps the earthquake a coincidence, and the power outage just the start of a bad day. It seemed the most likely that it was some kind of weapon, maybe something nuclear, that had exploded. Perhaps a large volcano. Ibrahim recalled what he had learned in university, about the explosion of Santorini, in the Bronze Age. That giant volcano had erupted, taking with it the Minoan civilization and perhaps spawning the legend of Atlantis.

That eruption had kept the eastern Mediterranean in darkness for days, after creating an explosion that the known world at that time would have heard. Ibrahim had noticed something else, that so far no one else had commented on. *It felt like it was getting warmer.* It was difficult to notice, both from the exercise of gathering wood, and the proximity of the fire they were sitting around. He had noticed when he was gathering wood. He hadn't collected much, and hadn't had to exert himself in extracting the wood he did recover. The air just felt … warmer, almost muggy and *humid*. Yes, that was it. It was humid. He hadn't felt air so thick with moisture in years; a great many years. The dry desert air was now so normal to him, that it was difficult to place how it now felt differently. They had seen a few falling stars pierce the cloud cover; bright flashes that quickly flared and then vanished in the sky. He had gone for a walk, excusing himself that he had to go to the washroom. He walked slowly in the darkness, watching the ground carefully, when he found his cache of supplies. He picked up the water, and a piece of fruit in as smooth a motion as he could, hiding it in his clothes, and then finding the shelter of a rise of debris. He drank cautiously, his eyes open, making sure he wasn't discovered. He drank a liter, and then hid the bottle under a flat stone that would be easy to find later. The water was warm and flat, but felt delicious. He ate his orange quickly, rubbing his hands into the dry dust to remove the scent of the peel from his fingers. He returned to the group, as another storm seemed prepared to break overhead.

Distant thunder had first gone unnoticed, and then drew near. Lightening had begun to pierce the clouds, staying above, discharging in the atmosphere, spreading out like the veins in a leaf. They could feel the strength of the storm increasing, the small hairs on their neck beginning to rise. Then the lightening began to come down in brilliant white bolts, lighting up the sky and making the ground shake with deep thunder.

With the lightening, came rain. It started with a few giant drops that fell onto the ground with a fat splat. They became more regular, and soon fell in a steady drenching downpour. The outsides of the fire began to sizzle, and Afshar scrambled to shelter the fire any way he could. A few people covered up some embers glowing under the building, keeping them hot and insulated, just in case their fire was extinguished. It became a scramble to save the fire they had, and to keep the hopes alive of starting another one it they failed. Ibrahim went to check on the two injured people while the others did what they could. They had already died, both of them lying on the ground, without moving since he had first seen them. He made sure their eyes were closed, saying one last prayer for their souls, and crossed their hands over their chests, before returning to the fire. A few saw him return, looking into his eyes. He shook his head, answering their question physically. They nodded, then turned away, tending to their tasks.

The few glowing spots under the building had been covered over, and Afshar had rigged a quick lean-to, which had been covered over with a few lengths of corrugated aluminum. The fit wasn't perfect, leaking all over, but it kept the worst of the rain off the fire directly, and the little that made it through was evaporated before it reached the embers. The aluminum became hot, and sizzled fiercely as the rain thunked loudly onto it, expiring in a furious hiss, the water dancing and bubbling on the hot metal. The rain was warm, and so they did not need to find shelter from it to keep warm; it was more of an annoyance, a mental discomfort. Nonetheless, they gathered around the fire, stacking the wood pile high to keep the stuff at the bottom as dry as possible. Those that were thirsty looked up into the sky with their mouths open, or tried to collect it in their cupped hands to drink. Ibrahim tried some, and grimaced. The water was slightly salty, and sulphurous, the sour smell unmistakeable. He rightly considered if it was even safe to drink. He spat out the little he had tried, and then wished he hadn't even tried. The foul taste remained in his mouth, feeling like it was drying out his tongue.

"What time do you think it is?" the quiet man asked to the group. No one knew for sure; Ibrahim tried to think back, to guess at least. He gave up; he couldn't be accurate within more than a few hours, perhaps as much as six or more. He didn't know when he had fallen asleep the previous night, or how long he had slept, or how long he had walked over to this fire. He thought it must be later in the evening, but he had no way of knowing. He had heard of prisoners who had been locked in darkened detention cells, or solitary confinement, who had sworn they had been locked up for weeks, when in fact it had been mere days. The mind could not be trusted to be a timekeeper, not when familiar patterns had been removed with nothing to reset them.

"Where are the authorities? Where is help?" A young man named Peyman asked the group. He had curly hair, and thick glasses that were covered with rain drops, causing his vision to be terrible, at best.

"They should be here by now; somebody, anybody! Where is the Revolutionary Guard?"

He was mad, clenching his fists at their situation.

"Maybe they can't get here. Maybe it's like this everywhere."

The voice was quiet, solemn. It was Ziba, a dark haired beauty with eyes that could drink in a mans soul.

"You don't know that! How can you say that!" His voice started to rise, on the edge of panic.

"You don't know anything!" he screamed, and she shrunk back, his loud voice unnerving her.

"Shut up, Peyman. Don't be an ass."

Peymans eyes widened, and he threw himself at Afshar in a rage, his arms ready to swing. Ibrahim was right about his strength. Peyman was down on the ground before he knew what had happened, choking and gasping for breath as Afshars' hand closed around his windpipe.

"If you are going to be polite, I will let you go. If you aren't, I will keep squeezing and you will go for a little nap."

Peymans' panicked eyes looked around in circles, looking for support, his own hands trying to pull the hand away from his own neck. Feeling his vision begin to blur, he nodded, agreeing to terms as he choked and gasped for breath, any air of dignity gone. When released, he rolled over gasping for air, coughing, his lungs taking in deep breaths.

"Ziba may be right. We have been here for a day now, long enough to have seen a helicopter, or plane. Something that would show that help is coming. We have seen nothing."

The older woman of the group shook her head, and then introduced herself to the group. She was in her early forties, a purple and red scarf wrapped tightly over her black hair. She wore a dress of a similar color, in a floral pattern.

"My name is Rasa. My husband was in the army, and Afshar is right. We would not be abandoned unless something else is wrong."

Peyman had recollected himself, and was sitting on the ground, next to the quiet older man. Ibrahim nodded, feeling the consensus of the group.

"We cannot expect any help," he said. "If it comes, then good, but we cannot rely on it, or expect it. We need to act like we are on our own, because we might be."

Afshar clasped his shoulder tightly, his fingers incredibly strong. He instantly felt pity, and respect for Afshar. If he had wanted to, he easily could have done far more damage to Peyman than he had done.

"Our Imam is right."

Ibrahim was surprised, at being called 'our'.

"If it is Allahs"' will to send help, He will. It may be His will to test us. We must keep strong, and together, if we are to survive."

Afshar must have been in the army, or some similar position of authority. His leadership was unquestioned by the group already.

"Allahu akbar!"

The group repeated the phrase. *God is great!* It lifted their spirits, and drew them together. Even Peyman felt better, his outburst forgotten. Afshar knelt before Ibrahim, piously, on one knee, his head lowered.

"Lead us in prayer, Imam." He dropped to both knees, and waited.

The others soon followed, kneeling at his sides before Ibrahim, tears in their eyes, hopes of rescue, every emotion written as if on a white wall. Ibrahim sat quietly for a moment, thinking fondly of Mohammed, of his singing voice, wishing he was with him now, wishing him well, hoping he had died painlessly. He cried for his family, and for those he knew were dead. He began the prayer, hidden tears streaming down his face, mingling with the rain. His voice, constricted with emotion, relaxed, and unused for so many years, rang true and clear, and he sang the Call to Prayer, feeling his spirits buoyed, feeling as if he sang before Almighty Allah Himself. A raven sat in the dark, its black feathers fluffed out, the rain sliding off its body in beads. It had been flying over the city, looking for food, when it had seen the light in the distance. It flew low and came to perch on the remains of a house in the distance, and now sat listening.

When they woke the next morning, they felt better than they had expected. Ibrahim had returned with a small amount of fruit, enough for each of them to have a small breakfast. The food had done wonders to cheer them, and they had eaten it quickly, down to the cores. Ziba ate her entire apple, core and all. Seeing that she had done it, Peyman had followed suit, and then the rest had followed. They did not know what they would eat next. The day was no brighter than the last, and their fire had burned low, but was still hot. Peyman had thrown in a few boards that had promptly ignited, lighting the area a bit more than they had woken up to. The rain had stopped for the moment, and the ground had quickly dried. It was getting warmer, and it wasn't just the humidity. It felt like it was noon already, under a sunny day. It wasn't hot, but no one had wished for blankets as they had slept, and no one had spooned for body heat, either. In the desert, one of the few certainties was a hot day and a cold night. Certainties seemed to have been changed, almost overnight. Ibrahim was surprised at how quickly the group had accepted the new facts of their existence. No doubt that they harboured a deep hope of rescue, but their ability to adapt to this unique situation amazed him. All of them had dead loved ones, of that, he was certain. As they had lain in the dark, trying to sleep after prayers, he had heard a few people crying softly in the night, but no one had come unglued, or seemed to have lessened their grip on reality.

"Ziba and I are going to look for food," said Rasa.

"Where are you going?" Peyman asked.

"We're going to follow the road first, that way." She pointed north.

"If you can, mark the buildings you search, so we don't waste time looking through them again later," said Afshar.

Ibrahim also spoke up.

"Try to look for ruins that have a high point. In my house, the fridge was the tall point. I don't know if that will be common, but it might help."

The women nodded, and then went up the street, their shadows quickly blending into the dark.

Peyman went into the dark as well, in another direction, presumably to find more wood. They had a good-sized pile by now, enough to last at least a day, maybe two if they burned the fire lower. They were using the fire for light, not heat. Ibrahim had noticed the old man was waving his face with a thin piece of wood, trying to cool himself down. He was sweating less, which wasn't good, a sign of dehydration, and the foul rain had probably worsened the situation. Its smell still lingered in the air, worse where the water was able to pool or collect. Then it began to rain again, a drizzle that felt like it came from nowhere; suddenly, with no warning until it landed on their skin. It felt cool, but the rain was still warm, and it increased the humidity in the air. The three sat around the fire, their thoughts their own, as they waited for the others to return. The women returned hours later, in what would have been the evening.

They were carrying baskets, which raised their hopes when they first saw them, their stomachs growling. Peyman had not returned since the morning, when he had come back with a few armloads of wood.

Rasa looked weak, her face haggard, her eyes red. Ziba was helping her to stand, her face also strained.

"What is it? What's wrong?" Ibrahim asked.

At first they were silent, and he thought they might not have heard him. Then Ziba replied, her voice low, and shaking.

"We found a family in a house, where we found the baskets."

Afshar lifted a basket lid, seeing the bread and cheese within. His mouth watered, but he resisted, waiting until they were settled.

The women sat down together, their arms around each other for support, both physical and emotional.

"We found a woman, and her children, all dead." Rasa gasped, her voice breaking. Ziba continued for her.

"The children were dead in her arms, under her. She was over them, trying to protect them, when they were killed. They were little. Oh, so little." This time Ziba sobbed, wiping tears from her face.

"I didn't really think of it earlier," continued Rasa. The darkness, the ruins, all of it really hides what is around us. We are surrounded by the dead. *Thousands of them*, all trapped in their homes, while we sit here around the fire, talking about being rescued. We are sitting in a necropolis, a city of the dead. All I can think about, is that we are surrounded by dead people, people that are going to be rotting in their tombs, while we dig through them, digging through their belongings. I don't think I can take that. Seeing more dead children.

Rotting children. The smell was...," she dry heaved, "the smell was terrible. I thought it was the rain. The rain. It isn't, at least not all of it. It's the smell of the dead."

She leaned over, and began to cry, hiding her face in her hands while Ziba also wept, rubbing her back with her hand, trying to console her.

Ibrahim and Afshar looked at each other, while the old man seemed to stare off into space. She was right; they hadn't given it any thought at all. Ibrahim had assumed that the victims had been blown away in the wind, as had Afshar. Rasa was right; the bodies were buried in the rubble, hidden from sight, and so they had been forgotten. Some corpses had been blown away, but surely not all, and in the thousands of people that had lived there, that meant a lot of people were stuck in what was left of their homes, their homes that had killed them, and would be their graves. He noticed the smell; there was a faint rancid smell under the sulphur, a smell he hadn't noticed.

The air was warm, and wet. The city would become a breeding ground of disease, the decay of so many bodies posed a serious risk. He would have to talk about it later with Afshar; in private, to weigh their options. He was also getting concerned about Peyman. They shouldn't have let him go alone; he could be injured and dying in the street, maybe only a kilometre or two away, and they would have no idea, no chance at all of finding him. They waited for another hour, waiting for Peyman to return before they shared the food in the basket. Eventually, they gave up, their bodies needing the food, the knowledge it was there driving them mad. Ibrahim wondered how to bring it up, when Ziba had settled the matter quite simply. She had stood up, taking the basket on her arm, and made her way around the group, breaking off hunks of cheese, and tearing the bread as fairly as she could, giving each person their share. As with breakfast, they ate quickly, not wasting a crumb. Afterwards, with the edge taken off their hunger, they succumbed to sleep, one by one.

Afshar was the last to sleep, forcing himself to stay awake until everyone else was asleep. He wanted to check the basket, to see if Peyman had been left a share, or if they had eaten everything in the basket. He walked to it slowly, to be as quiet as possible. He opened the lid, and found it empty. He was glad Peyman had not returned. If he had come back hungry, and seen evidence that they had shared food, the situation in the group could become very tense, perhaps even violent.

He considered throwing the basket into the fire, to remove all traces. In the end, he decided against it, stashing the basket in the shadows where it was very unlikely anyone would find it. They might need the basket later, so destroying it could prove to be an unwise option. Satisfied, he returned to the fire, putting a few thick pieces into the flames where they would burn through the night. The wood was soaked with oil, and burned with a thick black smoke that rose in a billowing cloud. Fortunately, it wasn't windy, and so the burning oil didn't prove to discomfort anyone. He settled onto the ground, watching the fire dance, the crackling and snapping of the burning wood soothing.

When they woke up, sometime in the morning, the air was warmer still, to the point where clothing was getting uncomfortable. Water was soon going to be a big problem, as they were sweating profusely.

They heard a clunking sound, and the approach of footsteps, walking slowly and steadily. There was no food for the morning, and the thin dinner of the previous evening was only a fond memory. Peyman emerged from the shadows, carrying a bucket in each hand that sloshed with promise.

"What did you find?" Rasa asked, eyeing the bucket with keen interest.

"Water," he gasped, placing the buckets down on the ground. They were large white soup buckets, the types used in restaurants. They had thick blue lids that snapped shut over the top, sealing them well.

He was shaking with exhaustion, and rubbed his aching arms, sitting down on the ground, enjoying the feel of the rain on his skin now that he had stopped walking.

"Fantastic," stated Afshar. "Where did you find this? Is there more?" Peyman nodded, breathing deeply.

"I think it was a hotel kitchen. I walked and walked, making sure to keep the fire in sight, at least knowing where it was so I could come back easy. I didn't want to return with nothing, so I kept going."

"We were concerned that you were hurt, going out alone," said Ibrahim. Peyman nodded.

"I thought of that later, after I had been walking for a while. By then it was too late, so I just made sure I was very careful, and hoped for the best."

"It is good to see you again," said Afshar, genuinely. He evidently bore him no ill will from the previous confrontation.

"You as well. I was getting paranoid that I might return to find you all had left. The darkness is getting to me."

"What about the water? Where is it?" asked Ziba, her voice sharp and demanding.

"It will take us a day to get there, maybe less, depending on things. There is a broken pipe sticking out of a wall. It might be attached to a well, but somehow the water just keeps coming out, not a lot, but enough to drink steadily from. And its clean." He snapped open the lids, but kept the buckets covered to keep the rain out.

"Drink."

They gathered around, three to a bucket, taking turns from one person to the next, drinking slowly, cautious to not waste a drop.

They drank their fill, settling back to the ground with their bellies sloshing with clear water. Peyman snapped the lids back on each bucket, before sitting again.

"I heard the water, splashing on the ground. Do you have any idea of how hard it was to find? The splashing was echoing, and it was just

quiet enough that when I took a step I drowned out the sound. I had
to step, and listen, step and listen. I was going crazy; thirsty, hungry,
with that shitty water taste in my mouth. When I found it I drank as
much as I could." He had attached his mouth to the pipe, feeling the
rust and grime on his teeth. It didn't matter; he drank and swallowed
the water as fast as it had left the pipe. He drank his fill, feeling his
stomach cramp and ache. He had thrown it up after fighting to keep it
down, and then drank again, this time more slowly, taking breaks to let
his stomach get used to it.

"When I was full, I looked around for a place to sleep and found a
square building behind what was left of a wall. It was the fridge of the
restaurant, or hotel, whatever it was. It was smooth to touch, all steel. I
walked around and found the door, with those big handles you have to
push to open. It was full of food. Bread and cheese and crackers and dried
meats and sausages." Everyone's mouth was watering, just hearing the
words. Rasa was in tears.

"I ate and then fell asleep, making sure I didn't lock myself in the
room. Then I filled the buckets, and came here."

Rasa stood immediately.

"When do we go?" she demanded.

"Not so fast, Rasa. We need to be careful, to think this out."

"Think it out?" Her voice was incredulous.

"Think what out? Whether or not to stay here and starve or go where
there is food and water? I've decided already; I'll go if Peyman points
the way!"

"What about the fire? How do you propose we take it with us? Peyman
didn't say there was a fire where he found the water." Afshar stood,
waiting for an answer.

"That's what I thought. I'm just as hungry as you are, but we can't rush
off and find out we made a mistake later."

"Did you see any matches, Peyman?"

He shook his head.

"It was too dark."

"We can't just pull out a stick and hope it burns until we get there."

Rasa sat back down, thinking.

The best solution was to carry an ember, or a hot coal with them, in a leather pouch. Except they had no pouches, nothing to carry something hot in.

Ibrahim hit upon an idea almost immediately, and waited until the tension had died down. The heat was getting everyone on edge.

"Some could go ahead, piling up wood along the way, to burn. Then, say in a day, the rest can follow, setting each fire as they went. It would take longer for everyone to get there, but we can take turns."

The idea floated out there for a bit, as people tried to come up with a reason why the plan wouldn't work. Peyman took a piece of wood from the fire, something that was burning well, and lifted it into the air, a few sparks floating off into the distance. He walked away from the group, holding the wood high. He walked slowly, and they watched as the flames slowly faded, leaving a glowing ember and a wisp of smoke. He only made it one hundred feet before the last of the flame extinguished. Peyman returned, throwing the wood back into the fire.

"It will take us days if we try it that way. We need to make a torch, to keep the fire burning longer," he said.

"We need to find some gasoline, or oil. Something we can put on the wood."

"If you want to go look, Ziba and I will watch the fire," said Rasa.

The men each went in different directions, looking for something, anything, that would help. In the dim light, their search wasn't going to be easy, and their concern was growing over the health of the old man. The heat was getting to him, his breathing was shallow, and he occasionally stumbled as he walked, more from disorientation and dizziness than because of the loose objects on the ground.

Ibrahim followed a gap in the rubble, the remains of a lane that gave a relatively easy path to follow, as long as he went slowly and picked his route. The sky was a little brighter than the ground, so it gave him a rough idea of where to look, and where he could go. He tried to keep lower to the ground, not standing fully upright so he could see forms against the sky. He wanted to find a car, or a truck; something that would be easy to recognize. He could not count on finding fuel in a home; the odds of finding something in a house were too remote.

His stomach growled at him, reminding him that there was real food not too distant. He had thought he knew what hunger was before, the deep rumble in his belly constantly gnawing at him. This hunger was something else, a feeling with the sharp edge of a knife. He was beginning to dream about food already, and it had only been, what, he wondered? A couple of days? Maybe three? It was getting difficult to remember how much time had passed. He walked until he saw what he was looking for; a round shape in contrast to the sky. The car had been flipped over, and rolled onto its side where it had come to rest leaning up against the corner of a building that hadn't fallen. A dense mound of wreckage had collected in the corner, and the car sat nearly on top of the mound, the outline of the tires in the sky unmistakable. The car looked like it had been through a crusher, the metal bent and twisted, the doors torn off. Ibrahim climbed towards it, feeling his way along the underside of the car until he reached the engine. He found the oilpan, and tried to twist the bolt.

It wouldn't give. He could feel the slickness of the leak around the bolt, the thick oil coating his fingers and making them greasy. His fingers slipped on the bolt twice, each time causing him to bang his knuckles on the engine. He grimaced, let the pain passed, and then tried again. It was no use. Without tools, there was no way he was going to remove it. He laughed out loud.

"And how did you think you were going to hold the oil?" he said to himself, suddenly realizing that he had nothing to carry the oil in, even if he had been successful. He shook his head at himself. On a hunch, he felt his way back to the trunk, and found it open. The rolling and twisting of the car had disengaged the lock, and the trunk had released. He felt around, remembering what his own father usually stored in the back of his car. He found a box that had been emptied, and he threw it out over his shoulder. His hands closed around a smooth plastic bottle that tapered to the top. It was full, or nearly so. He could feel the weight of the bottle in his hand. It was a liter of oil. He tucked the bottle into the corner so he knew where to find it, and felt around some more. There were some cloths, a few empty bottles, and some magazines. He tossed the empty bottles out, hearing them bounce clearly down the pile, the plastic sound crisp. Then he felt another bottle, this one a thick heavy plastic with a handle that was set in the top. Elated, he took it out, and then took the smaller bottle he had cached. His father used to keep extra oil in the trunk of his car, just in case of an emergency. The owner of this car had done the same thing. Smiling, Ibrahim traced his way back to the group, each hand holding a bottle.

Rasa and Ziba were the only ones in the camp when he returned. They were sitting on the ground, looking into the flames and talking about something in quiet tones. They turned around to see him come.

"Any luck?" Rasa asked.

He held up the two containers into the air. Rasa smiled.

"Can you find me a stick? We need to try this out."

Rasa motioned to Ziba to find something. A moment later Ziba returned with a piece of wood about two feet long and a few inches wide. Ibrahim cracked the seal on the smaller bottle, hearing the plastic snap as the tabs broke. He pocketed the cap, and found the bottle to be new. He had to peel the plastic seal off the top of the neck.

"Hold the wood out, so I can pour some of this on."

Ziba held it up to him. He carefully tilted the bottle onto the widest piece, pouring out a small amount of oil. He recapped the bottle, and rubbed the oil over the wood, smearing all of the sides with it, keeping one end dry. He nodded, and then rubbed his hand sin the dirt to try to clean his hands as best as he could.

"Try it now," he said to Ziba. Rasa watched intently; all of her hopes clearly pinned on this. Ziba walked towards the fire, and stuck the oiled end into the flames. It caught quickly, and the end of the wood was all flame and smoke. Rasa cheered.

"Now we see how long it burns for."

The flame was cool, burning orange and yellow, and the thick smoke was acrid, but it burned steadily and well. Ziba held it as it burned away, while Ibrahim and Rasa sat in silence. After what Ibrahim guessed to be about twenty minutes, the flames began to flicker and dim, before finally expiring leaving the end of the wood thick with black soot. Rasa clapped her hands.

"That does it then, doesn't it? We can go now."

Ibrahim nodded, cautiously. He wasn't sure it Rasa meant to go now.

"Yes, as soon as the others get back we can go."

Rasa clapped her hands again, her smile wide, and in spite of her dirty face, the excitement and happiness was plain to see on her face. Ibrahim suddenly found her hugging him, her feeling the need to celebrate. He hugged her back, until she broke it and went to hug Ziba. He couldn't help but smile.

It was hours before anyone else came back. The first was the old man. He was empty handed, and he was exhausted. Rasa told him the good news as he laid down on the ground, her hands shaking his shoulders. He had nodded in understanding, and then closed his eyes, and quickly slept. Rasa sat near to him, and when Ibrahim looked over to Ziba, he also saw the concern in her eyes. Peyman returned an hour later, holding a few sheets he had found, rolled up tightly in his hands.

"Good," he had replied to Rasa, when she told him they had oil to burn.

"You found it, Ibrahim?"

Ibrahim nodded.

"Then perhaps Allah has not forsaken us. Where did you find it?"

"In a car. I found it in the trunk."

Peyman nodded, and then leaned back onto the ground, sighing when he laid flat. He could feel the tense muscles in his back unwinding and relaxing, still sore from carrying the water back to the group.

"Then we are only waiting for Afshar, and we can go."

"Why don't some of us go now?" Rasa said.

Ibrahim winced. He was afraid she would say something like that. She was excited, and she tended to be impulsive when she was excited.

"We have to wait for everyone, Rasa. We don't have a lot of oil, and we might want it for later."

"Someone can go ahead, and start a fire where Peyman found the food and water."

Ibrahim shook his head.

"We will go as a group, with each of us carrying something to lighten the burden. We need to carry the oil, the buckets, and extra wood for torches. It will be best to wait."

Rasa's eyes narrowed, thinking of a persuasive argument she could counter with. She had clearly been hoping to get support for her idea, but wasn't getting any. Her forehead was furrowed as she thought, still trying to find some compelling reason she could use to go.

"But…," she began.

"No, Rasa."

It was Peyman.

"We wait for Afshar."

Defeated, she sat quietly. Ibrahim was grateful Peyman had spoken up, and he turned to nod to him, in thanks. Peyman saw it, and nodded back. Peyman was Rasa's hope, as he knew where to go. Without his support, she had no choice but to wait. Ibrahim followed Peyman's example, and laid down. It felt fantastic, and he couldn't help but close his eyes and enjoy feeling his muscles relax. It almost made him forget his hunger. Almost. His stomach had given up rumbling. Ziba placed some more wood in the fire, and came to lay down between the two of them. Only Rasa sat upright, her knees pulled up to her chest, her arms over her knees, with her forehead resting on her arms.

"What are we going to do when we get to the food?" Ziba asked.

Ibrahim answered, with his eyes closed.

"We will wait for help," he said. There was nothing more to say; nothing more they could do.

An hour later, the old man had begun to mumble loudly in his sleep.

He kicked out, and waved his arms at something in his dreams. Rasa had come over to him, only to catch his arm on her face. She stumbled back, holding her nose, her eyes welling uncontrollably from the pain. She wiped them clear, and holding her nose, she went back to him carefully, sitting up near his head, further away from his arms.

His mumbling had quieted, but he continued to ramble. He was shivering, and talking low. Rasa leaned over him, running her hand over his head, trying to soothe him. After a while, he was still, and Rasa stayed with him. The air was getting very hot. It felt like he was breathing in a sauna. Each breathe was hot and thick, almost to the point where he had to consciously inhale and exhale. With each breathe he could feel the heat in his nostrils, the hot air in his lungs.

Afshar returned later in the day, his arrival noted with the sounds of cans and bottles clinking together. When he came out of the dark, the group was watching for him, wondering what was making all of the noise. He had slung a sheet across his body tied together over his shoulder and looped over his head. The sheet was bulging with oddly shaped lumps; the sheet was clearly heavy; Afshar was sweating and each step he took was slow and measured to counter the weight he was carrying. When everyone saw him coming, they stood and came to his side, lifting the sheet off from his neck. They put it down carefully, hearing the objects in the sheet settle against each other, while he knelt on the ground, breathing deeply and turning his neck to stretch the muscles suddenly freed of the weight they were carrying. Ibrahim rubbed his shoulder where the knot had been tied, and Afshar winced, but didn't stop him.

"Did...did you find anything, Imam?" He panted the sentence, swallowing loudly at the end of the question.

"Yes. I found a few liters of oil in a wrecked car. Ziba burned a stick to try it out, and it worked fine."

Afshar nodded, his chest rising and falling in deep breaths.

"I don't know...," he swallowed again," I don't know how much longer I could have gone."

Ibrahim patted his back.

"It doesn't matter. You are here now. What did you find?"

He took a few more deep breaths before responding; Ibrahim waited patiently. Rasa was untying the knot in the sheet, while Ziba and Peyman were taking out some of the bottles and cans, sorting them neatly on the ground.

"I fell into a room. I was walking when I heard some boards creaking under me, and I fell. It was a small storage room, dug into the ground. The house was all gone; I couldn't even tell I was standing where a house was. Anyways, I was lucky, I fell straight through and landed on my feet, just like I had jumped down. I found that," pointing to the food.

"Most of the jars had broken, in the earthquake, but some were okay. The sheet was in there, so I filled it with enough I could carry."

Peyman opened a jar, the lid making a shhh sound as the seal was broken. He fished out a piece of the canned fruit, and chewed it hungrily. Ibrahim salivated, and his stomach came back to life, twisting in his belly.

"Let's eat, and then we can get ready to go." He slapped Afshar on the back to get him moving, and the food was passed out to everyone. There was canned meat and fruit for everyone, and there was no talking as they all ate with urgency. Only the sounds of cans and jars opening, along with their grunts of pleasure from eating could be heard. Rasa fed pieces to the old man, whose head rested on her legs. He kept his eyes closed as he ate, but at least he was eating. Most of the cans were the type with peel open lids, and the ones they couldn't open were kept on the sheet for later. It seemed like they ate for hours, and each mouthful tasted delicious, as if it was fine cuisine. Afterwards, they all laid on the ground, holding their gurgling stomachs, the area around them littered with opened cans and jars.

"When are we going to go?" asked Rasa, her eyes drooping, trying to stay open. Peyman was already sleeping, his snores loud.

Ibrahim yawned deeply, the type where you can feel your muscles quiver. He rubbed his eyes.

"After we wake up. We will feel better after we sleep." Ibrahim could barely keep his own eyes open. The combination of the heat and a full belly was overtaking him. Rasa nodded, her eyes closed. She had turned to her side, her head resting on her hands. They slept.

Ibrahim woke up last, to find the remaining cans had been sorted into two piles, ready to be carried in the sheets they were already slung in. There were a few piles of wood, and Ziba was coating a few pieces of each with oil, being careful to not use too much. He stretched and rose, looking around. It looked like they were ready to go. Even the old man was up, Rasa rubbing his back in small circles.

The heat was oppressive, intimidating and seemed to hang over their heads, a silent restraint to their first step. Ziba handed Peyman an oiled piece of wood, which he held over the fire. When it caught, he took the lead, looking around to make sure everything was in order. Ibrahim and Afshar had done the same. Ibrahim carried the oil and a bucket. Peyman carried the torch and another bucket with some of the remaining cans of food. Afshar had taken another sling around his shoulder with the remaining food. Ziba and Rasa carried several torches, each one already soaked with oil to replace the one that Peyman was carrying when it burned low. The old man carried a torch in each hand, walking behind Peyman and in front of Rasa. Afshar took the rear position, ahead of Ibrahim and Ziba. It began with a step. Peyman started out, and the rest followed. Only Peyman had the faintest idea of where they were going, but the promise of food and water was enough to entice them to follow his lead. The torch provided virtually no light past the first few people, but Ibrahim, Afshar and Ziba found that the close proximity made progress relatively easy; at least faster than if they were walking alone. With the heat in the air, the men had soon stripped down to their bare chests, and Rasa and Ziba had even removed some clothing. Ordinarily they might have caught the appreciative glances of the men, but the heat was too overbearing. Ibrahim felt his tongue drying in his mouth; the feeling if thirst overcoming his hunger. He tried to breathe through his nose, to keep his mouth moist, his throat bearable. Rasa had passed Peyman a few torches in the time they had been walking, the spent ones being carried for use later. They would have to be re-oiled when they ran low, and then again when they had reached the cache, to give them enough time to find wood to create a new fire. They began to slow as they marched, the initial energy and enthusiasm dampened by their dehydration and the heat.

Ibrahim found himself not thinking, simply walking, his mind clear of thought beyond the next step. Their surroundings remained the same; piles of rubble and twisted heaps of metal. The smell of decay in places was overpowering; the sharp odour of rotting flesh unmistakable. They tried not to think of what they were passing, of what was creating the penetrating smells. Flies buzzed thickly in the rubble, adding to the chaos in the darkness. With their hands full, they couldn't raise their hands to cover their noses. All they could do was bear it, to take the steps that would take them away from the smells, holding their breath for a step or two, just long enough to pass the worst of it. When they reached the summit of a hill that had peaked over a field, they could see an intense fire burning on the horizon. The flame soared into the sky, revealing the structures around it. It was, or had been, an oil refinery. The large storage containers were clearly visible; their round cylindrical shapes obvious in their size. One was on fire, its contents illuminating the facility.

The view was apocalyptic, the bright flames amidst the buildings and piles of rubble, the sky black and filled with billowing smoke that was highlighted from below. They could not help but stop and watch for a few minutes, like drivers going past an accident, their necks craned to catch a glimpse of the wreckage.

"This is new. That wasn't burning when I was here before." Peyman stood transfixed, his feeble candle a pittance in comparison to the gouts of fire in the distance.

"There is no one there. No one fighting the fires." It was true. If there was anywhere that they should have seen organized help, it would have been at a point of the national infrastructure; but there was nothing. No lights, no helicopters; just fire.

"God help us." They stood and watched, the heat temporarily forgotten. As they stood and watched, a second tank went up into the sky. The horizon grew bright, as a pillar of fire roared upwards, climbing into the very sky. A moment later, the clap of the explosion reached them, along with the breeze of the displaced air blown outwards. Burning oil and gasoline spread outwards, covering yet more tanks, a blanket of liquid fire. The torch was now useless for light; the burning refinery provided more light than it provided. It was useful only to carry their flame. They moved onwards, watching the fire burning far away. Although their path was clearly lit, it seemed darker than it had before, their steps heavier. They walked down the hill, towards a hope that seemed less promising than before.

The old man collapsed later that afternoon. They had been walking as before, in a familiar rhythm of step after step, when suddenly Rasa had fallen over, Ibrahim only catching himself from falling over Ziba at the last moment. Peyman stopped, hearing the commotion behind him. Rasa turned him over.

"Hold the torch over us so I can see him better," she said. Peyman moved the torch to the side, giving her some more light.

"Hamid. Hamid, wake up."

"Hamid?" said Ibrahim. "I didn't know you knew his name."

"He told it to me the other day, after you came back."

She tried lightly slapping his face, trying to wake him up.

"Hamid." He didn't move. She peeled back an eyelid, to reveal the whites of his eyes. He was pale, his mouth hanging open. Rasa put her hands to his neck, searching for a pulse. She moved her hand a few times along his neck, before grabbing his wrist and pressing down. She frowned, and shook her head, and then placed her hand over his forehead.

"He's cool, and his pulse is weak."

"What's wrong with him?" Afshar asked.

She shrugged. "He could have a medical condition we don't know about, but otherwise I'd say it's a combination of dehydration, the heat, and stress."

"So what do we do?" asked Peyman. "We can't carry him."

There was a moment of silence, as everyone thought.

"Either we leave him, or someone has to stay with him until we can come back."

"I'll stay with him. The men need to carry the supplies to where we are going. When you are settled, come back with food and water," said Rasa.

It seemed so obvious that no one objected.

"Okay then, " said Peyman. "We'll leave you some food for a couple of days." Afshar fished out some cans, placing them near her.

Rasa looked up at them.

"If he doesn't make it, I'll come look for you, so keep a fire going."

Ibrahim nodded.

"Allah be with you both."

They hugged her, and turned, walking away, looking back at her once, to see her raising his legs, checking his pulse again. She waved back at them, to give them encouragement to go on.

No one saw Rasa or Hamid again.

The four of them kept going, their spirits dampened with leaving two of the group behind, but their progress was faster. The oil fires on the horizon were burning lower; it didn't seem like the other tanks were going to explode after all.

"How much longer so you think?" asked Afshar.

Peyman kept walking, a new torch in his hand.

"A few more hours, I think. This is looking familiar."

Ibrahim thought everything looked familiar. Everywhere he looked it was black and dark and destroyed. There was precious little to use as a landmark, except the burning refinery. And when Peyman had come this way originally, he didn't have that to go off of. He was concerned they might be going in the wrong direction, but he had to trust Peyman.

"I kept going straight; I didn't turn, so if we keep going in this direction, we should find it alright."

And so they kept going. Afshar passed out a few cans of food, which they stopped to eat only briefly. They dropped the empty cans in the dark, and then resumed their march, feeling a little better for the bit of food in their bellies. They didn't feel very hungry even before they ate; their bodies craved water.

When the sky grew darker, which they assumed was night, they were exhausted, Ibrahim had never been so thirsty, and he was no longer sweating. His throat ached, and all he could think about was water.

His hunger had abated, to be replaced by something that was far worse. His previous hunger had been a minor inconvenience when compared to his thirst. His mouth felt swollen, and tasted salty, his lips dry and cracked. By the looks of everyone else, they felt the same way. Everyone looked tired and thin, ready to stop and rest but internally driven on by the hope of finding water. They stopped briefly and re-oiled the torches, grateful for the respite but wanting to go onwards. Peyman lit a new torch, and held it high.

"We are getting close. I recognize this spot."

It was a bit of a clearing, perhaps a previous intersection in the street where there was less rubble.

"Yes, yes I do." His voice was getting excited, which quickly rubbed off on everyone else, making them want to go faster. Peyman began to walk faster, almost running. There was little debris in the clearing, the torch clearly showing the flat ground with very little in the way.

The wind had scoured this place clear, blowing away whatever had been here. A broken stump was all that remained of a power pole; the pole itself was gone, no where to be seen. The electrical cables lay on the ground, like thick black snakes, coiled in loops on the road.

The ends of the cables were frayed where the cables had torn away, the layers of wire and insulation shredded and torn apart in ragged strands.

"Wait; I see it ! There it is!" Peyman cried.

He ran forwards. The others ran with him, in a line behind him. They dropped their supplies, except for a few torches so they could keep up with Peyman. If they were this close, it wouldn't be hard to find where they had dropped them. Their hunger for water, above all else, drove them. It was all they could do to run, but the promise of something to drink kept them going.

"Do you see it? I see it! Straight ahead." Peyman pointed forwards with his other hand holding the unlit torch. Ibrahim and Afshar squinted in the dark, trying to see over each other and to where Peyman was pointing and leading them to. Ibrahim did see something; it looked like a square building just down the road; it wouldn't have caught his eye in particular if he hadn't been shown where it was. Peyman was hooting and hollering, and began to pull away from them, running faster than they could. Both of his arms were raised above his head, pumping into the air victoriously. Ziba followed close behind to his side, while Ibrahim and Afshar jogged side by side, going as fast as they could. Looking forwards as he ran, he saw a few flashes of light from the direction of the building, and then Peyman fell flat, followed by Ziba a heartbeat later. They fell as if their legs had been cut out from under them, hard and suddenly. Ibrahim wondered what going on, and then he felt a sudden sting in his chest, and then another. He stumbled forwards for a few more steps, and felt his legs go weak, unable to support his weight. He fell to the ground, feeling his vision blur. Afshar fell at his side, face down, arms outstretched. A moment later Ibrahim heard the reports, a cracking staccato sound that shattered the quiet of the streets. He lay on his back, gasping, feeling short of breath, feeling his heart beating irregularly in his chest, fluttering within him.

Somebody shot us he thought, dumbfounded. He should have known; *they* should have been more careful. They had gone so long without seeing anyone else they had assumed that there was no one else. Somebody else had also found the spot Peyman had discovered a few days earlier, and they weren't too eager to share.

He coughed, tasting his coppery blood in his mouth. Whoever was there had heard them running down the street, yelling like fools, and he had taken care of them. He felt cold, and a little numb. He had always thought that being shot would hurt more. He had barely felt it, just a couple of stings and that was it. Peyman and Ziba were dead before they hit the ground, by the looks of it. So was Afshar. He felt tears running from his eyes; to come so far and fail at the very end. Rasa and Hamid would be left alone, waiting for them to return. Ibrahim heard stones crackling, footsteps coming towards him. He heard something metallic getting pulled, and a clicking sound. Whoever was coming was in no rush. He coughed some more, feeling his breath hitch and his chest burn. The footsteps came closer, and he opened his eyes, to see a man standing above him, his gun resting in his arms across his chest. He used it to poke at Afshar, who was limp and still. He guessed correctly that he had also poked at Peyman and Ziba in the same way. He stood above Ibrahim, his body dark and unlit, only a shadow in the sky above him.

His arms were now down at his sides, the gun barrel resting on the ground.

Farzam looked down at the man, who was breathing his last at his feet. The other three were already dead, and this one would soon join them; he could hear it in the way he was breathing. He wondered if he should shoot him again, to speed up the process.

No. It would be a waste of a bullet. He watched down the lane, wondering if anyone else was following these four. He was hasty, he had to admit, to blow his cover so quickly after shooting at these four. He should have waited. He would just have to be careful now; it was too late to change what was done. His rifle was cocked, just in case, the safety off, and he kept his finger on the trigger, ready to pull at a moments notice. It was a shame he had to shoot them. He would have liked to have learned where they had come from. They were the first people he had seen in several days, since he had come across the building he was sheltering in. He knelt down, and listened intently, keeping his eyes on the road. The man had stopped breathing. He muttered a quick prayer for his soul, and ran his hands over his face, closing his eyes.

He was genuinely sorry for the four of them; but he had no choice. This was about his own survival. He stood up, and turned to walk back to his shelter, keeping wary of the shadow around him. He walked past the girl, and shook his head. She was a pretty one. He regretted killing her. He had simply shot at the two closest people first before taking aim at the last two. He didn't have the time he would have preferred to select his targets; they were running too fast. He shouldered the rifle, and trotted back down the road, settling into the small dugout he had built in the side of a pile of rubble, leaning the gun barrel up against the side, under an overhang.

He had been part of a small troop that had been driving through the city on the way to a training exercise in the outlying bush, the engineer of the group. They had stopped for fuel and food before they left, parking on the street in a wide lane that truckers often used as overnight parking spots. It was unpaved, but the earth had been packed down over time and so was just as solid as a finished road.

They had spent the morning walking through that part of town getting some souvenirs to bring home to their wives and girlfriends and mothers, and when they had tried to leave their armoured personnel carrier wouldn't start. In fact, all of the other cars and trucks on the road had begun to hitch and jerk, coming to stop at haphazard angles on the side of the road. Not a single vehicle was running, and none of them would restart. Farzam had opened the service hatch of the APC, tracing his way along the battery to the start button inside the crew compartment. He didn't see anything irregular, so he pulled his head out of the hatch and yelled to the rest of the soldiers that were standing aside, or leaning against the side of the vehicle.

"This might take a while."

One of the newer members of the group groaned, putting out his cigarette under his black boot.

"Son of a bitch. The captain is going to chew us out for being late."

"Shut up, Behrooz. This isn't our fault. If we need witnesses, we have them." He pointed at all over the other stranded motorists on the side of the road. A few were looking around, seeing that everyone else was strangely having car troubles, and a few that had their hoods popped, bent over looking into the engine compartment.

The rest of the group milled about, kicking the tires, smiling as they watched a pretty girl walk by, or caught up on some reading inside the vehicle. They didn't know when Farzam might have it fixed, so they stayed close by. He stuck his head back inside the access panel.

"Hamim!"

Hamim appeared.

"Yes?" he asked.

"Get my tools from the back."

Hamim had nodded, and walked around to the back of the APC, releasing the toolbox from the side with a few clicks as he unlocked the restraints. He took a breath and lifted the toolbox over the side, walking with a noticeable lean to where Farzam was tinkering.

They waited patiently, expecting at any moment to feel the engine start up. A few had looked at their watches to check the time, only to find their watches were dead, too. They didn't mention it to anyone else, and so failed to make the connection that something else was strange. After about twenty minutes, Farzam had walked around to the back, his hands covered in grease that he was trying to wipe off into a thick towel.

"If anyone is hungry, feel free to go get something to eat."

Nabil sat forward in the cab. He was always hungry, so to have another opportunity to eat good food before he was back on army rations was an unexpected bit of good news.

"No luck, huh?"

Farzam shook his head as he scrubbed at his thumb.

"Go eat in the hotel there," nodding his head in the direction across the road.

"Then I know where to find you when I get this bucket running again."

They had all nodded in agreement, and started across the road. They checked for traffic out of habit, but there were no cars running.

Nothing was driving down the road, except for an old man on an old silver bicycle; a loaf of bread tied across the front in a wire basket. He was going down the middle of the road, quite happy to have the four lanes to himself.

"Do you want anything?" asked Abdullah. He was the explosives specialist; a short stocky man that was solid muscle without having ever lifted a weight in his life.

"Naaah. I'm good." He waved them on.

"I'll get something before we go."

Abdullah and the others had waved back, and went into the hotel, a twenty-story building designed for tourists and their kids.

He turned back, leaning on the truck. They might really be stuck, he was thinking to himself. He thought it out in his mind, tracing the vehicle components in his mind, thinking what he could check next. He also had to consider the strange coincidence where no other vehicle was running either. Not even a moped. He was about to lean back inside the access panel when he heard a rumbling sound, low, like a jet, and a series of squawks as a group of birds that had been resting on a power line suddenly took flight. A split second later he was thrown to the ground as it heaved beneath him. The APC bounced on the road as well, the heavy armour keeping it from moving around too much, but it still traced a few half circles in the dust, seeming to glide down the road.

Farzam had dug his fingers into the earth, trying to find something to hold onto as the ground shook beneath him violently. He heard the shattering and tinkling of glass raining down into the street, and the screams of terrified people. The din was incredible. He had never experienced a large earthquake, and although scared, was also fascinated. He knew he was in no immediate danger, and his army training had kept him relatively calm. He heard a large crack, and then several more in a quick sequence, like a series of giant knuckles popping, and then a roaring sound. The small shops, brick and wood alike, that were near the lane collapsed into themselves, a few screams coming from within that were quickly cut off. He saw the sky darken, and he was suddenly covered in a dense envelope of dust that blew over him, covering him and everything around him as it swept forward. He covered his nose with his shirt, pulling it up with his hand, squinting through the maelstrom to try to see what was happening. The shaking stopped suddenly, leaving an eerie quiet that was only broken with the faint hissing sound of falling debris.

Otherwise, all was silent. He waited a few more minutes until it seemed that the worst of the cloud had passed, and the sunlight came out again, and then rolled over onto his buttocks, leaning back on his hands. He could not believe his eyes. Nothing was left standing, except for a few power poles that were leaning in the ground at strange angles. A few power lines had snapped, and lay on the ground. He noticed that none of them were arcing, and none of the transformers had blown.

A few fellow stranded motorists stood in the middle of the road, wandering around aimlessly in shock, trying to absorb what they were seeing. They were covered in thick dust from head to toe, their clothes caked in a layer of ash. Farzam had blinked a few times, trying to remove the grit coating his eyelashes without rubbing it into his eyes. The dust burned, and he had to rub his hands over his face to remove the worst of it. It fell thickly from his hair, clumps that dispersed into the air as they fell and then were carried off into the breeze. He rubbed his eyes carefully; removing the dust with his fingers, feeling it stick to the corners of his eyes. He could feel the dust on his teeth, a fine grit that he could not remove. He stood, and and swept the dust from his uniform as best he could, brushing off his shoulders and patting his clothes with his open palms, each swat releasing a small fine cloud of particulates. He walked around the APC, seeing that every building that was nearby had fallen. He could see a few high rises in the distance that were still standing, but they were not in good shape. Both had a precarious lean to them, and he could see large pieces falling from the structures even at the distance he was away from them. The depth of the destruction amazed him, rendering him speechless as he gazed upon the remains of the street around him. He had been in a smaller earthquake in his youth, a small event that had barely caused the paintings on the family home to sway more than a few inches. This one had been enormous. He had actually felt the ground wave under his body, as if it were water.

The road was cracked and lined with fissures along its entire length.

Several larger areas of asphalt had broken free and lay flat on the ground, near where they had broken free of the road. Cars and trucks had been flipped over and rested on their sides, or even their roofs. The heavy weight of the APC had given it some resistance, but even it had moved several meters down the road. He ran his hands through his hair, and then took a deep breath and crossed the road, towards the large pile of rubble that had been the hotel where his comrades had gone for lunch. It was a mass of shattered concrete and twisted rebar; the floors of the hotel were clearly visible, laying nearly flat on one another in an angle in the direction the hotel had first collapsed. It lay nearly across the street, the upper floors cutting into the remains of another building that had fallen on top of it.

Paper and sheets fluttered in the wind, and wires dangled in the air. He could not hear any screams, or even any calls for help. He heard a crackling sound, and a faint rumble, and turned to see the last moments of one of the distant high rises coming down, the building disappearing behind the cloud of its own dust. He thought about walking over the wreckage, to try to find survivors or give help where he could, and then decided against it. One man alone would not be able to give any help; heavy machinery would be needed to work through the ruins, and teams of rescue personnel and dogs. He risked his own life, if he tried to search for others. He stayed in the street, and returned to the APC. He jingled the keys in his pockets, to reassure himself that they were still there. He locked the driver and passenger doors, and went around to the back, opening the double doors of the crew compartment. The other people he had seen were gone, presumably trying to make their way home on foot. He was alone in the street, a few birds flying overhead surveying the damages from above. He wondered when help would arrive.

He climbed into the APC, locking the doors behind him. He went forward to the radio, and tried to turn it on. It was dead. He returned the handset back into the cradle loudly, releasing some of his frustration at his inability to do anything. He was stopped for a moment by a necklace that was swinging off an overhead storage locker. The necklace had a small square locket fastened to the chain. It was Abdullah's. Inside the locket he knew there was a picture of his wife on one side, and his children on the other. He put his head into his hands, shaking it back and forth slowly. Their father was now dead, their mother certainly a widow. Once this was all over, he would have to return it to his family in person, to give his condolences. He owed that favour to all of the men he was with, to give their families whatever comfort he could, as the last one who had seen them alive.

He beat his fist against the side of the car, a surge of anger suddenly rising within him that needed an outlet. He felt his skin split on the second punch. The pain was good; it was real and certain. He punched the wall a few more times, screaming, and then sat back down, holding his bleeding hand out, fist clenched and shaking. He took several deep breaths, and then opened the medic supplies, wrapping his injured hand in a few layers of gauze, and then tying it off past his wrist. The bleeding had already stopped, and when he moved his hand, the bandages remained tight and secure.

He closed the cabinet, and lay down on the bench, trying to relax and calm down. He could still feel the adrenaline surging in his blood, his senses acute. He felt like a spring, ready to release at a moments notice. He had to calm down; mistakes were made at moments like this; when emotions were in control. He put his feet up, and put a rolled blanket under his head, his arms over his chest, and focused on his breathing. One thousand one, one thousand two, one thousand three, exhale. His breath released, and then he tried to inhale slowly, still feeling his heart beating fast in his chest. He continued his breathing exercises, closing his eyes to reduce the amount of distraction. Inhale, and release. Inhale, and release. Minutes passed, and gradually he felt his heartbeat slow, until it was nearly normal, a pattern he could no longer easily feel in his chest.

He needed to work on something; he needed to use his hands and get his mind off what had happened. He sat slowly, stretching his neck to one side, feeling the taut muscles resist the motion. With two sharp turns he unlocked the doors, and went back outside. After being in the darkness of the crew compartment, the sunlight was blinding, and he had to raise his arm to cover his eyes. The brightness had stabbed at his head like a knife, making his eyes water. He kept his eyes to the ground, letting them adjust. He walked to the side, and opened a few access panels, revealing the engine underneath. If he couldn't do anything in the ruins, he would at least try to fix the APC.

He went back to work, his mind oblivious to the passing time. His stomach growled at him, for a few moments a steady gurgle under his ribs. He pulled his upper body out of the compartment, putting his tools down on the frame inside the hatch. It was getting dark out, the sun beginning to go down and an evening breeze was picking up, occasionally gusting through the ruins, kicking up dust devils that whispered down the road, throwing bits and pieces into the air. He dug into his coveralls, and found his cloth, wiping his hands onto them to clean his hands as best he could of the grease and oil that coated them. He had some satisfaction in working on the vehicle; he had been able to quickly rule out that anything was mechanically wrong with it; and had traced his way through the electrical system for the better part of the afternoon, following a maze of wires through various parts. When he had finally stopped, listening to his growling stomach, it had become evident the problem was electrical. It looks like the system was fried. Some kind of surge had cooked it. Maybe the alternator was defective? He wondered. He wouldn't know until he was able to replace some parts, but he did know it was unlikely he was going to be able to fix it where it presently was. The parts he needed were going to be at an army base, the nearest of which was a few hours away. He slowly walked back to the rear, looking up into the evening sky where a few stars were coming out in the darkening blue sky. He looked around, seeing nothing in the streets as he rubbed the grease from his hands.

The sky near the horizon was dark, and he stopped to look at it. Actually, it wasn't near the horizon at all; the sky itself was dark, like a giant curtain was being drawn across it. He could see the separation of the sky between it, and the clear sky that was currently overhead. He had seen storm fronts like that before; a large high pressure system moving in, neatly pushing everything away before it. He took a few more steps forwards, hearing the gravel crunching under his boot heels. He looked up again, and realized he could actually see the storm front coming in his direction. Maybe it was a sandstorm?

In his earlier army days he had been caught in one; he had been in a convoy that figured it could beat an incoming storm before it got to its destination. It had caught up to them an hour before they were due to arrive, and he had never been so scared in his life, up to that point.

The storm had pounded the convoy, flipping over lighter vehicles and stripping the paint neatly off every surface. Glass was etched to the point of obscurity, windshields and windows rendered opaque. If this was a sandstorm, it was very unusual. It was the wrong time of year, and it seemed huge, climbing high into the sky. Maybe the darkness was playing tricks on him; fooling his eyes with longer shadows. The way the wind was beginning to howl around him, he wasn't so certain. It was getting gusty, in fact; the wind pulling at his clothes and pushing strongly at him. He watched the cloudbank come closer, and then decided to listen to his instinct and get inside the APC. He climbed into it, locking the doors behind him. He heard the wind blowing at the side of the truck, but felt secure now that he was inside a familiar space. He found a water bottle, and cracked the seal with a twist of the cap, drinking the warm water within. The bottle empty, he threw it under the bench. His stomach rumbled again; it wanted food, not water. He opened a small trunk near the end of the bench, lifting up a small tin latch. He pulled out a small block of cheese, breaking of a wedge and popping it into his mouth. He felt the truck shake with another wind gust; it was beginning to shake steadily, rocking back and forth on its thick springs as much as it could between gusts. He could hear objects blowing away outside, clanging down the street. Something hit the side with a loud thump. He startled, and then took another bite. He untied his boots, and slid them under the bench, stretching out his toes.

The APC began to shake. He finished his cheese, and laid down, his head back on the rolled blanket. The noise outside was getting raucous. The roar was getting continuous, and he could even feel the air pressure changing inside the compartment. He crossed his arms over his chest, and prepared himself to ride out the storm in the APC. He looked up at a window in the side, a small bullet proof portal. The sky was utterly dark, and he saw nothing through it. The wind suddenly got louder, and he felt a shaking feeling, as if some great irresistible force was making known its presence. The hairs on his neck stood up, and the APC was suddenly slammed forwards with a loud clap. Farzam felt his ears pop, and he was thrown against the back doors. They held, and for a moment he was pinned against them. The APC leaned forward, and then fell over, and he fell down to the nose of the compartment, along with everything else that hadn't been secured. His body slammed against the metal wall, and he felt the APC pushed to its side, when it began to roll. He wanted to cover his ears, but couldn't, being forced to try to protect himself as he was tossed around the inside of the truck like a rubber ball inside a lottery machine. He yelled, a token resistance to something he was unable to resist. He felt his bladder release, and he was suddenly ashamed and afraid. The air sounded like a jet engine, shrieking and howling with immense power. The vehicle rolled onwards; being pushed end over end.

Farzam tried to roll himself into a ball, to protect himself as he was tossed around the compartment. He heard the bench come free of the floor with a popping sound as the bolts broke free, and he raised his arms to his face as he saw it fly towards his head. He felt it hit his forearms, and then he felt his arms slam against his head. He was thrown back, his head hitting the outer wall, and all went black.

When he woke, his eyes flew open in terror, his arms flying out to hang on to anything he could feel. He sat up quickly, gasping, and then fell back, his head swimming and thudding with pain. His vision swam darkly, and he wanted to throw up. He rolled over, kneeling, fighting back the nausea, and breathed deeply through his nose. His head ached terribly.

Still kneeling, he held his head in his arms. He could feel a large goose egg at the back of his head, and his hair was matted with a thick crusty coating. He realized it was blood, and he felt his face, also feeling dried blood scales on his skin. He scratched them off, and then felt around the rest of his body. He was sore nearly everywhere, but nothing seemed to be broken. He slowly extended both legs, and then both arms, and then slowly turned his head to the left and then to the right. He leaned back slowly, sighing, wincing as his head thumped. His ears were muted; he could hear a static sound, and his ears were ringing faintly. Leaning back against the wall of the APC, it was then he realized that he could barely see anything. The interior of the compartment was black, save for a couple of lighter patches that were the windows, that provided only enough contrast to see where they were, and not enough light to see by. He stretched out his arms, and found he was sitting on the roof of the vehicle; it had come to rest upside down. He ran his tongue over his teeth, and swallowed. His mouth was pasty and full of grit. The underside of the roof was covered with everything that had come loose from the interior as it rolled. He felt the water bottle scatter away to the side when his hand brushed against it, and then he felt the side of the bench. He unlocked the doors and then pushed. The hinges resisted his efforts, and the doors remained shut. He pushed harder, hearing the doors grind open an inch, and then stop. He could smell the dusty air outside, the breeze coming into the compartment. The gap in the doors was only just visible in the dim light.

He reached for his boots, finding them after several minutes, and tied them tightly to his feet, pulling the laces snug, and tied them over in a double knot. He turned around, putting his legs on the doors, and then after taking a deep breath, kicked forward. The doors flung open with a raspy screech, and then stuck open, the hinges clogged with dust. He looked out in silence, gazing at the dark scene that greeting him. The land was dark and shadowed, covered with even darker mounds of jagged rubble. The ground was dotted with piles of ruins, in between smaller amounts of loose debris that sat scattered over the ground. The skeleton of a building loomed in the sky.

Farzam could see, even in the darkness, that the building had been scoured and stripped in the storm; that it was a nothing more than a concrete shell. Somehow it had remained standing, while everything else around it had been lain to waste, blown across the ground and scattered in the winds. He got to his knees, and then his feet, standing in the dark, leaning against the undercarriage of the APC. Without any standing buildings, he could see a further distance than he could have hoped, although everything he saw in every direction was black and muted. It was very difficult to judge distance, except for his immediate surroundings. On the horizon, ahead of him, a huge lightening storm was playing out, illuminating the ground with period strobes of intense light. It hurt his eyes, but it allowed him to get a better idea of his surroundings.

The APC had come to rest up the incline of a small hill, getting stuck and then partially buried against a dune of wreckage that had accumulated on the hillside. His downward view gave him a commanding view of the area of the city, and a clearer idea of the devastation that had occurred. The air smell of rain, a smell that he normally found fresh and invigorating that was somehow tainted; a slightly bitter smell carried in the breeze. He could see the downpour that was off in the distance when the lightening flashed, the rain falling in a deluge by the look of the clouds. The thunder was nearly continuous as the lightening flashed both overhead in the clouds, and to and from the ground. He grew used to it quickly, and soon ignored it. He fished around the inside of the compartment when the lightening struck, finding the food and beverages that had fallen out of the bench. He sat and ate his fill on the edge of the doors, his eyes looking out into the city below him.

He wondered how long he was out for, and had to assume it was night. He couldn't see the sun or the moon, and his watch was shattered, the crystal broken during his tumble in the storm. When the lightening flashed, he could see that the storm had blown piles of debris to the west, like sand dunes, stretching from the piles of buildings outwards in a tapering wedge, sometimes overlapping into other dunes or just coming to a gradual end. He could see the criss-cross pattern of the streets in the remains of the city, partially buried in places from the ruins, and in other places completely clear where the debris had been blown away. In spite of the devastation, and the sureness of the huge loss of life, he also found the situation enormously interesting. Whatever had happened it was catastrophe, and he was witness to what had occurred. He knew he needed to remember whatever he could, as it could prove valuable to people that would surely interview him later, once order had been restored.

That might take some time, depending on how widespread the situation was. It might take days, or even weeks, but help would come. In the meantime, it was his duty to stay alive, to preserve his recollection of what he had seen.

Farzam sat in a brick shelter he had dug out of a pile of ruins he had come across, cradling his rifle in between his knees. He was no longer convinced that help was coming. By his best estimates, it had been roughly two days since the storm had come, and he had seen no indication of any kind of organized rescue or relief effort. He had seen nothing at all. He had realized that when he woke up after the storm it was actually day, as the sky had darkened further, and he adjusted to completely black nights, and dim daylight hours, if they could actually be called daylight. The rains had fallen continuously for days, with fierce lightening storms, and they were tart and bitter, surely unfit to drink for a prolonged period. He had been forced to drink it, cupping it from rancid pools on the ground when his own water had run out, and there was no other alternative. As foul as it was, it was better than his own urine. He drank it reluctantly, grimacing, but having no other choice in the matter. His food had run out the first day, and he was famished, his stomach empty as never before. He felt himself weaken, and had already cinched his belt tighter by a notch.

Whatever had happened had turned day into night, had fouled the rain, and it showed no immediate sign of coming to an end. He had struck out from the APC when the food had run out, taking a rifle, some grenades, and all of the ammunition he could sling over his shoulders. He had stumbled in the dark, marching blindly, trusting to luck and fortune. Judging by the smell in the air, there had been a great many people that had not been so fortunate. The smell of decay was thick in the air; a sickly sweet smell that he could not escape, but only endure in greater or lesser amounts. He tried to keep upwind of large ruins, where the smells were worst, but he was at the mercy of the winds, and sometimes when the wind blew and changed direction the odor that it carried would drop him to his knees, clutching his mouth and nose. If he had eaten, he certainly would have vomited. He had come across several bodies, bloated and rotting and gassy, being picked over by birds and other animals. He had seen no other survivors, not even an indication of other people. Along with the decay, was the growing heat. It had been slight at first, something that was barely noticed and unimportant. As the days passed, it grew, and the air became thick and humid. It was getting to the point where it was difficult to breath. Since yesterday, he had removed his shirt, and had rolled up his pants in an effort to feel cooler. It helped somewhat, but the heat was oppressive and taking a severe toll on his body. His tongue had swollen in his mouth, his lips cracking and dry. His dehydration was getting acute; the feeling of thirst overriding his desire for food. When he peed, it smelled strongly, and it had begun to burn. He had stopped sweating the day before, and felt nauseous constantly, with a headache that he was certain was caused by his need for water. When he had stumbled around the corner of the ruins, he had heard the water bubbling and gurgling as it splashed onto the ground. He couldn't see it, but his trusted his ears, homing in on the promising sound as surely as if it was broad daylight. He followed the sound like a bloodhound on a scent, his animal instincts driving him feverishly forward, his attention and focus single minded. When he saw the pipe, he had cried out in delight and relief, dropping the rifle and bullets without a moment of hesitation. He had drunk his fill, savouring the clear water as it rushed down his throat. His stomach had reacted without the same enthusiasm, and he had quickly thrown it all back up, the water gushing back up in a few gasping heaves that left him trembling and faint. He drank his fill again, slowly this time, letting his stomach adjust. It stayed down, and he went back to find his gun and bullets when he was confident his belly had accepted it. He found them quickly, and investigated a building that was sheltered in the leeward side of a mass of wreckage. When he opened the door, pulling out a large steel handle, the smell of the food hit him instantly. His mouth found what little water was in his body, and he began to salivate. He stumbled into the dark of the storage room, and his hands found a loaf of bread, still smelling fresh and sweet.

Resisting the urge to eat it quickly, he chewed slowly, taking small bites and taking the next only when he thought he thought he was ready for more. There surely never was better tasting bread, and he ate the entire loaf at a sitting, his eyes searching the dark for danger, guarding his newly found food. When he was done, he shut the door, and leaned against the exterior wall, feeling the bread and water return strength and energy to his body; he felt revitalized and rejuvenated. He would wait here for help, of that he was certain. He wouldn't leave unless he had no other choice, and with his gun, he was prepared to fight for his find. He searched the area, and found a small cavity in a pile of bricks. It had a small overhang, and had a curve that was relatively comfortable to sit in. He had sat back into it, leaning the rifle against the wall with his ammo, and relaxed in the darkness. The dark and shadow concealed him perfectly. For the first time in days, he felt comfortable. He leaned back, and slept.

When he woke up, the sky was orange and red, a little brighter than before, the ruins cast in long dim shadows that sat in long angles along the ground. He crawled out of the cavity, and stood, to see a large fire bursting on the horizon. Huge arms of flame were reaching skywards, giving the land its orange and red hue. He could see the outlines of the oil refinery in the flames, the large cylinders of the containers unmistakable. He wiped the sweat from his brow, and went for a drink, letting the water run over him to help cool him down. He was concerned the water would run out, but at least so far the water pressure seemed constant, and it was still drinkable. He would have to find some buckets or some other container to store some, just in case. He returned to the food locker, and almost immediately found a stack of a dozen or so white buckets tucked into the corner. Elated, he took them outside, and placed one under the stream of water, catching it as best he could. He placed the others nearby for when the first one was full, and then returned to the room. He found a pile of blue lids for the buckets, stacked on a ledge. He left them where they were, his mind concentrating on his hunger. He would get the lids after he ate. He went to the back, smelling spices and coming across lengths of sausages hung off several large hooks, draped down the back wall. He broke off several with a twist, and bit into the first one with relish. The casing popped in his teeth as he bit through, and tasted the cured meat. It was delicious, and he fought to eat it slowly, his hands suddenly shaking with hunger.

He walked out of the room, taking the lids as he went, his other arm holding the sausages. He dropped the lids into the empty buckets, and sat into his nook, relishing the sausages. Each one tasted just as good as the first. Normally after eating something delicious, the next item, although maybe just as good, is somehow diminished by the memory of the first thing that was eaten. In this case, this was not so; each link was just as fantastic as the first, and when he was done, he sat in his dark shadow with a full belly and the satisfaction of a delicious meal. A week ago, eating a link of cold sausages in the dark would not have been so appealing, Farzam reflected, but now, it was an experience that had few rivals. Hunger was a great equalizer. He watched the light from the fire dim in the sky, the shadows around him growing dim once again. He sat in the dark holding the rifle like he once might have caressed a lover. It was a great advantage to him, and he kept it near. He heard a clap in the distance, and saw the sky brighten again, even brighter than it was before. He didn't move to investigate. Another container had exploded; he didn't need to see it to know it. Sitting in the dark, he wondered how long the food in the locker would last him. It was not refrigerated, so whatever it contained would last longer. He would have to took a careful look at it, to see what he should focus on first. Breads should be eaten first, with the preserved meats last of all. It would be the most efficient use of the resource, and he would be a fool to eat the preserves while the bread spoiled. He got up to check on the water, and found the first bucket was nearly full. He watched it for several minutes as it rose to the rim, and then replaced it with a second bucket.

The water splashed loudly in the drum for a few moments before quieting. He took a lid from the inside of the other buckets, positioned it over the full one, and snapped it into place, pushing down with his palms around the edge to make sure the seal was good. He left it where it was, not wanting to carry it back to the locker, and satisfied it was secure where it was. With the lid in place, the water would be potable for some time. He returned to the cavity, wondering how he was going to start a fire. With the heat in the air, it wasn't something that was a necessity, but it would provide him with extra light if he needed it, as well as expand his menu if he found something that needed to be cooked. It may help a rescue team locate him, but it also might bring unwanted attention to his location.

Still, if he built a small fire, and kept it hidden, he would reduce his risk of announcing his location to others. He would have to give it some serious thought. Starting a fire was the least of the problems; there was plenty of wood to choose from, and finding fuel was not an issue with all of the wrecked vehicles in the ruins.

He turned his head, thinking he had heard a sound up the lane. He heard nothing at first, thinking his mind was playing a trick on him.

Perhaps it was a rat or a dog. Then he heard it again, getting nearer. He looked into the street, trying to make out anything in the shadows. He was glad he was hidden in his hole; it would make him nearly invisible as well.

He brought his rifle up to his shoulder, his finger tense on the trigger. He looked down the barrel, looking along the sight as he aimed it around. He flicked off the safety with his finger. He heard some shouting, and tensed. He could hear running feet, getting close quickly. Suddenly, out of the shadows, a figure emerged quickly, running straight at him, yelling loudly. Two more became visible, a few meters back, also running in his direction. They were holding something long in their hands; in the dark it was difficult to tell what it was. He had only a moment to make his decision. He squeezed the trigger twice at the one in front. The shadow fell to the ground without a sound. As it fell, he saw a second fall directly behind him.

He had not seen that one; it must have been directly behind the one in the lead. The bullets he had fired had gone through the front person and also struck the person behind. A half second later he targeted his sights on the last two figures, and fired three times at each, in quick succession. One dropped quickly, the other first went to his knees, and then slowly fell over onto his back. He stayed motionless, smelling the gunsmoke linger in the air, keeping the rifle aimed down the lane. Three of the figures were motionless, the fourth was moving slightly. He waited until he felt sure that no one else was following these four, waiting to spring a trap on him. He discharged the clip, and inserted a full one into the rifle, sliding a round into the chamber with a click. He stepped out of the cavity, the rifle held at his hips, his finger still on the trigger. He came to the first person. He lay flat on his stomach, arms outstretched. One hand held a torch that was burning steadily, the other held two more sticks that had cloth wrapped around the ends. He hadn't even seen the fire as he was running. The stranger had solved that problem for him.

He put one of the extra torches on the one that was burning, just to make sure the fire didn't extinguish while he was inspecting the bodies. It lit quickly, and gave a strong flame. Satisfied, he went to the next, the person that had he hadn't seen. She lay on her back, her eyes open wide.

One of the rounds from the man in front had caught her in the chest. By the looks of it, it had gone straight through her heart. She was a pretty girl. He shook his head, and walked to the other two. The third had fallen much like the first, straight forward, arms out, twisting a bit as he came to a stop.

He lowered the rifle, and went to the fourth, the one lying on his back. He was still alive, and looked upwards at him, silent except for his breathing. It was rapid and shallow. He stood over him, keeping wary. He looked back down, to see the man had died. He was older, and looked similar to his own father. That these four had survived was impressive; he had seen no one else alive, and now he had killed them. He bent down, and closed his eyes, muttering a prayer for him, and then again for the other three. He walked back down the street, to his hiding place, where he sat back with a deep sigh. He would get the torches soon; he wouldn't let them go out; he needed time to reflect.

He came out an hour later, when the torches were getting low. He wasn't ready to just yet, but he had no choice. Now that the initial adrenaline had passed, and he had time to absorb what had happened, he was wracked with guilt. He had acted rashly. He should have stayed in the dark. They would not have seen him; he would have had time to watch them, to see if they would be a threat to him. He shouldered the rifle, slung over his back, and collected some wood, stacking it over the torches somewhat randomly. He collected wood for over an hour, building the fire into a raging pyre that sent flame and sparks high into the sky. He wasn't thinking; he just needed something to do physically. It was a routine that kept his mind clear. When his mind cleared, he saw the size of the fire raging, and he stopped and shook his head. He had acted rashly again. The fire could surely be seen for some distance. For not wanting to attract attention to himself, he had just done so in splendid fashion. He stopped adding wood to the blaze, and instead threw it into a pile for later use.

He went to the bodies one by one, piling bricks around and over them in a makeshift grave. He owed them at least a proper burial, so he gave them that decency. When he was done, he was exhausted, both mentally and physically. Sweat dripped from his body, and he could feel his limbs shaking. He went to the locker, when he was done, and ate, filling himself on bread, and washing it down with water from the pipe. He watched the fire burn down as he ate, finally to a point where he would be able to conceal it soon. A benefit to the large blaze he had created was that he had a thick bed of coals to work with. They glowed a deep bright orange, and when the wind blew over them, they flared nearly white. He gathered more stones and bricks, and pushed them into the edges of the fire with a pole, into a circular shape around the bed of coals. He built up a small wall around the fire, and as it cooled, and the stones blocked some of the heat from reaching him directly, he built it higher. When the embers were behind a wall nearly two feet high, he stopped, satisfied the fire was sufficiently concealed, and that the wall would insulate the coals enough to keep them hot for some time. He added more at the base before stopping, creating a small irregular cone that went up to the lip of the pit. He drank heavily when he was done, until his belly sloshed with water, and he could feel his swollen stomach. He went back to his hidden cavity, and settled in, trying to get as comfortable as he could. The heat was making him groggy and listless. He gave up trying to get more comfortable, closing his eyes and crossing his arms over his lap. He fell asleep quickly, his eyes twitching as he dreamt of better days.

He woke a couple of hours later, after sleeping restlessly. He was exhausted and groggy, and the heat in the air made sleep feel impossible; it was too uncomfortable. With every inhale he could feel the heat in the air go into his lungs; it was hot and dry, and his body was sweating profusely. He drank as much water as he could swallow without bursting, his stomach was swollen with water. He could not get cool. He undressed down to his underwear, piling his clothes near the water pipe in case he needed them later. He stood under the pipe, letting the water flow over his body, trying to cool himself off. When his muscles started to seize, he walked around the area, not wanting to sit any further. The fires from the distant oil refinery had nearly died off, and the sky had lost its reddish glow, returning to its more familiar black.

The smell of the rotting bodies buried in the ruins had become omnipresent, inescapable. He stopped walking, feeling dizzy in the heat.

He could feel his heart beating in his chest, thumping wildly as if he had just completed running an all-out sprint. He had to lie down, if just for a little bit, to try to relax. He laid down on a clear patch of street, closing his eyes and trying to breathe deeply, concentrating on slowing down his heartbeat. It didn't work; his heart continued to race, and he could feel it becoming irregular, every little bit he could feel it flutter in his chest, rapidly pumping a few beats, and then returning to its stressed pace before fluttering again. He stood up and went back to the buckets of water. His stomach didn't feel so bloated as it had before, and he was concerned that in the extreme heat that he would become dehydrated. He needed to be able to sweat, to cool himself off. The sweat was pouring out of him, and he could taste the salinity on his skin. It wasn't as salty as it was before, not nearly as much, but he wasn't concerned; his goal was to drink as much water as he could hold. Once the heat passed, he would be okay, he just couldn't get dehydrated. He knelt to the ground and raised handfuls of water to his mouth, drinking it greedily, whatever he missed running down his chest into the dry soil. His stomach was soon full, like he had eaten a large meal, and when he tried to sit upright, he found it too uncomfortable, and had to lie down. He burped, and felt a bit up water come back up, into the back of his throat. He reflexively swallowed, and grimaced at the slight taste of vomit in his mouth.

Now that he was laying on the ground, he felt a little better when the dizziness returned. Feeling the ground at his back helped him keep calm, reassuring his mind that it was only a feeling. If he had been standing, the dizziness would have had him on the ground. By looking and concentrating on objects around him, it also helped combat the feeling. When his eyes began to flutter, it became an annoyance. He would be looking at a wall or a brick to reduce his dizzy feeling, and then his eyes would just start to close involuntarily, twitching and contracting. When he squeezed his eyes closed, he could feel the muscles continuing to contract. He tried rubbing his eyes, and then opening them wide. For a moment, it was normal, and then it started with his left eyelid, and a minute later, his right.

Swearing under his breath, he closed his eyes, preferring to see nothing than having his eyes close on him. He dug his hands into the earth, to feel more secure, to convince his mind that he was not actually spinning. His heart began to flutter again, the steady beat becoming irregular, and quivering inside him. He breathed deeply, inhaling the hot air, fighting to calm himself. Then his body pulled tight, his muscles contracting and pulling him backwards. His jaws clenched tight, and every muscle in his body was flexed and quivering, his back raised off the ground as his spine curved backwards. Farzam groaned loudly between clenched teeth, breathing loudly from his clenched mouth and nose, gasping for air.

His hands scrabbled in the dust, seeking something to grab and hold onto, and finding only loose dirt and small pebbles. He could feel his heart thumping wildly in his chest, and his vision began to blur, his sight going grey at the edges. His eyes clamped shut, and he fought to keep them open, even as his vision faded. He knew he was losing consciousness, and the thought terrified him, of laying there, helpless. He gulped in air, and then gasped it out, his body tense and rigid and not allowing him to relax and breath normally. The tendons in his neck were flexed like cords under his skin, and were burning with exhaustion. Mercifully, when he lost consciousness, it was sudden, and nothing he sensed. His eyes quickly rolled up into the back of his skull, the whites showing as his eyelids opened and closed involuntarily. His body arched in rictus as his mind no longer fought for control, every muscle taut and shaking. He shook on the ground for minutes, and when his body finally collapsed to the ground, a deep sigh of air emanated from his lips, and he vomited in several large contractions, the fluid bursting from his mouth and nose, pooling around his head and neck. The vomit in his mouth stuck in his throat, and when his lungs tried to inflate, they drew it in, and he gasped and choked instinctively, his body trying to clear the airway.

He gurgled and coughed, and threw up a little more, and tried to inhale, and his face began to go blue, his body going tense with its need for oxygen. He lay on the ground, bubbling foam running over his lips. His body seized, going tense from head to toe, and then fell to the ground one last time, a gurgling exhale belching from his mouth in a spray of froth. His bladder and sphincter let go simultaneously, and his fisted hands slowly unclenched, his head falling to one side, the contents of his mouth draining into the dirt.

Rasa heard the gunshots clearly, distant though they were. At first, she hadn't realized what they were, only suddenly aware of a new sound in the distance, a few quick pops and cracks in the darkness.

Then she heard several more shots a second later, perhaps another four or so; she couldn't tell. She ducked to the ground, covering Hamid with her own body, suddenly fearful that she was being shot at. She lay terrified over him, shielding him with her body. He groaned at the pressure of her on him, but did not wake or stir. She lay on him for a few minutes, daring not to breathe, trying to keep as still as possible, any moment expecting to feel a rifle at the back of her head. It did not come, and she eventually rose, cautiously, looking around slowly. All she could see was the glow of fires in the distance, and shadow. The others had been shot at, she finally concluded. With the number of shots she had heard, they may all be dead. Poor Ziba, and Peyman. The Imam and Afshar.

She wiped tears from her cheeks, suddenly more scared for what was going to happen to her. Previously there was hope that the others would return with food and water and bring her with them; now there was little she could do. She could go in their direction, to see what had happened, but then she also risked being killed, and she could not leave Hamid alone in his condition. She felt trapped, wanting to run, but afraid she would run into the jaws of the beast itself. She stood, shaking, chewing her fingernails in the dark, her eyes roving in the dark while her mind raced for a solution. She brushed a strand a dark hair from her face irritably, her arm flicking it back quickly. It woke her from her trance, and she looked down at Hamid. He was staring back up at her, his eyes wide open with his mouth partly open. She knelt down quickly, her hand to his forehead. It was still warm, but his eyes did not blink when her hand went over his face. She placed her palm over his mouth, expecting to feel the slight breeze of his breath on her skin. She felt nothing, and nervously spread her hand over his face, the fingers shaking. His eyes never moved, and she lowered her fingers to his eyelids, waiting for him to react and blink. He remained still, and when her fingertips touched his eyelids, she only felt the softness of his skin, and not the reaction of his blink that she had hoped for. Her hand recoiled quickly, suddenly nervous that she may have hurt him, and also in partial revulsion that she had touched someone that was dead. After a few moments of collecting herself, breathing deeply and nervous fidgeting, she lowered her hand back to his face, and closed his eyelids, pulling them down over his blank eyes. Her skin crawled as she did so, her arm tingling, wanting to not be touching him. When his eyes were closed, she held her arm close to her chest, clutching it at the wrist, while she looked down at Hamid, breathing loudly with emotion. She knelt there for a few minutes, and then crossed his arms over his chest, hand over hand. She collected her things in a shawl, and stood, wondering what to do next. She already knew, but was afraid of taking that first step, making the commitment to what she had to do.

To walk around in the dark, aimlessly, was foolhardy, and she knew that it would be certain death. She knew roughly the direction the others had gone in, and in that direction there was food and water.

Taking a deep breath, she took the first step, and then another, each one firming her resolve to continue, to face the risk that certainly lay ahead, over the certain outcome of going any other way.

She lay in the ruins on her stomach, her mouth parched, her eyes wild and hungry. A piece of stone dug into her ribs, but she ignored the pain. Compared to her thirst, the stone was an inconvenience. The huge fire glowed in the darkness, the sparks and embers floating high into the sky before drifting off into the wind. She had wandered roughly in a straight line by her reckoning, using dark shapes as landmarks as she walked quietly through the streets. The fire on the horizon continued to burn, the outlines of the refinery clear in the backdrop of the flames. Some of the tall structures were sagging in the extreme heat, the metal melting. She had seen the fire from a distance; it was already roaring when she had seen it, and she had watched it closely to see if there was any motion. She hadn't seen anyone or anything moving around, so she proceeded cautiously, trying to use the darkness to her advantage, staying the shadows, out of the light of the fire. She picked her steps closely, putting her weight down slowly to not make any rubble come free, revealing her position. Whoever had fired the shots she had heard was around here somewhere, and she did not intend to make an easy target.

She went slowly forward, and at last had seen somebody moving around. All she could see was an outline of a man. He was moving around in the ruins, and she followed him with her eyes, watching him like a predator stalking her prey. She dared not move, seeing now where he was. In the light of the fire, down the street, she had seen the four irregular piles of rubble in the street, staggered and spaced out. He had killed them, she had seen the evidence. They had fallen within a stones throw of making it to their goal. She didn't feel any anger or sorrow; she was too hungry and thirsty. Her friends were dead, killed by this moving shadow. All that mattered now was the food and water that was in the dark. She couldn't see where it was, but he kept returning to a built up shadow in the dark, a pile that resembled the building that Peyman had described. It was hard to tell from her angle, but it must certainly be it. Somewhere in that darkness was food and water. Her stomach growled, and her tongue rasped in her mouth, her lips a cracked leathery skin, caked with dust. She saw him struggle into the darkness, wandering unsure on his feet, staggering over the ground. He vanished in the darkness, and she could not see where he was from her point.

She waited for what seemed like hours, before deciding to get closer, to see more for herself, being driven on by her needs. Perhaps, if she caught him sleeping, she could steal a few bits of food and a few mouthfuls of water, before making it back into the dark. If she was quiet, she could do it. She had to try. She would die if she didn't make the attempt. She covered the ground slowly, her heart beating with excitement and adrenaline. She was scared out of her mind, her senses on high alert. She felt as if she could see and hear everything; the sudden clarity in the darkness increasing her confidence and boldness.

She walked up the lane out of the direct line of the fire, not creeping from shadow to shadow as she had planned. She had her hands out to her side, her fingers spread, ready to catch herself, prepared to fling herself to the ground to hide at a moments notice. She could hear the water bubbling, splashing, as if it was a fountain; the grandest fountain that had ever existed. The sound was driving her mad, making her feel ill with need. Her mouth tasted salty, the promise of water making her feel her dehydration and weakness. Her limbs were trembling in spite of her feeling of strength, her body using the last of its energy to press forward. She crept around the corner, her face peering around the side of the building, her eyes searching for him. She could hear something in the dark, like the ground was being scratched and torn, a gritty dry sound. She saw his legs first, his feet tensed, the muscles in his legs shaking, and then dropping to the ground. His feet fell to the sides, quivering and twitching twice, before laying still.

She rounded the corner more, slowly, taking each step with extreme precision. He came into view, laying on the ground. The dirt to his sides had been torn at by his hands, the dirt clawed at by his fingers, the shallow furrows of earth criss-crossed at all angles. His hands lay palm up at his sides, the fingertips bloody and torn. His head lay to one side; she couldn't see his face. She came forward, rounding the corner into the opening where he lay, and was struck by the smell of his urine and excrement. She gagged strongly, raising her arm to her nose to try to shield herself from the smell.

She walked around him, the sudden need to eat and drink momentarily forgotten, the heat only a sensation. His eyes were closed, and she suddenly feared he was only sleeping, or laying in a trap for her, that he would suddenly wake and go for the rifle leaning against the wall. She watched his chest, to see if it would rise and fall. It didn't move, and after a few minutes, emboldened, she walked around to where his face lay hidden. A thick foam clotted his mouth, the vomit drying around his face, already drawing a host of flies. In spite of everything, she felt badly for him. She looked at him for a few moments, and then heard the water clearly, roaring in her ears, her body reminding her what she was looking for.

She found the source quickly, finding the overflowing bucket under the pipe. The clear water bubbled over the lip of the bucket, soaking into the ground. The smell of the water, its freshness driving her to her knees. She almost plunged her hands into the bucket, to drink from it, and then stopped at the last moment. She took the time to move the bucket over, and then let the water fall on her face, washing away the dirt and grime that had soaked onto her face, rubbing her hands over her skin to remove the last of it. She scrubbed her hands together, cleaning them, enjoying the feeling of the water drying on her face, cooling her in the heat, feeling her pores opening like a thousand mouths. She opened her mouth, letting the water run over her lips. The dried skin cracked when she smiled, and she ignored the pain, spitting out the first few mouthfuls of water, rinsing her mouth of the salty paste. When her mouth was clean, she swallowed a few mouthfuls, feeling it flow down her throat and into her stomach. Her stomach cramped, and then relaxed. She swallowed the water slowly, letting most of it flow over her body. She removed her clothes, feeling the water flow over her, soothing her raw skin. She ran her hands over herself, cleaning herself as best she could, and then rinsed her clothes, wringing them as dry as he could, before dressing herself only slightly, covering her privates but leaving as much as she could bare.

Feeling clean, with water in her belly, her stomach roared for something more substantial. She found a few baskets of bread in short order, and grabbed the closest loaf, cracking it in half, the thick crust flaking away to reveal bread that was still sweet and moist within. The air filled with the smell of it, and her mouth watered as never before. She bit into it, and shovelled it into her mouth, as fast as she could chew. The bread was like an elixir, the flavour unrivalled, the texture incredible. It was plain bread, and it was the best meal she had ever eaten. She ate the entire loaf, and a few wedges of small cheese found in the corner.

She slumped to the ground, feeling full and refreshed. Her arms were still shaking from hunger, but she could feel the nourishment spreading through her. With it, came the need for sleep. The heat and a full belly proved overwhelming, and she curled to the ground in a fetal position, her knees tucked high into her chest, her hands under her head. With the fire dying in the street, her eyes closed slowly, watching the fire flicker and dance, and when they closed at last, she slept soundly, as if all was well in the world.

When she woke, she felt rested, and uncomfortably hot. The heat was making her feel groggy, and sick to her stomach. The body of the man that had died on the ground had already begun to bloat, his stomach swollen, the skin pulled tight. She drank some more water, enough to fill her, and let it wash over her face for a minute, letting it soak into her hair. She went to the body, took a hold of it by the feet, and dragged it out into the street, away from where she would see it.

He was heavy, and it was hard work, and the sickly smell of rot and shit carried from him, making her want to throw up. He farted twice as she pulled him along, the gasses making her eyes water. When she was done, her skin crawled, and she ran to the pipe, rinsing herself furiously with her hands, trying to remove the memory from her mind. She shuddered a few times in recollection, and then heard the pipe begin to gurgle. The water pressure was slowing, and as she watched, the water went from a steady trickle, to an irregular wave, the water spurting from the pipe in small gouts. It bubbled a few times, and then stopped, a single drop clinging to the lip. Rasa stared up at the pipe, horrified. She had a few full buckets to use, but they would not last forever, and they were too heavy to carry around while she looked for another source. She sat back onto her heels, wondering what she was going to do. She wiped some water from her face, and then sat on the ground, her head in her hands.

Her head was pounding, her stomach rolling. The heat was unbearable, weighing down on her, every breath a conscious action.

Sweat was pouring out of her, and she felt tired in the oppressive warmth. She lay on the ground, limbs outstretched, wishing to feel a cool breeze wash over her. She needed to sleep, to have an escape.

The pipe was dry; she had tried shaking it and bending it, only to be rewarded with a few hot drops that had run down the length of pipe to her hand. Whatever source had been driving the flow had finally failed, the water pressure was gone. The horizon was black; the fire at the refinery had finally consumed itself, starved of fuel it had died.

Rasa had let the fire the man had built die. She did not need the fire for warmth or cooking, and the coal bed was deep enough that she was sure the coals would be hot for another day, if she had a change of heart. The tops of the coals still glowed red, so there was time.

Laying on the ground, she could not imagine why she would need fire. It was too hot already. She had begun to drop in and out of sleep, the heat affecting her mind. Twice in the dark she had yelled out, calling for her husband, a man that lay dead in the ruins of their home, their daughter crushed beneath him. She had seen him clearly, walking around her, and she had yelled at him to bring her some water, a cool glass of water, just one. He had vanished, and reappeared later, so she had asked him again. He had not come back. She woke from her delusion, shaking her head, missing him terribly, feeling the pain in her chest. She had not had much time to grieve for the loss of her family, and in the brief time since the earthquake, she had been too busy to be overwhelmed by her emotions. Now that she was alone, her mind had time to wander, and it returned over and over again to her family. In the heat, her emotions fed her delusions, blurring what was real and what was imagination, reopening her wounds. And the worst of it was that she knew she was delusional; when she woke up, she felt the need to go to the kitchen, except the logical part of her mind that was still in control told her that there was no kitchen to go to, and she knew it. But the rest of her mind was convinced she was wrong, that it really was there. All she had to do was go around the corner, and it would surely be there, just as clear as day. She felt dizzy and disorientated, waking up once feeling the world around her spinning. She knew it wasn't, but oh it felt so terrible, and she had sat up, trying to make the feeling go away, that it was wrong. When at last everything had stopped whirling around her, she saw Nima, her husband, in the distance.

"Nima!" she cried out to him. He turned, and began to walk away.

"Wait!" she yelled. She jumped to her feet, and ran towards him.

He disappeared, and then would reappear, and she ran onwards, trying to catch him, always nearly catching up, only to have him vanish again. She knew he was close; she could smell him; she could *feel* him in the air. She missed his scent; she had always found it comforting; something that made her sleep easy at night if he was away. She felt her tears flowing in frustration. She just couldn't find him. The heat was so bad, so terrible; if she could just be with him it wouldn't be so bad, he would know what to do, or where they could go and escape this. She saw him again, down the street, their daughter holding his hand, waving at her, a broad smile on her face, her favourite dress curling in the wind.

"Ghazal!" she screamed, her throat thick with emotion. Her daughter stopped, and waved back, her small hand motioning her forward.

Rasa cried aloud, sobbing, and ran forward, watching as Nima and Ghazal walked around a corner, disappearing again from view. She ran as fast as she could, and when her foot caught the edge of a curb, she barely felt it. She plunged forward, her hands out, trying to break her fall. Her arms hit the ground hard, her skin scraping on the concrete, and her head caught the edge of a pipe, a thick metal drain that had cracked in two in the earthquake, and then broken free from the ground, sticking above the surface of the road. She lay on the ground, dazed, in pain, her vision swirling and full of stars and bright images floating in the darkness.

Her cracked skull bled furiously, the warm blood flowing over her face. She lay there, her eyes wandering, looking along the surface of the road. She heard footsteps, and her eyes focused on two small sandals that suddenly stood before her, the sweet lavender scent of Ghazal's soap filling her nostrils, and then she saw Nima's shoes next to the sandals.

"Ghazal," she whispered in the dark.

"Nima."

She could feel her daughters small hands stroke her hair, and then a small warm kiss on her cheek.

"Mama." She heard her voice clearly.

"Rasa." It was Nima, and his voice sounded so strong.

"Rasa. You can come with us now. Come, our family is waiting."

She felt his hand on the small of her back, comforting her, giving her strength. She smiled, feeling his strength flow into her, her tears mixing with her blood in the street, glad to have caught up with them. And when she stopped breathing at last, closing her eyes for the final time, the smile stayed on her face. The darkness held no more fear.

Ixtab

Ixtab and Bacab watched as the sun set to the West. The sky had faded from blue to orange, and then finally slipped into hues of pink and red as the sun disappeared below the waves of the sea. The time had passed surprisingly fast. When dusk came the grounds slowly became lit by more and more campfires, and the lights of the surrounding tourist facilities. A few stars came out, dim points of light in the sky of the setting sun, until the sky faded to black and they became dominant. The stars of the Orion came out, the three stars of the belt an obvious constellation to the most ignorant of people.

They drank periodically from small gourds of water they had carried to the top, and Bacab kept the sacrificial fires burning, placing fragrant plants into the embers once the heart and burned into ash.

Ixtab stood nearly motionless, only moving enough to drink and occasionally shift his weight from one foot to the next. When the sun descended to the horizon, he began to pray, exalting in the last sunset of the Age. Bacab stood nearby, watching Ixtab praying to the Gods and Ancestors. He could feel their ghosts hovering around him, his skin prickling into gooseflesh and the hairs on his neck standing up. He felt comfort in their presence, knowing his people of old were there to celebrate with him, that they in turn could witness the ceremony with one of their own. When the sun had set, Ixtab kneeled onto the stone in a posture of penitence, his arms upraised in alternating gestures of forgiveness and worship. He prayed quietly, the words meant to be heard only by the Gods. Bacab knew what he was saying, but made certain to stand far enough away to not hear the words being spoken.

The prayers were meant only for the Gods; to eavesdrop would be blasphemous.

Bacab checked his wristwatch, a silver Timex that was badly scratched and beaten, the face so worn in some places the dial underneath could scarcely be seen. It was the only technology he owned. The masses of people below had erected a large digital clock that was counting down to midnight, and the end of the day and of the Age. More and more people gathered around the front where possible, until there were too many people to do so. A helicopter flew in the distance, its search spotlight occasionally highlighting them in the dark. He could see the reporter crews down below with their cameras, all lit with small blinking red lights as they recorded the event for posterity. Some were recording the crowds with the large clock, and others were aimed at them. The helicopter did a slow circle around the entire area, surveying the scene below. The clock counted down to three, two and then one, and the crowd below erupted in a cheer as they clock stopped at zero. His Timex showed two more minutes to go.

The people below celebrated in various ways, some had small fireworks, others lit up their doobies, determined to get as stoned as possible in as little time as possible. Others lit ceremonial fires and wafted the smoke over themselves in a cleansing ritual. Ixtab had prostrated himself on the stone, his arms outstretched and his head bowed, his forehead pressed to the block he knelt on. He was silent. Bacab said a silent prayer to the night sky, looking up at the hundreds of stars that twinkled down at them, the fuzzy caul of the Milky Way easily visible in the clear sky. The partying below continued as he finished, but still Ixtab would not move. He knew he would not move for hours, not until the pain had numbed his joints and he needed aid to stand. He must kneel there and endure. He felt privileged to have been born into such a time, and he wondered if anyone below him felt the same way.

He turned around to face the East, to where the new day would dawn, seeing the distant electric lights fade off to the horizon. As he watched, the very furthest away went off. And they continued to go, the far horizon now totally black and creeping towards them. The lights continued to go out, and as he watched, the city began to go dark, then the grounds, and within another minute all of the lights failed, and the pyramid was plunged into darkness. Only the flickering orange flames of the fires

444

below cast light into the celebration that suddenly went quiet. It was a sign. The Gods were showing themselves. The Age of Center had come! He trembled in excitement, to see what would unfold, to be a witness to Their actions! He could hear a few people on the grounds complaining the power was out, a few of the more rowdy crowd took the darkness as an opportunity to become more boisterous, and a few fights broke out. He noticed the cameras were off, their red lights no longer blinking in the dark, and he could hear swearing from where he knew they were. The helicopter that had been flying around them suddenly sounding different; he could still hear the rotors cutting into the air, but they were losing power, the sounds becoming less and less forceful. The aviation lights were no longer blinking on its fuselage. He knew where it was by sound and by its silhouette against the night sky.

He heard it slow, and could see it losing altitude, high over the forest. He watched as it suddenly lost its little remaining lift, and plummeted to the ground. A few trees cracked loudly as the chopper struck them, its blades cutting into the branches, tearing themselves apart.

With a crunch of metal the aircraft hit the ground, and then a gout of flame burst through the forest canopy and spent itself into the night sky. A cry rose from the people below, and a few groups ran towards the explosion, aware of what had happened. Ixtab did not move, could not move. He had to remain still. Bacab stayed with him.

"What do you mean, the god dammed camera is off? Turn it on!" Cyndi was furious, and Greg was pole axed. It had been recording fine one moment, and the next it had simply shut down with a faint whirring sound. He couldn't figure it out. She was standing next to him, pacing on the ground and swearing under her breath, arms crossed under her breasts.

"Fuck, Greg, we are missing out here!" His temper began to rise.

Every camera around them was dead, too. Whatever had affected his camera, had affected every camera. They heard the chopper going down, and then the crunching of branches and the explosion as it hit the ground.

"You're an idiot! The helicopter crashes and we missed it!" That was enough. He grabbed her by the shoulders and shook her.

"Listen here."

His voice rose in anger as he spoke each word.

"If you have finished your tantrum, you will notice every camera here is dead. EVERY fucking one! No one caught the chopper going down, so unless you're going to be helpful, you can shut your fucking trap!"

She stared at him, her eyes indignant with fury. She struggled against his grip, glaring at him as he glared at her, confident he would back down first. He didn't. She blinked and dropped her eyes. He let her go, and she stepped back, rubbing where he had held her arms. She turned around, fuming, but not saying anything. Her mind was racing. *How dare he speak to me like that!*, she thought. *He should be grateful he was working with her; in fact, he should be groveling! If it wasn't for me, he would be working in some flyspeck shithole in the middle of nowhere.* She knew that wasn't true; he was talented and could work anywhere he wanted, but at that particular moment, she was too furious to admit it. She glared off into the distance, content that by turning her back to him she was delivering another message to him, something that was sure to infuriate him. He didn't even notice. His back was turned to her as he inspected his camera. There was little he could do in the near darkness, so he had gone to the nearest fire where other camera crews had gathered, all looking at their equipment that had suffered the same sudden failure.

As she glared into the crowd, she noticed a few people had their cell phones out, and were trying to turn them on. They were having no luck, either. The phone screens stayed dark, not even the keys lighting up on the keypad.

In the darkness, someone distinctly cried out, "Hey man, what the FUCK happened to my phone?"

"Mine is dead, too," another voice stated, and then more and more voices joined in as people tried their phones.

"What is going on?" she whispered under her breath. *Something is very wrong.* She turned around, expecting to see Greg behind her. No one was behind her. Everyone had collected around the fires like moths to a flame. One crew from CNN had their camera nearly completely disassembled. The operator was shaking his head.

"What the hell?" He was holding a component of the camera up to the light, turning it to catch different angles.

"Here, check it out," he said, passing it to the man next to him.

He squinted, looking at the electronics. Cyndi came up behind them, where Greg had also leaned in. The board was clearly fried. A black mark stained the micro circuitry like a small bomb had gone off on it, the familiar green of the panel charred.

"What the hell causes that to happen? I ain't *ever* seen anything like that." A few other operators were suddenly inspired, and began to breakdown their cameras further. Every one had a fried board. Some were worse than others, but the link was unmistakable.

"It's like an electromagnetic pulse, or something. Something happened that fried everything electronic." That was when he noticed the sky was even darker than he had realized. He hadn't noticed the electrical lights were out also. He grabbed Cyndi's hand, pulling her toward the pyramid.

"What are you doing?" she yelled, suddenly mad at him again.

"We are going to the top to get a look around. Something is very wrong here."

They got to the first step, and started to climb. Before long she was wheezing for breath, panting for air. He was surprised. For someone with a hot body, she sure was in shitty shape. If she didn't watch it, she was going to balloon at some point.

"Come on, keep going." He pushed her backside. Normally he would have given her a quick squeeze while he was at it, but he wasn't in a joking mood.

"Hey!" she exclaimed, mad at being pushed.

"We don't have time to sightsee. Get your breath at the top."

Suddenly mad at him again, she forced herself upwards on pure will, her legs and lungs burning with the effort. If she could have spared the energy to swear at him, she would have. Instead, she gasped for breath. When they reached the top, Greg was panting hard, sweat dripping from his body. He had pulled Cyndi up the last few stairs, her legs having finally given out entirely, and she shook with exhaustion. He saw Ixtab and Bacab some distance away, by the looks of it Bacab was standing and Ixtab was kneeling. They paid them no notice. He stood up, taking deep breaths that filled his lungs, while Cyndi was laying flat on the summit, gasping heavily.

"I feel like I'm going to puke,' she gasped between breaths. A moment later, she did, retching on the stones, kneeling on all fours.

"Shit,' he thought. The only thing worse than puking, was the sound of puking. He waited until she finished, and then he stood her up, leaning her against himself. She was still shaking with exhaustion, and her breath had that sickly sweet small of vomit. She clung to him without saying a word. He looked around, and saw nothing but the horizon outlined against the sky, the black forest meeting the twinkling stars at some point in between. The only light, the only manmade light, came from the fires below. That settled it; something was very seriously wrong. For the city to also be out of power, it had to be large electrical disturbance. His mind worked to find a possible solution. A nuclear blast would do it, but that seemed too unlikely. To be affected, the blast would have to be close, and there was no flash of light or explosion. A normal power failure wouldn't cause their electronics to fry. The helicopter crash suddenly didn't seem so random. Whatever had happened had also brought the chopper down. It had *lost power*. Cyndi was beginning to stir, starting to feel better.

"What did we come up here for?" she asked, her face pressed to his chest. He lowered his mouth to her ear, talking through a wave of her hair that still smelled like her shampoo.

"There is no power anywhere. All the lights are off."

She turned around, to see what he was talking about, seeing for the first time the near perfect blackness of the night.

"What happened?"

He shook his head.

"Dunno. Not likely to be a nuke."

"A nuke!?" she exclaimed, raising her voice a little higher than conversational.

"We would have seen the blast. Whatever it was created an electromagnetic pulse. It fried everything electronic. It explains the cameras, the lights, the chopper, *everything.*"

"What else could it have been then?" she asked.

"I don't know. Maybe an explosion in the atmosphere. There was no lightening, the sky is clear. I don't even know if lightening could do that."

"What do you mean; an explosion in the atmosphere?"

"I mean something came into the atmosphere and exploded, something fairly big, and the explosion made an electrical disturbance that caused this." He waved his hands in the air, showing the darkness around them.

"How often does that happen?" she asked.

"Explosions in the atmosphere happen probably more than you want to know. NORAD gets several explosions a year in the upper atmosphere that are nuclear in size. Early warning satellites pick them up. And in 1908 there was the explosion in Russia. The forest for miles around was flattened and burned. If it had happened over a city, everyone would have died. Only then, our technology was too basic to be affected by things like that. Electrical, I mean."

"What do you mean?"

"I mean, basic electronics, like things with vacuum tubes are largely unaffected. Things with smaller circuitry are the most vulnerable. The Russians even used tubes in highly advanced aircraft, to make them less vulnerable in case of a nuclear war."

She stood there, thinking about what he had said, wondering if it was possible.

"But wouldn't we hear something like that?"

"Not if it was very high up. With all of the cheering and noise that was going on down there before the power went out, it would have been really easy to not notice."

He looked over where Bacab stood. He was evidently aware of them, but made no move to leave the spot where Ixtab was seemingly frozen.

He stood there for a while, enjoying their shared body heat, feeling her breath on his neck. He watched the shadows on the ground moving through the firelight, their long shadows stretching over the grass. A few people had tried to start their vehicles, only to find they would not start.

L

People had started to gather in larger numbers around the burning fires, or to make their own, seeking comfort as the heat of the day faded away. Others had begun to walk down the road, back towards the hotels that stood as rectangular shadows off in the distance. It would take then some time to reach them, but there were few options otherwise. No one else had thought to climb the pyramid, although several people were sitting or laying down on the first few rows of stones that made up the base of the structure.

"What do you want to do?" He felt her voice against him.

"I dunno. We might as well sit here for a while, or lie down. We might see the power come back on sooner from up here."

He felt her nod.

"You don't want to go back to the hotel?"

"That would take us a few hours, and I'm not keen on walking in the dark. We're safer up here, too."

"Let's get out of the wind."

He hadn't felt it before she had said anything. A light breeze had sprung up, and the air was cool on his face. He nodded, and they walked towards where Bacab was standing, in front of the smaller structure that sat atop the pyramid. They could sit at its base, where there was a small recess, and get out of the wind completely. Greg saw Bacab tense and reposition himself between them, unsure of what they planned to do. He motioned with a pointed hand to the base where they were walking. He saw Bacab relax, a little. He kept an eye on them as they found the small opening, and then sat inside it. Greg lined the floor with his jacket, and then he sat inside, getting comfortable. When he was ready, he took Cyndi's hand, and led her down, where she snuggled between him and the wall. The stone was still radiating the heat of the day, and with the wind no longer able to touch them, they felt warmer almost instantly. Bacab watched them move about, and then relaxed his guard when he watched them settle into the building. Watching Bacab, his still shadow motionless against the night sky, Greg tried to think about how much time had passed since the power had failed. Everything happened so fast. He guessed maybe fifteen minutes since the power had failed and the chopper had crashed, followed by their quick ascent of the pyramid.

He must have been running on adrenaline to make it up so quickly. No wonder Cyndi had been breathing so hard. Fifteen minutes. The space inside the stone was comforting, and he felt himself begin to relax. Birds began to chirp and call in the forest, and he could hear a low rumble, not coming from anywhere in particular. The white bison began to bellow, and by the sounds of the people yelling below, it had broken free of its modest restraints. Bacab was looking around, aware of something. The bird calls rose to a din, and the ground heaved. The pyramid began to shake violently; he quickly pushed Cyndi out of the recess, and then quickly scrambled out onto the open platform on his hands and knees. A roaring sound filled his ears, and as he made his way out he could see the shadows of birds flying in the night sky. Bacab dropped to his knees, and went over to where Ixtab was trying to stay in place. The giant stones of the pyramid crackled as they shifted against one another, popping like gunshots. The recess where they had been hiding began to loosen, and a few capstones shifted and then fell, hitting the other stones with a loud clap. Smaller stones in the structure began to break free of their mortar and fell to the ground, rattling and crashing as they rolled down the slope of the pyramid. He could hear screaming from down below, but couldn't see anything that happened on the ground from his vantage point.

Bacab was swaying back and forth on his knees, keeping an eye on Ixtab but not touching him, staying by his side. Underneath the roaring sound of the earthquake, he could hear the metallic scraping of the vehicles down below, being moved over the rolling ground. He counted as the seconds passed, knowing earthquakes generally don't last too long, perhaps a couple of minutes. Underneath them, the stones of the pyramid began to separate, small gaps opening where previously none had existed. Some blocks on the outer wall vibrated away from the core, and then toppled down, hitting each layer of stone as they fell with a sharp crack sound. More screams came from below, the growing cries of utter panic. And then the violence came to an end. The roar of the quake reached its peak and then subsided and quit, and the ground fell still. Cyndi uncovered her ears, and Bacab stood cautiously. After the fierce rumbling, everything seemed unnaturally quiet, the sudden calm ominous.

Leaving Cyndi sitting, Greg stood and walked cautiously to the edge of the platform, walking only where the blocks had moved the least.

The edge was no longer a smooth line of hand cut stone, but a jagged row of cracked and loose rock. He peered over the edge, witnessing a scene of violence. The few vehicles that had been down on the grounds had been tossed around, and three were even resting upside down, their roofs partially collapsed and window glass shattered. A few of the fires were out, and a few had spread as their embers had been shaken over the ground, igniting small grass fires that were slowly creeping forwards. The blocks that had fallen off the pyramid had left white impact marks of rock dust on the side they had fallen down, and buried themselves in the earth below. A few had rolled as they landed, finding only hard earth. Two people had been crushed by the falling stones, and the groups on the ground were in the process of covering the remains that had been splattered like a bug on a windshield. A few other blankets had already been used, covering other victims that he could only guess had been killed by the vehicles being tossed around the site. He could not see the bison; the fence structure that had enclosed it was flattened and torn apart, no match for the strength of an animal reacting to its survival instinct.

Several people were wounded, sporting self made bandages or covering their injuries with their hands, being supported or helped by others. One older man sat under a nearby tree, blood running freely from his forehead, the blood black against his skin in the darkness.

His right hand held a large bottle of something, and he was taking regular gulps of whatever was in the bottle.

"What do you see? What's down there?" Cyndi asked.

"A lot of hurt people. It's a mess."

"Can't we go help? Shouldn't we?"

He nodded mutely.

"We could, but we might also get in the way. There are a lot of people down there, and we don't have any supplies. We are better off staying up here looking after the four of us."

It was selfish, and he knew it, but he was more interested in keeping Cyndi safe from harm. Bacab stood watching them, nodding in agreement at what he heard, but keeping silent over Ixtab.

Greg motioned to Bacab, who came over slowly, after giving Ixtab a furtive glance.

"How long will he stay like that? On his knees?" Greg asked in a whispered voice.

Bacab replied quietly.

"He must pray until sunrise."

"What is he saying in his prayers?"

Bacab was silent for a moment, trying to think about how to explain and streamline the prayers for him.

"He is praying to the Gods of this Earth, and to the ghosts of our people for forgiveness of our ways, and in praise. He is seeking to show we are worthy of our Creators."

He started to stand, to return to Ixtab, when Greg quickly grabbed his heavily muscled forearm. It was hot and sweaty, not cool like he expected.

Bacab stopped quickly, his body tense and ready to strike. Greg released the arm, unconsciously sensing his tension.

"What do you think happened? All of this?"

"The Gods are speaking to us."

He returned to Ixtab, saying nothing more, leaving Cyndi and Greg to sit next to each other.

"The birds are still flying," Cyndi said.

"What?"

"The birds. They haven't landed."

She pointed up into the sky.

It was true. The air was filled with birds.

"Aftershocks?"

"Maybe," he replied.

"It wouldn't be unusual. I have never been in a quake before, but I know enough to know that one was a doozy."

"Is that a technical term?" she laughed, and he smiled back, glad to hear her sense of humor returning. Off in the distance, they heard a few sharp cracks, and then a soft rumble that ended in a few moments. The silence returned, and they listened intently.

"That must have been a hotel," Cyndi said. "Collapsing."

They tried to look in the direction of the hotels, but the sky was too dark, the hotels too far away. Greg looked at his wristwatch, fumbling at the small recessed button to light up the LED display.

"Piece of shit. These buttons are made for elves." Then he got it. Nothing. Even his watch was dead.

"It is nearly four."

They both jumped, not expecting Bacab to say anything.

"How do you know?" Cyndi asked.

He pointed to his wrist, where a gleam of metal reflected dimly in the night.

"Wait a minute," she said, perplexed, "how is yours working?"

Bacab made a winding motion, but said no more.

Greg chuckled.

"What's so funny, genius?"

"His watch. It's a wind up. It doesn't use batteries or electronics. Its just springs and gears. You don't see those very much anymore."

Off to the horizon, the sky was brightening, the midnight blue beginning to fade with the promise of sunrise.

"Oh, thank God," said Cyndi, her eyes hopeful seeing the beginnings of dawn. The night somehow made everything seem more repressive, more absolute. With daylight, they could see and walk for help. Her stomach growled. And get food. She was starving, after having puked up her dinner on the top of the steps hours earlier.

A breeze began to blow behind them, beginning so faintly that they did not even notice. It steadily picked up, and soon began to blow at their hair, brushing it in a steady wave.

"Jesus, that's cold."

Cyndi shivered, rubbing her arms for extra heat.

Greg nodded, agreeing. He looked forward to the sunlight as well, his body craving the heat. They sat together, sharing body heat.

The breeze continued to build over the next few minutes, occasionally gusting, howling in their ears and pulling at their clothes.

"Let's get back into that shelter," Greg said.

Cyndi agreed, and they went back to the wall, moving the fallen rocks out of the way so they could sit comfortably, brushing the gravel and mortar away with their hands.

"The birds," she pointed up.

Greg followed her arm into the sky.

They were hovering in the sky, their heads pointed into the wind, wings outstretched riding the air. When the wind gusted, they flapped their wings to try to stay stationary and to not be blown downwind.

The wind continued to build. And soon the sound of the wind blowing through the forest was distinct, the rustling of leaves and branches becoming louder. The sky continued to brighten, minute by minute, and the wind continued to pick up speed.

"Now what is going on?" Cyndi asked.

"Was there a storm in the forecast?"

Greg shook his head.

"Not that I remember." He was beginning to have to yell to make himself heard clearly. Bacab repositioned himself as a wind block for Ixtab, using his body to shield him as much as possible.

In the shelter of the small building on top of the pyramid, the wind did not touch them directly. Instead, they were being buffeted as the winds swirled and eddied around them, showering them with dust and small debris. They were forced to shield their faces with their arms, crouching low for protection. Underneath the sound of the howling wind, came another, more ominous rumble. It was deep, the kind of sound you felt in your guts more than you heard. The birds in the sky disappeared, turning with the wind and allowing it to push them away and high into the sky. The howl of the wind began to roar, and larger and larger debris began to be thrown into the air, branches snapped and shallow rooted trees fell to the ground, their crash muted.

Greg stood and cautiously went to the side of their shelter, carefully peering around the side, bracing his body into the wind. The deep rumbling sound was getting louder. He peered into the wind, shielding his face with an arm, trying to look into the storm. His eyes widened, and his stomach dropped. On the horizon, and moving quickly, he could see a wave of debris flying towards them, a black swirling cloud that rolled and churned in the air, carrying more and more with it, towards them. He turned back quickly and retreated against the wall. Cyndi leaned into him, yelling something in his ear. He couldn't make it out, and he tried to read her lips. He could see her frustration. He pointed at his lips. She understood, and repeated, over-emphasizing her words to try to make it clear.

"What….did…you…see?"

He thought about how to reply. Bacab was now kneeling headfirst into the wind, barely providing any shelter. His skin was getting cut from the objects breaking against his body.

He didn't reply, instead using his hands, trying to show a wall of wind coming their way. The brightening horizon began to darken as the blowing debris covered the sky. The wind began to shriek, Cyndi and Greg covering their ears, and Bacab settling down deeper, determined to shelter Ixtab. In the next moment, Greg and Cyndi felt the air get pulled from their lungs, and the wind exploded around them. The air clapped like a thunderstorm, and behind the shelter of the wall the air pulled Greg and Cyndi flat to the ground, pinning them down, barely able to breathe. Dust and leaves were sucked into the air, and then disappeared as the wind crashed over them. They watched with horror as Bacab and Ixtab were blown off the surface in an instant, neither man able to react. One moment they were there, and in the next the wave of air shattered around them and they were carried off into the sky, tumbling. The air was filled with the forest and anything the air could carry. Loose stones were torn out of their shattered mortar. Greg and Cyndi tried desperately to cling to each other and the ground, to find something to give them purchase, anything to hold onto. Then the wind that held them down began to swirl under them, breaking the vacuum that held them down. They were pelted with sand and debris, their skin cut and bleeding. Cyndi clung to him, her hands digging into his flesh with all her strength. He held onto a small stone that protruded just an inch above the rest. His hands burned, the wind pulling at him. He felt a fingernail crack as his hold slipped, the pain galvanizing him to hold on just a little tighter. A sudden undercurrent blew underneath him. Cyndi buckled in the wind like a kite, and was gone with a scream he never heard. She just wasn't holding onto him anymore. He screamed into the wind, suddenly lighter and more vulnerable. He felt the sweat on his fingers weaken his grasp, the flesh sliding on stone, and then nothing. He grabbed at empty air, and was himself carried off into the wind.

The pyramid grounds were scoured bare; the land left ravaged and windswept, a deep silence untainted by the sounds of Man or Beast. Trees lay flat, a few slim ones standing, stripped of leaves and branches, their bark peeled and cut. A few birds flittered through the devastation, seeking insects. The pyramid of Chichen Itza stood proud, high above the devastation, the bare stone cracked and broken in places, but otherwise holding steadfast, a monument to times past. The same was true for the pyramids of Palenque, Kukulkan, and Cholula; and countless others; islands of stone alone in the remains of the forest. When fire rained from the skies, the forests burned, and the temples were cleansed of their sins in purifying flame.

Kuljit Parmar

The tree crashed to the ground nearby, just outside the ring of thorn bushes that guarded their make shift camp. It was a large arjuna tree, tall and thickly leaved with wide branches. When it fell, it tore through the forest canopy with a roar of rustling leaves and crackling branches, before hitting the ground with a thunderous clap that boomed through the undergrowth. The men were startled awake, jumping out of their blankets with an instinctual jump, eyes wide and ready to run. Kuljit found himself leaning up on his elbows, torn from a dream where he was walking through Mumbai with his family. The spray of leaves and other debris from the forest floor spread out in a cloud that fluttered down to earth, the rich smell of kicked up soil hanging thick in the air. Janesh snorted and rolled over in his blanket.

"How did he sleep through that?" asked Amit, his heart thumping in his chest.

"At least he didn't shit himself again," Pawan muttered under his breath, trying to get comfortable on the ground.

Kuljit stayed sitting up, hearing the wind blowing loudly through the trees. He could see their dark silhouettes moving against the backdrop of the starry sky, the treetops swaying in a westerly direction. The logs had shielded them from the wind as they slept for the most part, keeping the worst of it off their backs. In a sitting position, Kuljit felt the wind blow his hair back, the gusts buffeting his shirt. Everyone else had settled back down, wrapped in their blankets and trying to fall asleep. Kuljit let them rest, and listened to the sound sin the dark. He could hear leaves being blown through the forest, and the treetops shaking loudly as the wind passed through the branches. In the distance, there was another crash, although muted and dull. Another tree being blown over in the night. The wind was blowing over them, catching the top of their fire pit and stirring up the ashes only slightly, stirring up the embers and making them glow with a bright orange light. He couldn't recall a wind like this before, in this time of year. It would not be unusual if it was the monsoons, but for this season it was odd. He felt a chill, and lowered himself to get out of the wind, behind the shelter of the log. He was now wide-awake and could not sleep, his mind working as he stared up into the sky. He could see leaves being blown through the sky high above him, blocking the view of the stars for an instant as they flittered past in a rolling and twisting course. The moon had moved across the sky, higher over the forest. It was a ruddy color, reddish, not so bright or crisp as it would be on a clear evening, or even as clear as it had been earlier in the evening.

He shifted his position, putting his back to the fire so he could look up over the log that was behind him. At first, his vision was dark and tinged orange, the image of the fire impairing his sight. Slowly, his eyes adjusted, the dark shapeless lump that was the log came into view, its features becoming visible in the low light cast by the fire and the moon above. He could see the leaves and dust blowing towards them over the treetops that were only slightly distant, just up the hill from where the creek fed into the lake, perhaps a kilometer away. At that distance, the debris formed a dusty haze that partially blocked the view of the sky Kuljit shifted his eyes upwards, trying to see the night sky above the fuzzy view of the blowing leaves. There was a line in the sky, where a black curtain of cloud suddenly blocked the clear night. He sighed, suddenly wishing he had pitched a tent, and he hoped it wouldn't rain before morning. He watched the wall of cloud, seeing it eating up the stars in the sky. The wind continued to rise in strength as he watched the front approaching. He frowned, watching the blackness spread towards them. It was coming quickly, creeping across the night sky with a rapid fluidness. He watched it over the horizon, and then as it neared, taking up a larger and larger amount of sky, now almost a quarter of the sky, and still growing quickly. The wind began to flow over the logs, and whistled through the gaps near the ground. Kuljit wondered if he was going to be able to pitch a tent in the darkness. It didn't smell like rain, but it was sure to come in a storm front like that. It was now over a third of the night sky, and by the way it was spreading over the sky, it would soon be over them. He pulled the blanket past his neck, pulling his legs up. He knew he should make a tent, but he didn't feel like he had the energy to do it. He would have to go deeper into the forest where he would be able to drive the tent pegs into the soil, for starters. And that meant they would have to try to get a perimeter together in the darkness in case Aryana came by on the prowl, or another of her kind. He hedged his bet, opting to hope for the best. The clouds were spreading incredibly fast he thought, watching the stars disappear bit by bit, until finally the limb of the moon was covered, and he watched as it quickly faded from view, plunging the landscape into a far greater darkness. He sat up, surrendering his hope to catch any more sleep for the time being. He wrapped the blanket around himself, covering his head and held tightly with his hand at his neck. He sat, back to the fire, watching the storm approach their camp. It was on him before he fully realized it. He sat in the dark, watching the clouds, when it seemed the forest before him was pushed flat, and a boiling cloud rushed over the land. For a brief moment, the wind died and fell flat, and then reversed direction. In the next, he felt the air being pulled from his lungs, and then the cloud surged over them, peeling them from the ground and pushing them forward in an instant. Amit alone woke just before he felt the wind die, sensing the change in air pressure, seeing Kuljit sitting with his back to him. He saw the mass of clouds rushing towards them, his eyes widening in disbelief and shock. In the next instant he was lifted from the ground when the wind hit him like a moving brick wall, pushing everything forwards end over end with immeasurable force. Trees were torn from the ground, blown flat or carried forwards, tumbling over the ground like giant rolling pins.

Amit and Kuljit watched the blackness rush towards them, dying before they could scream, their bodies lost in the boiling mixture of earth and wind. The clouds relentlessly carried onward, consuming the earth and sky.

Adelle Bäcker

The television went black, the screen image condensing into some weird shape before it went blank. For a moment, the emergency lights in the hallways and above the doors struggled to come on, the lights dim, and then they too failed and stayed dark. Adelle found the entire process very amusing, it had been a long time since she had seen a power failure like this. The last time was when a car had lost control up her street and ran into a power pole, bringing it down enough to damage the lines and cut power to a few blocks of her neighborhood. Then she heard the respirator hiss as the valve closed, the machine silent. It was then she noticed that there was no power at all, the hospital was completely silent and dim, the morning winter sun giving little light. *Where was the back up? There must be some kind of generator?* A nurse ran down the hall, trying to use a phone mounted on the corner of the wall. She held the receiver to her ear, clicking the hang up switch a few times, testing it. She hurriedly tried to put the handset in the cradle, but missed, and ran away as it fell to the ground, clacking loudly as the hard plastic hit the floor and bounced.

The nurses shoes were nearly silent on the floor as she ran down the hall, yelling for a doctor.

Adelle began to feel her lungs ache for air. Panic was rising in her, and she was powerless to do anything, she was trapped in the bed with no way of doing anything. She couldn't even scream. Her lungs burned, and she could feel her heart began to pound in her chest, needing oxygen, trying to feed her body. She began to sweat, her body reacting to the stress, and she could feel her eyes begin to swim, her vision blurring. The pain was incredible, she had never thought that suffocation could be so terrible.

Her heart hammered inside her, and began to palpitate, beating wildly, trying to stay alive.

Her lungs were screaming for air, they felt like they were on fire.

She felt her heart fluttering within her. *Oh God, no! I don't want to die* she screamed in her mind *I don't want to die*. She thought of her parents as her vision dimmed, the intense pain and need for air slowly fading. She felt her heart stop, and she saw a comforting light open before her eyes, a brightness that overpowered everything but did not hurt her eyes. A long tunnel formed, and she thought she could hear Joseph calling to her, she could see him. No, *she could hear* him, he stepped from the light. She yelled his name, her eyes filling with tears of joy to see him. He looked wonderful, so handsome, so glad to see her.

"Hallo, meine Leibe."

His voice was musical and rich.

She ached for him, hearing him again. He was unblemished and unscarred; looking as though he had that fateful morning that felt so long ago.

"Come with me."

She nodded, and reached out her hands. He took them, holding them softly, helping her to rise from the bed. She felt his warm touch, she could feel *everything*, a endless river of energy flowing through her body. She looked into his eyes and saw the delight in them, the the secret glee of some untold wonder. She knew she would never leave him again. Together, he led her into the light.

In her dim room, all was silent. Her dark lifeless eyes stared unblinking at the ceiling, a slight smile traced upon her lips. The motionless clock was frozen just past eight.

Antarctica

Their sleds buckled almost in unison, their engines coughing and stuttering, the sleds coming to a quick stop. They had both been startled, and jerked at the handlebars in surprise, steering away from each other until the shock had passed, coming back together as the sleds slowed.

Jess pulled off her helmet, adjusting her wool hat.

"What the hell was that?" she asked.

Neil had his helmet off, and was trying to restart his sled.

"I don't know. Bad gas?"

She tried her sled.

"Mine is totally dead. Same as yours?"

Jess nodded, holding her MP3 player in her hand.

"Even this is dead." She held it out to him so he could take a look.

He pressed the power button, and had no response.

"Weird shit."

"That really pisses me off," she said, taking the player back from him.

"I just bought the thing before coming out here."

Neil had popped the hood, and was checking the engine as best he could in the cold and wearing thick gloves.

"Jess."

She looked up from her MP3 player that she was trying to will back to life.

"Give camp a shout. They need to know we broke down."

She nodded and stood, looking through the supplies, pushing them aside until she found what she was looking for.

Jess positioned the radio in her hand, and squeezed the trigger.

"East Camp, come in please, over." She released the button, for a moment, and then repeated the call, this time for Vostok Station.

She turned the volume knob on the top of the handheld, and pressed the button twice in quick succession, and then pressed the page button. Nothing happened.

"They're dead too, Neil."

"What? How can that be?" She passed them to him, and he tried as well.

"See? Toast."

She looked up at the sun, where it was nearing its low point in the sky for the day, still well above the horizon. Habitually she checked her watch. The crystal was dead, the screen blank.

"Even my frickin' watch is dead."

"Something is seriously screwed up here," said Neil, sitting on his knees on the ice.

"How long of a walk to Camp?" he asked.

Jessica sat for a moment before making a guesstimate.

"Twenty klicks or so."

"Shit."

She nodded.

"If we walk steady, we could make it in about six our seven hours, maybe less," she said.

"Shit," he repeated.

"Think of all the fresh air you're going to get," she said, getting off the sled.

"You're enjoying this, aren't you?" he asked.

"Not particularly," she replied, "but it could be worse."

He nodded, agreeing with that. They would be noticed as overdue in a couple of hours, so they wouldn't have to walk the full distance.

"What's that?" she asked, pointing to the horizon. The ice was flat and they could see perfectly for kilometers. It looked like the glacier was fracturing; the ice was breaking in a wave shape, rushing towards them. A moment later there was a sharp crack following a deep tremor, and the ice rumbled beneath them, throwing Jessica off her feet and making Neil jump away from his sled. The ice shattered around them, the smooth surface exploding with pops and cracks as the ground heaved.

"Earthquake!" Neil yelled, trying to pull himself along the ice towards Jessica who was trying to hold her position on her stomach.

The sky was filled with a light dusting of ice particles, exploding upwards where the glacier was splitting. It looked beautiful, but at the moment they scarcely noticed, being more concerned with riding out the quake. Neil made it over to Jessica, and they held each other tightly as the last of the quake passed, the ground finally coming still.

"It was a wave!" said Jessica, breathing heavily.

"What? I don't follow..."

"You didn't see it? The ice was breaking like a wave was passing through it. I only just saw it, it came so fast."

"I didn't see a thing. One minute I was looking at the sled and the next I was doing the funky chicken on the ice here."

He ran his gloved hand over the surface of the glacier, sweeping away piles of shattered ice. They sat there for a minute, reliving the experience mentally before gathering themselves.

"Ready for our trek?" he asked Jessica. She took a deep breathe, and then nodding, rising to her feet. They took whatever clothing they could wrap around themselves, enough food to last for a meal or two, and started out.

"How does that go? Something about a journey starting with a single step?"

She nodded.

"Let's go."

They took a step.

The staff of East Camp and Vostok Station were scrambling trying to figure out what had happened. One moment, everything was fine, and in the next, everything was fucked. Absolutely nothing was working.

"What about the generators?" yelled Clive.

"They're down!" replied Ivan. "We can't get them to start."

"What is going on?" Clive wondered. Everything electronic seemed to fail simultaneously at both camps.

"Has there ever been a record of an electrical anomaly like this in the past?" He was hoping this had maybe happened to the Russians before; that there was a precedent to this.

Ivan shook his head, no.

"Magnetic, yes. Electrical, no."

They weren't in serious trouble yet. If worse came to worse, they could always use the gas ranges for heat, and they had lots of food, so there were options.

"Have we heard anything from Neil or Jessica?"

Ivan smiled, having already been filled in on the gossip.

"Nyet. The radios are down also."

Clive exhaled. They could only hope that they were okay. If not, they were stranded until they could regain radio contact. The odds of that were slight, but they existed. Luckily, the weather was good.

Clive suited up as quickly as he could. He wanted to go outside and see what he could find, if anything, that might give him a clue as to what happened. Ivan was already waiting for him, having come in from outside when their systems initially failed. His zipper linked with a quick metallic buzz, and he gave his hat one last adjustment, pulling his gloves up under the elastic band of his jacket sleeves.

He took a deep breath, and opened the door. The cold bit into his face. It was always a shock going from the relatively warm innards of the base to the outdoors, and it was what he liked least of all about living here.

Ivan chuckled seeing the hesitation on Clive as he stepped outdoors.

"You still haven't adjusted to this, have you?"

"I never will, Ivan. I'm not meant for this."

"You picked a strange profession, my friend."

"I should have listened to my guidance counselor."

"So what are we looking for?" asked Ivan, curious to know what Clive was looking for outside.

"I don't know; maybe a down transformer? Something that could have caused a spike. I don't know. I'm just hoping someone else solves the problem while we are out here."

Ivan heard the rumble first.

"What is that?" he asked. Clive heard it, too, and turned around where he stood trying to locate the sound. He looked up first, thinking it might have been a plane approaching the camp.

When he was pulled to the ground, he didn't even realize what had happened. All of a sudden, he was lying on the snow and ice next to Ivan, while an immense and deep rumbling sound filled his ears.

He at first thought there was a plane crash, and the impact had thrown them down to the ground. But the roaring continued, and the blue sky remained clear, free of the smoke he expected to see at any moment.

The ground cracked and shattered under them, the ice unable to resist the immense pressures from the ground far below.

The building behind them made a loud snapping noise, the walls buckling inwards as the foundation heaved. With a rush, it fell down, the roof coming down with a crunching sound over the remains of the walls. They heard other buildings collapsing, and the chaotic sounds of falling machinery and other items tumbling over themselves, and screams.

The screams were the worst part. They could do nothing at the moment to help, pinned to the ground that was waving under them. The worst screams were the ones that ended suddenly, cut short when still loud and powerful. The trembling continued for minutes that seemed to last forever, one wave being followed by the next, all the while the air filled with the violent sounds of the event.

It stopped suddenly, the ground coming still and the roaring sound that filled their ears gone, only a dreadful silence remained. Clive moved, hearing the fabric of his jacket slide against the ice, grinding in the teeth of his zipper. Ivan got on his knees, looking around him at the destroyed complex, his eyes not comprehending what he was looking at. Clive tapped him on the shoulder.

"Ivan, you okay?" he asked.

Ivan looked at him mutely, nodding but remaining silent. He got to his feet, standing next to Clive who was gazing around the landscape, his face a mixture of confusion and determination. Not a single building remained standing; they were surrounded by the remains of the base; only the Russian flag remained standing, the American flagpole leaning over at a forty-five degree angle.

"Hello!" yelled Clive, his hands cupped to the sides of his mouth.

They listened together, trying to hear the slightest response to his call. A puff of smoke suddenly broke through the wreckage, the smoke starting white and then changing to brown and black as it found fuel to burn.

"Hello!" they yelled together, in different directions.

The ground trembled beneath their feet again, a low steady vibration that slowly rose and then faded, different from the last event. They froze where they stood, waiting for another wave to knock them down.

Ivan quickly stood upright, listening intently.

"Did you hear that?" he asked.

Clive shook his head.

"Pozdravleniya!" he yelled. *Hello!*

The reply was faint, but clear.

"Pomogite mne." *Help me.*

Ivan ran in the direction of the voice, shouting instructions to whoever was calling for them.

"Prodolzhajte govorit' tak, ya mogu sledovat' za vashim golosom." Graf i prodolzhayet rasschityvat.' *Keep talking so I can follow your voice. Count and keep counting.*

The voice began to count.

"Odin." *One.*

"Horoshij! YA mogu uslyshat' Vas!" he replied. *Good! I can hear you!*

"Dva." *Two.*

They followed the voice as it counted, running through the narrow corridors between the buildings that had collapsed. They were surprised that no one else was calling for help yet, and also fearful.

The voice grew stronger, until they located the sound.

Ivan and Clive stopped where the voice was loudest, suddenly dumbfounded at what to do next. The building was a pile of ruins, and it was going to be extremely difficult to get to whoever was trapped removing the debris by hand.

"My - zdes'! Vy mozhete videt' chto - nibud'?" *We're here! Can you see anything?*

"Nyet. Tol'ko temnota." *Only darkness.*

The burning building was behind them, gratefully, and separated from this building. Flames had begun to appear at the top of the pile, burning low in the cold dense breeze that was flowing through the grounds.

The ground began to shake again, a slight tremor that made them pause. Waiting a moment, they stepped into the rubble pile and tried to grab something that would pull away, testing pieces of the building to see what would lift or move if they tried. A few boards came free quickly, and they were tossed aside, held carefully to not injure themselves on the protruding nails or the jagged edges of the boards.

The small tremor continued, rattling broken glass and trembling through their boots.

"What is that?" he asked Ivan, pausing for a moment from trying to remove a section of broken drywall.

"What do you think it is?"

Ivan tried to continue working, his face a betrayal of his effort to pretend he hadn't heard the question, and the answer that lay beneath the surface. He kept his eyes down, trying not to look Clive in the face.

"What is it, Ivan? What don't you want to say?"

The rumbling increased slightly, becoming a deeper feeling than a sound.

Ivan stopped working, pausing in a bent over position to wipe at sweat that was beading on his forehead. He looked up at Clive with a grim determination, and muttered one word.

"Vulkan."

His Russian was still a work in progress, and would probably offend the average Muscovite, but he had heard the Russian geological teams mention it enough to learn its meaning.

Volcano.

Lake Vostok was thought to be the creation of a nearby volcano, perhaps several, but the nearly four kilometers of ice that lay between them was an obstacle to knowing for certain. It was a theory that was likely to be correct, but as of yet could not be proven.

Ivan saw the look on his face, and nodded sullenly, returning to his work.

Clive stood in place, uncertain as to what would be the best thing to do. If there was a volcano under their feet, a prudent course of action would be to get to safety as soon as possible, to find some sort of refuge. His instincts told him to run, and to get away as fast as he possibly could. The persistent rumbling was making the hairs on the back of his neck stand out, an innate warning that he was in danger.

He succeeded in tearing out the piece of drywall, and threw it away with a flick of his arm, sending it spinning like a deranged Frisbee.

It hit the ground with a puff of dust, sliding a few feet and coming to a stop in a snow bank. Ivan kept talking to whoever was trapped in the building, while the fire behind them grew, putting out a glow of heat.

He began to talk under his breath as he worked, trying to think about when they might expect a rescue.

"McMurdo would have detected the quake," he reasoned, which should send a seismological study to the area, and if the ground kept shaking, it was certain to get attention. It would be a volcanologists dream to be able to take advantage of the geological activity.

"They might fly in on the Hercules…," thinking that if the resupply flight from McMurdo hadn't flown back to New Zealand yet, it might be sent back this way. All in all, it seemed highly probable to expect some kind of contact within a day, two at the latest. The logic cheered him, thinking that if they only had to spend a day in the outdoors, then that wouldn't be so bad. There was enough to do to keep busy, and keeping the fire going would keep them warm. They might even be able to pull some people out of the wreckage before help arrived. When Neil and Jessica returned they would have more help and be more effective at searching the camps. He pulled at a piece of insulation, hearing it tear on something further under the rubble. The pile wasn't as dense as he thought it was; as pieces came free he could see pockets in the fall that were surprisingly large. They had to be very careful where they were standing; one misplaced foot and they risked falling into the pile and being injured. A sudden and piercing crack shot through the air, sounding like an artillery piece. They both looked up at the sound, familiar with the noises of the glacier moving and ice shifting and splitting. Ivan had found another piece of the insulation, and was doing his best to pull it out, wiggling it from side to side. It didn't seem to be snagged, just held down under pressure. After a few minutes, he succeeded in pulling it free, throwing it down behind him.

"I think I can get down from here," he said to Clive, pointing at a hole in the pile that only he could see from where he was standing.

"Is there anything sharp in the way?" asked Clive, concerned about Ivan maybe being stuck with a rusty nail.

Ivan shook his head.

"No; it's clear. I can fit not too bad."

"But can you get back up?" he asked, more concerned now if he would get stuck underneath.

"There is a big space. It should be all right."

He had to trust to Ivan's judgment and nodded.

"I'm going to go down head first."

Clive came over to where he was standing, one cautious step at a time, and saw the hole that Ivan was about to descend. It was large enough for him, half again as wide as he was, and the sunlight penetrated far enough to allow them to see bits and pieces of the pocket of space that was below them.

"You see?" said Ivan.

Clive could only agree with him; there was plenty of space, and there didn't seem to be anything sharp or protruding in the way, at least from this point of view.

"I am going to take my jacket off when I go down. Pass it to me when I'm at the bottom."

"Okay."

"Here I go, then."

He unzipped his coat, handing it to Clive and quickly lowering himself to the opening. He shivered comically in the cold air, and began to pull himself down the gap.

"I want my jacket as soon as I get to the bottom!" he yelled.

Clive could only laugh, imagining how cold it must be. He was still wearing a sweater and thermal undershirt, but in the cool Antarctic air layers meant warmth.

There was another abrupt crack; Clive felt the pile he was standing on shift downwards, his stomach dropping slightly as he fell a few inches suddenly. He took a deep breath, waiting to fall into a gap he must be standing on. It didn't happen, and as Ivan quickly scrambled down the hole to get on solid ground, he exhaled with relief.

"I would like my jacket now!" he shouted up from his hole.

"Coming right up!"

Clive bundled the jacket as best he could in one hand, and threw it down to where Ivan was waiting, his hands open ready for it.

Ivan put it on in record time, zipping it up to his neck and pulling the neck up around his chin.

"What can you see?" Clive asked him, waiting as Ivan looked around.

"There are lots of spaces in here; I am going to check where I can go."

Clive heard him talking to the trapped Russian teammate, trying to get closer to the voice. In the meantime, he stayed outside, working on the pile and ignoring the ever-present rumbling sound.

Clive noticed the ice around the base that he could see was crisscrossed with jagged cracks and small fissures, distinct white lines that caught the light. The ground shifted quickly, dropping downwards. Clive put out his hands to catch himself as he went down. It stopped just as suddenly, although the air was filled with the sounds of ice cracking and splitting. The fissures in the ice were a little more pronounced after the last drop, the gap just a little wider than it had been before.

"Are you okay?" he shouted to Ivan.

"Yes," he replied, and Clive allowed himself to relax a little, concerned he would be stuck alone trying to rescue Ivan until help appeared.

He stayed where he was for a minute, testing his footing.

From the corner of his eye, he caught a faint wisp blow past in the air, and he turned to see what it was. The fire was to his left, but was putting out very little smoke, burning low and steadily. From a narrow gap in the ice, came a low but steady haze; a fog that rose quickly into the air and was carried away. He stared at it for a moment, and then decided to have a closer look, stepping slowly down the pile to the ground. His boots made a rasping sound on the cracked ice, the sounding a little like Styrofoam rubbing together with little snapping pops. He knelt at the crack, running his hand through the fog as high as he could reach, and then lowering it closer to the ground. When he was near the surface, he could feel the warmth on his palm, the condensation on his skin. He pulled his hand out, wiping the water on his thigh. Looking around, he saw that a few other fissures were also venting, although none so highly as this one, the fog keeping low to the ground and dissipating before it went far. Getting closer, sniffing, the fog had a foul odor to it. Rotten eggs. Sulphur. It was faint, but present nevertheless. He grimaced instinctively at the smell, and backed away from it. The rumbling went silent, the ground solid beneath his feet once more, although the steam continued to vent from the many fissures in the ground.

"Ivan, how are you making out in there?" he yelled.

"I'm almost there," he replied, his voice faint in the pile. He could hear them talking to each other, and the faint sounds of things being moved around or pulled out of the way. He heard another voice calling from the camp, this time calling in English.

"Where are you? Keep calling!" He went forward, trying to pin down where the sound was coming from. He paused, and returned to where Ivan was, telling him he heard someone else, and he was going to look for them. Ivan told him to go, and Clive walked quickly back to where he had heard the voice the first time, and listened. The voice called again, counting.

He had taken a few steps forward, when the earth fell under his feet, dropping him to the ground. The rumbling started up again, this time intensifying and shaking the ground. Steam began to vent from the fissures with greater strength, billowing from the cracks instead of a slow fog. The stench of sulfur was unbearable, and Clive covered his nose to try to block it out. The ice cracked again, and the ground developed a lean to it, slight but perceptible. He heard more yelling coming from the fallen buildings; people waking up or no longer content to be quiet while waiting for help. The cracking sounds became more ominous, deeper and more numerous. Clive wanted to get to high ground; he looked around for something that was sturdy, and saw only the Cat. He ran to it as quickly as he could on the shaking ground, slipping twice and falling to his chest. He climbed to the top of the Cat, and looked around. In every direction he could see the ground was shattered and shaking; the depression in the ground more visible from his point of view. He could see how the terrain had sagged, dropping off to a point maybe a kilometer away, outside of the base camps.

The rumbling grew stronger, and he had to grip the frame of the Cat for stability. He couldn't see Jessica or Neil anywhere on the horizon. Suddenly, off in the direction of where the depression was deepest, a wide fissure split open, releasing a large vent of gas that shot high into the air. Around the edges, the fissure began to crack and fall inwards, the hole widening slowly at first. He watched it, unaware of what to do next and also fascinated by what he was witnessing. The narrow fissure became a gaping crevasse, and it began to collapse ever faster, the edges vanishing into the steaming hole, blasts of steam and smoke belching from the cavity. He was no longer unsure of what to do. He climbed down the Cat as fast as he could, and began to run away from the base. Behind him, the pattern of collapse escalated, with large pieces of glacier falling from sight, the hole widening ever faster, the ice shattering as the hole grew, the cracks spreading outwards in a chaotic zig-zag, looking like a broken sheet of glass.

Clive watched the cracks spread past him as he ran. His lungs burned in the cold air, his eyes watering. He felt a huge push from behind, the force knocking him flat to the ground. He felt his ears pop, and turned over on his side as he tried to stand back up. A large shadow dropped over the land, the bright sunlight disappearing. Clive saw the sun vanish behind the immense cloud that was belching upwards, and rushing towards him. He felt heat on his face, and as he rose, the cloud enveloped Vostok Station. He saw East Camp falling into the pit, and he turned to run, his legs shaking. Ash began to fall around him, the shadow growing darker, a hot and rushing wind blowing at his back. He felt the heat grow, the wind pushing at him, and the roar of the eruption filling his ears. Gasping, and running as fast as he could, he turned his head to see what was happening. He turned just in time to see the pyroclastic flow reach for him. He raised his arm in a gesture of defense, and was consumed as the hot gas surged past him. The charred remains of his body fell to the ground, where it was entombed in ash. The eruption consumed the glacier, the open caldera vaporizing the ice as it fell, the intense heat of the lava flowing from its slopes consuming the ice from below.

Neil and Jessica felt the new tremor under their feet, causing them to stop their march as they waited to see if another large earthquake would knock them down. They crouched, waiting for a few minutes, and then Neil stood up.

"It must be an aftershock. Anything bigger would have hit us by now."

He extended his hand, and helped Jessica to her feet. The camp was still some distance away, beyond what they could see. They resumed their march, feeling the ground continue to shake as they walked.

"Any earthquake would be over by now," said Jessica, after walking for several more minutes.

"Maybe it isn't an earthquake. Maybe it's the glacier moving from the last one."

It was possible, she conceded, although it was unusual that there were no more large fissures or crevasses opening up if indeed the glacier had come a little loose. The rumbling varied in strength, ebbing as the minutes past, and then returning as before. They heard a few loud cracks, feeling the ice splitting under them. The sound was deep, the pressure of kilometers of ice suddenly releasing and grinding on bedrock far below.

"Hungry?" Neil asked.

Jessica nodded.

"I'll get something from your pack."

"The energy bars are in the middle pocket." She pointed with her gloved hand to roughly where she meant.

He unzipped the bag, and fished out a bar.

"You might as well get one for yourself."

He grabbed another one, and read the silver packaging.

"Are they all chocolate and peanut butter?"

She nodded.

"My favorite."

"You have something against Granola?"

"I'm a confessed chocoholic; sue me."

He zipped her bag shut, and passed her a bar, opening his with his teeth. He took a tentative bit, and chewed it slowly. It actually wasn't too bad. The peanut butter seemed a little dry, but chewing it more thoroughly helped that.

"What do you think?" she asked.

"Better than I expected," he admitted, taking another small bite.

"Although I suspect they would be better if they weren't frozen solid."

She laughed.

"Yes, they are better that way."

They walked and ate in silence, and then balled up the thin wrappers, tucking them into the side pockets of their packs.

"I would kill for a glass of milk right about now," said Neil, smacking his mouth for effect.

"And none of that watered down skim milk crap. Real milk, like two percent. Or Homo."

"Or chocolate milk?" Jessica added.

His eyes widened.

"Even better; I hadn't thought of that. I know what I'm having when we get back. Genius."

"Always ask the chocolate addict. Always."

The shaking ground ceased, becoming still.

"Well that's better," said Jessica.

"Strange how quickly you get used to something. Now it sounds too quiet," said Neil. Their boots bit into the ice with a sharp crunching sound, and their jackets and pants zipped together with each motion they made. Otherwise, the air was still and clear. The breeze was light; enough to feel pleasant as long as you were moving.

The ground started to rumble again, a little stronger than before, waxing and waning in strength and intensity.

"Shit, I jinxed it."

"It's a bit different now."

They could feel the trembling through their legs, vibrating through them. It felt deeper, quivering their muscles.

Near the horizon, a cloud bloomed, seeming to pour from the very ground straight into the sky.

"What the fuck?" muttered Neil, his hand raised over his eyebrows in an effort to reduce the glare from the sun.

They took a few more steps, and then stopped, both looking at what lay ahead of them. A ripping sound passed through the glacier; deep cracks tearing through the ice filling the air with violent commotion.

The cloud rolled from the ground, exploding upwards, unfolding as it spread upwards into the sky. The air was quiet and still a minute longer, and then began to fill with the sounds of the explosion, a deep booming sound filled with crashes and sudden snapping reports. The loose snow and ice fragments resting on top of the surface of the glacier slid in all directions. A deep rumbling came from underneath and grew in strength by the moment, the low vibration trembling deep within their bodies.

They stood and watched helplessly as the explosion unfolded. The eruption continued to climb into the sky, and then spread outwards from the base, a dark plume cascading over the glacier with ferocious speed.

"Holy shit," Neil muttered, his guts turning to jelly as it became apparent the cloud was coming towards them. His professional observation and detachment ceased as his bodily instincts told him to run. They turned and ran together, blind to the small fissures in the ice cracking open under foot and the darkening skies. They kept their eyes on the ground ahead, where they could place their next running footstep. Jessica did her best to keep up to him, but slowly lost ground, the weight of the thick winter boots dragging at her legs.

Neil could hear her boots crunching into the ground next to him, slowly falling behind. His mind was screaming at him to go as fast as he could, to just *run*, while he was torn with staying with Jessica, to help her as best he could.

"Neil," she panted, her lungs burning, "I can't keep up."

He turned as he ran, seeing her a few steps back, her face red with exertion and lined with fright and worry. The flow was rushing across the glacier towards them as he watched her, gaining on them by hundreds of yards each moment. Escape was impossible. The glacier was virtually flat at this point; he could not go any higher to escape the blast, nor would the flow be diverted away by the natural course of the landscape, which was their best hope. He slowed and stopped running, resting his arms on his knees as he gasped for breath. Jessica quickly caught up to him, falling to her knees with her thighs burning. Her back was to the explosion, and she paid no heed to the increasing vibration, being too tired to do more than gasp for breath. He knelt in front of her, one arm leaning on her back for comfort as he watched the surge rushing towards them. Jessica had her head down in fatigue, taking deep breaths and rubbing her thighs.

"Oh God they're cramping up."

She massaged them faster, trying to work the muscles deeply.

"Are we okay?" she asked, oblivious to the urgency of the situation.

Neil watched the cloud over her back, swallowing hard in fear. He knew what was coming their way; the cloud was a superheated explosion of gas; measured in the hundreds of degrees, the same sort of storm that had entombed hundreds of Vesuvians on the shores of the Mediterranean centuries earlier.

"We'll be all right," Neil answered, not wanting to upset her, hiding the truth. He watched a few seconds more, until the front was a mass that loomed large and menacing before him. He closed his eyes, clenching his fists, and together they were overcome, the gas rushing into their lungs and baking their flesh. Their clothing melted instantly to their skin and burst into flame as their bodies contorted in the extreme heat. They fell dead, and were blown along the ice, their bodies buried deep in the strata of the ash.

Dr. Sam Tse

Out at sea, the small fishing boat had weighed anchor for the evening, and the crew had already hauled in their nets and were repairing them, getting ready for the next day while their was still sunlight in the sky. The sea was relatively calm, although the air was brisk with winters chill, although not so cold as to set ice growing on the ship. As it was, the men sat in the shelter of the fore of the ship, the wind breaking over the bow and losing its coldest grip flowing past them. They could feel its chill, but were spared the worst of it.

A small garbage can had been set on the deck, where a small wooden fire burned deep within. The can had nearly rusted through, and was brown with age, with thin flecks of metal peeling off in layers like an old petrified onion. It was somewhat of a miracle that the fire hadn't burned through the metal just yet, although in places the orange of flame could be seen in small pinholes that were growing in the shell of the can. The ship was named the Khan, the family name of the Captain and her crew, the father and his three sons who had spent their lives at sea, while their mother and sisters had remained at home. The four men ran their fingers through the nets expertly, trained and deft fingers nimbly repaired small tears in the netting with speed. The catch of the day was already below in the hold, the deck had been washed, and dinner was cooking in the galley. A bit of rice, and a fish for each of them in the oven. The fish smelled good, and they were looking forward to getting out of the wind and getting below deck for a hot meal. The Khan was a couple hundred kilometers out at sea, in their normal fishing route, beyond the sight of land where from horizon to horizon stretched only open ocean. The waves were scarcely more than a foot high, and slapped at the bow lazily, making the Khan rock slowly in the water. The anchor held them in place easily, the chain rattling as the links sat loose in the guide off the bow.

Sook stood slowly, allowing his back muscles to stretch slowly as he stood to go check on dinner. He would let his boys finish the nets while he warmed up below and finished cooking. He went toward the door, when the sky began to brighten overhead. It was one of those days, where the sun was hiding behind the clouds, only to come out for a few minutes and warm things up a little bit, only to disappear again and have the cold air bite at you, scolding you for enjoying the warmth in the air. He would have preferred it if the day had remained cloudy. It was easy to feel warmer if you didn't have the sun coming out reminding how cold it really was. The sky brightened quickly, and a loud roar filled the air, a boom that made the surface of the sea shake with a series of miniature ripples in all directions. At the sound of the boom, Sook stopped to look around, and his boys looked up into the skies, the netting forgotten as they wondered what they had heard. It was certainly not a horn from a tanker. They had felt the tremble of the boom within themselves, in their very core, a deep bass that made their guts quiver. A moment later, the Khan and her crew were incinerated, vaporized along with the ocean in which they had earned their living.

It kept getting brighter, and within a few seconds, the room was lit up as though the sun was directly overhead, a fine summer's day with no cloud cover. Except that it wasn't summer. It was a winters evening on a partially cloudy day. While Kim was studying a variant, Doctor Tse stood up and turned around to see when to expect a cloud would cover the sun. He had to cover his eyes to shield them from the brightness. He mouth dropped open as he looked towards the east. A giant fireball was rising from the sea, an immense white pillar that was climbing upwards into the sky, and outward across the sea. He could see the ball expanding outwards, rapidly, the forefront of the shockwave rushing over the ocean surface in a white ring. The fireball continued to grow and climb, and finally Kim had turned to see what his mentor was looking at. The clipboard fell to the ground with a harsh chatter, the pen rolling under the hydroponic assembly. He shielded his eyes as well, squinting in the fierce light, unable to believe what he was seeing unfold before him. The city before them was being destroyed as if it were dust. As the shockwave passed over buildings they were torn down, falling forwards with the force of the blast, and then becoming a part of the churning cloud. They could see clearly that behind the shockwave, nothing was left standing. The white glare in the sky became reddish and orange as it grew, a wave of fire creeping over the ground at incredible speed.

A moment later the glass of the building shattered and was blown inwards in a hail of razor sharp debris, and the ground shook violently, tearing the very foundation apart, and shattering the deep granite below with fierce and sudden cracks. The two men screamed as their bodies were pelted with glass, and then thrown violently backwards, tumbling and then vanishing into the sky. The metal frame of the greenhouse buckled, and blew apart, dispersed into the winds. The shockwave passed, and following it came a rush of superheated air. The ground began to steam as water was boiled out of the very ground, the soil desiccating, and a moment later all burst into flame. The wall of fire followed the shockwave inland for hundreds of kilometers, igniting everything, burning all to ash and bare rock, leaving nothing in its wake. Where the Khan had once floated peacefully, a foaming orange and red crater steamed and hissed on the ocean floor, an immense wound upon the world, a scar that dug deep into the crust of the Earth. The vaporized earth had been thrown into the sky, rushing upwards and outwards, blotting out the sun and spreading across the atmosphere, crossing the equator and spreading into both hemispheres. The winds carried the ash and soot and vaporized rock to all the four corners of the world, hiding the sky behind a thick black shawl through which very little would shine, bringing perpetual night to the world. The ocean that had not been vaporized had been thrown back and outwards, creating a wave that sped away from the explosion faster than the speed of sound, a mighty crest that grew and broke ashore in places over a kilometer high, roaring inland with all the fury of hell. When the ocean flowed back into the crater, steam exploded into the skies as the waters were boiled and evaporated, feeding giant clouds of vapor that exploded outwards, pushing the explosion forward.

Kai Kwong Mok

Outside the glass of the skyscraper, the sun was setting, the eastern sky already growing dark. It had been a long day, and he stretched out in his chair, hearing the leather creak under him as he shifted and flexed. He yawned, enjoying the view over the Pacific. As he watched a few evening stars begin to shine in the sky, he watched in disbelief as the evening sky lit up with a glowing ball that raced across the sky. He saw it skip across the atmosphere a few times, and then brighten considerably, vanishing over the limb of the horizon. He stood and approached the window, looking out, wondering what it was he saw. It had happened so quickly, perhaps taking no more than five seconds. The horizon suddenly lit up, as if the sun was rising. The dark sky went bright, a white glare spreading outwards and growing as he watched it. The power in the building failed, and as he watched, the city went dark around him. He reached back to grab the phone on his desk, his hands fumbling to pick up the handset. Shaking, he placed it to his ear, and heard nothing. He dropped the handset to the desk, where it bounced and then fell onto the carpeted floor. He squinted as the fireball grew, dominating the horizon and growing quickly. He heard screams in the office, and people running down the hallway, desperate to find a way to escape. He stood fast, knowing there was no where to run. The explosion grew, climbing into the atmosphere, and he watched steadfast as the fireball appeared over the horizon, rushing towards him. He lowered his head, and said a quick prayer for his family, and for himself, and then he closed his eyes and waited for the end.

The heat blast was nearly instantaneous. He felt himself catch fire, erupting into a torch within seconds. He heard others begin to scream and yell in pain. The windows burst in the sudden heat, and he screamed in sudden agony as his flesh sizzled and burned. He ran to the window, through the frame, and out into the air, his limbs waving as he tried to put out the flames flowing over his body. He twisted as he fell, plummeting to his death twenty-two stories below. Qingdao burst into flames, the screams of the dying rising into the sky. When all in the city lay dead and burning, and the buildings were engulfed in flame, the earthquake struck, reducing the city to ruins. Homes collapsed into themselves, and high rises toppled and fell to the ground in a cloud of ash and dust. Not a building was left standing. The winds arrived afterwards, shrieking across the smoking and burning remnants, scouring the land bare, carrying the ruins far beyond and across the world.

Randy Palmer

The light went off, and he was plunged into nearly complete darkness.

At first he was surprised, his body instinctually reacting to the sudden darkness with a quick feeling of fright. His eyes were used to the bright glare of the lamp, and when that was suddenly removed, the room went utterly dark like someone had pulled thick curtains over his eyes. He stood, leaning on his shovel, and waited for his eyes to adjust. He looked outside to where the beehive was glowing, small sparks issuing from the top and then going out in the sky. He realized the familiar rumble of the mill was gone; he couldn't feel any shaking through his feet, or in his guts. He listened intently, trying to hear anything other than his muted heartbeat through the earplugs. There was nothing. He looked up at the lamp, where the bulb glowed dimly; the heat slowly dissipating in the night air. He pulled the cuff of his gloves, pulling the elastic off the arm sleeves of his coveralls, and taking his hand out of the gloves. They were sweaty and hot, and in the cool evening air, it felt grand and refreshing. He pulled the earplugs out, holding them in his palm. There was no sound at all, except for his co-workers yelling at each other through the walls. He parked his shovel back into the sawdust pile, and poked his head outside, looking around to see what he could see. The yard was black; if it hadn't been for the beehive burner, he wouldn't have been able to see anything except forms and shapes against the night sky. The light from the beehive was ruddy and dim, and didn't go far, but it was better than nothing.

"Everybody outside!" he heard someone yelling.

"Come on, everybody. We need everyone outside of the building. That's the rules." It was Glen, the night manager. He had worked at the mill his entire working life, working his way up the ladder into senior management.

Because he had actually worked in the mill, proving his worth through sweat and hard work, he was one of the few bosses Randy had even showed grudging respect for. He had done everything in the mill, at one time or another, and knew how to do a job, so if he said someone was a dog fucker, he likely was right, and if he said that someone was doing something wrong, he was likely to be right again. He blew a whistle, a tiny shrill sound that somehow seemed comical in light of how loud the mill was when it ran normally. He made his way down through the building, climbing down a few flights of metal grate stairs that had thick angled grips on them, designed to keep work boots from slipping if they got wet. He was outside a moment later, seeing the crew standing in an approximate line in the yard, a few bright cigarette ends glowing in the dark.

"Randy! Where you 'bin?" asked Richard. He was normally a forklift operator, or he was helping the carpenter do some repairing in the building.

Tonight he was running the debarker, covering a vacation leave.

"I was up near the chipper, shovelin' a pile of sawdust into the beehive."

"Gary and I was figuring you were whackin' off to one of Donald's calendars in the john."

Donald piped up quickly.

"All of my calendars are still on the wall."

There were a few chuckles, and a few other muted conversations that had come to a brief stop to see how this would act out.

"Naw, I was whackin' off to a picture of your missus that she gave me."

Gary roared, slapping Richard hard on the back. The rest of the guys were laughing loudly as well, enjoying the burn delivered without even a moments hesitation.

Richard's face dropped at first, and then he smiled, pointing at Randy.

"This guy always has a good come back."

Glen came around the other side of the planer, clipboard in hand and a small Browning xenon flashlight in one hand. The bulb was bright white, and in the darkness they had already adjusted to, it was murder on the eyes.

"Jesus Christ, Glen; point that thing someplace else. I'm gonna go blind," exclaimed Gary.

"You already are blind, Gary. We all know you couldn't find your ass with a map and a compass and a third arm."

There were a few chuckles, but otherwise everyone else was doing their best to not look near the flashlight and screw up their night vision.

"Randy, there you are."

He checked off something on his clipboard.

"Now that everyone is here, try to stay together. We have the millwrights going through the place trying to see why the power quit on us. Hopefully it won't take too long."

"Any chance we can go home?" someone asked.

"Maybe, if it looks like we won't have any luck. But it won't be paid time."

There were a few grumbles, but only a few. No one really wanted to go home, anyways. They were enjoying the rare occasion of a shutdown. The rare times the mill was down, it was maybe for an hour at the most.

"All I ask is if you do split up, go in pairs. Just in case."

"Sure thing boss," said William, who was chewing a long stalk of grass in his front teeth.

"So how did it happen?" asked Randy.

"How did what happen?" replied William.

"I was just shoveling when the light went out."

"Same with me. The chain just stopped, same time as the lights went out."

"So it's just a power outage?" asked Randy.

Richard replied. "Something like that. All I know is this; I have a big ass log stuck in the debarker, and it's going to be a bitch to get her out."

The night sky was incredibly dark; there were more stars out than Randy could remember seeing for some time, probably since he was a kid.

"I'm going to take a look up top of the chip silo. Who's coming?"

At first no one did. The silo was a one hundred a thirty foot tall cylinder that was kept about three-quarters full of sawdust to run the drying kilns when they weren't running any logs through the sawmill. It had a narrow metal ladder running up one side of it, enclosed in a small grating meant to catch someone if they started to fall.

"I'll go," said William, spitting the grass stalk down to the ground.

"See you guys later," he said to the rest of the crew.

"Have fun," replied Richard. Inwardly he shuddered. He hated heights; he would have rather run his ball sack down a sharp cheese grater than climb to the top of the silo.

William and Randy made their way to the silo using the glow of the beehive and the tall shadow of the silo in the night sky to lead them. Finding the ladder still proved harder than they thought, even though they knew roughly where it was. Randy eventually found it by bumping into it with his arm. The ladder was on the opposite side of the silo, facing the forest, and so was in near perfect darkness.

"Found it," he called to William, who then came over, nearly bumping into it with his head.

"Careful, Will. You almost walked right into me."

They laughed. It was really dark. Randy had seen William walking from the other side, but he had been hidden in the shadow, and blended in completely. William ushered him upwards.

"Age before beauty."

"Is that what your boyfriend tells you?" He laughed, and climbed up the first rung, testing his grip on the metal. It was cool, and was already starting to get some dew on it.

William didn't reply, but Randy had heard him snicker.

"Careful on the ladder. It's got dew on it."

"Kay."

He climbed the silo methodically, one rung at a time. He always liked the view from up here, seeing the mill drop away from him as he climbed. It made everything else look so much smaller, even at one hundred and thirty feet. As he climbed, he also looked upwards, seeing the stars above him shining clearly. There were so *many* of them. It wasn't just the bright ones, but there were so many faint small ones that seemed to be just a part of a larger blur. The caul of the Milky Way was nearly overhead, and the sight gave him a slight feeling of dizziness. He got to the top, and walked into the middle of the silo, hearing his boots drum on the empty space beneath him. Far above the mill, in the darkness, with almost no light, Randy felt like he was floating. It would be extremely easy to walk right off the side of the silo in the dark. He looked for the edge, finding it only after looking around for a bit.

"Careful, Will. You could be right near the edge and walk right off the side before you knew it."

"Sure thing," he replied. William climbed off the ladder, and stepped in beside him.

"No shit." He hard a hard time finding the edge as well.

"Creepy." He stayed in the middle. He might not have been too bright, but he had plenty of common sense, unlike other people who seemed to be the opposite. All the way off to the horizon, the ground was dark. Only a faint line was visible separating earth and sky.

"You know what's missing?"

"What?" asked William.

He pointed to the north.

"There are no lights from Charleston. Or Atlanta." Normally the city glow was visible from here, the light pollution drowning out the night sky.

"There are no lights anywhere." He looked around in a circle, the highest point for miles around, and could see nothing at all. No city lights, no cars, no street lights. Zero. Zilch. Nada. Not even the lights from a tanker running up the coast,

"What the fuck?" he wondered aloud.

"That's some big power outage," agreed William.

Far down below, he could see Glen walking the far side of the yard, the intense xenon light of his flashlight standing out like a sore thumb.

From what he could see, he would have guessed the entire eastern seaboard, or at least the northeast, was out of juice, and he wouldn't have been wrong.

He stood atop the silo, looking out over the landscape, enjoying the darkness and the night sky, while William quietly stood near the middle of the silo. Randy had gone ot the ladder, holding onto it as looked up and around. He liked the view from the edge better, but wanted the reassurance of feeling the metal guardrail at his side. The evening breeze was cool at the top, the wind blowing in off the coast from the south. As he stood and watched, the breeze slowly came to a stop, and then began to blow from the west, out to the black waters of the Atlantic. A few birds flew out of the trees, chirping, and as Randy turned to watch them flying, he heard a moment of a deep rumble that filled his ears and seemed to make his guts vibrate, and then the ground beneath him rolled. The trees and forest were shaking and rumbling, and the silo sounded like a giant empty drum booming, rocking on its concrete slab foundation. The slab cracked almost immediately in three large portions, the snapping sound as it cracked a sharp report like an artillery piece firing. Randy felt his feet pulled from under him, and he reflexively grabbed tight to the guardrail, falling to the roof of the silo, his eyes wide with terror. William fell to his feet as well, his arms and legs splayed out in an attempt to stabilize his position. He screamed in fright, his hands clawing at the smooth metal of the silo for something to hang onto to.

Far below, Randy watched in amazement as a thirty thousand pound Caterpillar forklift was bounced across the yard; the shaking ground bumping the thick pneumatic tires steadily forwards. He heard some yelling, and saw Glen's flashlight moving erratically, the beam covering an area sporadically. He assumed Glen was also thrown to the ground, and the flashlight was rolling in small semi-circles in the dirt.

"Help meeeee!" William screamed.

Randy turned to see him sliding towards the edge of the silo, inch by inch, his arms and legs unable to find a purchase on the roof and hold his position. Randy tried to stretch forward, leaning out from the rail as far as he could, but he was still more than five feet away from William, and could not safely reach him. After stretching out as far as he could without letting go, he retreated to the rail, hanging on tightly. The silo was bending in places, the long curved sheets of metal bending and folding slightly as the earth below it rocked and surged.

"You baaaastard!" William screamed at him.

"I can't get you!" he yelled back.

"I can't reach you!"

William was slowly creeping towards the edge, only a foot from the lip and getting closer.

There was a tremendous crunching sound, and a squealing of metal, and a portion of the planer collapsed into itself. A three foot saw blade came loose of its mount, and rolled free into the woods, where it crashed its way into the undergrowth before burying an edge into a tree, coming to a halt. A gout of sparks flew high into the sky with another crunching sound, as the beehive fell apart, at first a few sections falling inwards, and then, mortally wounded, it fell into itself with a grinding protest of shrieking metal and the popping of countless bolts and rivets. When the structure fell into the flames, a cloud of orange and yellow embers was thrown into the sky, where they floated for a moment, before falling back to earth at the edge of the yard and into the surrounding scrub. In the yard, the embers died on the cool barren earth. In the forest, they found dry grasses and beds of fallen springs leaves, and caught quickly, spreading from grass to shrub to tree in minutes. The dry tinder burned fast and true, and soon an acre of scrub was burning furiously, the trees candling as they went up in flames, catching from one tree to the next. A water main blew near the parking lot, marked where a geyser of water boiled from the ground and foamed several feet into the air.

William screamed again, this time more shrill. His feet were now off the edge, and he was fighting for all he could to get back over the edge fully. His legs scrabbled in vain, finding no purchase, no where to get a grip. His fingers grabbed at the surface, a several fingertips started to bleed as he scratched them against the metal. He slid further, his hips at the very lip of the silo, and then over, only his upper body and arms still flailed at the top.

He had stopped screaming; the realization that he might actually die had focused his mind on staying at the top, overriding his panic. His face had gone pale, his lips thin and his mouth as dry as chalk. He fought another fiver seconds, before another bump shook the structure, and pushed him another inch further. His nails began to slide, and he began to go over the edge. His mind snapped, suddenly sure he was not going to make it, and the silence was broken; he screamed to the very edge when his head disappeared, and with a flurry of arms, he was gone. His scream changed to a despairing wail as he plummeted the one hundred and thirty feet to the concrete slab below. As far as Randy could tell, he screamed the entire way down. Randy heard his scream distinctly, as clear as could be through the raucous sounds of the earthquake and the mill falling apart.

"AAAAAAaaaaaaaaaaaaaaaaaaa."

It ended suddenly, with a thick wet thud; the sound a soaking wet towel makes when it drops and hits the kitchen floor. He closed his eyes and shook his head. The ground shook another ten seconds, and then stopped, coming to a halt; the rumbling sound fading away as the quake continued on into the ocean, disappearing under the waves.

For a few minutes, he clung to the rail, terrified the shaking and booming might start again. The fire at the end of the yard was spreading through the forest, lighting the grounds with a flashing yellow glow and twisting long shadows that danced on the ground. He finally came to, with an urgent need to get back down to solid ground, as fast as he could. With his arms and legs trembling, he climbed down the slippery rungs one by one, until he felt his feet dangle off the final rung, and then rest on the flat concrete under the ladder. He fell to his knees, running from the silo, wanting to be away from the structure and in the middle of a field where nothing could fall. He didn't look back to see where William had fallen, or where he lay in a twisted broken heap. He ran to the parking lot, where cars and trucks were scattered like children's playthings, randomly deposited where the quake had left them. Once there, on the crushed gravel, he sat on his knees, shaking and trembling, his hands clutching the ground for reassurance and comfort. He felt a hand on his shoulder, and he screamed.

"Randy; it's okay man. It's me, Dennis. You're okay, man."

Randy looked at him as though he were crazy. The last thing he thought was that he was okay. It still felt like the ground was rolling under his feet, and he was trapped up high. The silo still stood, although bent in a few places like a partially crushed soda can.

Dennis was hunched over at his side, trying to figure out if Randy was going to sit there calmly or take off screaming into the woods. It looked like he could do either.

"Randy, I'm gonna go help the guys with the fire. You gonna be okay?"

Randy stared at him, seeing his mouth moving and hearing his words, but not really understanding what was said. He moved his head, and Dennis took it for a nod.

"All right. I'll be over by the fires, if you need someone." He pointed over to the far side of the yard where the brush fire was spreading in all directions. The wind was pushing most of the fire east towards the sea and away from the mill, but the structures in the yard made the wind eddy and swirl, carrying the sparks into different areas. The collapsed beehive was showering the grounds with more embers with each gust of wind, as the fractured structure was no longer contained. Dennis slapped him on the back, and then took off down the lane, his boots crunching in the pea gravel.

Randy watched him go, seeing his shadow grow smaller until he could no longer distinguish who was who in the distance. He could see people moving against the firelight, dragging around the thick firehoses over the ground, trying to lay down a stream of water into the blaze. The mill had two water lines, and was now trying to extinguish the blaze with only one hose, with compromised pressure. The second line continued to bubble and churn from the fracture in the ground. He sat in the dark, his knees drawn into his chest, feeling the cool dampness in his jeans where he had pissed himself.

Dennis reached the others, grabbing a hold of the fire hose and helping to drag it along the ground. Richard and Gary were holding the nozzle, trying to direct the flow of water into the deepest and hottest parts of the flames.

Glen was attacking the ground with his shovel, along with Donald and Robert, trying to clear a line in the soil and dig a small firebreak. The sounds of the metal biting into the dirt were harsh, the edges frequently catching rocks, biting into them with an abrupt clang. It was slow going, but they continued.

"How's Randy?" shouted Richard over the rush of water, looking back over his shoulder.

"He doesn't know if he's coming or going," replied Dennis, pulling up another few meters of hose to give some slack. Richard nodded, and Gary shook his head. They had seen William fall, his legs dangling over the edge, kicking furiously, and then his fall; a small shape rapidly plunging to the ground, his arms flapping for all the world as if he were trying to fly. He couldn't, and they watched his fall until he disappeared into the shadows.

Gary had suggested that someone should go look to see if he was okay, if by some miracle he was still alive. He had read stories, of parachutists who had survived falls when their chutes had failed, somehow alive against all the odds. Maybe William would have got lucky.

"If you're so eager, go for yourself," said Donald. "And don't forget to bring a bucket so you have something to yak into when you see what's left of him." Gary looked around, to see if maybe Richard or Robert were going to volunteer. They had kept silent, riding out the last of the earthquake that had suddenly quit as if someone had thrown a switch. Gary decided against going, not wanting to see if Donald was right about what he would see. Glen had come running out of the dark a moment later, his flashlight aiming everywhere.

"Thank God you guys are okay!" he exclaimed. He shone the light on them all, doing a mental headcount. They covered their eyes from the beam, as they had done earlier.

"Where's Randy and Will?"

"They went up on the silo, just before the quake hit."

"Well, hopefully their okay, then."

No one had the heart to tell him about William.

"We need to get to work on that fire, before it spreads too far. It might be some time before we can get a proper fire engine out here, or a water bomber."

"I'll stay here and wait for Randy," volunteered Dennis. He didn't mention William, and got a few glances from the rest of the guys. It went over Glen's head.

"Okay, good idea," said Glen. "When they come down, see how they are and come join us."

Dennis nodded.

"You betcha," he replied, wondering how Glen would react when he showed up with just Randy.

"Let's go," said Glen cheerily.

"Time's a wastin'!"

They got behind Glen, and followed him away towards the bush fire;

Dennis could hear him giving directions. Dennis went to lean against one of the trucks in the parking lot, and waited for Randy.

When Glen saw Dennis arrive, he looked around, and asked the question that Dennis knew was coming.

"Where's Randy and William?" He held his shovel out, leaning against it while he caught his breathe. His face was sweaty, and darkened with streaks of soot and dirt. Dennis grimaced at the smell of the water issuing from the fire hose. It was fed from a nearby lagoon, an old marsh that had never been drained and stood deep enough to drown a man, if he was careless enough. A few summers back a local kid by the name of Richie had gone swimming in the marsh, and when he was out near the middle, he stopped and put his legs down, to stand on the bottom to catch his breathe. His feet had gone straight into the mud like it was cooled pudding, and it held him like a vice grip. He was a foot under a moment later, the mud stopping mid-shin, and it refused to let him go. When the local highway patrol had found his car, following up on his missing persons report, parked next to the marsh, the constable had retrieved himself a twelve foot aluminum boat on a hunch, and pushed it into the still waters. He had paddled out into the lagoon, and found Richie ten minutes later, drowned, standing straight up in the mud like it had caught him, and dead as a doornail, his arms floating up at his sides. He hung there like a grotesque floating marionette, a few crayfish already digging their way into the flesh of his legs. The bottom of the marsh was thick with a dense grey mud that stuck to anything with a fierce suction, and it smelled riper than a bag of used diapers left to spoil in the summer sun. It was rich with rotting marsh life, and it stunk to high heaven. The water they were pumping out over the fire came from the lagoon, its pipe laid flat over the bottom, on top of the mud, with an aluminum grating at its mouth to filter out the big stuff that might clog the intake. As a result, the water stunk just like the mud.

"Randy is a basket case. He's sitting down in the parking lot."

"And William?" asked Glen, breaking a silence as Dennis wondered what to say.

"Will fell from the silo. He didn't make it."

Glen's eyes grew wide.

"Will's dead?"

Dennis nodded. Donald and Robert had planted their shovels into the ground, watching the conversation take place.

Glen let his shovel stand in the ground, and he began to walk away, towards the silo. He turned at the last moment, startling Robert and Donald who were still leaning on their shovels.

"Keep digging!" he shouted at them.

They jumped, startled at being caught unawares, and immediately began digging again, throwing some dirt over top of a few fingers of flame that were creeping towards them. Dennis watched Glen march off, and then twisted his shovel free, preferring to help out with the fire than to go check on William. A moment later, he was to the left of Donald, kicking the shovel into the ground.

Glen walked towards the silo, pissed off as all hell. The ground changed from packed dirt to the pea gravel of the lane, and he could see where Randy was sitting on the ground, cross legged, his head bowed down, his hair disheveled. With the flames behind him, the top of the silo was well lit, the bottom was cloaked in shadow from the buildings in the mill yard. He could see the silo was leaning a bit, and he could see the normally smooth expanse of the foundation had some huge cracks in it that run under and away. He wondered if he was going to be in trouble. If Will had died, sure as shit there was going to be an investigation, and that would tie up the place for a while. It had been years since there had been a fatality at the mill, the last had been Randy's old man. Prior to that, it had been a millwright who had crept inside a strapper, crawling over the stack of lumber, to get at a hose he was inspecting. He had somehow pushed the button with one of his feet, and had a few seconds to think about his impending death as the strapper laid four metal bends across the stack, before tightening them fast against the wood. When his body had been found, he had been neatly quartered, the metal bands cutting through his body and holding it securely down to the stack of lumber. He had been found by the other millwright who went looking for him at lunch time, when he hadn't shown up and was more than a little late. He had seen the green light flashing on the strapper, indicating the stack was ready to go. He would be interviewed over and over again to check for consistencies in his story, to see if he was in any way at fault. He knew he wasn't. He had told everyone to stay together, or to go in pairs, and they had listened. It wasn't his fault that the earthquake had struck. That was extraordinarily bad luck, akin to winning the lottery. He wondered if the person that would be assigned to investigate him would find him at fault for not telling the crew to stay on the ground. Anything was possible, and the insurance company might look for any way out to absolve themselves of the settlement legal troubles that were certain to arise. He felt his stomach roll.

He could only hope he didn't get an investigator that was out to look for a patsy.

He went around the side, and was struck by the smell. It was coppery, and also smelled like a mix of urine and feces. When he saw the body, he knew that he was right. William had split open when he had hit the ground, like an overstuffed bag of groceries. He stared at the corpse for a moment, taking it all in, and then his stomach contracted violently. There was no warning at all. He bent over from the force of the contraction and spilled his lunch over the concrete. When that smell mixed with the rest, he barfed again, this time less forcefully. He dropped to his knees, catching his breath that had been pushed out of him, and then wiping his mouth. He adjusted his hardhat that had slid forwards, using both of his hands to reposition it on his head. There was certainly no doubt as to the cause of death. He stood back up, turning around, feeling his knees buckle and tremble, feeling another stomach contraction coming. He managed to force it down, breathing deeply, trying to fill his lungs with fresh air. Looking over to the other side of the yard, it looked like the fire was moving away from the mill, towards the highway. At least he might get some credit for saving the mill from burning down. The earthquake had pretty well torn the mill apart, where it was weakest. Most of the building was framed with two foot steel I beams, and they had stood firm. The concrete underneath was shattered and cracked, but at least the steel seemed to be in good shape. He walked towards Randy, who seemed to be in bad shape. He hadn't really moved since he had seen him last.

Out in the Atlantic, the earthquake rolled forward, the shockwave triggering faults and slips as it sped around the world. Off the eastern seaboard, not too far from Charleston, the shockwave broke free a two hundred and four kilometer long piece of the continental shelf. It flowed to the bottom of the Atlantic; an immense landslide that no one had any idea of; millions of tonnes of rock crumbling and sliding downwards, displacing an immense volume of water that rushed in to meet the void created by landslide far below. If anyone had been standing on the coast, they would have seen the shoreline quickly recede far out to sea, the waters pulling away in the span of a few short minutes to a level far below what low tide would bring, exposing kilometers of the seafloor.

He sat down beside him, staying silent for a few minutes, letting him get used to the idea that he wasn't alone.

"You okay, Randy?" he asked after a bit.

He had shook his head briefly, still buried under his arms.

"That mean yes or that mean no?"

"Okay I guess," he finally mumbled.

Glen nodded.

"Do you want to talk about what happened?"

"Not particularly," he responded in a low voice.

"It will help you feel better, if you talk about it."

They sat in the dark for a few minutes, bathed in random firelight.

When Randy began to talk again, Glen nearly jumped, not expecting him to say anything just yet.

"I watched him go over the side. I just watched him."

"You saw him fall?" he asked.

Randy nodded. Glen shook his head.

"Can you describe it?"

"I was h-hanging onto the ladder," his breath stitched, "Everything was shaking. I COULDN'T REACH HIM!"

Glen was quiet for a moment, letting the emotions calm down a little further.

"If you could have helped him, everyone knows you would have."

"He just kept s-sliding closer and closer to the edge, and he j-just w-went over. I'll never forget the look in his eyes. Oh God; I'll never forget that look."

He drew a deep breathe; Glen could hear Randy's chest quivering as he inhaled. Glen sat there next to him, keeping his mouth shut; just letting Randy slowly accept the fact of what had happened. He heard another low rumble building, and instantly perked up, a shot of adrenaline in his blood. A few seconds passed, and the sound grew louder, but it definitely was no earthquake. It would have struck by now. Randy leapt to his feet, his eyes wide and panic-stricken. His sanity was hanging by a thread, a moment away from snapping and sending him screaming into the bushes.

Glen looked over the hood of the truck they were sitting beside, peering into the darkness, trying to see what was causing the noise. It seemed to be coming from the entire seaboard, not just a small local noise like a truck driving down a road. The sound was coming in all directions from the east.

Randy was standing next to him, clutching the rear view mirror assembly, white knuckled, his breathing becoming light and fast. He aimed his flashlight into the bushes, trying to see anything by aiming it into the deepest gaps of the tree line. It didn't show anything; the light just vanishing in the dark. He frowned, trying to see as far as he could. He looked over his left shoulder, seeing if the other guys could hear anything. They were still working on the yard fire, apparently unaware of the sounds that he and Randy could hear, their shovels and fire hose blocking it out. There was a rail line nearby, but it didn't sound like any train he had ever heard, and the sightline from the mill down to the coast would show any locomotive running down the tracks. There were no lights at all; the night was a dark as it could be. The sound quickly grew more ominous; the sounds of crackling and rustling brush becoming audible, like a muted jet. The others had stopped shoveling, and had put down the fire hose, also looking to the east, trying to see what to make of the sound. Against the darkness of the sky, Glen could make out the uppermost outlines of some trees in the distance. The furthest ones he could see began to shake, and then began to fall as others closer to them also began to shake; their branches violently rocking back and forth. Whatever was coming their way was moving terribly fast, and the sound seemed to double second by second.

Glen turned, to see that Randy had run for it, running down the lane as fast as he could; a run of panic and fear, not control. His arms flailed wildly by his sides, trying to pump back and forth ever faster, trying to make it somewhere else could feel safe. He tested the door of the truck he was looking over, and finding it unlocked, he climbed in, rolling the windows shut and locking the doors for the mental security that motion provided.

He watched from the cab as the others began to get second thoughts about standing where they were. The shovels were dropped, and the fire hose turned off, and the men ran in various directions, their escape unplanned and random. Glen found the truck keys in the visor, and stuck them in the ignition. He turned the keys over, and got nothing. Not even the seatbelt light came on; the truck was totally dead.

"Fuck!" he yelled, feeling bad about using the profanity. He used to swear like a longshoreman, and had fought to clean up his mouth after his son had commented about Daddy always swearing. He had gone deep red with embarrassment, and set to work immediately to clean the vocabulary from his language. It surprised him how much it had become a part of his vernacular, once he actually had to make a conscious effort to filter his speech. Once he began to think about what he was going to say, before saying it, the task became a lot easier. It was like teaching yourself to not stutter by putting rocks in your mouth, to force yourself to slow down and think about what you were going to say, and how you were going to say it. At first, it had made his responses slower than usual, and a few people had wondered if there was something wrong with him, like he had a stroke or he was on a medication that made him slower than normal. After a few months, he had cleaned up his speech, and now typically only swore when something was reflexive, like when he hit his thumb with a hammer or stubbed his toe. In the building tension in the air, the failure of the truck to start had triggered him; his emotion getting the better of his control. He could feel his hands starting to shake, and feel the energy of the adrenaline surging into his bloodstream. He felt like he could run a three minute mile, and then do it again. Robert was banging on the glass on the passenger door.

"Lemme into my truck!"

Glen reached over, and pulled the door lock up.

Robert pulled the door open, and slammed it shut behind him. The door made a deep metallic thud as it locked into place. It was a '62 short bed Chevy, a solid lump of metal where even the doors were heavy and seemed to be made out of cast iron. Robert had restored it a great deal, and painted it Bahaman Blue. And now it wouldn't start.

"Let's go!" Robert cried, not seemingly upset at all that Glen was sitting in the drivers seat.

"I already tried; it won't start!" he replied.

"Bullshit; I just put a new battery in her with enough cranking power to start a battleship. Do 'er again!"

He cranked the key again. Nothing.

Robert stared at the instrument panel, the wind taken out of his sails.

"You're doing somethin' wrong!" he yelled, trying to explain why the truck he had put a few thousand hours into wouldn't even light up, much less turn over.

"Sure," he replied sarcastically, "I turned over the key wrong. You want to explain that one to me?"

The roaring sound was looming; the sound of trees crashing becoming all too clear.

"Move over! Lemme do it."

Robert and Glen switched positions as fast as they could, struggling and puffing as they crawled over each other in the cab.

Robert settled into the seat, pumped the gas pedal twice, and turned the key.

"Nooooooo!" he screamed.

"You fucking piece of shit! Turn over!"

He tried it again. Nothing. He proceeded to hit the steering wheel with his clenched fists, which did nothing but hurt his fists.

"You whore! You motherfucker!" He tried again.

Nothing.

Glen would have laughed at another time, seeing Robert go into a fit at the wheel of his truck, but not now, not this time. He wanted the truck to start just as badly as Robert did, and he was getting a big old knot in his stomach, and the knot was telling him to get a move on before it was too late. Richard and Gary had fled into their own cars that also apparently weren't starting. He had seen Dennis run into the mill, but he didn't know where Donald was. He might be running down the road right behind Randy, trying to see who might set the land speed record for men running in steel toed work boots. Richard got out of his car, slammed the door shut and began to run down the road as well. As Glen watched, while Robert tried to convince his truck to start by swearing at it, the fire that had crossed the road suddenly went out. It was only a couple of hundred meters down across the road, and it had gone out just as quickly as if someone had blown out a match. He could feel the truck shaking and vibrating. No small feat for a truck that weighed as much as it did.

"What the hell?" Glen whispered. Looking out past the passenger window, he could see something moving. It was dark and rushing, and a moment later, it was on them. The surge of water crashed into the truck with a loud boom, shaking them back and forth in their seats. The water foamed up against the window, and they could feel the truck being picked up and carried in the flow, striking objects on the ground with jarring bumps. The passenger window began to crack, and then something hit the underside of the truck hard, making it stall in the flow. The broad wide surface of the side, suddenly stuck on the ground, began to roll over, being pushed inexorably over by the power of the water. The truck, for all of its weight, was inconsequential compared to the energy of the water that pounded against it and flowed around it.

"Oooooh shit!" cried Glen, feeling the right side lifting in the water.

Robert clutched the steering wheel, his body clenched, trying to hold himself in one position. The truck began to go over slowly, but once the water had the underside exposed, she went over like a paper hat. They cold see the water churning around them, bubbling around the glass, and they could see the ground rushing past them. Then the passenger window broke. It started quietly, the glass fracturing with the sound of a twisted ice cube tray, and then it popped, spraying inward with the force of the water pushing it aside.

Glen yelled," Aaagrble," as his mouth was filled with water; Robert took a deep breathe, his cheeks puffed out like a squirrel with a load of nuts. The vehicle struck something hard, and spun under the water and then came to a bone-crunching halt, pinned against something. The bump made Robert exhale his breathe in a series of violent bubbles, and he suddenly fought to escape, trying to get out of the water. Glen released his seatbelt, his lungs burning, and was pushed against Robert to the side of the door. He was fighting to roll down the window, succeeding only slightly. He had managed to get the glass down a couple of inches before Glen crashed into him, disorienting him and knocking his hand off the window lever. Glen felt himself pushed against the wall, and fought for all he was worth to get out, lashing out with his arms and legs, trying to break free, swinging and kicking. An elbow caught Robert in the nose, driving his head backwards, and making him exhale reflexively from the pain. The water flowed down his throat and into his lungs, filling them with cold salt water. His body hitched as he tried to replace it with air, but succeeded only in sucking in more water. He could feel his chest burning as if it was on fire, his heart beating wildly, thumping for any oxygen it could get. He could feel his thinking getting foggy, the pain getting less intense. His body lashed out in a final effort to break free, to get some air, and then with a few final twitches, it stopped. Glen fought for a bit longer, the raw physical exertion of his struggle using the last of his oxygen. It felt like his lungs were being ripped out of his chest, and he fought to control the reflex to inhale, his body crying and screaming for a breath. He lost the battle, and felt the water pour down into his body, where the cold shocked the last of the adrenaline out of him, giving him a few more seconds of fight. When it was over, the water pinned him next to Robert, his extremities shaking slightly as they struggled to deny death for just a moment longer.

Randy had taken off down the road, feeling an indescribable need to run, to get away from all of this as fast as he could. It was another earthquake. He could hear it coming, and this time he was going to try to get somewhere that the ground wouldn't shake, where he wouldn't see William fall from the roof screaming and landing with a sickening thud. All he had to do was run, run as fast as he could. He used to run a lot as a boy, but his times as a boy were long past, and his lungs began to ache, painful stitches in his side making inhaling painful. He kept running, his hand holding his ribs, his mouth dry from over exertion. He could hear someone else running behind him, and in his panic he concluded it must be Will, chasing him down, coming to get revenge for his own death, screaming at him as he neared.

"I'm gonna get you Randy! I'm gonna push you off the edge, so you can feel what it's like!" He could hear him cackling wildly, anticipating meting out the justice of the Dead. He ran harder, looking over his shoulder to see who was running behind him. All he could see was a shadow, and hear the thick crunching of work boots running down the lane. He ran faster, determined to not get caught. All he had to do was get home, and he could lock himself in his bomb shelter. It was only a few hundred more meters down the road. A few hundred more meters and he could relax. A few hundred more meters and that terrible rumbling sound could go fuck itself, he would be safe. He only made it another forty-three meters when the bushes to his right shook violently, suddenly exploding with a crest of water.

He cried out as he felt the first of the surge pull his feet out from under him, tossing him towards to ground. A moment later he was overwhelmed and picked up in the wave, mixed in with so many other branches and rocks, tumbling wildly. The air was knocked out of him almost immediately when he was rolled over in the wave, ass over tea kettle, somersaulted end over end. With a painful crunch he was pinned to a tree, his arms and head wrapped around one side, his legs around the other. The water pressure crushed him against the rough bark; the tree refused to yield, and he was ground between the hard wood and the incessant crushing force of the water flowing over him. He felt his ribs crack, and the urgent need to breath become dire. The pain was incredible; he couldn't tell what hurt more, the aching fire in his lungs, or the grinding of his crushed ribs. He was pummeled from behind, being struck by rocks and other loose debris being carried along in the flow. He didn't want to drown, he hated water, he would have preferred a death in a roaring fire than to drown. As it was, the Fates had no mercy, and he inhaled a lungful of water a second later. Donald was already dead; he had also been knocked down in the initial wave when it broke free from the forest and swept over the road. He had been carried a short way, when he was caught up between several large rocks being carried in the wave. He was ground between them, his body shattered in seconds and torn apart, caught up in natures own rock tumbler. When the storm surge ran out of steam, the retreating water picked up their remains, and carried them out into the deep waters of the Atlantic.

Dennis had run for the mill, trying to seek safety amidst the building. He could feel the ground shaking and hear the roaring grow louder and loader, a terrible low sound that made the hairs on the back of his neck stand up. Donald had elected to run down the road, following Randy who had shot down the lane at a sprinters pace on a few seconds before. He had seen Robert run for his truck, and Richard and Gary go for their cars. When he had reached the mill, he had climbed to the first floor, a steel grating supported by giant steel I beams and pillars. A few sections had popped free in the earthquake, but the thick steel structure had weathered the quake quite well. He had run over to a high observation walk that oversaw the chain, and kneeled down on it, trying to catch his breath as he gasped for air. He was not used to running, and the short distance he had covered, driven by fear, had winded him. He watched Robert and Gary trying to start the truck, hitting the steering wheel in frustration, and then he also saw Richard get out of his car. He could see the trees shaking and falling in the distance with a speed that rapidly coming towards them. He gripped the yellow railing tightly, feeling reassured and comforted. In a flash of steam and smoke, the fires that had spread to the other side of the road went out suddenly, casting the mill yard into near darkness. His eyes widened as he saw a wall of water suddenly burst from the brush, churning and roaring in a fury.

"Get away!" he yelled at the top of his lungs, trying to warn everyone. They never heard him, his cries lost in the chaos. He saw Gary's low

Pontiac get covered in water, disappearing beneath the waves, and a second later Richard was pinned to a silver Oldsmobile, his own car driven forward in the wave, crushing him against the side of the Olds. His arms were raised defensively into the air as he saw the car coming towards him, striking him forcefully at the hips, and then he sank beneath the waves, as the cars were twisted around and washed forwards. He watched in terror as Robert's Chevy was pushed forwards with ease, the water breaking and swirling around it, flowing over the cab and box. In a moment, it came to a sudden halt, and then neatly flipped in a smooth motion. He could see Robert clutching the steering wheel, and Glen's hand pressed to the glass as they went over. He tried to wave to them, to show them where he was.

"Git out git out git out!" he screamed. A moment later, the surge hit the foundation beams of the mill, kicking up a thick fine spray of sea water as it broke around the steel. He could feel the power trembling through his feet as the steel fought the onslaught, the metal grating shaking on the rails. He gripped the railing, wrapping his arms around the tubing for support, listening to the roar of the waves and the groaning of the building. He heard the Chevy bite into the I beam underneath where he stood, grinding as the water pushed it against the steel. The truck bent slighty, and stopped, held neatly in place, upside down. He could see the black tires glistening, and the water flowing over the underside of the truck, but he could see nothing of Glen and Robert, who he assumed were still trapped in the cab. He barely heard the glass explode, a muted tinkle that was abruptly lost in the rumble.

The water continued to flow and rise; churning under his feet. With a loud tearing squeal, the silo was torn of the foundation slab, and was sent rolling with thunderous echoing booms, crashing into the planer and vanishing into the dark. The beehive was extinguished in a raging hiss that screamed loudly and was extinguished a moment later. Dennis hung on, watching the river of ocean flowing underneath him.

When the water stopped rising, and slowly began to ebb, he was still clutching the railing, his hands fixed like claws. The wave had slowly come to a standstill, and as he watched, fascinated, it reversed direction, flowing back out to sea, carrying with it everything it had torn free from the ground, returning east with its spoils. The surface of the water was littered with objects of all kinds, only some of which he could make out, but which covered the surface nonetheless. There was so much rubble and flotsam that it looked like you could walk across it all over the water, to get wherever you wanted to go. A strong wind had picked up from the west, brushing the surface of the water and kicking up a fine spray. He had heard Roberts truck come free of the post it had been pinned against, and heard it rumble a few times as it rolled away under the waves, going end over end. He did not see Glen or Robert, for which he was thankful. Eventually, the silo came into view, rolling down the slope, smashed and battered, crushing the few trees that had remained standing, before fading away. Exhausted, Dennis leaned against the railing, trembling and cold, his arms crossed over his chest, his legs drawn up. The grating was not the most comfortable thing on his ass, but compared to everything else he was overwhelmed with, it was a minor inconvenience that he could tolerate. He closed his eyes and dozed, his body quickly falling into a deep slumber.

He woke up when he heard the roof peeling away from the walls; the bolts coming free, sounding like gunshots as they snapped. He blinked a few times, and saw the water had fallen several feet already, and it was still flowing strong. The wind was something else. Living on the coast, he was familiar with hurricanes, and had been through several good ones in his time. Hurricanes though came from the south or the east, not the west, and there hadn't been any hurricane warnings in the news that he had seen, not even any strong wind warnings. The weatherman had fucked up badly this time to have missed this. The wind was turning into a fine gale; he could feel his hair being whipped about when it gusted and howled. He watched the roof lift away in the air, and then fall into the retreating water with a metallic splash. Bits and pieces were blowing past him, and he could see all sorts of debris flying through the air. Leaves and dust, paper and bags. All the usual light stuff you saw in a storm that got picked up and carried high in the sky. His crouched up, massaging his butt. It hurt something fierce from the grating, and was tingling and numb as well. The wind howled through the mill; with portions of the roof gone, and the walls torn away in the waves, the wind was free to swirl and gust through the building, carrying away anything that was exposed and light enough. The evening sky was getting lighter; he could see the eastern horizon brightening with the coming day. How long had he been asleep for?, he suddenly wondered. A few hours for sure. He definitely felt better for it. But he sure was hungry. His muscles felt sore all over, no doubt from being on edge for so long, and his leg muscles were stiff and aching. He was no member of the track and field, and it had been some time since he had last run to anything, even a short distance. He rose, feeling his muscles protest and his joints crack here and there. In spite of it all, he felt good. It was a grand thing to be alive after seeing so much devastation. With the brightening sky, it was a little easier to see what remained around him. Most of the forest was gone, or still under water, and he could see the silver shimmering of the water flowing back all the way to the sea. The mill was in shambles, having collapsed in a few places, bent in others, or completely gone. Even the Caterpillar was gone, and that thing was no light weight. Across the eastern seaboard, as far as his eyes could see, there were no clouds. Not even a speck of the stuff. If it wasn't for the wind that just didn't seem to quit, and the aftermath of the night before, it could have been a very pleasant winters day. With the mill being the highpoint of the area, now that the silo had been removed, he looked around looking for a spot where he could climb and get a better vantage point. He went around the walkway, which covered the main planer area, and found a ladder that went up to a hatchway for roof maintenance access. The roof was gone, but the ladder was still there, clinging to the side of the wall, seeming to lead up to the very sky. He gripped the sides, and tried to give it a shake, to see it was still securely attached to the wall. It didn't budge, so he stepped onto the first rung, and made his way upwards, slowly, paranoid that it would suddenly fail, sending him backwards. He made it to the top, finding a wide steel beam that he could step out onto. He climbed off the ladder cautiously, and found the beam to be solid and secure as well, if not just a little bent here and there at the joints where it was fixed to others, making up the shell that supported the roof. The beam echoed as he took a few gingerly steps along it, the sound carrying down along its length. Satisfied, he looked around, seeing the view to the east, and to the west, a familiar dark sky with a marked delineation where a thick bank of clouds was in contrast to the clear cloudless sky to the east. He felt the wind buffet his body, a couple of times pushing him slightly, making him a little less sure of his footing, and of his idea to be standing on the roof. The storm was moving towards him; he could see it flowing across the sky; it looked like a wall on the horizon, pushing its way forward. It was moving with incredible speed. He had seen clouds blowing by quickly before, and had wondered how fast they were going. He had read somewhere that sometimes wind speeds could pass a couple hundred kilometers and hour; it depended on the altitude. The higher you were, the faster they went. Down here, near sea level, the fastest clouds were in hurricanes, or tornadoes. That is what it looked like; a giant hurricane blowing in from the west, from overland. Quickly, the wind seemed to pick up intensity, and Dennis found himself wanting to get down, to find some cover. By the looks of it, he had only a few minutes to go before the edge of the storm reached him. He took hold of the ladder, flipped around it, and made his way down, watching the clouds coming his way as he went, his eyes growing wider the more he saw.

He jumped down the last two rungs, hitting the floor with the ring of the grating under his boots. He needed to find a corner. Corners were the safest places, somewhere there was a lot of structure coming to meet in a relatively small location. A spot like that was stronger than the rest of a building. He couldn't be to fussy, having little time to spare, and settled on a spot where a series of pipes came down and then branched out, all within a few posts and beams. He settled in the spot, his back against the wall, and waited. The wind grew louder and louder, and then it felt like all of the air had suddenly been sucked away, an immense vacuum opening up filled with nothingness and silence. With a gigantic clap that popped his eardrums, and blew his hair forward, the atmosphere bore down with all of its might behind it.

The walls shuddered, buckling forward, and Dennis felt the wind slide behind his back, creating a suction that threatened to pull him free of his refuge. The air was filled with debris, and he could scarcely catch his breath, the air feeling as though it was being pulled from his lungs. He screamed into the maelstrom, his voice lost in the fury. Pieces of the mill were tearing free, bolts snapped or tearing away, the pieces falling down into the water of being cast off into the wind. The trees that had remained standing during the flood were gone, blown down and torn away. He heard another series of pops and snaps, and watched in horror as the joints of the beams that had so far sheltered him began to wobble. The nuts splintered, and the bolts feel free. Suddenly loose, the structure around him began to crumble, weakening what remained. Dennis felt the wall began to go, leaning forward, shivering in all directions. He held on and prayed that it would hold together, please God let it hold together. In the space of a heartbeat, the corner posts fell over, the walls cracked, and the wind that had been held off his back surged through, exploiting the opening. He was flung into the air, screaming, the wind pushing him into the sky like a kite as the wall behind him disintegrated and shattered, Edison's Mill falling into ruin, being scoured from the very Earth.

Ryan Speer

He was wakened an hour later by the sounds of Lucy whining at the door. The sound was so unusual that it had woken him up quickly, without the usual grogginess. He got out of bed and went into the living room.

"What is it, Lucy?"

She only whined, and looked at him, her insistence to open the door plain to see. Maybe she had the shits or something. If that was the case, better she have the sense to go outside than have an accident in the house.

"Here you go."

He opened the door, and she had squeezed herself through before the door was even fully open. He watched her run off to the yard, and then felt a wall of freezing cold air slam into his face.

"Have fun."

He shut the door and locked it up again. One nice thing about having a Husky was that you didn't have to worry about them in cold weather. He'd let her in when the morning came. He suddenly felt tired, his body relaxing after the initial adrenaline surge for a false emergency. Taking the opportunity, he put out a few more logs into the fire, keeping it stoked, and went back to bed. He slid into his sheets, reveling in the warmth still held by the thick duvet. He was asleep almost instantly.

The trembling woke him up. He had heard it first, like a freight train bearing down on the house. For a moment, it was only the loud onrushing sound. A few small things began to vibrate, and then it felt like that train he had heard ran into the house. Everything buckled.

He heard the concrete foundation crack loudly, and saw the cement in the rock wall crack, a few stones falling out of the mortar and clacking on the floor. The floor tiles had shattered and popped free, and the window panes first cracked in their frames, and then fell apart, crashing onto the sills and floor. He couldn't hear anything, the rumbling was so loud. He had jumped out of bed, hanging onto his duvet, and was knocked to the floor. *Holy fuck it's an earthquake* he thought.

"RYAN!" he screamed.

He couldn't hear anything, it was just to loud.

He yelled again and couldn't hear any reply. He couldn't stand either, the floor was buckling and heaving, so he tried to crawl. He heard the timbers and walls of the house creak and moan, swaying back and forth. He put his head down, blanket over his back, and crawled. He never saw the roof fall in on him.

He woke up seeing nothing but blackness. He felt something pressing down on him, something huge, and he felt cold. He suddenly remembered the earthquake.

"Ryan!" he shouted, coughing. Dust swirled around his face, and something cold. It was snow. He heard nothing. Looking around, he realized it wasn't all black. If he craned his neck up, he could see the sky. He paused and took measure of the situation, moving his arms, then his legs, trying to see how much room he had. His head ached, and he felt a large goose egg swollen just above his neck. It was a little wet, the blood scabbing over already. He realized the duvet was still across his body. It was a lucky break, the thick insulation keeping him warm while he was out. There were no sounds except whatever he made of his own.

"RYAN!" he yelled again.

Nothing. He lowered his head, fearing the worst. He felt around, and recognized his pile of clothes from the day before. He had put them near the foot of the bed. He struggled to put them on in his narrow confines, feeling the cold cloth on his skin giving him goosebumps. He recalled something.

"Lucy!"

He paused, listening for anything. She had known, he realized. She didn't have the shits, she felt the earthquake coming.

That's why she was hollering to get out of the house. *Good for her*, he thought, glad to know that wherever she was, she was certainly safe.

There was a small placer mine on the property that she had sometimes visited when she was on her own, maybe she was there.

He pulled on the last of his clothes, and pulled the blanket around him for added insulation. He pulled it cautiously, and found that it was free. A few pieces of rubble weighed it down, but it wasn't pinned under anything. He wrapped it around himself, and crawled for the hole where he could see the sky. It was slow going in the dark, he kept getting snagged on things he couldn't really see, but had to feel for. His head was pounding, and he felt nauseous. *Moderate concussion* he thought. He kept pushing, he had to get out and look for Ryan. Hopefully he was unconscious, and not...his eyes filled with tears, and he fought them back. *No, I have to stay calm.* He knew he needed to remain logical and in control. If he let his emotions get in control he could do any sort of stupid thing that could endanger both of them. He kept pulling, and soon found himself half free, his torso emerging from the ruins like a bug emerging from a cocoon. The god dam blanket kept getting stuck. Losing his patience, nearly free, he pulled, feeling and hearing the cloth tear.

No matter, it wasn't feather filled; it was foam, so it wouldn't fall out.

He looked about and saw the ruins of his home. No part of the structure was left standing, everything had been tossed on the ground like a child's toy, strewn about and jumbled. Steam rose from the remains of the fireplace, the stones keeping anything from catching fire. His truck was the only thing of normalcy. It sat as he had parked it in the driveway. It had been moved, sitting on an angle, but otherwise it was undamaged. He felt a sigh of relief seeing it; it meant he had shelter. Standing there in the dark, he looked around the countryside, seeing no lights from other farms. Off in the distance, a fire raged out of control; he could see the flames engulfing something. He got his bearings. The Weston farm. It had been destroyed, just like his place. God only knew if there were any survivors. He navigated through the rubble, trying to find Ryan. Where his room had been it was an indistinguishable pile of the remains of the house. He didn't know how he was going to find him in this mess. The dog was nowhere to be seen, at least she might have been able to sniff him out. She must still be spooked, hiding out somewhere she felt was safe. He began moving pieces of debris, pulling randomly in the dark at objects he couldn't easily see. He wondered how long he had been out for under the roof. He struggled over to his truck, searching underneath the rear spring assembly for his spare key. The metal was bitterly cold, painful to touch. He found the magnetic box, and slid the key out, fumbling with his numb hands.

He opened the truck door, the cab remained black, the cabin light not coming on. He hopped in, hoping to start the truck and aim his headlights at his house so he could see what he was going through.

He slid the key into the ignition, giving it a quarter turn. The panel did not come on, nor did the ignition chime. He turned the key all the way over. Nothing happened. Not even a click or an emergency light. He sat in the truck trying to figure out his next move. It was clear that for some reason, the truck was dead. The Weston farm was a few kilometers away down the road, but he didn't even know if anyone was there. And it would take him about an hour to walk there in sock feet. An hour that Ryan would be lying trapped in the cold. He hoped he had been lucky and still had his blankets around him.

"Hang on, Ryan. I'm trying to figure something out." he said aloud, just in case he could hear him but not be able to respond. He wrapped the blanket over his head; his ears were becoming painfully cold. All he could do was dig by hand and hope for the best, he couldn't think of another possible solution. There was a long chain and pull in the shed he could use for really heavy parts, but it was heavy and difficult to use by yourself in the best of times, never mind alone on a winters night. He walked back to the pile, and began throwing things off, one by one, tossing them over his shoulder into the field behind him.

"I'm coming, Ryan. You just wait."

He would have to get to the fridge and grab some food pretty soon if he was going to try to stay warm and have energy. It stood where the kitchen had been, the roof falling in around it, leaving it standing there like a steel coffin. Ironically, the insulation of the fridge was keeping his food *from* freezing, instead of freezing. He kept going, feeling warm as long as he kept up a decent pace. His vision swam a couple of times, his balance wavering. He knew his doctor wouldn't have recommended heavy physical exertion with a concussion, but then the situation was more than a little unusual. The pile barely seemed to move; the small bits of debris he had cleared were now revealing large pieces of the wall and roof that were going to prove to be considerable obstacles. He felt a breeze pick up, and hoped it wasn't going to last too long. Standing in the cold working was one thing, you could generate enough heat to stay warm. Throw in the windchill factor, and it didn't matter what you were doing or what you were wearing; the wind stole heat from the body faster than it could be produced. The breeze continued to grow, and he noted that it was going towards the mountains. He had never noticed wind going in that direction before, it always came from the mountains and blew down over the plains below, from the winds coming off the Pacific to the west. It was what sometimes gave him snow in July, or twenty-five degrees Celsius in the dead of January. The wind continued to pick up, fluttering the blanket around his body and stirring up the lighter pieces of debris, sending them scattering across the field behind him. He hunkered down to reduce the wind speed around his face, trying to keep warm. It took a lot of energy to move cold air, it was heavy and dense, so it meant there must be a strong storm front coming in. He didn't recall seeing any weather warnings in the paper; it was supposed to be clear and sunny for the rest of the week, through past Christmas. Stupid weathermen. He kept low, feeling the air really begin to flow over the ground. A few larger pieces of the home began to fly off, heavy shingles and chunks of insulation. He was going to have to get out of the cold; he could feel the wind robbing his body heat.

"If you can hear me, Ryan, stay where you are. It's getting really windy and I need to get warmer."

If he was okay, being under the pile could be the best thing right now; all of that debris would be good shelter from the wind. He made his way back to the cab of the truck, closing the door behind him. Although it was well below thirty in the cab, the still air felt warm, and he sighed at the feeling, curling the blanket around him. He watched the wind picking up, and he could hear it whistle through the vents of the truck. Maybe they were going to get a December Chinook; a blast of warm air after this earthquake would be great timing. In the distance, he saw what looked like a cloud descend the mountain slope, a huge bank of rushing air and snow. It looked like a video he had once seen of a desert storm in the Sahara, where the entire horizon was filled with blowing sand. This looked the same, except is was snow and blowing throughout the mountains. And it was coming incredibly fast. The mountains were a good hundred or so kilometers from the homestead across a flat prairie that curved up to meet it, so it was easy to see. The storm was eating up the distance; he could *see* it surging towards him. Something was terribly wrong. He locked the doors, and put on his seat belt, staring with wide eyes. He couldn't do anything to help Ryan, except stay alive and come back to help. *Jesus Christ look at that thing coming*, he whispered to himself. He hoped Lucy had found a good hiding spot. In about five minutes the giant storm front had covered half the distance to him. The wind outside was growing shrill; the truck began to rock on its suspension, the occasional dull *thunk* as something blowing in the wind struck a body panel. A few pieces of roof were beginning to lift in the wind, the flat surface area catching the wind like a sail. A few others were being forced down, the mass of air pressure pushing objects flat against the ground.

"Here it comes," he said, closing his eyes. The front of the wall of air was a churning mass; he could see the objects being blown down and carried before it. He sat and waited. The noise grew tremendous, like listening to a jet at the airport. He heard objects striking the truck and windshield, no longer dull *thunks* but hard impacts, and something cracked the right top of the windshield with a glancing blow from something that was a blur. The roar reached a crescendo, and he felt the truck move, and with a blast of air, it was upon him. It was a thunderclap, the sound went from incredibly loud to unbearable in a moment, and the truck bounced, and with a drop in his stomach, he realized it was being lifted, and then the world went upside down. The truck was blown through the air, the windows blowing out spraying the cab with glass shards that embedded themselves in whatever they struck. He sat within his blanket wrapping, feeling the air being swirled around him, being blown past him faster than he could breathe. The truck was still airborne, and he felt it coming down, rolling slowly. It crashed into the ground and rolled violently, throwing him from left to right inside the cabin, the seatbelt straining to keep him in place. He struck his head against something, and his headache intensified. He had no sense of direction from being thrown about indiscriminately, the truck rolling in the air mass as if it weighed nothing. He could feel himself blacking out from the g forces. He was terrified, so scared he couldn't scream.

He began to pray.

"Our Lord who Art in..." and then the truck came to a screeching halt, crushing itself against a large boulder deposited at the end of the last ice age. The truck had wrapped itself around the huge erratic with a squealing crunch, the protest of metal compressing and bending in a split second, shaped around the stone like a piece of foil in a stone rubbing. Steve Speer stopped worrying.

When the air burst had passed, Lucy came out of hiding. She felt the earth begin to shake under her paws, and knew she needed to get out of the house where the man and boy lived quickly. She knew he didn't understand, that he couldn't feel what she felt, so she had run for her life, tearing across the snow to get *away*, away from what was coming. Every fiber of her being told her if she failed, she would die.

As she was running, she felt the ground beneath her begin to shake and roar, and she whined in terror, feeling the ground shift beneath her. She lost her footing and rolled in the snow, where she stood and rode out the shaking. The grasses around her shook, and it took all of her concentration and her four legs to keep standing. She heard the house down the road collapse and then the *WHAP* as it exploded, The screams from within clearly audible. The people in that house were going to die, of that she was certain. She hoped her people wouldn't die. There was no fire in her house that she could see, so she had hope. When the ground stopped shaking, she could still feel something bad, something in her belly told her to find somewhere safe. It was the feeling she got when she was chasing rabbits, and they had run into their holes, listening to her sniff from above. She could smell their fear, smell their desire to find somewhere safer. She knew for certain that she felt what they had felt. She did not return to the house, it was not safe there. She covered the few kilometers in no time, enjoying the run in spite of her fear of what was happening. The fact she was doing something to protect herself made her feel better. She needed to run, to be safe, to protect her young growing within her. The air was cool, she could feel it as she breathed deeply, and it helped to cool her down. She took a mouthful of snow as she ran, chewing and swallowing it on the go.

She came to the spot, where she had gone a few times with the boy. The boy was not allowed there, from the man, she could tell from the tone in his voice and the smell he had when he had found them there. But she returned once in a while. It gave good shelter, and was cool in the summer. And there were lots of rabbits close to it. Rabbits she could chase and chase until they went tharn and froze in the grass, just waiting for her to kill them.

She sniffed the hole and entrance, finding a few rocks had fallen from the entrance and roof, but the rock was solid. She squeezed herself into the opening, and crawled down into the mineshaft, the old placer mine running about fifty meters deep into the ground. It narrowed out from the entrance where the men who had dug had tried to hid its existence, but further back it expanded broadly, and she could walk around in comfort. She had stashed quite a few of her bones here, a few treats, and a few rabbits when she had felt her brood stirring within her. She knew the man had wondered what was happening, he smelled confused, but he kept buying her more bones, and she hid them here. She sat down and whined softly, hearing the wind begin to pick up outside, fearing for what was coming. She was safe, she knew it, but it made her unease no less intense.

When the wind had passed, she had come back to the entrance and sniffed about. She had looked about the land, and saw that all the loose snow had been blown away, except for blocks of ice that clung to the ground. She could see snow farther away where it had collected in giant drifts against hills and in the dips in the earth. She sniffed along the ground, making her way back to the house where the man and boy lived. She ran the rest of the distance, curious to see what was there. She whined when she came to the house, what was left of the house. On the ground, all that remained was the concrete slab that had been poured into the earth itself, and a few places where the wall had been sunk into the concrete. The rest of the house was gone. She could smell where the man had been, smelled his worry, but he was gone. She couldn't find any trace of him, only his scent. She smelled the concrete, finding where the boy had been. She could smell his death on the ground, the odor unmistakable, a mix of fear and urine, and something else unique to that act, something that came from the body as it expired. She sat on her haunches, licking her muzzle as she looked around the property. The house that had burned in the night was gone, but a pipe stuck from the ground, and fire still blew into the air from it, the flames rushing into the air.

A glint of metal caught her eye, and she ran to investigate. The fridge had been blown into a small gully, where it lay on its side, doors askew and dented. Other pieces of the home had been blown into the gully. The stove was smashed and crushed; the door had been torn off and was missing. The freezer was nearby, it's contents spilled and strewn against the hillside. She smelled food, and ate her fill, finding bacon and other meats and people food she had as treats. With nothing else to hold her to the area, she emptied the fridge and freezer, making multiple forays to cache their contents in her den, saving the food for later. It would last for months frozen in her den.

She scouted the land, scenting the earth and laying claim to this ground. She could smell the rabbits, their fear scent strong after the ground shaking and the howling wind. She saw the sun begin to rise, and she suddenly felt tired. The fear from the night before, and the multiple treks to store the food, along with her full belly had all cumulated to make her tired, more tired than she had felt in a long time. She sat at the front of the mine briefly, watching as the rising sun was blotted out from a black cloud that flowed across the sky. It came from beyond the mountains and crossed overhead, across the opposite horizon. She could feel the thunder building, the air thick with humidity and electricity. She crawled inside, and slept.

Colonel Dwight Petersen

He sat at his desk with his elbows planted on the desktop, his fingers massaging his temples that were beginning to go gray at the sides. The rest of his hair was still glossy black; a flat top haircut keeping it low maintenance. He sported a few days worth of growth on his chin and face, his facial hair coming in salt and pepper. Given a couple of weeks, he could sport a thick beard if given the chance. He might have the chance now. The desktop, a thinly grained walnut stained in a deep reddish brown, was lightly dusted with a thin layer of concrete powder, dust the system had so far been unable to scrub from the atmosphere entirely. He had ignored the dust, his attention being more directed to more pressing issues than if his desk was dusty. The monthly calendar was still in place, the leather corners holding it in place, the days of the month crossed off as they had passed with a blue line that ran in a downward slash from corner to corner. Around the periphery of the calendar, a series of notes and phone numbers framed and decorated the large page like a fancy border. His desk organizer sat at the front left of the desk, the Inbox and Complete sections clearly labeled with a black on white laminated tag. The Inbox section was full, the Complete section was empty. A few pens rested in the holder on the side, another fancier chrome pen, a Cross, sat tucked in the small leather sleeve at the side of the calendar. It had been given to him as a gift when he had earned his promotion to the complex, and he had always kept it near and in his sight. The side of the pen had been engraved with his name and the date of his promotion, three and a half months earlier. The fluorescent lights in the complex flickered intermittently, more because of a few loose connections and damaged ballasts than anything. The earthquake had given everything a fierce jolt, threatening to destroy a complex that had been designed to withstand anything that a conceivable enemy could throw against it, concentrated, within today's foremost weapons technologies. He would have to get a crew in place to go around and repair the lights. It would be crucial to morale overall if it looked in the least bit like they were not going to be able to sustain operations in any meaningful way.

The facility, known as Firefox within the confines of the North American Aerospace Defense Command, had started construction in the early nineteen sixties, built as an upgrade to the Cheyenne Mountain Facility, although under complete secrecy. Cheyenne Mountain would become the ultimate decoy, and sacrifice, in order to keep Firefox operational. It had taken twenty years to dig out the structure and install the hardware, deep underneath the granite mountains of the Mojave National Preserve. It was in fact nearly a kilometer straight down, in a bed of granite that was selected for its density and uniform structure, a thick slab with virtually no faults or fissures in its length for kilometers at a time.

The command center had been carefully blasted out of the rock with controlled directed explosions, designed to focus the energies of the detonations in specific patterns. Firefox was known to select few, the top brass of NORAD and NATO being the primary directors of its information and resources. The elevator shaft that ran down to the base had only two corridors, one shaft for those going down, and another only for those going to the surface. Both had points where they could be stopped and assaulted if necessary to prevent intrusion to lower depths. The insides of the shaft were lined with ten meters of specially hardened concrete, designed to work with and strengthen the bed of granite surrounding it. It was incredibly dense, and was inlaid with a dense network of fibrous rebar webs to add to its strength and resistance. The surface of the base was concealed at the base of a large granite outcropping that had been cluttered with piles of of weathered granite, a natural camouflage in the hues of the desert that would not lead to any unwanted attention. When the base staff was changed over, it took months, the replacement staff being driven in by Jeep in pairs during the night in vehicles equipped with night vision hardware so that lights were not required, as they would potentially attract interest. The mandatory tour of duty in the base was two years, with a bonus paid out if it could be extended to four.

The slow staff turnover kept the area around the base pristine, and helped reduce the chances of vehicles leaving tell tale tracks in the desert. Wherever possible, the vehicles drove on solid rock so as to leave no tracks in the surrounding environment. The Jeeps had also been fit with especially soft tires to reduce their impression and create less noticeable tracks. With the length of time of a tour in the facility, candidates had to be single, preferably with no family ties that might wonder where their relative had gone. Contact with the outside world was explicitly forbidden; it was as if they had been erased from the world itself. Paychecks were deposited into bank accounts that saw no withdrawals. Infrared cameras scoured the terrain around the base, watching for people that came too close for comfort. The cameras were attached to hidden sniper rifles that had been hidden within the granite outcroppings, remotely controlled from deep below. The base had orders to shoot first and ask questions later, the threat of lethal force authorized to prevent discovery at all costs. So far, in the time since the base had been operational, the system had only been used once, to remove an individual that had taken his metal detector into the desert to look for hidden wealth. He had come virtually to the hidden doors of the mountain, when his detector had gone off, sensing the metal of the base and its infrastructure just below. He had come closer, parking his truck in the shade next to a rocky tower, and he began to dig. When his shovel had revealed a thick cable of power cords, and he had pursued interest in seeing where it led, the order had been given, and a rifle had barked silently from above; the puff of smoke invisible in the rocks. The round was designed to penetrate the body smoothly, leaving minimal exterior visible damage, and the shot taken had been aimed to miss as many bones as possible. When the bullet had been fired, the man had jumped, not from the sound, but from the feel of the bullet passing through his body.

He had staggered, putting his hands to his torso, the sight of blood a surprise. He had gone back to his truck, falling just shy of the door, with a small spray of dust kicked up into the air.

As soon as he was down, the body was examined for evidence that might give away a bullet wound if it was forensically analyzed. The flesh was removed messily, to prevent straight cut marks in the flesh, and to avoid bone, and then hidden in the mountains where only a thorough search would have found the body. At a later date, after it had been picked over by coyotes and vultures, and desiccated in the desert sun, it had been recovered and dumped at another location, chosen for its desolation, and outside of the search area that had been mounted by the civilian authorities. A small portion of gold had been left with the body to provide a cover story, and the truck driven a few kilometers away from the body, in a sheltered ravine dug out by flashfloods. The starter had been replaced with a dead one, to give a story of a lone prospector who had died out in the desert when his vehicle had broken down. So far, the remains of the body still lay out in the desert, and the truck had been nearly covered over by layers of desert sand, deposited by successive floods. The family still searched for him periodically, but to the authorities, the case was closed, and he was presumed dead.

At the base of the elevator shaft, the entrance opened into a wide domed room, and dug into the far wall a three meter thick blast door was set into the granite. Shock absorbers were built into the door to help keep them stable, and fixed and sealed within the hydraulics of the sliding mechanism. On the outside of the doors, twin machine gun emplacements were fixed on the elevators, with the option for remote control use if the manned operators were disabled. Explosive and gas charges were built into the wall, permitting the area to be selectively detonated, or filled with an unfriendly atmosphere. Behind the doors, a long corridor ran one hundred meters to yet another door, along with more weapons were aimed if a foe was fortunate enough to make it that far. Past that final door, was the operations and living areas of the facility, complete with food, water and fuel storage, enough for a tour of duty. It was comprised of one hundred thousand square feet of space, with a four meter ceiling in most places; enough to alleviate the potential claustrophobia encountered by some of the stationed inhabitants. The main operations center had a domed ceiling that was tem meters high, to allow for multiple screens to be affixed to the wall, each able to show one particular set of information, or variations of a larger screen, depending on what wanted to be seen. In calm situations, the panel wall generally showed one image, that of a political map of the Earth, showing each country outlined, the placement of its largest cities, in a Mercator projection style, as if the globe had been laid flat and made into a large rectangle. The image skewed the proportions of the landmasses, but it worked well enough in most instances.

The entire facility was built on a shock absorbing pad, to offset vibrations that would be caused in the cause of a nuclear exchange, or a potential earthquake, based on historical averages. Thousands of immense coiled springs supported the floor, each inset into a rubber composite. Firefox was built as an emergency operations center, to facilitate global communications in case of a potentially devastating nuclear exchange. It was built to survive a direct attack, and then direct resources to counterattack. It's electronics had all been constructed and designed to resist damage caused by severe electromagnetic pulses; electrical discharges in large explosions that rendered electronics useless, either incapacitating them temporarily, or destroying them entirely. Each system had multiple back ups and redundancies, and could be readily accessed and repaired with parts designed to be removed easily and replaced with a minimum of manpower. Within the mountain, Very Low Frequency and Ultra Low Frequency transmitters had been buried at strategic locations, allowing special military satellites to transmit and receive information to and from the center. The satellites themselves had been constructed with the scenario in mind that they may be the last lines of communication, and so they too had been built to withstand significant electromagnetic discharges. They had been placed in very high orbits, ranging from one thousand kilometers, to the extremity of ten thousand kilometers, in order to make neutralizing the satellites very difficult, as well as to keep them from reentering the atmosphere any time in the not to distant future. They were also powered with RTG's, radioisotope thermal generators, and a significant array of solar panels, allowing them to operate under severe power requirements. All were equipped with multiple sensing devices; cameras that operated from the microwave spectrum up to the ultraviolet, allowing images to be seen in any condition, anywhere in the world, to a resolution down to one meter for the farthest satellites, to a centimeter for the closest. They truly were eyes in the sky.

The satellites were primarily designed to watch for the launch signatures of rockets from various parts of the globe, as well as to detect the explosion signature of nuclear weapons, using electromagnetic sensors to detect the initial detonation, and then using the other optical options to analyze the data as it unfolded.

On a typical shift, the warning system would trigger an alarm, which would be routed to the primary command desk for verification. When the system had first gone online, the initial warnings were taken for a developing Soviet assault, and had triggered several mobilizations of the Armed Forces to prepare for the next world war. Instead, each case turned out to be a false alarm, with the seemingly affected areas showing no damage whatsoever; only the satellite detecting an atmospheric explosion of a nuclear scale. When the system was found to be working properly, the warnings thought to be software bugs, they had no choice but to look for other options to explain what was triggering their early warning system. Upon closer inspection of the data, the explosions were found to be incoming meteors that were exploding in the upper atmosphere. Most of them were relatively small, explosions in the kiloton range, Hiroshima sized blasts high in the upper atmosphere, but occasionally a megaton-sized explosion would be detected. The heat and friction of Earths atmosphere caused the meteors to explode, their huge energies dispersed as they tore apart. The Colonel had found it surprising, considering their frequency, that none had yet made it closer to the surface, exploding near a populated center. Such an event would devastate a city, perhaps erasing it completely from the landscape if it were large enough, incinerating the lives within it. With the frequency of the events, the protocols were changed to reroute the first emergency call to a secondary station. The event could be analyzed quickly, and then forwarded on to the primary station if necessary.

There was a faint knock at the glass window set in his door; three muted taps. He looked up with his eyes, his head still down facing the document he was scouring. He waved, nodding her in with a quick motion of his hand.

"Sir."

She saluted smartly, a brief held in the other hand. Her uniform was crisp and neat, the creases sharp, her brown hair professionally tied back into a bun at the back of her head. She had not let the current situation relax her standards.

"Lieutenant Pritchard."

He saluted back, and she let her hand fall to the side of her hips. She had a good figure, he noted, not letting his eyes wander, keeping eye contact with her. He wondered if her family had some Norwegian ancestry. She had prominent cheekbones, and her eyes were a light blue.

"The latest reports, Sir." She handed the briefing to him, a bright blue paper folder with a small stack of papers inside, neatly stapled in the top left corner.

"Have you had a look at these?" he asked her.

"No, Sir." He noticed she was still standing at attention.

"At ease, Lieutenant."

She relaxed a little bit, but not much.

"Have a seat." He gestured to a seat at the right of his desk.

"Sir?"

"Have a seat, and take a look through these yourself."

"Sir, the reports are your eyes only," she protested, her eyes briefly going to the folder.

"There is nothing in these reports that you aren't going to know soon enough, and maybe this will keep the rumors and speculation to a minimum." He knew that with everything that had happened, there was due to be gossip, even in a military operation. It was human nature.

"Sir, I…"

"If you don't, I will order you to read them."

He held the report back out to her. She looked at it warily for a moment, the large white and red label 'Eyes Only' prominent on the cover. Then she accepted it, and sat down in the chair, crossing her legs, the leather creaking as she sat into it. She opened the folder, and he watched her begin to read the documents. He appreciated her calves for a moment, and then returned his attention to the documents already on his desktop. He still couldn't believe how quickly everything had transpired.

He had been walking through Operations, visiting each station as was part of his routine. He went from one to the next, making sure everything was operational, and also making chit chat with whoever was manning the post. He made a point of getting to know as many people on his team as he could; if he was going to spend two to four years with these people, he was going to know them inside and out, seeing what made them tick. It made him an effective leader. He was good at motivating his staff, praising wherever he could, and effectively addressing needs in a manner that was educational and created a strong atmosphere of learning. It built a team that was fiercely loyal, and proud. The room had been built like a small theater, with stations descending downwards over a few flights of stairs. This allowed each post an unrestricted view of the monitors on the wall. He had checked his watch when it had begun to beep, signifying midnight. He pressed the small round button on the watch, muting the chime, and looked at the monitors on the wall. Currently they showed a combined image of the entire world, a clock ticking at the top right corner showing the local time, combined with the date,

21:12:2012:12:00:05.

His shift was currently nights, a rotation that lasted for a month, before he would go back to days. He had taken a few more steps, the hard soles of his shoes clicking on the concrete floor, when the monitor had showed a flaring image. The system adjusted as it was programmed to; it minimized the larger image and created a larger screen that was focused on the area that had triggered the alarms. He turned to face the screen directly, watching the computers analyzing the data in real time. Around him the control posts became highly active, the communication from one to the other being handled both by computer and by headset. The chatter was sudden, but quiet and controlled. He put on his headset, to hear what was being communicated.

"...eastern Asia; bogey being tracked by two GIDSAT locations."

The Global Image Detecting Satellites had been staggered, to overlap their sensing areas.

"Confirm, repeat confirm velocity..."

The information that was coming from the satellites was a blur, each station and post receiving its own specialized information; the location of the detection, the energy estimates, velocity information, altitudes, and other posts that cross analyzed the data. The flicked through his receiver to select different channels, each post having it's own internal frequency. He kept flicking through the channels with the hand controller.

"...explosion confirmed. Thermal sensors detected flare, enabling GIDSAT One..."

The Colonel turned off his headset; the information that was coming in was too preliminary, and too scattered to be able to glean any good information by randomly selecting frequencies. He would have to wait until more information was streamlined. He looked back up at the screen, where the computer was updating the information being downloaded from the satellites. It was definitely a meteor; the satellites had already calculated the trajectory and angle of the body, confirming it could not be an inbound missile. The trajectory had it travelling over Asia, in an easterly direction, at a forty-five degree angle. The velocity estimate was amazing; nearly seventy-three kilometers per second. If it was big enough, it could be through the atmosphere and at the ground in under three seconds. Good thing that was very unlikely. Most of the objects they detected were small, only a few meters across.

"Give me a report, people. There's a lot of chatter going on and I want an accurate update."

He saw several people nod, typing furiously at their keyboards, or their hands holding their headsets close to their ears. A moment later, the screen above the Pacific zoomed in, and showed an outwardly spreading white circle. The circle represented a detected explosion; there was no altitude information yet; the satellites would still be working on the energy output of the blast, watching it dissipate to arrive at final measurements.

The circle continued to expand. He watched the screen, waiting for the circle to begin to fade as the explosion died away.

"Where is the event?" he asked the room in general, his voice high, shouting instead of using the headset.

The global map indicated a general location; he wanted specifics.

"That information is coming, Sir. One more minute and we should have it." It didn't normally take that long to pinpoint the location.

"What is taking so long?" The same station replied.

"Unusual energy discharge, Sir. The readings are taking longer to process."

"What do you mean exactly by unusual energy discharge?" He walked over to the station, to see the numbers flashing and updating on the screen. The soldier at the post continued to examine the numbers, his hands flying over the keyboard as he worked to streamline the data. The Colonel looked up at the wall; the circle was continuing to grow.

"Sorry, Sir. I'll have something in another few moments."

He watched the expanding circle.

Another station reported in, the voice urgent.

"Sir; GIDSAT Four is indicating ground impact readings."

"Bullshit! That can't be right. Reanalyze your information."

"Yes, Sir."

Ground impact? he thought; that was crazy; the odds against that were so improbable that it wasn't even considered a training scenario.

"Sir; energy discharge estimates have been completed."

He walked briskly over to the post.

"Well?" he asked, leaving the question hanging in the air.

"GIDSAT estimates are off the chart, sir. Primary logarithms are calculating results in excess of a billion megatons."

The size of the number was incredulous, and his face showed what he thought of it.

"Run it again."

"Yes, Sir. Right away, Sir."

He walked back up to the top step of the platform, where he could see every post in front of him.

He clicked on his headset.

"Communications."

A female voice replied.

"Sir." There was no question; she was awaiting directions.

"Contact bases in Korea. I want a report from actual people, not satellites."

"Yes, Sir." The link was disconnected with a faint snap.

He continued to watch the monitor; the spot was continuing to grow. He could see it creeping outwards as he watched. It had to be incorrect data. A software glitch of some sort. He could feel sweat under his armpits. He could feel the adrenaline pumping as he surveyed the Operations room. He would get to the bottom of this; all he needed was time. His headset clicked twice; an incoming connection. He pushed the receive button.

"Peterson." His voice was curt.

"Ballistics, Sir."

"What have you got?"

"Bogey estimates, Sir."

"Proceed."

"Based on the infrared flare the satellites detected in the atmosphere, the bogey had an approximate diameter in excess of twenty-five miles. Precise measurements aren't available with atmospheric interference."

"Twenty-five miles!" he exclaimed.

"Yes, Sir."

"Something that large should have been detected," he mumbled under his breath.

He didn't mumble quietly enough; the officer at the station heard him clearly enough.

"With the velocity the bogey was moving at; if it had a low albedo, it is not unrealistic that it was missed by ground observation facilities." The Colonel didn't reply; he stood there absorbing the information he was receiving.

"Do we have any visual feeds? Something we can actually see?"

His headset clicked twice.

"Peterson."

"Communications, Sir."

"Proceed."

"I have been unable to confirm with Korean facilities, Sir."

"Does that mean they didn't see anything?" he asked.

"No, Sir. I was unable to establish contact with them to either confirm or negate our alarms."

"You couldn't reach them?"

"That is correct, Sir. It's like they weren't there. I didn't even receive a message acceptance verification."

"Try again. And try other bases, maybe in the Philippines, or Japan."

His headset clicked twice again.

"Peterson."

"Visual coming up, Sir. From GIDSAT One."

"Excellent," he muttered, looking forward to seeing nothing but ocean and clouds and the limb of the globe.

He stood watching the monitor, seeing the white circle now covering Korea, and moving into mainland China. He shook his head as he watched, trying to understand what was happening. Some software geek was going to get an ass chewing after a fiasco like this.

Another screen opened up on the monitor, replacing the western hemisphere with a large pop up window. For the moment it was black, as a video buffer was built from the downloading transmission.

"How close to real time is this?" he asked the room.

"Approximately two seconds behind, Sir."

He nodded, waiting, and then the screen came to life.

There were a few startled gasps, and the Communications officer that was trying to reach bases in Japan dropped her headset. Someone whispered *ohmygod*, and then the room went still. The image was slightly off center, but unmistakable. An immense mushroom cloud dominated the view, climbing rapidly through the atmosphere and towards space. The shockwave could be seen travelling through the air and over the ground. Cloud formations were suddenly erased, the sky swept clear, and then went solid white; an opaque mist materializing as water was shocked in the air. They watched in disbelief, seeing the explosion rush outwards and upwards, the very ocean being turned aside and vaporized, and a wall of fire spreading outwards concentrically. He didn't ask for a follow up from the officer that was recalculating the energy readings. The Colonel stood and watched as the reality of the situation struck home, that this was no software glitch. A moment later, he took a deep breath, realizing he was holding it, his lungs beginning to ache. He clicked his headset.

"Programming."

"Sir."

"I want an immediate global simulation based on data to this point. Extrapolate and playback asap. Convert the timeframe for forty-eight hour playback within sixty seconds."

"Understood. Programming out."

"Communications."

"Y-yes, Sir." Her voice was trembling.

"Sound a General alarm. I want every person at their post, I want everyone that is off duty called on duty, and I want this base sealed airtight." His voice was tense, but exact, his face red.

He waited for a response for two seconds.

"Yes, Sir. Sounding General Alarm." Having orders to follow, her voice sounded more confident.

A klaxon suddenly sounded, the normal lighting switching off, to be replaced with red. The horn was piercing, a shriek that repeated every two seconds. With the activation, an automated voice system came live, playing back from a recording made years earlier.

He began to play through the checklist in his mind, everything that must be done to properly secure the facility. Something he hoped that he would never have to do.

He switched his headset to intercom, so everyone could hear him. Every second counted.

"Engineering."

"Engineering reporting."

"I want all systems cut off from the external grid. We are going to internal power. We are self-isolating; I repeat, we are self-isolating. Do you copy?"

"Engineering copies. Standing by."

"Reactor online." Go. With each GO reply, the engineering team was activating a series of emergency switches, bringing systems online that would internalize every function of Firefox, making them self-sufficient and closed off from the outside world.

"Ventilation." Go.

"Hydro." Go.

"Exterior entry." Go.

"Blast doors." Go. A deep rumbling grinding vibration emanated from the floor as the immense doors came together, their locking mechanisms closing fast.

"Elevators." Go.

It took only moments, and then the facility was shut off from the outside world.

"Engineering, verify when all systems confirm."

The monitor opened another pop-up, this one labeled *Impact Extrapolation*. He watched as a mouse arrow scrolled across the window, and pressed the PLAY icon. The buffer opened, and the simulation began with the impact itself. Compressed to a sixty second window, the explosion unfolded with terrible rapidity, sweeping across the globe in a smooth motion. By the end of the simulation, the Earth had vanished behind a dark curtain of roiling clouds.

He took a deep breath.

"Communications."

"Yes, Sir."

"Transmit this message to all bases, no ciphering, top priority. Send through all channels, including UHF, VHF, ULF, VLF, and ELF in all used frequencies."

"Proceed, Sir."

"Identification Colonel Dwight Peterson, Firefox Base Command, United States, Security Code Tango Alpha Charlie Violet four six seven. Firefox facility has confirmed impact of a large meteor into the Pacific Ocean, Northeast of Japan. Impact information indicates extinction level event, low survival probability. Proceed with all necessary measures to facilitate your survival. Firefox Command has initiated complete self-isolation protocols. May God be with you all. Ending transmission."

K-448

The lights flickered quickly, plunging the vessel into sudden momentary darkness before coming back to life. In their training, the eighty-five crew members had remained quiet, and focused on their tasks. Those that were off duty and sleeping never noticed the aberration, and the crew that was on duty paused only briefly, waiting for the lights to come back on.

"What the Hell was that? Engineering, report."

The Captain spoke with authority into the intercom, and waited patiently for the response. His First Officer, Adrian Zhukov, stood at the map, plotting their course with the Navigator Konovalev as he waited to hear back from the engineering room. He was closest to the com station, and so had picked up the handset first. His First Officer had kept at his task, looking up only once as he worked on their course.

The Kirov had been at sea for four months, having left Severomorsk to put in for supplies. She was venturing out under the pack ice at the Arctic Circle to make detailed maps of the areas under Russian claim in the high Arctic, helping to add credence to their sovereignty claim with their presence. She had been commissioned in 1992, stationed in the Northern Fleet, a Victor III Class attack submarine with a little over seven tons of submerged displacement.

She had been running at a little over ten knots, keeping her speed slow and quiet to not interfere with the scanning equipment onboard.

The Kirov had been sticking close to land, to avoid the pack ice that was deepest at the Pole. Their mission was to measure and map the continental shelf, and so by necessity in some cases they had to come close to land. They were under orders to remain submerged, to prevent detection by other navies or ships that would report their presence if detected. The benefit of staying close to land was that the sea ice would be thinnest, if it existed at all, so close to land. She was an attack submarine, and so her hull was not designed to withstand surfacing through ice, like an ICBM boat, and so the sudden lack of power was of immediate concern to her Captain. If they were under ice and required rescue, it would be extraordinarily difficult to mount a salvage operation.

"Engineering reporting, Captain."

"Proceed."

"Everything seems to be functioning normally. We had a small spike in the reactors a second or two afterwards, but nothing shows them decreasing power."

The Captain nodded to himself.

"Run a diagnostics, Chernov."

"Already started a systems diagnostics. I'll report to you personally when its done."

"Very well." He put the handset back in the cradle, severing contact with the Chief. He would have to be patient.

"Bring us to periscope depth."

"Yes, Sir," Zhukov replied.

"Helm. The Captain wants us at periscope depth."

"Helm, aye. Going to periscope depth."

Tokarev and Sokov took control of the dive planes; the two seamen at the helm pulled back on the control sticks, pivoting the submarine at a gentle upwards angle.

"Prepare to blow the ballast."

"Ballast ready." The seamen looked up at the First Officer, waiting for his order. He nodded, and he pushed the button, venting the ballast water out of the boat into the sea, displacing it with highly pressurized air.

"Poushkin."

"Sonar aye."

"Any surface contacts?"

"No surface contacts, Captain. Sonar is clear."

"Last contact?"

"Last contact was at thirteen hundred hours, at fifteen degrees. Contact barely detectable."

They were currently in American waters, running between the Bering Strait, and he was concerned they might be within range of an icebreaking vessel.

"Helm; bring us to periscope depth and come to a full stop."

"Aye, Captain."

He stood holding on to a guide rail near the Conn, feeling the boat rising under his feet. They rose from three hundred meters steadily, coming to a gradual cruise just over twenty meters in depth. As they rose the boat acclimated to the lighter water pressure, the hull expanded slightly under the lighter load. He could feel the boat level off, and the screw coming to a halt as the vibrations slowly faded and then ceased.

"All stop, Sir."

"Maintain this position until we have a full report from Engineering."

"Aye, Sir."

He went to the periscope tower, and engaged the motor, bringing the periscope up to the surface. Placing his face within the viewer, he looked around twice, before disengaging the tower. He walked over to the map table where the First Officer was standing; the Navigation Officer to his right.

"Our position?"

The navigator immediately went to the table with the Captain.

"We are holding position at this position, Captain. He tapped the surface where a small 'X' had been written in thin black felt on the plastic. They were in the lower portion of the Chukchi Sea, Northwest of Nome, and nearing the International Date Line, on a course that would bring them parallel to Alyatki, on the eastern shores of Siberia. They were north of the Strait, approximately a hundred kilometers, where the water was deeper and less well known.

"Captain, sonar contact."

"What is it?" He was perplexed. He had just looked through the periscope; there was nothing around them.

"I…I don't know, Captain. I'm picking up loud clutter from a southerly direction."

"Can you tell us how many screws?" asked Zhukov.

"No, Sir, " replied Poushkin. "It doesn't sound like a ship. I can't hear any screws, and the computer can't identify."

"Perhaps an earthquake?" Zhukov asked the Captain.

"Possibly," he replied. An earthquake could trigger a landslide.

"Put it on speaker."

"Aye, Captain."

The speakers in the command clicked on, and in the distance a roaring sound could be heard, like a loud static only with a denser quality. The Captain went back to the periscope, and activated it, spinning around to look south. He focused the controller, slowly turning the scope from the left to the right. The sound was slowly increasing in volume.

Through the periscope, the Captain had a difficult time making out the horizon at first. The night was already dark, and he had to try to use the stars in the sky as a backdrop to see anything.

"Range?" he asked.

Poushkin typed a few commands into the computer.

"Difficult to tell, Sir. The contact is not exact. All I can provide is an estimate."

"And what is the estimate?"

"Approximately three hundred kilometers, Sir. Definitely south of the Strait."

"Three hundred kilometers? And it's that loud? Did you hear it earlier?"

"Yes, Sir. Only then it was much quieter, further away. The computer diagnosed it as seismic activity, and so I ignored the contact."

"How much further away was it when it was first detected?"

"About fifteen-hundred kilometers, Sir."

"And how long ago was this?"

The sonar operator went through his print outs, scanning the records for more accurate information.

"Approximately one hour, twenty minutes, Sir."

The Captain chewed at his lower lip, looking through the periscope. The First Officer was looking at the map again.

"In an hour it's come over a thousand kilometers?" That didn't sound right. Maybe the power outage had affected the sonar readings.

"Run a diagnostics."

"Sonar, Aye." The screens in front of the sonar operator ran through their tests, and completed a minute later, printing out a confirmation page.

"Sonar is working normally, Sir."

The roaring sound continued to grow, minute by minute.

"Approximate time of contact?"

"Ten minutes, Sir."

The First watched the Captain, scanning the horizon with the scope.

The sound was not metallic; it was a blur of static and rumbling and the occasional cracking sound. The Captain stopped scanning, and began pushing the focus button on the handle, standing still. They stood and watched, waiting for his orders. He licked his lips and frowned, struggling to see.

"What?" he mumbled, thinking aloud. He kept stationary, looking in the same direction, while the crew watched.

"Speakers off," ordered the First.

The room became quieter, but the sound was still audible, and growing louder by the moment.

"Captain, I think…"

"Wait…wait…the Captain interrupted, one hand out, palm open. "That can't be right."

He stood still for another moment, and then spoke slowly and clearly.

"Emergency dive; all ahead full. Steer a course due north."

No one quite understood the orders, and for a few moments everyone stood where they were, waiting to make sense of the order.

"Helm; prepare for emergency dive; all ahead full." Zhukov repeated the order calmly, the sentence perfectly clear.

"Preparing for emergency dive; all ahead full; yes, Sir," replied Sokov.

"Switch to emergency lighting."

The white lights of the command flickered off and were simultaneously replaced with red lighting.

The Captain turned off the periscope, his face sweaty and his eyes stern. He went to the map.

"Konovalev."

"Yes, Sir."

"Is this our present position?"

"Yes, Sir. We are currently due west of the Northwind Channel.

"And what is the depth range?"

"Maximum depth is one thousand meters, Captain. "

"Helm; bring us to the bottom, Tokarev; as fast as you can."

"Sir." The reply was questioning. He was already putting the boat into a steep dive, the crew having to lean to compensate for the angle.

"Put us on the bottom, Sokov. And give me updates every one hundred meters."

"Yes, Sir."

"Poushkin; keep Sokov up to date on how deep we can go. I don't want us to nose dive into the ocean floor."

Poushkin swallowed hard.

"Yes, Captain."

Zhukov went to the Captains side.

"Captain," he whispered, "Maximum operational depth is eleven hundred meters."

The Captain nodded.

"That is exactly why we are going to the bottom, Zhukov. For our sake, we need to get to the bottom."

Captain Demeter went to the com system, removing the handset and holding tight to a support rail as he raised it to his mouth.

"Attention crew of the Kirov; this is the Captain speaking. We have gone into an emergency dive to seek safety from a tidal wave that is heading in our direction. We are trying to get into deeper water where I am hopeful we will be able to ride it out. Secure yourself to the boat. This is not a drill. I repeat this is not a drill." The handset clicked back into the cradle with a loud snap, and the Captain held onto the rail with his other free hand, holding it firmly in both.

"Two hundred meters, Captain," said Sokov.

"Zhukov."

"Yes, Captain."

"I want you to release a buoy with the information we have so far, in case we aren't successful. I don't want Moscow to wonder where we are."

"Right away, Sir." Zhukov made his way to a control panel to the left of Tokarev, and began typing into the computer, downloading and programming the buoy.

"Three hundred meters, Captain." The hull groaned slightly under the compression, the titanium hull adjusting to the quickly changing depth.

Zhukov flipped open a blue transparent cover, and pushed the button underneath. There was a small thump as the buoy was released.

"Buoy is released and is active, Captain." The buoy was rising quickly to the surface, where it would transmit location information in a broad radio spectrum, alerting naval vessels of its presence. It was crowned with a flashing LED strobe that would aid in visual detection at night.

"Thank you, Zhukov."

"Four hundred meters, Captain."

The Captain sat in his chair, and drew his seatbelt tight around his waist. The others saw it, and took note, tightening their own belts.

Zhukov sat in the nearest chair, and did the same.

"Captain."

"Yes, Konovalev?"

"We are receiving an incoming message, transmitted in ELF, seventy-six hertz."

"Seventy-six hertz?" It was an American transmission; the Russian Navy used eighty-two hertz.

The printer came to life, printing out a quick message that Konovalev tore off and handed to the Captain without glancing down.

He took it, adjusted his glasses over his nose, and read the message.

"Five hundred meters, Captain."

"Zhukov."

He was belted into his chair, watching the readings as they dove into the sea. Captain Demeter folded the message in half, creasing the middle of the page sharply with his fingernails, and held it out.

Zhukov unstrapped himself, and came over and retrieved the folded sheet.

"Captain?"

"Just read the message, Zhukov."

He nodded, returning to his seat and buckling the strap around his waist, and then unfolded the sheet. The system computer provided a nearly instant translation of the transmission.

"Polkovnik Identifikacii Duajt Peterson, Komanda Osnovy Firefox, Soyedinennyye SHtaty, Tango Kodeksa Bezopasnosti Alfa CHarli Vajolet chetyre shest' sem'. Sredstvo Firefox podtverdilo vozdejstviye bol'shogo meteora v Tihij okean, K severo-vostoku ot YAponii. Informaciya vozdejstviya ukazyvayet sluchaj urovn'a ischeznoveniya, nizkuyu veroyatnost' vyzhivaniya. Prodolzhite vse neobhodimyye mery, chtoby oblegchit' vashe vyzhivaniye. Komanda Firefox nachala polnyye protokoly samoizol'acii. Mozhet Bog byt' s Vami vsemi. Okonchaniye peredachi."

"Captain, this can't be correct. Surely the Americans are playing a joke on us."

"That message is no joke, my friend."

"Six hundred meters, Captain."

He balled up the letter, dropping it into a black wire mesh wastebasket.

"What I saw in the periscope is explained by that transmission, and that is why we are going to the bottom."

"The Americans sent us a transmission about the tidal wave?" asked Poushkin. The other officers and crew in the command area looked about, and at the Captain, seeking more information.

"The Americans broadcast a warning to anyone that might receive it, Poushkin." He gave no more information, leaving the crew to ponder the message while they were at their station.

"Seven hundred meters, Captain."

Poushkin switched off his headphones at the sonar station, sliding them down to rest over his shoulders. The sonar read outs were beginning to get overwhelmed with information, displaying nonsensical information on the monitors.

"Konovalev."

"Yes, Captain."

"Prepare to turn us around. Due South. Continue descent."

"Aye, Captain."

Konovalev barked the orders to Sokov and Tokarev.

"Hard to port, bearing one hundred eighty degrees, maintain all ahead full, continue present down angle."

Sokov repeated the order, confirming the command.

"Hard to port, bearing one hundred eighty degrees, maintain all ahead full, continue present down angle, aye."

"Eight hundred meters, Captain."

The Kirov began to lean heavily to port as she spun around in her dive. The Captain wanted to drive her into the incoming wave, to be able to use the boats power to drive them through the surge as they encountered it. If they tried to outrun the wave, they risked being carried along with it, out of control.

"Current depth approximately twelve hundred fifty meters," said Poushkin.

"Twelve hundred fifty meters, aye," confirmed Sokov.

"Begin to level us out, Sokov. Five degrees on the dive planes," ordered Zhukov.

"Leveling out, Sir. Five degree on the planes. Nine hundred meters."

The hull groaned at the depth, nearing her operational maximum.

The severity of her descent began to lessen as the Kirov began to level out.

"Bearing now one eight zero degrees."

Konovalev repeated it to the Captain.

"One eight zero degrees, Captain."

"Very well, Konovalev. Maintain present heading and speed."

"Zhukov; inquire to engineering about the likelihood about going to one hundred and ten percent on the reactor."

"Aye, Captain."

He wanted to be able to go through the wave with as much power as he could muster. The sound of the oncoming wave was becoming oppressive, building on their nerves.

"Engineering reports one hundred ten percent possible, but only for a short time." Good enough.

543

"Go to one hundred ten percent."

"Yes, Captain."

Zhukov repeated the order to engineering.

"What is our speed, Konovalev?"

"Present speed thirty knots, Captain. Bearing still one eight zero degrees."

"One thousand meters Captain."

"Level us off, Sokov. Hold at one thousand meters."

"Hold at one thousand meters; Aye, Captain."

The Kirov leveled off, running at an even keel.

"How long can we maintain present speed and heading, Konovalev?"

"One moment, Captain," he replied, going to the map and charting their location.

Poushkin yelled out to the Captain, "Tsunami impact in approximately one minute, Captain."

"Warn the crew, Zhukov." Zhukov nodded, removing the handset from the station.

"Captain, we can maintain present speed and bearing for twenty minutes at present depth," shouted Konovalev.

"When we have passed through the wave, bring us to the surface as fast as you can," replied the Captain. "Blow the tanks if you have to."

Konovalev nodded in reply.

Zhukov's voice came to life over the com system.

"Attention all crew. Brace for impact. Repeat; brace for impact."

He returned the handset to the cradle, and sat with his hands clutching his seat, prepared to hang on. The sea roared, and one by one they covered their ears to block out some of the noise that was beginning to shake their boat.

"Try to keep us level, Sokov. The wave will lift us, so compensate for our position and be prepared to counter correct once we pass through."

"Aye, Captain."

"Contact in approximately ten seconds," yelled Poushkin, who was reading the monitors, seeing the pressure wave driving towards them. The sonar was reading the tsunami as a solid object bearing down on them, flashing impact warnings.

"Nine…eight…seven…six…five…four…three…two…one…"

For a moment, there was nothing, only the deep roaring sound intensifying as the wave rushed towards them. They held their breath, and waited, wondering for a moment if that was it, that it was past and nothing happened. And then the bow rose as if lifted by a powerful invisible hand. They jerked in their seats as they were pushed down into them, emergency lights coming to life and an alarm began to shriek. Two pipes burst overhead, spraying the compartment with pressurized water that felt like a thousand pinpricks on their skin.

Tokarev unbuckled his seat, trying to close the valve and shut off the water. They felt the boat rising, her nose being driven upwards, and another klaxon sounded.

"Reactor breach, Captain!" screamed Konovalev.

"Coolant lines have burst in both reactors!"

"Seal the areas!" he replied, hanging on to his seat arms. "Shut them down!" Tokarev was hanging from the ceiling as the boat went vertical. Konovalev punched a red button, closing the reactor compartments behind hydraulic doors, and then another, draining the water from the reactors, effectively stopping the fission reaction from continuing, shutting them down.

"Reactors offline, Captain!"

"Go to batteries!" he replied, trying to keep power to Sokov to help control the boat as best he could. Kirov shuddered; the thick titanium hull being strained to resist the power of being swept upwards and back by the wave, while the screw was trying to drive her forward, the bow planes edged downwards.

Captain Demeter saw the batteries go online, supplying power to the single screw. Their forward momentum of thirty knots had been negated by the wave, and they were being driven backwards. The wave was too strong; it was coming too fast. The boat began to spin, and they felt a sharp jerk and a metallic shear. Another alarm sounded, a digital map of the boat appearing on the screen showing the stern failing.

"Captain! The stern has impacted the ocean floor; we are taking on water!" Captain Demeter shook his head in wonder. They were a kilometer under the waves under incredible pressure, and the hull was still resisting, holding together. The screw was lost, the Kirov rudderless. The one hundred and eight meter length of K-448 rolled over, spinning, and was driven onto the seabed a second time. Another alarm sounded, the display of the boat going red. The titanium groaned, and then bent, opening a gap in the hull that the ocean drove into, the immense pressure seeking to fill the small space within. For a moment, the Captain saw the water burst through the sealed bulkhead, the door flying from its torn hinges like a bullet, decapitating Konovalev neatly. The men began to yell, in defiance of what was to come, raging against the dying of their light. He saw the bulkhead begin to crinkle like tissue paper, the metal beginning to fold inwards, and he knew no more. With a crackling sound, the Kirov was torn asunder, strewn across the sea. A kilometer above, the emergency buoy flashed in the night, a tombstone for eighty-five souls far below.

Trevor Holmes

The air was thick and humid, rich with the fetid sweet smell of decay and mildew. The heat was stifling, adding to the discomfort and unease. A small scented candle threw off a dim yellow glow in the tunnel, the fruity apple odor misplaced in its immediate surroundings. The light illuminated a small portion of the brick walls, reflecting off the shimmering surface of the narrow stream of water that flowed in the channel. The moisture on the walls added a slivery sheen to the tunnel, contrasting starkly to the utter blackness that enclosed the small oasis of light on either side; a void that promised to swallow them if given the chance. Trevor sat on the thick red woolen blanket, his eyes blank and reflective, watching the small ripples dancing on the water. A small brown rat stared back at him, sitting on its haunches, whiskers twitching as it smelled the air. It sat at the exit of a small pipe where its effluent joined the main line, its thick pink tail wrapped around its body. It would come no closer, preferring to sit and wonder at the intruders in its domain. The car seat was to his left, between himself and the quiet form of his sleeping wife. Her breathing was low and deep, yet carried along the walls and tunnel in an eerie echo that was somehow magnified. There were no other sounds, and nothing more came from above. The manhole was ten meters down the sewer, and up a narrow access hole lined with a cold iron ladder. The manhole was in the middle of the street, across the driveway of their flat that had comprised a row of nearly identical homes stretching along its length. The silence was all-encompassing, a terrible harbinger of all that had unfolded above. The street was now a shambles of cracked and melted asphalt; the once proud row of new flats gone, replaced with smoking piles of ash and irregular debris. Cassandra slept deeply in her car seat, dressed in her pink sleeper with a floral baby blanket draped over the edge of the seat to keep the errant breezes off her as she slept. Trevor looked at her with no small wonder, his eyes sad and full of desire to keep her from harm. She was just shy of three months old, and already the changes he saw in her as she grew caught him unprepared. She was different weekly, and sometimes appeared to be so daily. She would have her mothers hair, he could see already, and possessed a strong will. So far she had been asleep for nearly three hours, a significant length of time as she had not yet given any indication of starting to sleep through the night. It was because of her very sleep patterns that they were alive at all.

He had heard her making snuffling sounds in her crib, sounds she made when she was getting hungry, but not yet at the point of being fully awake and crying.

"Is it your turn or my turn?" he asked his wife, his whisper sounding loud in the room. She didn't move, her sleeping form still under the blanket.

"Rebecca," he whispered. Nothing. She was either asleep, or pretending to be, refusing to stir.

"Nuts," he muttered, pulling the blanket off his legs and swinging them over the side of the bed. He sat there for a moment, rubbing his eyes, and then pulled his bathrobe from the bedpost, tying it snugly around his waist with a loop and a pull of the belt. Cassandra was sucking on her balled fist, still content in her crib, her eyes looking around the shadows of the room. He went into the kitchen and found a bottle in the fridge door. He unscrewed it, pouring the milk into a small glass and set the microwave for thirty seconds, and then waited as it counted down, looking outside the front window of the living room. The morning sky was still dark, the yellow sodium streetlights casting long shadows down the road.

The microwave beeped twice, and turned off. Trevor tested the milk on his wrist, finding it warm but not hot, and then poured it back into the bottle. He screwed the nipple back on, squeezed out the air, and went back to the bedroom. Cassandra was beginning to fuss, whining and kicking her small legs.

"Good morning, Princess," he cooed softly, reaching for her under the blanket. She squirmed and smiled at his voice, her hands and arms outstretched as he laid her against his chest.

"Shhh don't wake up Mommy," he whispered into her ear. She laid her head into the crook of his neck. He carried her into the living room, settling into his recliner with her cradled in the elbow of his right arm, Her arms reached out, looking for the bottle she knew was coming. He held the bottle loosely while she fed, listening to her suckle and swallow, while one of her hands gripped his index finger tightly, the other drooped over her forehead, palm up. She ate with her eyes closed, relaxing in the smooth rocking motion of the chair. Trevor watched her eat, marveling at his daughter in his arms, enjoying the quiet solace of this time with her. Before she was born, he had no comprehension of the depth of affection he could have for another person. He had looked forward to their first child, full of angst and excitement simultaneously. He watched Rebecca's stomach grow, month by month into an extended orb, watching her bond with her unborn child in a way he did not understand and could not relate to. He spoke to the lump, watching it and feeling it kick as Rebecca watched him, smiling with a maternal glow as he cooed and read stories. He came to memorize the children's tales quickly, reading them with pomp and great flair, exaggerating the exploits of Horton in the Jungle of Nool, or the annoyance of green eggs and ham. The pregnancy passed quickly, and he found he was strangely envious of the obvious bond that already existed between mother and child, himself feeling isolated and excluded. That all changed within a few short minutes. Rebecca was laying back on the hospital bed, covered in sweat and breathing hard with exhaustion, her legs still up in stirrups, when the nurse had passed his daughter to him, swaddled in a thick pink blanket and toque. He watched her birth, her head crowning as she was pushed out into the world, and then her small glistening body held in the arms of the doctor who pulled her free. The doctor had passed her to the waiting nurse, who was ready with a blanket.

"Congratulations, Dad," she had said, her voice slightly muffled behind the pale green face mask.

"You have a beautiful little girl."

He had caught himself from staggering backwards, the finality of her birth a shock to his reality and place in the world. He felt Rebecca squeeze his hand tightly.

"We have a little girl," she whispered, her voice hoarse and thin from the combination of emotion and fatigue. He had smiled back, his mind trying to filter and sort his own mix of emotions that were racing through his mind. He watched as the nurses cleaned her, wiping off the afterbirth and cleaning out her nose and mouth as she struggled and fought the sudden discomfort. She did not cry, but gasped and inhaled deeply. Her reflexes were tested, she was weighed and measured, and then she was wrapped in her blanket with expert efficiency. The nurse lifted her from the scale in a smooth motion, carrying her over to him, a broad grin on her face.

"Here you go, Dad." She passed him the bundle and he awkwardly held out his arms to receive her. The nurse had settled her into the bend of his right arm, watching his unease with a grin of familiarity. She patted him on the shoulder in an appreciated gesture of support, and turned away to return to her duties. He looked down at her for the first time, his gaze reading her expression, watching her as she tried to open her eyes in the bright glare of her new environment. He felt something click deep within him, an overwhelming surge of protectiveness and love that took his breath away and erased all conscious thought, his mind suddenly blank. His bond with her was instantaneous and consuming, a feeling he had never felt before but was true and recognizable. A fleeting thought crossed through his mind.

"If anyone ever harms you, I will kill them." It scared him, and yet was so certainly true he accepted the fact, watching her small blue eyes blink at him, studying his face intently. He had always felt up to that point that he would never be able to purposefully harm anyone, much less kill someone. That knowledge was erased in a surge of born instinct, the rules suddenly rewritten to protect his child from all harm and danger. For her, to keep her safe, he would certainly extract those pounds of flesh.

He suddenly felt Rebecca's eyes on him, and he raised his head to see her watching them as they bonded, her eyes warm and content seeing father and daughter together for the first time. He went to her side, regretfully passing their daughter into her arms with a kiss on the forehead. He watched as Rebecca settled her onto her chest, holding her close.

"Hello, Cassandra. Mommy loves you," she whispered softly. They had agreed on the name months earlier. Cassandra for a girl, Cassius for a boy. Upon hearing her name, the final pieces fell into place.

Cassandra.

He had a daughter named Cassandra.

All was right with the world.

He had finished feeding her, and was holding her on his knee, patting her back with her head held in his hand. He heard Rebecca getting out of bed, pulling her bathrobe out of the closet. She needed to pump more milk for the day ahead, and the morning routine began.

Cassandra burped, her back straightening and leaning back into his hand as it escaped her. She went limp in his hands as her rubbed her back in a circular pattern. Rebecca walked past them into the kitchen, waving as she went. He waved back as best he could, watching Cassandra dozing off on his leg. His gaze went to the street, watching the stars twinkle in the dark sky through the window. Low over the horizon, a twisting light rushed towards them, a narrow band of blues and greens, and subtle mixes of all the colors of the rainbow. It looked like the aurora borealis, the Northern Lights, only stretching from horizon to horizon in a narrow flexing band that pulsated and swelled as it travelled overhead. He stared at it in wonder. It was surprisingly bright, and moved across the sky with speed. He hadn't seen an aurora since he was a teenager and had spent a year travelling with his family across Canada from coast to coast.

He had first seen them at the age of sixteen, when they were driving through the middle of Alberta in the dead of winter in a rented motor home where they had spent the vacation. They had been driving at night in the dark of the Canadian winter; the sky was black and filled with immeasurable stars, the ground covered in a frozen blanket of snow that twinkled back at them, reflecting the glow of their headlights. He had been sitting in between the front seats, watching the endless highway unfold before them under the scrutiny of the headlights, the painted lines flickering past at ninely kilometers an hour. He couldn't believe the size of the country; the scale of the land was lost on a globe or in a map, the distances too great to comprehend. He didn't see how they could spend a year driving across the continent when he looked at the map. He was familiar with England, where the signs of humanity were ever-present and inescapable. Here, they drove and drove and could see no sign of civilization for hours at a time, except for the highway they were driving on and the fellow traveler. The distances between cities grew wider as they went west, the land in between expansive corridors of boreal forest and rolling plains that disappeared at the farthest edge of the horizon. The prairies were utterly flat, a landscape that gave him horizontal vertigo. The highway went over the land in very nearly a straight line for hours at a stretch, the sky meeting the horizon in some far off place. During one evening of travel, he had seen a light on the horizon, and presumed it to be a grain silo or a rail crossing coming up. It had taken an hour to reach it, and then it had become apparent the light was in fact the edge of a city, visible from so far away owing to the flat lay of the land. He had shook his head in disbelief. He stayed in the middle of the seats whenever he could, wanting to keep away from the worst of the winter chill that seeped through the windows and thin metal frame of the vehicle. The bottom of each window was encrusted with an inch of ice that bled water down the side of the wall. His father had leaned over the wide steering wheel, his gaze upwards, and then he had slowly begun to pull over, feeling the tires biting into the snow and ice piled at the side of the road, crunching under the cold rubber. He had killed the RV's lights, plunging them into the dark of the winter's night. His father had turned to him, pointing to the black sky.

"What is it?" he asked, wondering what he was doing.

He leaned over his sleeping mother in her seat, her head deep in a pillow tucked between the window and the seatbelt. If they woke her up, she would get a migraine headache; she always did if her sleep was disturbed, so they were cautious to not wake her. His father stayed silent, looking up out of the large flat windshield. His eyes adjusted to the darkness quickly, and finally he saw them. The aurora flexed and waved in the sky, like an ethereal curtain, shifting colors and curling as if blown by an unseen wind. They had sat on the edge of the TransCanada highway for an hour, watching the ghostly light shimmer overhead.

This light was very similar in appearance, only travelling across the sky in very nearly a straight line, and quickly. It disappeared from sight as it neared, growing too high in the sky to view from the window where he sat.

A moment later, the lights went out. Not just the lights, but everything went out. The microwave clock went from reading a perpetual 12:00 to nothing, and the lights in the street blinked out, casting the city into darkness. Only the stars in the sky cast any light. He laid Cassandra down into the chair, and run up the stairs as fast as he could, three or four at a time, using the handrail to pull himself along. He reached the ceiling access door, and pushed it open, kicking a small wedge of wood into the frame to stop the door from locking shut behind him. He saw the light in the sky receding to the east, and the lights of the city failing as it went. The lights went out in blocks, as grids failed; sections of the city losing power in great chunks, like some dark monster was taking bites out of the very city. He watched the aurora fade over the horizon, seeing the lights go out under it, the entire city plunged into darkness. An aurora was an electrical storm, the discharge of ions high in the atmosphere. This was not a normal aurora, that much was obvious. His mind raced, trying to reach a conclusion at what he had seen.

It was a form of an aurora; it had overloaded the power grid and shut it down. Natural aurora occurred nearer the northern and southern latitudes, where the solar wind reacted with the magnetosphere and channeled the ions into the upper atmosphere. This was too far south to be natural, and its directionality suggested something closer. An explosion? It seemed the most likely explanation. Something nuclear, and it had to be close by to have such an effect. An electromagnetic pulse from an explosion would explain the power outage, but a nuclear explosion would have to be close to have this effect on the grid. And if it was that close, then something was very wrong. Maybe a terrorist attack? He mind was settled, either way. Something was wrong, and they wouldn't be safe in their flat.

He saw the look on Rebecca's face as he ran down the stairs, nearly jumping from one floor to the next.

"What is it? Trevor, what's wrong?" Cassandra was awake and playing with her hair, holding it tightly in her fists.

"We're not safe here. Something is wrong."

"Wrong? What do you mean, wrong?"

"I don't have time to explain right now. We need to get out of here as fast as we can."

She stood still, her face confused.

"And what should I do?" She asked, bewildered by the strange happenings so early in the morning.

"Get things for Cassandra, food and water for us."

"And what are you going to do?"

"Get us a place to go to."

The nearest bomb shelter was nearly twenty minutes away, too far away for him to feel safe trying to reach. He punched the key fob for their car, trying to open the trunk. It was dead. He shook his head, partly at the dismay that the power outage had also affected his car, and secondly because it was slowing him down. He slid the key into the trunk, and popped it open. He felt for the crowbar he kept in the back, found it, and slammed the trunk shut. He ran into the middle of the street, a black flat expanse in the early morning. He found the manhole cover, and slid the tapered end into the hole in the lid with a grating echo. He pulled the crowbar down with all of his strength, and was rewarded with the cover sliding up and over the asphalt surface. He slid it over enough to allow him to fit, and then he ran back to the flat.

Rebecca was standing in the doorway, Cassandra locked into her carseat.

"Do you have any candles? And matches?"

"In the kitchen," she replied.

"And what about us, then?"

He ignored her for a moment, rustling through the kitchen drawers, dropping things he didn't need to the floor. Finding what he was looking for, he stuffed them into a plastic bag and returned to Rebecca who was waiting for him, arms crossed beneath her breasts.

"Good, let's go." He put his hand to the small of her back, and began to push her out of the door, grabbing the car seat and Cassandra in his free hand. They crossed onto the road, and he stopped at the open manhole.

"Go down, quick."

"What? Into the sewer? I'm not going down there, and neither..."

He cut her off, doing his best to resist throwing her down the open hole.

He was tingling with adrenaline, the small hairs on his neck standing upright.

"Go down the hole, or so help me God I will drag you down kicking and screaming if I have to."

Rebecca went down the hole, feeling for the ladder rungs with her feet, descending slowly. When she was at the bottom, Trevor followed, carrying Cassandra in his arm. He felt her take the seat from him when he was low enough, and then he scrambled down as fast as he could. He opened the bag he had slung over his forearm, grabbing the first candle he felt, and lit a match, feeding the small flame to the wick. It caught quickly, illuminating the small tunnel they were standing in.

"Let's go, down that way."

He passed her the candle, and followed as she went forward. The tunnel opened up to a sewer stream running between two ledges each wide enough to lay down on.

"Good enough. Let's stop here," he said.

"And now what?" she asked, kneeling down to Cassandra, rocking the carseat.

"Have you gone insane?"

He smiled.

"I hope so. If nothing happens, you can bug me about this for years. If I'm right...." He let the sentence trail off.

"I'll be right back."

He ran down the tunnel to the access way, climbing up the ladder as fast as he could, ignoring Rebecca who was yelling his name.

His first trip he returned with two large jugs of water from their kitchen water cooler. He stood them upright against the wall, leaving Rebecca to keep Cassandra entertained by candlelight.

His next trip was a suitcase full of as much food as he could carry, mostly cans and stuff that didn't need to be refrigerated. He was on the edge of panic, trying to get as much as he could as fast as he could, all the while wondering how much time he had. Rebecca had seen the fright in his eyes, and was doing her best to convince herself that they were going to have the best story to tell for all time. Trevor ran back to the flat, grabbing some blankets and a package of diapers. He stuffed them into a clear garbage bag, and then stuffed them down the manhole, running back to their home even as it fell into the sewer.

He found more candles, and rummaged through his closet, trying to find a loose piece of drywall above the door lintel. He pushed, and the drywall popped loose, revealing a small hole. He stuck his hand into the opening, and felt the cold metal shape leaning against the framing stud. It was a nine millimeter handgun, a Glock G36 model. Rebecca had allowed it, on the terms it was out of sight and hidden. It was preloaded with a six cartridge clip, a second clip next to it which he slid into he pocket. He slid the gun into his side pocket, making his way through the dark interior to the kitchen where he filled another bag with some fruit, and the extra candles, before running back out into the street. He started down the ladder, and when he was half way down, he slid the manhole cover overhead, where it clanged into the circular metal guide fit into the road. The sound echoed loudly through the narrow confines, making him wince. He waited for the sound to fade, and then made his way down, carrying the extra supplies over to where Rebecca and Cassandra were waiting. She had already spread out the wool blanket to cover the floor as best she could, folding it over itself to make it a little softer. He looped the bag over the neck of one water bottle, and then sat next to Rebecca, pulling her close to him, his heart pounding.

"What had gotten into you?" she asked.

"What has you so scared?"

He swallowed and looked at her, seeing the fear in her eyes.

He explained the light in the sky, and the coincidental power outage, trying to explain his hypothesis as best he could in as little time as possible.

He was almost done, when a roar filled their ears, and the ground leaped under them, rolling and buckling, the bricks cracking in the wall. They shook for minutes, the air filling with mortar dust from the cracking bricks.

When the quake stopped, the silence in the tunnel was surreal; a profound absence of noise. Trevor and Rebecca had robotically cleared where they were sitting of fallen debris, pushing the pieces of brick and earth into the sewer channel with their hands. When the shock faded, they stopped, and held each other tightly.

"What happened?" Rebecca sobbed into his neck, her fingers digging into his back.

"I think it was a bomb. It had to be a bomb."

"What do we do now?"

"We'll wait here. It's safer than being above ground."

She nodded against his chest while he held her, before Cassandra began to cry.

"I'm going to take a look up top."

Rebecca tended to Cassandra, taking her out of her car seat and holding to her chest.

He climbed up the ladder, and pried the manhole cover loose, peeking out of the hole cautiously. The air was thick with smoke and dust, and the sunlight of dawn revealed a scene of destruction. The row of flats was gone, knocked to the ground into a twisted pile. He could see the road was lined with cracks, rough shards of asphalt jutting up from the ground in places where the road had separated and lifted. He didn't see anybody. He turned in the other direction, to see a fire furiously burning in the ruins that were across his street, a thick black smoke billowing out of the ruins, nearly concealing the red gouts of flame that were bursting from the wreckage.

A car was burning, trapped under the ruins. Its tank had ruptured, spilling gasoline across the ground that had quickly lit, spreading the fire down the lane. He watched for a few minutes, and then shut the cover over him, climbing back down the ladder.

"How is it?" Rebecca asked, holding Cassandra to her breast as she fed. He shook his head.

"Everything was knocked down."

"I can smell smoke. Is there a fire?"

He nodded.

"The Williamson's place."

"Did you see anyone?"

"No. Nothing." The enormity of what had happened suddenly hit home, making him feel like everything was in slow motion. If they hadn't moved, they would be dead by now. Dead, or trapped in the ruins of their home.

He shivered, and his skin prickled with goosebumps. How many of their friends and neighbors were dead, or trapped?

When the winds came, they could hear the air whistling through the holes in the cover, shrieking at them with a loud piercing wail. The candle flickered ominously, threatening to go out as the air in the sewer gusted and sighed. They sheltered the candle with their bodies, and stayed close together, holding each other as they listened to the chaos above. They could hear debris blowing across the street, banging on the road, and the unmistakable sound of glass shattering and crunching metal.

"Those are cars, isn't it? That crunching sound is a car. Cars are being blown around?"

"I think you're right."

If cars were being blown in the wind, a bomb must have gone off even closer than he had thought. Or perhaps a second one; one closer than had caused the light in the sky.

"Is this World War Three? Are we in a nuclear war?" Rebecca asked.

He could only shrug in painful ignorance.

"It doesn't make sense," he said. There were no international tensions that could have lead to this. And terrorists couldn't have access to create multiple weapons. And then to target this particular part of England made no sense either.

When the wind had died down, he took another look topside. The street was littered with wreckage, and the piles of rubble that had been on their street were lower, flattened and compressed by the wind. Cars had been tossed into the ruins, blown into the mess by the wind and caught in the debris.

The fires had spread, consuming the row opposite the lane down to a black skeletal framework.

"I want to see."

He winced, trying to think of a reason why she shouldn't take a look. He couldn't think of one, and climbed down. He took Cassandra as Rebecca passed her to him, and watched her climb up, seeing her freeze as her head peeped above the surface of the road. She covered her mouth in shock, and stood there, looking mutely out at their street. He waited for her to climb down to close the street cover, and then followed her to the blanket, where she sat silently, her knees pulled up to her chest, her face pressed down to her thighs.

He put Cassandra in her car seat, and began to rub Rebecca's back.

She started to cry, but did not change her position; her sobs muffled and blurred.

The next few days passed slowly, with periodic checks to see if anything was happening above. They heard no sounds of rescue, no sirens or calls for help or assistance. The sky had gone black at some point, as dark as night without features or distinguishable clouds. It had rained several times, and the water running through the sewer rose appreciably, but did not crest above their platform. The water stank with a sulphurous stench that burned the nose and eyes. They had tried to cover their noses by breathing through their shirts, anything to reduce the reek. Several storms had passed by, rumbling thunderclaps shaking the ground, the flashes of lightening piercing the sewer like a strobe light, momentarily outshining the candle in a blast of whitish blue light. And the temperature had begun to climb. At first, they had found it more comfortable; the air was warm and they had even slept well, the chill in the air gone. A few more days passed, and it had got hotter and hotter, to the point where sleep was difficult and the air had become thick with humidity. And then the fires had started. They had seen the reddish glow poking through the manhole, and Trevor had gone to investigate. He had climbed the ladder, and peered through a hole, to see sheets of flame rising from the ruins in the street, great pillars of yellow and orange fire soaring into the sky. He had touched the cover, and pulled back his hand quickly at the heat of the metal, burning his fingertips. He could smell the asphalt burning as well, a thick oily smell that bit into his sinuses.

They had huddled together, waiting in the near-darkness for the fires to die.

Trevor was becoming concerned at their supplies situation. Cassandra was not a problem, being breastfed, but keeping her supplied with breast milk was going to be a problem if they ran out of food and water. He could see that Rebecca was concerned as well, her eyes watching the level in their water bottles slowly drop. It had taken over a week, nearly two, for the worst of the heat to pass, long after the fires had extinguished. He had tentatively touched the manhole, finding it warm but not hot, and then leaned his weight into it. It refused to budge. He put his shoulder into it, pressing upwards. It gave slightly, pushing upwards, but would not pop free. He came back to it with his crow bar, and slid the tapered end into a channel under the cover, and pulled down using his body weight to his advantage. There was a faint sucking sound, like almost dried glue tearing at itself, and then the cover came free, long gooey strings of asphalt clinging to the sides of the metal plate. He lifted it aside, hearing it stick to the road with a crunch of gravel, and stuck his head out.

Everything was burned; the dark landscape was filled with the charred remnants of the homes, the black drooping frames of vehicles, and thick piles of ash and soot. The sky was still black, as black as night, giving only enough light to see the silhouettes and outlines of the wreckage in the street.

He climbed out of the sewer, and stood on the road, feeling the hot wind blowing at his body. He went forward to his flat, kicking at the remains on the ground. The ash broke apart and was lifted into the wind, blowing away in the breeze. His foot hit a blackened brick that had made up the lower part of the outer wall. Next to it, a ceramic garden gnome stood buried to its beard in ashes, its face also stained with a grimy coating of soot. Their car had melted in the heat; the metal frame sagged in half at the roof, the metal frame drooping in a pronounced curve that touched the ground. Anything that could burn, had burned. There was nothing left to salvage, nothing he could use. Nothing they could use. He felt despair creep up on him and crawl up his spine, settling into his mind with a chill. In spite of the heat, he felt cold. He did not know what they were going to do. He had never felt so afraid.

The plate was stuck to the road, and so he left it there when he returned to the sewer. He walked quietly, not wanting to disturb Rebecca who was sleeping quietly, or Cassandra who was also dozing. He sat down on the blanket, aware of a rat that had come to the edge of a small pipe and that now sat watching him, it's small black eyes reflecting the light of the candle.

He stared at the water, trying to find a solution, trying to find a way out of this. Their water was nearly gone, and they had at the most a few days left of food, if they stretched it out and went hungry. He felt sick to his stomach, full of doubt and angst. A thought had slowly crept into his mind, one that he had first ignored, and then slowly began to listen to. They would have been better off if they had not fled their home. They would be dead, but not forced to deal with the mental anguish of what lay ahead. Death by starvation? Death by dehydration? Exposure? The finality of his mortality had never been more clear. They were not the lucky ones. The lucky ones had perished weeks earlier. He removed his Glock from his pants, and laid it next to the car seat, removing an uncomfortable lump from his backside.

It was his duty to keep his family safe. Or to keep them from suffering.

He mulled the thought over and over in his mind, wondering if he had missed something, something that was obvious that could flood light on their predicament. Each idea came to a dead end, the surety of each conclusion so final and absolute that he felt the doors of his mind closing with each one, his possible solutions streamlined and narrowed. Hope faded, and was lost.

He reached for his pillow, and pressed it down over Cassandra. She woke instantly, he felt her body tense and fight under him. He pressed the pillow down, tears of pain dripping from his face as he felt her weakening. The pillow muted her cries, and he endured her struggle moment by moment, fighting the urge to pull back and let her breath, to let her live. He could not.

This was the only way; he owed her a fast death, over the one she surely faced otherwise. He would face whatever penalty was due to him afterwards, his only hope lied in the fact that he was doing it out of his love for her. He would not see her suffer. He could not see that. Better this way, than something he had no control over. She stopped struggling, and went limp under him. He gasped in nausea and emotion, feeling his heart tearing at him in his chest, trying to overcome the sense of betrayal that was coursing through him.

"I'm so sorry, Cassandra," he whispered deep into the pillow.

"Daddy loves you. Know that he loves you. Be at peace, please."

A sudden scream pierced the air, and he jumped up to see Rebecca's horrified face staring at him, her face a mask of rage and agony. He watched her eyes go to him, and then to the car seat, where a tiny hand lay outstretched, the arm covered under a pillow.

"NOOOOOOO!" she screeched, her face going red and eyes flooding with tears, her motherly instincts pounding at her skull. She saw the gun lying on the blanket and scooped it up, shaking in her hand as she raised it.

Trevor raised his hands defensively, imploring her to wait.

"I had to. I'm sorry Rebecca oh God I'm so sorry," he cried.

She fired three times in quick succession, each shot driving him backwards, the final one catching him in the heart, pushing him over the edge of the platform. He fell into the water with a loud splash, his eyes rolling up into his sockets as he sank out of sight and was carried away slowly in the lazy current.

She dropped the gun to the blanket and frantically dug into the car seat, throwing the pillow into the water, clutching Cassandra to her chest. She was still warm, and hung limply against her, lifeless.

"Oh God NOOOOOOO!" she screamed, her heart knowing her daughter was gone forever. She sobbed into her hair, and then laid her down, covering her mouth and nose with hers, trying to resuscitate her.

Her chest rose as the air filled her lungs, and then dropped as she exhaled. She was breathing frantically, her limbs shaking with emotion and she tried repeatedly to bring Cassandra back. Her eyes stayed closed, her small body motionless.

"M-my b-baby," she stuttered.

"M-my little girl!" she knelt over her, crying, holding her tiny hands in hers as she wept, hoping beyond hope she would suddenly feel her breathe against her cheek and everything would be okay.

She didn't.

Rebecca knelt upright, crossing Cassandra's arms over her chest, and then laid her blanket over her, tucking it against her sides.

She kissed her on the forehead, and then whispered softly into her ear.

"Mommy is going to see you soon, sweetheart."

She picked up the Glock, keeping her eyes on her child, and placed the barrel to her temple. She smiled faintly, her face a mixture of pain and love. She wiped the tears from her cheeks once last time.

She pulled the trigger.

Colonel Dwight Peterson

He watched her quickly type the message as he relayed it to her, and then press a green SEND button. His wide spectrum transmission was a breach of direct orders; he had effectively broadcast the existence of secret facility to the entire world. In normal times, he would have been tried for treason, and likely even executed.

"Message transmitted, Sir. Shall I keep the systems open to receive verification of reception?"

"Negative. Cut the line."

"Copy that. Cutting the line."

She entered a brief code, setting her post offline to exterior channels.

A voice played out over the facility intercom.

"Engineering confirms facility isolation complete. All systems are running within normal parameters."

The Colonel nodded, satisfied with their quick response. The Engineering team was excellent.

"I want all relevant teams to coordinate intelligence gathering of the impact. I want as much information as you can collect, real or implied, based on data we have to date. Let's get moving, people."

"Security."

"Security, Sir."

I want MP's stationed at every point of exit of the facility. No one has authorization to leave; isolation must be maintained at all costs. Use of lethal force authorized."

"Understood, Sir."

"Systems."

"Systems, Sir."

"Bring every satellite we have access to online. I want to use every bird we have available. If necessary, override current users and applications."

"Yes, Sir."

"When can we expect the shockwave to reach our location?"

An officer near the front stood up, handing him a print out on a thin white paper, with perforations on the side to guide the sheet.

"Sir; an estimation of the impact."

He took the sheet with a nod, looking at the print out closely.

The top of the sheet consisted of the estimated data from the initial observations.

Estimated Velocity: 44.71 MPS / 72 KPS
Diameter: 30 miles / 48 km
Impact Angle: 45 degrees
Target Density: 1000 kg / cubic meter (water)
Projectile Density: Unknown

The bottom of the sheet was where the computers had generated the estimated results of the impact. It read:

At Distance from Impact: 6 210 miles / 10 000 km

Seismic Shaking: 2000 seconds
Richter scale Measurement (Approx.): 12
Air blast: 30300 seconds
Maximum Air Velocity: 380 m/s
Sound Level: 100 dB+

Looking at the print out, he did a quick mental calculation. They could expect the seismic shockwave to reach them in less than a half-hour.

And now, a few days later, he sat at his desk, going over the reports that were being generated. They had fastened down as much material as they could, and had to hope that the dampeners built into the facility would absorb much of the vibrations. It had, but the earthquake had still proven too strong to be ignored, and they had too little warning to take meaningful preventative action. There had been several fatalities as a direct result of the damages, and one indirect death. Falling concrete had claimed the lives directly; reinforced concrete being unable to weather the shock completely, and falling free in large pieces. Several shock absorbers had broken free of the floor, collapsing sections of the complex that were suddenly unsupported. One officer had apparently suffered some form of a heart attack, brought on by a combination of fear and emotion. There was damage everywhere one looked, from cracked walls and ceilings, to equipment strewn about the floor. The elevator shafts had taken the worst of the damage, and were rendered unusable. Nearer the surface, where the movement was more severe, entire slabs of concrete had broken free, and fallen to the base of the pit, to be followed by pieces of the mountain itself. One individual had run for the blast doors when the earthquake had stilled, his eyes full of fear, and he had ignored the calls of the stationed MP's. He was gunned down while trying to input his security override pass into the door security panel. The engineering teams had begun repairs on the most critical items first, itemizing their task list and providing regular reports as progress was made. Cosmetic repairs were so far down the list as to not yet even appear. The habitability of the facility was paramount; life support needed to be maintained at all costs. Once those systems were verified, less critical repairs could commence, within reason.

He had already seen much of the report that he had just turned over to Lieutenant Pritchard, who was reading the information within slowly and carefully, her eyes wide, her fingers gripping the paper. Later, when he filed the report, he would find that she had left creases in the pages, where she had held it firmly, crumpling it slightly. The latest batch was a summary of what he had been seeing gradually over the past one hundred and twenty hours. The view of the satellites high in orbit had proven invaluable to see what was happening globally. They had lost several low orbit platforms within the first day, as ejecta material had been thrown into space, and striking satellites. They were even able to watch the International Space Station get torn apart within the first few orbits. It had crumpled as if it shot from a shotgun, and then exploded violently when it suddenly depressurized. It was possible the oxygen tanks had been punctured, but they would never know. As for the satellites that had ceased to answer commands, they didn't know if they were still in orbit, or just so badly damaged that they had failed to function. The high altitude reconnaissance units were fine, well beyond the ejecta spread, and had been spared from the electromagnetic pulse of the explosion. Their special construction had proven resistant to the pulse, and it enabled them a birds eye view of the spreading devastation. They were able to confirm that nothing electronic had survived the pulse; there were no communications of any sort going on that they were able to detect. The globalized connected world was suddenly cut off; populations and cities having no means of communication. The Colonel had hoped that some military units would still be transmitting, but they were quiet, so he had been forced to assume they were lost in the following air blast that had circled the world in less than a half-day.

The blast moved faster than the speed of sound, and possessed incredible energy. They were able to witness the clouds spread over both hemispheres, crossing the normally impassable equator. They had seen the giant tsunamis race across the seas, flooding vast portions of the globe. Low lying areas like the Amazon basin, and the American Southeast were particularly hard hit, as the waves were able to travel for hundreds of kilometers inland, stripping the ground bare, down to bedrock. Once the cloud cover concealed the world, they had been forced to change all of the GIDSAT units to non-optical wavelengths, in spectrums that would allow them to see through the clouds that normal light could not pass through. They witnessed giant lightning storms pass over the world, and see the impact crater, a glowing wound almost six hundred kilometers across, and three kilometers deep. The heat from the crater, and the explosion, heated the atmosphere steadily. When the ejecta began to fall back to earth, the many millions of particles heated up, each carrying extra energy back to the surface, and the temperature of the world climbed to just over six hundred degrees. The world burned, adding to the already thick and toxic black cloud that encircled the planet. Very few in the facility were given complete disclosure as to what was happening to the world above them, and those that had access to the information were operating under extreme orders to remain silent, at this point.

The fires were now spent; there was literally nothing left on the surface of Earth to burn; everything was ash and dirt. The next steps they were waiting to unfold; the cooling of the planet, and the creation of the next ice age as temperatures would quickly plummet to below zero in most places. They could expect to see a narrow band of clear ground at the equator, or where ocean currents carried warm air, but most places were going to freeze solid, and be buried under kilometers of ice. The amount of rainfall and snowfall that would precipitate as the vaporized seas condensed out of the atmosphere was going to be extreme; the air temperature only needed to cool. The rains the world had experienced so far would be highly acidic, and warm, perhaps even hot. The extinction percentage of species was going to be near total, very likely in the high nineties. Some species would survive, but they would be small, and foragers, and very likely able to hibernate or sleep for extended periods between foraging. And it would have to be below ground already, or hiding. Anything caught on the surface was already dead. The ocean ecosystem was going to be wiped clean as the lack of light would topple the food chain there as it would on the ground. The only plants that would survive would be those that had already gone to seed, or who produced tubers, and whose seed was buried, or needed heat to germinate. Some officers had wagered, rather grimly, that the extinction rate was going to be as high as 99.5 percent. It would be something they would never be able to verify. With the analysis of what was happening in the world above, it had gradually dawned to his team, some slowly, some quickly, that the above ground population of *homo sapiens sapiens* was going to be in danger of being rendered extinct in a very short period. There would doubtless be some survivors, of both the initial impact and earthquake, and then of the air blast and global firestorm, the benefit of having a global population in the billions, but the numbers were going to fall suddenly with each event, the death toll was going to be staggering.

Survival would favor the lucky, and he was not so sure that those that had survived would want that kind of luck. To survive, you would have to be underground; it was the only way to survive the firestorm. So now he sat at his desk, opposite the Lieutenant, whose face had gone a lighter shade of pale, and whose hands were shaking slightly, the paper shivering in her grasp, wide tears running openly down her face; tears she refused to wipe away, or did not feel in her state. He read down the page, seeing the nuclear reactor was running again at one hundred percent. It had scrambled after the earthquake; a normal safety precaution that forced an emergency shutdown. The engineering team had given it as thorough an inspection as could be performed in their timeline, and restarted the initiation sequence, their nerves tense as they potentially waited for the worst possible outcome. Instead, it had come on routinely, lights on the control board slowing activating as sequences were successfully passed. There had been more than a few cheers when the reactor had gone into a normal production range, with no apparent damage. The slightest damage would have been a severe impediment to their situation. They were on their own, and had to be completely independent if they had any chance of survival.

"Tissue?" he asked, leaning forward and pushing a Kleenex box towards her. She had nodded quickly, taking two tissues out of the box in quick sequence, and then rubbing her face as dry as she could get it, dabbing under her eyes.

"This is accurate? Every bit?" she asked him, hoping for better news.

He nodded slowly, unsure of how she might react. So far she was behaving as he expected. The staff knew that something was happening, but no one had any real indication of the depth of their situation.

"Have we been able to raise anyone? To get any contact?"

"No. The severity of the EMP on the surface wiped out virtually everything. We haven't heard from anyone."

In truth, they weren't really listening either. If they had contacted a survivor, there would be a certainty that someone might raise the suggestion of a rescue attempt, and that would compromise the security of the facility. They had to remain isolated; for as long as possible. They had enough uranium in the reactor to last them a good thirty years; food was a different situation, but for the moment that problem had remained dormant.

"So what are we going to do?" she asked.

"We are going to get this operation back in order, and take each day one at a time. We are still alive, and I mean to keep it that way."

She nodded, and tried to straighten herself out.

"I can't go back out there yet. I'm sorry; I didn't expect this."

She handed the sheets back to him, where they sat slightly crumpled on his desk. He picked them up, shuffling them together and then sliding them back into their folder.

"Take your time. There's no rush."

"Th-thank you." She sniffed twice, and wiped at her eyes again.

They sat in silence for a moment, listening to the clock tick on the wall.

"Do you know what I keep thinking about?"

He shook his head, crossing his hands over his stomach as he leaned back into his chair.

"I keep thinking of all the places I've been. They are all gone, aren't they? Everything is just gone." The way she pronounced *gone*, it sounded even more final, more certain.

"The huge trees at my family's old farm. Los Angeles. Rome. They just aren't there anymore. What do you think it looks like up there?"

He didn't have to try very hard to imagine it.

"It's dark. The air smells bad. It's getting cold." He kept it simple, trying not to push her back over the edge. She was calming down, and he wanted her to relax. She shivered.

"Do you think anyone will make it up there? With everything that has happened?"

"I think the odds are against them. Whoever they are."

She nodded quickly, having already come to that realization and expecting the same answer. She stood up, and straightened her skirt with a few downward strokes of her hands on the fabric.

"Sir." She saluted him, and he saluted back with a quick sweep of his hand. She closed the door quietly behind herself, and walked away, turning around a corner and going out of sight. He sat in his chair, staring blankly at the wall, listening to the clock faintly tick away the seconds, his eyelids growing heavy.

He was startled awake by a faint knocking at his door. He had jumped, his eyes wide and his body alert. His right hand had gone for his holster, only to find it empty. A second later, he remembered where he was, and he settled back down into his chair. He hadn't fallen asleep in his chair for quite a while. He stretched, feeling his back crackle in a few spots and a few muscles pull tight, stiff from his sleeping position. He waved at the door, motioning the doctor into the room.

"Sir."

"Good morning. At least I think it's morning."

He glanced at the clock. It was a little past ten.

"What do you have for me?"

The doctor sat in the chair opposite the desk, and produced a thin red folder, handing it over the desk.

He took the folder, and opened it, finding page after page of photographs of the base personnel, along with a detailed medical file after the photograph.

"Personnel records?"

The doctor nodded. Her hair was cut short, exposing a neckline he found attractive, leading to a softly muscled shoulder. She was taller than he was, something that he found intriguing. She had graduated medical school at the top of her class, and was recruited fresh from its ranks. She was twenty-four, having an extremely high IQ and beginning her medical training when most of her peers were still in high school.

"Were you ever informed of the Eve Protocol?" she asked the Colonel.

"The Eve Protocol? No, I haven't heard of it."

The doctor nodded.

"I expected as much. I was briefed on the program when I accepted the position here, with the understanding it was known only to myself and my immediate medical team."

The Colonel leaned forward in his chair, his interest piqued.

"Well, Doctor Mokele, you have piqued my interest. I assume you are going to educate me on the Eve Protocol?"

Doctor Mokele nodded, and smiled slightly, the bright white of her teeth contrasting sharply with the near black hue of her skin.

"The Eve Protocol is a repopulation program…"

"Excuse me; did you say repopulation?" cutting off Doctor Mokele. The Doctor nodded.

"If you suggest you were directed to have us leave this complex in this situation I will advise you now that we are going nowhere. No where for a while if I can help it."

The Doctor shook her head.

"The Eve Protocol is nothing of the sort, in fact. At least, not initially."

"Not initially."

"Correct. Let me explain the program. The staff in this complex were chosen for many reasons, most of which you are aware of. The ability to operate well in a military environment, a good education, no issues with isolation, no immediate surviving relatives or family, all of the things that you were briefed on when you were considered for your command."

He nodded. The list of aptitudes that were required to be selected for this facility was long. Most of them were inherent traits; behaviors and personality characteristics that were innate and could not be learned. If a candidate had those traits, then the screening process delved deeper into education and family situations.

"There was also a deep medical inquiry of which you would have had little insight."

He remembered his own evaluation; the blood tests and physical examinations.

"There was the standard battery of tests that you expected, but there was another series that you would know nothing about. The blood work was extensively screened for all of the normal filters.

Inheritable diseases, degenerative conditions, substance abuses, and the like. What you weren't informed of was the DNA analysis of each candidate. Each of us was selected based on our genetic variance form one another, with a high focus on selecting candidates representing a wide field of human diversity. European, Asian, and African stock for example."

Dwight nodded, steadily becoming very interested in where this was going. He was very aware of the ethnic diversity of the facility; it was blatantly obvious at the moment you arrived at the base.

"From these genetic backgrounds, only those with the most genetic variance were selected, providing they carried no inheritable diseases either dominant or recessive. And then the selections were based on gender ratio, one-fifth male, four-fifths female."

He had noticed the ratio was skewed as well, not representing the normal ratio of nearly fifty-fifty, but had paid it no attention. His only concern was ability.

"Homosexuality was a large concern, not out of political concerns, but strictly in terms of attraction to the opposite gender, and therefore, successful reproduction."

"Wait a minute here; what you are telling me is that this base is some kind of zoo?" His tone was incredulous.

She looked at him, her eyes level with his.

"Not a zoo. Breeding stock. We are a self-contained breeding stock for the human species.

Have you ever noticed that there is no one here that is considered to be old? You, I understand, are the oldest person here, and still well within your prime."

He squirmed, feeling a little uncomfortable at the distinction of his age, and that he was being scrutinized as a potential sperm donor.

"There are no females past thirty, all for sound principles of human reproduction. This facility, while used in a military application, was also conceived, if you pardon the expression, to harbor a young and healthy population of the human race."

"What are you proposing?" he asked.

"The situation above ground is obvious to everyone that has seen the information; the human species has been, or will be, rendered extinct. I am proposing nothing; I came here to introduce you to the Eve Protocol, so that we can implement the strategy."

He sat in his chair, digesting the information presented to him.

"I presume you have the Directive issuing the Protocol to be executed?"

She laughed momentarily, the laugh fading off to a chuckle.

"I assure you, Colonel, implementation of the Protocol will be nothing more than allowing human nature to take its programmed course, within a few guidelines. You may give the order if you like, but nothing so official is necessary."

She was right, of course. There were strict guidelines in place in the complex about cohabitation. Relaxing the guidelines would naturally lead to more natural and intimate relationships developing.

"What are the guidelines?" he asked.

"Firstly, and the most unnatural portion of the early phase, is the controlled pairing of groups within our population. Our population is small, and therefore, even within the genetic diversity we possess, the risk of inbreeding exists. Steps must be taken to insure that the initial *result* of children is as genetically diverse as possible. The human race, in fact, is quite genetically limited. There is more genetic variance in a single troop of chimpanzees than there is in the entire human race. Monogamous pair bonding will not be able to occur for sometime. For some people, this will not pose a problem as they will be more inclined to polygamy or the avoidance of pair bonding anyways; but for others, it will pose a challenge."

"How is this going to be controlled?"

"How is what going to be controlled?"

"The early phase. What needs to be done?"

"Each male will be paired with five females. The initial matching has already been completed so that we have a group list to work with. The few deaths we encountered during the incident will change this slightly, but we can incorporate the changes into others groups."

"Excuse me? Each male will have to ...err...mate with five women?"

"Correct. Before you imagine indulging a pre-pubescent fantasy, this is strictly to create a core group of children to base future matings on."

He leaned back in his chair, rubbing his temple as he tried to imagine how the staff in the complex would react.

The doctor continued.

"Each of these women will need to bear five children from their initial male. The gender of the offspring is irrelevant; the genetic mix within the children is what is crucial. Once these children are born, perhaps more traditional methods of mate selection will be allowed to unfold. Within guidelines."

"But with so few males how is that going to be possible?"

"It isn't going to work entirely traditionally. There aren't enough males to go around. So although a male-female bond might develop a man and wife relationship, he will still be needed to father other children with other women within certain groups. His genetic code cannot be diluted. We may lose one or two women in childbirth, or afterwards from complications arising directly from childbirth, and in those cases it is imperative that the child be saved where it is obvious the mother cannot. Her genes must be preserved."

"That sounds cold."

She nodded.

"Our situation is extreme."

"So the purpose is to create groups with genetic distinctiveness, rather than have them averaged out? Or diluted, to quote you?"

"Precisely."

They sat silently for a moment in the room, the Doctor watching him think out the protocol and the ramifications. It was a bit of a surprise to hear he was expected to sire at least twenty-five children.

Finally, he broke the silence.

"And how about you? What do you see yourself doing in all of this?"

"Other than the fact that I am going to deliver one child a year until menopause, I am going to work with the medical team in this facility to document our gene pool. And train the next generation."

"There will be some resistance to this program."

"Undoubtedly. But these are military people, and they will follow orders. Especially once they are given the reasons behind it. If we do this properly, we will save our species and all of our accumulated knowledge. Fail, and we will perish from the Earth."

His throat was suddenly dry, with an itch that threatened to make him cough.

"Coffee?" he asked, gesturing to the Braun coffeemaker sitting on the desk under his clock.

"Love some," she replied.

She waited as the brew percolated, and then sipped the hot liquid carefully as he handed her a large white mug. It tasted good, and she took another sip.

He swallowed his quickly, feeling the coffee burn the itch from his throat. He licked his lips, and placed the mug down on his desk, forgetting the coasters near the coffee pot.

"How do you recommend we begin?"

She started.

Time passed inexorably, daily tasks rolled into routine, and the day to day activities kept everyone busy, purposefully. The repairs to the facility had been completed as scheduled, fresh patches of reinforced concrete lining the wall where pieces had fallen, and the lighting attended to. The radio waves had remained quiet and still, with no contact with the topside world. They did not broadcast, but instead listened for all the hours in the day. They had received a few short desperate broadcasts that had spanned seconds months earlier, pleas for help filled with static and garbled interference. The messages were not repeated. The world above passed from a time of heat and flame, to one of cold and snow and creeping ice. They watched in isolation from the vantage point of the satellites as the polar caps froze, and the oceans began to follow suit, thick pack ice creeping ever southward and northward, towards the equator. They could verify that the thick cloud layer in the atmosphere was beginning to thin, slowly clearing as time passed. The upper atmosphere was choked with fine dust that would stay airborne for years, and reflect sunlight back to space. The lower dust had been cleared first in the sulphurous rains, and then in the thick snows that followed. It would be years, nearly a decade before sunlight in any strength once again touched the surface of the world. It would slowly brighten, without heat, for some time.

The facility had received the Eve Protocol with the acceptance that Doctor Mokele had predicted. There were those that found the plan difficult to accept, on moral grounds, but with the understanding of the reasoning behind it, and irrefutable data that the world topside was barren and spoiled, they came around, suspending their prejudices in light of what they faced. The Colonel stood watch over the monitoring team, watching as they scanned the airwaves for the unlikely transmissions from above. If they had detected a signal, they could not have rendered aid. Their task was to monitor and observe.

Every woman was pregnant, all performing their tasks with growing bellies and the promise of the next generation within them. He could not help but smile with amusement, seeing so many pregnant women concentrated in one place. He felt a warm hand on his neck, fingers tracing along his jaw line. He turned to see Doctor Mokele looking into his eyes, a smile on her face, one hand on her belly.

"What are you smiling at?" she asked, feeling his hand running over her round stomach.

"So many pregnant women. I'm sure there is a good joke here somewhere."

She chuckled, seeing what he saw.

"How are we doing today?" he asked her.

"Your child likes to make me sick, but it's getting better."

"How was the amnio?"

"It was fine. She is healthy and strong."

"She?"

Doctor Mokele nodded.

He smiled, kissing her. The news he was having a daughter cheered him, somewhat lightening the load he felt on his shoulders. He felt her hand on his and he caressed the curve of her belly.

"How are the rest doing?"

"We had to abort one yesterday; the fetus was developing abnormally."

He nodded.

"How is the mother?"

"She is upset, of course. But she is determined to try again. At her age, it's very unlikely to repeat."

"Is everyone asking about the gender of their babies?"

"No, not everyone. A few want the surprise. We know, of course; it's part of planning the next phase, but we aren't telling the parents."

"How about mine, then?"

"Promise not to tell Chiang or Dhaliwal?"

"They don't want to know?"

The Doctor shook her head.

"Promise."

"Girls, and one boy."

He grinned. The knowledge of having four little girls and a boy was heartwarming.

"Who is carrying my son?"

"Dhaliwal. She probably has a suspicion, because the heartbeat is lower for her than the rest of our group, and she saw the recordings being taken. Remember, not a word."

He pantomimed his lips being zipped shut.

"What is the ratio for the first batch?"

"Almost equal. Rodriguez is having four boys and a girl, so he averages you out."

"Almost equal?"

"There are three sets of twins, all girls."

"Three?"

She nodded.

"A high percentage in our population, but they aren't identical. Fraternal twins."

"Try to imagine this place in several months. It's going to be full of babies."

She nodded.

"You are going to have to suspend some normal operations when that time comes."

He agreed. They were going to have to operate a bare minimum, with a lot of rotating schedules, with the men doing much of the basics as they weren't going to be as tied up as the new mothers.

A bank of yellow strobes suddenly came alight, flashing on the walls in a circular motion, shadows running in all directions.

"The reactor!" he shouted.

The yellow strobes were dedicated to the reactor systems, indicating only when there was as issue with the core.

He punched a comm link on the panel in front of him, getting direct access to the engineering room.

"Report!"

A klaxon sounded, escalating the urgency.

A voice came through the speaker on the other end, shouting.

"The coolant system has failed! We are losing the reactor!"

His mind raced, furious to find a solution.

"What happened?"

"A series of pipes suddenly fractured. They must have been damaged in the quake, something the team missed during the inspection!"

He nodded. They did not have a x ray scanner, something that would have detected structural issues in the piping. They could only trust to a visual inspection, and monitor the reactor performance. Over time, a hidden weakness had failed.

"Get anyone not critical to the reactor into isolation! We can't risk anyone if the system contaminates the base."

He looked at Doctor Mokele; she nodded, and quickly left, taking with her others into the direction of the quarantine rooms. They were cut off from the rest of the circulation units, and were not linked to areas that radiation could reach if there was a breach.

"Shut down the reactor! We can't have a breach; at all costs prevent a breach!"

The lights dimmed and pulsed as the power from the reactor fluctuated. He punched a button on the desk, killing the resounding drum of the klaxon so he could think, and he ran towards the reactor bay in the Engineering quarter. They could not fail; everything was depending on it.

Everything.

At a speed of over fifty kilometers a second, the leading edge of the asteroid flirted with the upper atmosphere, causing it to spin faster and also slightly slowing it down. The friction overcame its forward momentum, and with an immense sonic boom it entered the atmosphere. The air around it burst into a white light of searing plasma as releasing heat and energy stripped atoms of their electrons and protons, For a brief moment it sped through the upper atmosphere, creating an immense contrail. Ground underneath its path burst into flame, and then was vaporized in the growing heat. In the next moment its white hot surface punched through the ocean below, instantly vaporizing the water and sending it outwards and upwards as a giant explosion of steam and charged particles. With its great speed and mass it continued downwards, its mass being converted into enormous amounts of energy from the impact, and with a cataclysmic and deafening roar it exploded into the crust, tearing deep into the mantle itself, peeling back and throwing outwards the outer skin of the planet. Gasified rock was blasted from the explosion and was ejected into space, as a giant shockwave sped around the wounded world faster than sound. As it raced around the globe, it triggered immense earthquakes as continental shelves were suddenly jarred, and volcanoes released the deep pressure from below.

Behind the shockwave a wall of superheated air flowed over the surface, igniting and vaporizing all it encompassed. Within a thousand kilometers of the impact, the surface was reduced to molten rock, glowing red like the hot blood of the world. Beyond another thousand kilometers, the ground was shattered and broken with immense faults and fissures covering the surface, steam venting from anything holding water as the intense heat boiled water away, as magma rose to the surface between the fissures. Entire forests steamed in the heated air and then spontaneously blazed, the crowns of trees exploding in fire. Animals ran, flew, or dug for cover, only to be overcome from the heat and then to burn with the forests. The surface already scorched bare and hot by the pyroclastic flow, now rumbled and shook as earthquakes dispersed the energy of the shockwave. The superheated flow of air and rock covered over a half of the planet before finally running out of energy.

Tsunamis sped away from the explosion, a wave of water rising a kilometer high traveling faster than sound. The giant waves crashed over continental shelves and coastlines, breaking inland and rushing over once dry land, wreaking devastation as the water flowed over the surface. In places the great waves were stopped against the steppes of mountains, boiling with churning power, and then with restless pressure from behind they were channeled through valleys, which compressed the flow of water, accelerating its speed as it tore through the countryside, allowing it to travel even further deeper inland. Over flat plains the surge of water carried hundreds of kilometers before coming to a standstill.

Once the outward pressure of the explosion was lost, the seas rushed into the impact crater, vaporizing columns of water into the atmosphere and dousing the open wound in the crust. Pieces of earth and asteroid that had been blown into space from the explosion now began to fall back to earth, and carried by their own orbits sometimes fell on the opposite side of the planet, creating minor craters and explosions of their own, where others were vaporized in the atmosphere as they were crashing to the planet below. Across the world death continued to rain down. Tens of thousands of meteorites fell back to the Earth, each one releasing heat and energy into the air, and together they raised the temperature of the atmosphere by hundreds of degrees. Vast clouds of steam and dust and ash filled the sky, spreading and covering the planet within a day, concealing the devastation below behind a dense cloud as dark as sack cloth, that flashed with lightening and roared with thunder, a scene from Dantes Hell, were devils and demons fought in the skies above for domination of the world below.

The ashen cloud covered the globe and the sun and light disappeared, and night reigned supreme over the world. Once the rain of meteors had largely ceased, the surface began to cool rapidly, and the vaporized oceans began to fall as rain, which cooled the surface further and doused remaining flames and open lava flows. The rains washed over the charred remains of the world. The impenetrable clouds prevented any sunlight from reaching the surface, and as the Earth continued to cool over the course of weeks the rain began to fall as dirty snow. Creatures that had survived the devastating fires and heat in the previous weeks were now faced with a cruel winter unlike any other. Vast amounts of snow fell to the ground, piling up in immense drifts and dunes that travelled over the surface under direction of the wind, a desert of snow, no less deadly than the Sahara, and no more forgiving. Depths of snow were compressed into ice, and glaciers spread through the mountains of the world. Wounded and cold, the planet beneath the clouds passed into a dark cold sleep, while Death stalked the land and claimed its bounty.

And the Angel poured forth the seventh
vial into the air, and a voice cried from Heaven,
"It is done."

–Revelation 16:17